NATHAN JOR

A
CROOKED
NUMBER

a novel

Flat Rock
Publishing

Published by Flat Rock Publishing
Fairmont, MN
www.flatrockpublishing.com

Copyright ©2011 Nathan Jorgenson

Distributed by Greenleaf Book Group LLC

For ordering information or special discounts for bulk purchases, please contact Greenleaf Book Group LLC at PO Box 91869, Austin, TX 78709, 512.891.6100.

Design and composition by Greenleaf Book Group LLC & Bumpy Design
Cover design by Greenleaf Book Group LLC & Dan Pitts

Publisher's Cataloging-In-Publication Data
(Prepared by The Donohue Group, Inc.)
Jorgenson, Nathan.
    A crooked number / Nathan Jorgenson.—1st ed.
    p. ; cm.
    ISBN: 978-0-9746370-3-7
    1. Dental students—Fiction. 2. College teachers—Fiction. 3. Teacher-student relationships—Fiction. 4. College life—Fiction. 5. College stories, American. 6. Love stories, American. I. Title.

PS3610.O65 C76 2011
813.6   2011920622

Part of the Tree Neutral® program, which offsets the number of trees consumed in the production and printing of this book by taking proactive such as planting trees in direct proportion to the number of trees used: neutral.com

United States of America on acid-free paper

TreeNeutral®

10 9 8 7 6 5 4 3 2 1

For my children.
The best thing I'll ever do in this life is be your Dad.
Dream big dreams. Never give them up and never let anyone steal them.

❖ CHAPTER 1 ❖

July 23, 1959

Just a dull green 1953 International Harvester pickup truck that rode like a lumber wagon, that was all it was. When it was brand new it wasn't exactly airtight; even closed doors and windows couldn't keep the dust out. But now with some age and a few hard miles the thing had become a dust factory. Clouds of brown road dust rolled into the cab through rust holes in the floorboards and settled over the metal dashboard in a gritty layer. Riding with the windows open actually seemed to help.

As Big Ole Thorson rumbled along the dirt road he glanced over to his right and smiled. Five-year-old Grant, the youngest of Ole's five sons, sat quietly with his arm around an aging springer spaniel. Grant's hair was cut short, a buzz cut, and he kept a red plastic water pistol in the pocket of his blue jeans. Just now the boy was consumed with the task at hand, catching the red liquid running off his cherry Popsicle with his tongue. The July sun and the little boy were locked in a spirited race to see who could devour the Popsicle first. Grant seemed to be struggling to keep up, but the issue was still in doubt.

Rags, the old springer, inched closer and closer, then began to lick the sweet red drips running off Grant's elbow.

"Dad?" Grant looked over at his father and Rags crept closer to intercept the steady drip of Popsicle juice running down his arm.

"Yeah?"

"Who's faster on the draw, Marshal Dillon or Paladin?" Grant asked. He waited for his father's answer as if the weight of the world rested on him.

"Well, I don't really know, son. They're both good guys so maybe they're both the same."

Grant furrowed his brow and thought about his father's answer while Rags continued to harvest the runoff from his elbow.

"Who's a better shot, Davy Crockett or Daniel Boone?" Grant asked after several minutes of serious thought.

"Don't know that one either, son. I don't think either one of those guys ever miss, so that's probably a tie, also," Ole answered seriously.

All the new information swirled around in Grant's head . . . it needed to be assimilated and organized somehow.

"Dad?" Grant asked. When he spoke he turned toward his father and moved the hand holding a nearly melted Popsicle. Rags could stand no more temptation and snapped the last of the Popsicle from Grant's hand. Grant's only response was to wipe his sticky hand on his shirt, then ask, "Does Robin Hood shoot his arrows with confidence?"

Big Ole Thorson could only smile at his boy's question. "Yeah," he said after a moment's reflection. "He couldn't be that good without confidence."

Grant stroked Rags's head with his left hand and let the dog lick his right hand clean while he pondered Robin Hood's self-confidence.

"Dad?" Grant asked once more.

"Yeah?" Ole responded again.

"I saw Rags eat a horse turd yesterday."

"Oh?" Big Ole said, trying to guess just how his son had shifted so quickly from Robin Hood's confidence to Rags eating horse turds.

Then, before Big Ole could find more useful insight to add to the conversation, Grant said, "I think I'm gonna be a professional baseball player when I grow up," as if that was the only logical conclusion that could be drawn from the discussion of cowboys, confidence, and turd-eating dogs.

"Well, good," Big Ole said, then drove on in silence for several minutes.

The truck swept a ribbon of dust into the dry summer air as it rolled along toward Big Ole Thorson's place. Big Ole was about to say something to Grant when he noticed several trucks parked in his neighbor's farmyard.

Ole Hokanson had lived on the next farm, about a quarter mile from the Thorsons', for fifty years. A small, wiry man, he was twenty-some years older than Ole Thorson, and through the years he'd become Ole Thorson's best friend and something of a father figure. The neighbors had dubbed him Little Ole as a way to differentiate between him and his constant companion, Big Ole Thorson.

Big Ole's dark eyes turned hard when he realized why there were trucks at the Hokanson place. He downshifted the old truck and jostled the boy and his dog when he stood on the accelerator. Rags and Grant bounced completely off the bench seat of the International when Big Ole roared into the Hokanson driveway. The truck slid to a stop and Grant's father jumped out even before the skidding truck came to rest. He slammed the door behind himself, and in the same motion he wheeled and barked at Grant, "Stay in the truck!"

Grant leaned forward and peeked over the dashboard as Big Ole sprinted toward Little Ole's machine shed. The boy grew fearful as the farmyard fell silent and his father disappeared through a thin haze of dust into the dark, open mouth of the corrugated steel shed.

Big Ole knew what he'd see when he burst through the open door of the old shed. Like a giant cave, the darkness of the shed swallowed him for a moment. All his senses screamed at once. The musty scent of the dirt floor mingled with gear grease and fertilizer and drove a familiar smell into his nostrils. His eyes needed more light, but they acclimated quickly when he charged into the maw of the shed. Little Ole lay on the floor, his face bloodied. He was trying to raise himself onto one elbow. Big Ole glanced to his left and, without breaking stride, grabbed an ax handle that rested against a workbench covered with greasy tools and tractor parts.

The four men standing over Little Ole flinched and stepped back while they raised their hands in self-defense, as Big Ole charged them like a snarling guard dog about to strike. But when he reached Little Ole's side he set his boot heels into the ground and skidded to a stop.

"I'll kill you sonsabitches!" He raised the ax handle as if he were about to do just that. "This is enough!"

Four scruffy young men, all heavily muscled, stared at Big Ole. Dressed in worn blue jeans and cotton work shirts, the surly men were reevaluating the situation. They'd beaten their father before, but never this badly. They'd come today with the intention of breaking some bones, maybe something more. But now Big Ole had come to his friend's defense.

Big Ole Thorson was not a man to be taken lightly. Those square shoulders and heavy arms were far too powerful for any one of Little Ole's boys. If there was one thing they knew of Ole Thorson it was that he kept his word. His reputation and the wild look in his eyes gave him a powerful psychological edge just now.

The boys calculated their chances. Four pairs of angry blue eyes sized up the situation, darting from Big Ole to one another, trying to estimate the damage they'd suffer in a fight. Maybe they could rush Big Ole? Certainly the four of them could overpower one man?

"One more fuckin' step, Lars . . ." Big Ole growled. He offered a fight with no reservation and no quarter.

Lars Hokanson, the oldest and biggest of the Hokanson boys, actually seemed to be considering a challenge to Big Ole, and silence settled over the shed once more.

Small footsteps broke the spell. Grant Thorson ran from the truck to the shed and stopped in the open doorway. Rags followed close behind, then sat down on the dirt just outside the large sliding door.

"Dad?" Grant called.

"Go back to the truck," Big Ole said calmly.

Grant and Rags were no more than a pair of timid silhouettes when Lars began to move his eyes back and forth between them and Big Ole.

No one knew what to do next.

Rags leaned to his side and used a hind foot to scratch his ear, then dropped onto his belly next to a confused Grant. "Dad?" he called again.

All the fight went out of Lars. He breathed heavily once, then lowered his hands and walked out of the shed, leaving Big Ole a wide berth as he passed by. The other three men followed at his heels. They passed by little Grant as if he weren't there, and went to their trucks.

"It's over, boys! Next time you touch this man I'll kill you!" Big Ole called out in a guttural voice.

Fresh tears mingled with the blood and dirt on Little Ole's face as he raised himself up on one elbow. He sobbed softly and let Big Ole try to dab the blood away from a mouse that was about to close his left eye.

"I'm sorry, Ole," Big Ole said softly. "This shouldn't be happening. Why don't you *tell* them?"

Grant walked tentatively toward his father and Little Ole, struggling to comprehend what he was looking at, Rags followed playfully at his heels. His eyes were filled with wonder and fear when he crept close enough to see the pain and shame ground into Little Ole's bloody face. Grant stepped closer and stared. He was afraid now, and confused. Grown men didn't cry. His dad would never cry, that was for sure. His father held the old man as if he were a child, injured on the playground, and the moment burned its way into Grant's memory. What had happened?

∾:∾

"You shouldn't have let him see it," Gladys Thorson said.

"I couldn't help it, Gladdy," Big Ole said, without looking up. "I didn't want it to happen either."

Gladys and Big Ole Thorson sat in the evening darkness of a screened-in porch off the kitchen of their farmhouse and listened to the rhythmic chirping of a million crickets.

"I was afraid," Big Ole said. He reached over and took his wife's hand. "Those boys meant business today."

"What were you afraid of? Would they have attacked you, too?" Gladys asked.

"They were thinking about it, Gladdy," Big Ole said softly. "I'd a stood my ground. I might have killed 'em."

"I don't like to hear you talk like that," Gladys said. She knew her words made no difference to Big Ole. She knew he'd have done anything to defend Little Ole. He always stood his ground.

They sat together in silence for a few minutes, each of them thinking of all the things that could have happened in Little Ole's shed.

"How can they do that to their own father?" Gladys asked after a long silence.

"He won't tell them. They don't know the truth," Big Ole replied. "They think it's all his fault."

The kitchen floor creaked softly and let them know they weren't alone. When they looked back into the dim light of the kitchen they saw Grant peering around the doorjamb. Ole said nothing. He simply made eye contact with the boy and held his hands open, inviting his son to come and sit with him.

Grant paused for a second. He'd taken a bath and was ready for bed. He wore black cotton pajamas that said ZORRO on the front and accentuated his long, skinny arms and legs. Before he left his hiding place in the doorway, he turned a questioning glance at his mother. When she nodded yes he ran to his father's lap and straddled him. He put his arms around Big Ole's neck, rested his forehead against his father's, and sighed.

As far as anyone could remember, the touching of foreheads had begun when Grant was a toddler, sitting in his high chair. Big Ole had made a face at Grant and the boy began to pump his arms, kick his feet, and smile. He'd reached out to Big Ole to indicate that he wanted to be picked up. When Ole lifted him from his chair, Grant slowly moved his forehead into contact with Ole's and held it there while he smiled. The little ritual had survived ever since that day, and had morphed into a special embrace for them. It was just what they did when they needed to be close.

"Dad?" Grant said after a moment.

"Yes?" Big Ole replied.

"Are you gonna kill those men you yelled at today?"

"No, son."

"Then why did you say that?"

"Because they hurt Little Ole, and I got mad. I shouldn't have said that."

"Are they gonna kill you?" Grant asked.

Gladys squeezed Big Ole's hand.

"No," Big Ole replied.

"Why did they hurt Little Ole?" Grant asked.

"It's really hard to explain, son. I don't think you're old enough to understand. I'll tell you all about it when you get a little older," Big Ole said.

"Dad?" Grant asked with his forehead still pressed against his father's. Then he reached his soft hand to his father's face and felt Big Ole's coarse black whisker stubble. He moved his hand over Big Ole's face and studied the sandpaper texture.

"Yes?"

"Can I stay up and listen to the ball game with you?" Grant asked, still softly rubbing Big Ole's whiskers.

"You're supposed to be in bed," Gladys said. "You got to stay up and watch *Gunsmoke*, now it's bedtime."

"Please?" Grant begged. "Paul has the game on his radio!"

Big Ole simply reached over and switched on the radio that always sat on an end table next to his chair.

The steady voice of a happy man calling a far-off baseball game raised itself through the static of an AM radio and restored order to another summer night. Crowd noise in the distant stadium could be heard over a faint crackling in the radio signal, and every so often a vendor called out, "Peanuts!" or "Cold Beer Here!" while the man on the radio talked about baseball.

"Harry Caray," Big Ole chuckled.

"He's a nut," Gladys said.

"I think he's got a snoot full," Ole replied.

Grant didn't know what it meant to have a snoot full, but it seemed that his parents liked whoever it was they were talking about.

Grant slid off to his father's side, still sharing the same chair, curled his knees under his chin, and began to stare at the handful of baseball cards he'd carried along from his room. Big Ole lifted a powerful left arm around his boy and tried to make out the names and faces on the cards, too. The light from the kitchen was all they had, and they both turned and tipped their heads to see the cards in Grant's hands. There were Willie McCovey, Jim Maloney, Willie Mays, Joe Adcock, Eddie Mathews, Warren Spahn, Whitey Ford, and Stan "The Man" Musial. Grant flipped the last card onto the top of the others and revealed the face on the special card. He stole an upward glance at Big Ole. "Paul gave it to me," Grant said proudly. He'd saved the best for last.

Looking back at them through the dim light of the porch was a smiling Mickey Mantle. "Mickey's my favorite player," Grant said in a reverent tone, and he stared at the card as if he thought Mr. Mantle might speak to him.

All was pretty much right with the world just now, for Grant. The Hokanson boys were forgotten, the friendly voice on the radio was calling a night game from San Francisco. It seemed as if the man on the radio was sitting right there with them on the porch. Mays got a hit. Musial got one, too. Some kid named Koufax was showing signs of greatness down in Los Angeles, but he couldn't find the strike zone very often. Harvey Haddix had fired a perfect game for thirteen innings a few weeks earlier, and people were saying that maybe it was the greatest day any pitcher ever had. Grant decided he'd have to keep an eye out for Harvey Haddix's baseball card, and that Koufax guy's, too.

Chirping crickets called through the stillness of a dark night on the northern plains and mingled with the radio static and the ball game. Grant didn't know what to think about the scary thing he'd seen at Little Ole's. That still bothered him some. But he was safe at home now, dreaming his dreams.

❧ CHAPTER 2 ❧

September 10, 1975

Maybe this hadn't been such a good idea after all.

Grant Thorson stood on the corner of Washington Avenue and glanced from side to side while he waited for the light to change. Everyone in the gathering crowd seemed smarter, better prepared, and more confident than him.

When he'd applied for acceptance to the University of Minnesota School of Dentistry he'd been told there were 1,500 other applicants, most of them well qualified, and that chances of being selected for the freshman class of 150 were pretty slim.

But here he was, and he couldn't help but wonder about the road that had led him here. Just being in college the past four years had been enough of a challenge. The war in Vietnam was over—he didn't have to worry about that anymore. Nixon said we'd won, but it didn't feel like it. Grant was just glad to have missed it.

College had come and gone so fast. Beer, baseball, and a steady girl-friend had been serious distractions, but he'd managed to get decent grades in spite of them. His days on the Gopher baseball team had ground to an inglorious end. He'd hardly played as a junior and senior. That career was definitely over.

The steady-girlfriend thing seemed to be unraveling too. For most of his college days he'd been pretty sure that he'd just marry Anne, his high school sweetheart, when he finished school and took a job. For a while there he'd guessed that it would be OK to be a coach and teacher. Practice teaching put an end to that idea; it seemed like he'd been put in charge of a day care center for children of the criminally insane. Teaching was out and dental school seemed like it was worth a shot. He had nothing else planned. Now a job was four years further down the road.

Anne had just gone on and taken a real job and a divergent path. She'd accepted a job teaching English and coaching basketball at Wayzata High School, way out in the western suburbs. She was busy with her new life and didn't seem to have much time to hear about what he was doing. Although she still claimed to be interested in a future with him, Grant suspected that a shared past was all that held them together anymore. Anne was beautiful, and good to him, but in those moments when he really thought about all this stuff, he knew that she'd come to feel like an old glove that didn't fit anymore. That fire had gone out. He tried to push that idea out of his mind whenever it appeared, but his life was here now, and it would be for several years.

His emotional good-bye with his father flashed through his mind, too. While Grant was piling things into the trunk of his car, about to leave for dental school, Big Ole had stood beside him. "I'm more proud of you than if you were going off to play for the Twins," he'd said. Grant had never seen his father weep, and he still didn't know what to think about that.

At least it was a clear September morning. The rising sun was splashing a little extra color onto the trees along University Avenue, and the familiar smell of burning leaves made him think of home. The sky would be a little bluer and the grass a little greener for the next few weeks while the seasons changed.

He could do this, he reasoned to himself, when he looked at the crowd gathering around him. He'd find a way to succeed here in school. He'd just work harder than everyone else, like he always did. And the thing with Anne? Well, he'd think about that some other time. Damn, how *had* he wound up here? Maybe John Lennon was right when he'd said that life is what happens while you're waiting for something else.

Just a shade over six feet one, Grant Thorson had the square, well-defined shoulders and narrow hips of a young man who'd only recently grown into his physical prime. His backpack full of books hung on one strap over his right shoulder, and when it began to slip he raised his shoulder to readjust the weight. He glanced to his right and saw that most of the other people standing there beside him wore blank expressions, obviously lost in thought, or maybe just stuck in neutral while they waited for a chance to cross the street.

The crowd began to push itself closer to the crosswalk. Grant recognized a couple of his classmates. He didn't know all their names yet, but one of them had worn leather pants to school a couple of times and Grant had overheard people making fun of the guy—his name was Paul Zoch. Grant looked away quickly.

Several pretty girls drifted into the crowd and Grant tried to get a thorough look at them without staring.

Then he shifted his gaze across the rest of the human flotsam that continued to coalesce by the crosswalk and noticed Will Campbell, the kid from Duluth that everyone liked so much. Everybody seemed to know Will Campbell. Grant had never spoken to him, but he'd heard that Will had graduated from Harvard.

Will was still about thirty feet away when he made eye contact with Grant, smiled openly, pointed at Grant, and nodded in recognition. Grant nodded in return, then looked away, wondering once again if everyone here was smarter and better than him.

The crowd began to close in and Grant felt someone pressing up against his left arm. He turned to look and found himself nose to nose with a woman. He'd noticed her twice during his first week of classes. Both times she'd been standing by a bank of vending machines, talking with several male professors. Her long, dark hair and happy smile had captured his attention from across a crowded cafeteria. She was young, not much older than him, and she was always sharing lunch with the graybeards on the faculty. She'd just seemed so out of place over there with those old men. Now she was inches away, smiling, and he didn't quite know what to do.

She had to be a doctor or a professor or some such thing. Their worlds would certainly never intersect, but nonetheless he'd found himself staring at her in the cafeteria and wondering what she might be like. Her light blue eyes were set in the soft white skin of her face, and surrounded by all that dark hair. She was nearly as tall as he was; she looked to be six feet. Now she smiled as if they were old friends. "Hi," she said.

"Hi," Grant replied with an easy smile, and the woman turned away from him. Well, that went pretty well, Grant thought to himself. She seemed to recognize him, and he'd spoken to her, sort of. He stared at the back of her head and thought she was even prettier now than she'd been a few minutes earlier, before she smiled at him.

The light changed and the woman stepped off the curb into the crosswalk. Grant stood on the curb for just a moment and watched her from behind as the second unusual thing about this woman captured his attention. When she walked, her left leg was stiff as a board. Her shoulders bobbed a little, and she swung the leg with each step. A steel brace extended from her pant leg and held her left shoe. She had such a beautiful face, with soft, pleasant lines, and he couldn't help but notice her full breasts, and that she had the posture of a runway model. But the leg thing. What was that?

She'd changed from simply a pretty face to an enigma. Who was she? The blue eyes, the long, dark hair, the soft skin, the figure, that friendly smile, and now the vision of her walking across the street were all juxtaposed in one suddenly mysterious woman.

The surge of the crowd pushed him into the crosswalk. He'd have to let go of this little pitter-pat in his chest. The dark-haired woman had simply smiled at him to be polite. He'd never talk to her again. His thoughts began to drift ahead to the 8:00 a.m. Dental Anatomy lecture, and the woman vanished into the crowd. He held the strap of his backpack while he wove his way through the human traffic. Biochemistry, Gross Anatomy, and the correct contours of the facial and lingual surfaces of the maxillary incisors drifted through his head as he crossed the busy street.

Hundreds of students, teachers, doctors, nurses, and clinic employees were moving about as Grant began to climb the concrete steps that rose from the Washington Avenue sidewalk to a small plaza just in front of the school. He was pretty sure that he'd have time to review yesterday's notes from his Dental Anatomy class, so he reached his left hand over his shoulder to his backpack and began to unzip the main compartment.

The zipper stuck for a second, then opened, and Grant reached into the backpack in an awkward twisting motion. As he withdrew a thick folder, his left foot failed to clear the third step from the top and he stumbled. He was out of control and headed for a hard landing on the concrete steps when he instinctively threw his left hand out to help regain his balance. Every sheet of paper in the folder flew into the air as he thrust his hand toward the step.

His Dental Anatomy notes were flapping about his head and shoulders while he watched his left hand strike the concrete. He saw his thumb roll over the back of his hand, and he felt the pain like a lightning bolt. "Fuck!" he yelped. At the same instant, his right foot failed to clear the next step. He landed with all his weight on his right elbow and right knee, and he felt the concrete erase skin from both as he tumbled to a stop.

The pain in his left thumb was breathtaking, and he knew his other hand was certain to be scraped and bleeding. But in that brief instant right after he'd fallen, the only thought that came to him was that two hundred people had just watched him fall like a clown, and they were trying not to laugh. He must have looked like he'd been thrown from a moving car.

He bounced quickly to one knee in a vain effort to recover some of his dignity. If he allowed the pain to show, that would only make the embarrassment more intolerable. He'd just pick up all the papers as quickly as he could, stuff them into his backpack, and tend to his wounds once he was inside the building.

His thumb hurt so badly he could hardly close his hand. Then, as he grabbed at some paper and winced in pain, the worst possible thing happened.

A brown shoe with a steel brace connected to it appeared beside his aching hand. "Are you all right?" the blue-eyed beauty asked in a motherly voice. She began to pick up the debris scattered around his crash site and her efforts only intensified his shame.

Oh shit! He wished he'd just been run over by a bus instead of this. It was bad enough to stumble. But he'd actually taken a fall, and he'd gone down flailing. Now it really hurt, and he was struggling to just hide the pain. Jesus, it was embarrassing.

Why did this woman have to be the one who stopped to help? She was the *one* person in the crowd he would have selected to miss the spectacle he'd just made of himself.

"Yeah, I'm fine," Grant gasped, as he closed his left hand over the paper. Neither his voice nor his eyes could hide the pain in his thumb.

"Here. Here's the rest of your stuff," the woman said as Grant stood up. She pushed his wrinkled notes into the backpack and then surprised him when she took his right hand in hers and looked at the open cuts that were beginning to bleed.

"I've got some bandages at my office on the sixth floor," she offered. Then she turned the blue eyes toward him. "I know you're a dental student, I've seen you around."

She did recognize him! That took some of the pain away. Her hands felt like satin. Her fingers were long and elegant and her touch was soothing. He wanted to just stand there for a while and have her hold his hand.

"Naw," he said with the best grin he could muster. "I think I'll just crawl under a rock somewhere and die of embarrassment. But thanks for the offer."

She smiled a warm, sympathetic smile and said, "I fall down sometimes."

They turned and walked together toward the glass doors for a few steps. The woman swung her leg as she walked, and she shifted the books she was carrying so she had her arms folded across her chest. "Yeah, I fall down sometimes," she said again without looking at him. Her tone was pleasant, but she'd shared a bit of her own pain. Maybe she hadn't meant to, he couldn't say for sure, but he liked her more with each passing second.

When they reached the school building Grant made a point to open the door for her, but he grimaced and whimpered softly when he used his left hand.

"Thanks," she said. "You're a gentleman. Hope your day gets better." She smiled that gorgeous smile and brushed past him.

"Thank you," Grant said. She was so close that he noticed her scent. He closed his eyes and breathed in heavily through his nose so he could hold on to her for a moment longer. Then he stopped in his tracks and watched her walk that irregular walk over to an escalator and glide away to an upper floor.

To hell with cadavers, and biochemistry, and molars, and his throbbing thumb. He breathed in her scent once more, then walked toward a different escalator. "Damn! Who is she?" he mumbled to himself, then stopped and glanced up for another look at her.

He made a fist with his left hand, to see if he could move his thumb without pain. Then he stretched his neck to catch one last look at the woman on the escalator as Will Campbell walked past him from behind.

"Smooth!" Campbell said, without stopping. He kept on walking and turned to look at Grant after he'd stepped onto the down escalator. "Get into some bad mushrooms, did you?"

Grant could only smile. Will Campbell was funny. He tried to give Will the thumbs-up signal with his left hand, then grimaced in pain. Campbell laughed and disappeared in the opposite direction from the dark-haired woman.

~: CHAPTER 3 :~

Several dozen subdued conversations mingled to create an easy background noise in the preclinical laboratory. One hundred forty-nine dental students sat at their assigned laboratory seats, elbows resting on the workbenches, working diligently but chatting with those nearby while they carved blue dental wax to duplicate the exact size and contour of a maxillary central incisor.

The two-and-a-half-hour laboratory period would be ending in about thirty minutes, and the students were anxious to finish the assignment and receive a grade for the afternoon's work.

One student, however, sat with his chair turned so that his back rested against the workbench, arms folded and staring into space.

"You OK?" Will Campbell asked when he slid his chair next to Grant's.

"No," Grant said, without looking or uncrossing his arms.

"What's the matter? You look like you're gonna cry."

"I just got my grade on this." Grant turned the side of his head toward the blue wax tooth resting on his lab bench. He hardly knew Will, but he was angry enough to say exactly what was bothering him.

"So?" Will smiled.

Grant looked at him. "That asswipe Dr. Rettig went out of his way to humiliate me in front of the other guys; asked me if I didn't understand the assignment." Grant leaned forward in his chair now. He was growing animated. "The miserable prick squashed the first tooth I took up there. Said it looked like a blueberry. Dropped it on the floor and stepped on it. Took me an hour to remake it. Rat bastard! Then he gave me a C minus."

Will leaned over and examined the project Grant had just completed. "Looks pretty good to me. Really good!" Will said as he looked at it from several angles. Then Will and Grant both stole a glance at Dr. Ebverret Rettig III.

Dr. Rettig sat at the center table in the laboratory, looking at a central incisor that had been carved from blue wax by a freshman dental student. Rettig studied the carving as if it were a microscopic crime scene while a terrified-looking young man stood next to him. The kid shifted his weight from one foot to the other and waited for Dr. Rettig to humiliate him, as he'd done to every other student so far.

Ebverret Rettig had been director of preclinical studies for as long as anyone could remember. His thin gray hair was cut short and he looked to be about sixty-five years old. Upperclassmen had grumbled their contempt for Ebverret Rettig since the day classes had begun. Will and Grant had already heard dozens of Ebby stories from sophomore dental students. He'd grown famous in the dental school community for mean-spirited appraisals of his students' work. Every dental student in the building referred to him disrespectfully, but behind his back, as "Ebby." The name was often breathed with palpable malice. Ebby never seemed to have anything to say that might help a student, only snide and hurtful criticism, and this freshman class had already grown to fear and loathe him.

"I thought maybe your work was suffering because of that face-plant you took on the way to school today, but hell, your work looks better than mine," Will said. He looked back at Grant, shrugged, then reached over and snatched Grant's blue wax tooth from his workbench. He turned and walked directly to the center table where Dr. Rettig was seated, then waited his turn to have an evaluation.

Suddenly it dawned on Grant that Will planned to present *his* work for a grade. If Will actually did this they'd both be guilty of cheating, wouldn't they? Will was about to hand in work that Grant had done. Somebody had to be guilty of something. This was not good.

While he was still seated at his lab bench, Grant made eye contact with Will. He turned his palms up and used his eyes to beg for an explanation. Will nodded, winked, and then passed Grant's work to Dr. Rettig when he extended his hand.

"Shit," Grant hissed as he turned back toward his desk and tried to hide his face. This guy just didn't get it! Now what? What if Ebby recognized the work as Grant's? Would someone get kicked out of school? Grant had to look away.

Grant began to snap his head sideways and steal quick glances at Ebby. The old man was taking a lot of time examining the wax tooth. He had to know what was happening. "Great. This is just great," Grant whispered to himself. "This guy is gonna get me kicked outa school, and I don't even know him!"

Minutes passed while Ebby turned the tooth back and forth in his hand. Then he said something to Will and returned the tooth to him. Grant tried to turn away, but he couldn't. He studied Will for clues as to what had just happened while he watched him return.

As Will walked back toward Grant he began to smile. He placed the tooth on Grant's workbench, sat down beside him, and said, "Thanks, Pard! I got an A."

"You're shittin' me!" Grant barked, and jumped up. Several heads, including Dr. Rettig's, spun quickly to see who'd said it.

Grant lowered his voice, but couldn't hide the anger when he added, "I'm gonna go tell that prick he just gave the same project two different grades."

"No you're not," Will said. Will put his arm on Grant's shoulder, then guided him back into his chair. Both of them had their elbows resting on Grant's workbench, and their foreheads were almost touching when Will began to share his insight on the whole incident.

"Here's the deal, as I see it," Will began softly. "There's a hundred 'n fifty A students in this room. If you weren't a top student you wouldn't be here. But the old-timers who run this place think that God wants them to grade us on a bell-shaped curve. You know, a few As, a few more Bs, a lot of Cs, then some Ds, and finally a few Fs. I know it makes no sense, we've all proven that we're A students." Will paused, then asked, "With me?"

"Yeah."

"Well, how do you get a bell-shaped curve if you have all A students taking the test?"

Grant stared, then shrugged.

"If you asked these guys straightforward questions, designed to teach them the principles you'd discussed in class, well, everyone would get an A, and we can't have that!" Will grinned. "So, instead you ask a bunch of stupid, ambiguous, trick questions designed to confuse the class, not educate them." Will raised his eyebrows and smiled. "And when you grade stuff like *this*"—he held up the wax carving—"well, it's pretty subjective, so you just make shit up! You just give good grades to whoever you want to, and you arbitrarily downgrade the others." Will shrugged. "Pretty soon that bell-shaped curve shows up and the professors are happy."

Grant's eyebrows tightened when he replied. "Yeah, but . . . Ebby . . . the prick . . ." Grant sputtered.

"He just doesn't like your face; he wants you to be one of the C students, so you're just fucked," Will said softly, smiling a devious smile. "Sounds like there're a handful of guys like that in each class. I'm guessing that Ebby just ignores the sheep, you know, the timid little followers who do whatever he says? But he really goes after guys like you who challenge him. Probably make things easier for you if you don't get in his face over the little stuff anymore." Will waited for that thought to settle in, then added, "Remember that little quiz we took last week?"

"Yeah."

"What grade did you get?" Then before Grant could reply, Will added, "I'll bet you got a C, right?"

"Yeah," Grant admitted grudgingly.

Will raised his eyebrows, nodded, and leaned back in his chair. "That's how Ebby decided to make you a C student, forever."

"That was just a five-point vocabulary quiz!" Grant spoke as if he were pleading now. "And the two questions I got wrong were both . . . well, I learned in elementary school that you can't use a word to define itself, and that's exactly what Ebby did, so I changed a couple answers, and . . ." His voice trailed off.

"That was elementary school, where the teachers are professionals. This is dental school, where most of the teachers are flunky dentists, losers who can't make it in the real world," Will said.

"Yeah, but Ebby . . . what a shitty teacher." Grant was mired in frustration, and he ground to a stop.

"You're a C student now, Pard. Nothing you can do about it. Ebby knew he was gonna give you a C before you brought your tooth up there. And now he's gonna ride your ass until the day you graduate. That's just the way it's gonna be."

Grant sighed heavily, then slumped into his chair. "What'd *you* get on that little quiz?"

"An A. I'm an A student." Will grinned.

"But you handed in my work, and got an A," Grant said, as though he might understand better if he heard himself say it. "Not fair, goddammit. Not fair! Ebby made me feel like shit, then gave you an A . . . for my work!"

"Listen, Pard," Will began. "A long time ago somebody apparently decided that the way to make dental students into great dentists was throw dog shit at them for four years, like a four-year fraternity hazing. You figure it out. I don't get it, either." Will gestured toward Dr. Rettig. "I think they had a contest to try to find the most miserable prick in the profession, and of course Ebby won. Then, after a brief satanic celebration ritual they appointed him director of preclinical studies, where he could do the most harm."

Grant looked up at Will and began to smile for the first time.

Will nodded his agreement with himself, then added, "Don't worry about it! You do nice work, better than I can do. You'll be fine. You're just gonna have to eat some shit and pretend you like it. 'Sides that, you know what they call the guy who graduates last in his class, don't you?"

"What?" Grant asked.

"Doctor!" Will said.

They both chuckled softly for a moment, as Grant's anger drifted away.

The kid from Duluth was a breath of fresh air for Grant. Will had just made him feel good about himself for the first time since classes had begun, and his explanation had provided some illumination; made him laugh, too. He could see why everyone liked Will.

Will straightened his back and was about to stand up when he noticed something across the room. He smiled, pointed with his glance, and said, "Just be thankful you're not her!" Then he gestured toward Darcy Wilhelm.

Darcy was one of a handful of women in the freshman class. She was short, a little pudgy, and not very attractive, but she seemed to think that all the men in class were lusting after her. She was not gifted with the good hands required for a delicate profession like dentistry, she talked all the time, and when she was with a group of classmates she never seemed to fully understand what the others were talking about or why they might be laughing.

Darcy's head was down, and she was talking to herself and working feverishly to complete the day's assignment when Will and Grant looked at her. She happened to choose that moment to look up from her workbench and make eye contact with them. Will and Grant nodded hello, and Darcy returned their greeting with a friendly nod.

"Nice. Really nice," Will chuckled as he waved to Darcy. Her face was covered with tiny blue wax shavings from the tooth she was carving, and she didn't know it. She looked like a happy toddler sitting in a high chair, eating blueberries with her hands.

Both men laughed softly and turned away when Darcy looked back at her project and started talking to her hands again.

"What do you think she's saying over there?" Grant asked.

Will stared for a moment, then broke into his impression of Darcy Wilhelm. "She's talking to her hands, like a football referee giving instructions during the coin toss. You know: 'Cap'n Right Hand, this here is Cap'n Left Hand. Cap'n Left Hand, this here's Cap'n Right Hand. Now I want each of you to pick up an instrument and start carving wax to beat hell. No stabbing each other, no slashing, and try not to poke me in the eye, or fuck up this assignment. OK, now let's get out there and have a good day in preclinical lab.'"

Grant covered his mouth and listened to Will while he watched Darcy work and talk to her hands.

"Wanna stop down to Stub & Herbs for beer later, Pard?" Will asked.

"Sure thing, Doctor," Grant replied.

A friendship had been born. No introductions had been necessary.

❧ CHAPTER 4 ❧

A crowd of students straggled into the lecture auditorium just before an 8:00 a.m. Dental Anatomy lecture. Most were carrying coffee cups and chatting while they looked for a place to sit.

Grant was sitting alone and flipping through notes from the previous day's lecture when Will appeared beside him. "Hey, Pard. Mind if I sit with you?" Grant was glad that Will had sought him out, and he moved his books to make room.

"Ready for the quiz?" Will smiled.

"Sure thing," Grant replied.

Twenty minutes later, however, when Dr. Rettig returned another five-point vocabulary quiz, Grant's face darkened. The class was looking over their own papers when Dr. Rettig spoke up. "All right, class. Let's go over these terms once more."

"Dr. Rettig!" Grant stood up and interrupted. "My second-grade teacher taught us that it was incorrect to use a word to define itself. But you've done it *again*. Twice."

Dr. Rettig looked up into the audience in the silent amphitheater and found Grant. He stared for a moment, then looked back at his own notes resting on the podium in front of him. He cleared his throat and began to review the quiz, as if he hadn't heard Grant's challenge.

After Dr. Rettig had spoken for several seconds, with his head down and staring at his notes, Grant understood that he was going to be ignored. He shrugged his shoulders, sat down once more, and folded his arms while a tiny murmur of subdued laughter drifted through the lecture auditorium. He looked to his right and noticed that Paul Zoch, the guy who wore the leather pants, was snickering, and he wanted others to notice him laughing at Grant.

A moment after Grant returned to his seat, Will leaned over and whispered into his hear, "Nice one, Pard. I told you not to do that shit. Next time why don't you just wind up and hit yourself in the nuts a few times. That'll get you about the same amount of satisfaction as talking to Ebby."

~:~

"Jesus, when it rains, it pours," Grant said several hours later, when Will found him standing next to the vending machines during lunch. Grant pushed a few coins into a machine, waited for a sandwich to drop, and scowled at Will.

"Why, what happened now?" Will asked, before turning his attention to the vending machine in front of Grant. "You gonna eat that shit? Those are World War Two surplus sandwiches, you know," Will said. He pointed at Grant's bologna sandwich while he put money into a different machine and waited for a paper cup to drop and then fill with coffee.

"You wouldn't believe it." Grant studied the sterile, bland-looking triangular assemblies of bologna and white bread for a second, ignoring Will's comment about his sandwich. "I went to see if I could test out of Histology. You know, I aced it last year as an undergrad, and the first week's material has been all review, so I asked if I could test out of it."

"Yeah?" Will didn't look up. He watched the coffee flow from the vending machine into his cup and waited for Grant to continue.

"So the prof said 'sure,' then gave me the same final exam he gave to last year's freshman class. Said if I got 75 percent he'd give me an A for the semester and I'd be done."

"Sounds fair," Will said as he blew on his coffee.

"Yeah, I thought so too. Then about ten minutes after I handed it in he called me to his office and told me I got a 74, so I'd have to take the course again."

"Bummer," Will offered. "Close but no cigar, eh?"

"Yeah, sorta pissed me off, but I figured that's the way it goes," Grant replied.

"So what's the problem?" Will asked.

"As I was leaving, Paul Zoch walked in and asked to do what I'd done."

"The asswipe with the leather pants?" Will interrupted.

"Yeah," Grant said. "Anyway, the prof gave him the same test he gave me, but told him he could use the book *and* his notes from last year. The guy got a 77; three more points than I got, *and* he got to use the book! He's out, but I have to take it over! *Not fair!*" Grant's voice was growing louder as he spoke. "Jesus, what do those guys do? Stay awake at night and think of new ways to jerk us around?"

"So what're you gonna do?" Will asked with a grin, and waited for Grant to reply.

Grant thought it over for a moment. Then his face bent into a smile and he shrugged. "Go off somewhere and hit myself in the nuts, I guess."

"Now you're talkin'," Will said, and the whole incident seemed to slide away from Grant. "Hey look," Will added. "There's Darcy Wilhelm over there all by herself. She's got a flower in her hair today, too. Very fetching. And look at that! She's sittin' there all alone, eatin' and talkin' to her lunch, just like she talks to her lab projects."

Grant turned so they were both facing Darcy's table.

"Now, what do you suppose she would say to a bagel and cream cheese?" Grant asked.

Will raised his hands in front of his face and began what Grant thought was another pretty clever impersonation of Darcy. "OK, Cap'n Bagel," he said to his left, "this here's Cap'n Cream Cheese. Cap'n Cream Cheese," he said to his right, "this here's Cap'n Bagel." He turned back to his left hand, "Cap'n Bagel, you have won the toss, would you like to receive?"

They both chuckled, but as he was about to open the plastic wrapper around his sandwich, Grant let on that he felt sorry for Darcy. "We shouldn't be laughing at her. She's got the hands of a blacksmith. Dentistry is gonna be hard for her." He paused for a moment. "She does seem to think she's a pretty hot number, but the guys in class laugh at her behind her back already. She's gonna go through four years of dental school and not make any friends," Grant said. "Let's go over and sit with her."

"Sure," Will replied, and he glanced at his own hands. "Cap'n Coffee and Cap'n Sandwich," Will said to his lunch, "please follow me."

"I'm guessing she could use a friend," Grant said while he lifted his book bag onto his shoulder. "I heard Ebby wipe his feet on her just before lunch. Almost had her in tears. Somebody should tell that miserable prick to lay off."

Before either of them could take a step toward Darcy, a voice from behind them joined the conversation. "He's standing right over there. Speak up a little and you can tell him yourself."

The dark-haired beauty with the blue eyes was standing so close that

Grant could smell her again, and she was smiling just as she had out on the street. "Might want to lower your voice a little," she said as she put her coins into the vending machine. She'd been standing behind them and overheard everything he'd said.

"Yeah, sure," Grant said as he began to slink away from the vending machines and toward Darcy's table. He didn't know just where the pretty woman worked, and now he feared that she was a friend of Ebby Rettig. "Thanks," he said over his shoulder with a sheepish smile.

"It's OK," the woman said. Then she leaned close and added, "Nobody likes Ebby." She looked at Grant for a moment, glanced at Darcy, and added, "You *are* a gentleman!" She took her coffee from the machine and turned back toward several professors waiting for her.

Darcy Wilhelm was still spreading cream cheese onto her bagel when Grant and Will sat down at her table. She had a peach-colored flower stuck in her hair and she appeared to be trying for the look of a native Polynesian woman who'd just paddled her canoe over to a three-masted wooden ship for lunch. Grant thought she looked ridiculous.

"Hi, Darcy. How's it going?" Will asked as he slid his chair next to hers.

She was thrilled that a handsome young man like Will would approach in such a way, and when she smiled, Will couldn't help but notice two small shavings of blue inlay wax on her cheek.

"Hold still," Will demanded. He reached over and flicked the blue wax shavings off her cheek. "You must have been carving up a storm, Darcy." He smiled and showed her the wax. "Probably walked right over here from the lab, huh?"

"Yeah," she said. She brushed her cheek in case any more shavings were left. "I got my project done just before lab ended, but Dr. Rettig wasn't in a very good mood."

"He's never in a good mood," Grant offered, before he started his sandwich.

"Yeah, that's true," she agreed, then changed the subject. "Hey, are you guys going over to the kegger tomorrow night at the Sigma Delta house? It's supposed to be a big one. I just heard they had four kegs of beer on ice already."

"Yeah, I was planning to take my wife over there and introduce her to some of the people I've been telling her about," Will said.

"You're married?" Grant blurted. "You never told me that."

"You never asked," Will replied.

"How long you been married?" Grant shot back.

"'Bout three months," Will answered.

"No shit. How 'bout that, Cap'n Sandwich?" Grant said to his bologna sandwich.

Will and Grant were lobbing questions and answers back and forth over the top of Darcy. And now Darcy was clearly disappointed that Will was already taken. She seemed to lose interest in him, and in the questions Grant was asking him.

"How about you, Grant? Are you married?" Her question carried the implication that she could accompany him to the kegger if he was, in fact, not already taken.

"No," Grant shook his head, "but I have a steady girlfriend." Then he turned his attention back to Will and fired another volley over the top of Darcy. "Married, huh? No shit?" He stared for a moment. "Maybe you and your wife would like to meet Anne and me somewhere before the kegger? We can get to know each other." Then Grant remembered his manners. "You should join us too, Darcy. Got a boyfriend?" He already knew the answer.

"No," Darcy replied as she slid her chair back and got ready to leave. She'd pretty much lost interest in Will and Grant. "I think I'll go a little early and mingle. See you guys in lab." She stood up and left.

Will watched her walk all the way out of the room before he spoke. "A frat house kegger; med students, dental students, and a couple hundred undergrad party animals. I'm looking forward to watching Darcy work that crowd in search of a boyfriend." Then Will looked back at Grant. "You never told me you had a girlfriend, either."

"Well, it's been sort of a rough stretch for us these last couple months," Grant said. "But we'll have fun tomorrow night."

Will chose not to comment on the uncertainty in Grant's eyes.

⁂

The smell of formaldehyde made its usual assault on Grant's nose when he opened the hallway door that led into Jackson Hall. He was a few minutes late for the start of Gross Anatomy Lab and his footsteps echoed in the hall as he hurried toward a large room filled with busy students and cadavers.

An unforgettable visual image had been burned into Grant's memory on the first day of Gross Anatomy lab, and it played over and over again whenever he walked down this hall.

The entire freshman class had been led this way on the first day of school. They'd been guided into a large room with a squeaky wooden floor. Every red brick in the old building smelled like it had been immersed in formaldehyde. As the students eased themselves slowly into the Gross Anatomy lab on that first day, they'd noticed long rows of stainless steel coffins. They crept through the open door and slowly dispersed themselves along the outside walls of the room while they waited for instructions from the professor.

A vague fear that just maybe the cadavers were going to start moving around in those steel coffins pushed the students against the outer walls on that first day as they inched their way deeper into the laboratory. A team of four students had been assigned to each cadaver. The teams all approached their cadavers tentatively, then peeked inside their assigned coffin and spent a moment staring in wonder while they introduced themselves to a deceased person who would shape most of their freshman studies. Grant would never forget that first day.

Today Grant was buttoning his white lab coat and looking around for his dissection partner, Ben Pribyl, as he approached the table where his cadaver lay. That first, scary day in Gross Anatomy lab now seemed to have happened long ago.

Grant's group had chosen to work in groups of two. Carol Knutsen and Jimmy Drahota alternated with Grant and Ben in about ten-minute intervals. One of them would do the dissection while the partner took notes and the other team observed. Then they'd change places and let the other team dissect.

"Hi, Grant," Jimmy said when Grant stood beside him. "You guys are up in about five minutes. Ben's over by the window, smoking." He nodded toward a bank of large old sash windows on the west wall of the lab. "He's going to get in trouble for smoking in here."

"I don't think Ben is too concerned about the minor rules, is he?" Grant answered. "I'll talk to him about it." Grant turned and walked toward Ben, then said over his shoulder, "Holler when it's our turn, Jimmy."

Ben Pribyl was emerging as the leader of Grant's dissection group. He helped the others on his team study and take notes, but he studied from his notes only. A little older than the others, he was meticulous at dissection, and he recorded his observations in an intricate system of notes and drawings. But when he was not directly involved with the dissection he often wandered around and studied other cadavers in the room, or went to a window and smoked cigarettes. He was unafraid of challenges, and he didn't seem to be bothered by the petty rules or vague motives of the faculty. Ben remained distant, slowly allowing those he'd selected to ease into his circle of friends. He selected Grant immediately, and each day he allowed Grant a little closer look at his world. Grant liked Ben and enjoyed the relationship that was developing.

"Hey, Ben," Grant said when he reached the windows. "We're up pretty soon."

"Hi, Grant," Ben said softly.

"You're gonna get in trouble for smoking in here, you know," Grant added.

Ben couldn't summon the energy to even roll his eyes to show his ambivalence toward the no-smoking rule. He simply stared at Grant for a second.

"Just trying to help," Grant shrugged.

Ben changed the subject. "I noticed there're some fine-looking young ladies in the Dental Hygiene class. I think you and I should go on up to the hygiene clinic and volunteer to be patients up there!" He nodded, then continued. "That'd be a purdy good way to meet some girls, wouldn't it?"

"I have a girlfriend," Grant offered. Ben looked at him as if he'd mentioned smoking again.

"So what? You know those young college girls; they can be a lot of fun. We're gonna have to go on up there and meet a couple of 'em."

"OK you guys, you're up!" Carol called to them.

Ben and Grant walked to the cadaver and studied what Carol and Jimmy had just done. Then Ben lit a cigarette, took a drag, and gently placed it between the index and middle fingers on the cadaver's right hand. "Hold this, will you?" he said to the cadaver, as he took a scalpel in his right hand and began to enlarge an already lengthy incision in the old man's chest.

"Jeez, Ben!" Carol said.

"It's OK, Carol," Ben said without looking up. "Cigarettes already killed this guy once. He's in no danger from that one."

"You're gonna get in trouble," Carol admonished.

"I don't think so," Ben replied. "OK, Grant," he continued without hesitation, "this here is the outer layer of the lung, and if you watch, I'll bet I can lift it away . . ."

Ben dissected and talked for almost fifteen minutes while the others took notes. He stopped several times to have a drag from the cigarette he'd entrusted to the cadaver. When he was done with his turn at dissection he stopped, looked at Carol, and said, "OK, you guys are up." Then he walked to the sash windows and rested his elbow on one of the windowsills while he looked down on the human traffic walking along the sidewalk.

"Hey, darlin'," he called down to a pretty girl on the street, and he waved to her.

"Nice work over there," Grant said when he'd joined Ben by the windows.

Ben didn't look up. He stared down at the street below them for a moment, then turned an agitated, angry face toward Grant. "You hear that?" he asked.

"What?" Grant shrugged and stepped back.

"That guy talkin' over there." Ben scowled and pointed.

Grant looked where Ben was pointing. "You mean Paul Zoch?"

"Yeah." Ben scowled. "The dipshit who wears the leather pants."

"That's the guy!" Grant smiled. "What'd he say? I didn't hear anything."

"Oh, he's over there tellin' his buddy, the big guy, all about Vietnam." Ben tossed a malevolent glance as if challenging Zoch to look back at him. "'Cept he doesn't know shit!"

"You were in Vietnam?" Grant asked.

"Yes," Ben answered. He was angry, perhaps insulted, that someone who hadn't been there would presume to tell others about Vietnam.

"What'd you do?" Grant asked, then added, "And forget that guy, he's a dickhead. What'd you do?"

"Special Forces," Ben replied.

"You mean the Green Berets?" Grant was incredulous.

"Yes."

"No shit?"

"No shit," Ben replied.

"So you ran around in the jungle blowin' shit up? Like John Wayne?" Grant asked.

"Not exactly." Ben almost smiled. He lit another cigarette. He thought Grant's reference to John Wayne was funny and he began to let go of his anger toward Paul Zoch. "Hi, darlin'," he called down to another coed on the street.

"How long were you there?" Grant asked.

"Two years," Ben replied casually.

"So did you ever kill anybody?" Grant paused. "Is it OK for me to ask you stuff like that?"

"Sure, you can ask about it," Ben said. "And yeah, I did my duty. He took another drag on the cigarette and then flicked it out the window. Before the butt hit the ground below he turned to Grant and said, "I'll be right back. I'm gonna go over to the hygiene clinic and make appointments for you and me to get our teeth cleaned tomorrow, so be sure to wear clean underwear," and he walked away. Grant was staring at Ben's back, trying to let the last incongruent parts of the conversation sink in, when Ben looked back over his shoulder and added, "I'll be back in ten minutes."

CHAPTER 5

Two dozen people sat in the sixth-floor lobby outside the dental hygiene clinic. Standard procedure required each hygiene student to step out into the lobby, call out their patient's name, and then escort the patient back into the clinic to take a medical history and clean their teeth.

Grant and Ben sat next to each other in overstuffed chairs, waiting for a student to emerge from behind the clinic doors and call their names.

"OK," Grant said. "I heard that in order to be in the Green Berets you had to know a second language. What was yours?"

"Think I was bullshittin' you?" Ben asked with a grin.

"Maybe," Grant replied. "What was it?"

"Norwegian," Ben said with a much bigger smile. "Didn't do shit for me, either."

"I suppose not." Grant laughed. "Not so many Norwegian-speaking Vietcong, huh?"

"Hardly any," said Ben.

Young women appeared through the clinic doors one at a time, then read names from pieces of paper in their hands and waited for their assigned patients to walk over and introduce themselves. Roughly half of the patients waiting in the lobby had been called when the clinic door swung open once again, and a petite, dark-haired girl entered the lobby.

Ben nudged Grant with an elbow. "Holy shit! Look at that," he whispered. The girl had dark brown eyes, a deep tan, and long hair. When she lowered her eyes to look at the paper in her hands, Grant thought she looked like a deer fawn. She looked so innocent, so beautiful. Her waist was tiny, but she looked as though her breasts might burst though the white clinical coat she was wearing.

"Grant Thorson?" she called out.

Grant turned a satisfied grin toward Ben, then stood up and walked over to meet his hygiene student. "Hi, Grant, my name is Tanya Miller," she said when she shook his hand. "Please follow me

Grant couldn't resist looking over his shoulder and flashing a farewell smile at Ben before he walked through the double doors into the dental hygiene clinic.

Thirty-two dental chairs had been arranged in groups of eight. The clinic was bright and bustling. As he walked and looked about the clinic, he brushed shoulders with a good-looking male student who was also wearing a white clinical coat. He didn't really think much about the young man; he was busy watching Tanya's rear end as he followed her to her dental chair.

Then, from out in the lobby he heard the young man in the white coat call out, "Ben Pribyl?" Grant smiled and he spun around just in time to see Ben shaking hands with the kid in the white coat. Poetic justice, Grant thought. He knew exactly what Ben's reaction would be to drawing the only male dental hygiene student in the class.

Tanya took Grant to a dental chair, sat him down, draped a paper napkin around his neck, and began to explain what she was about to do. Her long eyelashes and perfect nose and round face made it hard for Grant to listen to her. But he did notice the male hygiene student walking past in the hallway with Ben in tow, just outside the cubicle where Tanya had seated Grant. Grant looked at Ben, who scrunched his face up as though he was squinting into a bright light, and mouthed the word, "Fuck!" as he walked by.

Another good story to tell later, over a few beers, Grant thought. He settled back, tried not to laugh at his good fortune, and let the lovely Tanya place her soft hands on him while she counted his teeth, made notes about his old fillings, and then prepared her hygiene instruments.

"OK, Grant," Tanya said in her luscious voice. "You can tip your chin up and open wide now." Grant raised himself up in the chair and opened wide. When Tanya moved close to him he felt her breasts press against the top of his head. He thought of Ben briefly and wondered how his visit was going, but he decided not to think about Ben Pribyl now. He tried to concentrate on those perfect breasts that were massaging his scalp.

A lightning bolt struck in his gums! Then another! His body tensed and he couldn't help but flinch and grab at the armrests on the dental chair.

"Try to relax and stay open," Tanya coached. She stabbed him twice more in rapid succession. He could hear Tanya's steel instrument scraping along the side of his lower teeth. Then the instrument slashed at his gums again and he could taste his own blood. Tanya reached for the little vacuum cleaner, rinsed away what seemed like a pint of blood, and sprayed ice water on the newly exposed root surface of his lower front teeth. "Try to stay open," she repeated.

The instinct to flee and thereby survive was powerful, but Grant overcame it, adjusted his posture, and tried to make this easy for Tanya. Despite the little voice in his head screaming at him to run away, he repositioned himself, then opened wide once more. Tanya began to pound and stab at his teeth as if she had no idea there was a person attached to those shredded, bleeding gums.

From time to time Tanya would try to talk about the weather, or current events. She seemed to talk about herself a lot, too, Grant thought. He could feel himself flinch every so often, and he really tried to relax. But he had no control over the flinching and sweating. Although he tried not to shrink away from her heavy touch, he couldn't help it. She just kept stabbing him. He began to sweat profusely . He tried to join the conversation with a whimper or a groan every so often. For the most part he only spoke when he felt his survival depended upon getting this girl to remove those jagged little flesh-ripping instruments from his mouth. He could feel the curved steel snag his gums, then slash through them every few seconds. Tanya also seemed to have the ability to send high-voltage electrical charges into his teeth with her metal torture devices. It was simply impossible not to flinch under her heavy hand. "Try to stay open," she kept saying. He wondered if she was doing this procedure with a cattle prod. He was no longer aware of those breasts moving about on the top of his head. His thoughts centered on endurance, and he noticed that his back and the backs of his legs had sweat through his clothes onto the chair. He was almost ready to fake a medical emergency, or simply run away screaming, when Tanya announced that she was finished. Thank you, Jesus! Grant thought.

When she stood up and went to look for a professor to check her work, Grant was certain that the hand of God had reached down and driven her away. He'd been spared any more wrath at the hands of the beast.

Grant took several deep breaths in an effort to calm himself. It felt like battery acid was throbbing though his pulverized gums. He looked around in search of Tanya, but when he couldn't find her he reached over to the small saliva vacuum, brought it to his mouth, and watched it suck a red syrupy gob from between his lips and down a clear plastic saliva ejector tip. This wasn't supposed to happen, Grant thought. He closed his eyes and waited for Tanya to return with a professor. It felt like she'd cleaned his teeth with a six iron and a grain auger.

"Hey! It's you! How's your thumb?" came a voice from just behind him. It was the woman with the blue eyes and the leg brace. She must be the professor that Tanya had gone looking for, he thought. She sat down in the chair that Tanya had been using, and put some papers on the countertop beside her. Grant looked around, in search of Tanya, then answered before Tanya returned.

"The thumb feels a lot better than my teeth!" Grant tried to joke. He hoped this woman wouldn't notice the real pain in his eyes, or the fact that he'd been sweating profusely.

The woman tipped Grant's chair back and examined his mouth in order to check Tanya's work. After a thorough exam, she sat the chair upright so Grant could turn and look her in the eye. "Your gums are pretty inflamed," the woman said.

"They should be. I just took a beating," Grant said. "Maybe you should encourage Tanya to move on to an alternate career path. Perhaps counter-terrorism . . . you know, using her God-given talents during the interrogation of known criminals. Or maybe the construction business . . . I hear they're always looking for good bricklayers. She's a rough one!"

The woman smiled, then changed the subject. "My name is Kate Bellows," she said as she extended her hand. "Nice to finally meet you . . ." —she looked down at the papers on the countertop and searched for his name—"Grant."

"Nice to meet you, too," he replied. "You're a dentist?" The touch of her hand was even more soothing than before.

"Yes. I work in biomaterials. Doing some research. I also work here in the hygiene clinic one day every week. You'll have me for a couple lectures next year." She looked around briefly, then asked, "Did you come up here today to meet girls?"

"No, but my friend did, so he made me come with him," Grant replied, then he felt a sense of despair. He'd met the beautiful woman, found out where she worked, and now he knew her name. That was good. But she was older, and she'd certainly have male friends and male colleagues with money and position. She was already part of a whole different social stratum; she was connected. She was better than him, and now she probably viewed him as a contemporary of this young girl who'd cleaned his teeth.

"Well, you sure got to meet a pretty girl today. Tanya is a knockout," Kate said.

"I bet she wishes she was you," Grant blurted, then regretted his words immediately. People like him weren't supposed to say things like that to people like her.

Kate looked uneasy for a moment, like she didn't quite know how to respond. Then the male hygiene student appeared, said he was finished with Ben, and asked her to come and give him a grade for his day's work in the clinic also. Kate stood up, shook Grant's hand again, and smiled politely when she said, "Well, good luck with your studies. I'm sure we'll see each other around school. Watch your step!" Then she walked away.

She looked like one of those hair models on TV, the ones who would shake their heads to send their long hair swishing in slow motion. He breathed in and tried to hold on to Kate's scent. He wished he hadn't said what he'd said; he was embarrassed now. But for a fleeting second there, it seemed like Kate liked what he'd said.

~: CHAPTER 6 :~

Several missing bricks and several more broken ones out on the fraternity house patio gave it a disheveled appearance to match its reputation. Every light in the three-story brick house appeared to be on, and people carrying beer in plastic cups were wandering all over the front and back yards. Two large speakers outside the front door throbbed with loud music that drifted far out into the warm September night, while a group of ten or twelve young men stood around a keg of beer on the front porch.

"That guy there, the one standing by the door? I know him. He's a senior in dental school. He's the one we pay," Grant said as they walked up the sidewalk toward the well-worn old house. Grant was reaching for his wallet when Will stepped in front of him and gave the big man in the door six dollars.

"This is for the three of us," Will said, and then pointed to his wife, June, and Grant.

"Here's your cups, have all you can handle." The man raised his voice over the loud music, then handed each of them a plastic cup and filled it with beer from the keg. "How's it goin', Grant?" he said as he finished filling Grant's cup.

"Pretty good, Dommy. How 'bout you?" Grant asked.

"Really good. Think I might join the navy! If I practice for a few years in the service they'll pay off all the school loans. Not bad, eh?" The man grinned for a second then added, "Hey, how's Ebby treatin' you guys?"

"He's a dickhead, Dommy!" Grant said.

"That's no shit, eh? Stop back later and we'll talk," the big guy said. Then he turned to the half dozen new arrivals standing behind Will and Grant at the front steps and raised his voice. "Two dollars each! And try not to puke in the house, eh?" He turned his meaty face toward June and winked at her as she walked past him and into the house.

June Campbell was a fine-featured, petite young lady with sandy-colored hair. She had a pretty face, like the proverbial girl next door, and she looked a little out of place at a frat house kegger. She clung to Will's right arm but said nothing as she looked around at the loud, but as yet not too drunk, crowd of dental students. All of them could feel the vibration of the music.

"How do you know that guy?" Will asked Grant.

"Dommy?" Grant grinned. "Dominic Sabetti . . . Dommy! All those Italian guys have great names." Grant sipped his beer, then added, "He played hockey for the Gophers; he's a senior dental student. He was friends with a couple guys I played ball with. He's from Eveleth. Great guy!"

"You played football here?" Will asked.

"Baseball. Well, I was on the team. Didn't play much," Grant said.

"No shit! Me too! Well, I played for two years at Harvard, but the writing was on the wall. Everybody was better than me. So I just let it go. Quitting baseball was one thing I regret. I miss it."

June led them on a meandering path through the crowd and into the loud and smoky frat house living room where the couches had been pushed against the walls. She stopped and turned to Grant. "I'm really disappointed that Anne couldn't come tonight. I was looking forward to meeting her. I hope she feels better soon."

Grant sighed. "I think she was just tired. You know, she just started her teaching job about a month ago. I tried to talk her into coming over here and meeting my friends, but . . . you know." Grant looked away, and June shot a questioning look at Will. It was obvious to both of them that Grant was disappointed, maybe a little angry that Anne hadn't come. The look on Grant's face when he'd explained her absence hinted at the rest of the story: they'd probably argued because Anne didn't want to come with Grant tonight, and now he was making an excuse for her.

"Maybe next time," June offered. "Or maybe the four of us can do something together next weekend?"

"Yeah, that'd be good . . . ," Grant said without much conviction. His words hung, a sentence that hadn't been finished. Both Will and June waited for him to continue, or to change direction.

"Hey! You hosehead!" someone yelled from across the room, and Grant was spared the discomfort of a long pause. Will, June, and Grant all shifted their attention to the other end of the living room where two young men seemed to be greeting each other. The two clearly had been drinking for some time. They toasted each other and then chug-a-lugged until their beer cups were empty.

"That little guy would be Moe Babich," Grant said. "He lives here at the frat house with Dommy. That's how I got to know him. Also from Eveleth. Unusual for a little town like Eveleth to have two boys in the same class at the dental school," Grant offered as they watched Moe laughing. "I don't know who that other guy is."

"Moe?" Will asked.

"It's actually Deion. So naturally he became Moe," Grant said, shaking his head to indicate that he didn't get the nickname either.

"Makes perfect sense to me," Will said.

Moe spotted Grant and hollered, "Grant! How's it hangin', eh?"

Grant waved and nodded in reply. Moe was about to make his way toward Grant when someone grabbed his arm and spun him back to face the small group he'd been talking with. "No wonder I didn't feel good, there was puke in my stomach!" he hollered.

The group roared in laughter while Moe made his way over to greet Grant.

Will leaned over toward June and said, "He's an upperclassman, honey. So he's been studying all that digestive-system stuff."

June tried to scowl at the crude humor but she was having a hard time not laughing at Moe also.

Moe was still chuckling at the way he'd delivered the old joke to a new audience when he reached Grant, Will, and June.

"Great party, eh?" Moe bellowed.

"Oh yeah! Gonna have a big crowd tonight, Moe!" Grant reached one arm around Moe's neck, then introduced him to Will and June. To their surprise, Moe morphed into a perfect gentlemen for just a moment while he shook June's hand and welcomed her to the fraternity house.

Will looked Moe over for a split second, then asked, "You play hockey, too?"

"No, I abandoned the trappings of youth and decided to dedicate all my energy to the pursuit of academic excellence." He raised his glass to Grant, and both of them chuckled. "So how's Ebby treatin' you guys?" Moe added.

"Still a dickweed, Moe," Grant sighed.

"Yeah," Moe agreed. "I wouldn't piss on that guy if he was on fire! That reminds me. I gotta go drainna boa! I'll catch you guys later." With that, Moe turned and walked away.

"OK, honey," Will said so that both June and Grant could hear him. "Here's the Eveleth-to-English translation on that last colloquialism. 'I gotta drain the boa' actually means, 'I am great with urine and I must micturate immediately.'"

She put her fingers in her ears and looked away.

"It's getting too crowded and smoky in here; let's go out to the back-yard," Grant said, then he led Will and June to a short brick wall in back of the frat house where the crowd was, as yet, still fairly quiet.

Grant thought he was going to like June. She'd tried not to laugh at Moe, but he'd seen her give in and smile several times. Grant thought Moe was always pretty funny, but when he'd been drinking, the banter he served up often devolved into a string of obscene insults and suggestions for anyone within earshot. He'd been raised on Minnesota's Iron Range, and he'd spent his young life listening to some truly creative swearing by older teammates. He'd arrived at college armed with a spectacular vocabulary of dirty words, and he seemed to be on a mission to discover new and creative combinations. He particularly enjoyed discussions about bodily functions, sex, and fighting—preferably fights during or after hockey games. Grant thought he was a poet. He'd first come to think of swearing as an art form several years earlier when he'd heard Moe and Dommy trying to outdo each other in a barrage of filthy epithets during a frat party just like this one. He chuckled now at the memory of that night. He didn't understand why, but it made him feel good that his new friend's wife might actually appreciate the beauty of dirty language at a frat house kegger.

A September full moon was casting shadows across the backyard when the three of them found a quieter place to sit on the brick wall next to an alley. Grant took a sip of his beer and winced. His gums were still throb-bing from the beating he'd taken at the hands of the lovely Tanya Miller, and his teeth were now so sensitive to cold that he'd have to let his beer warm up before he tried another drink.

"So why did you decide on dentistry?" Grant asked Will.

"Dunno," Will said between sips of beer. "Guess I just wanted to do something that would allow me to come back and live in Duluth, and I didn't want to go to law school."

"Why not law school?"

"I value my soul, and I have personal integrity. The law was a bad fit for me."

June smiled at Grant, then sipped her beer.

"How 'bout you?" Will asked.

"I don't know, either. I guess it was because a couple buddies on the baseball team said it was impossible to get into dental school."

"So you did this because you thought it might be too difficult?" Will asked. "Like someone had dared you?"

"Yeah, I guess that's about right." Grant shrugged. "Didn't want to get a job just yet, either. Guess I wasn't ready to turn off this road just yet."

Will smiled, tipped his head back, and finished his beer. "Hey, Pard? You want another beer?" he asked Grant.

"No, I'm not done with this one yet," Grant said.

"Well, get me one too, will you?" Will said, with complete disregard for Grant's answer, handing Grant his empty cup.

Grant took Will's cup, smiled, gulped the last of his room-temperature beer, and asked June if she'd like something more before he walked to the keg.

The backyard of the frat house was beginning to fill up with partygoers when Grant returned with three more beers. "You'll never guess who I ran into," he said when he passed one of the beers to Will.

Before he could tell them, a familiar female voice called from the crowd on the sidewalk. "Hi, guys! What's happening?"

"That would be . . . Darcy?" Will said while he cupped his hand behind his ear and listened for more.

"You are correct," Grant answered.

"Hey! Here I am!" Darcy said as she walked toward them with a beer in one hand and a folding paper fan in the other. She'd decided to accessorize her outfit tonight. "You suppose she has blue inlay wax shavings on her face?" Grant said quietly, while he waved to her.

"No. But I think she wants to meet June, and then introduce her to Cap'n Beer and Cap'n Dorky Paper Fan," Will said as he waved to Darcy also.

"I don't get it," June said, then questioned Will with her eyes.

"I'll explain later," Will said.

Darcy's dress was, as usual, all wrong. She wore a skirt that was entirely too short and seemed to have been picked to accentuate her stumpy legs and thick ankles. Her white cotton blouse strained across her ample midriff and she'd decorated it with what looked like spaghetti sauce just above her left breast. To top it off, the paper fan didn't match anything.

"Hi, guys!" she repeated when she reached them. "I'm Darcy Wilhelm," she added when she made eye contact with June. "Will's probably told you about me."

"Yes. He has! Nice to meet you, Darcy. I'm June, Will's wife."

"Nice fan!" Will interjected. Grant felt a little catch in his throat when he tried to stifle a laugh at the same instant he was about to swallow some beer.

"Thanks. It's Korean."

"Humph. I'd 'a guessed Japanese. How 'bout you, Grant?"

"You look nice, Darcy," Grant said. The stain above her breast was like a flashing beacon and he couldn't look away from it. No matter where else he tried to look, his eyes darted back to her breast. "Do you have a date tonight?" he asked, then held his cup of beer up high enough that it blocked his view of the stain on her breast.

"No, I came by myself tonight," Darcy replied, as if tonight was an exception, and that she usually rolled into frat house keggers with her steady man.

All Grant could think of was the stain by her breast, and he tried mightily not to peek over his beer cup to get another look at it.

"Well, I have to go." Darcy smiled. "I guess there's supposed to be a whole bunch of upperclassmen here tonight! Nice to meet you, June. See you, Grant." And she was off to mix with the growing crowd.

"Jeez, did you guys notice that spaghetti stain by her boob?" Grant sighed. "I couldn't look away."

"Yeah," Will agreed. "It was hard not to stare. You know, she's a nice person. But she's a mess, and not much to look at. I'll bet her parents had to tie pork chops to her ears in order to get the dogs to play with her."

"Will!" June snapped. "That wasn't very nice!"

"Sorry, honey, but . . ."

"I know what you meant, " Grant smiled, then added, "This time you go get some more beer."

"So, I have to ask you something, June," Grant said when Will was out of earshot.

"What's that?"

"How do you feel about all this?" Grant looked around him. "I mean Will being in dental school, and busy all the time? And not home very much."

"Well," June started, "sometimes I resent the fact that you get to see him more than I do. And I don't always like it when he comes home from school and talks about you; he tells me how you're getting to be such good friends." She paused for a moment while she considered what she was about to say. "But we're trying to make an adventure out of this time in our lives." She looked at Grant and paused again. "Will's father took us aside when we told him we were going to get married before Will started dental school. He told us that it would be very difficult for us because we're both going to change, to grow up, over the next couple of years. And we'd better be careful to grow up together instead of growing away from each other. He said this would be hard for us, and to stay close. So that's what we're trying to do."

Grant had no idea how to respond to June's words. It was as if she knew he was seeking some insight into his issues with Anne. June had accurately described the thing that had already happened between him and Anne, and no amount of wishful thinking could fix it now. He nodded his head and waited for a moment before he changed the subject.

The crowd continued to grow for an hour while Grant, Will, and June sat on the brick wall and conversed. Classmates wandered by and chatted for a few minutes, usually about what an asshole Ebby Rettig was, then moved away when someone else drifted over.

"Hey, Pard. There's Ben Pribyl," Will said. He nudged Grant and pointed into the crowd. "Hey, Ben!" he called.

When Ben turned around he was holding hands with Tanya, the dental hygiene student. Just the sight of her made Grant's mouth hurt again. Ben waved and immediately began to walk toward the little brick wall where Grant, Will, and June were sitting. Tanya recognized Grant and waved to him.

"She's a doll!" June said.

"She's an ax murderer," Grant replied.

"What?" June and Will said in unison.

"She cleaned my teeth this afternoon . . . with a hammer and an ice pick. Beat the shit out of me. I'm getting the cold sweats just looking at her," Grant said. Then his tone changed completely when Ben and Tanya were close enough to hear him. "Hi, Ben. How's it going, Tanya?" he said pleasantly.

Ben introduced Tanya to Will and June, and when June asked Tanya something about herself Ben leaned close to Grant's ear and whispered, "You were right!"

"Huh?" Grant asked for clarification.

"She's a rough one! We went out for a drink after clinic, then went over to her place. She's a scrapper!" Ben smiled and flicked his eyebrows twice. "Thanks for setting me up with her." Then he added, "She thinks you're a pussy, by the way."

"Glad I could be of assistance," Grant said.

"You know," Ben said, as if he couldn't believe what he was about to admit, "that guy who cleaned my teeth was pretty good. Never hurt me once! Nice guy, too." Tanya began to tug on Ben's arm and let him know she wanted to move along.

"Nice to meet you," she said to Will and June. Then, over her shoulder, Tanya added, "Bye, Grant," and the new couple slipped away into the crowd.

"Bye, Tanya," Grant said. Under his breath, he sighed, "I hope I'm able to chew again in a week or two."

The party was gathering momentum, and Grant was about to walk over to the keg and ask Dominic Sabetti to refill his cup when the crowd parted for an instant and he noticed Kate Bellows. His back straightened and he bolted forward to be sure it was her. God, she was pretty! She was standing by the keg, talking to Dommy and holding a plastic cup full of beer. She was wearing blue jeans and a light blue jacket, and Grant couldn't look away.

The guy standing next to her put his arm around her waist and Grant stood quickly to get a better look. He was tall and well dressed. He had long blond hair and seemed to smile all the time. Just the kind of guy he thought she'd be with. But Grant suddenly felt like the guy was taking something away from him or using something of his that he had no right to. He felt a nasty rush of anger. Hell, he was jealous, and the feeling surprised him. He barely knew the girl's name, and she was way out of reach.

"I'll be right back," Grant said. Leaving Will and June, he started walking directly toward the keg, then he altered his course so he could approach the keg in such a way that Kate would see him coming. When she finally looked up and noticed him, she smiled and waved. His heart fluttered just a bit, and he tried to create the illusion that meeting like this, beside the keg, was pure chance. "Hi," he said. Then he moved as close as possible to Kate while he refilled his plastic cup.

The other guy still had his arm around her waist when Kate spoke to Grant. "How're you doing?" she asked, pointing to her mouth. "I mean, your teeth."

"Well," Grant started, "the bleeding has stopped." He finished filling his cup and shut off the tap. "But I'll need some therapy to help the nightmares. Tanya walked by here just a minute ago and I lost control of my bladder."

Kate tipped her head back and laughed out loud. Grant felt a wonderful sense of satisfaction he'd never quite felt before. He was responsible for that laughter. He'd put that smile on her face. Strange as it seemed, it felt like it might be one of the great accomplishments of his life.

When her laughter subsided she stepped toward Grant. Her date's arm fell away from her waist, and she brought her lips to the side of Grant's face. She was about to share something with him that she didn't want anyone else to hear, and he lowered his face toward hers. When her mouth was close to his ear he smelled her scent again. He loved the feeling that she thought he was special enough to move close to him in this way. He hoped others in the crowd could see them. When she was finally close enough to speak, he couldn't help but stare at the perfect way her shirt curved around her breasts. He moved a little closer to her, too, trying to stretch the moment. He noticed her long, thin fingers holding her beer, and remembered how soothing they'd felt only a few hours earlier when she'd touched him after his appointment with Tanya. He wanted to reach over and pull her close.

Kate paused as if she wasn't sure she should share what she was about to tell him, then said, "We call Tanya . . . ," she hesitated again "the Mauler." She was smiling again when she moved away from his ear.

"Yeah, well, that didn't work out very well for me, did it?" Grant pointed to Ben and Tanya, who were now fondling each other while they talked to some friends on the other side of the front yard. "But my buddy over there, he likes it when she's rough with him!" Kate laughed from way down inside once more when she looked over and saw Tanya clutching Ben's arm. Grant hoped the people standing nearby were noticing that Kate Bellows liked him.

Kate was about to say more, when the guy she was with hollered the punch line of a joke and laughed along with the others in his group. He still hadn't bothered to cast a glance in Grant's direction when he pulled Kate back toward her other friends. A moment later, when Kate looked back to say good-bye to Grant, he'd turned away from her and was talking to Dommy.

"Do you know her, Dommy . . . that girl I was talking to?" Grant asked.

"Kate? Sure. She was in the class ahead of me. Really quiet, nice girl. She's on the faculty now."

Grant held his cup out for a refill. "'Zat her boyfriend, or what?" As he asked the question he turned to look at Kate. In that instant her date slid his hand down over the perfectly round curve of her butt and pulled her close. Grant wanted to run over there and punch the guy.

"His name is Rod Muir. Nice guy. Comes from a rich family. They own a bunch of barges on the Mississippi and Lake Superior. Lots of soybean-processing plants, too. A real shitpile of money. You wanna meet him?" Dommy asked.

"Hell no," Grant said. He turned to rejoin Will and June.

Grant had to pick his way carefully through the crowd to keep from spilling his beer. The front and back yards were filled to capacity and the crowd seemed to be swelling. Grant turned and twisted his way back to Will and June, but the unwanted mental image of some guy's hand on Kate's behind would not leave him alone. He began to think he'd rather go home than see any more of that.

"Judging from the current tempo and volume of this little soiree, I'd say it's only gonna be about an hour till somebody invites the police over here," Grant said, as he looked over the crowd. He truly didn't want to see that guy holding Kate, but he could not overcome the urge to look for her. Maybe she'd smile, or laugh, or brush her hair behind her ear. It didn't matter; he just wanted to look at her.

"Yeah, we should probably wrap it up here pretty . . . ," Will started.

"Her name is Kate Bellows," Grant interrupted, still scanning the crowd, oblivious to what Will had been saying.

June turned quickly toward Will, then raised her eyebrows and grinned.

"I just talked to her." Grant still hadn't looked away. He was bobbing his head and trying to catch a glimpse of her through the crowd, still unaware of the way Will and June were looking at him.

"Do you want to go talk to her some more?" June asked.

"Nah, we should go." Grant stood up, then added, "She's with some guy," as if that fact spoiled the end of his evening.

Grant, Will, and June were edging their way through the crowd when they came face to face with Moe Babich once more.

"You guys leavin'?" Moe barked, as if to accuse them of a crime. "Party's just gettin' started!" He began to weave slightly. The beer was causing some turbulence on the sea of Moe Babich.

"Yeah, well, I think we're gonna go home," Grant offered.

"You should stick around . . . ," Moe started, but he was interrupted by a small commotion near the keg, and the crowd noise receded noticeably when everyone turned to look.

Several huge young men were standing by the keg and they seemed to be talking to Dominic Sabetti. Judging from the size of their necks and shoulders, Grant thought it was pretty obvious that they were Gopher football players, probably friends of Dominic's. But there was an unfriendly air of confrontation, and a wiry little kid was squaring off in front of the biggest of the men. It seemed that some sort of a challenge had been issued.

"This is gonna be good," Moe said softly. "That's Dommy's little brother, he's a junior in high school."

"The big guy is gonna kill him," Grant said.

"No way in hell," Moe replied. "Just watch."

The big guy was probably six feet six and about 275 pounds, Grant guessed, while Dominic's brother was about five feet ten, maybe 160 pounds. They stared at each other for a moment, then the big guy pushed at Dominic's brother and caused some beer to splash out of the cup in his right hand. It didn't seem right for a high school kid to be drinking like this at a college kegger, and Grant stepped closer for a better look.

"Hey!" the little guy barked. He raised his left hand and pressed his index finger onto the big guy's chest. "You can kiss my ass, right where da sweat makes it red!"

"OK, honey," Will leaned over and said quietly to June. "I'll have to paraphrase this for you once again. What he really meant was . . ."

"Shut up, Will!" June said, then she smiled at Grant.

That was it for the big guy. He couldn't let some runty little high school kid talk to him like that. He lurched toward the Sabetti kid and tried to throw a punch with his right hand.

The little guy jumped back, dropped his cup of beer, reset his feet, and launched his left hand. The punch was lightning, and young Sabetti was up on his toes when it landed. When his hand connected with the big man's face, it sounded like a pot roast hitting a concrete floor. It may have been a one-punch knockout, but they'd never know. When the football player's knees buckled, Dommy's little brother hit him two more times with the same frightening speed before he could fall down. The big man toppled to the grass, holding his bloody face.

His two friends stepped toward Dommy's brother, who was now issuing them a challenge, too.

"That's enough!" Dommy said. He rushed in front of his brother and showed his palms to the other men. "Tark! Get outta here!" he barked over his shoulder. His little brother stood for a moment with his fists in front of his chest, motioning for the other big men to keep coming his way.

"You guys want summa that too? Well c'mon." He nodded and gestured for them to keep coming. "C'mon! I'll kick yer ass till yer fuckin' nose bleeds!"

"Tark!" Dommy bellowed. "Get outa here, or *I'm* gonna kick your ass!"

Still brandishing a defiant sneer, the little guy walked belligerently to the beer keg, filled his cup, and strolled into the frat house while the two big men tended to their bloody friend. The fight had simply been a hole in the party. It had opened briefly, and now the party closed round it again. In a moment it was as if the fight had never happened.

"Told ya," Moe laughed.

"Jesus! Who was that?" Will asked.

"Paladin Sabetti," Moe replied.

"Paladin?" Will chuckled.

"Yeah. Remember that old TV show, *Have Gun, Will Travel?*" Moe said. "Dommy's old man really liked that one, so he named the kid Paladin. I liked Lucas McCain better. You know, *The Rifleman?* Cool fuckin' gun."

"Stay with me for a minute here, Moe," Will begged. "Didn't his brother call him something else just now?"

"Yeah. Tark. That's what they call him. Tark," Moe answered with a nod.

Will scrunched his face and shrugged. "Why? He's Paladin, but they call him Tark?"

"We started playin' hockey back when we were little kids. He was just a tagalong runt kid brother, but he was faster and better than everyone else. The Gophers are all over that kid, by the way. They want him to play hockey here, bad! Anyway, his old man thought he looked like Fran Tarkenton scrambling around out there." Moe shrugged. "Started callin' him Tark, and it stuck." Moe finished yet another beer, then smiled. "Get it?"

"Makes perfect sense to me," Will said.

"Good. I didn't wanna 'splain it again," Moe said, as he turned to go talk to Dominic Sabetti. "See you guys later, eh?"

"Beer and testosterone make a volatile mixture," Will said to June and Grant. "I don't think that's gonna be the last fight here this evening."

"Yeah, it's time to go get a pizza," Grant replied, and they began to make their way toward the street. "After what Tanya the Mauler did to me, though, beer might be all I can chew for a while, but I'll give it a try."

When Will and June reached the quiet sidewalk and started walking away from the party, June took his hand in hers and smiled. "That was quite a party."

"Yeah. I'd say the big guy with no neck is gonna be looking for some aspirin about noon tomorrow," Will said. "Quite a party!" he added. Holding hands with June, he walked toward his parked car. "Moe, Dommy, and Paladin, too! How 'bout that, Pard?" he called over his shoulder. "Great names, huh?"

Will and June assumed that Grant was walking right behind them. But when he didn't reply to Will, they both stopped and looked back for him.

Grant was staring across the street, watching Kate Bellows walk away holding hands with her date. The handsome young man opened the passenger door of a silver Porsche, helped Kate get into the car, and then drove away. Grant stood and watched as if he'd been abandoned by an old friend while the Porsche's taillights disappeared around a corner.

~: CHAPTER 7 :~

During the first weeks of school, as Will and Grant became fast friends, Will developed a morning ritual that allowed him to ease into the two-and-a-half-hour Dental Anatomy laboratory sessions. He'd bring his coffee to Grant's lab bench and visit with him for a few minutes before he moved over to his own bench and go to work himself. The morning conversations usually moved back and forth from sports to sex, then maybe current events, and sometimes even dentistry.

On this morning, Will was offering a persuasive argument that Grant was trying to ignore. Will sipped his coffee, then put the cup down near Grant so he could share. Grant took a sip while Will started talking once again.

"It'd be easy to do it, you know. We'd just have to skip one Friday session up in Gross Anatomy lab and one Physiology lecture. If we left after school on a Thursday, we'd have all day Friday and Saturday. The fishing is great this time of year!"

"Yeah, but how do I make up the time I miss from class?" Grant never looked up from the blue inlay wax he was carving to create a mandibular first molar.

"Look," Will began to explain, yet again. "We're talking about one lecture and one lab." In need of something to do with his hands while he tempted Grant to skip class with him, he picked up Grant's wax spatula and held it in the flame of the Bunsen burner. He gripped the steel instrument by one end so as not to burn his fingers while he held it in the flame, then he continued with his rationale for a September weekend in northern Minnesota's lake country. "Besides, my parents have a cabin on the lake, where nobody goes. We'll have the place to ourselves. Night fishin' under the September moon. Big walleyes lardin' up for winter! Some people would pay big bucks to have an experienced guide like me."

"Not gonna happen, Pard. I wish I could do it, but I just can't miss any school. 'Sides that, you just want me to come along so I'll tell you secrets about fishing . . . and sex," Grant said, still concentrating on the wax tooth he was carving.

"We'll talk about it more," Will said. The wax spatula he'd been holding in the fire was glowing, and he set it down next to Grant's other waxing instruments without giving it another thought. Heating the wax spatula had been the equivalent of doodling with a pencil. He was certain Grant had seen him heat it nearly to the temperature of the sun. "We're going fishing, Pard. So start packing your stuff!" Will said, as he pushed his chair back and prepared to return to his own bench.

"Leave the coffee," Grant said without looking up.

"Start packing," Will reiterated over his shoulder as he walked away. The lab was filled with a low undertone from a dozen other small conversations.

Mired in a painfully laborious quest, Dr. Rettig was sitting at his center table, evaluating a blue wax tooth while stress oozed from a young man standing beside him. Twisting and turning it back and forth under his bifocals, as usual, Ebby was searching for some microscopic defect he could use to humiliate the anxious student waiting beside him. Will glanced over at Ebby and marveled at the man's diligence. He'd study that tooth until he found something to criticize, or else he'd just make something up. But he'd never hand it back to the student and utter something simple like "Nice work." He just couldn't do that.

Will slid his chair up to his bench and began to assemble the waxing instruments in front of him. He'd just propped open a book so he could study a large drawing of a tooth, and then he reached for his own wax spatula when a loud cry knifed through the quiet lab.

"Yeow! Fuck!" Grant yelped. He was standing up, actually jumping, while he shook his right hand. Everyone in the lab, including Ebby Rettig, stopped what they were doing to watch him.

He'd picked up the glowing hot wax spatula that Will had heated, then he'd thrown it reflexively, and it was now stuck in the ceiling of the freshman preclinical laboratory. Initially, Grant's dance had the appearance of some tribal ritual, but in short order he'd regained enough composure that he could walk in a tight circle and mutter swear words to himself while he shook his right hand. "Shit! Fuck! Goddamn!" he hissed.

He finally looked over at Will, who stared back blankly at first. Then, as he began to understand what had just happened, a smile spread over his face. He raised his left hand to cover his mouth, but made sure to let Grant see the laughter in his eyes.

"Asshole," Grant whispered when he sat down at his own bench again. Then he looked back at Will, and started laughing himself.

About one hour into the lab session, students began to stand up and move about. People would leave, one or two at a time, to get coffee or simply stretch their legs a little, then wander back in, so someone always seemed to be entering or leaving the lab.

Grant heard Will's familiar footsteps coming his way, but he didn't look up from his project, even when he knew Will was standing next to him.

"Burn your fingers?" Will finally asked.

"This one feels pretty good." Grant held up his middle finger, but still wouldn't look up.

"It's OK, I covered for you. I told Ebby you had Tourette's syndrome," Will offered.

Grant held up his middle finger again.

"Ah! Sign language. Like an Indian . . . with Tourette's!"

Grant began to chuckle, but still wouldn't look at Will.

"Wanna go get some coffee?" Will asked.

Grant nodded, then stood up and started walking, and Will followed at his side. "You're an asshole!" Grant said when they reached the doorway. He began to laugh, slowly at first, when he thought of the scene he'd caused. Before they reached the fourth-floor coffee shop they were both laughing out loud and recounting the incident.

~:~

Morning laboratory was nearly over when Grant began to put his things away and prepare for lunch. He'd had a productive morning, in spite of the blisters that had risen on his fingers. He smiled now, when he thought of Will, and those blisters, and his own fit of swearing.

Will had been right. He could do this work as well as anyone. He was going to make it. His grades were, in fact, among the top half of the class, and he was about two days ahead of his classmates in his laboratory work, despite the incident with the wax spatula.

Grant stood and walked to Will's lab bench, then waited for Will to put his instruments away. "Hey, Pard," Will said, closing several small drawers full of his supplies, then locking them. "I'm thinkin' we should go down to the Steak House for the ninety-nine-cent special today. How's that sound?"

Grant opened his wallet and looked inside. He had two one-dollar bills. "Nah, I better just eat what I brought."

"Peanut butter and Wonder bread?" Will grimaced.

"Everybody loves that. It's . . ."

Grant was interrupted by a growing disturbance on the other side of the lab. In a moment, scattered laughter began to spread across the room, but Grant could see no reason for the laughter as he looked around.

"Oh Jesus, look at that!" Will finally said with no humor in his voice.

Darcy Wilhelm had been using the dental drill at her lab bench while she worked on her project for the day. The dental drills used in the preclinical labs had only one exposed moving part, a small button that rotated in a clockwise direction at whatever speed the operator chose to run the drill. The rheostat controlling the dental drill rested on the floor, and Darcy had been using her right foot to control the drill when she'd leaned too close and caught her hair in the rotating, exposed button.

In the same shocking and sudden way that a powerful vacuum cleaner might accidentally suck up a cat's tail, the little button on the back of Darcy's drill had apparently snagged a strand of hair, and in a heartbeat the drill wound other hairs around itself, and then shot up to her skull, wrapped in a huge tangle of hair.

Darcy was hunched over and whimpering. She was still holding the drill in her right hand. The whole mess of hair, the dental drill, and Darcy's right hand were pinned against the side of her head. She was stuck.

All she could think to do was step on the rheostat again and again, which made the drill twist tighter. She looked like she was using the drill to lift herself out of her own chair every time she stepped on the foot control.

A mean-spirited rumble of laughter drifted through the male students sitting around her. If she'd been on fire, Grant doubted that any of her classmates would have thought to put her out. Will was still seated at his bench, staring, when Grant walked to her lab bench, surprised and disappointed that no one else came to her aid before he did.

"Darcy," he said calmly, when he reached her chair. "Relax. I'm gonna flip this switch so the motor on this thing runs backwards, and we're gonna roll it out of your hair."

Laughter had spread through most of the lab by now, but Grant could see that Darcy was crying. He knew that she was in pain from the little drill pulling at her hair. But more than that, Grant knew that Darcy could sense the way her classmates felt about her. This little incident was forcing her to face that reality.

She sobbed softly and waited for Grant to remove the drill from the snarl of hair on the side of her head. He simply rolled the little button by hand and unwound her hair from the drill. Several times he had to stop to pull a long brown hair loose from the drill, or from her head.

"There," he said when Darcy was free from the drill. He brushed her tangled hair with the palm of his hand. "Good as new."

Darcy put both hands over her face and ran from the lab, sobbing.

As Grant returned to his own bench he walked by the table where Ebverret Rettig III was seated, and one of the students next to Dr. Rettig said, "God, what a klutz!" Grant stopped in his tracks and spun to see who'd said the words. Paul Zoch returned his glance with a sneer. He'd been the one who'd been laughing the most while Grant was helping Darcy. She'd heard everything Zoch had said and she'd understood the contempt in his voice.

Grant walked to Zoch's chair. "Shut up!" he said. Then he put his index finger on Zoch's forehead. He pushed his finger as if it was the barrel of a gun, and Zoch's head rolled back about an inch. "She has feelings, you prick!" he said angrily.

The laboratory was absolutely silent as Zoch steadied himself in his chair, about to stand up and challenge Grant.

"Stand up!" Grant said. "Do it," he dared, "and I'll drop you like shit from a tall cow!"

Every student in the silent laboratory stared and waited for several agonizing seconds to pass. Grant was livid, ready to let the anger boil over. Then Zoch settled back into his chair after a moment of cautious reappraisal.

"That's what I thought . . . you're all hat, and no ranch," Grant said, and he walked away.

∽ ∶ ∾

A noisy lunch-hour crowd had almost cleared out of the fourth-floor coffee shop when Grant made his way down the empty hall. He'd spent an hour talking with Darcy, and he'd missed his lunch. Now he only had a few minutes before a 1:30 lecture in Biochemistry, and then a two-and-a-half-hour Gross Anatomy lab.

Darcy seemed to have recovered pretty well. He'd underestimated her. Grant could see that she'd spent a lifetime resurrecting herself after incidents like the one this morning. That was why she'd made it this far; she had the strength to come back from the kind of humiliation she'd suffered in lab. She'd be OK.

Grant went to a coffee machine and put his money in. When he had his coffee in hand he turned and walked, head down, toward the tables. He'd sit down and have his peanut butter sandwich and coffee by himself.

The cluster of empty tables over by the window seemed like a good place to sit, but when he looked up, there she was. Kate Bellows was sitting by herself at a small table. In fact, she was the only person in the coffee shop. For a brief moment, he thought about saying a pleasant hello and then sitting at a different table. But this was his chance. He had to sit with her.

He was still several paces away from her when she glanced up and noticed him. She grinned in recognition, and then reached over and started to reposition her papers and books to make room for him to sit.

"Join me!" she said when she looked at him the second time.

God, she was gorgeous. He feared he was wading into water that was over his head, but this was an opportunity that might not come again.

There were two chairs available at her table. One was directly across from her; the other was right beside her. She'd think he was trying too hard if he sat close to her, so he went for the chair across the table from her.

"So how's your thumb?" she asked.

"Pretty good," Grant said. He stood beside the table, wiggled the thumb for her, and smiled.

"And your mouth?" she asked. She was teasing now, and her eyes twinkled.

"Should be back to solid foods in a week or so," Grant said, pulling back the chair. As he sat down he added, "I felt like that detective in *Psycho*, you know, when Norman Bates was stabbing him and he was falling down those stairs?"

"She wasn't that bad," Kate said.

"I guess not," Grant admitted. He leaned forward and moved some of her things so as to get a better look at the four record albums mixed in with her schoolbooks. "What do you have here?" He lifted the albums and looked at them. "Paul McCartney and Jackson Browne. Who do you like best?" he asked, while he turned them over and looked at them.

"I don't know," she replied.

"Well, Paul McCartney is pretty good," Grant began. He spoke as if he'd given his own question years of thoughtful deliberation. "He seems like a nice guy, too. And he sure makes a pile of money. But on his best day, I mean the very best day he ever had, he's not Jackson Browne. There's a guy with some passion, makes you *feel* something."

Grant slid the LPs back underneath Kate's papers, then changed the subject. "So, are you friends with Dr. Rettig? I mean, I see you talking with him and a couple older guys all the time."

"No," she started, "I wouldn't say we're friends, and I didn't like him when I was a student, either. I just graduated last spring, so all the memories from preclinical laboratory are still fresh. But right after I graduated he started to treat me like I was a human being. He's really not such a bad guy once you get to know him." She leaned forward and rested her elbows on the table to emphasize what she was about to say. "In fact he was just here, sitting right where you are." She raised her eyebrows and grinned. "He told me what you did in lab this morning, with that Wilhelm woman in your class . . . the one who's kind of odd."

"So what'd he say?" Grant leaned forward, unable to hide a little fear and curiosity in his voice.

"Well, he wasn't very pleased," she replied.

Grant rubbed his forehead for a second, then asked, "So I'm in trouble?"

"I don't know," Kate replied. "Well, maybe," she teased.

"Great." He sighed and sipped his coffee.

"I caught my hair on one of those things when I was a freshman," Kate said. "It really hurt. I was so embarrassed. Everyone laughed at me, too. I felt like they all laughed because I was a woman, and they didn't think I belonged there in a class with all men. You know, like getting my hair caught in that thing proved to them that they were right in their feelings about me." She paused while she remembered the moment.

"Were you the only woman in your class?" Grant asked.

"No, there were two of us in the beginning, but the other girl dropped out right away."

"So why did you choose dentistry? I mean, it's sort of a man's world."

"Oh, I had some interest." Kate shrugged. "And maybe something to prove." She stared at the paper plate in front of her for a moment, then returned to her story about getting the drill stuck in her hair. "Anyway, I tried to act like it didn't hurt, like I wasn't embarrassed about having that thing stuck to my head, but it hurt me. I can laugh about it now, though." She looked up and noticed a smile spreading across his face.

"What?" Kate asked.

"Well, I was just wondering what you thought was funnier, you catching your hair in the drill, or me flopping around like a fish out there on the Washington Avenue sidewalk?"

"Oh!" Kate's face blossomed when she smiled. "You flopping! No doubt about it. *That* was funny. You know, you didn't just fall. You staggered, and skidded, and waved your arms!" She was laughing out loud. "I knew you were really embarrassed, and that just made it funnier." She leaned back and laughed. She was always so pretty when laughter curled the corners of her blue eyes and lifted her lips over those perfect teeth. And then in an instant her eyes filled with compassion once more and he caught a glimpse of who she really was.

Something had changed. Something subtle, to be sure, but something was there now, between them, that hadn't been there before. He'd seen it in the way she teased him. She'd taken a little extra joy in the teasing, the strange joy that people get only from a friend's embarrassment. Kate was offering something more than a passing conversation or sympathy to someone who'd fallen on the sidewalk. No doubt about it. A door had opened, maybe just a tiny bit, but it was open. Maybe Kate didn't even know it.

Grant was staring at her, just enjoying the view, when Will called to him from the hallway. "There you are! Pard, we gotta go! We're gonna be late for Biochemistry lecture." Will waited at the coffee shop doorway. "You comin'?"

"Be right there, Will," Grant said as he stood up. "Well, Kate Bellows," Grant said, "I'm glad I could brighten your day a little. Maybe we can meet like this again and pick at some of my other emotional scars." He smiled and added, "I gotta go."

"Wait," Kate said. She reached forward and took his hand. "That was a nice thing you did for the Wilhelm girl. You *are* a gentleman."

"Thanks," Grant said when he turned to leave.

"You're funny, too," she added.

Grant nodded, shrugged, and slid his chair back under the table.

"I'm sorry I laughed at you," Kate said.

She was arranging her things, getting ready to go back to work, and Grant stood there, watching. Before he could say anything, Kate began to laugh again. "No, I guess I'm not so sorry about that." She chuckled.

No wonder the old men on the faculty seemed to gather around her, Grant thought. She was gorgeous and funny and she made him feel special just by teasing him.

It was time to leave. Will was waiting for him. He could feel Will's eyes on him, and the pressure of Will's impatience.

No way, not just yet, he thought. Dr. Kate Bellows, the lovely lady dentist who would be his teacher next year, the dark-haired beauty who ate lunch and mingled with all the gray-hairs on the faculty, had just hinted that maybe, just maybe, he wasn't completely under the radar.

He turned quickly, pulled back the chair next to Kate and sat down close to her. "Can I call you sometime?" he asked with all the confidence he could muster. It was the most impulsive thing he'd ever done and his body temperature began to spike. If he thought about it a second longer he'd have been undone by his own self-doubt. Suddenly he wasn't sure if he'd made an embarrassing blunder. He knew his anxiety was showing while he waited for her answer.

"You're asking for my phone number?" she said slowly. She leaned her head back and to the side while she smiled. She was teasing again, and enjoying his fear of rejection. But she was trying to verify the request, too.

He pursed his lips and nodded. What if she told him to take a hike? That little whisper of encouragement still lingered on her face, but there was so much more that he just couldn't decipher in those eyes.

She slowly tore a scrap of paper from a notebook. Her eyes narrowed in a playful grin while she wrote her phone number. "I never gave my number to anyone before," she said as she offered him the folded paper. Oh Jesus, the door was definitely open. Definitely! It was all over her face, now.

"Yeah, well, I never asked for one before, either," he replied, as he stuffed the paper in his wallet next to his two dollars.

When he stood to leave he made eye contact with her. He planned to say something witty and clever, but no words would come. Instead, a relieved and triumphant grin tugged at the corner of his mouth and then spread. All he could do was bring his hand to his chest and pat it against his beating heart as he turned away and left. "Whew," he sighed, and then made a point to let her see him wipe imaginary sweat from his brow.

Several steps out of sight and walking briskly to get to the lecture on time, Grant turned to Will and laughed out loud. "I can't believe I just did that!"

"What 'ja do?" Will asked.

"Talked to her! Got her number." Grant shook his head.

"You mean like, 'Here's my number, call me sometime'?" Will asked.
"Yup!"

Will spun his head to look back at the coffee shop. "No shit! Nice work!" he said. Then he moved an incredulous stare up and down Grant and added, "She must live a lonely and desperate life."

~: CHAPTER 8 :~

The professor seemed to be talking about something, and apparently he thought all those molecules and equations he was drawing on the overhead projector were pretty interesting, but all Grant could hear was Kate Bellows's laughter. He tried to take notes, but the Biochemistry lecture going on in front of him was little more than a distraction. All he could see was Kate's face. As the class filed out of the auditorium, Grant looked over at Will and said, "Can I borrow your notes? I have no idea what I just heard."

"Sure." Will gave Grant his notebook. "Havin' a little problem staying focused?" he asked.

"Just thinkin' about Kate, I guess," Grant said, as he slid Will's notes into his book bag.

"I was gonna give you a nudge there a couple times," Will replied. "Looked like you might'a slipped into a coma. But I was afraid I might come down with diabetes if I touched you."

Grant looked back at Will and questioned him with his eyes.

"Sappiest, most lovesick, sorry-ass look I ever saw plastered onto anyone's face," Will said. "Every time I looked over at you my blood sugar spiked."

"I'll get your notes back to you tomorrow," Grant replied, and he drifted back to thoughts of Kate Bellows. He wandered along with the rest of the students toward the next class, and he grinned when he thought of Will's comment.

The familiar smell of formaldehyde confronted them as they turned into the hallway leading to Gross Anatomy lab. Most of the students already had their cadavers ready for the day's dissection and study when Will and Grant entered the room. There was a low murmur of quiet conversation, and someone laughed at something over on the other side of the room, but no one seemed to notice them.

"Hey, Pard, you know the lab is open after supper tonight for anyone who'd like a little extra study time. You think we should stay late tonight and go over some of these other cadavers so we'll be ready for the test next week?" asked Will.

"Sure," Grant replied. Then he walked directly toward the window on the west wall, where Ben Pribyl was preparing to light a cigarette.

"Gotta thank you for setting me up with Tanya last weekend," Ben said. "We hit it off right away. I didn't think I'd be interested in somebody that young, but I sure like her. We spent Friday and Saturday night together!"

"Sounds like true love, Ben," Grant offered.

Ben took a long drag on his cigarette and changed the subject. "We've gotta start reviewing the abdomen and the chest cavity before next week. Big test on Friday, you know."

Before Grant could reply, Will joined them at the window. "You OK, Pard?" he asked.

"I'm fine!" Grant replied.

"What's the matter?" Ben asked, unaware that Will was teasing Grant.

"Nothing. I said I'm fine," Grant said.

"He's in love," Will joked.

"You too? With who? I thought you already had a . . ." Ben's eyes narrowed in thought.

"It's the lady dentist," Will offered.

Ben's eyes narrowed further. "Really!" He stared for a second, then asked, "Dark hair? Brace on her leg?"

Will nodded.

"She's a professor, isn't she?" Ben asked. "She's the one from the hygiene clinic."

Will nodded again.

Ben exhaled a cloud of smoke. "She's gorgeous. What would she want with you?" he asked, as if Grant were nothing more than an old tire on the side of the road.

"Well, I believe that her status would still technically be 'The Other Woman,'" Will explained. "Although I'm still waiting for clarification on that, too."

Grant stared out the window and remained a nonparticipant in the conversation while Ben nodded, smiled, and looked him up and down. "Ah, one of *those* deals, huh? The eternal triangle, and somebody's gotta go, eh?"

He flicked his cigarette out the window. "Time for one more," he said while he lit yet another. "Hi, darlin'," he called to a pretty coed passing by on the street below.

"OK, lemme see if I understand this situation," Ben said. He leaned against the window frame, sat on the sash, and tried to look introspective. "This lady dentist from school here makes your heart go pitter-pat, doesn't she?"

"Pretty much," Grant said, without looking at him.

Will began to smile, and glanced back and forth between Grant and Ben. "I believe the word 'infatuation' might be a good fit here, but he's on the fast track to 'pussy whipped,'" he interjected.

"And the other chick," Ben started in again, "your old girlfriend, she's nice, but it's over with her. 'Cept she doesn't know, or suspect any such thing, right? You just don't want to tell her that it's time to stick a fork in the whole thing between you and her because, well, because you'll hurt her, and there were a lot of good times. Happy horseshit like that, right?" Ben stopped, then continued before Grant could respond. "*And*, you feel guilty because you've felt that way for a while but you didn't tell her because . . . ," he hesitated for effect, ". . . you're a chickenshit. 'Zat about it?"

Grant validated the truth in Ben's words with a steady stare.

"OK." Ben took a long drag while he composed his next few sentences and prepared to solve Grant's problem. "Can o' corn here, Grant." He exhaled a cloud of smoke and watched it drift out the window. "Here's what you do. You tell the old girlfriend it's over. 'Thanks for the memories; I'll always remember the good times, blah, blah, blah.' Tell her any kind of shit you have to. But get it done. You know it's a dead horse, now shoot it!"

Grant nodded. Will grinned.

"All right. Now here's the part you don't realize." He took another drag to emphasize what he was about to say. "She'll be happily married within a year after you drop this bomb. You're not the only guy on earth. She'll find some guy that'll make her eyes roll back in her head and forget all about you. Well, maybe she'll think about you when she gets into one of those warm and fuzzy moods that women do, but that's about all. And although you *do* want her to be happy and move on, you *do* want her to remember you, right . . . 'cuz you're a guy and you're kinda vain about stuff like that? So it works out good for everyone. Go tell her she's history! She'll thank you someday." Ben flicked the cigarette butt out the window and walked back toward the cadaver. Then he called over his shoulder, "Successful relationships? I've been in hundreds of 'em. I know how this shit works!"

Will grinned and waited for Grant to say something when Ben was gone.

Eventually, Grant shook his head and pointed at Ben with his thumb. "This morning over coffee he was showing me the carpet burns on his knees, from pushin' Tanya the Grim Reaper all around his love nest. Probably not the most sensitive guy, huh?"

"Yeah," Will nodded, "but I think he's got your situation figured about right."

Before Grant could reply, a young woman approached him from behind. "Are you Grant Thorson?" she asked.

"Yes," he replied

"Dean Muckinhern wants to see you in his office," the young lady said.

"Now?" Grant asked.

"Yup. That's why he sent me down here." She looked at him for a second, then added, "Eighteenth floor. He's waiting for you." She turned on her heels and walked out.

"Great." Grant sighed as he shook his head. "S'pose this is over the little confrontation in Dental Anatomy this morning?"

"Bet the farm on it, Pard." Will said. "You still want to stay here late and study tonight?"

"Yeah, I'll be back when he's done with me, if I don't get kicked out of school."

"It'll be OK, I'll be here waiting. We'll go have a couple beers when lab closes at 9:00, and you can tell me all about your love life, and the ass chewing you're about to receive," Will said.

∾⦂∾

The sign next to the door read Office of the Dean. Printed beneath was the dean's name, Dr. Frederick Muckinhern. The door was open and Grant took a deep breath before he walked through it. The woman who had walked all the way to Gross Anatomy lab to summon him was seated behind a large desk in the middle of a spacious outer office. "He's on the phone," she said, without much enthusiasm. "Have a seat and I'll let you know when he's ready to see you."

Grant nodded, but chose not to sit down. The walls of the outer office were covered with an odd mixture of trappings from northern Minnesota. An old pair of snowshoes hung on one wall, along with several nice fish, an ancient bamboo fly rod, and an even older canoe paddle. A large map of the Boundary Waters Canoe Area was posted on the wall behind a leather couch.

The outer office and the secretary were apparently shared by several other faculty members, but no one else seemed to be around. The place was silent, like a morgue . . . no students around, no talking, no laughing, just a surly secretary. A separate hallway led to two other offices, and Grant wandered slowly down the hallway to read the names on those doors. The first door had no name on it and was open, so Grant peeked through the opening.

Scattered across three small desks were spools of colored thread, patches of animal fur, and dozens of dried chicken pelts with multicolored feathers still attached, along with various intricate tools. Somebody up here, probably several somebodies, had been tying flies in that office for quite some time, judging by the clutter.

"You looking for somebody?" boomed a large voice just behind him. The man had approached so quickly and so silently that Grant hadn't heard him, and he flinched when the man spoke to him.

"I'm waiting to see the dean," Grant said.

"Well, you found him, son!" The man extended his hand and Grant took it. He was big and round and about fifty-five. He had sharp eyes and a pink, bald head. His handshake and his voice were warm and friendly. He seemed like the guy who lived down the street, like he might wander over and chat while you were outside cutting the grass.

"Joe Ruminsky," the man said. Grant recognized him as one of the men that he'd seen several times, talking to Kate.

"Grant Thorson," Grant said as he shook the man's hand. "But I'm waiting to see Dean Muckinhern."

"Oh. I thought since you were standing outside my office you were looking for me," the man said. Then he stuck a key into the other doorknob and unlocked it. He swung open a door that read Dr. Joseph Ruminsky, Dean of Admissions/Chairman—Oral Surgery. He hung his suit coat on a hook on the wall and sat behind his desk. "Looks like Fred's busy. Would you like to wait in my office?"

"Well . . . I . . . sure," Grant stammered. He stepped into Dr. Ruminsky's office.

"I saw you looking at our fly-tying room. Do you tie?"

"Yeah, but I was just wandering around. I'm a freshman dental student, and . . ."

"I know who you are. I processed your application last year. You're the baseball player," Dr. Ruminsky said. Grant liked this man immediately. He had power and status and yet he made Grant feel like an old friend.

"What are you doing up here?" Dr. Ruminsky smiled and arranged some things on his desk. He seemed genuinely interested in Grant.

Grant lowered his eyes. "I think I'm in trouble."

"Dean Muckinhern will see you now," the secretary said from just outside Dr. Ruminsky's office door. "He'd like you to join them, Dr. Ruminsky," she added. Ruminsky stole a quick glance at the nervous young man on the other side of his desk. He stood up, walked to the door, and said, "Follow me."

Dr. Fred Muckinhern was seated at his desk, waiting for them, and he motioned to the chairs in front of the desk. When Grant and Dr. Ruminsky were seated, he got right to the point. "Dr. Rettig called me over the lunch hour. He said that you threatened another student this morning? Is that correct?" Dean Muckinhern leaned back in his chair and waited for Grant's response. He was a little geek, Grant thought. Not much over five feet six inches with a slight build, thin graying hair, and square black frames on his glasses. Fred Muckinhern did not look like a man who should be the dean of a dental school at a Big Ten university, until he started talking. Then he looked like a man who knew that significant power had been placed on his shoulders and he wasn't afraid to use it. Grant saw no humor in his eyes.

"That would be true," Grant said. "Sort of."

"Would you like to explain?" Muckinhern asked. He didn't seem to have a lot of time for chitchat, either.

"Well, my classmate, a girl, caught her hair in her laboratory hand piece . . ." Grant stopped. "Did Dr. Rettig tell you that?"

"Yes. And it's happened before to female students," Muckinhern replied.

"Well," Grant started to explain, "you know how that kind of thing is funny sometimes, but sometimes it isn't?" Grant waited for Dean Muckinhern to answer, but when he simply stared, Grant continued. "Well today it wasn't funny. Darcy, that's her name, was crying. I'm sure it hurt her, it was really tangled up. I could see that she was crying, and really ashamed." Grant paused, and once again Dean Muckinhern waited for him to continue. "Anyway, a classmate said something fairly mean-spirited, and I, well, I did what I did. I threatened to kick his ass."

"Is she your girlfriend?" Muckinhern asked.

"Oh, jeez, no," Grant responded immediately and with a grimace, as if a foul smell had been brought into the room, and then shook his head. "She looks like ten miles of bad road, and sometimes I think she's dumb as a bag of hammers. But she's a decent person, and her feelings were hurt."

Dr. Ruminsky raised a hand over his face to cover a smile.

"Well, I guess it's commendable that you stood up for her," Dean Muckinhern started. "But Dr. Rettig recommended some sort of disciplinary action be taken. Can I assume that if we just let it go with this meeting, I've heard the last of this whole incident? This will be the end of it all, correct?"

Grant thought for a second, nodded yes, repositioned himself in his chair, and then spoke. "Probably, but if the same thing happened again tomorrow, I'd drag that kid outside and kick his ass. I just won't let that slide. I don't want to get in trouble, Dean Muckinhern. But I . . ." Grant stopped and looked at his feet. "You'll have to do whatever you think is right, too." His tone was neither defiant nor argumentative, but he remained steadfast in his promise to defend a woman's feelings, and he diverted his eyes from Dean Muckinhern after he'd spoken.

Fred Muckinhern took his glasses off and tossed them onto his desk. He rubbed his face with both hands, and shot a glance at Dr. Ruminsky. He was looking down at his desktop and still rubbing his forehead when he spoke again. "I'll tell Dr. Rettig that you and I talked it over. I don't want to see you up here anymore, Grant Thorson. Understand?"

"Yes, sir."

"Go on back to the lab," Muckinhern scolded, then added, "Thanks for your candor, young man."

Grant nodded and quickly left the room. When he was safely out of earshot, Fred Muckinhern turned to his old friend Joe Ruminsky and said, "I wish Ebby would just handle this stuff on his own and not send it up here for me."

"I like that kid," Ruminsky offered.

"Me too," Dean Muckinhern agreed. "He didn't try to bullshit or brownnose his way out of this. That was a breath of fresh air. And he wasn't afraid of me. That was unusual."

"I don't know, Fred. I think he was plenty scared of you. He just wasn't afraid to tell you the truth. That boy has some integrity." Ruminsky stood up and left Muckinhern's office, then turned around and thrust his round face into the doorway. "Know what else, Fred?" he asked.

"Huh?"

"Sometimes I think Ebby is dumber than a bag of hammers!" Joe Ruminsky turned and laughed all the way back to his own office.

~: :~

"Long damn day, huh?" Will asked Grant. They were the last students left in the Gross Anatomy lab. He looked at his watch and added, "Shit, it's after nine. I'm studied out and tired. I just wanna go home. Let's go for beer some other night, OK?"

"Sure," Grant agreed. "See you tomorrow." He watched Will walk out of the dissection room and listened to his footsteps as he made his way out of the building. All the other dental students were gone. Grant was alone with forty cadavers and one teaching assistant who was closing up for the evening. "See you tomorrow, Evan, thanks for staying late."

Evan, the teaching assistant, didn't reply but continued tending to all the cadavers before he lowered them back into their steel coffins.

The hallway was dark and silent as Grant made his way to the Washington Avenue exit. The only thought in his mind was the memory of Kate's face when she'd given him the scrap of paper with her phone number. As if on cue, he noticed a phone booth near the glass doors ahead of him, and when he drew near he reached into his wallet and took out the small piece of paper. "What the hell," he whispered to himself. He put a dime into the slot, dialed the number, and listened while it rang.

"Hello," came a woman's voice from the phone.

"Kate?"

"Yes."

"This is Grant Thorson." He could hear Jackson Browne's "Late for the Sky" playing in the background.

"Oh, hi!"

"I hope I'm not calling too late?" He knew he'd surprised her.

"No, I'm just reading."

"Would you like to have coffee, or something? I just thought . . ."

"Now?"

"Yeah, I'm just leaving school. I stayed late to study Gross Anatomy." A bit of anxiety came over him; what if she really didn't want to see him? "I remembered several other times when I humiliated myself. I thought maybe you'd want to hear about them," he said.

"Yeah," she said with some uncertainty. After a second she added,

"Yeah. Sure!" Grant could hear the idea of a late-night coffee break gaining momentum in Kate's voice, and he breathed a small sigh of relief. "That would be nice." She laughed. "Meet you at a little spot called Benny's Deli, over by Lake Harriet."

"I know the place. Meet you there in fifteen minutes," he said.

All the great smells of an old-fashioned deli rolled over Grant when he swung open the front door of Benny's. The place was mostly empty, but he spotted Kate immediately when he stepped inside. She was sitting at a small booth, waiting for him, and she waved and smiled the instant she saw him. She wore a plain red sweater and blue jeans, and once again Grant felt himself slowing down just to look at her.

Kate already had a cup of coffee when Grant slid into the booth across from her and motioned to the waitress that he'd like one also. A covered dish of pickles sat on the table, next to an array of condiments. "This place has classic ambience, huh?" he said as he warmed his hands around a steaming coffee cup.

"How are your classes going?" she asked.

"OK. Well, pretty good, actually. I was just leaving Gross Anatomy lab when I called. Big test in a few days," he replied. "I guess I can do the work. But I don't understand why so many of the old-timers, like Ebby, think they need to wipe their feet on students."

A tired-looking waitress wandered up to their booth. "Would you like to order something to eat?" she asked.

"I'd like a slice of cantaloupe with my coffee," Kate said.

"Just coffee," Grant said.

The waitress left and Kate continued. "It's always been that way, they say. It's kind of funny. There were several instructors who were really hard on me, too. Merciless! Then, the day I graduated they treated me like we were old friends, colleagues. Now I just can't make myself like them."

"Is that how you got to know Dean Muckinhern and Dean Ruminsky? I mean, being part of the faculty and all. I see you talking to them all the time," Grant offered.

"No, that's totally different," Kate said. "Dean Muckinhern is a special friend."

"Jeez, you mean like a boyfriend?"

"No." Kate laughed. "When I was twelve years old my parents were killed in a car accident. I went to live with my older sister, who had been married for about a year. Turns out that Dean Muckinhern lives two houses down the street from my sister and her husband." Kate shrugged.

"He's the one who influenced me to go into dentistry. He kept telling me I was smart enough and that I could do it. You know, for a long time there, the only careers open to women were nursing or teaching." Kate stopped for a moment and stared at her coffee cup. "I guess I had something to prove, too." Then her eyes cleared and she went on. "Anyway, he likes me, and he sorta looks out for me, like a surrogate father. In fact, I probably got this job because he pulled some strings for me."

"I'll bet you were the best candidate," Grant replied.

"So what about you? How did you wind up here?" Kate changed the subject.

"Grew up in Halstad, a little fart of a town up near where the world drops off in northwestern Minnesota. Lived on a farm. I have no idea how I wound up here."

They talked of the little things in their lives for an hour. Each of them gave away small secrets about their families and their expectations for their own lives yet to come, then asked for the other to reveal some small bit in return. They laughed about Grant's fall once again, and they each shared a couple of stories about Ebby and Ben Pribyl and Tanya the Mauler.

"You were right about something you said earlier today," Kate said, while she worked on the slice of cantaloupe.

"Really? What was that?" he asked.

"Jackson Browne. He's better. He writes beautifully about love, and longing, and fathers and sons. The water's a lot deeper out there on his end of the pool." Kate nodded. "You were right. He has passion."

Grant tried to hide a satisfied little grin. Kate had been thinking about something he'd said, not just the small talk. She wasn't simply an attractive woman. The water was pretty deep over there on her end of the pool, too.

He saw something else in Kate's eyes, also. The mood was still playful, but he was certain that she liked him. She was interested and she liked being here, like this. The door was definitely open.

The bored-looking waitress refilled their coffee cups several times, then tossed their check on the table.

"Wow," Kate said when she looked at her watch. "It's almost midnight." She began to reach for her jacket on the seat next to her.

Grant swept up the check and opened his wallet. Then he calmly closed his wallet, hunched his shoulders, reached across the table and took her hand. "Kate, I have to tell you something," he said seriously, as if he were about to confess a crime.

She stopped fumbling with her jacket, looked into his eyes, and squeezed his hand in case he might need some support with a personal crisis. "Yes?" she said, both curious and afraid of what he was about to share with her.

"This bill is for $3.25. I have two dollars in my pocket. Can you help me here? I don't wanna stay and wash dishes." Then he scrunched his face into a ball as if he couldn't understand how this had happened. "If you can't help me out with a couple bucks, maybe you could just sneak over there and open the door? I'll make a break for it! I think I can outrun the waitress. She's kinda fat anyway. I think she'll quit chasing me after a couple blocks."

"You're serious?" Kate grinned.

"It's true." Grant nodded. "I just forgot to check my cash position before I came over here. Go ahead and laugh, maybe you should try to imagine that I have a dental drill stuck to my head, too."

She leaned back in the booth and let her face bunch up in a smile, then leaned forward again, sliding her elbows across the table toward him. "You asked me out for coffee, and now you can't pay?" She was teasing again, and she was prettier than ever.

"I specifically asked you out for *coffee*," he corrected. "I had no idea you were such a big eater! I'd be OK here if it wasn't for that cantaloupe."

She took five dollars from her purse, gave him the money, and walked to the door. Grant listened to her laugh all the way to the street while he stood at the cash register and paid the check. Her playful reaction to his faux pas was so pleasant that he never had time to be truly embarrassed. He was having too much fun with her.

She was waiting with her hands in her pockets when Grant joined her on the sidewalk in front of Benny's.

"You really know how to impress the ladies!" she said.

"Let me make it up to you?" he asked. "Do you have a boyfriend?" He braced himself for the answer he suspected was coming.

"Yes," Kate said hesitantly. She tilted her head, questioning his motive for asking such a question.

"Wrong answer. But I think we can work around it, for now. Would you let me take you out for dinner?"

She stopped smiling and stared at him for a moment. "Maybe."

"We'll go to a quiet place I know." He raised his eyebrows.

"Where's that?" She asked.

"Metropolitan Stadium. Should be about forty thousand empty seats.

The Twins' last home game for the season is tomorrow night. Supposed to be a nice night, best food in town, it's a great place to talk. I'll be witty and clever."

"I'm sure of that," she said, and she began to smile again.

"So, I'll pick you up right after classes are over?" He raised his eyebrows several times and nodded yes to help her answer the question. "We'll go early, for batting practice?" He nodded again and waited for her reply.

"Will I need to bring cash?" she asked.

"Oooo, good one!" He winced and pretended to be hurt by the question. "But no. I'll bring extra cash in case you have another feeding frenzy. We'll have fun."

"OK," she said, and then, still smiling, she walked to her car. She waved and shook her head when she drove past him.

CHAPTER 9

"So what's up?" Will said, as he turned a chair backwards, swung his leg over it, and sat down next to Grant's preclinical laboratory bench. He sipped his hot coffee, but before he could set it down, Grant took it out of his hand and tasted it.

"Got a date with Kate Bellows tonight," Grant said with childlike braggadocio, as he spread his instruments across the workbench and prepared to begin the day's assignment. He couldn't wait to share the good news with his friend.

"Where you taking her?" Will asked.

"Twins game."

"Good call," Will said. "Chicks dig that stuff."

Grant lit his Bunsen burner, propped an open book on his bench, and took several more instruments from a drawer under the bench. "I called her last night after Gross Anatomy lab. We had coffee at a little deli." He looked at Will but patted his own chest when he said, "Oh, man, I really like her."

Will lifted the coffee cup from the lab bench and said, "I thought she had a boyfriend."

"Yeah," Grant sighed, "there is that problem."

"And I thought you had a girlfriend."

Grant put his instruments down and rubbed his face with both hands. "Yeah, well, there is that problem, too." He looked at Will and was about to say something, but he lost the words and grew frustrated before he could speak. With his elbows resting on the lab bench and his chin resting on his hands, he gave up and stared down at the bench. A moment earlier he'd been excited to tell Will about his conversation with Kate.

But that excitement had been sidetracked by the complications of other relationships.

Will leaned forward, picked up Grant's wax spatula, and held it over the flame of the Bunsen burner again. "OK, forget the date for a minute. Tell me about your meeting with the dean yesterday," he said.

"I guess that little chat was about what I expected," Grant said. "It sure could have been worse." His face brightened and he took a sip from Will's coffee. "Dr. Ruminsky is a good guy, and they have a well-stocked fly-tying bench in a little office up there! Those guys are fishermen; the whole office up there is decorated like somebody's cabin at the lake. I think Dean Muckinhern might be OK, too. He just made it pretty clear that they didn't want to see me anymore."

"Yeah, well, I suppose you're used to people telling you things like that," Will said.

Grant ignored the remark and changed the subject when he remembered something. "Hey!" he said. "Kate is good friends with Dr. Muckinhern. That's why we're always seeing her talking to those old guys."

"I'll bet Kate is pretty well liked by all those older guys," Will replied, as he rotated Grant's wax spatula in the flame. "You know, they see a pretty girl with a charming personality, it's hard to miss that she's a doll. But they also see something innocent and vulnerable. She's the type they like to protect, like a father would." He rotated the wax spatula again and waited, without looking away, for Grant to reply.

"Yeah, you probably got that about right," Grant said. "I think she's charming. She makes me laugh, too. But I'll give it to you straight." Grant shrugged. "I want to do *all* those things that those old guys are trying to protect her from."

Grant smiled to himself and read through some notes while Will held the wax spatula over the fire. "I understand," Will said, then added, "Hey, I just saw your buddy Dommy out in the hallway, between classes. He was all dressed up. White shirt and a tie. What's he doing?"

"He's taking the inlay practical today," Grant replied.

"What's that?"

"Apparently it's a clinical exam. He has to do an inlay today and get a superior grade, just to prove that he's mastered the procedure, or else he can't graduate. I think we have to take several of them during our senior year," Grant said. "At least that's the way he explained it to me the other day."

"So what's with the shirt and tie and polish on his shoes?"

"Sorta goes without saying that if you dress up and look good, then maybe your instructor will see you as something better than you really are, maybe give you a better grade," Grant said.

Will put the glowing wax spatula down on the workbench, then slid his chair back and prepared to go to work at his own lab bench. Before he left Grant's side he leaned over and said, "So you'll be wearing a tux to the ball game tonight?"

"Leave the coffee," was all Grant said in response.

Will returned to his bench, spread his instruments out, and was about to say something to the student seated on his left when he heard Grant erupt.

"Yeow! Fuck!" Grant screeched.

An instant later Grant's wax spatula bounced off the ceiling and ricocheted back down. The steel instrument made a rapid series of tinging noises as it bounced across the laboratory floor.

Grant was up again, stomping the floor, pacing in tight circles, shaking his burned fingers, and cursing, when he made eye contact with Will. He was hissing small swear words—"Shit, fuck, shit!"—when Will began to laugh at him. Grant returned to his bench, stuck his index finger in his mouth to soothe the new blisters, and looked back over his shoulder at Will.

Will was waiting for him to look. He rolled his eyes and shook his head as if to say, "I can't believe you're that stupid. You watched me heat that thing until it was glowing, then picked it up?"

With his index finger still in his mouth, Grant raised his middle finger to Will, and began to smile.

~:~

The huge parking lot at Metropolitan Stadium was nearly empty when Grant pulled in and began searching for a place to park near Gate G, where he could buy two-dollar tickets for left-field seats.

The small talk on the way to the ballpark had been nice. Just the fact that the lovely Kate Bellows was sitting in his car, talking with him, made him feel special. But when he'd gone to her home to pick her up after class, she'd created a visual image that he could *not* get out of his mind.

She'd swung open her front door wearing a black turtleneck that strained against her full breasts, and then disappeared into the tiny waist of her blue jeans. Her long, dark hair was pulled back in a ponytail that highlighted the delicate lines of her face.

And on her left hand she wore a baseball glove! She pounded her right fist into the glove, smiled her great smile, and said, "Play ball!"

It was a cheap old hardware-store glove, probably one she'd had since childhood. Grant and his brothers had had a box full of them when he was a boy. But now she held it like it was an old friend. She slapped her right fist into the pocket several more times and asked, "You ready?"

Kate still wore the glove as they walked across the stadium parking lot and up the ramps that ran behind the left-field seats.

They emerged from the walkway behind the stadium seats and stepped out into the full glory of Metropolitan Stadium on a cool fall evening. The color and the sounds of the ballpark swallowed them. Players in white uniforms ran across the green outfield. They threw white baseballs back and forth. They talked and laughed with one another and signed autographs. The crack of white ash on horsehide called out through the crowd noise as if to welcome them.

"Think we'll catch one out here?" Kate asked, still pounding her thin white fist into the parched old glove.

"Did you play a lot of baseball?" Grant asked when they sat down and waited for a batting-practice home run to come their way.

"Sure! Mostly right field. Not so mobile, you know." She tapped the brace on her leg. "We usually had a real right fielder . . . and me." She glanced over and watched a player chase a ball into the outfield corner, then throw it in to second base. "Jeez! That guy can throw! Did you see how far he threw that thing?"

"He's a major-league outfielder. He's got a cannon," Grant said. Her words replayed in his head. She'd said, "a real right fielder . . . and me." She couldn't even be allowed to play right field by herself in a children's sandlot game. How demeaning that must have been. But apparently she was resigned to it.

"Wow! These guys can all throw it," she said. Her eyes roamed across the field and she seemed to drink it all in while she watched the players prepare. Grant loved the excitement in Kate's eyes. It was far more enjoyable to watch her than the action out on the field.

"I never could throw it very far," Kate offered. "But I could catch pretty good, if they didn't throw it too low." She was lost now, somewhere far back in her memory, and she stared across the outfield. "Remember on the playground, when they used to throw the bat up in the air and one of the boys would catch it? And then they'd each put a hand on the bat, one hand above the other, until one boy held the top of the bat, and he got to choose first?" She paused but didn't wait for an answer. "I was always the last one chosen."

Her words took his breath away. She was still smiling the wonderful smile that he was falling in love with. But her eyes had flickered and revealed a hint of pain. He watched out of the corner of his eye while she kept on pounding her fist into that glove.

He'd always been the first player chosen. He'd wondered from time to time what it must feel like to be the last one chosen, to have a friend look at you and say grudgingly, "OK, I guess we have to take *you*." He couldn't bear to think of Kate dealing with that pain. The pain of others less fortunate than him, like Darcy Wilhelm, or children on the playground who got picked on by childhood bullies, or laughed at by classmates because of the way they looked; that had always bothered him. But this? This was something new. The pain hidden behind Kate's smile stabbed at him as if it were his own.

Grant knew Kate had been whisked back to her childhood, and she appeared to be loving the feel of it. He understood that baseball had the power to do that—to restore a person's childhood—if only for a moment.

He tried to imagine Kate as a little girl struggling to keep up with the other kids at play. He saw a joyful little kid with pigtails. No, French braids, and that same glove, and the brace on her leg. He saw her laughing and hobbling around, playing with all the kids in her neighborhood in spite of always being the last one chosen, and then standing out there in right field, pounding her fist in that glove and waiting for a chance.

"I did some checking on you," she offered, without looking up, interrupting his vision of her as a child.

"Oh? Did you place a call to your friend Ebby, or perhaps Dean Muckinhern?" he asked, while he leaned back and put his feet up on the empty seat in front of them. The image of eight-year-old Kate trying to keep up with her friends lingered for a moment, then vanished.

"Well, your name has come up in recent conversations with each of them," Kate said. "But I was talking about Dommy. After I saw you talking with him at that kegger I called him and asked about you."

"Really? You noticed my rugged good looks and charming personality, didn't you?" Grant asked.

"Well, I thought you were cute."

"Men don't want to be cute." Grant made a face and shook his head. "Handsome. Not cute."

"Well, anyway, I called Dommy," Kate continued.

"And what did he say?"

"He said you were a nice guy and a baseball player for the Gophers."

"Did he say anything else?"

"He said you never got to play very much, but you worked really hard." She smiled.

"That would be about right," Grant chuckled.

"I'll bet you were as good as those guys down there." She pointed to the major leaguers warming up just in front of them.

"Nope. Not even close. But it's a nice thought."

"Don't you still want to be a ballplayer? Don't all little boys hold on to that dream?" she asked.

"Sure I do. I love that dream, but some things are just meant to stay dreams." He paused. "All I really want is just to be a little boy for a while longer, that's why I come back for more baseball." He looked at her for a moment, then asked, "You know what I mean, don't you?"

"Yup," she said.

A small commotion began to stir amid the thin crowd in front of them along the outfield fence. When they looked up where everyone was pointing, they saw a ball high in the sky and headed their way from the batting cage. The ball seemed to hang in the twilight for a moment, then grow bigger and bigger with each passing second. Kate raised her glove as if she wanted to catch the ball, but her posture soon took on the look of self-defense. Grant put his left arm around her shoulder and watched the ball close in on them. It struck a wooden seat a few rows over their heads, bounced straight up about ten feet, struck another seat, and bounced directly into Grant's outstretched right hand while several little boys chased after it.

"Here's your ball," Grant said when he gave it to Kate. She looked it over as if it were a moon rock. Then she instinctively began to pound it into the pocket of her childhood glove.

"Thanks!" she said while she studied it. She read the printing, sniffed at it, pounded it into her glove once more, then put her arm over the back of his neck and pulled him close. She kissed him softly on the lips and whispered, "Thanks," a second time.

He was fascinated by the kiss, and the way she held the ball, and he wondered just what was going through her mind. Her touch was so soft, and the kiss carried a subtle promise of so much more. This was good, all good, Grant thought, while a strand of her long hair tickled his cheek.

"You hungry yet?" he asked. Kate had turned her attention back to the ballplayers and began to pound the ball into her glove again.

"Yeah," she nodded.

"Well, let's sneak over there to the concession area behind home plate, grab something to eat, and watch the game from those empty seats."

As they walked along the concourse on the way to the concession stands behind the first-deck seats, Kate dropped her hand to her side and took Grant's hand in hers. The idea that she was willing to claim him in such a public way seemed innocent enough, maybe even playful, but it sent a charge through him. He wanted to shout and point out to strangers that Kate Bellows was holding his hand. Just the way she moved her thumb softly over the back of his hand was thrilling. He *definitely* had a chance with her.

Grant bought each of them a bratwurst and a beer, and they walked over to one of the condiment tables. Kate unwrapped the paper from her brat and was about to spoon some ketchup onto it.

"Whoa! Wait. What the *hell* are you doing?" he said with all the feigned indignity he could muster.

"Huh?" Kate said, totally off guard.

"Are you gonna put ketchup on a brat?" He stared at her like he'd just caught her stealing.

"Yeah." She began to smile.

"Nobody, I mean *nobody* is allowed to come to a major-league park and put ketchup on a brat!" Grant looked at her as if she'd stepped in something. "You can't do that. Well, maybe a five-year-old kid, but not a grown-up, not you." He shook his head in disgust, and she waited for him to continue.

"Look around you," Grant said. "Do you see anyone selling cantaloupe, or vegetables, or shit like that? No! This is a ballpark. We eat baseball food here! You know, hot dogs, brats, beer, Cracker Jack, Eskimo Pies. Real food. And there are rules! Proper decorum must be observed."

"Oh?" she said.

"Would you like me to help you?" he teased, then extended his arm and waited for her to hand over the brat she'd been about to desecrate. "OK, first you spread mustard all over this bad boy." She watched while he did so. Then Grant asked, "Do you like sauerkraut?"

"Yeah, sure." She smiled.

"Not a very enthusiastic answer, but it was correct," he said, as he covered the brat with sauerkraut.

"OK, how 'bout onions? They're optional. The only reason I ask is because I plan to do whatever you do as far as onions are concerned," he said.

"Why?" she asked.

"'Cause I'm gonna try to kiss you later, and I don't want to blow onion breath in your face if, well, you know."

"No onions, then." She nodded, very businesslike.

"Good call," Grant said. He handed her the brat and prepared the other with the same loving care. "OK," he said when he was finished. "Let's go down in front and try to look like we belong in those expensive seats."

They sidestepped their way across a row of empty seats to a vacant section about twenty rows up from the Twins' dugout and sat down in the middle of it. "Looks like we're gonna have a paid attendance of about eight thousand tonight. Should leave about 35,000 empty seats. We'll be fine here," said Grant. They sat down in the midst of several thousand people, but saw only each other for the next two hours while they ate, drank beer, and got to know one another.

"So why do they keep bringing in new pitchers?" Kate asked during a pitching change.

"'Cause the old ones are getting pounded." Grant chuckled, then he thought for a minute and asked, "Do you understand about the righty-lefty thing, when they change pitchers?"

"Not really."

"OK," Grant started. "When a right-handed pitcher throws a curveball to a right-handed batter, the batter starts to wonder if maybe the pitch might be about to hit him in the head. So he hesitates, just for an instant, and then the ball curves right in there for a strike before the hitter can figure it out. It's just too late to swing at it. Strike three and you're out! With me?"

"Yeah."

"OK, the other way to make a curveball effective is when the pitcher throws the ball right over the plate to begin with. The batter thinks it's going to be a strike, right down the middle, so he swings. But just as he swings, the ball curves away from him, nowhere near the plate. He misses badly and looks like a fish flopping around out there. Make sense?"

"Sure."

"It's just a big advantage for a right-handed pitcher to pitch against a right-handed batter and for left-handed pitchers to pitch against left-handed batters." He paused for a second, then tried to explain further. "It works the other way, too."

"What do you mean?"

"Well, you know when one team takes a time-out and brings in a pinch hitter?" he asked.

"Yeah."

"That almost always means that the manager of the team who's batting is trying to create a righty-lefty matchup that favors his team instead of the pitcher's team. You know, they want a right-handed batter up there hitting against a left-handed pitcher, and vice versa. Get it?"

"Sure," Kate said. "So what's a change off?"

"You mean changeup, not change off," he corrected. "A changeup is just a real slow fastball. You throw it the same way you throw a fastball, but you start out by gripping it way back in the palm of your hand. No matter how hard you throw it that way, it just won't go very fast."

"Why would you want to throw it slower? Doesn't that make it real easy to hit?" she asked.

Grant smiled for a minute, trying to think of a way to explain. "OK," he started. "It's been said that hitting is all about rhythm, and pitching is all about the disruption of rhythm. That's the best I ever heard anyone describe pitching. If a pitcher can change the speed of the ball, and make it curve a bit, he takes away the hitter's rhythm. The really great pitchers can get most hitters to feel real clumsy up there. But then the really great hitters have the strength and coordination to make lightning-fast changes and adjust to subtle changes in their rhythm. Does that make sense?"

"Sure. Can you hit a curveball?" she asked.

"No." He shook his head. "Not a good one. Well, not even an average one, if I don't know it's coming." He thought for a moment, then added, "I faced a pitcher a couple summers ago who had a big-league curveball. I was playing town ball. And this kid was from a little-bitty town down by Austin, and he was the best pitcher I ever saw. He's in Triple A ball now, that's just one step down from the majors."

"What happened?" Kate asked.

"Well, my first time up I hit two pitches real hard. Both of 'em went foul. Then I grounded out to the second baseman. Pretty good at bat, I thought."

"What happened your next time at bat?" she asked.

"He struck me out—made me his bitch!" Grant blurted. "Everyone laughed, even the umpire. I looked even clumsier than when I fell down on Washington Avenue!"

Kate laughed out loud too, and the game ebbed and flowed while they shared peanuts, Eskimo Pies, beer, and bits and pieces of their lives.

The action on the field interrupted their date less and less as the innings came and went. The ball game devolved into a sideshow, and their conversation grew easier with each story. A funny story from childhood, an anecdote from dental school, maybe a comment about a celebrity who'd made the news recently; everything seemed to bring them a little bit closer.

"So what's town ball?" Kate asked, as she cracked a peanut in half. "You said something about town ball earlier."

"It's just amateur baseball." Grant shrugged. "A few years back it was a big deal, actually. Every little town had a team. The heyday was back in the fifties. There was no major-league baseball west of the Mississippi yet. There were a lot of good players around, people had a little more money after the war, and so they had some leisure time too. Nobody had air-conditioning in their homes yet, and even if you had a TV, there wasn't much to watch. The only thing to do on a hot summer night was to get out of your house and go watch your local town team play. They say it was a real social experience, everybody in town was there. The baseball was actually pretty good, too, so they say."

"And you still play town ball?" Kate asked.

"Yeah, sure, but it's not the same anymore," Grant said. "Nobody goes to the games, just girlfriends and mothers, maybe a handful of fans. The players are an odd bunch. It's mostly college boys mixed in with some older guys who just can't give it up."

"I'll bet you're a pretty good player," Kate said, then touched his hand and looked into his eyes. "No matter what you say."

"Well, I surely do love it," Grant said. She was holding his hand now, right there in her lap where anyone could see it, and it was time to tell her what he'd been thinking for the past hour.

"You're the prettiest girl in this ballpark," he said bluntly.

Kate had no idea how to respond. No one had ever said such a thing to her. "Well, the place is almost empty," she joked. "There aren't many girls here."

Grant stared at her, challenging her to acknowledge the compliment differently.

"Thank you," she said, and the happy little girl with the French braids smiled back at him and squeezed his hand.

She had been beautiful a few weeks before, even when he'd never spoken to her. But now when she laughed, or smiled, or shared some personal insight, she really began to shine. He studied the blue eyes and the soft skin and he breathed in her scent. Even on a night when Metropolitan Stadium was packed, she'd still be the prettiest girl in the ballpark.

Kate saw the way Grant looked at her, and she loved it. Grant Thorson was a good man, he was handsome and clever and he had integrity, anyone could see that much. He was many things—an athlete, a scholar, a gentleman—and he was smitten with her. But he had another quality that drew her: he was still a little boy. Kate guessed that Grant still walked through the middle of mud puddles. In fact, he probably stomped through them just to see how far the water might splash. Kate was growing to adore that little boy.

The Twins game was tied in the top of the seventh inning—a pretty good game, actually. But Kate and Grant were lost in their own world, oblivious to the goings-on in front of them.

"Yeah," Kate started, while she held an Eskimo Pie in her hand, "one time . . ."

The crack of a bat interrupted her, and the crowd began to rumble. A slow, heavy-legged base runner came plodding into third base while an outfielder chased after the ball in center field. The third-base coach began to spin his right arm like a wheel, telling the runner to hurry and try to score. Everyone's eyes were on the runner now. The runner huffed and wheezed around third as the cutoff man, in shallow center field, took a throw from his teammate in the outfield, then wheeled and fired a bullet toward home. The crowd, such as it was, roared when the base runner and the catcher collided like a train wreck at home plate.

The catcher was picking up his gear, and the runner was smiling and walking back toward the dugout while his teammates congratulated him, when Grant spoke. "You know, one of the great things that comes back to me in my baseball dreams is just that. What we just saw. Rounding second base, running like the wind, and then somewhere in no-man's-land out there between second and third you make up your mind to try to score. But you know when you're rounding third and heading for home, there's gonna be a play at the plate. There's nothing like that in any other game."

"Yeah, I'll bet." Kate sighed and looked away. "I guess I can run when I get to Heaven."

He was thunderstruck. Kate was pounding her fist into the glove again when he looked over at her, and his life turned in that moment. Something in his soul twisted, then locked into place. She was the one, and he knew it. He'd marry her and love her forever. That thought had been there, born in the wind, but unspoken, maybe from the first time she'd touched him, out there on the Washington Avenue sidewalk. He couldn't say for sure, but he knew it had been drifting around in his thoughts, waiting to be recognized. He peeked over and saw the woman who would lead him to a better life.

She wasn't some professor anymore. All that disparity over her lofty position at the university and his lowly one had gone out the window with a batting-practice home run and a bratwurst. She was the one.

Metropolitan Stadium was nearly empty as the final inning of another game and another season came to an end. Grant watched other people filing out of the ballpark, and he stole sideways glances at Kate. He wished he didn't have to take her home.

Traffic was light, and when they rolled out onto I-494 he reached over and took her hand in his. She held his hand and softly stroked it while they talked about the academic challenges waiting for him over the next year. He heard the words but all he could think about was the smooth skin of her fingers and the way she kept moving her thumb softly over the back of his hand.

"Thanks for taking me to the game. I had a great time," Kate said when she stood on the front steps of her house.

"Can I see your glove?" Grant asked. She gave it to him and he immediately dropped it on the ground next to his feet. "Your hands are gonna be full for the next few minutes." He reached his hands around her tiny waist and gently pulled her close. "What are you thinking?" he asked when they were nose to nose.

"Glad we left the onions off," she said.

Grant leaned forward and gently touched his forehead against hers.

"So, in the parlance of baseball, are you thinking that you're gonna get to first base tonight?" she asked.

"Yep," he whispered. He rubbed the tip of his nose on hers.

"Maybe I'll just give you an intentional walk," she whispered in reply.

"No way," Grant said softly. "I was charming and clever tonight. I earned my way to first base. I hit the ball hard! In fact, I'm thinking about trying for second base."

"Well, that's not gonna happen. But I can tell by the way you're holding me that you've got pretty good wood!" Then she gasped at what she'd said. "Oh God, did I just say that?" She buried her face in his shoulder and laughed. Grant wrapped his arms firmly around her and let her laughter shake them both.

When their laughter subsided he continued to hold her close, then whispered, "What're we gonna do? I mean, neither one of us . . ."

Kate lifted her head away from his shoulder and put the tip of her nose against his once more. "Like you said, we'll have to work around that for now." She raised her eyes to meet his, then closed them and kissed him. Her tongue was warm and wonderful, and Grant let the kiss linger. When it was over he put his cheek against hers and held her for a moment.

"So what are you thinking about now?" Grant whispered.

Kate brought her mouth to his again. She pulled him close and kissed him softly. "I think you know," she breathed, then kissed him again.

Kate's body pressed against Grant while the tip of her tongue flirted gently with his. He could feel the hunger inside her growing. Then she turned her face to the side and held her cheek against his. "Whew," she sighed. "You'd better go."

"I'm never leaving, Kate," he teased. "In case you didn't notice, I've been in love with you since . . ." He stopped himself and tempted her with an unfinished thought.

"Since when?" she whispered. He could feel her face smiling.

"Mmm," he said softly as his lips brushed her ear. "Bottom of the fifth . . . top of the sixth?" He kissed her ear and smiled. "I'm not leaving, Kate. You're gonna have to break somebody else's heart."

Grant stroked the back of Kate's head and slowly moved his hand down her back. She rested her head on his shoulder but said nothing for several minutes. The lovely Kate Bellows was holding him, kissing him. She liked him. Just how much better could life get?

"Not kidding with you, Kate," Grant said. Another silent moment drifted away before he added, "I'm gonna want another turn at bat." He kissed her ear again and she nodded in agreement, but still said nothing.

"Can I see you this weekend?" he asked.

"No. I have some things to take care of," she said without taking her head from his shoulder.

"What's the matter?" he whispered.

"I don't want you to leave either," she said. She stepped away from him. "But you have to go. We'll see each other next week."

Grant picked her baseball glove up off the ground and gave it to her. As he placed it in her hands he stole a kiss. "In my next turn at bat I'll be swinging for the fences. Now, you understand that in the parlance of baseball that phrase has a strong sexual innuendo, and . . ."

"See you Monday," she said, smiling.

Grant sighed, stole another kiss, then turned and walked away. He was halfway to the street when she joked, "Watch your step!"

Grant wheeled and pointed at her. "I'd take a fall like that one on the street outside school every damn day of my life if I thought you'd be there to pick me up. And if I ever had the chance, I'd choose you, Kate Bellows. I'd choose you *first*!"

Kate smiled and waved good-bye, and when she opened the front door she thought she'd never be able to stop smiling. He'd asked her what she was thinking about, then listened to her answers. He'd laughed and teased, and looked at her with hungry eyes, too. He'd kissed her so softly while they whispered and giggled on her front steps, and he'd made her ache for more. She'd never been clever, and pretty, and sexy, until Grant Thorson let her. "I'd choose you, *first*." He'd actually said that!

❖ CHAPTER 10 ❖

The phone beside Will's bed exploded. He rolled over and groaned when he read 5:00 a.m. on his alarm clock. "Hello," he muttered, as he emerged from his sleep.

"You awake?" Grant barked.

"Hell no." Will sat up, swung his feet over the side of the bed, and arched his back.

"Scratchin' your nuts?" Grant asked.

Will looked out the window as if Grant might be looking in at that very moment, then began to scratch his nuts. "Good idea," he said sleepily. "Why did you call me so early?"

"Because I haven't slept, I'm sitting at an all-night gas station about five blocks from your house, and I've got one word to say to you," Grant said.

"What's that?" Will asked.

"Road trip!"

"That's two words," Will replied.

"Get your ass out of bed and put some coffee on, I'm coming right over. We're going fishing!"

June wore a terry cloth robe when she swung the door open to greet Grant five minutes later. She stared through sleepy eyes for a second, then tried to smile.

"What's for breakfast?" he asked, as if he actually expected something. "Waffles and whipped cream would be good."

"Talk to Will about that," she said as she turned away. Her slippers scuffed along the floor when she walked. "Coffee's ready. C'mon in."

She sat down at a tiny kitchen table. She was trying to let the steam from her coffee warm her face when Grant sat down next to her. "So what's going on?" she asked.

"Long night last night," Grant said. "I took Kate Bellows to a ball game, then broke up with Anne." He poured himself some coffee and tried to sip it, even though it was still too hot.

"You've been up all night, haven't you?" June asked.

"Yeah. The thing with Anne was really hard." He looked away and added, "Really hard."

"That's too bad. I'm sorry," June offered.

"It's OK. It had to be," Grant said softly.

"So what happened, exactly?" June asked. Will emerged from a small bedroom fully dressed and carrying a duffel bag. He poured himself some coffee, then sat next to Grant, combed his hair, and waited for him to answer June's question.

"Well, this had been coming for a while. And then, last night after the time I spent with Kate, I just had to go and tell Anne." He gazed into his coffee cup for a moment. "She cried. It was awful. I hurt her."

"What did you tell her?" June asked. The ease with which Grant could walk into her kitchen, pour himself some coffee, and then talk to her about something this personal surprised June.

"The truth; that I'd met someone else." Grant looked at June and seemed to be trying to justify everything when he continued. "It hurt me too, you know. I left something behind in this thing too." He looked down at his hands again. "We held each other for a while. That made it worse. We both cried. Jesus, how do you tell someone what I told her? I'll never forget the look on her face. She looked sort of lost. I felt like I'd stolen something from her. Then for a moment there, it seemed like we were gonna have sex and try to make believe that it wasn't happening. You know, I wanted to do it, sort of. I wanted to climb under the sheets and hold each other like we used to. Maybe I thought there was still something safe and familiar that I didn't want to leave behind. It seemed like there was about to be a death, and we could prevent it if we could just . . ." Grant stopped, and June stole a sideways glance at Will, then took hold of his hand under the table.

"It hurt me, too, to think that I was gonna walk away from, from a friend; someone who'd been my best friend. But it was already over. We both knew that." Grant drew in a deep breath, then let it out slowly. "Nonetheless, I dropped a bomb on her."

He stared at his coffee, then stood up and put two slices of bread in the toaster on the kitchen countertop. "Wasn't easy for me, either," he said again, perhaps trying to justify what he'd done. "Then she said she could smell Kate's perfume on me. How do you think that made me feel?" Grant stared down into the toaster. "I told her the truth. I wasn't unfaithful, was I?"

Grant had been animated when he'd arrived a few minutes earlier. In only the short time that he'd been telling the story of his evening, he'd come to look haggard and weary.

"Do you still love her?" June asked.

"No. I haven't for a long time. I just want to be free from her."

"Did you come straight here from her place?" Will asked.

"No. I went home. Decided to skip school today. Then decided that we *do* need to go fishing. I made a pot of coffee, packed my stuff, and thought about all this." He extended his cup for more coffee.

"What about not wanting to miss any classes?" Will asked.

"The world turned for me last night. This is stuff that needs to be worked out over a campfire. You know how this works. Besides that, Kate's busy this weekend—I already asked."

"So you're ready to go? Really?" Will asked. He looked at his duffel, then back at Grant.

"Yep." Grant nodded.

"Wait a minute!" June insisted. "You told me this fishing trip was off. Something about needing to study. Remember?" She furrowed her brow and scowled at Will.

"Well, honey, we *did* decide not to go. Remember? That was *after* we'd already gotten several days ahead in our studies." He paused, making a pathetic, pleading gesture with a twisted face. "And now that Grant has had this happen . . . well . . ."

June turned an exasperated grimace at Will, then stared over the top of her glasses at Grant. "Have fun. Be careful," she sighed.

"Let's roll!" Will said. He kissed June on the lips, picked up his duffel, and pushed Grant to the door. "Bye, honey! See you Sunday night," he called over his shoulder.

"That worked out *great*! Nice work, Pard!" Will said. Once they were in his car, he turned north onto Snelling Avenue and accelerated, then added, "Pour me some coffee from the thermos?"

"She sounded a little pissed off there at the end, Will, and it seemed like she was pissed at *me*, too," Grant said.

"Yeah, I told her this whole fishin' thing was your idea," Will replied.

"Huh? Why?"

"'Cuz I wanted to go fishin'! If it was my idea she'd never let me go, and for a while there I thought it just wasn't gonna happen either. But when you started in with that stuff about needing somebody to talk to over a campfire? Well, women really like that needy, sensitive stuff. That cinched the deal. That was brilliant! Nice work."

"Well, it was true. But now she hates me," Grant said.

"Better you than me, Pard." Will shrugged. "Don't sweat it, though. All she wanted me to do was stay home and stare at the side of her head and talk about our feelings." He shrugged again. "You know, stuff like that."

"Glad I could be of service," Grant said.

"Yeah, it'll actually work out good for everyone. When we get home on Sunday she'll still be pissed 'cuz I went fishin'. Then 'bout Tuesday, maybe Wednesday, she'll get over it. We'll talk about our feelings for a while, then we'll make up and have monkey sex." Will nodded, proclaiming the wisdom in his words and the accuracy of his prediction. "Like I said: works out for everyone."

"What about me?" Grant asked.

"Well, it's not quite so good for you." Will chuckled. "She's just gonna hate you, because you take me away from her and make me do stuff like this. No doubt about it, Pard, she is gonna hate you, but that's what friends are for."

Rush-hour traffic hadn't reached its peak yet, but the going was slow when Will's car rolled onto the interstate. "Man, it's gonna take us five hours to get there, Pard!" Will sighed as he looked at the gridlock ahead of him. "So tell me about the ball game." When he looked over, Grant was crumpled against the passenger door with his head hanging over the back of his seat, mouth open, snoring like a chain saw.

～∶～

"Hey, Pard, wake up, we're here," Will said, as he turned off a narrow tree-lined gravel road and onto an even narrower forest trail. Two ruts to guide the car tires and some short grass between the ruts was all that could be seen of the trail that wound through a dense forest of mature hardwoods and conifers.

"Jeez, my neck hurts," Grant said, as he stretched and looked about. "Where are we?"

"Spider Lake Duck Camp," Will replied.

"Huh?"

"It's my parents' cabin, that's all. It used to be a duck camp for a bunch of rich guys from Minneapolis about fifty years ago," Will said.

Grant rubbed his eyes and stared into the woods. Every oak and maple and birch tree in the forest was in its full autumn splendor. Red, yellow, and orange leaves rustled in a light breeze, and the afternoon sun bathed them all in a golden hue. Scattered among the fiery hardwoods were thousands of tall pines thrusting green spires into a clear blue sky.

"Jesus," Grant whispered. His mouth hung open as the car inched along.

"Not bad, huh?" Will said.

The narrow trail wound through unbroken forest for nearly a mile before it opened into a large clearing that surrounded several log buildings. A lean-to made of planks gave shelter to several cords of firewood and two small boats. Not far from the lean-to was a large storage shed with a garage door facing the clearing, and about fifty feet from the large shed sat a much smaller, much older log shed, which was tucked back into the forest.

Resting on the crest of a hill, and surrounded by virgin red pines, sat a massive rustic lodge made of logs.

"This is no cabin in the woods. It's an estate! Your family is rich. You're rich, aren't you?" Grant asked.

"Yup. Pretty much," Will said as he parked the car.

They both stepped out of the car, and as Will began to carry bags up to the lodge, Grant walked around and tried to take it all in.

About forty feet below the lodge, at the bottom of a long slope, Spider Lake sprawled in every direction. Grant kicked at fallen leaves as he walked around the place. He'd seen a few homes like this before, but only from the road. Most of the leaves still clung to the trees, but with each gust of wind a few more decided to cut loose and fly. Grant craned his stiff neck to look up at the third story of the huge house, then shook his head in amazement.

"Not bad, huh?" Will said, as he walked out the porch door and down the front steps.

"Wow," Grant answered.

"The walleyes will be bitin' out by that island, way out there." Will pointed across the lake. "It's called Christian Island. Pretty good duck huntin' there too, when the ducks are movin'."

"Wow," Grant said again, as he scanned the blue lake and its immense sparkling surface.

"All right," Will said. "Let's go put some gas in the boat and get our gear ready. I think we should get out there and start fishin' as soon as we can. We'll fish till after dark, then come back up and have fresh walleyes for dinner, or breakfast, or whatever."

"I haven't eaten since I had toast at your place. I'm hungry," Grant protested.

"Don't get your shit hot. We've got all kindsa time to eat. We gotta get out there, c'mon," Will said. "We're gonna hammer the walleyes!"

~:~

"Well, that sucked," Grant said, as he trudged up the long hill from Spider Lake to the lodge. The surface of the lake had calmed to glass when the afternoon breeze died away. Not one fish had been brought to the boat in six hours of fishing, and now all that buoyed Grant's spirits was the thought of food.

A crescent moon hung in the silent sky and lit their way back up to the cabin.

"Can't remember the last time I got skunked out there," Will said.

"Skunk?" Grant said. "Sounds good! I could eat the ass end out of a dead skunk."

"Never fear. We'll whip up a midnight snack," Will assured him, and they walked on through the half-light until they reached the lodge.

"God, this place is spectacular," Grant said as he plopped down into a large overstuffed leather chair. "A huge-ass stone fireplace, leather furniture, the logs, an open stairway, deer heads and fish on the walls! And look at that view from the porch. Even at night you can see the lake shimmering."

Will said nothing. He headed across the porch and went inside, through the great room and into the kitchen.

Grant got up and wandered around, looking at all the things on display, then stopped to examine some old photos on a bulletin board near a door that led out to the porch. "What's for supper?" he called out while he squinted at the photos. "I'm hungry!"

He heard cupboard doors slamming and pots and pans clanging, but Will didn't answer.

"What are you making?" Grant called again. After a moment of silence he called again. "Hey! Is this you in this picture, holding this big trout?"

Will appeared in the great room wearing a stricken look. "Did you bring any food?" he asked.

"Was I supposed to?" Grant replied, with a hint of malice.

"Well, I . . ." Will stammered.

"There's no food?" Grant asked.

"My mother must have cleaned out everything when they were up here last week. You know, sorta like closing up for the winter. I thought for sure . . ."

"So there's no food?" Grant asked, this time with plenty of malice.

"Sorry, Pard." Will shrugged. "I just thought . . ."

"Well let's drive into Walker," Grant suggested.

"Nothing will be open at this time of night," Will replied.

"I sure hope you turn out to be a better dentist than you are a fishing guide," Grant whined. "No fish, no food. Jeez, Will . . ."

"Quit your bitchin'," Will interrupted. "We're OK. We're not gonna starve. The lake is full of fish. We'll catch 'em tomorrow! And for tonight? Well, we've got this." He held up a quart of Christian Brothers brandy. "I know where Dad hides it."

"Brandy for dinner?" Grant asked.

"Fruit of the vine!" Will answered. "I'll grab some ice and we'll go outside and talk about this over a campfire."

A single line of wood smoke drifted into the night sky ten minutes later as Grant dropped several more pieces of jack pine onto the flickering campfire. "I like the way pine crackles in a fire, and I like the smell, too," he said.

"See, this isn't so bad," Will chided. He clinked the ice cubes in his glass and sipped his brandy. "We'll just have dinner with our Christian Brothers."

"Where's *my* glass?" Grant held out his hand.

"I only brought one glass. Oops," Will said as he handed his drink to Grant.

Grant was too tired to complain anymore. He took the glass from Will and rolled his eyes.

"You never told me about your date, or the ball game last night," Will said. He leaned back against a log.

"Well, let me put this in terms you might understand," Grant began. "Remember when you were in eighth grade, or thereabouts? There was always one special cheerleader. Basketball! She was always a basketball cheerleader. She was a senior and all the big jocks in your school were always buzzing around her like flies around shit?"

"Not the metaphor I would have chosen," Will said. "But yes, I remember such a girl."

"Anyway," Grant continued, "she had perfect hair and perfect skin and she was the prettiest girl in town. When she wore her cheerleader sweater she had perfect snow cone tits, and that little skirt sorta flapped when she walked . . . didn't hide anything. She was gorgeous and every time she passed you in the hallway you had to use your books to cover that roll of dimes that sprouted in your pants. But she didn't know you were alive. You with me, Pard?"

"Yeah, her name was Susie Pautchnik, and it was a roll of silver dollars, not dimes. Gimme that brandy," Will replied, acknowledging a similar experience. "Keep going," he added, after Grant passed the drink to him.

"OK, now you've got the picture. So just imagine that one day she's about to pass you in the hallway, and you're all set for her to just walk right by and not see you again, but this time she stops and smiles at you and says 'Hi,' and you can't believe how great it is that the prettiest girl in school actually knows who you are. Are you with me?"

"Yeah." Will grinned. "It was that good, huh?" He seemed happy for Grant.

"Oh, it was way better." Grant sighed. "She kissed me, and said she could feel that roll of dimes in my pocket, and we laughed." He stared into the fire. "She likes me."

Grant threw another log on the fire. "I think Kate's the one, Will."

"Really?" Will said. "Do you think she knows that yet?"

"Probably not." Grant poked at the fire. "But there was something sorta cosmic going on there. I know she felt it too. Know what I mean? You must have felt something special about June, too?"

"Yeah," Will said, "sure, and it was great. It still is." He raised his knees up under his chin and threw some scraps of pine bark into the fire. "But . . ." He stopped himself.

"But what?" Grant asked.

"Gimme the brandy," Will said. When he'd taken a sip and chewed on an ice cube for a moment he was ready to continue. "Here's the deal. You get to a certain point in life and you look around and ask yourself, 'How in the hell did I wind up here?' And you look at your wife and ask yourself, 'Out of all the women in the world, how did I wind up with this one?'"

Will stared at Grant for a second, and Grant returned the stare.

"That sounded bad, didn't it?" Will asked.

Grant nodded. "Sorta."

"I didn't mean it that way. I think what I'm getting at is that sometimes I wonder what was waiting for me if I'd taken the other fork in the road. I wonder where that would have led me. 'Zat sound better?" Will asked.

Grant took the empty glass from Will's hand, scooped some ice from a cooler, and filled the glass with more brandy. "Well," Grant groaned, as he sat down by the fire again. "Maybe our Christian Brothers can give us a little deeper insight on that topic. And yes, I do wonder about that sort of thing, just the same. But then I wonder if all those forks in the road might not have led me here, too. You know, like destiny?"

"Jeez, you're a philosopher! A poet! Gimme the brandy," Will said. He poked a stick at the fire, thought for a moment, then began slowly, "I never told June about this." He stirred the fire again. "When I was a freshman at Harvard I met a girl. My roommate, Thom Hutchinson, was a rich kid from Michigan who seemed to know everybody, and he introduced me to this girl. Anyway, she was a senior. Gorgeous, clever, money. She would flirt with me at parties." Will sipped brandy and gazed into the past. "I thought that's all there was to it. I would have called her and asked for a date if I'd thought I really had a chance. She was so popular, everybody had a crush on her."

Will had talked himself into a trance now. He poked at the coals and watched the sparks swirl away into the night sky.

"On the day before she graduated I stopped by her house. Just thought I'd help her and her roommates move out. They were carrying stuff out to their cars, you know? Anyway, after a few minutes Jeanie, that was her name, Jeanie Amundsen, she took me aside and said something I just can't forget." Will stared into the fire as if he was searching for the answer to a riddle. "She got a little choked up and she said she'd waited all year for me to call her. She asked me what was wrong with her . . . why I hadn't called her. She said it just about broke her heart that I never called."

Will sighed heavily. "I woulda thrown June away. I woulda." Will nodded. "I wouldn't do it now. That's not what I'm trying to say. But on that day I would have, for sure. I woulda taken that other fork in the road.

"So whatever happened to Jeanie Amundsen?" Grant asked.

"She died. 'Bout a year ago. Cancer, I heard," Will answered, still staring into the fire.

"You never saw her again?" Grant asked.

"Nope. Makes me feel good and bad at the same time whenever I think of her."

"Well, it's a sad story," Grant said.

"I wasn't tryin' to make you feel bad. I just wanted to tell somebody. I never told anyone before. And I don't know that there's a point to the story, either, just something to wonder about."

"I guess that's how it works, huh? We see bits and pieces of other people's lives, and then we use what we want, or what we need, to build our own life. But every now and then one of those other lives sort of splashes onto us and we can never get it off." Grant sipped the brandy, then sighed. "Crazy shit, huh?"

"Well said," Will sighed.

Grant stood up and collected an armload of firewood, then returned to the fire. "Hey! It was Kate's first time at the ballpark. Remember your first Twins game?" he asked, as he fed the fire.

"A Saturday," Will replied. "'Bout 1963, maybe '64. Twins were playing the Orioles. It was a sunny afternoon. I remember the color. The grass was so green, and the orange on those Orioles uniforms was so bright. Awesome!"

"Remember who won?"

"The Twins! Tony Oliva knocked in the winning run in the bottom of the ninth, jacked a double into the corner. Crowd went wild. How 'bout you . . . your first Twins game?"

"1961. I'll never forget. It was the Twins' first season. I was just a little kid. But the Yankees were in town for the first time. Dad got some tickets and took the whole family. Jesus, what a spectacle. Gimme the drink." Grant took a sip and stared into the fire while he chose his words. "There must have been a thousand little kids pressed up along the fence waiting to get a look at Mickey Mantle during batting practice. Roger Maris was standing there taking some swings in the on-deck circle when Mantle came out of the dugout. Every kid in the place started screaming 'Hey Mickey!' in our high-pitched little voices. Mantle smiled at Maris, then turned and waved to us. I swear to God, every kid there thought Mickey was waving at them." Grant sipped again. "But it was me. No doubt about it. He was waving to me!" Grant chuckled and nodded in agreement with himself.

"Who won?" Will asked.

Grant shrugged, admitting that the winner of that game was of no consequence. "Know what I *do* remember, even more than that first game?" Grant asked, not waiting for Will's reply. "We used to have a little screened-in porch just off the kitchen. My Dad would sit out there at night, in the dark, and listen while Halsey Hall and Herb Carneal called the games on the radio. Did you have a place like that?"

"My Dad's study." Will smiled at the memory. "Walnut paneling and bookshelves all over the place. He kept a little lamp on, next to his big chair. Read the box scores and listened to the Twins."

Grant nodded. "Thought so. You know, I can vaguely remember ball games even before the Twins. We used to pick up some Cardinals games, and some White Sox and Cubs games. But man, when the Twins came to Minnesota, that was a big deal! We had our own team, and they were actually pretty good. We'd sit out there on that little porch and hope to catch a breeze. Then Dad would turn the radio dial until Halsey and Herb would come crackling through. Sometimes Mom would make cookies, maybe some lemonade, maybe if we were really lucky we could have a bottle of pop. Dad was always out there till the game ended. Every now and then we'd play checkers while we listened. Just my dad and me."

"Remember the Twins fight song?" Will interrupted.

Grant lifted a smoking stick from the fire and began to tap a familiar rhythm on one of the rocks in the fire circle, and both of them raised their faces into the moonlight and began to sing. "We're gonna win, Twins. We're gonna score. Crack out a home run, shout a hip hooray! Cheer for the Minnesota Twins today." Grant lowered his eyes and looked into the glowing embers while Will finished, singing softly to himself, "We're gonna win Twins, give it our all. We've got boys who'll knock the cover off the ball. Let's hear it now for the team that came to play, cheer for the Minnesota Twins today." The fire crackled softly for a few minutes while they stared into flickering light and remembered things that they couldn't or wouldn't share with anyone.

"I was too young to understand it then . . ." Grant interrupted the silence. "I think my dad spent a lot of time worrying about work and money and his family. But for a few minutes out there on that porch on those summer nights, baseball sorta set him free."

"Yup," Will agreed.

"Where do you think you'll live after you finish school?" Grant finally asked. "Wait!" he said immediately. "Before you answer that, I'd like to hear some more from our Christian Brothers." He held up the empty glass and passed it to Will.

Will took his turn and filled the glass with brandy and ice once again.

"Duluth, definitely Duluth." Will said when he returned to the fire. "How 'bout you?"

"Somewhere up around here, I guess."

"So, can Kate walk without that brace on her leg?" Will surprised Grant and nudged the fireside chat around a sharp curve. Their conversation had acquired a perfect incongruity and tempo that only the precise mix of alcohol and wood smoke could lubricate.

"Yeah, I did ask her about that. She says she can do it, but it's pretty awkward," Grant answered. "What made you think of that?"

"I dunno," Will replied, then tossed out another totally unrelated question. "Do you remember the day when you realized you weren't gonna be a big leaguer? The day when it sort of dawned on you that you just couldn't make it?" Will pushed the conversation around another sharp curve, back to baseball.

"Do you?" Grant asked.

"Freshman baseball at Harvard," Will responded without a second thought. "Oh-for-four in the first game of a doubleheader. Didn't play in the second game. That's when the light clicked on. You?"

Grant thought about his answer for a long moment. "Gonna give it to you straight, Pard," he started. "I still think I've got a chance. Not shittin' you! I'm not done dreamin' that dream yet. Whataya think about that?"

"I think you're crazier than the proverbial shithouse rat." Will pointed the glass of brandy at Grant, and some of the brandy splashed out. "Oops," he added.

"You gotta dream big dreams, Will. Hell, I got to first base with Kate Bellows last night!"

Will laughed out loud and gave the brandy to Grant. "First base! I haven't heard anyone brag about getting to first base for years. Remember those days? Remember when we used to huddle up in the locker room with several buddies and talk about how far we got with some girl after the junior high dance? First base, second base . . ."

"Yeah, I sometimes lied about my total bases," Grant admitted.

"Sure seemed like a helluva long way from first to second, didn't it?" Will said.

"We had a few arguments about just what counted as gettin' to second base." Grant raised his knees under his chin and pointed the glass at Will.

"Second base was under her shirt, Pard. Everybody knows that," Will said.

"That's the same point of view my buddies all took when I told them I'd felt up Mary Jane McCarthy. Mary Jane had a reputation for being sort of frigid. So when I told the guys I'd felt her up on Friday night, they'd needed details."

"Please continue," Will urged.

"Well, I told the guys we were ridin' around in the backseat of somebody else's car after a basketball game. Really cold winter night, you know? Anyway, I explained that she was wearing a heavy sweater and a winter coat and we were cruisin'. So we're kinda makin' out a little bit and I put my hand on her boob."

"You were wearing gloves, too, weren't you?" Will asked, then covered his eyes and shook his head in contempt.

"Sure, it was cold!" Grant replied.

"And you were bragging about feeling Mary Jane up over the top of her sweater *and* winter coat while you were wearing winter gloves?" Will accused Grant, but he already knew the answer.

"Yeah."

"She probably didn't even know she was being felt up, and if the girl doesn't even know it's happening, then it doesn't count. You were still on first base!"

"That was the very same point of view my buddies took," Grant chuckled.

"Probably feeling up the armrest on the car door!" Will said. After a moment of silence, he asked, "So whatever happened to Mary Jane? Still frigid?"

Grant furrowed his brow and pointed at Will. "No, last I heard of her was sometime during the summer after we graduated and she'd learned to work with several runners on base at the same time."

"Ah, great use of symbolism, too. You *are* a poet." Will stretched out and looked up at the sky while he laughed and savored the image of Grant and Mary Jane Whatshername. "I've got a pretty good buzz going here," he offered.

Will was an easy drunk. His hair got mussed, magically, without even touching it, after a couple drinks. He didn't slur his words; he just needed extra concentration to complete his sentences. "It's extraordinary, almost mystical . . ." Will put his hands behind his head and leaned back, ". . . the way that the proper mixture of ice and brandy can enhance a man's insight and sharpen his focus as to the workings of the cosmos." He belched with his mouth open, then nudged another piece of wood into the fire. "The first time I got to second base . . ."

Like most friendships tempered over the heat and glow of a campfire, the already strong bond between Will and Grant found its way to higher ground. As they told stories and watched a crescent moon slip through the autumn sky, they learned to read another man's open heart, and perhaps to understand things left unsaid.

∾ CHAPTER 11 ∾

Clanking dishes and the morning chatter from a milling crowd filled the air in the dental school cafeteria before classes on Monday morning, while several freshmen students stood shoulder to shoulder and moved through the line at a busy counter.

Grant carried his tray to an empty table and sat alone while he waited for his classmates to join him. An eight o'clock lecture in Gross Anatomy was still forty minutes away, and the boys would have a chance to visit for a few minutes before classes started. Grant used his foot to shove a chair out of the way, and Ben Pribyl sat next to him.

Ben stuffed half of a jam-covered English muffin into his mouth. "Heard the fishin' was pretty rough," he said, the words muffled by his breakfast.

"Yeah, we got skunked. Never caught a fish. Didn't even need the fillet knife," Grant said.

"Well, a good knife is all you need sometimes." Ben pushed the other half of the English muffin into his mouth. "I had a little narrow-bladed one, like a fillet knife, when I was in Vietnam."

"Oh?"

"A little blade like that can be pretty handy," Ben said. He leaned forward and grabbed a napkin. "You just stick it up through the foramen magnum, into the brain, like pithing a frog. People die real quiet that way." Ben appeared to be a million miles away as he moved the napkin over his lips. For the first time since Grant had known him he wore an expression that Grant didn't understand. He seemed to be fascinated by the things he was remembering, and he'd offered something extraordinary with no prompting.

"You really did that stuff? No shit?" Grant asked, spreading cream cheese on a bagel. His own father had been unwilling or perhaps unable to tell him much about his experiences in World War Two, and now this guy that he was just getting to know seemed willing to share some graphic details.

"Yeah," Ben nodded. "Remember when we were dissecting a while ago in Gross Anatomy? It was the day when we were looking at our guy's lungs. Well, right up there behind the sternum, that's where you want to cut a man. You just put the knife in like this." Ben pointed his three-inch plastic knife into the air. "And you slice this way." He flicked his wrist and the knife moved in a small arc. "Cuts the aorta, the pulmonary artery, and maybe the heart. They die real quiet." Ben's tone was calm, as if he was explaining an equation from a biochemistry lecture.

"Why would you do that? Why would being quiet matter?" Grant asked. He leaned forward with his arms resting on the table and waited for his answer.

"Well, think about it. Say you've got a prisoner, but you're out there in Injun country where he might call out to his friends and get you killed. He's gotta go," Ben said calmly. "He wouldn't think twice about killin' you either, you know."

"You did that? Really?" Grant asked.

Ben looked at his English muffin. "We did a lot of things. You do what you have to, and you try to survive." He dragged his spoon around in his coffee cup and continued. "One time we were dropped way out in the bush, then we walked for about two days, until we found what we were sent to destroy. It was a large building, like a dormitory, and we waited till night. We snuck down there and blocked all the exits except one, then we torched the place. We had several machine guns set up and we shot everybody who came running out." Ben drank from a Styrofoam cup, then continued. "Killed about four hundred Russians. I think we were in Cambodia." He set the coffee down and glanced casually at Grant. "Spent a lot of time on ambush, too. Sometimes we'd wait for twenty, thirty, forty minutes for several bad guys to line up so we could shoot 'em all with the same bullet."

Grant found himself staring, openmouthed, when Ben finished. "I gotta ask you, Ben," Grant started slowly, "does any of that stuff bother you? That you killed all those people? Can I even ask that? I'm just curious. You seem to be OK with it all. Are you? I mean, we hear so much about Vietnam vets having all kinds of emotional problems after they did stuff like that." Anyone who could recount stories like this should be trembling at the awful memories, Grant reasoned. But Ben told the stories as if he was remembering his walk to school this morning. Grant could see no sign of lingering trauma or dread. Ben shared his experiences easily. He wasn't boastful, and he didn't trivialize the things he'd done, either. When Grant watched him speak, it was clear that there were many more stories to be told.

"I told ya, I did my duty." Ben shrugged. "I was well trained and I did my duty. I just wanted to come home, and that was what I had to do in order to come home. I'm OK with it. I was serving my country. I just decided to be proud of the fact that I was good at what I did." He lit a cigarette and leaned over his coffee cup. "But sometimes I think about all that shit, and wonder how I wound up here."

"Talking about Nam?" said Andy Hedstrom, a baby-faced kid from Pelican Rapids, who placed a lunch tray on the table and sat next to Ben.

"Yeah," Ben said. "Were you there?"

Before Andy could answer, several more classmates followed him to the table and sat down for breakfast.

"No, I was in the air force, never went to Vietnam," Andy said, as he stirred the cafeteria oatmeal with a plastic spoon. "It was actually like I'd stayed in school, though. I spent a couple years sitting in missile silos in North Dakota, waiting for orders to blow up the world. I read a lot, took almost a full load of college classes while I was out there. What did you do, Joe?"

Joe Paatalo placed his tray on the table and sat down beside Andy. Joe seemed to have a smile permanently built into his face. "I went to Nam. Ordnance disposal," Joe said, ever-present smile in place. "I saw some shit. Pass the salt, would you, Andy? What about you, Mitch, were you there?"

The only person at the table who hadn't spoken was Mitch Morgan. No matter what clothes Mitch wore, his posture and mannerisms created the impression that he was sporting a bow tie and suspenders. He was one of the top students in the class, and everyone listened when Mitch spoke. He arranged the food on his tray, but said nothing while everyone waited for him to share his Vietnam experience.

"C'mon, Mitch. I heard you tell Andy you were there for a while. What'd you do?" Ben asked.

Mitch seemed to be ignoring Ben's question. He looked much older than he really was. Middle age had claimed him far too early. Based on the way Mitch's shoulders were rounded over, and the way he shuffled when he walked, Grant guessed he'd never been an athlete. Finally Mitch began to grin, but he was still reluctant to answer.

"C'mon. We're waiting, Mitch," Ben said.

"Rough duty. I don't like to talk about it much." He paused and looked at his classmates. "I played the sousaphone in the Marine Band," Mitch said, then he laughed along with the others.

When the laughter subsided Grant leaned forward and offered, "I stayed in school. Just seemed like the thing to do. Thought I might get drafted, but it never happened." He looked right and left, then added, "I was afraid. I was afraid of everything I heard about Vietnam. The jungle, bugs, snakes, booby traps, bad guys, everything. I didn't want to go over there and be part of that. To tell you the truth, I was afraid of dying. Weren't you guys scared?"

"Scared shitless," Ben replied.

Joe Paatalo nodded his agreement while he arranged his breakfast tray. "No shit. Every day. Every minute." The table grew silent for a minute.

"I remember the day I got my lottery number. They were broadcasting the draft lottery on TV over at Coffman Union," Grant said. "A buddy came walking up with a big smile and told me I'd drawn number 350. So just for the hell of it, I asked him what day had been chosen first. He said that if your birthday was March 6, you were the first-round draft choice of the United States Army!" Grant leaned back in his seat and held on to the memory for a moment. "There were four other guys standing in that little group, and two of them were born on March 6. What are the odds of that, huh? Man, you could feel the wind comin' out of everyone's sails. I tried to hide what I was feeling, my own relief. But one of those guys died in Vietnam, and the other was back in school two years later. It's sorta like you just said, Ben, sometimes I wonder how I wound up here, too."

"Ever make any political statements around campus?" Ben asked Grant.

"You mean did I protest the war? Stuff like that?" Grant asked.

"Yeah, that's what I was getting at," Ben said.

"I had no idea about the politics of the times. In fact, I was always amazed when other college kids, about my age, would stand up and explain how to solve the country's problems. I wondered how they'd learned all that shit in only a year or two of college, when all I'd learned during the same time was that I was still afraid of the war, and how to tap a keg," Grant said.

"You're an honest man, Grant," Ben said.

"Everybody was afraid," Joe added. "No shame in that. I remember watching B-52s return after a bombing run with a five-hundred-pound bomb hanging from the bomb bay door. I wondered if I was watching my own death coming to get me every time. I just couldn't help thinking that it would really be a bummer to get killed by one of our bombs that forgot to fall out of one of our bombers.

Andy Hedstrom looked up from his oatmeal, and took his turn. "We used to move the nuclear missiles around from one silo to another at night, so the Russian satellites couldn't see us, and wouldn't know which silos were armed. We'd put a missile on a semi trailer and take off for a different silo. The local cops had strict orders not to stop us. No speeding tickets or shit like that, just get out of the way," Andy said.

"So one dark winter night—it's colder than a witch's tit—some city cop in a little town pulled our caravan over. I was ridin' in the lead jeep, and when that cop came struttin' up to our vehicle, the guy sittin' next to me chambered a round in his .45 and then unzipped that little plastic window on the jeep's door while he waited. I just about shit my pants."

Everyone at the table leaned forward.

"When that dumb cop stuck his face in the window there was a very large pistol about an inch from his nose, and I know that the driver was willing to use it. 'Hit the fucking ground!' was how that conversation started. When he had the cop facedown on the freezing blacktop he put his knee right in the cop's back and held the muzzle of that gun on the back of his head. He leaned way down to that cop's ear and said, 'I can't believe you're stupid enough to stop a convoy carrying a nuclear missile!' He was so angry his voice was shaking. Then he says, 'My name is Captain Dean Libra, and my commanding officer is General Glenn Leimbach, in case you're stupid enough to call headquarters over at Grand Forks and tell them what you did, and complain about the way you were treated.'"

No one at the table had taken a bite of breakfast while Andy had been talking. "So what happened?" Joe asked.

"Captain Libra kept his knee in the cop's back and the gun at his head while he waved the convoy back onto the road. That cop just lay there with his eyes shut. Man, there was a cold wind blowin' that night! I'll bet it was 40-below windchill out there. But that cop never moved. When the convoy rolled out of sight, the captain growled, 'Don't fuckin' move. Just keep your face and hands flat on the highway.' Then he stood up and said, 'I still don't know if you're a terrorist, or a spy, or just a fuckin' idiot, but I have every right to shoot you and I just might. Now I'm gonna get back into my vehicle and rejoin my unit. Corporal Hedstrom here will be watching you, and if you even move before we're out of sight I *will* turn around and shoot you.'"

Andy pointed a plastic fork at Ben, and finished with, "When we were about a mile down the road the captain turned to me and said, 'I'm kinda glad I didn't shoot that guy.'" Andy shook his head. "I wonder whatever happened to that cop," he said. "Sometimes I wonder whatever happened to Captain Libra, too."

With that, the conversation about Vietnam and all the absurdity that led them to this moment evaporated. It was just over.

"You got my notes from Biochemistry?" Ben asked Andy.

Grant noticed Kate walk into the coffee shop and stand in front of a vending machine. He stood up immediately and walked directly toward her.

"Hi, how was your weekend?" she asked without looking at him. He wanted to sneak a kiss, but after a quick look, Kate turned her eyes away from him. Her body language and facial expression just weren't right, and she certainly didn't seem glad to see him. Given the way they'd parted a few days earlier, he'd expected to see that wonderful smile this morning.

"You OK?" Grant asked.

"Sure." She smiled half a smile. "How was your weekend?" she repeated, then looked at her feet.

"It was all right. I'd rather have been with you. Will and I had a good time at Spider Lake. The fishin' was terrible. Can I see you tonight?"

"I have a curriculum meeting after work," she said.

Something wasn't right. This was not the same woman who'd laughed at his jokes and kissed him several days earlier.

"How 'bout after that?" Grant asked.

"I have some work to do at home."

Something definitely wasn't right.

"Well, maybe we could plan to go out on a real date Friday night? I've got some midsemester exams this week and I should put in some extra time studying at night. Can we go out Friday night?" He wanted to stand closer to her, maybe hold her hand, but she seemed to shrink away from him.

"OK," Kate said, as if she was giving in just to make him stop asking. Her eyes lingered on him for a moment, then she turned away.

"What?" Grant asked. "What's wrong?"

"Aw, nothing," she sighed. "I just need to get up to the clinic. I'll see you later."

As Grant watched her walk away, he knew he'd seen something he didn't want to acknowledge, but he let himself ignore the body language and facial expressions that had been all wrong. He simply wanted to believe that things between him and Kate had remained unchanged since they'd laughed and kissed on her front steps.

Staying focused during Gross Anatomy lab or Biochemistry lecture should have been fairly easy, but no matter what the task at hand was, whether dissecting the cadaver's abdomen or memorizing equations in the Krebs energy cycle, somewhere just beyond the academic challenge in front of him there was an image of Kate Bellows drifting slowly by.

He might be lifting the hepatic artery, searching for the place it disappeared into the liver, when he thought about the way Kate's smile had energized him during the Twins game. Or he might be taking notes about the production of adenosine triphosphate at the cellular level and then lose track of biochemistry for a moment while he remembered how wonderful it felt to have her pressed up against him.

But tethered to every beautiful thought about Kate was the memory of how she'd looked away with no joy in her eyes when they'd spoken that morning. He tried not to think about that.

Kate never showed up at the coffee shop on Tuesday, so Grant went to her office after class, only to find it locked. When he asked a secretary in a nearby office if she'd seen Kate recently, the woman said Kate had locked her door and gone home about thirty minutes earlier.

He tried to call her every half hour that night until 11:30 p.m., but there was no answer. Kate was a no-show at the coffee shop again on Wednesday, and Grant had to work at suppressing the fact that she was avoiding him.

Over in a darkened corner of his conscious mind, an idea that he didn't want to acknowledge began to emerge from the shadows: her feelings had changed over the weekend while he was at Spider Lake. He was out. He tried to stay with the thought that she was excited about another date with him, and they'd just pick things up where they'd left off when he'd said good-bye to her after the game. But if that was true, if she felt the same way he did, she'd be looking for him during the day, she'd want to see him after class. She'd certainly be home and answering the phone. The painful suspicion evolved into a grudging acceptance after a day or two to think things over. She must have decided that it was better to stay with her old boyfriend. Surely that was what had happened. Now she was just afraid to tell Grant to his face that their evening at the ballpark was the beginning *and* the end of their relationship.

Nevertheless, he couldn't stop looking for her around the coffee shop.

He couldn't stop hoping. He called her home several times Wednesday evening, and again Thursday night, but when she never answered it was impossible to deny what was happening any longer.

He'd been able to hide the disappointment and heartache from his friends all week, but he couldn't deal with it any longer himself. It was consuming him, and he had to have some resolution.

Friday after class, a small stream of happy dental students filed out of the lecture hall after the Gross Anatomy midsemester exam was finished. "Hey, Pard," Will called to Grant. "We're all going down to Stub & Herb's for about twenty beers. C'mon."

"I'll catch up with you," Grant replied. "I've got some things to do first." He had no intention of joining Will and the others for beer and bullshit. He felt terrible. He thought his world had turned a week earlier. He'd thought he had a date with the girl of his dreams tonight. And now, well, the date had to be off. She'd just hidden from him for a week and he knew what that meant. He felt empty inside as he walked toward the elevator.

"Hey!" Will called. "Have your ass down there in twenty minutes or I'm comin' to get you!"

"Be right there!" Grant lied. He had to find Kate.

"Hi, Grant!" Tanya Miller said when she rushed past him in the hallway outside the dental hygiene clinic. She was hurrying to leave the building. "Aren't you coming to Stub & Herb's? Sounds like everybody's going to be there."

"Yeah. I'll be right there. Hey! Is anybody still in the clinic?" he asked.

"I don't think so," Tanya said over her shoulder. Then, unable to bridle her enthusiasm, she actually started to run for the exit.

Tanya was right. The dental clinic was empty when Grant stepped in and looked around. Kate's office was just around the corner. He'd try there one last time.

A seam of light spilled into the darkening hallway through a small opening in Kate's office door. Grant approached as quietly as he could, put one eye next to the doorjamb, and peeked inside. He watched her make some notes and arrange the things on her desk for a minute, then he pushed the door open slowly, until she noticed him.

"Hi," he said when she looked up at him.

"Hi," she said with no sign of emotion.

"I thought we had a date for tonight," Grant said.

She nodded softly, then looked down at her desktop.

"You couldn't do it, could you?" Grant said.

"Huh? What?" Kate replied.

"Break up with your boyfriend. It wasn't worth the risk, was it? Or maybe you just came to your senses? You could have just told me, Kate."

She stared at her desk and said nothing, letting her actions confirm his fears.

"I looked for you all week. I thought . . ."

Kate looked at him, then looked away. She could only look at him for a second before she had to avert her eyes.

"Kate," he begged softly, deliberately. "Talk to me."

"I never had a date in high school," she said, while she stared at her desktop. "I never had a date in college. I never had a date in dental school. I think you know why. Men never quite see me as a whole woman. Nobody does. Rod was the first boy—man—" she corrected herself, "that I've ever been with." She held his gaze for a moment before she continued. "I met Rod at one of those keggers at Dommy's house last spring. He was nice to me." Kate took hold of Grant with her eyes. "He wants to marry me."

This was not what Grant wanted to hear. She was trying to take back all the things she'd said at the ball game. She was about to tell him she was really sorry, but she'd chosen someone else.

"I should just go, Kate. I'm sorry I caused problems for you." Grant turned to leave.

"No. Don't." Kate said. "Sit down. You don't understand."

Grant took a seat near Kate and waited for her to say something. He sat quietly and waited, but he soon grew uncomfortable with the silence. He needed to get out of there. He was pretty sure he understood the situation completely. "I don't want to be your friend, Kate," he said. "I have lots of friends. But you? I don't want to be your friend, and then see you with someone else. I couldn't do . . ."

"Rod is so good to me," she interrupted, and the anguish in her face deepened. "I was ready to settle for that. I was ready to marry him, I think." Kate pursed her lips and shook her head. "And I think there was a time when I could actually have settled for that, and been happy. Maybe." She drew in a huge breath, then let it out slowly. "Then you started talking to me, and you made me laugh. You made me feel pretty, and special. You ruined all that."

"Sorry," Grant said.

"Don't be," Kate answered.

"So are you gonna marry him?" Grant asked. "I'm a little confused here."

"It's not right to 'settle' for someone," Kate said.

"So what are you gonna do? I thought you said he was . . ."

"I broke up with him, Grant," she interrupted. "He didn't like it very much, either. He got really angry."

Grant stared at her and tried to understand.

"I knew I should never have gone out for coffee with you, or to that baseball game," she said.

"So why did you?" he asked.

"I thought you were cute, and a gentleman, and funny. I was curious. Oh, shit, I don't know. Going out for coffee that night was just one of those things that you do sometimes, but never understand *why* you did it." She looked down at her feet, suddenly unable to share any more.

His spirits lifted. There might still be some joy in the world. It was nice to hear her say those things, but now what? This wasn't at all what he'd expected to hear.

"Men don't want to be cute," he said.

"Huh?" Kate turned quickly.

"You said I was cute. I don't want you to think I'm cute. I told you that before," Grant answered. "I want you to think I'm handsome, like a movie star, not cute, like Opie. When you look at me I wanna make your knockers throb."

Kate softened, then replied, "Knockers don't throb, and women like cute."

"Well it's my fantasy, Kate, and some knockers are gonna throb!"

That did it for Kate. The smile he'd been hoping for appeared at the corners of her eyes, then spread. "That's it! Right there!" She pointed to the grin on his face. "That's why I was drawn to you," she said. For the first time since he'd come to her office, she relaxed.

"Kate, I don't know what to say here. I mean, I can't compete with Rod, you have some history with him, and he's handsome, and rich, and nice . . ."

"Rod is a nice guy," Kate interrupted. "And he was good to me, and he is handsome, and he does have a lot of money, and that might have been enough to make me happy once." Kate looked at her hands for a moment. "But on his *best* day, I mean the very best day of his life, he's not you! You make me laugh, and I loved the way you held me. Whenever I see you I want to stand close to you. You make me *feel* something. I could never settle for something less, now."

Grant turned a confused smile toward Kate. "So what's the problem here?" He sat down on a chair next to hers and held her hands. "I don't understand."

"I'm afraid to believe the things I feel for you," she whispered.

"Why?" he asked.

"I guess I don't think I'm entitled to feel them."

"That doesn't make sense," he said.

Kate looked into his eyes, afraid to explain further. Then she said it, coldly, with no emotion. "I don't want someone to settle for me, either."

He watched those perfect blue eyes fill with tears, and he saw the whole story.

He let things come into a final, clear focus for a moment before he spoke. She was slumped over slightly in the chair next to him, and she'd left it for him to be the one to speak next.

"This is about something more than walking away from an old boyfriend. This is about being the last one chosen, or not being chosen at all, isn't it?" Grant started. "This is about a lifetime of standing out there in right field watching others play the game and not letting you join in. You're afraid that maybe I'm gonna do what everyone in your life has done, leave you standing there and choose someone else! Right? In fact, you're trying to give me a chance to sort of back out of all this before I feel trapped into settling for you. That's what this is, isn't it?"

Kate wiped her tears away and nodded.

"Kate, you've just spent too much time out there in right field, that's all. This brace on your leg? Well, that's just gonna have to represent your dreams that are meant to stay dreams. God knows I have mine, too. We all do. It's too bad you can't let something else define you—your beauty, brains, charm, anything. Look what you've done. You're admired and respected by students and your colleagues on the faculty of one of the finest grad schools in the world. You're OK! Think about that for a minute." Kate sat there motionless and stared at her hands.

"And one more thing," Grant added. "When we walk outta here tonight I'm hoping you might hold my hand and claim me in front of anyone we meet, like you did at the ball game. I just can't imagine anything that could make me feel more special than that."

He stood up and took her in his arms. He stroked her dark hair and felt her tears run onto his cheek. He rocked slowly from side to side and whispered, "We'd never have met if it weren't for all that. It's what kept you available until I came along. I guess I should be thankful. Maybe it was meant to be."

She sobbed, then laughed, then buried her face in his shoulder and tried to make herself stop crying. Grant kissed her hair and held her while they swayed side to side a minute longer. Eventually Kate exhaled, as if to punctuate the end of an unpleasant experience.

"You're the most complete person I know, and you're a better man than I am. Well, you know what I mean." He placed his finger under her chin and gently lifted it until her eyes met his. "And that never having a date thing? I don't get that. I'll tell you something that I probably shouldn't. We *are* gonna go out for dinner tonight, but I want to be around for breakfast, too. I want you to rest your head on my shoulder and whisper promises in my ear. I want you to make me laugh like you did the other night. I want to stand close to you and I want people to see us together. I choose you . . . *first!*"

Eye makeup had run down both of her cheeks. He'd said all that he could say. Now she'd have to step out there onto what she feared was thin ice and see if it would hold her up.

With one hand on the small of her back, he pulled her close and kissed her. But the warmth of the kiss was soon undone by an unusual taste, and he felt Kate begin to smile as she recognized the taste of the mascara that covered both of her cheeks.

She stepped away and began to clean the smeared makeup.

"C'mon, Kate. Let's go have dinner at Benny's. Sky's the limit. Order some cantaloupe if you want," Grant said. "I told you, you're the one!"

"OK," she said. She leaned over and used a mirror next to her desk while she cleaned up.

When Kate finished with her makeup and turned to get her jacket, Grant noticed a freshly opened package of stationery on her desk. The University of Minnesota School of Dentistry logo was printed across the top of the stationery, and Grant's thoughts slipped instantly from Kate to Will Campbell. A wicked scheme to get even with Will for scalding his instruments came to him with lightning speed. He knew what he had to do, and while Kate was standing with her back to him he took several sheets of stationery and placed them in one of his books. By the time she turned around, the deed was done. He'd deal with Will Campbell later.

"Ready?" Kate asked.

"Yup!" Grant replied.

She leaned forward and kissed him softly on the lips. Then she took his hand in hers and they walked out to Washington Avenue.

᪰ CHAPTER 12 ᪰

An invisible dome separated the corner booth at Benny's from the rest of the world when Kate and Grant seated themselves. Clinking dishes, the comments of passing waitresses, and conversations from neighboring booths all went unnoticed under the hemisphere of yellow light flowing from an old fixture suspended above their table.

Grant moved a dish of pickles off to the side of the table and reached across toward Kate. He gestured for her to give him her hand. He then held it gently while they talked about all the things that had been brushed aside during the previous week.

He shared the stories of his weekend at Spider Lake. He tried to explain the hollow sense of desperation he'd felt all week during her absence. He complained about some of the vague questions on his midsemester exams. He laughed along with her when he told some stories about Ben Pribyl. But he never stopped stroking the back of her hand with his thumb, nor did he try to hide his infatuation.

Kate told a story about Tanya the Mauler's rough treatment of another patient, and she shared some frustrations regarding her job and the inflexible management policies of a large university. Then, as if to separate all that had come before this moment from all that was to come, she breathed a contented sigh and smiled when she confessed, "I missed you."

"I was sure you'd decided to stay with Rod and forget about me," Grant said.

"No. I dropped him . . . ," she hesitated, ". . . like shit from a tall cow!" Her face twisted and she laughed with her mouth open for a moment. It was the first time she'd been able to joke about ending her relationship with Rod, and her laughter had a cleansing quality. "Dr. Muckinhern really liked that line, by the way," she said, then she added, "but you didn't hear that from me."

"He knew I'd said that? And he told you about it?" Grant asked.

"We're kind of close," Kate explained. "We had a little chat earlier this week. Apparently Ebby told him exactly what you'd said, and then he told me."

"Hmmm," Grant said, still unsure of his status with the dean and the head of Preclinical Dentistry. Then he remembered something. "Hey, I went and tried to apologize to Paul Zoch, the guy who I had that little head-bangin' incident with. Dean Muckinhern was pretty clear about not wanting to see me up there again."

"That was nice," Kate said. "Good move."

"No, not really. The apology thing didn't go too well. He's a jerk, for sure. Made me want to kick his ass all over again. He made me feel like a fool for trying to apologize." The waitress brought a glass of beer for both of them. When she'd left the table he leaned forward with a tentative expression on his face, and said, "Tell me about your chat with Dr. Muck-inhern. How did I fit into that conversation?"

"Oh, after the curriculum meeting on Monday he took me down to Stub & Herb's and we had a sandwich. He could see that something was bothering me, and he asked about things. I told him about Rod, and this other guy I'd been seeing. He was pretty surprised when I told him just who that other guy was. That's when he laughed and told me all about your visit to his office. He likes you. He thinks you have integrity. I don't think you're in any trouble over that incident in lab."

"Really?" Grant grinned.

"But I wouldn't try him again if I were you," Kate smiled.

The waitress returned with two large deli sandwiches and French fries. Grant let go of Kate's hand, picked up a fork, and reached across the table to her plate. He carefully picked some onions off her sandwich and pushed them to the side of her plate. Kate questioned him with her eyes.

"I'm hoping for a turn at bat here in a little while, and, you know, onions," he said.

"Good call," Kate replied.

The clatter and bustle of Benny's Deli went on all around them while they ate and talked, and laughed, and flirted with each other.

An hour later the pickle dish clinked against Grant's plate when he slid it forward and leaned back from the table. He was about to say something when Kate moved her plate to the side, reached for his glass of beer, and drank the last swallow. "I like beer!" She raised her eyebrows and grinned. "Want to split another one?"

"I've got beer at my place. Let's go see if there's a movie on TV."

"Sounds good," she said.

While they were gathering their jackets from the coat hooks on their booth seats, Grant said, "Would you like to go to the Orion Room sometime— you know, the restaurant at the top of the IDS building—and have a special dinner?"

Kate, standing next to him, zipped her jacked and said, "It's really expensive."

"You've been there, haven't you?" Grant said, unable to hide his surprise and disappointment. "I can tell by the way you said that."

"Yeah," Kate said. She suddenly wished she hadn't said anything. Grant's disappointment was palpable. "It wasn't that great," she added.

"That's not the point. I just wanted to take you someplace special and show off my date." Grant took her hand and they began to walk to the door. "How 'bout Murray's? That's the other place everyone talks about. Been there, too?"

Kate nodded. Grant slumped.

"Rod?" Grant asked.

Kate nodded once more. "Really, it wasn't *that* great." Grant was stung, first by the fact that he didn't have the money to take her to those nice restaurants anyway, and also because Kate was obviously trying to backtrack and protect his tender feelings.

"Well, shit," Grant sighed. "I wanted to take you someplace special. You know, so we could say it was our *place*."

"Oh, but you did! Metropolitan Stadium! In case you didn't notice, it's the largest restaurant in the world. We had a great dinner. They had live entertainment, too. Not a crummy comedian, or some guy playing a violin, but fifty of the highest-paid celebrities in the country."

Grant smiled, held her hand, and let her continue.

"They played a big-league ball game for our entertainment, and we sat with the rich people!" Kate said. She leaned close and kissed him on the lips. That can be our place: Met Stadium. Nobody ever took me there before." She paused. "And I had *way* more fun than at the Orion Room, or Murray's."

She took his hand and they walked out the front door of Benny's Deli, into the cool autumn night. The softness and sincerity in her words were comforting for his shaky ego. The kiss and the way she was holding his hand were more than enough to let him forget the Orion Room and Murray's. Those two-dollar seats out in left field last week just might have taken them both someplace special.

~:~

"Love what you've done with the place," Kate joked when she peeked into Grant's apartment. Ivory-colored walls that had been painted and repainted dozens of times gave contrast to the dark oak trim. The building was a well-worn brick sixplex a few blocks from the St. Paul campus. Grant lived in a tiny one-bedroom apartment on the third floor.

"Well, thanks." He hung his jacket, then hers, on coat hooks behind the oak door. "I've tried to stay with the impoverished-student theme."

A rickety card table stood in the corner nearest the door. Patches of colored fur, feathers, and other miscellaneous materials covered the top of the table. A fly-tying vise was fastened to the table in front of a rusty folding chair.

"Fred, I mean Dean Muckinhern, would love to see this," she said when she glanced at the table. "And I see that you have a Maytag box for a kitchen table. That's a nice touch."

Another rusty folding chair, the mate to the one by the card table, set next to a huge cardboard box near a small kitchenette. A hole had been cut through the side of the box so that the person sitting in the chair could move in close and sit with his feet under it, something like a real kitchen table.

Grant turned and examined his kitchen table closely. "I believe it's a Lady Kenmore box," he corrected, sarcastically.

The remainder of the room was furnished with a 1950s vintage avo-cado-colored couch flanked by two aluminum-framed lawn chairs, both sporting frayed vinyl webbing, and an RCA color TV console that was only a shade smaller than the couch. A broken set of rabbit ears rested atop the TV. Tin foil had been wrapped around both of the rabbit ears, then stretched toward the ceiling and fastened to the wall with thumbtacks.

"My folks gave me the couch from our basement. The rest of this stuff I just found," Grant said.

"Nice TV," Kate joked.

"Yeah, it's an oldie. The streetlights go dim every time I fire that thing up!" He laughed, then he opened his refrigerator. "Would you like a beer?" he asked.

"Sure," Kate replied. She followed him into the tiny kitchenette, then peeked over his shoulder and laughed out loud. "All you have in there is beer and ketchup, and you gave me hell for using ketchup!"

Grant found an opener in a kitchen drawer and opened a bottle of Leinenkugel beer for each of them. He gave her one, then clinked the neck of his bottle against hers.

"That's not exactly true," Grant started. "I gave you hell because you were about to desecrate a ballpark brat by using ketchup on it. Ketchup is a fine condiment. I use it regularly." He opened a cupboard door, pointed inside, and added, "I do have some food, too."

"Let's see here," Kate said as she peered inside. "Macaroni and cheese . . ."

"Ah, yes, Orange Death. It's a dish I prepare several times a week. I learned how to cook mac and cheese when I was in college," he said proudly. "You just cook the noodles, then add the cheeselike stuff . . ."

"Never mind." Kate shook her head and looked beyond the saltines. "What's this? Spinach . . . and basil . . . and olive oil, and pine nuts? Do you actually cook, instead of just eating boxed meals?"

"Sure, that's for a dish I learned from Dom Sabetti and the other Italian guys from Eveleth. You just grind all that stuff up and put it over pasta. It's great! I call it Mayfly Hatch 'cuz it looks like the front of my car on a summer night when there's a mayfly hatch. You know, about two pounds of mayfly guts stuck on the bumper."

"Everyone else in the world calls that pesto, I believe," Kate said as she closed the cupboard door.

"I knew that." Grant smiled. "I just wanted to see if you . . ." He stopped himself. "I don't wanna talk about food. C'mere." He leaned back against the kitchen countertop, reached his hand behind her waist, and pulled her close. Then he took the beer bottle from her hand and set it on the countertop beside his.

Arms around each other, they stood silently for a moment, touching their foreheads together and allowing a tender caress to stir something. Then Grant brought his mouth to hers. The kiss settled softly on her lips and she invited him to linger there. He held her gently and let his hand wander under her sweater, onto the soft skin on the small of her back. When his hand began to creep beneath the waist of her blue jeans she shuddered, then buried her face against his neck.

"What are you thinking?" Grant asked softly.

Kate slowly raised her lips to his ear, then ever so slowly she breathed, "My knockers are throbbing."

Grant laughed out loud, just as Kate did. She'd delivered a great punch line where there had been no joke. Neither of them could stop laughing. While his shoulders were still shaking he put his arms around her and squeezed.

Dr. Kate Bellows was in his apartment, in his arms. She was gorgeous, and clever, and whatever it was that they were doing, she clearly wanted it to continue.

They held each other cheek to cheek for a while and let the moment last.

"Do you ever worry that this is all moving too fast?" Kate whispered.

"I don't think like that," Grant said. "Besides that, I had this in mind on that first day out there on the sidewalk in front of school." He moved his hand under her sweater again. "And I can't think of one thing I'd do any differently if we had to do it all over again. Can you?"

She shook her head.

"Would you like to see if we can't do something about that throbbing?" he whispered.

Kate nodded and put her head on his shoulder.

His hands moved under her sweater and began to fumble with the hooks on the back of her bra. Her mouth was moving delicately over his when she realized that he'd never unfasten the bra without some help. She reached around and unfastened it for him, then brought her mouth back to his. "Smooth," she teased, kissing him.

"It's a long way from first base to second base," he offered, as an apology for his clumsiness, then he felt her lips curl into a smile as she kissed him. "Does this help with that awful throbbing?" he asked after a moment.

"A little bit," she replied, then she added, "Is there anything else you can do?"

She was joking, but she wasn't joking. She was exhorting him to continue with the seduction, and the provocative way she'd asked the question was thrilling. Something new and wild was happening in the silence of his kitchen. His heart was trying to hammer its way out of his chest.

A flush of sexual tension rolled over both of them as Grant reached for the button on Kate's blue jeans. When he began to slide her pants down over her hips she stepped back away from him and slid them off herself. She hesitated for just a second, then removed the steel brace from her leg and laid it on top of her clothing.

Grant looked down at the brace, now on the floor. It seemed as if Kate had discarded a whole separate person and dropped it there in his kitchen.

She stood before him wearing only her sweater and panties, and she let him stare for a moment. Then she reached behind him, flipped the kitchen light off, buried her face against his neck, and held him.

Grant put his hand under her chin and lifted it so that he could kiss her. "You're beautiful," he whispered, then gently moved his hands over her.

She held her cheek against his for a while, then grew a bit rigid. Something had changed.

"You all right, Kate?" Grant asked, when he sensed that something might be wrong.

"Yes," she replied, without taking her cheek away from his.

"Do you want to stop, or, go back?" he asked.

"No," she said.

"Is this your first time?" he guessed with a whisper in her ear.

"No. Kind of. Well, yes," she said, still unwilling to show him the uncertainty on her face.

Grant kissed her ear and held her close, then moved his hands up from the roundness of her behind and lifted her sweater over her head. "I think it'll be fine," he said.

She stood before him and looked at him, wanting him to want her but afraid of what he might think. A street lamp and a gnarled old boulevard cottonwood combined to throw muted blue shadows over her body.

He took off his pants and lifted his sweatshirt over his shoulders, then pulled her close and let his bare stomach press against hers. Her scent, the way she held him and whispered to him, the feel of her long, dark hair cascading over his arms as he embraced her, and the extraordinary softness of the skin she pressed against him was exciting. He made a point to hold her in such a way that she'd notice something else was throbbing.

~:~

Her long hair lay about the pillow when at last he slumped forward onto his bed and lay beside her. She drew in a deep breath and let it out, then kissed him on the neck. "Something is wrong," she whispered, with a rising sense of panic in her voice, then she began to shake both hands.

"What? What do you mean?" He turned his face toward her. "Are you OK?" Grant's mind began to race. Maybe the sex had triggered an irregular heartbeat? Maybe she was about to have a seizure? Now what?

While she lay on her back, Kate thrust both hands straight into the air. "I can't move my thumbs," she said, then she started to shake both hands as if she was trying to dry them off. "I have a charley horse in both thumbs!"

Grant rose up on his elbow and watched, smiling and relieved, while she shook her hands in the air for nearly a minute.

"There, that's better," she said finally. She began to laugh.

"What were you doing? You scared me." Grant chuckled, then pulled her close. The bedclothes only covered them below the waist now, and the curious blue shadows from the street fluttered slowly over her bare chest. A few minutes earlier she'd been reluctant to have him look at her. Now she wanted to feel his hungry eyes on her.

"What were *you* doing?" she whispered.

She'd begun to make small gulping noises while they'd been making love. The noises had changed into something like laughter as they neared the end. The noises seemed beyond her control. An avalanche of pleasure carried them along while they made love, then she'd arched her back and let herself be swept away.

"I wasn't thinking about my thumbs for a while there, that's for sure," she said. She hid her face against his chest and sighed.

"I love you, Kate," Grant said.

"I love you too," she said, as she raised her arms above her head and invited Grant to look at her naked body. She liked what they'd done, and she loved the way he looked at her now. "Mmmm," she purred, while she stared at the ceiling and let Grant slowly, gently move his fingertips over her. He was barely touching her as he moved from her forehead to her eyes, then her neck. He lingered on her breasts. She flinched and began to giggle when he touched the underside of her arms. Her hips began to move when he passed over her flat stomach, then her legs.

"You wanna do that again?" she whispered.

~:~

First light was only a few minutes away when Grant awoke and looked over at Kate. Her breathing was soft and regular and her face was peaceful. She'd spent the night with him, and everything had been perfect. It was still perfect. Ever so softly, he lifted the bedclothes to look at her. He kissed her nose and her eyes opened. She smiled when she understood what he wanted, and they made love again.

The warm sunlight of late morning flooded Grant's apartment when he shuffled into the kitchen and began to brew a pot of coffee several hours later. He wore only his boxers, and he flinched at the bright light every time he turned toward the windows. When the coffee was ready he poured a cup for himself and shuffled over to the TV while he rubbed his eyes.

The picture tube on the ancient TV set took nearly two minutes to warm up, but by and by Grant began to recognize the sound of somebody's marching band playing. Good, must be a football game on already, he thought. As the picture came into focus he could see that Michigan was playing but he couldn't make out who the other team was. Didn't matter. Today was a beautiful day. Kate Bellows had spent the night with him. Life was good. He sipped coffee and started to come awake.

"Wanna go get something to eat?" he asked over his shoulder, without looking away from the TV when he heard Kate coming out of the bedroom.

"I guess we'll have to," she said. "I'm not hungry for kippers or pesto."

Grant turned to smile at her and noticed that she was wearing one of his Gopher baseball T-shirts, and only that. It pretty much covered Kate.

He kept his eyes on her as she walked toward him without her brace. She could walk, but it was difficult for her. She looked awkward, really awkward. Her left leg was withered to about half the size of her right, and she had to sort of flop it out in front of her, then hop so that her shoulders heaved when she shifted her weight. She looked as if she was about to collapse with each measured step.

"Good morning," she smiled, then kissed him softly as she walked past him toward the kitchenette.

"Good morning," Grant replied, watching her from behind. He'd never seen her like that. Never even wondered what it might look like to see her that way. She walked a little different than everybody else he knew, and he wondered if anything hurt to walk like that. He stared, and thought, and wondered.

When Kate reached the kitchen countertop she stood straight on her right leg and looked though Grant's empty kitchen cupboards.

She reached up to the highest cupboard door and opened it while Grant watched from behind. The T-shirt rode up and exposed her bare backside. "We're gonna have to go get you some groceries," she said, while she tried to peer into the uppermost cupboard.

She probably wasn't trying to tempt him, Grant thought, but that didn't matter now. The half-naked woman in the kitchen was Kate Bellows, the object of his infatuation, and man, that T-shirt wasn't hiding very much anymore. He stared for a minute until he could stand it no longer. When he moved to the kitchen and reached his hands under her shirt she knew exactly what he wanted. The need for restraint was all gone now. They were lovers, each of them desperate for the other's touch.

Kate straightened herself out on the green couch when their lovemaking was finished and smiled at Grant. "We aren't gonna get much else done today, are we?"

"Nope," Grant replied. He could feel her shaking the charley horses out of her thumbs as he kissed her.

~: ~

"No onions, please," Grant said, as the waitress at Benny's Deli turned and left their table. A wry smile spread across his face, and when he made eye contact with Kate she covered her eyes and shook her head. "Think we can make it through dinner?" he grinned.

"I didn't think any urge could be that powerful." She laughed.

They'd made an attempt to leave Grant's apartment and buy some groceries around midafternoon. But somewhere in the produce section they'd both been overcome by their carnal fantasies and decided to purchase only what was already in the grocery cart and bolt for their love nest. Their appetites for the newfound joys of sex seemed insatiable.

"What do you suppose your parents would do if they knew about us?" Kate asked over dinner.

"I don't think they want to know about stuff like this. But they're gonna like you. When I take you home for the first time, my mother will try to feed you. She'll just keep bringing food to the dinner table and holding it in front of you, like she thinks you've been starving. When she gets me alone, she'll whisper and tell me that you're just a doll. Then she'll get you alone and tell you what a good boy I used to be, and maybe show you a few baby pictures. And Dad? Well, you won't meet many like him."

"What do you mean?" she asked.

"He's a stoic Norwegian. Tough as nails. Spent some time in a Japanese POW camp. He's indestructible. My hero. Only one I ever had, except Mickey Mantle." Grant smiled. "My mother saw him throw a horse right through a fence once, too. It's a long story . . . the horse bit him on the ass and he sort of lost control for a minute there." Grant paused for a moment, afraid that he'd made his father sound like a monster. "He's really a gentle man, just not a guy you want to aggravate. He gets down on the floor and plays with my brother's kids. Loves to tease 'em. Loves to hold the babies till they fall asleep, and then walk the floor with 'em and whisper to them. Just a unique man. All I want to do is live my life so people might say I was like my dad. I guess you just have to meet him."

Kate recognized Grant's affection for his father, and she liked that. She was conscious of the fact that she already saw Grant as the man she might spend her life with, and she liked the idea that he was so fond of his family. Grant Thorson would be a good husband and a good father. She let that thought linger for a moment, before his next question blew it away in a puff.

"So tell me about your parents," he said.

"My parents, my home? Well, I don't think it was like yours." Her smile faded instantly.

"What do you mean?" Grant asked, with a puzzled expression. "How bad could it be?"

"Pretty bad," Kate replied.

Grant waited for her to explain, but when she seemed reluctant to continue he asked another question. "The other day when you were talking about choosing dentistry, you said you had something to prove. Did that have to do with your parents?"

"Yeah," Kate sighed. "My dad. I felt like I had to accomplish things in order to gain his love. Maybe it was the polio, I don't know, but I always felt I needed to earn his love. He seemed so distant and detached. Then I guess when he died I never lost that need to prove myself. I wish I'd gotten to know him better. I'll always wonder . . ." Her voice trailed off.

"How about your mother?" Grant asked.

"That was never right either," Kate replied. "Once, when I was at school, maybe about third grade, a button came off my dress. It just came off, you know how they do that sometimes? Anyway, I was afraid to go home. I stopped at a little playground and sat on a swing for an hour before I walked the rest of the way home. I knew I was gonna be in trouble." Kate stopped.

"Over a button?" Grant asked.

"Yup," Kate replied. "And I was right. When I told my mom about the button she started ranting. She said she just didn't know why she'd had children, we were just a bother."

"Over a button?" Grant asked again. "Really?"

"That's what it was like at my house, all the time," Kate responded, as calmly as if she was sharing a weather forecast.

"How 'bout your dad?" Grant asked.

"Well, he had two daughters, so it worked out pretty well for him. He didn't have to spend much time with us because we were just girls, you know?"

"That's not the way it should be," Grant offered. This look at Kate's childhood was unpleasant, not at all what he'd expected her to say. He imagined her as a little girl again, just like he'd envisioned her on their first date at Metropolitan Stadium when she'd described standing out in right field. But now Grant saw a scared little girl with a cotton dress and a button missing. She still had French braids, and that brace on her leg, and he could see pain in her eyes once more.

"Your dad let her talk to you like that?" Grant asked, incredulous at Kate's story. "Big Ole would never have allowed that."

"He was always out of town on business. He didn't want to be around her either," Kate said.

"What was he like when he came home?" Grant asked.

"He drank a lot," Kate said.

"Childhood isn't supposed to be like that," Grant said.

"I know that, now," she replied. "But it seemed normal for me then. What else did I know?" She looked up and added, "When I got a little older I began to see that some of my friends had families that were different, like yours." She thought for a moment, while she watched the steam rise from her coffee. "My sister married some loser when she was eighteen. She just wanted to get out of my parents' house. I was angry at her. I felt like she'd abandoned me, left me all alone with my mother. Her marriage only lasted a few months. But then she got lucky and met a nice man and . . ." Kate stopped her story and tried to smile at Grant. "That's enough." She sighed.

"So what do you think Dean Muckinhern would say if he knew about us?" Grant asked. It was time to change the subject away from Kate's childhood.

"I'm not sure," she said. "I know he already likes you, but he's pretty protective." She smiled at the mention of Fred Muckinhern.

"What about you, Kate? What do you think about all this?" Grant asked.

"I never knew it could be like this."

They talked of school, and people around school. Their conversation began to move to the future. Each of them shared vague hints and visions about how they saw their own lives unfolding. Every declaration of a dream for the future carried with it a subtle suggestion that their future would be a shared one.

Kate reached over and held Grant's hand on the drive back to his apartment. She talked of small things in their lives and stole glances at him while he drove.

The stairs in Grant's apartment creaked as they made their way back to their private place.

His hand was on the light switch an instant after he'd opened the door, when Kate reached over and stopped him. "Leave 'em off," she said. "I know I asked you this once before, but aren't you a little bit concerned about how fast all this is going?" She was holding his hands in the dark.

They made their way to the green couch and lay down together. They lay in the dark and said nothing for a while. Grant stroked her hair and kissed her cheek from time to time, and let the silence surround them.

"Nobody knows we're here," Kate whispered finally.

"Nope." He kicked his shoes off and listened to them thump onto the floor.

"I love you," he added after a moment.

They undressed and made love on the green couch, because it was a nice place for sex. They'd find their way into the bedroom before long, and that would be a nice place for sex, too.

Sunday evening finally came, and the lock on Kate's front door clicked when she opened it. She hadn't been home since Friday morning, and she really didn't want to come home now. She sighed and turned to Grant. "I love you." She kissed him softly. "I'll see you tomorrow." She kissed him again. "That was the longest date I've ever been on."

ᢓ CHAPTER 13 ᢗ

"I can do that," Ben Pribyl said casually. Carol Knutsen handed over what looked like a miniature power tool and stepped aside with a look of disdain, perhaps failure, on her face. "It's all right, Carol. I'll just do this part for you," he added.

The project for the afternoon was to use the small circular saw to cut their cadaver's skull in half in order to remove the brain. The saw had been passed from one dissection team to another when it wound up in Carol's hands. After sizing up the situation for a moment, she decided she couldn't or didn't want to do this job, so she asked if someone else would.

Ben held the saw with a steady hand and began at the back of their cadaver's skull, then moved it forward with no hesitation. Just doing his duty, Grant thought, as he watched Ben work. It was time to study the brain, and Ben Pribyl was the man to get things started. The whirring noise from the electric motor began to compete with an even more disturbing sound. The circular, two-inch saw blade chopped and gobbled its way through bone and scalp, moving across the cadaver's head at the rate of half an inch every few seconds. It sent tiny chunks of skull, brain, and scalp into the air above the cadaver. The efficient action of the saw blade opened a fault line between the hemispheres of a human skull as it pulverized bone and created yet another new visual image for every member of the dissection team. They all watched the blade go around, and wondered just where in their memory they'd file this picture. Ben glanced up at Grant and raised his eyebrows. Neither of them quite understood what to think about the procedure they were doing. The knowledge they gained at each session gave them new respect for the incredibly complicated human design and for the profession they were entering. But they'd never imagined that part of the learning procedure would involve splitting someone's skull and removing a brain.

Suddenly, during the brief moment Grant and Ben made eye contact, the noise from the saw changed drastically. The saw screamed and tried to jump out of Ben's hands, and when Grant turned his eyes back to the cadaver's head, he saw that the little blade was spraying sparks into the air like a small fireworks display. The screech from the saw had the same effect as a fire alarm; everyone in the room spun their heads around to look. Ben quickly shut off the saw, and immediately a crowd of curious dental students gathered around him. Evan, the teaching assistant, ran to Ben's side and began to look for the source of the problem. He hunched over the cadaver's head as everyone waited silently for him to speak. "Holy shit! This guy has a steel plate in his head. It's the size of my hand," Evan said. "I'll take over on this one, Ben." Ten minutes later Evan lifted a stainless steel plate from the cadaver's skull, finished the dissection, and explained to Ben, Carol, Grant, and Jimmy Drahota how they should continue. The other students wandered back to their own cadavers after a brief inspection of the steel plate. When Evan left the group, Ben turned to Grant. "Let's go have a smoke," he said. "You guys let us know when it's our turn again. I'll bet the excitement is over for today," he said to Carol and Jimmy, as he reached for his cigarettes.

Ben walked to the big sash windows on the west wall of the lab and threw one open. He lit a cigarette and turned to Grant. "How 'bout that one? Scared the shit outta me," Ben offered. "I'll bet that's why that old guy gave his body to science. Some doctor probably saved his bacon after an accident. Whataya think, Grant?"

"I think he probably had to wear a hat when he played golf," Grant ventured. "And you're probably right about leaving his body to science. I'll bet he had a close call with the Grim Reaper. Somebody over in the other section had a guy with an artificial heart valve. That was pretty interesting to see, but nothing like a steel plate, huh?"

Ben took a long drag. "Yeah, that was really something. Hi, darlin'!" he called to a girl on the sidewalk below. "That reminds me. I saw you talking to that lady dentist at lunch today." Ben smiled.

"Yeah?" Grant said as innocently as he could.

"That girl is warm for your form!" Ben said.

"Oh?" Grant replied, still trying to appear ignorant about Ben's line of questioning. Several weeks had passed since his first date with Kate, but he'd kept things a secret from everyone but Will.

"Been hidin' the salami?"

"That would be privileged information," Grant said.

"I'll take that for a yes. It's in her eyes, Grant. Can't miss it. Hi, darlin'," he called down to another coed below.

"Really?" Grant asked. "You can see that stuff?"

"Like I said . . . can't miss it. She's got stars in her eyes for you."

"Can you blame her?" Grant said.

"Hmph." Ben smiled, flicked his cigarette butt out the window, and lit another. Grant had come to think that Ben had a gift. He could walk into a room full of fifty women, and if there was one, and only one, looking for a good time, Ben would find her in five minutes.

"Hey!" Ben said when he remembered. "Will must not have opened his mail yet today. He woulda shit his pants by now!"

"Yeah." Grant grinned wickedly. "I saw him carrying the letter around at lunch. But he must not have opened it yet. He would have said something. For sure!"

That morning over coffee, Grant and Ben had written a note to Will on the official University of Minnesota stationery that Grant had pilfered from Kate's office. They'd found an available typewriter at the student resources center and typed a letter to Will explaining that he was failing Biochemistry. They'd gone on to remind him that any student who flunks *any* freshman class must repeat the entire year. Then, in closing, they'd added, "Please visit my office at your earliest convenience," and signed it, "Dr. Frederick Muckinhern, Dean of Students."

"Maybe he went out and stepped in front of a bus or something," Ben suggested.

"No, he'd come and tell me about it before he did that!" Grant said.

"OK, you guys are up!" Carol called to them.

Ben was using a tiny pointed steel instrument to separate layers of the external surface of the dura mater and Grant was taking notes when Will scurried up alongside them. "You guys fuckin' with me, or what?" Will barked the words as a challenge, but failed to explain any further.

Ben refused to look up from the cadaver's cranium. "That would involve a gender identification crisis of apocalyptic proportions. Your butt hole is safe on our watch," he said, then added, "What are you talking about?" Grant could tell at once that Ben was good at this sort of thing.

Will scowled at Grant. "Is this your doing?"

Grant kept a straight face and tried to crane his neck and get a look at the letter in Will's hand. Will quickly hid the letter.

"Looks like it's written on official stationery from the U," Grant offered. "What is it?"

"What's it say?" Ben asked, still not looking up.

"Says I'm flunking Biochem! That can't be. And it's from Dean Muck-inhern," Will exclaimed. "Did you guys do this?" Grant and Ben could both see that Will had taken the bait and was grasping at straws in an attempt to question the letter's authenticity.

"Jeez, that's the shits, Will. You know, don't you, that if a freshman flunks *anything*, even some one-credit class, he's takin' the whole freshman year over," Ben offered. Then he threw a knockout punch without looking up. "I thought you Harvard guys were all A students."

It was brilliant. His challenge to Will's declaration that he was an A student, his nonchalant explanation of academic policy, and the way he'd delivered the information were worthy of an Oscar. He'd almost convinced even Grant that he had no idea what was written in that letter fluttering in Will's trembling hand. He still didn't look up at Will. "It's probably nuthin'. I wouldn't worry about it," he added.

"He wants me to come to his office," Will said. His eyes narrowed in disbelief and disappointment when he lowered his gaze and tried to make sense of it.

Grant had to look away before he gave himself up and started laughing. "So forget about it. Just c'mon down to Stub & Herb's with us after class. We're all going out for beer," Grant urged. Will had most certainly taken the bait, and Grant's exhortation to forget about it all only set the hook a little deeper.

"Nah, I better take care of this." Will seemed to be melting as he spoke. His shoulders slumped a little lower with each step when he turned and walked back to his own dissection team. He never said another word.

"I'd say we got his attention," Ben said to the cadaver.

∼:∼

An early-evening crowd of college students had Stub & Herb's rocking when Kate walked in and joined Grant and his friends at a large table. Grant introduced Kate to everyone, even though they all knew who she was.

Carol Knutsen and Darcy Wilhelm were the only women sitting at the table. Carol was a regular; she drank beer, laughed, and told stories right along with her male classmates. Darcy, however, always seemed to be about one joke behind the rest of the bunch, wondering what she'd missed. Jimmy Drahota, Joe Paatalo, Ben Pribyl, Andy Hedstrom, and Mitch Morgan were all waiting for Will to appear. By the end of the day they'd all been let in on the prank, and they'd watched as a stricken Will trudged up to the dean's office after class to talk about his failing grade in Biochemistry.

By now there were several empty pitchers of beer and several full ones on the table as the anticipation grew. The group finished three more pitchers while they tried to guess what Will's reaction would be. The sun was setting in an orange sky at the other end of Washington Avenue when Carol finally looked out the window and called, "Here he comes!"

Will swung the front door open and nine pairs of eyes fixed on him. He walked to their silent table and looked directly at Grant. "You fucking rat bastard! It was you! Wasn't it?" The table erupted in laughter, and everyone present stood up to salute Will. Carol gave him a glass of beer and they all drank a toast to a good prank.

"So what happened?" Ben asked. "You have to tell."

"Well, I took this fucking letter up to the dean's office," Will started, amid the steady laughter of his friends.

"I just stood there in Dean Muckinhern's door until he noticed me. His secretary had already gone home. He was sitting there at a little table tying flies." Will turned to Grant and calmly added, "They *do* have a nice table and a lot of fly-tying materials up there by the way, you asshole."

"Keep going," Joe Paatalo redirected.

"When he finally noticed me, I said, 'Dean Muckinhern, I'm Will Campbell.'" The group grew silent, waiting for Will to continue. "So he says, 'Yes?' But what he really meant was 'Big fuckin' deal!'" The table erupted once again, and Will waited for the laughter to subside before he continued. "So I said, 'I'm a dental student . . .'"

Will looked around the table and paused for emphasis. "Finally Dean Muckinhern says, 'Well good for you, Will! Now what can I do for you?'" Once again the table erupted. Will finished his beer while he waited for quiet.

"So I just came right out and told him I was flunking Biochemistry. He looked at me and said, 'So?'" Will extended his empty glass toward Grant. "Pour me another one, will you? You asswipe!"

"So I dug myself in a little deeper," Will continued. "I said, 'You wrote me this letter about repeating my freshman year?'" Laughter circled the table again; Grant and Ben tapped their glasses in triumph.

"He looked at me and said, 'No, Will, I think someone is having some fun with you.' And then he said a strange thing." Will paused, then spoke deliberately at first. His voice quickened as he spoke, and opened into a booming crescendo by the end of his sentence, "Yeah, the dean says to me, 'Do you know that asshole Grant Thorson? I'll bet *he* did this to you!'" Will was hollering to be heard over the laughter of the crowd when he finished. "Good one, Pard," Will yelled, and raised his glass in salute.

~:~

Kate reached over and touched Grant's face a little after midnight. They spent every night together now, and they were holding each other in the quiet shadows of Grant's tiny bedroom after they'd made love. "I never did things like that before," she said.

"Like what?" Grant asked.

She kissed his bare chest and said, "Like that little party at Stub & Herb's. I never got included in that stuff. I always went home and studied."

"Well, you're in the mix now," Grant said. "Can you see that all my buddies have crushes on you?"

"No they don't," Kate said.

"It's probably better if you can't see it," Grant said. He moved his hand over the curve at the small of her back, then pulled her closer.

"I never had a friendship like you have with Will, either. I think *he's* got a crush on you!" Kate laughed.

"Yeah." Grant sighed. "I'd take a bullet for Will."

Grant thought about what he'd said for a moment while Kate softly twirled the hair on his chest.

"Well . . . ," he added, pausing, "it would have to be a small caliber . . . and in the foot." He laughed at his own joke, then wrapped his arms around Kate, held her close, and forgot about Will.

It was good to be Grant Thorson just now, and he knew it. In just a short time he'd come to understand with certainty that Kate Bellows was the love of his life. This beauty with the dark hair and blue eyes made him laugh, helped with his studies, and shared insights and feelings that no one else ever had. She'd saved up a lifetime of sexual energy and she was anxious to spend it all on him. He kissed her ear and thought of her excitement during their lovemaking.

The little apartment had become the incubator for a special love and a great friendship. When they rose in the morning they ate breakfast on the cardboard table and talked about the day they were about to conquer. When they returned after school, they shared stories of the things they'd done. They sat together on the old green couch and read to each other, or they watched TV, or they made love with a joy and haste that only young lovers know. When they were together here they felt safe from the rest of the world, and each of them wondered privately if anyone else had ever discovered a love like theirs.

ᴄ: CHAPTER 14 :ᴗ

It was going to be difficult to stay awake this morning. Dr. Jamshad Gopnaith would be starting his morning Biochemistry lecture in about fifteen minutes. Dr. Gopnaith was well liked by most of the students—he just didn't happen to speak English very well. His halting and awkward mispronunciation of chemicals, microorganisms, and metabolic processes made his lectures impossible to understand. He delivered about one-quarter of the lectures in Biochemistry, and the students never knew who would be lecturing until they arrived in class. When they entered the auditorium and saw him at the lecture podium, preparing his lecture, about half of the students sighed heavily and gave up for the day. The other half groaned and dug in for an hour of difficult note taking . . . they'd begun to call it code breaking. The lecture auditorium was beginning to fill up as weary dental students drifted in one and two at a time. Most of the students wandered in with a Styrofoam coffee cup in one hand and a book bag in the other. When they noticed Dr Gopnaith, they either grimaced or smiled, then sat next to a friend and make small talk in subdued tones while they waited for the rest of the class to arrive.

Grant arranged his notebook, although he knew there wouldn't be much note taking in the next hour. He raised his coffee cup to his lips and thought about how pretty Kate had looked when he'd kissed her good-bye ten minutes earlier in the coffee shop.

"Aw, not another hour with the Gopper," Will groaned when he took a seat beside Grant. He lifted a notebook from his book bag and then swiveled the folding writing platform up from the arm of his chair and settled back into his seat. He opened his notebook and pointed to his notes from the previous lecture. "Look at that," he moaned to Grant. The page was blank when Grant looked over at Will's notebook. "Pretty hard to study from *that*!" Will pointed at the blank page and scowled. "Gimme a hit of your coffee, will ya?" He reached across Grant's notebook and took the cup from his hand. "Thanks, Pard."

"Shit. We got Jump Shot again today?" Ben Pribyl grumbled as he side-stepped in front of Grant and Will, then sat down next to Will. "Oh well, at least I'll get some reading done this morning," he said when he slouched into his chair and opened a paperback. The realization that Jamshad Gop-naith would be lecturing had brought about an abrupt change in Ben's attitude. One minute earlier he'd been a dedicated student, ready to accept the day's assignment. Now he looked like a man who'd just finished a hard day's work, taken his shoes off, and stretched out in his favorite chair. Ben searched for his page and slid farther down in his seat as he started to read.

"Hey." Will nudged Grant while he arranged some papers. "S'pose you and Kate might like to spend a few days at my parents' cabin over the Christmas break?"

"Sure." Grant shrugged. "That place was great! Kate would love it. Won't it be all closed up for the winter?"

"No. We keep it open all year. There'll be a lot of snow on the ground, though. Actually, it's pretty romantic up there." Will flashed a fiendish smile and raised his eyebrows twice. "We thought you guys might like to come and join us for a couple days."

"Yeah, that'd be fun," Grant said. "What should we . . ."

"Hey, hey. Listen to this!" Ben demanded their attention. He'd com-pletely immersed himself in his paperback while Grant and Will were talking. He sat up in his chair and pushed his index finger onto the printed page in front of him. "'Dirk lowered her gently onto the satin sheets,'" he read, then interrupted himself. "You're gonna love this!" he added, with a twisted grin. "'He kissed her alabaster skin once more, then thrust his throbbing love cudgel deep into her quivering quim.'" Ben looked up with mock wonder in his eyes. "This guy is a wordsmith!" He held the book up for Will and Grant to see. It was entitled *A Hard Man Is Good to Find*. "That tears it!" Ben exclaimed. "If I ever have a son I'm gonna name him Dirk!"

Will nodded and pointed a finger at Ben, signifying that he approved of the name Dirk.

Grant raised his coffee cup to his lips, then stopped and posed a ques-tion to his friends. "I'm not familiar with the word 'cudgel.' Are either of you?"

"Well yes, as a matter of fact, I am," Will replied, now feigning academic pomposity and clearly enjoying what he was about to say. "The word 'cudgel' comes down to us from an ancient Teutonic dialect. The exact translation is simply, 'a short angry Nazi who wears a turtleneck!'" He waited for Grant and Ben to laugh before he continued. "But I'm a bit uncertain as to the exact linguistic derivation of the word 'quim.'" Ben and Grant shook with laughter while they waited for Will's next punch line. "I believe the word 'quim' comes to us from—"

"Grant, can I see you for a moment?" A stern voice from the aisle next to Will's seat broke the spell. All three were still chuckling when they looked up and saw Dr. Ruminsky standing in the aisle, staring at Grant. "You might want to bring your books," he added, then he turned and walked up the thirty steps to the back of the lecture auditorium.

Grant couldn't hide the anxiety in his heart when he looked at his companions. He shrugged his shoulders and stepped into the aisle carrying his book bag in his right hand. The dean of admissions at the dental school didn't often attend freshmen lectures, and he *never* came down from the back of the auditorium and spoke to students. Dr. Ruminsky waited for him by the large wooden doors at the back entrance of the small amphitheater, and then stepped back through the doors and into the hallway outside when Grant reached him.

Was he being expelled from school for some unknown reason? This couldn't be a good thing. The dean didn't come and pull students out of class unless they were in trouble.

"Your father had a heart attack," Dr. Ruminsky said, when Grant was close enough. The words hit Grant like a hammer, and the obvious question began to form in his eyes immediately.

"He's all right," Dr. Ruminsky said. "I just spoke with your mother a few minutes ago. He's going home from the hospital today."

The confusion began to register in Grant's eyes. "When did it happen? And why did she call you?" Grant asked.

"Sunday," Dr. Ruminsky replied.

"Five days ago?" Grant asked.

"They thought your studies were too important. They didn't want to worry you," Dr. Ruminsky explained.

Grant dropped his book bag onto the floor, put both hands on his head, and stared at his feet. "They didn't want to *worry* me?"

"Your mother called my office to get permission to tell you about this." Dr. Ruminsky almost smiled. "They, your mother and father, thought your studies were too important to be interrupted."

Grant drew in a huge breath and let it out all at once, then lowered his hands. "I'm the first one in my family to do anything like this, Dr. Ruminsky. My mom and dad think I'm down here looking at smoking test tubes while nurses dab the sweat from my brow." Grant stopped, then looked directly into Dr. Ruminsky's eyes and questioned him. "Last Sunday?"

Ruminsky nodded. "Take a couple days and go home. Your grades are fine, I'll see that . . ."

Grant heard footsteps in the hall behind him. He turned to see Fred Muckinhern and Kate walk around the corner, coming toward him. He marshaled himself, trying to stifle his emotions. Kate was walking faster than she should have been. She swung her left leg awkwardly and bobbed her shoulders as she accelerated toward him. She was trying to run to him. Her face was wired with concern, and she didn't care that others might see her clumsy strides or the fear in her eyes. She meant to find her best friend, right now.

When she stepped into his arms the full weight of the moment registered.

His mother had let the two most powerful men at the University of Minnesota School of Dentistry know that she felt what they were doing for her son was more important than a heart attack. He could only imagine what his mother must have sounded like when she'd asked Joe Ruminsky for permission to tell Grant about this. She'd paid them an odd compliment that no written word could convey.

Ruminsky and Muckinhern had apparently been quite moved by Gladys Thorson's phone call. Joe Ruminsky had made a point to tell Grant about his father's heart attack personally. And Fred Muckinhern must have known about Kate's involvement with Grant. He'd been the one to track Kate down and pull her out of class to tell her about this. Both of these men were offering something very personal.

A few minutes earlier Grant had been joking with his friends. Now, suddenly, his father, who'd always been an unbreakable rock and his only hero, had morphed into a mortal, an old man. And Kate had just let Fred Muckinhern, her surrogate father, know *exactly* how she felt about Grant.

His mother's phone call, a heart attack, Muckinhern and Ruminsky, the look in his lover's eyes—it was a lot for a young man to deal with. This stuff happened to other people, not him.

Kate stroked the back of Grant's head, and the back of his throat tightened. His eyes filled with tears. Don't start to cry, he commanded himself. Keep a stiff upper lip; no one should see a man cry. He swallowed hard several times and managed to push it all back. Kate gave him a Kleenex and he wiped his eyes. He was embarrassed about leaking a few tears in front of Muckinhern and Ruminsky, but there was no stopping it.

"You should go see your father," Dean Muckinhern said to Grant. "Go now. Your mother said your whole family will be home for a few days."

"We'll see that you have notes to study from all the classes you miss," Joe Ruminsky added.

"Thank you," Grant said softly.

"And Kate, if you're going with him, I'll cover for you while you're gone," Dr. Muckinhern offered.

Kate wiped her own eyes dry. "Thanks, Fred . . ."

"Get going." Muckinhern smiled.

~: CHAPTER 15 :~

Empty fields, harvested recently and stripped down to the black earth, had been drifting past the car windows for hours when Grant and Kate finally turned north onto U.S. Route 75 and rolled out of Moorhead. Then, Kate thought, the world got *real* big and empty. The farm fields were barren; some were covered with a dusting of snow. Miles passed without a curve in the road, or a hill, or a valley, or a tree. The tiny towns they drove through seemed to have been evacuated years earlier, or maybe deserted after some natural disaster.

"Cat got your tongue?" Grant teased, when at last they drove past a tiny road sign that said HALSTAD. Kate looked right, then left, as Grant drove slowly down Main Street. She seemed stunned by the lack of activity and the small, rundown brick storefronts. It was nearly dusk on a gray December Friday afternoon, and Grant's hometown appeared to be deserted. Two old pickup trucks turned onto the street ahead of them, then pulled into diagonal parking places in front of a neon light that flashed BUCKY'S in a dingy little window.

"That's our town bar," Grant said, pretending to be proud of the little establishment. "Church is over there, and the school is over there." He pointed with his thumb. "And the grocery store is over there." He pointed with his other thumb. "And that's about it." The car rolled right through town and back into open fields. "My folks' place is a couple miles farther."

"That was it?" Kate chuckled. "Your hometown?"

"Yeah, pretty nice, huh?" Grant joked. "We can come back tomorrow and I'll show you the rest."

"I think I saw it all," Kate said, as she looked back over her shoulder.

"Not much, is it?" Grant said. "But it was a great place to be a kid."

The December sky darkened, and Grant grew noticeably more anxious as they left the little town behind them. Kate reached over and took Grant's hand in hers. "You OK?" she asked. She knew Grant was thinking of his father, now that they were only minutes from the farm.

"Yeah. I'm all right."

Twilight was nearly gone when Grant and Kate eased into the Thorson farmyard. All four of Grant's older brothers and their families were already there, and the gravel turnaround in the center of the farm was cluttered with cars.

The gravel stopped crunching under the wheels as Grant parked. He shut off the ignition. "We're here!" he said. "Ever been this far out into rural America before?"

"Not even close," Kate replied.

The chill of an early winter evening reached under their collars when they stepped out of the car. Grant led her up a narrow sidewalk and through the gate of a heavy woven wire fence surrounding the large, white, square, two-story farmhouse. A row of overgrown lilac bushes reached over the fence and followed it all around the yard.

Two black-and-white cats crept close, cautiously examining the visitors. They scampered away when Kate and Grant neared the concrete steps leading up to the back door. As Kate watched the cats disappear around the corner of the house and into the darkness, a door swung open. The silhouette of a small woman was backlit by a yellow glow from what Kate assumed was the kitchen, and the cacophony made by Grant's family rushed outside. Several other heads appeared above the woman's shoulders as a crowd began to gather at the kitchen door.

"Grant's home!" came a child's voice from somewhere in the kitchen.

"Welcome home!" Gladys called to him. She reached up and hugged her son. Before she had a chance to say anything more, another pair of hands reached out from the crowd standing just behind her and jerked Grant into the kitchen.

"And you must be Kate! I'm Grant's mother. We've heard so much about you!" She stooped over and reached out to Kate as if she might need help with the front steps, then hugged her like a lost puppy. "Welcome! C'mon in and meet the rest of the family!"

Gladys took hold of Kate's hand and led her through the door and into the noisy kitchen. She stood silently and waited for her family to quiet down before she spoke.

"Everyone . . ." Gladys held up her hand and the biggest kitchen Kate had ever seen fell silent while fourteen strangers stared at her like she was a museum exhibit. "This is Grant's . . ." she paused, ". . . friend, Kate Bellows. Now Grant, you introduce your family."

Kate's eyes darted around the room while she smiled and tried to make eye contact with everyone. The soft light was friendly, and the thick aroma of fresh bread and roast beef filled the room.

Grant stood about three feet from Kate, with one arm draped over the shoulders of an attractive but very pregnant woman, and a can of Hamm's beer already in his other hand.

"Kate Bellows," Grant started, this is Linda, she's David's wife." Grant pointed to his brother David, who nodded and smiled. "And this . . ." Grant used the beer can to point to the man standing next to Linda, "this is John, and John is married to Sarah." He pointed to Sarah next, then introduced James and his wife, Mary, and then Paul and his wife, Beth.

"And those two little guys over there?" Grant pointed at his eight- and six-year-old nephews. "That's Todd and Jay; they're John and Sarah's boys. And that guy with the blonde hair right there, that's Jason . . . he belongs to Paul and Beth. That little girl with the beautiful red hair?" Grant continued. "That's Rene; she belongs to James and Mary." Rene, about six years old, buried her face in her mother's leg.

"And last but not least . . ." Grant stooped over and picked a toddler off the floor and held him in one arm. "This is James Thorson Junior. We call him The Jimmer." The child's eyes widened and the plastic pacifier in his mouth began to vibrate. "I think that means The Jimmer is glad to meet you," Grant said.

With James Junior resting on his arm, Grant moved close to Kate, put his other arm around her, and faced his family. "This is Kate Bellows."

In the midst of the small silence that followed Kate's introduction, from somewhere in the back of the crowd, a declaration of the obvious came from John Thorson's lips. "She's not bad, brother, not bad at all!" John was trying to tease both Kate and his little brother. Like most big brothers, he'd always seen it as a birthright, an obligation, and he did it well. Kate blushed immediately while the men chuckled and the women groaned.

"John!" Sarah scolded, "Can't you ever behave like a gentleman?" Then she turned immediately toward Kate. "Don't mind him," Sarah said to Kate. She touched Kate's arm and added, "There won't be a quiz on all these new names and faces, but stick with me and I'll help you keep everyone straight."

"Where's Dad?" Grant asked his mother.

"He's taking a nap. He should be about ready to get up."

"I'm right here," came a voice from somewhere behind the Thorson clan gathered in the kitchen.

Big Ole Thorson emerged slowly, as the crowd in front of him parted to let him pass through. Smiling while he let Paul and James step aside, he walked directly toward Grant and extended his right hand. "Hello, son," was all he said.

This moment would fix itself in Grant's memory forever. One of the unyielding cornerstones of life revealed itself to him with a sudden bluntness.

Big Ole Thorson, the indestructible head of this family, the man who'd survived a Japanese POW camp, the handsome man with the square shoulders and powerful hands that had built this farm and raised this family, had turned a corner. Big Ole was still alive; he looked pretty good, actually. But he'd changed. His youth and strength were gone now. He wasn't ten feet tall and bulletproof anymore. How could he have changed this much in only a couple of months? Had the changes been there all along, slowly piling up over the past few years, and Grant had just failed to notice? Ole's hair was mostly gray now, and he moved with a frail uncertainty as he approached Grant. Maybe it was his heart attack, maybe it was just grains of sand slipping through an hourglass. Life would not bestow many more blessings on this man; it would only take them away.

Grant felt a sense of remorse over the loss of all that had come and gone through his father's life and left him here, like this. But there was a symmetry in all this, too, and he felt that he himself was part of it all, for the first time. He'd never seen his dad like this. He'd just assumed that things around this home would always remain as they once were, and that's the way he'd managed to see things, until now.

He brushed his father's hand aside and bent over and pressed his forehead against Big Ole's. Grant sighed before he hugged his father. "You scared me, Dad. How do you feel?"

"Pretty good. A little tired maybe," Ole answered in a weak voice, while everyone watched. Grant held his father close and allowed himself to enjoy the moment. His dad was all right after all, and his whole family was together. But everything felt a little bit wrong, like the first time he'd come back to the farm after he'd gone off to college and realized that this place wasn't his home anymore.

These changes in Big Ole and Gladys, well, they were just the next thing he'd have to accept. Big Ole Thorson *had* gone around a bend in the river, and he'd left part of himself behind. Grant didn't feel the thick muscles under his father's cotton shirt anymore. Instead, he thought Ole felt small and brittle. Grant understood for the first time that he was much bigger and much stronger than his father. Others may have noticed the changes in father and son several years earlier, but tonight was the first time Grant had seen things as they really were.

"Gonna introduce me to your girl?" Ole asked, as Grant held him.

Grant stood back and grinned while his father and Kate looked at each other. In that brief instant, before either of them moved or spoke, Grant knew that he'd just delivered a change into his father's life, too. Kate Bellows was *the one* for his youngest son, and Big Ole knew it the moment he looked at her. Grant saw it all in his father's eyes, then let another one of life's singular moments pass with no comment. "Dad, this is Kate Bellows. Kate, this is Big Ole Thorson." Ole raised his hands and gestured for Kate to come closer. When she was close enough, he put his arms around her. Kate stood several inches taller than Big Ole as she returned the hug.

"Welcome to my home. It's nice to finally meet you," Ole said into her ear, while his entire family listened and watched. Then, with his arms still around Kate, he turned to Grant and added, "John was right. She's not bad."

While the others laughed, Gladys scolded Big Ole for teasing, and Grant couldn't help but notice Kate's reaction. She loved the way Big Ole teased her. She smiled as she had on the night he couldn't pay the bill at Benny's. She'd made an instant connection with his father.

"OK." Gladys began to wave her arms. "Everyone out of the kitchen while I get supper on the table."

Sarah took hold of Kate's arm and conducted a friendly debriefing about her relationship with Grant while they assisted Gladys with the final preparations for dinner.

There didn't seem to be room at the enormous oak table for another spoon or fork or dish of any kind when Grant's mother called the family back into the kitchen. As the Thorsons each searched for a place to sit at the family table, Kate snatched Grant's hand and squeezed, then gestured toward the milling crowd when Grant looked at her.

John and David were talking about their jobs. Paul and John were laughing about an incident that happened on a golf course years earlier. Sarah and Beth were helping Gladys bring more food to the table. Mary was explaining the differences between her two pregnancies to Linda. Todd and Jay were slapping each other, and Big Ole was seated at the head of the table and seemed busy with the The Jimmer on his lap. He'd taken The Jimmer's pacifier away and substituted a dill pickle, and he was laughing at the face his grandson was making.

"What a great family," Kate whispered into Grant's ear.

"Thanks," Grant replied. "My dad likes you, by the way. Don't you feel like some great treasure that I brought to show-and-tell . . . like a dinosaur bone or a plastic replica of the Statue of Liberty? Everyone wants to look you over pretty close."

"Yeah," Kate nodded, "and I like it."

Kate's first meal with the Thorson clan was a slow meander from one dish and one anecdote to the next. Grant's brothers took every opportunity to embarrass him with stories from his past. She heard all about the time he shot at the wrong basket in a high school basketball game, and the time he drove a lawn mower over the garden hose, and the time he peed on the electric fence. Fact and fiction seemed to blur from time to time, and most of the tales about Grant diverged into entirely different stories about someone else seated at the table. Each story seemed to stimulate the recollection of another even more outrageous story, and was soon followed by modifications, denials, or rebuttals.

The Thorsons conversed in volleys fired back and forth across the dinner table, sometimes firing several questions at one time.

"Pass the potatoes there, Sarah? Where you from, Kate?" John asked.

"Stop that, Todd," Sarah scolded, while she passed the potatoes. Todd took one last swipe at Jay, his younger brother.

"Minneapolis," Kate replied, ignoring the ruckus.

"Knock it off, Todd!" John cuffed the boy on the back of the head, then continued his questions as if he hadn't just whacked his own son. "What high school?"

"Edina," Kate answered.

"Cake eater, eh?" James interjected. "Are you rich?"

"Todd, now it's your turn, slap your uncle James," Sarah groaned. "Leave the poor girl alone, James," she added. Todd looked around and wondered if he should actually obey that strange command from his mother.

"Just curious," James grinned.

"David used to go out with a girl from Edina," Big Ole said. "She was beautiful!" He turned a devious smile to David. "Whatever happened to her, anyway?" Ole looked directly at Linda, David's wife, and waited for her to answer. He loved to tease Linda about David's old girlfriend.

"She got fat. Really fat. Looks like she sat on an air compressor," Linda answered, then she turned toward Kate. "All the Thorsons have this need to tease others." She rolled her eyes and shook her head. "It stems from their insecurities. It's his fault." She pointed her thumb at Big Ole, who wore a contented grin.

Big Ole enjoyed teasing Linda more than the others, and Linda apparently loved it, too.

Dishes clinked, people drifted in and out of multiple conversations being carried on at the same time, and Gladys got up periodically to bring more food to the table.

"So what do your parents do?" John asked Kate.

"They were killed in a car accident when I was about his age." Kate pointed at eight-year-old Todd. "Oh, I'm sorry," John stammered.

"It's OK. I lived with my sister and her husband. That's how I wound up in Edina."

"What happened to your leg?" Todd blurted.

"Yeah, she walks funny," Jay added.

John reached over and cuffed Todd's head once again. "Sorry," John said. He forced a grin during the uncomfortable silence. "Some people's kids, you know."

"That's OK." Kate smiled. She turned to Todd and answered his question. "I had a disease called polio when I was about your brother's age, and my leg never got better."

"Does it hurt?" Todd asked.

"No," Kate replied.

"Do you have to wear that thing all the time?" Todd asked.

"No, not all the time, but I can't walk very well without it," Kate answered.

"Are you gonna marry Grant?" Todd asked, with his chin nearly resting on his plate and ketchup smeared on his cheek. He'd lost interest in the brace on her leg and wanted to get right to the next question.

John cuffed Todd instantly, then offered, "He gets that from his mother." Everyone at the table chuckled, but they left the embarrassing question alone.

Gladys and Sarah cleared the dishes, then served cake and ice cream while the conversation wandered once again. When the younger children finished eating, they were excused from the table and they left to play in the next room.

"So how did a pretty girl like you get mixed up with Grant?" David asked when the kitchen fell silent and the table was ringed only with adults.

"Well, he volunteered to be a patient in the dental hygiene clinic. I think he did it to meet girls." Kate smiled and looked around the table. "You know, he had a dental hygiene student clean his teeth."

"Ooo! Good idea!" David said.

"Didn't work out too well for me," Grant offered. "I got a hygienist who should have been an assassin. She beat me up!" He laughed. "But Kate was the teacher in clinic that day and we sorta became friends."

"You're a teacher?" David asked. "In the dental school?"

"Yeah." Kate nodded.

"Kate just graduated from dental school last spring, David. She's a dentist," Grant said.

This was new ground for the Thorsons, and some barriers had to fall. As far as anyone could recall, there had never been a college professor in their kitchen before this evening. And there had most certainly never been a doctor sitting at the kitchen table. Now, this pretty woman with the long, dark hair was a doctor, and a professor at the university, and she had that brace on her leg, and she seemed to be in love with Grant, the kid brother.

For a moment it seemed that several mouths might actually fall open. No one knew what to say.

"You're the only woman dentist I ever met," David said. He grinned and sat back in his chair, and he wore a mystified expression.

"You wanna touch her?" Grant laughed. "You look like you're standing outside the monkey cage at the zoo!" The others all laughed as Grant pulled Kate close and kissed her cheek.

"I'd like to touch her," John said, as he reached a hand toward Kate.

"Stop that," Sarah scolded. "Stop teasing." She slapped at John's hand.

"Hmmm," Big Ole said, with a twinkle in his eye. "Did you hear that, Linda? Grant's girlfriend from Edina is pretty, *and* she's a doctor." Ole had seized another chance to tease Linda, and maybe shift the spotlight off Kate.

"Hold on there, Ole," Linda said, as she wrapped her arm around Ole's shoulders. "You can't tease me about *Grant's* girlfriend. It doesn't work that way." She shook her finger and added, "You can only tease me about *David's* old fat-faced, twelve-sandwich-eatin' bimbo girlfriend." She puffed her cheeks out and looked around while they all laughed.

As dishes were carried to the sink, then washed and dried, an easy conversation continued at the table. The clan remained seated while they took turns with kitchen chores. Big Ole was the first to grow weary and retire for the night, then Gladys, then The Jimmer and the other children. The Thorson boys and their wives remained at the table, lowered their voices, and talked with each other late into the night.

~:~

Grant spoke in a tiny whisper as he eased the bedroom door open. "How come you get a single room? My old room, as a matter of fact. Everybody else is packed into little family groups, and I'm sleepin' on the couch!" He slid the door closed behind himself, tiptoed across his childhood bedroom, and sat on the oak chair in front of the writing desk where he'd done his homework, years before.

"I'm the special guest," Kate said. She'd been lying under the covers in Grant's bed and reading while the Thorson house fell silent for the night. She closed her book, rolled onto her side, and propped her head onto her hand. "This room is like a shrine to you. I'll bet your mother hasn't changed a thing since you left home."

The room was small and plain, but it was still decorated with icons from Grant's life at home. The same brown-and-white plaid bedspread still covered the twin bed. A bookshelf displayed a few baseballs, some Minnesota Twins memorabilia, and several model airplanes, along with a copy of *The Last of the Mohicans*. Grant's high school letter jacket hung on his closet door, and a bulletin board above his desk still had newspaper clippings from his days as a baseball player. Tacked to the wall at the head of his bed was a faded blue pennant that read "Minnesota Twins 1965 American League Champions."

Grant gave the room a cursory glance. "This room used to be a lot bigger," he offered. He leaned back and put his stocking feet on the single bed, next to Kate. He raised his eyebrows and pointed to the bed where Kate lay. "I used to lie there in that bed, and wonder about things."

"Like what?" Kate asked.

"Oh, when my grandpa died, I wondered if he could look down from Heaven and see what I was doing and know that I was a good boy. Wondered the same thing about my dog, too. And naturally I worried about the monsters under my bed and boogeymen outside my window." He pointed toward the barnyard outside, beneath his second-story window. "A little later on, I wondered just what I was gonna find if I ever got my hands under a girl's dress."

Kate covered her eyes and shook her head.

But I think I spent most of my time lyin' there and just dreaming my dreams," he said.

"What dreams?"

"Hmph." He smiled a faraway smile. "I was pretty sure I was gonna be a big-league ballplayer. I used to sit on that little porch down there by the kitchen and listen to the Twins on the radio and tell my dad that I was gonna be a great pitcher someday, and pitch for the Twins, and win the World Series."

Grant looked away, far away, into his childhood. "Summer nights were so hot, and dark. When the day's work was done, Dad used to wander out onto that porch and listen to the radio." Grant smiled at his soft memories. "Herb Carneal and Halsey Hall callin' those games on the radio. Jesus, those summer nights were magic." He looked all around him. "And this little room was my safe harbor."

Kate nodded and thought of Grant's apartment at the university. She understood what a safe harbor was.

"See that?" Grant pointed to the pennant on the wall above his bed.

"Yeah," Kate answered.

"Minnesota Twins 1965 American League Champions." Grant read the words proudly. "They just about broke my heart." His tone fell with the words.

"Really! Why?"

"World Series, game seven. At home . . . they shoulda won." Grant shook his head in despair. "But Sandy Koufax just blew 'em away. He was just better than they were, and it took me a long time to forgive Mr. Koufax. Broke my heart." He sighed. "Sorta left something unfinished, too. Now I don't see how it'll ever get finished. The Twins are terrible and it looks like they're gonna be terrible forever."

"Maybe they'll win the World Series someday, you never know," Kate offered.

"Fat chance," Grant sighed. "I grieved for a long time over that. Know what my dad finally said to me?"

"What?"

"He said that's just life, some things just gotta stay dreams," Grant said. "Ever heard that before?"

"I can see why you're so fond of him." Kate leaned forward and pointed at Grant. The mention of Big Ole had jogged her memory and she wanted to ask Grant something. "He kissed you!" she started. "He kissed all your brothers, too! You're all grown men, and he kissed you. Does he always do that?"

"Sure." Grant shrugged.

"He's so cute," Kate said.

"Yeah, he can be cute. Fathers can be cute, but—"

"Were all your meals like that, like the meal tonight?" Kate interrupted.

"Yeah, pretty much." Grant shrugged. "'Cept we were doing the fighting, my brothers and I, like Todd and Jay were tonight. Isn't that how meals go for everyone?"

"No, not really," Kate answered. "My *parents* did the fighting. They used to start arguing as soon as my dad got home from work. By supper time they were usually pretty loud. I saw things like dinner rolls and glasses of milk get thrown across the table. It wasn't good," Kate sighed, as she recalled her own past. "I thought it was my fault."

"Why would you think that?" Grant asked.

"I dunno. I was a little girl. I thought if I did better at things and behaved better, maybe they wouldn't fight."

Grant touched Kate's leg with his stocking feet. "I'm sorry, Kate. It shouldn't have been like that."

"I want a family like the one I saw down there tonight," she said.

Grant let one foot rest against her leg for a moment, then raised himself up as if he were about to lie down with her. "Know what I want?" he asked with a wicked smile.

"What are you doing?" she asked.

"I think you know," he teased.

"What if your mother walked in here and found you in bed with me?" Kate bristled. Concern that was about to morph into panic rose in her voice, and she straightened her arms to keep him away.

"She'd know you were a loose woman, trying to drag me asunder." Grant laughed as he lifted himself off the bed. "She'd know you put impure thoughts in her little angel's head. She knows her little boy could never . . ."

"Exactly! You go on down to the couch," Kate whispered, as she pushed him away.

Grant smiled, took his legs off the bed, then bent over and kissed Kate. "I love you," he said.

"I love you too," Kate said, as she pulled the covers up to her chin.

He turned to leave, and when he was about to shut the door behind him he looked back at Kate. "Some dreams do come true."

Kate listened to her lover's footsteps disappear down the creaky flight of stairs, and then she shut off the bedroom light. In the moment after the yellow light flicked off, she felt alone in an ocean of darkness. But slowly, as her eyes began to acclimate, she could see that the small bedroom was awash with moonlight, and the objects and icons from Grant's childhood began to show themselves again.

The old house was silent now; all the little sounds were done. No crying noises from cranky children, no subdued conversations down at the kitchen table. Everyone was safe in their beds. *This* was a good dream—a large, loving family all tucked in their beds on a winter night. She'd spent her whole life dreaming this dream. It had been there all along as she'd listened to her parents argue, and then while she'd grown up without parents, living with her older sister. It had been a vague longing, drifting though her other dreams with no face or definition.

But was it really safe to dream that one day she could have this and keep it for herself? She wished Grant would come back now, and lie down and hold her, and reassure her that they'd make it come true, together.

~:~

Grant's mother was baking something, and the friendly aroma of fresh pastry mixed with the smells of coffee and bacon coaxed Kate from her sleep. She drifted along for a few minutes, not quite awake, but warm and secure in Grant's bed, until muffled voices and soft noises from the kitchen beneath her bedroom assured her that a new day was beginning. She dressed quickly in the half-light of the December dawn and then tiptoed toward the yellow glow in the kitchen.

A large pot of cowboy coffee simmered on a well-used stove top. It looked like Gladys was making fresh doughnuts, too. Men's voices could be heard out on the porch, but the kitchen was empty.

Gladys must have begun to prepare a large breakfast, then gone to the cellar for something, Kate reasoned.

She poured herself a cup of coffee then peeked through a little window that opened onto the porch. She tried to determine which of the Thorson men were sitting in the cold and watching a pink sun inch its way into the morning sky.

"Warm enough, Dad?"

It was Grant's voice, and Kate stopped in her tracks.

"Yeah. I like to come out here and greet the day. I like the cool air," Big

Ole replied. Kate could see their warm breath condense into thin clouds in the cold morning air.

Kate took a seat at the kitchen table as quietly as she could, and decided not to interrupt their conversation. Only their backs were visible when she looked out onto the porch, and she began to eavesdrop on them.

"That's a big pile of wood, Dad. Did you cut and stack all that?" Grant asked, as he pointed to several cords of firewood stacked neatly just outside the kitchen door.

"Lars Hokanson did that," Ole replied.

"Really?" Grant couldn't hide the surprise in his voice. "The feud is over?"

"Nah. It wasn't like that," Ole answered.

"Well, what was that all about, anyway?" Grant asked. "Everyone knew there was sort of a grudge between you and those boys for all these years." Grant pulled the stopper from a well-used thermos and poured more coffee into his cup. "I still remember that day, you know. I remember Little Ole lying there bleeding. And I remember you threatening to kill the Hokanson boys. You always said you'd tell me about it when I got a little older, too. I should be old enough to hear about it all now. C'mon, Dad. What was all that about?"

Kate stole a cautious peek out at the porch and saw Big Ole turn to his right and then his left before he answered, as if he needed to be certain that no one was listening.

"Goes way back, son," he started.

Kate leaned a little closer to the porch window.

"Emily, that was Little Ole's wife, was a beautiful woman. But she took up with a lot of men. She ran off with other men a couple times, too." Big Ole shook his head, still unable to understand Emily's actions. "Little Ole was always trying to explain to those boys. They never knew why their mother was gone so much, and he never told them the truth. He'd just make up some story, then stick with it until Emily came home again."

Big Ole stopped and looked at his son for a moment, uncertain if he should continue. "She propositioned me one night," Ole said, with no expression.

The thought of another woman batting her eyes and flirting with his father sent a smile across Grant's face.

"Don't laugh, boy. I was a fine figure of a man back then," Ole said.

"Go on," Grant said, still smiling.

"Anyway," Ole started again, "I told her that maybe she should just go away and let Little Ole and the boys get on with their lives. 'Bout a month later she called and asked me if I'd drive her to the train station 'cause she was gonna run off with some salesman."

"Did you do it?" Grant asked.

Big Ole Thorson looked right and left once more, then answered, "Yup, and you're the first person I've told since 1939."

"Really! You never told Ole?" Grant asked.

"No."

"Why?"

"Woulda broke his heart, I b'lieve. She just didn't want any more to do with him. And he'd have wanted to know where she went. Maybe he'd have chased after her. He just didn't need to know all the truth."

Grant thought about his father's words and actions for a long moment. Big Ole had kept that secret since 1939, and now Grant was the only other person who knew the truth about Emily's disappearance.

"So what ever happened to Emily?" Grant asked.

"Don't know," Ole replied. "She did send the boys a couple letters." Ole's face tightened while he remembered it all. "She just sorta let those boys believe that Ole threw her out, and that's why she left home." Big Ole took the last swig of coffee from his cup and stared across the backyard. "Bitch."

"And that's why those boys hated their father?" Grant asked.

"Yup."

"Why didn't he tell 'em the truth?"

"I asked him that very thing, many times," Big Ole said. "Know what he told me?" Ole asked, then shook his head in disbelief. "Said no one should know that their mother was a whore."

"Wow," Grant said softly. "So those boys never knew the truth? He let them grow up with a lie, in order to protect a woman who'd abandoned them?"

"That's about it. He even made me promise not to tell the boys." Ole sighed. "As the years went by he finally divorced her. That was really hard for him. He was so hurt and ashamed. I asked him once if he was lonely after she left him." Big Ole swallowed some coffee, then returned his gaze to several decades in the past. "Know what he said?" Ole sighed yet again, but didn't wait for Grant to reply. "He said, 'Not as lonely as I was before she left.'" Big Ole rocked in his chair several times, then added, "He was a good man. He didn't deserve a life like that."

"So Little Ole went to his grave with no resolution to all this?" Grant asked.

"No." Big Ole shook his head and confessed something more. "Right there at the end, when Ole was really sick, I went and told Lars the truth, some of it, anyway. I broke my promise to Ole. Lars seemed to understand everything pretty well. I guess he should have, he was almost an old man himself by the time I told him. He must have suspected something like that. Sometimes I wonder if he didn't know about things all along in some unconscious way, like he just needed someone to say the words in order to make it all be true. Anyway, he went and made peace with his father at last. We've become friends now, too, Lars and me. That's how the wood got stacked. He came over to help out after the heart attack." Big Ole thought for a moment. "All those years . . ." His voice trailed off.

"Ever wish you'd have told Lars before Little Ole was so sick?" Grant asked.

"Yes. Yes I do," Ole said. "But I thought my integrity was at stake if I broke my promise to Little Ole." Grant's father sighed heavily again, and poured the last of the coffee into his cup. "Life isn't fair, son. What happened to Little Ole shouldn't happen to anyone. And you know, through all of this, the only person who did one honest thing was Emily. She just ran away, and she had no integrity. But Little Ole told a huge lie in order to protect someone else. I guess integrity doesn't have much to do with honesty, huh?" Ole asked.

Kate stretched her neck to look at the man who'd just said those words. What an odd insight, she thought. All she could see of Big Ole Thorson was the back of his head, and his words condensing in the cold air. She wondered about Big Ole's life; the hard times on this small farm, a Japanese POW camp, the richness of a fine family. She didn't think she'd ever known anyone like this man, but before she could organize her thoughts in any way, Ole broke the spell.

"How's school going, son?" he asked Grant.

"Good. Really good, Dad."

"Getting good grades?"

"I'll be fine."

Big Ole nodded his approval. Then, as if he'd been waiting for a chance to take the conversation in a different direction, he offered, "You sure brought a nice young lady home."

Grant nodded and smiled. "I love her, Dad."

"You be good to her," Ole said.

Kate liked to hear them talk about her in such a way, but she didn't have long to think about it. She heard footsteps coming up the wooden stairway from the cellar and she turned to face the cellar door.

"Oh, you're up!" Gladys said with mild surprise when she emerged from the cellar. "How did you sleep?"

"Fine. Just fine," Kate answered. "I poured myself some coffee." She raised her cup to show Gladys, then asked, "Can I help you with anything?"

"No, no, you just relax." As Gladys spoke, Kate could hear the floor in the living room creak, and in the next moment Sarah and Beth appeared in the kitchen.

The entire Thorson family drifted into the kitchen in the next few minutes. The adults wandered around with coffee cups in one hand, snitching samples of the big breakfast Gladys was preparing with the other hand.

The growing commotion in the kitchen soon put an end to Grant and Big Ole's conversation on the porch, and they rose to join the others. When the porch door swung open and Big Ole stepped into the kitchen, Kate happened to be the one standing nearest to the door, and Ole smiled a wry smile, as though he couldn't believe his good fortune. He flicked his eyebrows to the middle of his forehead twice, shuffled toward her and held his arms out to Kate, requesting another hug. As he wrapped his arms around her he asked, "How'd you sleep?"

Even as Kate answered, "Fine," Big Ole was turning from her. He made his way through the milling crowd toward Gladys, and patted her behind when he finally stood beside her at the kitchen stove. She smiled, gave him a soft, quick kiss on the lips, and then turned back to the breakfast she was preparing.

Kate watched the exchange between Big Ole and Gladys, and she didn't know what to make of the gentle man who kissed his wife and children. She stared at Big Ole as if he were a star athlete who'd stopped in the middle of a ball game to sign an autograph for her. Grant's father was a good man. He'd given Gladys and all the boys a fine place in the world.

"So, Dad," John Thorson asked when the whole family assembled around the breakfast table and sat down, "What did the doctor say about your cigarettes?" He knew the answer, but he wanted to hear his father repeat the doctor's orders.

Big Ole was holding The Jimmer on his knee, feeding him grape jelly on a spoon, when everyone at the table turned his way, fell silent, and waited for his reply.

"He suggested that I cut back a little," Big Ole said innocently.

Big Ole's sons all leaned back on their chairs and laughed at their father's outrageous lie, while the women straightened their backs and shrieked.

"Mmmmm!" The Jimmer added, as he waved both hands and kicked his feet. Whatever was happening, he wanted to celebrate along with the others.

"You liar!" Sarah laughed. "He *ordered* you to quit."

"I can't believe you said that!" Beth blurted, as if she was shocked Big Ole could attempt such a huge lie, even as a joke.

"The doctor said this was a warning!" Gladys said. She'd stood up from the table and retrieved a plate covered with homemade doughnuts covered in powdered sugar. "He said Ole can recover and be just fine, but he'll have to quit the cigarettes!" She put the plate of doughnuts on the only empty place at the table, just in front of Kate, then added, "How can you tell such a lie to your children?"

Ole smiled, pleased that his lie had triggered such an enthusiastic response.

The Jimmer locked onto the doughnuts with both eyes, straightened his back, and slid off his grandpa's lap.

"It's no joke, Ole," Gladys scolded. "The doctor said they'll kill you if you don't quit."

Ole shrugged, then winked at Kate. He'd said what he'd said just to trigger this very response from Gladys and the others.

Big Ole was so cute, Kate thought. Then she noticed two very tiny and very busy hands pulling at her pant leg. The Jimmer had crawled under the table in his quest for the doughnuts, and he'd surfaced at her side. He couldn't walk just yet, but he pulled himself into a standing position alongside Kate's chair and now he held his hands up in the universal gesture for "Pick me up?"

Kate lifted him onto her lap and he immediately reached toward the plate of powdered sugar doughnuts. "Can he have a doughnut?" Kate asked Mary, as The Jimmer leaned as far as he could, strained his short arm, and groaned, trying to reach the prize.

"Sure," Mary said with some resignation. "He's just gonna scream if he doesn't get one now."

"I thought your father would have given up cigarettes after Todd got sick in the car," Gladys said, scolding Big Ole again for something that had happened years earlier.

"Huh?" Grant and James said in unison.

"Didn't you hear about that?" Gladys asked.

"No," Grant and James replied, leaning forward now, waiting for a story.

"Oh," Gladys started. "The poor thing wasn't much older than The Jimmer is now. We were taking him home to his parents after he'd spent a week here with us." Todd began to smile and revealed his missing front teeth. He knew the story his grandma was about to tell.

"I told Ole to stop smoking in the car!" Gladys continued. "Little Todd just kept getting greener and greener. Finally he tried to tell me he didn't feel good. He burped once, and . . ."

"Looked like a goat exploded!" Ole interrupted. "Barfed all over the car. I didn't think the little shaver could hold that much vomit!"

"Ole, that's not acceptable table talk," Gladys scolded.

Todd's chin barely showed above the tabletop, and he looked right and left to see who else was laughing at the funny thing he'd done. All the Thorson men laughed, and the women groaned. Todd grinned a huge toothless grin and thought it was great that everyone was talking about him.

As James Thorson chuckled at his father's description of a goat exploding in the front seat of his car, he glanced over at his own son in time to witness yet another memorable family moment unfold. While Big Ole and Gladys had been telling the story of their grandson Todd throwing up in their car, The Jimmer had been sitting in Kate's lap, minding his own business and shoving most of a powdered sugar doughnut into his mouth with both of his tiny hands.

The doughnut was good, and The Jimmer's cheeks were stretched tight when he noticed Kate's ample breast straining against her black sweater. That nice round breast was right there, about an inch from his eye, when he finally took note of it and gave it the serious attention it deserved.

The Jimmer's father, James Senior, looked at his son in time to understand what The Jimmer was about to do. Kate was about to get felt up by a toddler. Unable to do anything in time, James could only watch his little boy do the crime. The Jimmer reached a tiny hand coated with powdered sugar up to Kate's breast and gave it a firm squeeze. All five fingers. Several times.

Kate's face turned crimson, and her ears burned with the blush.

"Nice one," James sighed, then he put both hands over his face and waited for his family to notice The Jimmer's handiwork.

The entire Thorson family forgot about Todd throwing up in Grandpa's car and turned toward Kate, whom they'd known for only twelve hours.

The Jimmer smiled a huge smile and showed them the doughnut, stuffed in and around his mouth.

Kate was mortified, looking from one Thorson to the next with a burning red face and a perfect white handprint made of powdered sugar on the black sweater covering her left breast. While everyone stared, The Jimmer decided to squeeze the other one, too.

"Mmmm!" The Jimmer said, and he kicked his feet while everyone laughed. Even Gladys had to wipe tears from her eyes when Sarah whisked The Jimmer off Kate's lap.

Sarah nudged Kate, shook her head, and observed that apparently all the Thorson boys were the same.

When the commotion died down, John stood up and reached across the table with a napkin, ostensibly offering to help Kate brush the powdered sugar handprint off her breast, until Sarah slapped his hand and passed another exasperated glance to Kate. "See what you're getting yourself into here?"

Kate laughed along with the others, even before her blush faded. But she hoped Sarah was right, that this was what she was getting herself into.

CHAPTER 16

"Mornin', Pard. How's your Dad?" Will said, as he took a seat next to Grant in Monday morning's Biochemistry lecture.

"He's good, he looked a little weak. The doctor says he'll be fine. Sure scared me, though," Grant answered. "Here, let me help you with that coffee," he added, as he took the Styrofoam cup from Will's hand.

"We probably won't be seeing Ben today," Will said, while he arranged his papers and settled into his seat. "Did he call you?"

"No, what happened?" Grant asked.

"Oh, man! It's the kind of thing that could happen only to Ben," Will started. "You'll never believe it. Gimme back the coffee." Will took the cup from Grant and took a sip. "OK, you know how we're not supposed to take our typodonts home? They're supposed to stay in the building, right?"

"Yeah," Grant nodded. Every dental student knew very well that the typodont, the set of teeth and jaws issued to them on the first day of school, was not supposed to leave the building under any circumstances. Students were to learn operative dentistry techniques in preclinical laboratories only. If students were to take their typodonts home, instructors feared they might unscrew the individual teeth and modify their laboratory work under magnification in order to improve it, and then receive a higher grade. Taking a typodont home was tantamount to cheating.

"Well, you know how Ben thinks the rules are for everyone else?" Will continued.

"He took his typodont home?" Grant guessed.

"Yup," Will replied.

"And he lost it?" Grant guessed.

"Well, sort of, but worse than that." Will began to chuckle. "He took his stuff home Friday after school. I told him not to. Anyway, Saturday night rolls around and he's sitting in front of his TV. He's been working on the typodont, has the teeth all unscrewed and lying around on the coffee table in front of his couch, like so much loose change." Will laughed and shook his head. "So he gets up, grabs himself a beer and some potato chips, and while he's up he feeds that stupid dog of his. Well, the dog is kind of happy and excited at that point, and he follows Ben back to the couch, where he spots the potato chips and all those little ivorine teeth strewn across the coffee table, and he thinks they look sorta like the dog food he just ate . . ."

"You're shittin' me!" Grant laughed. "The dog ate his homework?"

"Yup! Slurped it right up. Ben said it happened so fast he couldn't believe it. Said the damn dog stood there and looked at him, sort of smiling and thanking him for the treat," Will said.

"Then what?" Grant asked.

"Well, he can't very well show up here with half the teeth missing from his typodont. But then he remembered his favorite passage from the Bible: 'This too shall pass, sayeth the Lord.' So right now, as we speak, he's waiting for his dog to shit out those teeth."

"He's home right now, skipping class, so he can watch soap operas and feed his dog Ex-lax while he waits for a package to arrive?" Grant summarized.

"That's about right," Will said.

"Unbelievable," Grant said.

"There was a little bit of excitement last night, though," Will offered. He waited for Grant to ask for more details.

"Oh?" Grant asked.

"Yeah. He said he usually takes his dog over to a nearby park when it has to shit. Naturally, he's been keeping the dog on a leash so when it finally drops a turd with some teeth in it, he'll be right there. Well, it turns out the dog suffers from stage fright and doesn't like to shit with Ben watching. Anyway, the pooch got loose from Ben after dark last night and ran behind some old lady's house to do his business. Ben wound up crawling around the lady's yard with a flashlight looking for fresh dog shit around midnight."

Will stopped, took another sip of coffee, and shook his head. "You couldn't make stuff like this up! So, after a few minutes he finds some fresh stuff. It's the really loose, stinky stuff, and he goes to steal the old lady's garbage can lid so he can scrape the steaming pie onto something and then take it home and examine it more closely. He's got the flashlight in his mouth and he's starting to wretch from the stink of it when the old lady turns on a yard light and starts to scream about how she just called the cops." Will was laughing so hard he had to stop telling the story. "Then he gets up and sprints down the street with a garbage can lid full of dog shit above his head, like he's delivering drinks at the country club."

"Any prizes in the shit?" Grant asked.

"Nope. He said he was gonna sneak back to the old lady's house tonight and return the lid, though."

A comic vision of Ben Pribyl sneaking through an old woman's backyard lingered with Grant and Will while they unpacked notebooks from their book bags and prepared for the morning's Biochemistry lecture. It was time to forget about Ben.

Dr. Sigfus Torvik strolled up to the podium in front of the lecture hall and began to organize several books, along with the text for the lecture he was about to give. Torvik spoke English very well, and had a charming sense of humor. Everyone liked him.

"Well," Grant started, "at least we don't have to listen to Jamshad Gopnaith today. That's . . ."

"Hi, Will! Can I sit with you?" a woman's voice interrupted. When Grant turned to see who had joined them, a dark-haired beauty had already settled into the seat next to Will. She was a visitor, not a classmate; that much was apparent at a glance.

"Hi, Kathleen. Did you find the place all right?" Will said.

"No problem!" She hugged Will, then thrust her right hand toward Grant. "Kathleen Monahan. Will's friend from Harvard. Here for my interview at the School of Dentistry." She smiled and pumped Grant's hand with a strong handshake.

"Grant Thorson." Grant took stock of her while he held her hand.

The woman turned all her attention back to Will. "It's so nice to see you again, Will. I'm glad I could attend a class with you before my interview. It's at eleven o'clock with Dr. Joseph Ruminsky. Do you know him?"

"A little bit," Will said.

The woman smiled a beautiful smile and grabbed Will's arm as if she thought he was about to blow away. "It's so nice to see you again," she exclaimed, then snuggled up next to him. She was beginning to irritate Grant.

All the little conversations in the lecture room ended when Dr. Torvik cleared his throat and began to speak. Kathleen let go of Will's arm but leaned close to him for the entire hour.

She was undoubtedly an attractive woman, Grant thought. And she sure had an outgoing personality. Just the look of her screamed East Coast and Harvard. Her long hair was perfect; it bounced when she turned her head. Her clothing oozed Ivy League. Grant figured that the outfit she was wearing cost more than his car. She looked like some rich guy's girlfriend.

Will and Kathleen left the lecture auditorium arm in arm, as if strolling down a flower-lined path in a quiet meadow. She walked with him all the way to his bench in the preclinical laboratory, pulled a chair up next to him, and stared like a puppy waiting for a scrap of food to fall from her master's table.

Grant was arranging the instruments on his lab bench when he heard a familiar voice behind him. "Hey, Grant. How's your dad?" Ben was standing at Grant's side, grinning like he'd just won the lottery.

"Hi, Ben. Dad's gonna be OK!" Grant said when he turned around. "Will said you were looking for a hidden treasure this morning?"

"Sure was!" Ben held up his typodont with all thirty-two teeth screwed into place so Grant could inspect it. "Did Will tell you all about it?"

Grant nodded.

"Yeah, Watson, that's my dog's name, he came through for me this morning. I could see a couple teeth in the pile he dropped. Had to run water on 'em for a while, you know. But they're good as new now."

"I don't really wanna know any more," Grant laughed.

"Yeah, I gotta get to work, too. Can I borrow your notes from the Biochemistry lecture I missed?"

"Sure, Ben. I'll see you in lab, huh?"

⁓ ⁚ ⁓

Ben's cigarette smoke drifted out the sash window and into the December breeze. It was several hours after the morning's Biochemistry lecture, and Ben was gazing, arms crossed, toward the other side of the Gross Anatomy laboratory. "Who's the RB?" he finally asked Grant.

"Huh?" What's an RB?" Grant had just walked over and joined Ben by the window after watching Jimmy and Carol dissect for a few minutes.

"Rich bitch. An RB is a rich bitch," Ben explained. "Who's the RB hangin' all over Will?" Ben pointed across the room with his cigarette.

"Some girl from college. A friend of Will's. She's trying to get into dental school, had her interview with Dean Ruminsky just before lunch," Grant said, while he watched traffic move past on the street below.

"Does Will's wife know about her?" Ben asked.

"I don't know. Why?" Grant turned around in time to see Kathleen giggle at something Will said.

"'Cause that girl wants a ride on the baloney pony." Ben tipped his head toward her. "Look!" Kathleen laughed again, and then rubbed her breasts against Will's arm.

"Nah, they're just friends," Grant said.

Ben looked at Grant with unbridled skepticism, as if he were peering over the top of imaginary bifocals. "'Fraid not, buddy. That girl is craving an injection of vitamin C, for Campbell." Ben flicked his cigarette out the window and started back toward their cadaver. "We're up."

"No way," Grant insisted as he followed Ben back to their cadaver. Then he let a bit of uncertainty creep into his voice. "You think you can tell when a woman is . . . ? Besides, he wouldn't . . ."

"Yeah, well, I don't think you want to argue with *me* on this one," Ben said confidently. "Personally, I think she's way too perky. But sometimes the perky ones can be real scrappers!"

"Ah, she just wants to look around the school, talk about dentistry some with Will, and see if it's for her," Grant insisted.

"The only dentistry she's interested in is polishing Will Campbell's probe!" Ben scoffed. "Don't believe me? Ask Carol, she knows." Carol Knutsen and Jimmy Drahota had been listening to Ben and Grant's last couple of exchanges while they stood next to the cadaver.

"Carol," Ben said. "Have a look at the way that girl over there next to Will is acting. What do you think is on her mind? Really."

Carol studied Will and Kathleen for a moment, then said, "I think she'd like to make an appointment at Will Campbell's private office to have her uppers pulled and her lower filled." Then Carol shook her head. "I've been around you guys too long. I can't believe I said that."

"See," Ben said to Grant. "Told you so. Now let's get to work."

∽:∾

The big booth in the corner of Stub & Herb's was still available at the end of the day when the group made their way in after Gross Anatomy lab. Andy Hedstrom stopped at the bar and ordered three pitchers of beer while Grant, Kate, Joe Paatalo, Jimmy, Ben, and Carol slid over the leather seat and arranged themselves in the booth. Before everyone was completely settled, Carol put her arm around Grant's neck and pulled his head low so she could whisper in his ear. "Kate is so pretty, and such a nice person. Everyone, I mean *everyone*, likes her, you know. How did someone like *you* get your foot in the door with her?" Grant smiled at Carol and then looked over at Kate, who was listening intently while Andy Hedstrom told her some story about his day in Gross Anatomy.

"Well, Carol, I guess she just has low standards," Grant said. He poured glasses of beer for himself and Carol. He raised his glass and tapped it against Carol's before he drank.

"Apparently!" Carol agreed.

"You're a pretty girl, too . . ." Grant nodded, struggling to hide his smile ". . . and you have something that men find very attractive."

"What's that?" she asked.

"A dirty mind."

"Well, look who I hang around with." Carol shrugged and pointed around the table.

"What are you talking about?" Ben asked, as he shoved his face into their conversation. "I missed that." The background noise of happy hour was beginning to grow.

"I was just telling Grant about how I caught you harvesting your nose yesterday." Carol laughed and took the conversation in a new direction. She shook her head in an effort to embarrass Ben.

"Couldn't be helped. I had a bear in the cave!" Ben said seriously. "Besides that, you snuck up on me. You stalked me in order to watch me perform personal hygiene tasks. Are you infatuated with me?"

"You were picking your nose in the hall outside the men's locker room when I walked by, and you showed the booger to *him*." Carol pointed at Andy Hedstrom. Everyone at the table was suddenly listening, and waiting for Andy's response.

Andy stared at Carol, then furrowed his brow as if he had something profound to say. "Yeah . . . ," he nodded, ". . . and it was a nice one, a real trophy!" He reached over and tapped his beer glass against Ben's. "Great snag, Ben. Winner winner, chicken dinner."

The men all cheered for Ben's booger while Carol shook her head in disgust and Kate covered her eyes.

"OK, here's what I wanna know," Ben called out over the laughter and groans of his friends. "Why do you persecute a man for picking his nose when he sticks a finger in there?" He looked around to emphasize the question he was about to ask. "But you think it's all right for a woman to do that *thing* women do?"

"OK, I'll take the bait," Carol said. "What *thing* are you talking about?"

Ben placed his right elbow on the table, then held his index finger in the air. While everyone watched, he lowered a napkin over his finger, slowly and deliberately. Then he stuck the finger, and the white napkin covering it, in his nose and looked around the table. "Now, how is this *not* picking your nose? But girls do this all the time! Do you think this tissue on your finger changes something? Do girls think they're magicians? Do they think the rest of us don't know they've got a finger rammed up their nose because the finger is covered by a tissue?" He glanced around the table with his napkin-covered finger buried in his nose and defied everyone seated at the booth to look away from him.

Carol slowly lowered her face and shook her head while the others laughed at Ben.

"Hey. Where's Will?" Joe Paatalo asked. "He should be here by now."

"I saw him walking the other way with that girl who was with him all day," Andy Hedstrom answered.

Ben shot a quick glance at Grant, as did Carol. Grant shook his head slowly, in silent defense of Will, then looked away and pursed his lips.

"Hey, Ben?" Joe asked. "Does your dog know any new tricks?"

Joe's question was all the prodding Ben needed to launch into another dramatic retelling of the adventure with his dog's digestive system. His story took twenty minutes to review, and when he was finished Jimmy Drahota got up and bought three more pitchers of beer while Carol filled a paper dish full of peanuts for everyone.

The conversation at the corner booth never strayed far from professors, other students, and problems at the dental school, for the next hour.

Grant was preparing to nudge Kate and let her know that he was ready to leave when he noticed Will strolling through the bar on his way to join them.

"Where have you been?" Grant called. "Party's almost over."

Will edged his way into the small space still available next to Kate and put his arm around her. He picked up the half-full glass of beer in front of her and drank it all, then refilled it with the last of the beer in the pitcher nearest him.

"Go ahead. Finish my beer," Kate smiled.

"Thank you," Will said, and he started picking though the plate of peanuts in front of her.

"Where you been, Pard?" Grant asked again.

"I took Kathleen back to her hotel and had a little something to eat with her. She's flying back to Boston tomorrow morning," Will said, while he searched for peanuts.

Ben made eye contact with Grant, then raised his eyebrows. He could just as well have hollered, "I told you so!"

~: :~

The deepest, darkest time of night had settled over Grant's apartment when he leaned back from his chair at the rickety card table. The rest of the apartment was quiet, and the entire city seemed to be sleeping.

He'd been studying and reading over his notes for several hours. Then fatigue, like an invisible force, began to push him into his chair and he grew restless under his own weight. No matter how hard he tried to refocus, he was done studying. He slid his chair away from the card table and rubbed his face with his hands.

Kate was still awake, sitting on the couch, reading. He looked at her while he packed his books and notebooks into his backpack. Grant expected her to look at him and smile, like she normally did, but she kept her face in her book.

He'd asked her a question about Biochemistry earlier and she'd given him a short answer, something like, "It's been a long time since I studied that material, figure it out for yourself." It was actually a pretty good answer but it was the first time she'd spoken to him that way. Then, roughly an hour after that, he'd asked a question about Dental Anatomy and she'd walked over to the table and drawn a few pictures to help answer him. She'd helped, but there'd been no caress, no kiss on the cheek, no joking, like other times. Something was bothering her.

Kate's bare feet were crossed and resting on a coffee table Grant had made from peach crates. He pulled one of the cheap lawn chairs close to her and began to rub her feet while she read.

"Jeez, your feet are freezing!" Grant said. He quickly leaned back in the chair and took his socks off, then slid them onto her feet. "There, that's better," he said. He continued to briskly rub his hands over her feet, as if he were trying to start a fire.

"What's the matter, Kate?" he asked.

Kate closed the book and stared a hole in Grant. "Is Will having an affair with that girl?" she asked. She'd been waiting for an opportunity. "I saw Ben look at you when Will sat down at our booth tonight."

"Well, everyone seems to think so," Grant admitted. "But I don't. I just don't think he'd do that."

"Everyone said she was beautiful, and rich," Kate offered.

"She is, but Will has integrity. He wouldn't do that." Grant paused for a moment. "I know him. He just wouldn't do that."

"People betray one another. We both did it to someone else."

Kate's words stung and surprised him. "You don't really feel that way," he answered.

"I don't know what I feel." Kate closed her book and tossed it on the couch. "Do you think Carol Knutsen is pretty?" she asked.

Grant leaned back and questioned Kate with his eyes.

"I see the way she talks to you! When will you lose interest in me?" Kate asked flatly.

"So this isn't about Will, is it?" Grant asked, still softly rubbing her feet.

"You could have any woman you want," Kate said.

"I want you," Grant shrugged.

"You'll grow tired of me and move on. I'll just be an ex-girlfriend that you tell your buddies about!" Kate put her hands on her face and struggled to stay in control of herself. "I'll just be the crippled girl you had a fling with, like dating a midget or a freak." She'd been holding something back and now it boiled over in a trickle of tears.

"You can't believe that," Grant sighed. He lifted her feet from the coffee table and spread her legs. Then he knelt on the floor in front of her and lay forward so that his head was resting on her chest and his arms were around her waist. "Never say that again."

"That's how life is," Kate said. She began to stroke the back of Grant's head.

"I don't think either one of us knows how life is, Kate." He kept the side of his face against her chest and let her hold him close. "Isn't that what we're all trying to figure out, how life is?"

Kate closed her eyes and let her cheek rest on top of his head.

"Your demons are back, aren't they? They're trying to convince you that you're not worthy. Right?"

Kate nodded.

"What can I say? I'll be there for you. You don't have to prove anything to me. You know that," he said.

She nodded, then kissed the top of his head.

"Strange, isn't it, that you can't see yourself the way others see you?"

"It's more than that now, Grant. Much more."

"What do you mean?" he asked.

"'Sometimes I'm afraid I'm going to lose you . . . ," she paused, "your friends, your family, this." She stroked his head. "I hear you and your friends talk about all the crazy things that happen. I don't want to be the centerpiece for another story about how crazy life is twenty years from now. I'm so afraid I'll lose my best friend. I couldn't bear that now."

"Not gonna happen, Kate. Everybody worries about stuff like that. I guess that's how you know you love someone." Grant sighed, then nuzzled his face deeper into her bosom. "You know, when you're over at school you just exude this easygoing charm and self-confidence. But sometimes when you're alone with me it all goes away. Why?"

"Because you're the one I need," she whispered.

"That's the greatest thing anybody ever said to me," he replied. The yellow light of a small table lamp was all that lit the apartment, and they lingered on the couch and let the silent minutes tick away. Kate leaned back on the green couch and Grant kept his head resting against her chest. Neither of them needed more than the gentle reassurance of a lover's touch.

CHAPTER 17

"Where's Kate?" Ben asked when he looked up from his newspaper. "She's coming along to Petrowiak's today, right?"

"She had some stuff to do up in her office. She just took her coffee and went right up there," Grant answered. Morning coffee in the coffee shop had become a ritual for quite a few freshman dental students. Kate and Grant started almost every day at a table with Will, Ben, and the others. Someone always seemed to have a story to tell, now that the first semester was coming to an end.

"Where's Kate?" Andy Hedstrom asked when he ambled over, took a chair next to Grant, and started to spread cream cheese over a bagel. "She's coming along today, isn't she?"

"Busy right now," Grant answered without looking up from his Gross Anatomy notes. "But she's comin'." He glanced at Ben and noticed the open newspaper on the table in front of him. "Aren't you gonna look through your notes once more, Ben? The final exam is in twenty minutes."

"No. I got 'er pretty well studied up," Ben answered. "I'm gonna let my mind rest for a few minutes . . . just read the paper and go in there fresh."

"Me too," Will added. "Gimme the sports page, will ya, Ben?"

"I'm readin' the sports. But you can take this." Ben handed Will another section of the paper, and the group at the table settled into silence, each of them preparing for the semester final exam in their own way.

Darcy Wilhelm found her way over to the table a moment later. She was stirring her drink in a large cup when she sat next to Andy Hedstrom and greeted everyone. "Hi, guys!" No one looked up, but Andy answered with a monotone. "Hi, Darcy."

A few seconds later, Andy's head whipped around and he covered his nose. "Jeez, Darcy! What is that you're drinkin'? It smells like my gramma's shoes!"

"It's herbal tea. It's supposed to be good for you," Darcy replied.

"Chrissakes! It smells like you're soaking a mouse nest in there," Ben groaned.

"Hey, listen to this!" Will interrupted, engrossed in the newspaper article in front of him. "Says here the fire department was summoned to a fire in a fish house on Lake Minnetonka yesterday. Turns out a couple of high school kids were in there screwing when a chimney fire started. Apparently they'd been drinkin' and smoking pot too. They were running around naked on the ice, and the cops found some drugs. Sounds like a bad day all around. Newspaper guys must love writing stories like this." Then Will turned abruptly toward Darcy when the vapors from her tea reached his nose. "Jeez, Darcy, that shit smells like hot garbage!"

Everyone at the table reached for their books and stood up to leave, to escape the stench of Darcy's tea.

"OK, guys, remember!" Andy called out before the group split up. "We're leaving from here, en masse, for Petrowiak's, after the Biochem final! Right?"

The group cleared out in only a few seconds, except for Darcy and Ben. Ben stared straight ahead with a look of serene enlightenment, as if he just cracked the DNA code and discovered the secret to the double helix, then looked at Darcy. "In a fish house! They were screwing in an ice-fishin' shanty," he said to a confused-looking Darcy. "I never thought of that."

∾ː∾

The waiting line stretched from the front door of Petrowiak's Bar all the way around the corner, and shivering dental students stood with their shoulders hunched, trying to hide from the December chill.

"Shit! We've got a long wait," Andy whined, while Ben parked the car.

"That's why we come here, Andy," Kate said. "We stand in line and drink beer! Well, then there's the food, too. Iron Mike Petrowiak makes the best beef sandwich in town." She went on to explain that dental students had been marking the end of semester studies with group outings to Petrowiak's Bar for years.

The oak doorway of the ancient bar swallowed small segments of the waiting line every few seconds, and the group of students inched their way toward Petrowiak's, one tiny, frigid step at a time. When Grant finally swung the heavy door open, a din of crowd noise and polka music rushed out from the dimly lit bar. As their eyes acclimated to the darkness inside, the group noticed that the waiting line snaked around the tavern's interior and was still about two hundred feet long.

Iron Mike Petrowiak stood at the far side of a large room, wearing an enormous white apron and making sandwiches one at a time. He leaned over a banquet table, shaved thin slices of meat off a giant slab of beef, and dipped the slices into a gurgling caldron of beef juice and spices before he plopped a hungry man's portion of beef onto a jumbo hamburger bun.

"Jeez, that guy is huge! I bet he weighs four hundred pounds," Will said.

"Yeah, he was a professional wrestler back in the '50's," Kate replied.

Joe Paatalo and Andy Hedstrom had been involved in an ongoing discussion of possible answers for various questions on the final exams they'd just finished. The whole thing was turning into an argument, and the others were being drawn into the fray.

"OK," Joe started once more. "On question number fourteen, the one about the pulmonary artery. The answer was the left ventricle."

"Bullshit," Andy whined. "You didn't read the question properly! The only answer could be . . ."

"The aorta," Carol interrupted.

"What?" Andy and Joe groaned in unison.

"Of all the answers, the aorta is the dumbest choice. The aorta . . . ," Mitch Morgan began to explain, and so the discussion went. When the talk moved on to the Biochemistry final, emotions revved up.

"Know what really pisses me off?" Joe asked at one point, when the test question being discussed had to do with the mechanism in which enzymes break complex starches down into simple sugars. "We had class three times a week for fourteen weeks. Think of all the material we covered. And then some lame-ass professor like Dr. Schneider gives a final with twenty-five multiple-choice questions. He was just too lazy to write any more questions. And the ones he did come up with were really poorly written and ambiguous."

"That's what I've been saying all along!" Will interjected. "They have to ask stupid, ambiguous questions or we all get perfect scores. Actually," Will continued, "that biochem final was beautifully designed. The lack of questions gave too much statistical significance to each one of the questions, *and* the questions were vague and misleading. A perfect test if your plan is to skew the results."

"Shit," Joe Paatalo moaned, "I had higher expectations for the university. Everybody on the faculty here is a loser."

Like a cat leaping on a mouse, Kate reached through the crowd, grabbed Joe's ear, and began to twist. "Listen, young man," she blurted, "I'll keep you after school clapping chalk dust off my erasers and writing apologies on the blackboard until your ass falls off!"

Frightened, and caught off guard by the swiftness of Kate's response, Joe flinched and then froze when Kate brought her nose about an inch from his cheek. But it didn't take long until he realized at the same time everyone else did that she was joking, and contorting her face the same way Ebby did when he examined wax carvings. "Present company excluded," Joe managed to whimper, as the entire group dissolved in laughter. Joe had been caught by a faculty member while he criticized the faculty, and that was funny enough in its own right. But Kate, the one person here who was still a bit of an outsider, had done something entirely uncharacteristic, and claimed a place in the circle of friends. Kate had been quiet and reserved when she mingled with Grant's friends at first. She'd known full well that she was an observer, nothing more, in the beginning. Then, after all the beer and good times at Stub & Herb's, she'd gradually been brought into the fold, but just within the outer circle.

Now this. She was in! Joe put his arm around Kate's shoulder and confessed, "You scared the shit outta me."

Kate laughed at her own joke. She laughed with her mouth open and her whole body shook. Grant watched as Joe squeezed her, then kissed her cheek. He remembered the complete lack of self-confidence from only a few days earlier, and wished she could feel like this all the time. She looked so happy. Somebody had finally hit one out to right field, and she'd caught it.

"The scary part is that you actually kinda looked like Ebby for a second there," Joe added, and the laughter escalated once more.

Ben turned toward Will and spoke softly into Will's ear. "Look at her, she's changed." He gestured toward Kate.

"Whaddya mean?" Will asked.

"She laughs and jokes. She never used to. She's a flower that's blossoming."

"Very poetic." Will grinned. "But I know what you mean. I see it, too." Will pointed at Grant. "And look at him. He's changed, too. That boy's in love."

"Yeah, he sure has been steady these past few weeks, not so much bitching about all that trivial shit Joe and Andy were just whinin' about," Ben offered.

"Well, I think he and Kate have been pretty busy." Will raised his eyebrows.

"Yeah," Ben sighed. "She's a beauty, isn't she?"

Kate was holding Joe by the ear once again like a disobedient grammar school student and teasing him while Ben and Will watched.

"Look around us." Ben nudged Will in the ribs. "Look at all the men in this bar right now that are staring at Kate."

Will made a quick survey of the tables and booths in the bar and nodded. "I saw four guys peekin' at her."

"More than that," Ben corrected. "But the point is that she's givin' off some sort of vibrations that she didn't used to. Men are noticing her. She's the matter/antimatter opposite of Darcy."

"Well, I guess you would be the expert on that sort of thing," Will said.

"You guys want something to drink?" came a husky voice from behind Will. The waitress confronting Ben and Will appeared to be about forty-five years old and was one of several hard-looking women serving drinks to the people waiting in line. She wasn't waiting on tables; she just moved up and down the long line of thirsty customers and brought them drinks while they talked with one another and waited to buy a sandwich.

"Well hello, darlin'," Ben said when he turned to face her. She wasn't pretty anymore, but she once was. She didn't seem to be particularly happy to be here, either. A lifetime of cigarettes, hard work, and hard men had shaped her, Ben guessed.

"Our throats were gettin' awful scratchy here, darlin', could you bring us . . . ," Ben paused while he pointed to everyone in the group and waited for them to nod yes if they wanted a beer, ". . . ten beers?" Ben nodded and winked at the waitress. The woman turned on her heels and walked toward the bar with no facial expression.

"Jeez, Ben, if I didn't know better . . . ," Will started, then stopped. He studied Ben's eyes as they moved over the waitress's narrow hips.

"Look around you," Ben interrupted. "There's a bunch of half-drunk dental students in here, and the rest of the people are lawyers and downtown businessmen, maybe a few secretaries and girlfriends."

"So?" Will said.

"So she'd damn near invisible to this crowd. Nobody here would notice her unless she caught fire or something," Ben replied.

"So?" Will asked again.

"So, she's a person, maybe a pretty soft-hearted one at that. She gets treated like shit on somebody's shoe all day at work, and I'll bet her only crime in life was that she trusted somebody, probably several somebodies, through the years. She trusted a couple men to make her life better, and they let her down." Ben lit a cigarette. "Her parents probably had pretty low expectations for her, too."

"You sound like you know her," Will said.

"Maybe I do, sort of," Ben replied. He watched her backside as she weaved her way through the crowd back to the bar.

Several minutes later the waitress returned with beer for everyone and a pleasant smile for Ben.

"Thanks, darlin'," Ben said when he paid for the beer, and he gave her a nice tip.

The waitress's smile broadened and for a moment Will thought she was pretty and young again. But when she turned her head her broad smile exposed a missing bicuspid on the side of her mouth, and Will thought her beauty disappeared in a puff of smoke. Then he felt sad for the woman and her hard life, and for the way he'd judged her.

"See, she's kinda pretty, isn't she?" Ben said.

"Yeah, she is," Will admitted. "But you aren't gonna . . . I mean, you're not interested in her, are you?" he stammered.

"No. I'm not gonna." Ben finished his cigarette while Will studied him and tried to guess what memories might be swirling around inside his head. After a moment Ben looked back at Will and put a punctuation mark at the end of their discussion of the waitress. "She just wants to be happy too," he said. Ben was a good friend and a good man, but Will couldn't help but notice that he saw life, and lived life, a little differently than anyone else he knew.

Ben and Will rejoined the rest of the group's conversation as they celebrated the conclusion of the first semester. The small circle of friends inched along toward Iron Mike Petrowiak and a huge beef sandwich while they joked and looked back on their past fourteen weeks of graduate school. All of them bore a huge sense of relief. They'd made it. One semester down. They could do this.

They joked about Ebby and about a few of the more unpopular faculty members. They joked about classmates, and then their own mistakes and failures over the first semester. But the prevalent feeling was one of triumph. The most difficult semester was out of the way.

A deep sense of camaraderie had grown between them, too. They'd survived together, like a combat platoon on the front line. They'd taken everything the enemy could throw at them and they'd made it, each with some help from the others.

The waitress returned several times, always with more beer and a warm smile for Ben, and the conversation grew louder as the group moved slowly toward Iron Mike.

"You know," Carol Knutsen started, in a voice just loud enough to call everyone's attention to herself, "my favorite moment of the semester was watching Grant holler 'fuck' and then throw those red-hot instruments at the ceiling!" She walked stiff-legged in a tight circle and shook one hand while she imitated Grant. "Fuck!" She scowled and shook her hand. "Shit!" She shook her hand. "Goddammit!" She shook her hand.

"That was pretty good," Joe said over the laughter. But I liked watching Will tell the story about reporting to Dean Muckinhern's office!"

In the midst of all the laughter and commotion, the waitress with the broken smile appeared at Kate's side and offered her something. When the group's laughter subsided the waitress handed her a bottle of Champagne and ten paper cups. Then she said, "It's from him," and pointed across the bar to a young man sitting at a table with several other young men.

Kate glanced at the bottle, then at the man across the room, and an uncomfortable smile crossed her face. She showed the bottle to the man who was looking at her now, and then nodded and mouthed an exaggerated "Thank you."

The man nodded in return.

"What's with the Champagne?" Andy asked.

"It's sort of an inside joke," Kate answered, but she didn't seem to think it was very funny.

"I think I know that guy," Joe said, "He's a clinical instructor up in crown and bridge, right?"

"Yup," Kate said. "He's a couple years older than me."

"Another old boyfriend?" Grant asked, trying to make light of something that he hoped wouldn't evolve into a clumsy situation.

"No, not at all," Kate answered. "Nothing like that."

"I know!" Joe interrupted again, when he remembered something more. "He's the clown that just bought a red Corvette and spends all day bragging about it in clinic. The upperclassmen all hate that guy! Miles Clark, that's his name!"

"Yup," Kate answered.

Ten heads turned toward Miles Clark's table. He was handsome and a bit over six feet tall, with long blond hair, broad shoulders, and blue eyes. He waved and nodded.

"He's not bad!" Carol said. "Not bad at all."

"You can have him," Kate replied.

"So what's the story here? C'mon, the suspense is killing me," Will begged.

"Well," Kate started, "we had a party the day we got the results back from our national board exams. It was a big deal and we were all glad we passed. The atmosphere was sort of like today, with you guys." She gave the Champagne to Ben before she continued. "To make a long story short, the party wound up at his house. Everybody was handing me glasses of Champagne, so I drank 'em all. I just never did stuff like that." She shook her head. "I got really sick. You haven't been sick till you've been sick on Champagne," she smiled.

"So that's the story?" Joe seemed disappointed. "That's nuthin'."

"Sorry," Kate said. "But I guess the end of the story is that he wanted my girlfriends to just leave me at his house to sleep it off." She glanced suspiciously around her circle of friends. "*That* didn't happen!"

The cork exploded from the Champagne bottle with a loud pop and hit the high ceiling in the old bar. "Well, we're still gonna drink his Champagne!" Ben said, as he began to pour some into each of the paper cups. Then he, too, nodded his thanks to Dr. Miles Clark, who nodded back.

Carol Knutsen inched closer to Kate. "Do you think he had ulterior motives? Do you think he would have taken advantage of you?" she asked.

"Well, let's just say that I knew his reputation, and even as sick as I was, I wasn't going to stay there," Kate said.

Grant passed her a paper cup filled to the top with Champagne. "Ooo, get that away from me. Just the smell of it makes me sick, still," Kate said, as she pushed the cup away.

Mitch Morgan plucked the cup from Grant's hand and tossed it back with one gulp. "Don't mind if I do."

"Funny thing is . . . ," Kate paused and the group standing around her closed in a little to hear what she had to say, ". . . I've hardly talked to Miles for a couple years. I didn't know he was here today. I can't figure why he'd send over a bottle of Champagne."

Ben cast a knowing glance at Will, then nodded. Miles Clark had noticed a flower blossoming, too. Ben pursed his lips and said, with his eyes, "I told you so."

All thoughts of Miles Clark were gone a minute later with the last of the Champagne. The group was inching closer to Iron Mike Petrowiak and they began to eye the huge chunk of beef he was carving.

Mike Petrowiak never spoke. Never. He cut slices of meat, dunked the slices in the cauldron of gurgling spices and beef juice, and then assembled every sandwich, one at a time, while the hungry patrons watched.

From time to time, people tried to cajole Mike and draw him into conversation. Maybe he didn't talk to his customers because he didn't want to slow the line down and irritate patrons at the end of it. Maybe he was just tired of half-drunken businessmen asking him stupid questions. In any case, he never spoke.

As they neared the table where Mike was steadily working, Grant put his arm around Kate and kissed her cheek. "Got all your stuff packed?" he asked.

"Yes," Kate answered. "But are we gonna be warm enough? It's s'posed to snow up there today and tonight."

"We'll be fine, Kate. You're gonna love Spider Lake Duck Camp."

When it was her turn, Kate stepped up to the carving table, held out a heavy paper plate, and waited for Mike Petrowiak to plop a man-sized sandwich onto it. His huge fingers looked like sausage links, but with the proverbial hands of a surgeon he assembled a spectacular beef sandwich on her plate.

"Thanks, Mr. Petrowiak," Kate said, before she moved along with the others in line, sidestepping to pick up a small salad.

Iron Mike Petrowiak looked up casually to see who'd offered the pleasant thank-you, and then did a double take when she smiled at him. "Enjoy!" he grunted, and his one-word sentence surprised everyone nearby.

Then, as he was assembling Grant's sandwich, he stopped. "Hey, kid. You with her?" he asked.

"Yes," Grant answered.

"Good boy," Mike said clearly, then plopped an extra helping of beef onto Grant's plate. "Good boy," he repeated. He snuck one more sideways glance at Kate and let the tiniest hint of a smile curl.

"Thank you, Mike," Grant said. Mike Petrowiak didn't look up again.

Ben noticed the exceptional break in Iron Mike's silence and the twinkle in his eye, too. He took his sandwich and followed Kate and Grant to a table where the others waited for them.

"Sorry June couldn't make it today," Kate said when she sat down beside Will.

"Well, somebody's gotta work." Will smiled. "But she'll be ready to go after school. We're planning to pick you guys up as soon as she gets home, and then head for Spider Lake. Should be fresh snow on the gr . . ."

"Hi, Kate, still drinkin' Champagne?" A strange voice interrupted. Miles Clark stepped in front of Grant, his back inches in front of Grant's face, and sat down in the chair next to Kate's that Grant was about to sit in. He sat with his back to Grant, ignoring him while he addressed Kate, unconcerned that Grant and Ben were standing there, sandwiches in hand, waiting to sit down with their friends.

"No. I can't stand the smell of it," Kate replied. She made a point to look behind Miles Clark and suggest that he move along so Grant and Ben could sit down.

He ignored her gesture. "Haven't seen you in a while." He smiled as if he was doing her a favor. Clark wore pleated khaki pants and expensive loafers with leather tassels. His pastel yellow golf shirt was covered by a light blue pullover with Hazeltine Golf Club embroidered on the left breast.

"Yeah, well, I'm pretty busy," Kate replied, then deliberately peeked at Grant and Ben once more.

"I've been teaching up in crown and bridge," Clark announced, apparently impressed with his own position and still oblivious to the traffic piled up behind him.

"Yeah, I heard that," Kate said.

"We should get together sometime," he suggested. He waited briefly for a reply from Kate. When none was forthcoming he made an offer. "Maybe we'll try Champagne again?" The others at the table were mortified. Was this guy trying to pick Kate up; to ask her on a date? Was he on a mission to insult Grant? Maybe he was just trying to cause a problem between Grant and Kate. Or was he just so full of himself that he thought Kate might be grateful for a chance to jump in the sack with him?

"Well, I . . . ," Kate started, clearly uncomfortable now.

Clark leaned back in the chair Grant was waiting for. He appeared to have plenty of time on his hands. All the others at the table were embarrassed and chose to look down at their sandwiches. "I'll give you a call . . ."

"Hey! We're hungry back here!" Ben called out.

Clark glanced over his shoulder and stared blankly into Grant's eyes, then Ben's. He turned back to Kate as if he hadn't noticed anyone back there.

"So the new job is working out OK?" he asked.

"Hey, Jack!" Ben called, and he glowered at Clark's back before Kate could reply.

"I'll give you a call," Clark said once more. He winked at Kate, then stood up slowly and rejoined his friends across the crowded bar without looking back at Grant and Ben again.

"What a puke," Mitch Morgan offered, as Grant and Ben seated themselves once Miles Clark was out of the way.

"Asshole," Joe Paatalo said between bites of his sandwich.

Ben sat down and smoldered, but said nothing.

"Sorry about all that," Kate apologized. "He's just one of those people who thinks he's entitled to . . . something."

"He seems to think he's a pretty close friend of yours," Grant teased. "Should I be jealous?"

"He's cute! No doubt about it," Carol Knutsen said before Kate could answer.

"No," Kate grimaced. "He's the kind of person that likes to know something bad about others, like maybe they cheated, either at work or in their personal lives, so he can hold it over them and maybe have some power over them. If we had ever . . . you know . . . he'd have mentioned it just now for your benefit. Does that make sense? I guess he's just a dented can."

"He's an asshole," Joe reiterated.

"Yeah, but he's still cute," Carol said again. As if no more needed to be said on the topic of Miles Clark, she then asked, "Is everyone going to the kegger over at the frat house tonight?"

The conversation at the table returned to the usual issues—plans for the evening, plans for semester break, even plans for the summer—then circled back to some of the ambiguous test questions from earlier in the day. Everyone at the table joined in the renewed atmosphere of celebration, and thirty minutes passed while they joked with each other.

Ben was listening to Joe Paatalo whine, yet again, about another obtuse question on the Biochemistry final when he noticed movement over by Miles Clark's table. He turned slightly and watched Clark stand up and walk to the men's room.

"I gotta toss a whiz," Ben said to Will. "I'll be right back."

"Good idea. I'll go with you," Will said. He was unaware that Ben was stalking Miles Clark as he followed his friend to the men's room.

Ben's eyes fixed on his prey and he remained about ten paces behind when Clark swung open the door to the men's room and disappeared inside.

The men's room, like the rest of Petrowiak's Bar, had been built around 1930, and nothing had been changed since then. Clark stood at a urinal trough which was about ten feet long and could accommodate four men at the same time. The floor was covered with white ceramic tiles, each about one inch square, and the walls featured black and white ceramic tiles in a checkerboard pattern.

Clark was alone in the men's room, and when the door swung shut behind Will, Ben tapped a finger sternly on Will's chest. "Watch the door," he said. He walked to the urinal trough and stood next to Clark for a second.

Will recognized something malevolent in Ben's eyes and he froze by the door. He stood there now, waiting, but waiting for what? His question was answered in less than a heartbeat.

Ben swung his left hand into Clark's groin, grabbed his testicles, and used his thumb to pinch Clark's penis against the metal zipper of his khakis. The swiftness of his attack was startling, and Will could only step back and watch.

Clark's back stiffened with pain and shock, and Ben immediately drove his right thumb into a pressure point beneath Clark's left ear, then he shoved him against the checkerboard wall.

"I'm not gonna hurt you," Ben growled. "But you need to learn some fuckin' manners." He paused and brought his face close to Clark's. "Blink your fuckin' eyes if you know what I'm talking about."

Clark blinked, but his face was drawn tight with fear and pain.

"If you want to call Dr. Bellows and ask her for a date, you go right ahead," Ben hissed. "But if you ever embarrass her, or Grant Thorson, like you did a little while ago, I'm gonna rip your dick off and ram it up your cannoli. Understand?"

Clark blinked again.

"Good, now I'm gonna wash your piss off my hand and then go finish lunch with my friends. If you want to continue this discussion outside behind the bar, you know where you can find me. Don't move, and don't talk to me when I let go of you. Understand?"

Clark blinked, and Ben released him. Ben washed his hands while Clark gasped and tried to compose himself. Will stared openmouthed, first at Clark, then at Ben, and back and forth until Ben was ready to return to their table.

As they walked back to rejoin their friends at lunch, Ben put his arm around Will's shoulder. "Probably be good if you didn't tell anyone what you just saw."

"I didn't see anything," Will replied. "But I gotta ask you a question."

"What?" Ben replied.

"Wasn't it sort of icky to be holding on to some other guy's pecker like that?"

Ben grinned, then he laughed off and on for the next twenty minutes. The group finished lunch, and their first semester of dental school, with no further interruptions.

❦ CHAPTER 18 ❧

A sloppy winter snow shower descended over the Twin Cities just after sundown. Wet snowflakes melted into rivulets of water on the car windows and shattered the streetlights and automobile lights into a million sparkles. When Will eased his car onto I-494, all they could do was roll slowly along with rush hour traffic.

"It's gonna be slow going for a while till we get out of the cities," Will said, as he squinted to see the cars moving in front of him. "Then it's supposed to get cold and snow some more."

"Sorry I was a little late," June said. "It would have been nice to get moving a little earlier."

"No problem," Kate replied from the backseat. "We've got plenty of time. We're on vacation! I can't wait to see your place up north. Grant's been telling me all about it for weeks."

Grant sat in the middle of the backseat with his left arm around Kate and his right arm on the weary head of Watson, Ben Pribyl's homework-eating dog.

"You didn't tell me we were bringing Watson," Grant said, as he scratched the dog's ears.

"Didn't know myself until yesterday," Will replied. "Ben decided to take a little road trip with Tanya the Mauler and he asked if I'd take Watson for the weekend. He's not much of a problem, *usually*." With the word "usually" he glanced at June, then over his shoulder at Grant.

"I told you to close the door better," June said in a motherly tone.

Ben had dropped Watson at Will and June's house twenty-four hours earlier, so he and Tanya could hit the road right after the party at Petrowiak's.

Only two years old, Watson was an odd cross between a blue heeler and a black Labrador. He had a charming personality but way too much energy, and he was an enthusiastic garbage hound. There were just too many tempting smells in a garbage can, and Watson had never learned to resist.

Will and June kept their garbage in a little room off the kitchen until the garbage man came on Tuesdays, but this week they'd taken a seventeen-pound turkey from the freezer and let it begin to thaw in the cool little room next to the back door, so they could have a turkey dinner while they were at Spider Lake Duck Camp.

When he'd left for school that morning, Will had neglected to close the door of the little room securely and a curious Watson had been unable to restrain himself. He'd pushed open the door and then eaten all the garbage *and* the entire seventeen-pound turkey, bones and all.

"He sure looked guilty when I got home," Will laughed.

"He looked like a fifty-pound wood tick, about to explode from over-eating," June added.

Watson now lay with his head resting in Grant's lap. Kate reached over, scratched Watson's neck gently, and said, "He still looks like a great big ol' sausage that's about to pop."

"Well, I can tell you this," Will said. "That dog is gonna be sleepin' in the garage tonight. It's gonna be nasty when that turkey makes its way through . . ."

"Will! Let's talk about something else," June interrupted. "OK?"

"Sure, honey," Will smiled.

Kate took the cue and asked about June's first semester of teaching.

The car eased its way through a slurry of creeping vehicles and gradually emerged from the traffic when they turned north toward St. Cloud. Other people's headlights and taillights drifted off onto other roads, and before long they were all alone, driving through a Hollywood snowfall on a quiet night while the temperature dropped.

Anticipation over spending the weekend with good friends at a special destination kept the conversation lively while they rolled along for several hours, but eventually Kate lowered her head onto Grant's shoulder and let herself be overtaken by sleep. June slumped against the car door and did the same while Grant and Will continued to chat about school, baseball, ducks, and trout.

About an hour from Spider Lake, even Grant grew sleepy and laid his head against Kate's. Road noise, music from the car radio, and the steady thumping of the tires on the road surface were about to carry Grant off to his dreams. All was quiet and dark for a few monotonous miles. Abruptly, a hideous and foul stench seared his nostrils. Kate woke up, covered her nose, and groaned.

"Will!" June called out. "What is that smell?"

Will rolled his window all the way down and let the bracing winter cold rush into the car. "Dog fart!" Will laughed.

Kate covered her head with her coat, as much for protection from Watson's fart as from the cold. Grant raised the neck of his sweater up over his nose.

After several seconds, Will closed his window and added, "Wow, that was a prizewinner."

A muffled voice came from under Kate's winter coat. "How much farther?" she groaned.

"'Bout an hour, maybe less," Will said.

"Step on it!" Kate laughed as she lowered her coat. "My eyes are watering."

"That's the thing with dog farts," Will said analytically. "You just never get much warning. Maybe in a quiet room you can hear a little air escaping, but . . ."

"Shut up, Will," June interrupted.

"Sure, honey," Will nodded. "Everyone should be prepared in case Watson drops another bomb. Be ready to open a window on short notice," he warned.

Most of the next hour was spent rolling windows down and seeking shelter from what Kate began labeling as "pingers." Laughter and fresh air were the only defenses against the relentless attacks, and no one fell asleep again before they reached Spider Lake Duck Camp.

"We're here!" Will said, as they came to to a narrow driveway that was nothing more than an opening in the trees, covered with a white blanket of new-fallen snow. The road into Spider Lake Duck Camp was a narrow, trackless ribbon of white winding through a forest of tall pines and lit only by a sliver of moon. It appeared as if had been lovingly placed there by the delicate hand of God. When Will eased the car into a moonlit clearing, the lodge loomed like a friendly giant and welcomed them after the long night of travel.

The roof of the lodge seemed to have been painted with fresh snow. Except for the swishing sound Watson made as he ran around frolicking in the snow, the woods were silent as the group stood on the porch and waited for Will to unlock the door.

The pine logs, the stone fireplace, the leather furniture, the snowshoes, deer heads, maps, and old photos on the walls gave the place a powerful and rustic link to earlier times.

Kate made her way inside and looked around with the same wonder that freshman dental students showed when they first entered the Gross Anatomy labs. The others each made several trips back and forth from the car, but Kate inspected the place as if she was visiting an ornate cathedral.

"Told you so," Grant said, as he placed an armload of firewood beside the fireplace. He stood up and put an arm over Kate's shoulder. "Could you live here, Kate? I mean, a place like this?" he asked.

Kate nodded yes, then she shook her head again in awe.

"OK," Will said a few minutes later, as he leaned back on the couch and put his stocking feet up on the coffee table. "The game is Great Baseball Names. You go first."

Kate and June had moved to the kitchen, where they were baking several trays of chocolate chip cookies in an added attempt to warm the lodge.

"All time, or the Twins?" Grant asked.

"All time," Will replied.

"Nicknames or just proper names?" Grant asked, while he struck a match and held it under the newspaper and kindling they'd just piled in the fireplace.

"Either," Will replied.

"Teddy Ballgame," Grant shrugged. "Ted Williams."

"Mudcat Grant."

"Catfish Hunter."

"Ducky Medwick."

"Ted Kluszewski."

"Rocky Colavito."

"Zoilo Versalles."

"I love Zoilo," Grant said. "I always loved that name." Then he added, "The Big Train, Walter Johnson."

"The Splendid Splinter," Will said.

"Pee Wee Reese."

"Duke Snider."

Each man spit out a name faster until Grant leaned back and said triumphantly, "Mickey Mantle! If I ever have a son I believe I'll call him Mickey Mantle."

"Yeah." Will tipped his head back and said thoughtfully, "Mickey Mantle Thorson. Has a nice ring to it."

"What if his mother has a different idea?" Kate asked as she carried a plate of cookies to the coffee table and sat next to Grant.

June followed closely behind, carrying a tray with four cans of Hamm's beer. She said, "Let's have a toast to celebrate the end of the first semester. Cookies and beer!"

"Who'd have thought that we'd all wind up here, like this, back on that first day of school, huh?" Will asked, as he clinked beer cans with Grant.

As Grant raised the beer to his mouth he turned toward his lover and saw her smiling in reaction to Will's toast. The road to this place had indeed been filled with surprises.

~:~

The bedroom was filling with the soft gray light of an overcast winter morning when Grant allowed one eye to open. The snow had stopped. The moon had made a brief appearance during the night, but now a slate sky had locked winter down over the dark woods and the white lake. Grant lifted his head from his pillow and marveled at the quiet.

He rose and sat on the side of the bed and he noticed that Kate was already up for the day. The floor felt cold on his bare feet, and while he cleared the sleep from his head he searched for his blue jeans, a sweatshirt, and some warm socks.

"Good morning!" the others said when he shuffled into the great room and found them all sitting by a fire, once again.

"There's coffee in the kitchen," Kate said. She wore an odd smile. "Will was just telling a story you'll want to hear," she added as he wandered into the kitchen. He poured himself some coffee and returned.

The leather couch groaned a warm welcome as he settled next to Kate and blew on his coffee. "So what's the story?" he asked.

"Well," Will started, "Ben asked me, told me actually, not to tell you guys about this. But I gotta tell you. I already told Kate."

"Sounds interesting," Grant said.

"Yeah, well, you know that guy who bought us, er, Kate, the Champagne yesterday?"

"Yeah," Grant said.

"Well, I followed Ben into the can yesterday, to toss a whiz." He turned toward June and said, "That means I went to the men's room in order to urinate."

"Shut up, Will," June groaned.

"Anyway, Champagne Man was standing there pissin' when I walked in. Ben was with me. But before I could even whip out Emile the Destroyer—that's what I call . . ." he started to explain.

"Shut up, Will! Just tell the story," June groaned again.

"So anyway, Ben and I walked into the can. Next thing I know Ben grabs the guy by the nuts, and not in a tender way, if you know what I mean. Then he does some sort of Green Berets, kung fu shit and smashes Champagne Man up against a wall. Tells the guy if he ever embarrasses you or Kate again, like he did, he's gonna rip the guy's pecker off." Will smiled and nodded. "Not shittin' you, Pard! It was a promise, not some idle threat. He meant business. He told Dr. Clark if he wanted more, he'd be glad to meet him out back. Then he told him to stand there and shut up while he washed the piss off his hands." Will shrugged. "We came back to the party and you'd never have known there'd been a ruckus."

Grant questioned Kate with his eyes.

Kate shrugged. "Miles is one of those guys who makes his receptionist tell patients that he's not in the office at the moment because he's teaching at the university, like that makes him something special. Truth is, they need instructors up in crown and bridge. They'll take anybody, and he has nothing better to do because his private practice is pretty slow. Miles just picked a fight with the wrong guy. He had it coming."

"Yeah, and now I have another instructor who hates me," Grant sighed.

"No, based on what I saw there in Iron Mike Petrowiak's shitter, I'd say that Dr. Miles Clark will be happy to step aside whenever he sees you coming," Will said. "OK, I just wanted to share that story, even though Ben told me not to." He changed the subject. "Now, June and I are going to do a little cross-country skiing along some old trails in the woods. We'll take Watson with us, see if we can run some of the energy off, not to mention a few dog farts. We'll be gone for a couple hours and you two will have the place to yourselves. If you want to put some birdseed in the bird feeders, it's out there in the little shed. There are books on the bookshelves and, well, I'm sure you two can think of something to do." He winked at Grant.

"Will, you're such a moron," June sighed. "Let's go." She turned to Kate. "We'll have our big meal this evening: Reuben sandwiches. You're on your own till then."

"Have fun," Kate said.

~:~

Will and June returned to a silent lodge a little after 2:00 p.m. Warm coals still glowed in the fireplace but Grant and Kate were not there. Will called out to Grant. "Hey! Where are you guys?" He knocked on the bedroom door where Grant and Kate had slept, then peeked inside when there was no reply.

"They probably went for a walk," June said. She took off her ski boots and warm clothes and put them beside the fireplace.

"How far do you think Kate's gonna walk in a foot of new snow?" Will asked while he looked out a window, searching the grounds for tracks. "It looks like they were poking around in the shed, and they *did* put some birdseed in the bird feeders."

June strolled through the kitchen and into the great room while she raised both hands to her head and began to pull her hair into a ponytail. "They've got to be somewhere close by," she said with a rubber band between her teeth. When she'd pulled her ponytail through the rubber band she readjusted her sweater and walked to the bank of windows facing Spider Lake. "What time do you want to eat supper?" she called out. She was scanning the small islands scattered across the frozen, snow-covered surface of the lake. "Are you sure you've got enough cheese . . ." She stopped and brought her hands to her mouth. "Will! My God! Come here!"

"What's wrong?" Will asked, as he ran into the great room.

"Look!" June said, pointing outside across the sheet of ice and snow.

One dark form, the silhouette of a man, was the only movement June and Will could see against the white snow all around. The overcast afternoon colored the world only in shades of gray, and the man trudged across the lake wearing snowshoes. A harness made of rope was fixed to his shoulders and he was pulling something across the lake. Will stepped closer, strained his eyes against the snow and the distance, then snatched a pair of binoculars hanging by the porch door and began to focus them. June stared with her hands covering her mouth.

"Jeez, honey. Look what he did," Will said, handing the binoculars to June.

Grant was pulling a toboggan and Kate was sitting on it, enjoying the ride as if she were the Queen of the Nile. Grant had discovered the snowshoes and toboggan while he'd been searching through the shed for birdseed to put in the bird feeders. He'd found an old red waterskiing towrope lying beside a long-forgotten pair of water skis. After he'd fashioned the towrope into a harness and secured it to the toboggan, he'd found some musty old flotation vests and tied them together to form a comfortable seat for Kate.

"He's pulled her through the woods like that for a mile, wearing Grandpa's snowshoes," June said, still peering through the field glasses.

"Two miles," Will said.

"I heard them talking this morning. He told her he wanted her to know what it felt like to walk through the woods on fresh snow. But I didn't think . . ." June stopped herself.

"He's got her bundled up like an Eskimo," Will said.

Out in the middle of the lake, on a sheet of ice covered with new snow, Grant stopped walking. He shed the harness and rested with his hands on his knees, then turned awkwardly and took the snowshoes off.

"Getting tired?" Kate called. "We didn't have to come way out here."

"Nope," he lied. Still huffing, he walked to the side of the toboggan and opened the neck of his parka, then took off his gloves.

"This is so beautiful," Kate said. She swept her eyes across the lake in all directions. "Look! Look back at the lodge. It's perfect, it's just like the movies. The roof is all covered in snow."

Grant lifted his stocking hat off and exposed his sweaty, matted hair. Heat rose from his head and condensed into vapors, so that his head appeared to be smoldering. He wiped huge beads of sweat from his red face with the sleeve of his coat.

"You look funny," Kate said.

"What do you think of a summer wedding?" Grant asked. "I'm thinkin' July."

She looked him up and down for a moment. "You're asking me to marry you?" she asked.

"Yeah," Grant nodded, then dropped to one knee, reached into his pocket and retrieved a small jeweler's box. "How'm I doing so far?"

"Pretty good," Kate said. She placed a hand over her face to cover her smile when Grant opened the box and showed her the ring.

"It was all I could afford," he said, as he slid it on her finger. "It's a pretty small diamond, but . . ."

"It's beautiful," Kate replied

The beads of sweat were reappearing on his face, and his head was still steaming when he took her hand in his. "All I've wanted since the day we met was to be with you. I love you, Kate, and I'm asking you to choose me. Will you marry me?"

She leaned forward and put her arms around his neck, then she pulled him close and squeezed, hard. She'd never held him like that and she kept the firm embrace for five seconds, then ten, then twenty. He could hear her sniffling and feel her chest heaving gently while she cried. "Of course I'll marry you," she whispered.

The embrace lingered for nearly a minute. Kate didn't want the moment to slip away.

"Wow," Grant said while she squeezed him.

"What?" she said. She released her grip and kissed him on the lips.

"I just asked Kate Bellows to marry me." Grant shook his head and seemed like he couldn't quite believe it himself. "And she said yes!" he added, still unsure if he should believe his own good fortune.

"Well," Kate replied, "I thought you'd never ask." She pulled him close and kissed him again. Then she added, "But I do have one condition; one demand."

"What?" he asked.

"I want you to promise me that I'll have a place in the world. I want that house with a picket fence, and neighbors who stop over and say hi, and kids, and dogs and cats; a place in the world. Do you know what I mean?"

"Sure. We'll have a place in the world. We'll have a good life," he said.

They sat together on a silent sheet of ice and snow, and planned their wedding and the next part of their lives.

A half hour later, Grant stepped into the snowshoes and reattached the toboggan harness so he could pull Kate back to the lodge at Spider Lake Duck Camp. After only a couple of steps across the frozen lake, he stopped and turned back toward her. "So how'd I do on the proposal?" he asked, then he waited for her answer.

"Good!" Kate smiled. "Really good. Nice work."

"Thanks," Grant said. He turned around and started pulling the toboggan again. "I thought it was some pretty fine work, too, if I do say so myself."

Kate and Grant returned from their walk in the woods but said nothing to June and Will about their news while they lounged about the lodge. Afternoon slid into a calm gray twilight, and then the outside world was dark again.

The four friends sat together in the rustic kitchen and assembled Reuben sandwiches while they laughed and joked. Grant warmed the corned beef in an ancient gas oven while he told about the long walk across Spider

Lake. Kate opened a can of sauerkraut and stood beside Grant while she heated it in a saucepan and laughed at his retelling of the story. Will sliced a brick of Swiss cheese and rambled on for a while about several professors at school. June fed pumpernickel bread into the toaster and told a few stories about the students in her school, but she also took note of the way Kate and Grant touched each other, and smiled at each other, and were never far apart. They were even more affectionate than usual. The couples ate together at a small table in the kitchen. They talked of everything and nothing while they ate, and when the meal was finished they slid their plates forward and let conversation continue over their dishes and food scraps and empty beer bottles for another hour. Eventually they adjourned to the great room, and June kept studying Grant and Kate.

They talked themselves into the deepest part of a silent winter night, and when the fatigue of a long day settled over them they agreed to get ready for bed and then return to the great room for a nightcap.

Will and June sat together on the leather couch and waited for Grant and Kate to join them. A yellow flame danced and flickered in the fieldstone fireplace, and June grew so warm she had to lower the Hudson Bay blanket she'd been covering up with. The leather couch groaned a bit when Will slid closer to her. "They're up to something, I tell you," June whispered in a low voice.

"What do you mean?" Will asked.

"Just look at them!" June replied, and pointed with her forehead.

Grant and Kate were standing nose to nose in the kitchen, almost thirty feet away. Kate wore baby blue silk pajamas and stood with an arm around Grant's waist. Her long hair fell past her shoulders as she spoke playfully with Grant. Her leg brace was nowhere to be seen and she was keeping her feet warm with oversize red wool hunting socks.

Grant's tattered gray sweatshirt and sweatpants hinted at the athletic physique underneath. His cotton sweats were a total mismatch to Kate's elegant pajamas. Will and June watched as Grant whispered in her ear, then pulled her close. He lifted the neckline of her pajamas away from her chest and tried to sneak a playful peak down the front of her shirt.

The gentle, angular lines of her face framed a joyful smile as she slapped his hand and scolded him.

June found Will's hand under the Hudson Bay blanket, gave it a squeeze, and turned a knowing smile his way.

"What?" he asked.

"Something's going on there," June grinned.

"Really, Sherlock?" Will grimaced. "How could you tell? Was it the moaning and the furniture thumping around last night in their room that tipped you off?"

"That's not what I mean," June said. "Oh, look at that." She swooned as if she was watching a puppy playing with a chew toy.

Grant slid his hand inside Kate's pajamas and squeezed her bottom in the same playful way that he'd peeked down her neckline. Kate responded by doing the same thing inside his sweatpants. He kissed her, just a peck on the lips, then brought his arm up and wrapped it around her waist.

He lifted slightly and both Kate's feet came off the floor. She put an arm over his shoulder and they locked together like two boxcars. He intended to carry her, instead of making her walk without her brace, and when Grant turned toward the great room he and Kate were moving as one person. With a six-pack of Hamm's in one hand and Kate held by his other arm, Grant walked into the great room and placed Kate on the leather couch across from Will and June, then sat down beside her.

"Well," Grant said as he fumbled with the beer. "I s'pose we should tell you first."

June squeezed Will's hand.

"We're getting married this summer," Kate announced. She held her hand up to show them the ring on her finger.

"Ohhh," June squealed. "Congratulations!" She jumped up to hug Kate and Grant. "See, I told you so, Will!" she added.

"Congrats, Pard, and Kate. Really happy for you," Will said. "When did all this happen?"

"Today, out on the lake," Kate beamed.

"Ohhh," June squealed again. "That's so romantic! I knew something was going on out there!"

Will looked at his wife, then turned a devious smile back to Grant and gave him the thumbs-up signal. "Romantic is good, isn't it, honey?" He flicked his eyebrows at Grant and Kate.

"Shut up, Will," June said.

"Sure, honey." Will flicked his eyebrows again.

Grant passed beer across the coffee table to each of them.

"Here's to a great life together!" Will said. "Congratulations!"

They talked for another hour while they threw more wood into the fireplace, sipped at several more beers, and discussed plans for a wedding and all that might come after.

Will's hair was mussed, and June seemed flushed and giddy from a little too much celebrating, when they stood up to go to their upstairs bedroom.

"Goodnight, you two," June gushed, as she was about to turn away. "This has been so special, and so romantic. You got engaged at our cabin!" She clasped her hands at her chest. "We'll see you in the morning."

As she turned her back to Grant and Kate, Will flashed a huge grin, winked, and again gave them the thumbs-up signal.

"Shut up, Will," June laughed, without looking.

"Sure, honey," Will replied.

"But stay close. You've got some work to do."

"Right behind you, honey."

One more thumbs-up from Will, and they disappeared up a flight of stairs.

"Did it feel odd to tell someone that we were getting married?" Grant asked.

"A little," Kate said. "How about you?"

"Yeah, a little," Grant said. "It was the first time I ever said the words." He slouched back into the couch and leaned against Kate. "Wow," Grant breathed. "We're talking about the rest of our lives."

"Does that bother you?" Kate asked.

"Hmph," he mumbled. "Not at all, just makes me wonder where it will take us. Don't you wonder about that? I mean, just what will become of us?"

"Sure," she replied.

Grant slipped an arm around her so they could lie together on the couch and stare into the fire. They looked at the flames and tried to imagine a home, and children, and what life had in store for them.

Kate thought about the times she'd struggled to prove to others that she was worthy of what she got from life, and the way she'd worked so hard to win things that no one would willingly give her. Now Grant was offering to simply give her love and a great friendship, things she could never win. The yellow flames danced and flickered, slowly rising and falling just above the glowing embers. Maybe there was understanding to be found somewhere in the fire.

Grant thought of his parents, and the farm, and his life at home. That was all behind him now, forever. Life would never be like that again. His future was out there, waiting, and Kate Bellows wanted to share it with him.

He moved his hand slowly over her silk pajamas, and when he passed over her breast he lingered for just a moment. She felt him press against her and she knew what he was thinking.

"We can't do it out here," Kate whispered. "What if they come downstairs and . . ."

He reached his hand inside the pajamas and felt her stiffen and resist, then he held her firmly and let her desire for sex compete with her fear of being discovered by Will and June.

"We can't," she tried to object. "What if . . ." She tried, halfheartedly now, to push his hand away.

He nibbled at her ear, and she felt herself give in and let her hips begin to move. The crackling fire, the old lodge, the warm couch. This was the day he'd proposed to her, and there could be no more romantic setting. They'd make love right here on this couch. It was perfect.

Her blue silk pajama bottoms lay on the floor a few minutes later, next to Grant's sweatpants. "I love you," he whispered, as he raised himself above her. Everything was perfect.

"FFFFFFTTT" came a noise from the floor by the fireplace. By now it was a familiar and disturbing sound, and both of them glanced just in time to see a weary Watson raise his blocky head off the floor and look behind himself to check and see what had happened back by his rear end.

The reality of a bizarre situation struck both of them in the same instant.

"Dog fart!" they both blurted, laughing and scrambling to get away at the same time.

Grant jumped up, swept Kate off the couch with one arm and threw the Hudson Bay blanket over them with the other. Both her feet were dangling just above the floor as she threw both arms around his neck and let him carry her away. They giggled and ran away toward their bedroom like two children who'd been caught stealing from a neighbor's garden. They laughed until their stomachs ached, they made love, and they lay in the darkness of a winter night and planned their future together.

∿ CHAPTER 19 ∿

August 30, 1977

Outrageous fortune. That's what Shakespeare had called it—the slings and arrows of outrageous fortune. But who cared? This was the worst thing ever. Outrageous fortune didn't cover this one.

Maybe this was the end of innocence. Grant understood that concept, sort of. Authors had written about it for ages.

Or a reckoning, maybe this was a reckoning. Perhaps there was some cosmic scheme to even the score. Maybe it just wasn't all right for Kate and him to have been so happy. Some people got drafted and then died in Vietnam. Some died in car accidents. Still others got cancer or another dreadful disease. Some just wandered through life with broken and lonely souls. But a reckoning? That made God a murderer, didn't it?

Grant sat on a hard chair in the small waiting room, put his face in his hands, and tried to dismiss all these thoughts. He'd never get his mind around this. A young doctor had just delivered unbearable news. They'd taken Kate into the little room across the hallway and it was quiet in there. This was the worst day of his life.

It didn't seem like such a long time since that day at Spider Lake Duck Camp when he'd asked for Kate's hand in marriage.

∿∶∿

When word got out that he was engaged to Kate Bellows, a huge dose of status arrived at his doorstep. He noticed older students and staff members pointing and whispering from time to time, and he knew that he was being pointed out as the guy who went with Kate. Several times during the semester, senior dental students or faculty members went out of their way to introduce themselves and tell him what a nice girl he was about to marry, and what a lucky man he was.

Kate of course moved to the absolute center of his life, too. They were seldom apart. Although Kate kept her own apartment, she never stayed there. Each day when her work was finished in clinic or the classroom they'd meet at her office and walk together down to Washington Avenue. They'd catch a bus and sit together on the ten-minute ride to his apartment.

The only exceptions to the routine came when there was something that the group needed to celebrate, or bitch about, in which case they all met at Stub & Herb's after school as they had from the beginning.

Love was an ember that had billowed, and its heat was thrilling. The short bus ride home could present an unbearable delay to their passion, and on some afternoons they couldn't get home fast enough.

A sideways glance or a gentle touch was all it took to fan the ember into a flash fire of lust. When the urgent need for sex became a roaring blaze, they found abundant pleasure in searching for new ways to extinguish the flame and then rekindle it.

They'd been married on a sweltering July afternoon. Fred Muckinhern gave the bride away. The long dress, the radiant smile—it had been a fine day. The entire Thorson clan had been there. It was great to see his brothers laughing and getting to know his friends from school. Everyone who mattered was there to see Kate Bellows choose him. Maybe it was the best day of his life.

After a short honeymoon in Duluth, they were back in school.

"You know," Kate said one day several months later, just after Christmas, "my breasts are kind of tender and I'm late." Grant would always remember the uncertainty in her eyes when she told him.

"You mean, like you might be pregnant?" he'd asked, as if he had no idea how such a thing could happen.

"Yeah," she'd nodded, unable to hide her indecision. She hadn't been quite sure if she wanted it to be true, and she needed his approval.

Then on the day of her doctor's appointment, Grant had hurried up to her office after his classes were over. He eased the door open and peeked inside to find her waiting for him. She'd nodded and let an apprehensive smile flicker in her eyes. "You're gonna be a father," she'd whispered.

They'd just stood in her small office for a few minutes and grinned at each other while they tried to understand all that they were feeling.

Were they ready for this? Would they be good parents? It was thrilling and unsettling at the same time.

They bought a used crib at a garage sale, and a couple of baby showers provided almost everything else they needed.

Sophomore year only strengthened the bond between Grant and his classmates. They'd spent another year in the same foxhole and it had been grand. He'd married the girl of his dreams. The good times would never end.

Kate was nearly nine months along. Everything was fine.

Until today.

"The baby hasn't moved for a long time," Kate whispered in his ear, just before sunup. They made a hurried trip to University Hospital, only to have the doctor confirm their worst fears.

"I'm sorry. Your baby is dead," Dr. John Schultzsaid, and the nightmare began. "We should induce your delivery immediately," he added. And that was that.

Kate fell to pieces when Dr. Schultz left his office to inform the delivery-room staff.

"Why?" she groaned, as her face twisted. "Why?" Something dark and frightful swallowed her whole, right there in the doctor's office. It seemed impossible that her face had ever held a smile, or ever would again. Grant watched her shed the bitter tears of a mother who was about to lose a child before she'd held it.

The hallway outside the emergency room was quiet when they stepped inside and looked for someone to help them check in as they'd been instructed. After a few minutes of filling out forms and answering questions, they were escorted down another long hallway to an elevator, then to the maternity ward, by a perky young candy striper.

"Is this your first child?" she asked with wide eyes and a big smile.

"Yes." Grant nodded, unwilling to provide any more information. Their footsteps were the only sounds in the hallway after that.

This was supposed to have been a happy day, one of the truly happy days in their lives. The chasm between what was and what should have been was so wide that neither of them could see back across to the other side.

When they reached the maternity ward, a friendly middle-aged nurse with a brightly colored uniform and a name tag that read Marsha greeted them. Marsha was polite, but all business. She said she'd spoken to Dr. Schultz and she'd help them get ready for their long day. She knew what was going to happen, and thankfully she kept the conversation brief.

"All right," Marsha said in a calm voice, after she'd placed the intravenous cannula in Kate's arm. "This will induce your labor. It usually gets to work pretty fast." She tried to comfort Kate by gently rubbing her arm.

Kate looked away, then covered her eyes with her other hand.

"It'll be OK, honey," Grant whispered.

"Now, Mr. Thorson, this hospital has only recently begun to allow fathers in the delivery room," the nurse started. "And because of the special nature of this delivery you won't be allowed to accompany Kate into the delivery room."

"No! He's coming with me," Kate pleaded.

"I need to be with my wife," Grant added.

"We have to follow the rules," Marsha replied, but when she saw the agony in Kate's eyes she relented a bit. "I'll talk to Dr. Schultz. Maybe we can get permission, but for now you'll have to step into the waiting room." She patted Kate's shoulder once more. "I'll be back and check on you in a few minutes."

"It'll be OK, honey," he said to Kate when he let go of her hand and left the room. It was all he could find to say, and it wasn't enough. But then, what would be enough? What could he say at a time like this? He took a seat in the waiting room, and waited. Someone he didn't even know had to give him permission to go stand by his wife in her worst moment. Outrageous fortune? Yeah, definitely. How had life led him here?

CHAPTER 20

"It's all right, Mr. Thorson. You can come in now," Marsha said after a short wait. She held the door open and invited him back. "I'm sorry to make you leave, but . . ."

"I understand," Grant said. He went to Kate's bedside and took her hand.

Ten minutes later the door to the labor room swung open and Dr. Schultz stepped in. He stood beside the bed and took Kate's other hand in his. A tall man, about forty, Dr. Schultz seemed to understand what Kate was feeling.

"Any pressure yet, Kate?" he asked.

Kate nodded, then wiped a tear away.

"It's gonna be a hard day for you, Kate. No way around that. But you'll get through this." He put the palm of his right hand on her forehead.

Kate nodded, wiped her eyes once more, and then winced.

"Contraction?" Schultz asked.

Kate nodded again.

"It'll get more and more intense." The doctor looked at her chart for a moment, then added, "Grant, you're going to be coming into the delivery room with us. You'll have to wear a gown and a hat. Just do whatever Marsha tells you to do, OK?"

"Sure," Grant said. Kate squeezed his hand, then sniffled again. She needed him, and he'd be there for her, but there was no joy in the moment.

"All right, then." Dr. Schultz turned to Kate. "Like I said, your labor pains will grow more intense and regular. I can't tell you how long it will take, but induced labor usually goes pretty fast. We'll be checking you frequently, and when you're ready we'll take you into the delivery room."

He nodded to Kate, and she nodded in reply.

"I'll see you later," the doctor said as he left the room.

The frequency and intensity of the labor pains did increase rapidly. In the beginning she'd just turn to Grant and announce that she was having a contraction. Then she began to flinch as though each labor pain arrived with a punch. She'd clench her teeth and try to hold on until it let up.

"You're dilated to about eight centimeters," the nurse announced from the foot of the bed when she checked Kate's progress after only three hours of labor. "We're gonna move you in just a minute."

"My god, honey. What can I do to help?" Grant asked at the end of one particularly powerful contraction.

"Just don't go anywhere." She breathed with her eyes closed. "Don't leave me."

"I'll be here," he reassured her, as he placed a cold washcloth on her forehead. He wished there was someone to reassure him, too.

Kate seemed to fall asleep between contractions. She could drop off from extreme agony to peaceful sleep in a split second. When the contractions let up, she looked calm, as if she'd been asleep for hours. Then her face would catapult forward, cloaked in misery when the next contraction struck. She'd clutch his hands and squeeze with a power that he didn't think she possessed.

She threw up twice during contractions. All that would come up was bile, and Grant helped to rinse the bitter taste from her mouth. He gave her cool water and then held a bucket in case she had to vomit again. Her hair was matted sweat and she looked exhausted. At the end of each contraction, before she laid her head back, she said the same thing, "Don't leave me."

Marsha, the delivery room nurse, arrived with two other nurses and began to move Kate onto a gurney so they could move her into the delivery room. As Marsha slid her hands under her back, Kate lurched forward and clutched both of Grant's hands. Her face was contorted beyond anything he'd seen yet, and she held on to him with a very real sense of desperation. Grant knew that his wife was being drawn into a whirlpool of agony and the only thing that could keep her from disappearing into it was her connection to him.

"You're almost ready, sweetheart," the nurse said when the contraction let up. They wheeled her down the hall and into the delivery room.

"She's dilated to ten and fully effaced," Marsha said in a businesslike tone to Dr. Schultz.

Grant looked on from Kate's bedside. It was his turn to be overwhelmed.

He saw her legs resting in the delivery stirrups, one lean and muscular, the other withered and weak. He saw her exhausted face as she waited for the next contraction. A helpless bystander, he stared at the grim faces of the doctor and nurses. No one spoke a word. They stood there and waited.

The end result of this joyous pregnancy and painful labor would be a lifeless child, and they all stood waiting for this terrible scene to play itself out. Jesus, how had all the winding roads in his life led him here? What should he do? What should he feel?

"Do you feel the urge to push, Kate?" Dr. Schultz asked.

"Uh huh," Kate groaned, without lifting her head.

"OK then, on the next contraction, you push, Kate. As hard as you can," the doctor said.

Her head popped forward when the next contraction began and the doctor repeated his exhortation to push several times. Grant thought something might burst in Kate's head. The blood vessels in her forehead stood out and she groaned and grunted as if she was trying to scare away the pain that held her captive.

"Here it comes. Here it comes. Push harder, Kate. One more time." The doctor waited a second. ". . . There!" He held something in his hands briefly. Then a nurse took it away from him and left the delivery room quickly.

"OK, you're going to expel the placenta with the next contraction, Kate, and then we're done." The delivery room fell silent.

Kate covered her eyes with one arm and released an unstoppable river of anguish in the silence after the last contraction. Long, terrible cries rose from a bottomless pit of despair. Every mother who ever lost a child cried out with her.

"Where's my baby?" she wailed.

"Kate. It's . . ." Dr. Schultz stumbled, surprised by her question.

"I want to see it!" Kate demanded, as she lifted her head from the pillow and stared at the doctor.

Grant saw his wife as if she was looking back at him through a broken mirror. She was shattered, and the pieces didn't seem as though they'd ever fit together again. She'd been reduced to human wreckage, and he had no idea what he might do or say to comfort her.

One small vignette in the human drama of a mother-and-child relationship was unfolding before his eyes. He understood now, for the first time, that Kate's loss was greater than his. It had to be that way, just as her bond with a living child would always be greater than his.

She covered her eyes with her hands while doleful cries lifted from her chest.

"I'm going to place several sutures to repair the episiotomy now," Dr. Schultz said after several minutes.

Grant softly stroked her face while Dr. Schultz worked at the other end of the bed. There was nothing he could say to give her comfort. The best he could do was simply be there.

Several minutes went by in silence before Dr. Schultz stepped back and pulled a sheet over Kate's legs and feet. He stripped off his latex gloves and threw them away. Then he removed his surgical mask, dropped it in a wastebasket, and went to a sink where he splashed water on his face. As he walked toward Kate's bedside he dried his face and hands on a towel.

"I'm so sorry for your loss," he said as he leaned against the bed. "Sometimes I feel like an old man." He sighed. "And even though I've been a part of many other births like this one I never get used to it. To tell you the truth, I still think it's a miracle that anyone is ever delivered safely into this world."

Kate nodded and wiped at her eyes.

Dr. Schultz sat silently for a short time, grieving with Kate and Grant, before he stood and left the room. He returned a moment later, carrying a bundle.

"You need to hold your son," he said, as he placed the bundle in Kate's arms. "When I was a young man, fathers weren't even allowed in the delivery room. So much has changed." He sighed. "We just . . . we just took care of things like this and never let parents . . ." He stopped. "Have this time together as a family. I'll leave you alone for a while." He turned and left.

Kate nestled the blanket covering her lifeless child against her, and began searching through the folds in the white blanket for what she knew would be her first and only look at him.

A tiny pale infant with wispy soft black hair seemed to lie sleeping in her arms. She looked for a moment but said nothing. One final tormented gasp twisted her face, then she reached through the blanket and found the boy's hands.

When she turned to Grant and closed her eyes she was pleading for some way to understand what had happened.

Kate wept softly, as if trying not to wake the baby. She unwrapped the blanket and looked at the feet, then the black hair on its head. She touched the child with her palm. She put her cheek against her baby's cheek.

Grant watched her for several minutes. He sensed that Kate was engaged in something timeless, something that a mother had to do.

A moment later, she turned to Grant, nodded, and gave him his moment with his son. He put his arms around mother and child and then brought his face down slowly until his forehead rested against the infant's. He kissed the baby, touched the tiny face with his hand, then stood straight and wiped his eyes.

A few minutes later Marsha returned and asked if she should take the baby. Kate and Grant stole a final look at the child, then covered his face and let Marsha take him from Kate's arms. They watched a stranger take their child away, forever.

Eight hours later, after Kate had been moved to her room, she was exhausted from her ordeal and coming down from the hormone-induced high of childbirth. She was about to drift off to sleep for the first time in thirty-six hours when Dr. Schultz let himself into the silent hospital room. Grant sat slumped over in a chair that seemed to have been designed to keep people awake. His neck was bent at an odd angle and he, too, was about to doze off, in spite of the chair.

"Sorry to disturb you," Dr. Schultz said softly, and he pulled a chair alongside Grant's. He crossed his legs, leaned back, and drew in a deep breath, then glanced at the clock on the wall next to Kate's bed and sighed. "Ten o'clock. Long day for all of us, huh?"

Kate and Grant both nodded and tried to smile, then tried to sit a little bit straighter.

"May I have your permission to speak to you about all that has happened today?" Dr. Schultz asked.

"Yes," Kate and Grant said in unison.

"I wanted to talk to you, both of you, because I've been where you are, and no one talked to me. In fact they, the doctors and staff at this hospital, did things to make my experience into a truly ugly memory," Dr. Schultz said.

"Twenty years ago . . . ," Dr. Schultz paused and flattened the front of his white coat while he let the memory come back to him, "I was a medical student and Mary and I showed up at the hospital just as you did today, knowing full well what was about to happen. Our child had stopped moving a day earlier. We knew, well, we suspected what had happened, and the doctor confirmed our worst fears.

"Fathers weren't allowed in the delivery room in those days. Never," he said, after he'd gazed into his past for a second. "Mary went through the delivery by herself." He glanced at Grant and added, "It was good that you were there today.

"There was a time, not so long ago, when they used to whisk a stillborn child away from the parents before they ever saw it. I'm pretty sure some of them were incinerated as medical waste. Terrible to think about it." He shook his head at the horror he was describing, then continued. "The thinking was that you needed to just keep it all hush-hush and then hurry up and get over it. But the thing is, that doesn't work. You need closure, just like you would with the death of any other loved one.

"I never saw my daughter," sighed Dr. Schultz. A twenty-year-old wound reopened as the doctor spoke. "I was just sent away to pick out a tiny casket. Then we had a quick burial service while Mary was still in the hospital. It was the worst thing we could have done. She didn't get to attend the funeral of her own child." Dr. Schultz stopped and looked at Grant.

"So, if you could do it again?" Grant asked.

"There are no rules, Grant. And everyone seems to have a different idea about the proper way to handle those things. If you're asking me what I think you should do, I'll tell you."

Grant nodded and then waited for Dr. Schultz to continue.

"Give the child a name. Let him be somebody. And then have a burial service. You'll probably want to keep it pretty small, and that's OK. But mark the end of this life like you would any other."

Kate and Grant both nodded their understanding.

"Let this be something to draw the two of you closer. It will be something that each of you will share with the other, and no one else, for the rest of your lives. If there is to be any good in this it will be that this loss may bind you together even stronger than before."

Each of them held their own thoughts and let the silence stretch out for a minute.

"And remember," Dr. Schultz continued, "to forgive the clumsy attempts that your friends will make to comfort you. They'll say things like, 'Don't feel so bad, you can have always more children.' They won't understand that you're mourning the death of a real person. They'll tend to think of this as little more than a missed opportunity and that you should just let it go and take the next one." Dr. Schultz sighed. "Just allow them to come to you and help you return your lives to normal."

Dr. Schultz stood up to leave and shook Grant's hand, then reached over and touched Kate's arm. As he swung the door open he stopped and looked at Kate. "You'll be going home tomorrow, Kate. I'll stop by." He paused for a moment, then said, "Life will go on. As the years go by you'll . . . well, you'll see."

The door clicked shut behind him, and he was gone.

~:~

Kate was still sleeping an hour after sunrise the next morning when Grant crept into her hospital room with a cup of gas station coffee in one hand and a bag of doughnuts in the other. He sat down beside her bed and nursed the coffee until she woke up a few minutes later.

"Did you sleep?" he asked when she sat up in bed.

"Some," she replied. "You?"

"A little." He shrugged, then he stood up and kissed her. "You're still the prettiest girl I ever saw," he whispered.

Her only response was to turn away and weep. "I heard the nurses bringing babies into the other mothers' rooms," she cried. There seemed to be no end to the nightmare.

A nurse let herself into the room a few minutes later as Kate was drying her eyes. She took Kate to the bathroom, asked a few questions, took her blood pressure, and said she'd be back with breakfast in a few minutes.

Grant sat quietly beside Kate's bed for half an hour while she ignored her breakfast. She was staring at the bland scrambled eggs and toast when he stood up, pushed the breakfast tray away, and sat down on her bed.

"I have a name," he said, and he took her hand in his.

For the first time since all this began, a faint grin lifted the corners of Kate's mouth. "Mickey Mantle?" she asked.

There was still some light left inside her! God, what a surprise, and what a boost that thought was for his flagging spirit. There were still very few things that gave him as much satisfaction as the knowledge that some little thing he'd said or done could make his lover smile.

"No," he said. He leaned over and kissed her lips. "I'm glad you remembered, but it's not what I had in mind."

"Good," Kate said. "I don't feel like arguing." Her eyes still smiled and she squeezed his hand.

"I've been thinking about it for a while, most of the night, as a matter of fact," Grant started. "And . . ." His sentence stopped as though he'd hit a wall. "Well," he tried again. "We're never gonna be able to give this child very much, so let's give him a good name. He should be Ole Thorson, after his Grandpa . . . best name I could give him."

Kate's smile vanished and her eyes swelled again. She wiped away another tear, then nodded with hesitant approval. "But what if . . ." She caught herself and stopped.

"What if we have another son someday, and what if we want to call him Ole?" Grant asked.

Kate nodded.

"I guess there are a lot of other good names out there. We'll find one if that day ever comes. But this little child needs a name that'll get him his place in the world, too. He's Ole Thorson, OK?"

"It's perfect," Kate whispered.

~:~

What next, Grant thought, two days later, when they stepped out of his car and walked across the green grass in the cemetery surrounding Six Mile Lutheran Church. The day Kate had been released from the hospital, they'd driven to a funeral home and picked out a tiny coffin, an ordeal that would linger forever in his memory. Now they had driven to Halstad for a burial service.

Big Ole, Gladys, and Pastor Jacobsen were the only others standing with them in the August sun beside the little brown coffin. The reverend said a few words and a short prayer, and then he left the Thorsons alone with their grief.

Over the years, Grant had attended half a dozen funerals at his family's church on the prairie. The others were sad affairs, too, with dozens of family and friends present, but there had always been time set aside for fellowship afterwards. Today there would be none of that. When the reverend drove away, the four of them were all alone, as a warm summer breeze moved through the row of pine trees surrounding the churchyard.

Big Ole stood solemnly in his Sunday suit for a few minutes, and he seemed to be praying. Then he did something Grant would never have expected; he took Kate by the hand and said, "Will you walk with me?"

Gladys and Grant sat down together on a bench in the shade of a pine tree and watched Big Ole and Kate stroll hand in hand. Ole moved slowly so Kate could swing her leg easily on the soft, uneven grass and keep up with him.

"Remember the first time you came to my home?" Ole asked.

"Sure," Kate said.

"I was so happy to see the kind of woman my son would choose. I knew right away that you were the one for him."

"You raised a good boy," Kate said.

Ole's hand was coarse and gnarled from a lifetime of hard work, but his touch was tender, like Grant's. Kate walked on, wondering just where he was taking her.

"Are you reading the stones?" Ole asked after a while.

"Yes," Kate replied. The names were all Scandinavian: Larson, Swenson, Hokanson, Jorgenson. She'd seen some with birthdates as far back as 1802. Some lives had been long, others very short. Some stones had single dates; June 1, 1921, or April 1933, and marked very short lives, like her son's. It was easy to imagine the rich and full lives of the old people who'd been buried here, but lying beside them were so many who'd had tiny lives that flickered for a moment and then went silent with no notice or fanfare, save the grief of a mother. Kate had never taken a walk like this one, and there was much to wonder about here.

Ole led her along for a while longer, then stopped in front of two small gravestones. "They're my brothers," he said flatly, and he held her hand while they looked at the markers together.

"Raymond Eugene Thorson, January 6, 1920 – January 20, 1920" read the message on one. The other stone was inscribed "Louis Arthur Thorson, July 7, 1929 – July 6, 1945."

"Louis died in a farm accident while I was in a POW camp in Japan, one day short of his seventeenth birthday. And Ray? All Mother ever said about him was that he was such a pretty baby, but there was just something wrong with him from the beginning; she said he never cried," Big Ole explained. He stood still and stared at the gravestones. He showed no grief, no sign that he might break down and weep. He was done grieving about his brothers. That had ended long ago. Now there was only a distant longing, a wondering about two lives that might have been.

"You know what the worst moment was for me on that night we were shot down over Tokyo?" Big Ole asked her after a while. "It was after my parachute opened and I was drifting though the night sky." He didn't look at Kate. "I felt so bad because somebody was gonna drive out to my parents' farm and tell my mother that I'd been killed, and she'd always wonder about it." Ole thought for a moment. "Then Louis died a couple weeks later. Can you imagine my mother's pain?" Ole sighed heavily and squeezed Kate's hand. "You never really know the meaning of the word 'vulnerable' until you bring a child into this world. But that's life, Kate. I'm guessing that only a mother could really understand. I just wanted you to see this, and know there have been others—in your own family—who may have felt what you're feeling." Ole and Kate stood there, holding hands for a few minutes. When they rejoined Grant and Gladys, the four of them left the cemetery together.

Grant and Kate made the long drive back to Minneapolis the next day. When they got home, they packed up all the baby things they'd accumulated. They boxed the items and labeled them in silence, then they got ready for bed.

They were spooning, holding each other close for the first time in days, when Grant whispered, "You awake?"

Kate nodded. How could she sleep? Every time she closed her eyes the nightmare started all over again. Everything she'd done, from the morning they'd driven to the hospital until they'd put away the baby things, played over and over in her mind.

"I love you, Kate," he whispered.

"I love you too."

Outrageous fortune, Grant thought.

❧ CHAPTER 21 ❧

The bus ride from St. Paul campus to the dental school felt wrong without Kate. Grant stared out the windows and wondered if Kate would be all right without him, while the crowded bus rolled over the potholes on University Avenue and carried him to school.

The Washington Avenue bus stop in front of the dental school was bustling when he stepped onto the sidewalk. A crowd of new faces bunched together at the stoplight, as on that day he'd first bumped into Kate two years earlier. In his mind's eye he saw her smiling at him. He saw her walk away into the crowd, and he saw himself falling. He remembered all of it and wondered if it could ever be like that again.

Grant meandered through the human traffic and made his way to his new lab bench on the eighth floor. All third-year dental students had been reassigned to new laboratory benches on the eighth or ninth floors, so they could be closer to the clinics where they'd be seeing patients for the next two years, and incoming first-year students would move into their old lab benches in the preclinical laboratory on the fourth floor.

He'd had his new bench on the eighth floor for only a couple of days when everything went wrong with the baby. He'd taken a week off to deal with his personal crisis, and now he felt like he was starting over.

He opened the padlock that secured his things under the lab bench, and he spread his instruments on the work surface in front of him. As he reached for his Styrofoam coffee cup, he felt a hand on his shoulder.

"Good to see you again, Pard," Will said, as he sat down next to Grant. "How're you doing?"

Grant had seen Will several times since everything had come undone. Will and June had made a point to stop over and express their sympathy, and Will and Grant had already had long talks about the healing process.

"Kate's really struggling," Grant confided. "She starts crying all the time and there's no consoling her. She can't eat or sleep. She walks around like a zombie. I think she's OK physically, but it's pretty dark over there on her side of the moon."

"Terrible thing for her," Will acknowledged. "But she'll heal. It's just gonna take time, I s'pose."

"Yeah," Grant sighed. He changed the subject. "Hey, thanks for helping with notes from the classes I missed, and with reading assignments, and thanks for picking up Kate's mail at her office."

"No problem," Will said. "Anything else I can do?"

"No, I think we're all right now," Grant replied.

Their conversation rolled to a stop, and they both began to work on the lab projects in front of them. Everyone else seemed comfortable in this new lab setting, and Grant hoped to settle in quickly. He felt like a newcomer, still a little unfamiliar with the new surroundings on the eighth-floor lab, and he knew he'd fallen a bit behind his classmates, too.

Another hand clasped his shoulder. "Hey, buddy," Andy Hedstrom said. "Glad you're back. I'm sorry for your loss." Andy squeezed his shoulder and tried to smile.

"Thanks, Andy," Grant said.

Andy was incapable of any more conversation. He squeezed Grant's shoulder once more and walked silently to his own bench.

"Hey, Grant," came the voice of Joe Paatalo a minute later. "I'm really sorry about your loss. It's nice to see you back in school." Joe patted Grant's back as he walked past him to take a seat at his own bench.

"Thanks, Joe," Grant said. A knot began to tighten in Grant's throat.

Others came in one at a time and extended condolences and greetings, but the expected murmur of voices and laughter never started up.

Ben Pribyl walked over and stood beside Grant for a moment, but he never spoke. When Grant looked up at him, Ben's eyes were puffy and he simply nodded before he went to his bench.

Carol Knutsen was the last to stroll into lab that morning. "Ohhh," she sighed, when she noticed Grant. She put her books down on her lab bench and then walked directly to him. She leaned over and hugged him, kissed him on the cheek, and whispered, "I'm so sorry," before she walked back to her bench. That did it.

Twenty-eight dental students sat together in the silence, and twenty-seven of them were staring at Grant's back, wondering what to do next. Carol had loosed something that he couldn't hold back any longer. His throat tightened, his eyes overflowed, and he struggled against a current that threatened to carry him away. He sniffled, then swallowed, and he even held his breath for a moment. He just couldn't break down in front of everyone, even though they could all see that it was about to happen. He knew they were offering to help with whatever grief they could lift from him. He wouldn't let his emotions get out of control. Finally he was able to draw in a few big breaths, dry his eyes, and blow his nose. Then, without looking up from his workbench, he offered one trembling word to everyone in the room: "Thanks." And that was the end of it.

Lunch hour on that first day back in school came with a familiar routine. The group walked together to the Greek steak house on the corner across from Stub & Herb's. As usual, everyone ordered the special, a ninety-nine-cent hamburger patty with a baked potato and a salad, and then they began to bellyache about school. Some order was beginning to return to Grant's life, and it felt good.

The healing was all his, however. After a lonesome bus ride home, Grant found Kate just as melancholy as she'd been when he'd left in the morning. She cried while he prepared macaroni and cheese. Then they sat together on the green couch and tried to talk while Grant ate, and Kate pushed her food around with a fork. After dinner they tried to watch TV for a while, but everything, every spoken word and every image in front of them, reminded Kate of her lost child and what she'd just been through. She barely spoke.

As one day rolled into the next, Grant grew frustrated with her moods. She seemed to enjoy moping, and sometimes he thought she was simply unwilling to let go of a millstone that was about to anchor her in a sea of depression. Several times he wanted to scold her, yell at her. She needed to snap out of this before it was too late.

But he gave her time, and whatever distance she needed, and sure enough, he began to see the glimmer of a smile every so often. She talked to him a bit more frequently, just small talk about work and school, or the weather, and every time she spoke to him he felt like the sun had peeked through heavy clouds. Several days after she went back to work, she touched him by resting her toes on his while they sat on the couch and watched TV. It was thrilling. A week later she asked for a hug several times. He wanted more, and he kept close to her like a flower turning to face the sun. But a hug, or maybe a smile, was all she had to give.

He wanted the laughter and good times to return, and he wanted sex, too. He missed the way things used to be, and then sometimes when he saw the way Kate still struggled, he felt guilty that he could let his own selfish desires creep so far into her healing process. Eventually she'd reengage with her friends, and her job, and her husband, Grant assumed. But Kate's melancholy state and Grant's uncertainty about when she'd emerge from it became a burden for him as the days and weeks dragged on.

∾:∾

Each new class of dental students was brought along slowly. When they'd finished studying something in a classroom, they were escorted into the clinic, and then instructed in the hands-on skills necessary to actually learn the profession. They needed only to look to their right or left to find their first patients—they learned on each other. They'd already performed diagnostic examinations, learned thorough X-ray procedures, and made plaster models of their classmates' teeth. Today they'd be learning to inject anesthetic into each other's mouths.

"Today's the day, Pard," Will said one morning during lab. "You ready?"

"Well, I hope *you* are," Grant replied.

Will and Grant had partnered up for this procedure, as they had for all the others. Exams, plaster models, and X-rays had all been easy first experiences for them. They'd learned quickly and done well with little or no anxiety. But today was different. They'd be doing something more invasive. They'd been joking about the experience for a few days as a way to deal with their apprehension, but in truth, they both expected this to be another small hurdle to step over. Some of their classmates, however, harbored genuine concerns about giving, as well as receiving, an injection.

"I see a little anxiety on some of the faces in here," Will said, as he looked around at the other students sitting at their lab benches.

"You know, that reminds me," Grant replied. "Do you know who got partnered up with Darcy? 'Cuz that person *should* be a little nervous about the things Darcy might do."

Will's lips parted in a sinister smile. "I guess Carol felt sorry for Darcy and said she'd be her partner," he said. "Look at her. She's sittin' over there at her lab bench right now sweatin' bullets. I'll bet she's rethinking *that* decision." Will flicked his eyebrows. "We should go over there and give her a pep talk. Maybe inquire about next of kin, or how she'd like us to handle any medical emergencies."

They both turned their attention back to the work on their lab benches and drifted to talk of the weather and sports for a few minutes, until Ben Pribyl burst into the lab.

"There you are!" Ben exclaimed, clearly thrilled to have found Grant and Will right where they were supposed to be. He leaned forward and almost ran to Will's side, then grabbed him by the shirt and lifted him from his chair. "C'mon! You guys hafta see this! C'mon!" he added, when Grant was slow to stand up.

"What's up?" Grant said, as the three men raced down two flights of stairs as if the building was on fire.

"Just follow me!" Ben insisted.

A small crowd of about twelve dental students stood just outside a men's room door on the sixth floor when Ben led them into the wide hallway.

Ben led them without hesitation and the crowd parted to let them pass. Another small group of dental students was smiling and milling around in front of a row of urinals when Grant finally stepped into the men's room.

While he tried to understand what was happening, a single dental student stepped out of a toilet stall. He shook his head and laughed out loud. "Call a priest!" he said. "It's a miracle!"

Ben grabbed Grant and Will by their shirts and shoved them both into the toilet stall.

Shoulder to shoulder, stuffed against each other by the narrow partitions, Grant and Will stared, dumbfounded at first, by the amazing thing in front of them.

A turd, almost a foot long and nearly four inches in diameter, floated peacefully in the toilet.

"Jeez," Will said just before he dissolved in laughter. "The thing looks like it's posing, like it wants to have its picture taken."

Grant backed out of the stall first, followed closely by Will, and two more new arrivals squeezed into the stall immediately after they'd stepped out. Every one of the dozen or so faces in the men's room was creased with a smile. Most of the young men were chuckling and waiting for a second look when Grant and Will stepped out of the men's room and into the hallway.

"Here's to higher education!" Will said, when they returned to their lab bench a minute later. "We just ran down two flights of stairs to look at somebody else's shit, and there was a waiting line, you believe that?" He hoisted a cup of coffee for a toast.

"It *was* pretty impressive," Grant countered.

"So what is it about that stuff?" Will asked, posing a deep philosophical question. "I mean, we're part of a fairly elite group, academically speaking, and I'll bet every guy in our class made at least one trip into that stall for a good long look at a *turd*. Hell, there were seniors in there, too! Why? What's the fascination?"

"Simple, Doctor," Grant replied. "Little boys find bodily functions—farting, belching, stuff like that—to be very funny, an endless source of entertainment."

"Boogers, too, don't forget boogers!" Ben said, as he rejoined them in the lab.

"The Turd," as the episode in the sixth-floor men's room had come to be known, occupied nearly every conversation among small groups of students, even as the class assembled in clinic later that day to give their first injections of local anesthetic. It proved to be an endless source of conversation for years to come, too.

After lunch, the entire class watched a video explaining the proper technique for administering local anesthetic. They broke up into smaller groups of eight and listened again while a clinical instructor repeated the same lecture they'd just seen. This time he spoke to them individually, face to face, so they could feel free to ask questions while they had his undivided attention.

Eventually they were sent to their assigned dental chairs in the clinics on the sixth or seventh floors. There were sixty-four dental chairs on each floor, and every dental chair was equipped with all the supplies necessary to do operative dentistry. Each of these dental operatories was set up with a tray containing two stainless steel anesthetic syringes and plenty of needles and anesthetic.

The operatory Grant and Will had been assigned was adjacent to the operatory where Ben and Andy would be working. Darcy and Carol would be on the other side of them, and the operatories were separated only by four-foot-high privacy partitions, so they'd all be able to hear each other.

Carol was the first one in clinic, and she had her operatory all ready when Will and Grant arrived. "You guys ready?" she asked, while she rested her arms on top of the privacy partitions and peered into their operatory.

"Sure thing. How 'bout you?" Grant asked, while Will arranged some instruments.

Carol looked skyward as if sending up a prayer, then rolled her eyes. "Pray for me?" She smiled then changed the subject. "Hey, how's Kate doing?" She was aware of Kate's struggles.

"Grant shrugged. "Good days and bad. But she's getting better. Takes time, I guess."

"Yeah," Carol nodded. "An injury in here . . . ," she tapped on her heart, ". . . is about like any injury anyplace else on your body. It just requires some time to heal."

"Yeah, I s'pose," Grant said.

"I haven't seen her around very much," Carol offered. "I hope she's planning to join us at Stub & Herb's after clinic today."

"She hasn't felt much like socializing lately," Grant said. "But yeah, she'll be there after class. It'll do her some good to . . ."

The instructor who'd been assigned to supervise their section of the clinic strolled into the room and called out, "OK, let's get to work! We're doing mandibular blocks with Xylocaine and epi. Get after each other." Then he added, "Call out if you have questions."

The party planned for Stub & Herb's was forgotten as the students busied themselves.

Novocaine had become the name that everyone outside of dentistry used to refer to local anesthetic. However, Novocaine, the actual drug, had been gone from the marketplace for some time, replaced by a wide assortment of other "caines," as the students called them. Lidocaine, Xylocaine, Carbocaine—they were all local anesthetics and they would all get the patient numb. The different caines just had slightly different chemical formulas. Some had vasoconstrictors added to their formula. Vasoconstrictors, as the name implied, were chemicals that constricted blood vessels in the area of the injection, which kept the anesthetic from being carried away by the blood supply, which in turn kept the patient numb much longer. The epi, or epinephrine, they'd be using today was a vasoconstrictor, the same drug as Adrenalin, which makes a patient's heart race if it's injected directly into the bloodstream. The faculty wanted the students to be certain to experience precisely what their patients felt. They'd all be numb for hours when this clinic session was over.

"Well, who's first, Pard, you or me?" Will asked, as he eyed the stainless steel syringes and small glass vials of Xylocaine on the tray in front of him.

"You do me first, Will. That way I'll know how gentle to be with you when it's my turn," Grant said, as he seated himself in the dental chair.

"Sounds good," Will replied. He set to work preparing the syringes after he'd washed his hands.

Grant slid into the dental chair and tried to relax, but he never took his eyes off Will's hands. About twenty inches from Grant's face, Will assembled the steel syringe with a long, 27-gauge needle and a 1.8 cc car-pule of Xylocaine with epinephrine.

While Will put the syringe together and Grant watched, they listened to the goings-on in the neighboring operatories. Although they couldn't see the others, they could hear the conversations all around them. Ben Pribyl and Andy Hedstrom, just off to their left, were doing pretty much the same thing as Will and Grant. Darcy Wilhelm and Carol Knutsen were trying to proceed in the cubicle immediately to Grant and Will's right, and the privacy partition couldn't obscure the confusion and height-ened stress level over there in Darcy land. Carol had decided to be the first to do the injection, and Darcy would be the patient. That way Carol could explain everything to Darcy, yet again, so that it might be easier when it was her turn.

"This could be good," Will said, when he'd finished assembling his syringe. He stuck a Q-tip into a small jar of cherry-flavored topical anes-thetic and grinned at Grant. The topical anesthetic was to be rubbed on the injection site, just above and posterior to the lower teeth on the left side of Grant's jaw.

Grant lay back in the chair and waited for Will to begin. As Will reached his hands toward his face, Grant readjusted his weight slightly, then looked up into Will's eyes and said, "Try not to fuck this up, OK? And I mean that in a very positive way."

Both men began to chuckle while Will used his left thumb to locate the injection site and then brought the Q-tip into Grant's mouth with his right hand.

After he'd held the Q-tip in place for about thirty seconds, Will tossed it in a wastebasket and reached for his syringe. With the needle paral-lel to Grant's lower teeth, Will gently penetrated the pink oral mucosa several millimeters superior to Grant's second molar, then inserted the needle smoothly until it touched the mandible where Grant's mandibular nerve branched from the fifth cranial nerve and entered his lower jaw. He depressed the plunger and began to express the Xylocaine into Grant's jaw. At the first feeling of pressure, Grant opened his eyes and stared into Will's eyes. He winked, then gave Will a thumbs-up. No problem, no pain, nice work, was the message in his eyes.

"I'll try to do a good job when it's my turn," came Darcy's nervous voice from the other side of the partition.

"You'll do fine," Carol reassured her.

A light came to Grant's eyes, and Will returned it. Will's needle was buried deep in Grant's mandible, and the two men smiled at each other while Will finished the injection. They calmly listened to the developing chaos in the next cubicle when he withdrew the needle.

"OK," Carol said, "I'm finished. Are you starting to get numb?"

"Yeah," Darcy replied. She sounded amazed that anything she'd been a part of might actually work, even if her only task was to lie there and receive an injection.

"Nice work, Doctor," Grant said while he rubbed his chin. "You musta been pretty close to the mandibular nerve. I'm getting numb already, left side of my tongue and everything."

From the adjoining operatory they heard Carol's voice again. "All right, Darcy, I'll show you one more time, then it's your turn." With that, Carol looked over the top of the privacy partition separating her from Grant and Will, then rolled her eyes.

Will and Grant returned the smile, stifled their laughter, and went about changing places.

"OK, Pard. Open wide," Grant said, when he'd cleaned the operatory, prepared a new syringe, and was ready to begin injecting Will. Will opened wide, Grant introduced the needle, depressed the plunger slowly, and asked, "You doin' OK, Pard?"

Will blinked and gave Grant a thumbs-up, just as Grant had. It was easy.

Suddenly a gurgling, gagging noise erupted over in Carol and Darcy's operatory, and they heard Carol run to the sink and cough and spit. "Jesus," Carol choked. "You didn't engage the needle properly into the anesthetic carpule, and you just let a whole carpule of that nasty-tasting shit drip onto the back of my throat! None of it went though the needle! Now we have to do it again."

Will and Grant locked eyes and smiled.

"OK," Carol sighed, "lemme show you *again*." And she began the explanation once more.

Grant withdrew the needle from Will's jaw. "Getting numb yet?" he asked, while he disassembled the syringe.

"Yup. I believe our day in clinic is finished," Will answered. "Let's go get Kate and head for Stub & . . ."

"Ouch!" Andy yipped from the cubicle on the other side from Darcy and Carol. He'd signaled his discomfort but was trying not to interrupt Ben's injection.

"Shut up, you pussy," Ben said calmly, making it clear he was not about to change what he was doing. They could hear Andy laughing, too, and trying not to move while Ben finished the injection.

Before Grant or Will could stand up and look over the partition at Ben and Andy in the cubicle on their left, another commotion erupted in Darcy's cubicle on their right.

"Ah shit, Darcy!" Carol said. "My heart is racing! You must have injected right into the mandibular artery!" Carol sat up with a panic-stricken look on her face, just as an instructor stepped into their cubicle.

"It's all right, Carol," the instructor said. "That extreme sense of anxiety will let up in just a minute and your pulse will slow down. You'll be fine. She just put a little epinephrine into your system." Then he turned his attention to Darcy.

"That's why we use an aspirating syringe, Darcy," he said, unable to hide his frustration with her. "I told you several times, after you've placed the needle where you think it should be, just pull back slightly with your thumb. If you've got the tip of the needle in the mandibular artery, the carpule will fill with blood and you'll know you should just move the needle tip a little bit before you inject the rest of the anesthetic. Do you understand?"

Darcy stared blankly, then nodded.

Will put his lips close to Grant's ear. "Cap'n Needle, this here's Cap'n Mandibular Artery," he said softly so that only Grant could hear him. "I believe Carol is gonna need a beer or two when this day is over."

Stub & Herb's was full to capacity when the last of the gang rolled in after clinic.

Carol hurried through the door and came quickly to the corner table where everyone waited. She looked terrible. Her lower lip hung on both sides of her face. From across the room her friends saw anger in her eyes, but as she drew near the anger morphed into a smile, such as it was.

"Where's Darcy?" Ben asked.

Carol rolled her eyes. "Deethus Cwist!" Carol slurred, due to her numb face. "I hope thsee havs to thtand with hew nose againtht the wow! The inthtwucto made hew keep thabbing me untiw thsee got it wight. Both fuckin thides! You bewieve that?" Carol raised both her index fingers as if they were pistols, and pointed to her mouth, then crossed her eyes.

Then Carol noticed Kate sitting with the group and motioned for her to stand up for a hug. "Weewee been mithing you!" Carol said. "Nithe to thee you again!" Compassion and comedy mingled for one brief absurd moment, and Kate's face lit up for the first time in weeks.

"Thanks, Carol," Kate said. "Sit down with me. Looks like you've had a long day."

"No thit!" Carol said as she sat down between Grant and Kate. Then she lifted a glass of beer to her lips and laughed right along with the others as beer trickled out the corners of her mouth when she swallowed.

~:~

Kate and Grant were lying under the covers and waiting for sleep to come when he reached around until he found her hand.

"Gotta tell you something," Grant said.

Kate squeezed his hand and let him continue.

"It was so great to see you smile again tonight at Stub & Herbs," he said.

"I had fun. It was nice," she whispered.

She rolled onto her side and invited him to spoon.

"Remember the night at the ball game when you said you could run when you get to Heaven?" he asked, after a moment of silence.

"Yeah. What made you think of that?" she asked.

"I think about it sometimes. And I've been wanting to share something I've been thinking." His words came with the lilt of a question, as if he needed permission to continue.

"OK," she said.

"Remember when I told you that I used to wonder if maybe my grampa was watching, you know, looking down from Heaven?"

"Uh huh," Kate answered.

"Well, I've been thinking that when our son got to Heaven that maybe Grampa Thorson was there, waiting for him to sort of welcome him, and watch over him until we get there."

"That's pretty good. I like that," Kate said.

"Or maybe your parents," Grant offered.

"Yeah, maybe," Kate said.

Another silent moment passed. This time Kate broke the silence. "Still awake?"

"Yeah," he replied.

"Gotta tell *you* something."

"OK."

"Three times this week somebody asked about our baby. The custodian up on the sixth floor, by my office; one of the cooks in the coffee shop; and then the woman in the bookstore," Kate said. She stopped her story and stared out at the streetlight.

"And?" Grant asked.

Kate shrugged. "I just told them all that we'd lost the baby. The two women got all embarrassed, and said they were so sorry. The custodian looked like he was gonna cry. I had to give *him* a hug."

"How did you feel about all that?" Grant asked.

"OK, I guess, and that's what I wanted to tell you." Kate stopped for a moment, then added, "Our friends have all moved on, you know. They've told us how sorry they are, and they've moved on. They'll probably never speak of it again." She stopped again. "That's what we have to do, too. But we'll still have each other to talk to."

"Yeah," Grant nodded. Kate kissed his arm and backed herself closer to him. He'd been waiting to hear her say something like that, and instead of adding anything he let the talk of healing come from Kate.

"Yeah, well," he whispered in her ear, "I just want my best friend back."

CHAPTER 22

The bus lurched to a stop on Como Avenue and Kate watched while several college students stepped inside, brushed the snow off, and found seats. One of them wandered up the aisle and plopped down two seats in front of her, and she watched the kid start a conversation with the girl next to him. Snow whipped through the gray December dawn. It was Friday, and the weekend would be starting in a few hours for all the students and faculty who were passengers.

As the bus lumbered back out into traffic, it rolled through a pothole and jostled all the riders to the right, then back to the left, and no one seemed to notice. It was still dark outside, and they were on their way to work, or school, and the bus ride was just part of the journey.

No one on the bus, except Grant, who sat beside her and tried to study, knew what she'd been through. Young people got on the bus, then got off, and never noticed her. People walked along the sidewalk, only a few feet away, busy with their own lives and problems. They hunched over against the cold wind and waited for another bus to carry them someplace. Everyone was going somewhere and none of them really cared where she was going. And that wasn't so bad; it was just the way of things.

She put her arm around Grant smiled when he looked over at her.

"Prettiest girl I ever saw," he said, and he stole a kiss before looking back at his notes.

He'd been a rock while she'd struggled to get over her postpartum depression. Always ready to listen, he'd been there whenever she needed to talk, and he'd known when to leave her alone. She'd been distant, sometimes unnecessarily so, and he was aching to be close to her again. He was hungry for sex and all the affection that came with it. She'd seen it in his eyes and his actions for weeks. At first she just wasn't interested in intimacy, then she began to deny him because it was about all she had any power over, and she needed that power. But every day he got up and tried to do the little things to help her find her way back. He did the best he could with dishes and laundry and odd jobs around their apartment. He'd been quick to tell her she was pretty, and that he loved her. He was still a gentleman.

She smiled now when she remembered the night he'd been unable to pay for her cantaloupe. He was so handsome, and he'd been so serious that night. She glanced over and looked at him again. Maybe the one time when it had really mattered she'd had some good luck. The man she'd chosen wanted her, too. She touched his neck softly and smiled again when he looked up from his notes.

"What?" he asked, unable to understand why she was smiling at him. He reached up and brushed his hand across his nose. "Do I have a booger hangin' out?

"You make me laugh," Kate said.

Grant brushed at his nose once more, furrowed his brow with a suspicious stare, and went back to his notes.

He'd been right about everything. All those times when she'd wept for no reason, with gloom settled over her, he'd been willing to sit and share it with her. "You'll heal. This will pass," he'd said over and over. "It takes time. You don't heal from something like that because you decide to just get back in the game. You heal when . . . when it's time."

As the weeks went by she had returned to her old routine at school, and she'd begun to feel better, more like her old self. Now the veil seemed to have lifted, and in spite of a blizzard, Kate was happy with the place life had taken her.

The short walk from the Washington Avenue bus stop to the dental school was treacherous today. Several hours of sleet had preceded a blustery snowfall that was now packing drifted snow across the sidewalks on campus. Grant took her arm and helped her across several icy patches on the plaza in front of the dental school.

After a quick stop at the fifth-floor coffee shop and a minute to shake the snow off their coats, Grant and Kate were about to go their separate ways, Kate to her office on the sixth floor and Grant to his lab bench on the eighth floor.

"I've been thinkin'," Grant started, while they waited for an elevator.

Kate looked through her purse and let him continue.

"I'd like to play some town ball this summer." He threw the words out there and let them settle around Kate. "What do you think?"

"Baseball?" she asked.

"Yeah, amateur ball. Mostly college kids, a few older guys, too."

"What if you get hurt? You'll be graduating in a year. A broken hand would . . ."

"But I love it, and I miss it, and you can't think like that," Grant replied.

"Sure you can, it's . . ."

In the distance a spontaneous chorus of men's voices rose up in a single boisterous cheer. Before either of them had time to say more, a second, louder cheer went up. Then a third.

Grant turned a questioning look to Kate and said, "C'mon, that sounds like freshman dental students, over by the preclinical lab. Let's go see what they're doing."

Cheers erupted every few seconds, each one louder than the one before, but they came with no regularity. Grant and Kate walked down a long hallway, then turned a corner and walked down another. More voices seemed to join in with each unruly cheer. Each outcry rose up with a bit more excitement.

When they turned a final corner and looked down the hallway just outside preclinical laboratories, they were greeted by an extraordinary sight. Dozens of dental students, maybe a hundred of them, stood shoulder to shoulder, staring out a large bank of windows that overlooked what had become a particularly slippery section of sidewalk between Grace University Lutheran Church and the dental school.

Beneath them, on the street, the first wintry blast had created an icy gauntlet that *no* pedestrian was able to navigate safely. Every student or professor or university employee who walked through that stretch fell down. Some of the crashes were spectacular, and the dental students sipping their morning coffee had begun to gather two and three at a time to watch the developing spectacle.

Twenty minutes earlier, a handful of dental students with coffee cups in their hands had lined up along the windows to chat before the day started. They noticed the unwary pedestrians down there on the sidewalk slipping and falling in silence. Sure enough, a few groans went up from the students after some ugly crash landings, and before long, the groans drew more and more dental students from their laboratory, and then the groans morphed into cheers.

Neither Kate nor Grant could keep from smiling, and when they placed their elbows on the windowsill next to the others, they found themselves standing next to Will and Ben.

"Mornin', Pard. Hi, Kate. Did you hear the cheering from way over by the coffee shop?" Will asked.

"Yup," Grant answered.

Another unsuspecting college kid wandered around the corner of the church and slipped exactly where all the other pedestrians had. He hit the pavement so hard that one of his shoes flew off, and the entire group of dental students cheered. Several of the students tapped car keys on the window to draw the kid's attention. When the kid looked up to see who was signaling him, he saw the long row of people laughing at his misfortune. About half of the students standing along the windows were now holding up large scorecards, as if they were judges in an Olympic competition.

The kid who'd lost a shoe gave the finger to everyone standing at the windows, which drew another loud cheer, and then he hurried away after he'd replaced his shoe.

The process repeated itself over and over again, without fail. Each pedestrian who slipped and fell—and they *all* slipped and fell—was greeted by a thunderous cheer and a panel of judges with scorecards. Some of the crash victims ran away, humiliated and angry. Most smiled. One kid took a bow and saluted the judges before he picked up the notes he'd scattered all over the sidewalk during his fall.

The whole incident took on a surreal quality. It shouldn't have been funny, but it was. Kate turned to her right and watched Grant, Will, and Ben laugh. They looked like five-year-olds giggling at cartoons on TV.

"Hey," Kate said, as she pulled Grant a few steps away from the others. He was still laughing at the most recent train wreck when he turned toward her.

"Huh?" he asked.

"I have to go to work," Kate said. "Good luck with your first patient in Removable Prosthodontics. That first denture case is always pretty memorable."

"Thanks, I'll see you later," he said, and he stole a kiss.

Before he could step back from her she pulled him closer yet. "I think you should play ball this summer, honey, if it's what you want."

"Well good. I'm glad it's OK with you. Will and I were planning to try out . . ."

"But!" Kate interrupted. "You're gonna need some batting practice tonight!" She raised her eyebrows twice.

"You mean . . ." A greedy, hungry grin spread across his face.

"I mean we're gonna work on baserunning for a while, then I'll expect you to be swingin' for the fences." She held his eyes with a seductive stare for a moment, then she turned and walked away. "I have to go to work. See you later!" she called over her shoulder.

Grant sidled back over to the window and pushed his way in between Ben and Will just as another cheer rose from the crowd.

"You really married up, you know that?" Ben said, without looking at Grant.

"Whaddya mean?" Grant asked.

"I mean she's better than you. How'd you wind up with her?" Ben said.

"I make her laugh," Grant said.

"You mean like when she listens to you read, or when she sees you naked?" Will asked.

"No, I mean . . ." Another outburst from the crowd silenced Grant.

"You back in the saddle yet?" Ben asked, before Grant could finish his sentence.

A flustered Grant Thorson began to stammer about not understanding the sexual innuendo in the question.

Ben exhaled a cloud of smoke. "Heh, heh, heh," he laughed to himself. "Saw it in her eyes just now."

~:~

"Holy cow, look at the sweat drip off the cook's nose today," Will said, when he and Grant took their places in the waiting line at the small Greek steak house. "Order please!" the cook with the sweaty nose hollered.

"Special," Grant replied.

"Special," Will added.

The sweaty Greek tossed their ninety-nine-cent specials onto the grill. Two hamburger patties began to sizzle, fire flared up underneath them, and smoke from the grill shot up in a cloud.

The smell of beef cooking over a fire always hung heavy in the little steak house, and Will and Grant let themselves be taken in by a familiar routine. They inched along with the other hungry students in line and watched the cook flip hamburger patties, holler at the new arrivals, and sweat. When he finally plopped their lunch on a plate and slid it across the counter, Will thanked him, then turned to Grant and said quietly, "Twenty-two drops of sweat."

"Huh?" Grant asked.

"That guy had twenty-two drops of sweat fall off his nose while he cooked our lunch," Will answered.

Grant glanced back at the cook. "I didn't count 'em," he said.

"I always do," Will replied. "Last week he had thirty-one drips, but that was a busy day." Will paid for his lunch and added, "So Kate's got plans for you tonight, huh?"

Grant took only a second to marvel at the incongruity in Will's comments, then he let all thoughts of the sweaty Greek drift away with the beef smoke.

"Well, she was teasing about it this morning," Grant answered. "I sure hope so."

"Here's the deal, Pard. If Ben Pribyl says it's so, then it's so. You better pick up some flowers," Will said, as they sat down at a small table.

Grant stuffed a patty of butter into his baked potato and then took the ketchup from Will. "Well, it's been a while. Kate just hasn't been interested in, you know, since the . . . for weeks." Grant raised a fork to his mouth and took a bite of the hamburger patty. "I just read in the newspaper—somebody did a survey—they said that men think about sex every twenty-three seconds. You think that's true?" He pounded the bottom of the ketchup bottle.

"Dumbest damn thing I ever heard," Will said between bites. "Every twenty-three seconds? You shittin' me? That's crazy!"

"I thought so, too," Grant added. He poked at his potato, content that he was in agreement with Will, but Will surprised him.

"I've *never* gone for twenty-three consecutive seconds without thinkin' about sex!" Will said as he reached for his coffee. "Never!"

Grant leaned back in his chair and laughed out loud. "Good one," he said when he picked up his fork once again. "So," he continued, "that leads to a question I've been wantin' to ask you."

"Five times in one day," Will blurted without waiting for the rest of the question. "That's my record. But it was a short day. December, two years ago. If you're asking about a twenty-four-hour period, well, that's different." He stared as if he was taxing his memory, and then began counting on his fingers, clearly overacting.

"No, that's not what I wanna know, not exactly anyway." Grant shook his head. "I gotta ask about Kathleen Monahan, the girl from Harvard, your friend who wanted to get into dental school. Remember?"

"Sure." Will took a sip from Grant's coffee cup.

"Well?" Grant begged.

"Ask me," Will demanded. "Ask me what you want to know."

"Were you having your way with her?"

"No," Will said. He took another bite with his fork.

After a short pause Grant pushed for a better answer. "This is an essay question, not a true-or-false quiz. I'd like the five-hundred-words-or-less answer."

"OK," Will started. He rubbed a piece of his hamburger patty through the ketchup on Grant's plate, then, while he chewed it, he continued. "You wanna know about Kathleen?"

Grant nodded.

"Well, when I was an undergrad, back at Harvard, she was one of those pretty girls that all the guys, *everyone*, fantasized about. Everybody wanted to be her boyfriend. I had a couple classes with her so I knew her a little bit, didn't really like or dislike her. She was so busy being noticed around campus that she never had the time to really get to know anyone. I suppose if the opportunity had arisen I'd have been willing to pork Kathleen's brain out. And I mean that in a very loving way." Will pointed his fork at Grant.

"Of course," Grant nodded. "A sensitive guy like you . . ."

"Remember Jeanie Amundsen, the girl I told you about?" Will sighed at the girl's memory.

"Yeah, sure."

"Well it wasn't like that. Not at all. Kathleen was just a gorgeous young woman with some money." Will stabbed a piece of potato with his fork and swirled it though the ketchup on Grant's plate while he thought about Kathleen.

"Anyway, nothing ever happened between us back in college," he continued. "And yeah, I knew she was making herself available when she was visiting campus here a couple years ago. But I knew she was just a social climber who wanted to be part of all this." Will glanced out the window toward the dental school, then across the street at Stub & Herb's. "And she wanted it right away, before she'd even finished the application procedure. She thought if I'd just give her a ride on the baloney pony she'd somehow own part of the experience. She didn't want me, she wanted this." Will took a sip of coffee. "I knew she'd get into school on her own, or probably change her mind and do something else. In any event she wouldn't want me anymore. And by the way, that's exactly what happened. She married some rich guy and I haven't talked to her since she was here that weekend two years ago." Will sighed heavily and looked at his plate. "I just wanted to see how it would feel to have her touch me and fawn over me like she did. And I wondered if I might actually, you know . . ."

"Pork her brains out?"

A slight smile turned the corners of his mouth. "Yeah," he nodded, "but what I really wanted was to know how it felt to have somebody, somebody really attractive, want me."

"How'd it feel?"

"Nice, really nice," Will said.

"So you never . . ."

Will shook his head.

"That was incredibly insightful, Doctor," Grant said.

"Thank you, Doctor," Will replied, "but don't tell anyone, OK? It's good for my image to know that all my buddies think I was porkin' her." He pointed his fork at Grant again and added, "And I mean that in a very loving and sensitive way."

"Of course, Doctor."

For the remainder of the lunch conversation, they speculated about the patients they'd be assigned when they started their rotation through the Removable Prosthodontics clinic that afternoon, and their plans to play amateur baseball in the summer.

A few minutes later, both men lowered their chins to keep the icy wind from blowing down their collars when they stepped out onto Washington Avenue and began the short walk back to school for afternoon clinic. "What do you think our wives would say if they could hear us talking?" Grant asked.

Will grimaced. "They don't want to know what we're talking about. They've convinced themselves that we're down here reviewing our biochemistry notes, or maybe talking about our feelings; stuff like that."

Grant smiled, nodded his agreement, and leaned into the wind.

"Seriously, Pard. They don't think like we do. And if they ever knew the stuff we talk about? Well, I think that could be bad," Will said.

"Yeah, probably," Grant agreed.

"But it's their fault, you know," Will added.

"Oh?"

"Well, if they didn't have such low standards, they wouldn't have married a couple of toads like us. I figure they deserve to be shocked and disappointed from time to time," Will said. "Let's get up to clinic, it's cold out here!"

Ben was waiting for them by the doors upstairs at 1:55. This afternoon they'd have their first experience in Removable Prosthodontics clinic. Each third-year student had been assigned to a patient who needed new dentures, and they'd spend every Friday afternoon for the next ten weeks with their patient while they made the dentures. They were to gather in the ninth-floor clinic at two o'clock today, introduce themselves to their patients, and then get to work.

"Holy shit!" Ben cackled. He'd just walked through the waiting room where their patients had been assembled, and he couldn't stop laughing. "There's a guy sittin' out there wearing a coffee can on his head, like it's a crown!" he said. "There's a couple other dandies, too, but that guy is the prize. I hope *you* get him," Ben said, pointing at Will.

The students entered the clinic and set about preparing their operatories and looking through their patients' charts. All that remained was to walk out into the waiting room, call out the person's name on the folder they'd been issued, and see who stood up.

"Well, the guy with the coffee can isn't mine," Grant said to Will and Ben. "My patient's a woman." He held up the chart in his hand and smiled. Will and Ben each smirked and groaned, ready to roll the dice. Both of them had been assigned male patients. It was hard enough to be doing all this for the first time, but to wind up with a nutcase for that first clinical experience . . . nobody wanted that.

The university dental clinic attracted patients by having much lower fees than dentists in private practice, but the university also made it clear that their patients would be treated by students, and procedures would naturally take longer. Patients would pay with their time. Some of the people who had plenty of time were retired, or they worked at night. Some of them were college students, and some were just nutcases. Students got patients through the luck of the draw. You got who you got.

Grant strolled out to the waiting room and let his gaze pass over the crowd. There were several nice-looking women sitting out there on the orange and lime green couches. This would be good. He called the name on his chart, Loretta Klitsche, and no one moved. He called it again and he saw a very large head covered with blonde curls turn his way. The woman made eye contact and smiled. She leaned forward in her chair and Grant walked over to meet her. When he was close enough to shake her hand he repeated her name and she nodded. Then a low rumbling began to rise somewhere deep inside her. She brought her hand up to her chest and the rumbling grew louder. Something in her chest was trying to get out. Surely she was about to cough up a sandbox? The coughing jag ended and she stood up.

"I'm Loretta," she said, as she extended her hand. "Excuse me."

Her voice was shocking. She sounded like a coal miner. No, the little girl in *The Exorcist*. She wasn't human.

"Hi, Loretta. I'm Grant Thorson. It's nice to meet you. Please follow me." He expected her head to spin around, but that wasn't the worst of it.

Loretta Klitsche was somewhere between fifty and ninety years old. A lifetime of chain-smoking and probably other bad behavior that Grant didn't want to think about made it hard to tell for sure. He'd look in her chart and check her birth date in a few minutes when she wasn't looking.

As she followed him into the denture clinic, he couldn't help but notice her most striking feature—the way she was dressed. She wore white patent leather go-go boots and a red patent leather miniskirt. Her horrendous blonde wig hung down onto a white cotton blouse.

Grant had to bite his lip as he walked past Ben and Will with Loretta in tow. Will crinkled his face as if he'd looked into a bright light, and Ben ogled Loretta as he would the female lifeguard at the beach, then winked and gave Grant a sarcastic thumbs-up.

"Have the guest-of-honor seat, Loretta," Grant said when they walked into the assigned dental cubicle.

She lifted a leg onto the chair and then shocked Grant once more when she sat down. As she lowered herself into the chair she passed gas. The vinyl cushion of the dental chair and her miniskirt combined to amplify the sound.

"Excuse me," the demon inside Loretta said.

"Oh, it looks like I forgot something, I'll be right back," Grant said. He turned on his heels and bolted for the men's room about one hundred feet down the hall. Something uncontrollable was about to explode inside him. Farts were always pretty funny, but this one was hysterical. There was absolutely no way to respond when a cartoon character farted in your dental chair. All he could think to do was send himself on an errand to retrieve some equipment or material necessary for the construction of dentures, and hope to control the laughter until he was out of earshot.

He was nearly choking when he burst into the men's room and unleashed the belly laugh he'd been holding back. Ben and Will were right behind him, laughing in the same way and trying to hold each other up.

"That was a five-second mud-sucker fart!" Will gushed.

"Jesus, Grant!" Ben blurted. "Sounded like she was droppin' wet cement off a twelve-foot ladder!"

"Ooo, this semester is gonna be interesting," Grant said, while tears of laughter puddled up in the corners of his eyes.

"Should I call a priest?" Will asked, then tried to imitate the raspy, malevolent timbre of her voice when he added, "Excuse me!"

After taking a moment to compose themselves, they returned to the denture clinic and Grant attempted a fresh start with Loretta while Will and Ben went out to meet their patients.

"You go first," Will said to Ben, and Ben took his chart out to the waiting room. He returned several minutes later and led a well-dressed, clean-cut man of about sixty into the cubicle next to Grant and Loretta. When he'd seated the man he looked over at Will and shrugged. His patient was pretty normal. Now it was Will's turn.

With his confidence bolstered by Ben's good fortune, Will turned and walked to the waiting room. The guy with the coffee can was still sitting there, but so were a couple of dozen other patients. On closer inspection, Coffee Can Man was fairly obese. His belly hung out under his T-shirt and he had about four days' worth of gray whisker stubble. Everyone else looked pretty normal. Will lifted his chart and read the name on the cover. "Marvin Bosshart."

The guy with the coffee can smiled and waved.

"Oh fuck," Will whispered to himself.

Coffee Can Man stood up, wearing his Folgers hat, and walked toward Will. He was still several feet away when Will realized that his patient was cloaked in a powerful force field of body odor.

"Will Campbell," Will said as he offered his hand.

"King Marvin, of Me," Marvin Bosshart replied, then shook his hand.

"Well, follow me, Marvin," Will said. He wanted to wash his hand right away.

As he entered the clinic with Marvin Bosshart in tow, Will made eye contact with Grant and rolled his eyes. He stole a glance at Ben and did the same thing.

Ben and Grant were both working with their patients, but they were listening closely to the conversation in Will's cubicle as Will got to know

Coffee Can Man. "Says here on your chart that you're the "King of Me?"" they heard Will ask.

"Yep," Marvin Bosshart, the Coffee Can Man, replied.

"Is that your job, or . . ."

"I don't work outside my realm."

"So what do your friends call you?" Will asked.

"Oh, Your Highness or King," he answered.

"Well all right, Your Highness," Will said. He knew Grant and Ben were listening closely. "Can I put your crown over here?" Will asked. "It's gonna be in the way while I make the royal dentures." Grant had to stand up and smile at Ben.

"Sure. But don't drop it," the king said.

"No problem," Will added. "It's a nice crown. Made by Folgers, I see. It's cool the way you've got these edges all carved, like King Arthur. I'll just put it over here, OK?" Will looked over at Grant and rolled his eyes again.

"Yep," the king said.

"So . . ." Will asked, as he looked through the impression trays and began to fit them in the king's mouth, ". . . is your castle nearby?"

∾:∾

Kate sat next to Grant in the corner booth at Stub & Herb's an hour after clinic was over. Her arm was draped over his shoulder and she listened to everyone's stories while she picked at some French fries and drank beer with her free arm. Her face was sore from laughing, and the stories kept coming.

"Grant, do you think your patient was wearing a wig?" Joe Paatalo asked. Everyone laughed at the obvious sarcasm. The long curls flowing down over her shoulders made for the worst wig any of them had ever seen.

"Well, the thing is, I think she's an English barrister and she's supposed to wear that," Grant replied.

Everyone in the class had made clandestine, unnecessary trips through denture clinic after the word got out that Will and Grant had drawn a couple of pretty colorful patients, and now the usual group was gathered to celebrate their first day in Removable Prosthodontics. It had been an unforgettable day for Grant.

The "King of Me" Marvin Bosshart had proven to be a pretty good patient for Will. He was a little weird, to be sure, but he was fine to work with and he made it easy for Will to take perfect impressions of his mouth and begin the new dentures.

Loretta Klitsche, the voice of Satan, had been quite another story.

"So just what happened over there, Grant? What was all the commotion about, anyway?" Carol Knutsen asked. She'd been assigned a cubicle on the far side of the clinic and she hadn't seen much of the episode Grant had endured.

"Well, first of all, she took out her old dentures." Grant looked around the table while everyone gave him their undivided attention. "She's been smokin' about four packs of Camels every day for her entire life, and those things were so brown they looked like she'd been keeping them in her ass."

The group laughed out loud, Carol rolled her eyes, and Kate dropped her French fry back on the plate.

"To make it worse," Grant continued, "she'd just eaten a box of glazed donuts and those brown choppers were coated with some filmy white shit."

Carol pretended to gag, and Kate covered her eyes.

"But the topper, the thing that really made my day, came while I was trying to take the impression of her lower jaw." He looked around him and shook his head in disgust while all his friends leaned a little closer. "I had the tray in her mouth, the putty was almost set, and she starts to cough. Now I can hear chunks of shit breaking loose in her chest, and I'm getting nervous that one of her lungs might just fly out her mouth." Grant paused and shook his head in disbelief. "But it was worse! She started getting this distressed look on her face and then she starts to gag. About that time she lost her grip and farted again." Grant paused for emphasis. "Serious moisture content!" Heads bounced back in laughter, then returned for the end of the story. "So anyway, she's still gagging," he paused yet again, "and she blew lunch! Everywhere! I'm guessing she had about a dozen scrambled eggs with that box of doughnuts."

The men erupted in laughter and Kate grimaced before she plugged her ears. Andy Hedstrom raised a glass of beer in salute and the rest of the gang joined him.

"Yeah," Will added before the laughter had died down. "That was when His Highness turns to me and rolls his eyes, like he thinks *Grant's* patient is just a bit off center."

"Well," Ben interjected, "I couldn't help wondering just what it sounds like when she's gettin' after it with her boyfriend . . ." Ben stopped himself and made a face that suggested even *he* was sickened by the thought of Loretta Klitsche in an amorous embrace. Then he looked directly at Carol, and with a bovine growl he began to imitate Loretta's voice, "'. . . Give it to me! Give it to me!'"

A burst of laughter drove everyone back in their seats, and Grant walked to the bar to get four more pitchers of beer. While he stood there waiting, he looked back at his friends. Joe Paatalo had his arm around Carol, Ben was emptying a pitcher into his beer glass while he laughed at his own joke, and Kate was sharing a story about her first denture patient. The world had turned, and his best friend was back.

❦

"Wow," Kate sighed, and she began shaking her hands.

"Your thumbs go numb again?" Grant asked, as he pulled the covers over himself and Kate once again.

"Yeah, there was some serious pent-up sexual tension there, huh?"

"I'd say so," Grant said.

"It happened about five times there, right at the end. One orgasm right after the other," she said, still shaking her thumbs.

"Just happened once for me," Grant said. "But I think I got whiplash from it."

Kate smiled, brought her nose to Grant's neck and breathed in deeply. "I love the way you smell," she whispered.

He moved his arm so she could rest her head on his shoulder while they lay together in the dark and stared at the ceiling.

"I love you," he said softly. "Prettiest girl in school." He stroked her hair. "I wish I could explain how special it makes me feel to have you sit next to me, like we did tonight at Stub & Herb's. When you put your arm around me, and claim me in public like that—I still want everyone in the place to be sure and notice that the beautiful smart girl chose me."

"You were so funny, telling those stories," she said.

"Does it seem like this was a *really* long day, like that bus ride over to campus was a week ago and not just this morning?"

"Sorta," Kate replied.

"Gotta tell you something," Grant said after several minutes of silence. "I feel kinda bad about my patient, Loretta."

"What do you mean?" Kate asked.

"Well, all that stuff happened today; the farting and puking, and I guess Loretta herself, she is kinda funny. But it's kinda sad, too. I mean, her whole life is a train wreck, and we laugh."

"Well," Kate sighed, "Mark Twain and W.C. Fields both felt that all humor is rooted in the misfortune of others."

"I didn't know that," Grant replied.

"Well, think about it," Kate said. "Even if Twain hadn't come right out and said it, just look at the characters in books and essays, and look at W.C. Fields's movie characters, they're all bumblers with nagging wives, or shysters, and we laugh when they fall down or get cheated." She paused a moment. "And think about our own lives. We have a lot of laughs at Darcy's expense, and just this very day we stood by the windows and laughed while all those pedestrians slipped and fell."

Grant pulled her close, kissed her cheek, and said, "Smart women really turn me on." Then he turned both of their naked bodies so they were spooning, pulled Kate close, and held her. "You thought it was pretty funny when I fell down, too."

"Yup." Kate sighed and then snuggled a bit closer to him.

Grant kissed the back of her neck and whispered, "My best friend."

~: CHAPTER 23 :~

The King of Me and Loretta Klitsche developed friendships with Will and Grant as the semester moved along. Friday afternoons in denture clinic became something that everyone looked forward to, along with the obligatory class meeting at Stub & Herb's afterward. King Marvin and Loretta got their new dentures right on schedule, and first semester rolled over into second semester.

Kate was her old self again, too. The horrific stillbirth had happened, and she'd healed, for the most part. Every now and then something would remind her of that day and a dark cloud would hover over her soul for a few minutes before it blew away. Sometimes while that dark cloud hovered, Kate and Grant talked about the things that had happened, and sometimes they didn't. From time to time they both took a few quiet minutes to wonder about things like that.

During second semester of that junior year, the students had only a few lectures each week, but they had a two-and-a-half-hour clinic session every morning and every afternoon. Initially their patients had been chosen for them. The faculty tried to match patients who had very simple needs with dental students who had very limited skills. With each new clinical success a student's skills and confidence increased exponentially, and before long students were allowed to schedule themselves into Operative clinic, where they could do whatever fillings their skills would allow. They were also assigned to other clinics: Crown and Bridge clinic, Endodontics (root canal), Pedodontics (children's dentistry), and Removable Prosthodontics (dentures and partial dentures).

Each department had strict rules about skills and procedures that had to be mastered before a student could graduate. At the start of each clinic session a student was given a starting check in a little logbook. When the clinic session was finished, the student was given a grade for the day, and the clinical instructor marked the student's progress in the little book. Students treated these logbooks like secret military documents; that book was a record of their progress through school. When it was complete, they were done. Every clinical department allowed students the freedom to move along and master the skills at their own speed.

Oral Surgery, however, was different. Students could do some real damage there without a little more direct supervision. The protocol for instruction in Oral Surgery was that each student would be paired up with another student and then report to the Oral Surgery clinic every day for a few weeks, where they'd be taught hospital procedure and basic surgery skills.

Grant and Will had been advancing through the other clinics at a steady pace. They'd been placing silver and gold fillings, dentures, and partial dentures, and they'd each finished several root canals.

When their turn came for a rotation through Oral Surgery they paired up, as usual. They were waiting anxiously in the hallway to find out which of the oral surgeons on the staff would be the supervisor for their time in clinic.

"Hope we don't get some dickhead like Ebby," Will whispered.

"He's over in Operative, not Oral Surg . . . ," Grant tried to reply.

"I know that. But there's no shortage of dickheads around here," Will interrupted.

"Hi, fellas!" came a large voice from down the hall. Joe Ruminsky had just stepped out of a small classroom and was walking toward them. "Looks like we're together for the next few weeks."

This would be good, really good. Everybody liked Joe Ruminsky. Grant had made a special connection with the dean back when Ebby had sent Grant for what he hoped would be an ass chewing a couple of years earlier. On Grant's wedding day he'd stood at the reception with Ruminsky and talked about fly tying, and fly casting for smallmouth bass, and then he'd watched as Ruminsky became friends with Big Ole. Now when they crossed paths around school, Joe Ruminsky and Grant always found time for small talk about one thing or another. As often as not, Will was close at hand, and the three had formed a solid friendship.

"All right, you guys, this is what we're gonna do," Ruminsky started. "Your patient today is a sixty-five-year-old woman." He handed the patient's chart to Will. "You guys go on out to the waiting room and bring her back.

Then, when she's seated in that surgical suite right there," he pointed to an operating room just beyond Will's shoulder, "one of you will take her pulse and blood pressure while the other one goes to the dispensary and gets whatever surgical forceps and elevators you might need. With me?"

Both of them nodded.

"If you look here . . . ," Ruminsky waited for Will to open the chart, then he held a stubby finger on the page with "Treatment Plan" printed at the top, ". . . you'll see that she's already had an initial exam and that her treatment plan has been written out for you." He tapped his finger on the page. "There it is. What does it say?" Ruminsky asked.

"Extract teeth number two and number three," Will said.

"That's right. Think you can handle that?" Ruminsky asked.

"Sure," Will smiled.

"OK then, go get her. You guys decide who's gonna take her pulse and blood pressure, and who's gonna get your instruments. You'll also have to decide who's the surgeon today, and who's the assistant. Tomorrow you'll switch roles." He paused for a moment. "Well, get to work. But come and get me after you've taken her blood pressure."

The old woman seemed was heavyset, with some gray hair, and she wore no makeup. When Grant escorted her to the surgical suite, she walked as though her feet hurt, but her medical history was good, and she said she was healthy as a horse. She smelled like mothballs.

When she was seated in the dental chair, Grant motioned that he'd take her pulse, so Will stepped out of the room to go get the instruments they'd need.

"So where'd you grow up?" Grant asked while he arranged her medical chart on a small table behind her chair.

"Up by Forest Lake, on a farm," she replied. Grant liked to visit with patients. They all had interesting stories to tell about their lives, and the telling of these stories always seemed to relax them. "Still live on the same farm," she offered. "It's been in my family for ninety years, Doctor."

She thought he was a doctor! That was so cool. Grant continued to prepare a little table behind the dental chair. It would be the place they'd keep all their instruments and anesthetic syringes once they began the extractions.

"Do those teeth on the upper right hurt you today?" Grant asked, still not looking at her.

"No, not so much today, but they were swollen up pretty good for a while there," she replied.

"OK. We'll have them out of there before long," Grant said, while he continued to search through her medical chart. "Why don't you just expose your right arm for me, and I'll take your blood pressure in a moment," he added. He put her X-rays up on the illuminated view box on the wall and picked up a stethoscope and a blood pressure cuff. He got the surprise of his life when he walked around to the front of her chair.

She'd slipped out of her dress and she was naked from the waist up, extending her right arm for the blood pressure cuff. Her hefty, pendulous breasts hung nearly to her waist.

He'd never seen anything like this before. He'd never even imagined that something like this could exist. He managed to not cry out from the shock of it, and he didn't jump backwards. But he couldn't look away from those awful breasts. What should he do? He was paralyzed for a moment. Then he was overtaken by another horrible thought. What if Will walked in right now, while he had the woman's dress half off and was staring at those hideous breasts? Or worse yet, what if Joe Ruminsky walked back in? Serious heat began to creep up from under his collar.

"Oh," Grant said as calmly as he could, "I don't think we need to take everything off. It's cold in here, and all I need is your arm. You can put yourself back together there. We'll just roll your sleeve up."

"OK," the woman said.

Grant watched as she slowly tucked those flabby breasts back into her bra, then slowly started to lift her dress back over her shoulder.

Hurry up, for Christ's sake! he wanted to holler. And never do that again! When she'd buttoned the last button on her dress, Grant stepped forward and sighed, "That's better." Then he wrapped the cuff around her arm and began taking her blood pressure just as Will reentered the room.

"How's it going in here without me?" Will asked, as he placed the tray full of instruments on the table Grant had prepared.

"Just fine, Doctor," the woman answered.

Grant wondered what his own blood pressure might be. He'd seen a crew of firemen put out a fire once, and he thought the woman's breasts resembled those flaccid fire hoses lying flat in the street after the fire. He couldn't get the image out of his mind.

Several minutes later, Dr. Ruminsky let himself into the surgical suite and supervised while Will injected the local anesthetic and then used a forceps to luxate the teeth. When the teeth had been extracted they were placed on a four-by-four-inch white cotton gauze pad on the tray with the instruments, as part of the routine. The recently extracted teeth were always to be placed on that four-by-four-inch gauze, and then the instructor was summoned to evaluate the extraction site and make sure that no roots had been left behind and that the patient was ready to be dismissed.

"Nice work," Ruminsky said to Will after he'd checked the patient.

Thirty minutes later, Grant and Will were cleaning the suite they'd used on their first day in oral surgery when Ruminsky stuck his head in the door.

"You guys had a pretty good day today," he said. The clinic session was over, the other students were gone, and the doctor was about to go home for the day also.

The surgical procedure had been interesting, Grant supposed. But he'd struggled to concentrate on things after the blood pressure incident.

"Hey, Joe?" Grant said before Dr. Ruminsky could leave the room. Grant and Will had reached an understanding regarding the way they addressed him. If there were no other students around, and if the topic they wished to talk about was personal, they called him Joe. In the presence of other students he was always Dr. Ruminsky.

"Yeah?" Ruminsky replied.

"You ever been to Stub & Herb's?" Grant asked.

"I'd say every Gopher game either starts or ends there," he answered with a grin. "And when I was your age we used to go there as a group, after class, and bitch about school."

"Huh! Some things never change, I guess," Grant said. "Can I buy you a beer, and tell you a story?"

∾: ∾

"Never thought I'd be sittin' here having a beer with the dean and tellin' a story like that," Grant said thirty minutes later, when he finished.

Ruminsky's belly still shook while he leaned back and laughed.

"But I guess I'd rather be sittin' here and telling you about it than having to explain it all up there in surgery while we stared at those . . . breasts!" Grant grimaced.

Ruminsky kept on laughing. The Monday night crowd was much smaller and quieter than the usual Friday night bunch. Will, Kate, Grant, and Ruminsky sat at a small table, shared a pitcher of beer, and were able to visit without the usual boisterous crowd all around them.

"Yeah, well, you'll see some strange stuff up there," Ruminsky said. "When I was a student, just after the war, we had a bum show up one day with a toothache. We called 'em bums in those days. Now they're homeless people. Anyway, the guy had one tooth left in his head, an upper canine, tooth number six." Ruminsky leaned back and grinned, then shook his head. "When I began to luxate the tooth I heard a crack. Then I noticed that his entire eyeball and cheekbone were moving when I lifted the tooth. Wanna guess what that was all about?"

Kate looked back and forth between Grant and Will, then they all shrugged.

"Fractured skull?" Kate suggested.

"Not really," Ruminsky grinned. "Turns out the guy had tertiary syphilis and the infection had settled in the sutures in his skull. His head was coming apart!"

"Really?" Will asked.

"Really." Ruminsky nodded. "He died a couple weeks later."

Will leaned forward and rested his elbows on the table. "You know, I've been thinking that maybe I'd like to go into oral surgery," he said. He waited for a reply.

"Well, you'd better have good grades, and then be prepared for another few years of school," Ruminsky replied. "How 'bout you, Grant?"

"I guess I'd like to get to work, get on with my life." He looked at Kate and added, "Our lives."

"And what about you, Kate? Will you make it a career at the university?"

"Don't think I want that anymore," Kate said.

It was the most decisive remark Grant had ever heard her make on the subject of their future. He turned and questioned her with his eyes.

"I don't think I can stomach the bureaucracy," she sighed. "We had another staff meeting today. Looks like we're gonna finish the year with $38,000 left over in our budget. I thought we'd done a good thing and we'd be rewarded for it somehow. But you should have seen everyone start to jockey for position."

Ruminsky nodded his understanding, knowing what she was about to say.

"Whaddya mean, Kate?" Will asked.

"Well, it was clear right from the get-go that we had to hurry up and spend that money. Somebody explained for the benefit of us newcomers that if you don't spend all of your budget allotment, you get penalized; they cut your budget by that amount for the next year." She shook her head. "That's just not right—hurry up and spend money on things you don't need so you can waste it again next year."

"That's pretty much the way it works, Kate," Ruminsky said. "As a life-time bureaucrat I can tell you that it is frustrating. All you can hope for is that somebody inside that cumbersome bureaucracy is a wise enough leader to build a fine university, in spite of the system. I've spent a big part of my life fighting that mentality."

"Yeah, well, life is short." Kate finished her beer and took Grant's hand in hers. "I've done the university thing, now it's time to move on. We've been talking about moving to Walker when Grant graduates next year." This was the first time Grant had heard Kate speak of that plan with no reservations or limitations. She squeezed his hand and smiled. "We're ready to move on."

∽ CHAPTER 24 ∾

The last day of Grant's junior year in dental school had arrived. There would be no more boring lectures from Ebby. No more incomprehensible ramblings in pharmacology, delivered by the Gopper or anyone else. The classroom portion of dental school was over and he'd passed the national board exams. From here on it would be all clinic. Real patients, real life. All that remained was to finish his clinical requirements and then graduate the following spring.

It was his final clinic session in Oral Surgery rotation. One more patient with Will and Dr. Ruminsky. It had been a good experience, but he was ready to get back to Operative and Crown and Bridge. That stuff was more fun for him. Will, however, seemed to have found his niche in surgery. He was putting all his energy toward a graduate degree in oral surgery, and was planning to spend three more years in grad school.

Grant sat in the locker room at school and remembered the way a spring breeze had blown so softly through Kate's long, dark hair that morning. As he got dressed for clinic, he let himself recall her face. He stood up, crossed the locker room, and stepped out into the hallway, but his thoughts were all of Kate. She'd been wearing a yellow spring jacket when she'd glanced back over her shoulder and said good-bye just a few minutes earlier. Her smile was back; she *was* the prettiest girl in school. So much had happened in the past three years. Sometimes it didn't seem real.

"Hey, Grant!" someone called from behind him, and he turned to see Paul Zoch approaching. He was dressed in surgical scrubs, about to finish his rotation through Oral Surgery today, also. "Wait a second," Zoch said.

Grant realized that he hadn't seen Zoch wearing those leather pants in a long time.

"Hey, Grant," Zoch lowered his eyes and shifted his weight slowly from side to side. "I just wanted to tell you how sorry I was about all that stuff that happened to you and Kate last fall. I know you and I sorta got off on the wrong foot and . . ." He shrugged. "Anyway, I'm really sorry." He extended his hand.

"Thanks, Paul," Grant said, as he shook hands and smiled at Paul Zoch for the first time. They chatted for a minute and somehow the ugly incident that tied them together slid away. Each of them wished they'd never been part of it now. Grant was surprised and relieved that Zoch had sought him out and spoken to him. They'd never be friends, but they didn't have to go on any longer with the weight of their old confrontation pushing on them.

Zoch said a pleasant goodbye and stepped into his surgical suite and Grant turned and walked to the suite that he and Will would be using for the day. As he walked, Grant wondered how many other classmates he'd never taken the time to know.

"Didn't see that one comin'," Grant mumbled to himself. He stepped into his operating suite and was startled to see Will already there, deeply involved in what appeared to be a serious conversation with Carol Knutsen. Each of them held a coffee cup and they were standing close to each other. They'd both obviously arrived early for clinic, and somehow wound up here, talking.

"I just don't get it," Carol said.

"What's not to get?" Will replied.

They looked at Grant when he walked in, but then returned to their spirited discussion.

"Well, why would you do that?" Carol asked.

Grant ignored them, also. He opened the patient's chart, put the X-rays up on a view box, and read through the previous entries while Will and Carol continued, oblivious to his presence.

"Look, they're called stirrups and they fit over your hose," Will explained.

They were talking about Will's baseball uniform, apparently.

"Your hose? Now you sound like Ben Pribyl. He's always bragging about his hose." Carol crinkled her face in confusion.

"No! Hose means sanitary hose; you know, the white socks you wear under the stirrups." He shook his head in frustration.

"Well," Carol rolled her eyes, "I didn't know those little baseball outfits were so complicated. But they are kinda cute."

"Men don't want to be cute," Grant interrupted, but he never looked away from the X-ray view box. "They're not outfits, they're uniforms, and there is an art involved in the wearing of stirrups. We think we're handsomer than shit in our white flannels, by the way, and when we step into our stirrups and button up our colors it's just one more connection that binds us to our national pastime and to all the heroes of our childhood." Finally he showed Carol a wide smile and asked, "Get it?"

She shook her head and moved toward the door. "I gotta get ready for clinic," she said.

"Well, just remember that real men don't wanna be cute," Grant said as a parting shot when Carol walked out the door.

She stuck her face in the open door a second later and asked, "Are you guys coming to Stub & Herb's after clinic today? You can wear your baseball outfits."

"Today's the first day of baseball practice," Will replied. "If you want to see our hoses you'll have to come to practice . . ." Carol was gone before he could finish. He turned to Grant and sighed, "Women."

"How'd you get into a conversation like that, with her?" Grant asked while he flipped through the patient's chart.

"Ah, just in passing I mentioned that today was the first day of practice for our amateur team, and that we had to buy our own hats and stirrups. So she starts with twenty questions about stirrups . . ."

"Did you see that our patient is a twenty-one-year-old college student?" Grant interrupted, no longer concerned with Carol's understanding of stirrups and hose.

"Huh uh," Will answered.

"With four impacted wisdom teeth?" Grant added. "Look at these X-rays. We've never seen a case this difficult."

Baseball stirrups and the party at Stub & Herb's were forgotten instantly, lost in a sudden swell of insecurity. Both men swallowed hard when they began to study the X-rays.

The patient turned out to be a pretty girl with short blonde hair and big blue eyes. She asked questions and visited with Grant and Will as if they were old friends while they went over her medical history. She knew they were dental students, and after a while she asked, "Am I your first patient?"

"Nah," Will answered confidently. "This is actually our last day up here in surgery, so we've seen about everything."

That was a whopper, Grant thought. They'd each extracted a couple of dozen teeth. That was it. Quite a few of the teeth they'd extracted were already loose; some of them seemed to be waving in the breeze. Will had even joked once about putting pepper on an old man's lip and having him sneeze his own tooth out. Whenever it had been time to extract a difficult tooth, Dr. Ruminsky had stood by their sides and helped every step of the way.

But Will's lie reassured the young lady, and she resumed her light-hearted conversation.

"Why don't you go get the instruments, Pard?" Will said. "I'll stay here and take her pulse and blood pressure." He winked at Grant as soon as the young lady turned away. Just as Will had hoped, Grant closed his eyes and grimaced at the awful memory of those sagging breasts he'd seen way back on that first day.

Thirty minutes later the pretty young patient had been anesthetized and was profoundly numb around all four of her wisdom teeth.

Dr. Ruminsky strolled into the room and greeted everyone. He washed his hands, put on a surgical mask and latex gloves, then stood close to the patient and looked directly into her eyes. "How're you doing, young lady?" he asked in his usual friendly tone.

"Weewee numb," she replied, then laughed at the way the anesthetic affected her speech.

"Well, that's good," Dr. Ruminsky said. "And you should know that these two men are fine students, the best we have." He said that to every patient, even Darcy Wilhelm's patients, so it didn't mean much to Will and Grant, but the patient was glad to hear it. "I'm just going to watch them today, and maybe share some insight."

"Gweat," the girl replied, then laughed nervously.

"All right, Grant," Ruminsky started, when he picked a scalpel off the tray and deftly hid it from the patient's view. "I'm gonna start this for you, then you're going to finish."

The patient opened wide and tipped her chin toward the ceiling. Ruminsky made a half-inch incision into the gums covering the upper right wisdom tooth, then passed the scalpel to Grant and watched while Grant completed the incision.

"Perfect," Ruminsky said. He picked up an instrument that looked like a small, pointed spoon and handed it to Grant.

"Now, reflect the soft tissue," Ruminsky said. He watched while Grant tried to push the gums away from the white tooth that was beginning to show itself. "Give it a little more muscle, Grant. That tissue on the tuberosity is really tough. Lean on it some. There! That's it."

Ruminsky took the pointed spoon away from Grant and then handed him an elevator, a hand instrument that resembled a screwdriver, all the while hiding the stainless steel instruments from the patient.

"How're you doing?" Ruminsky asked as he nudged the patient.

"Gaa," she replied.

"Did that mean 'Good'?" Ruminsky asked.

The young lady nodded, then smiled as best as she could.

"All right now, Grant. Just take that elevator and place the open side on the mesial of tooth number one. Then rotate the handle clockwise and raise the handle."

Grant did as he was told and tried to hide his astonishment as the tooth lifted itself and followed the elevator right out of the socket.

"Piece o' cake!" Ruminsky said. "Now we'll place a couple sutures and do the same thing on the lower tooth. Then it's Will's turn to do the other side."

Grant placed the sutures and did everything by himself on the lower wisdom tooth while Ruminsky and Will watched. He placed the final sutures on the lower extraction site, then he sighed as if a piano had been lifted off his back. He'd done it. The wisdom teeth were resting on the gauze pad behind the patient, where they were supposed to be, and everything had been easy.

Ruminsky then coached Will through the upper tooth on the other side, and things went smoothly. The incision was done on the lower tooth and Will was about to begin elevating when a nurse came into the room and asked Dr. Ruminsky to step out into the hall. "Go ahead and use the elevator just as you did on the upper tooth," Ruminsky said, then he ducked out into the hall and closed the door behind himself.

Will knew he would lift that tooth out in no time. He turned the elevator and lowered the handle. But nothing happened. No problem, he'd try again.

Ten minutes later he was still trying and the surgical light was getting warm. Nothing he did would budge that tooth. Sweat was beading up on his forehead, then his arms and hands. The patient began to question Grant with her eyes. Why is this taking so long? Is this guy no good at this? Where did the older doctor go? Why is this beginning to hurt me? Why don't you just show him how to do this . . . you got the one on your side with no problem. She was looking at Grant more and more all the time and he knew exactly what she was thinking. Hell, he was beginning to wonder the same things.

Grant could sense the desperation growing in Will. But Will didn't know what to do except keep repeating what Ruminsky had shown him. It was the only thing he could do. Another half hour passed, and Will had sweated through his surgical scrubs. Grant thought Will was about to throw something against the wall out of frustration.

Finally the door swung open and Joe Ruminsky burst in. "Aren't you done yet?" he blurted. He walked quickly to the sink and washed his hands, then slipped on some new latex gloves. He walked to Will's side and peered over his shoulder for a moment while Will continued to fumble with the elevator.

He reached a powerful, stumpy little hand toward the patient and then grabbed Will's hand, elevator and all. "Man, you're never gonna make any money in private practice," he chuckled. Then he redirected the tip of the elevator and gave Will's hand a mighty squeeze as he turned the elevator clockwise and lowered the handle.

At first nothing happened. A second later everyone heard a loud pop and something flew out of the patient's mouth. It flew past their heads and plinked against the huge operating light suspended just above them. A small, bloody smear appeared on the surgical light after whatever had gone flying struck the white glass reflector and made a pinging sound. In the next instant they heard a tap over on the instrument tray behind them. When Ruminsky, Grant, and Will glanced back at the tray, they all saw the same thing at the same instant.

The lower wisdom tooth that Will had prodded and teased for an hour had exploded from its socket at the speed of sound, banked off the surgical light on the ceiling, and come to rest on the same four-by-four-inch piece of gauze where the other teeth were resting, exactly where it was supposed to be placed. It was the bank shot of a lifetime. Ruminsky's firm twist over the top of Will's trembling hand had produced the most spectacular bit of dentistry any of them might ever see.

Ruminsky stared into the bloody socket, gave no hint of his own surprise, then looked at Will as if he did that sort of thing routinely. "*That's how you take teeth out!*" he said with a straight face, then added, "Put a couple sutures in there, go over postoperative care, and you can send this nice girl home." He walked out the door without a glance at Will and Grant. Then, he looked back at them from the hallway, shook his head, and started to chuckle at what he'd just done. It was one thing to extract a tooth so easily while he was holding his hand over another man's and using the instrument in *his* hand. It was quite another to have that tooth fly from the socket, ricochet off the surgical light, and then come to rest exactly where the surgeon was supposed to place it at the conclusion of the surgery.

"Heh, heh, heh." They could hear Ruminsky chuckling as he walked down the hall to work with Zoch and his partner.

~:~

When their car rolled to a stop at a local high school baseball field two hours later, Will was still talking about the extraction. But Grant forgot it completely as soon as they'd pulled into the ballpark parking lot. He took a moment to immerse himself in the joy of what he was about to do.

Baseballs made such a great sound when they came to a sudden stop in the pocket of a baseball glove. Grant shut the car off, closed his eyes, and listened for a moment. Men were playing catch only a few feet away and the sounds of baseball carried him away.

This was good, all good. A warm spring afternoon; green grass; the smell of leather; and the sounds, the comforting sounds of this game. Somebody was taking batting practice over in the cage—crack, crack, crack came the sound of bat on ball. Young men were spread out across the ball field, preparing for baseball practice. Some were sitting in short grass and stretching their legs. Others were playing catch. Their muffled voices drifted over and through all the other sounds, as they laughed and renewed old friendships.

Grant had left school giddy with excitement. Today he'd play ball with his buddies down at the park until sunset. Then he'd be with Kate, maybe for a late dinner at Benny's Deli.

As Grant and Will walked from their car over to the dugout where other players were getting ready for practice, Grant tried to ignore Will's obsessive ranting. Will hadn't shut up since Ruminsky had left them to finish up with that last patient.

"That tooth just wouldn't budge!" Will said for the hundredth time. "And then . . ."

"I got mine." Grant shrugged, clearly implying that he was a better surgeon than Will.

"Yeah . . . but . . ." Will stammered and tried to keep up while Grant lengthened his stride. ". . . well, that raises the question, fuck you!"

"Heh, heh, heh." Grant laughed and put his arm over Will's shoulder, then stuck another needle in him. "It's OK, Pard. Darcy needed a lot of help, too."

For once, Will had no reply; all he could do was laugh along with Grant. They walked together, laughing and kicking at the grass, just two little boys heading off to play ball.

Waiting for them in the dugout was one of Grant's former teammates at the university, Danny Austin. Danny gave them each a uniform and welcomed them to the Blue Sox. Then he introduced them to their new teammates and told them that this was an A division team, one with superior talent that would play a very competitive schedule.

The roster was no surprise to Will or Grant. The Blue Sox's best pitcher, their ace, was a thirty-five-year-old who'd pitched at a major college in the South, come up a bit short after a run in the minor leagues, but still had plenty of gas in the tank and couldn't give up on baseball yet. Every amateur team in the Twin Cities had one or two pitchers like him. The rest of the team was made up of boys who were currently playing on college teams and men who'd recently finished their college careers, had no shot at the pros, and were trying to squeeze in a couple more years of baseball.

There were no flamethrowers in the league. All the really good young pitchers were being paid to play ball in somebody's minor-league system. Town ball was for baseball junkies. Will and Grant would fit right in.

When the introductions were finished, the players got ready for practice. Everybody followed pretty much the same routine. They arrived at the park half-dressed for practice, then wandered over to the dugout, carrying a duffel bag containing their baseball shoes and glove. Some players wore tattered old baseball pants for practice, others wore baggy shorts, but they all finished dressing in the dugout and then went out to warm up.

Grant stood on the foul line and began to lob a ball softly to Will, who had taken a position about seventy-five feet into the outfield. The ball was fairly new, but it had a few grass stains and scuff marks. Grant smelled the ball every time Will threw it to him, before he threw it back.

His arm was a little stiff, but it felt *so* good to throw. Better by the minute. Will returned the ball with a bit more zip each time, and as their arms limbered, Will backed up farther and farther out toward center field. The drill was called long toss, and it was the time-tested way to warm up and build arm strength.

"You look nice in your baseball outfit!" Grant called to Will.

"Thank you, Doctor," Will replied.

Their throws grew longer. Each catch and throw required a little more effort, stirring something inside Grant. There was a simple joy in the ritual. When the ball popped into Grant's glove now, he began to crow hop before he threw it back to Will; he reset his feet with a little hop, like a bird. It was the way outfielders were taught to prepare their feet in order to make a strong throw back to the infield.

Grant threw the ball back to Will and it sailed into the timeless ether of baseball—then it returned to him. Little fantasies began to sneak into this familiar warm-up routine. Grant started to see himself as Mickey Mantle patrolling center field in the warm sunshine at Yankee Stadium. By and by, as the ball sailed his way, it became a scorching line drive off the bat of Willie McCovey, and suddenly Mays was standing there on third! He'd tag up and try to score! If he scored it would be the winning run and the Giants would win the series. That could not happen! Grant caught the ball, crow hopped, and made a throw to the plate. Will understood the game going on in Grant's imagination; every boy dreamed those same dreams. Will waited for the throw, guarding an imaginary home plate, just like Yogi Berra would guard the real one, then put the tag on a sliding Willie Mays. "Toast!" Will yelled.

Mantle, Koufax, Bob Gibson, Killebrew, all the great players of his childhood were there, moving in and out of his baseball dreams. Long-forgotten home runs and strikeouts played themselves over again in his mind. He caught the ball over his shoulder, just like Willie Mays, then turned and threw it back toward Will, and Will did the same.

CHAPTER 25

Hard to believe three years had passed, Grant thought. Autumn of his senior year was just around the corner. His last town ball game of the summer was tonight and fall semester would start in two weeks. He was in the homestretch now. He stood on the corner of Washington Avenue and Union Street once again and waited by that same stoplight where he'd first noticed Kate. It seemed like he'd known her all his life.

A new group of freshman dental students would be gathering at the light and hoping to find a friend just as he'd done three years ago. They'd be timid and worried about . . . The light changed and the crosswalk filled with people. Grant forgot about the new freshman class. They'd have to find their own way.

This summer had been spectacular. He'd been able to work on his clinical requirements during the day and play ball several nights a week. Kate's workload at school was much lighter during the summer, and they'd been able to spend every evening together—either at some ballpark around the Twin Cities, at Benny's Deli, or in their little apartment. They'd spent the entire summer talking about two things that both seemed to have limitless possibilities: baseball and their future together.

He picked up the pace and walked past the spot where he'd stumbled three years earlier. He was too busy to think about that now. Today was his final day in clinic for the summer and he had to get up there and get to work.

"Did you see who we have for our clinical instructor today, Grant?" Ben Pribyl asked when Grant strolled into clinic. It was clear that he knew the answer to his own question.

Grant was preparing his operatory for morning clinic, planning to place an amalgam filling for a very attractive dental hygiene student in her second year of study. Now Ben had interrupted his train of thought, and Grant looked a bit irritated when he replied, "No, who?"

Ben didn't answer right away. He meandered into Grant's operatory and peeked at the chart on the countertop. "She's back for more, huh?" Ben teased when he read the name on the chart, as if he'd forgotten his own question regarding their clinical instructor.

Grant's patient, Tina Hilgendorf, was a head turner. Long blonde hair, perfect cheekbones, alabaster skin, sleek, not too tall. Everybody, especially Ben, noticed her. She was a flirt, too, and she'd volunteered to be a patient in dental clinic for the same reason Grant and Ben had several years earlier; she wanted to meet somebody. She was working on her "MRS" degree, as the guys in his class liked to say. She'd been assigned to Grant strictly through the luck of the draw, and when he'd called from the waiting room for the first time she'd been unable to hide her approval. Grant Thorson would do just fine. Her eyes had widened in surprise just before she flashed a seductive smile.

During the course of their introductions Grant had made it abundantly clear that he was happily married to Dr. Kate Thorson, but that seemed irrelevant to Tina at first. She'd asked Grant out for a drink after clinic on two separate occasions. Then she'd slowly accepted the fact that Grant would be her friend, but nothing more, and began approaching him for small talk and introductions to his friends whenever she noticed him with a group of other students around school. She was seeing a sophomore dental student at the moment, but Grant's friends liked to joke that she was trying to upgrade to a senior, any senior who might be closer to graduation and a steady income. Grant had actually come to like her, now that they'd reached an understanding about his marital status.

"So who *do* we have for clinic today?" Grant asked Ben. He chose to ignore the impending sexual reference to Tina, but he knew Ben was incapable of letting such a moment pass without one.

"That girl has several cavities she'd like you to fill," Ben said.

"Yeah, well, can you blame her?" Grant replied. "Who's our instructor today?" he asked again.

"How come you always get the hotties?" Ben persisted.

"You know why, Ben," Grant sighed. "They try to match us up." He grinned, then he asked yet again, "So who do we . . ."

Dr. Miles Clark strolled into clinic.

"Oh fuck," Grant groaned.

Ben nodded, then he shook his head in disgust.

"How do you get along with him?" Grant asked. "I mean, after that scene at Iron Mike Petrowiak's a couple years ago?"

"He never speaks to me. I'm sure he hates me, but he's apparently smart enough to fear me," Ben smiled. "He checks my patient like he's supposed to, he gives me a grade, then he gets up and leaves the operatory. Never says shit. Pretty fair grader, I'd have to say, too. How 'bout you?"

"Only had him a couple times. Never says much to me, either, but he likes to jerk me around some. You know, just the little stuff." Grant sighed.

One hour later Grant signaled that he was ready to have his instructor, Dr. Clark, come over and check his work. He'd anesthetized the lovely Tina and prepared her tooth to receive a filling. Before he could continue and put a filling in the tooth, he had to have Dr. Clark evaluate the cavity he'd prepared, give him a grade, and then give him permission to continue and place the filling in her tooth.

Clark made Grant wait for twenty minutes before he came to check Tina's tooth. Grant knew, just as all other dental students knew, that one way for an instructor to make things difficult for a student was to waste their time and make them wait. Clark was a master at it. He didn't seem to like teaching. He didn't seem to like dentistry or anything else, for that matter. He only liked himself. There were a few other clinical instructors who appeared to have the same issues, but Clark was the most hated of the bunch. Dental students despised him and talked about him endlessly behind his back.

Clark finally came to Grant's operatory, then he made a point to ignore Grant's greeting, "Hi, Dr. Clark."

Clark spent several minutes fawning over the beautiful Tina. He asked questions about her dental hygiene classes and her hometown. She smiled and batted her eyes and laughed when she was supposed to. Finally, Clark picked up a mouth mirror and a dental explorer and took an excruciatingly long look at the way Grant had prepared her tooth.

"You didn't understand the assignment, did you?" Clark eventually sighed. "Have you been getting passing grades from other instructors?" Clark asked with a snide edge.

"Huh?" Grant stammered. He thought Clark was joking at first, but there was no humor in his eyes. Anger began to build in Grant's chest and he felt his pulse quicken. "Actually, I've been getting pretty good grades," Grant said through tightening lips.

Clark rolled his eyes. "Well, the gingival seat is *way* too high. Take it down a tenth of a millimeter and call me back to check it," he said, and he left the operatory.

Grant looked into Tina's twinkling blue eyes and shrugged. Clark was simply trying to humiliate him in front of a pretty girl. Tina knew it, too. Grant saw it in her eyes, but she kept her silence.

Grant nodded and let the familiar frustration settle over him. He'd been putting up with bullshit like this for three years, and he could do it a while longer. He happened to glance out into the hallway and noticed Ben Pribyl walk by.

"I'll be right back," Grant said to the lovely Tina. He walked out to the hallway outside the Operative Dentistry clinic.

Ben stood with his elbows on a windowsill, smoking a cigarette.

"Hi, Ben," Grant said, and he leaned on the windowsill beside him. "You done already?"

"My patient never showed. I did some paperwork and now I'm gonna head home. What're you doing out here?" Ben asked.

"Dr. Asswipe just told me to lower the gingival seat a tenth of a millimeter," Grant sighed.

"No one can judge a cavity prep down to a tenth of a millimeter with the naked eye," Ben grinned. "That prick is just jerking you around, isn't he? He wants to impress that little number in your chair, too."

"Yup," Grant agreed.

"So what're you gonna do?" Ben asked.

"Gonna eat shit and wait until you're done with that cigarette. Then I'll have Dr. Clark come over and check Tina's tooth again. That should be enough time for him to think I've modified the cavity preparation in a satisfactory manner." Grant rolled his eyes.

Ben and Grant chatted for a while, until Ben smashed the cigarette completely out. "See you tomorrow," Grant said, and he walked back into the clinic. He told Dr. Clark that he'd modified the prep and asked him to please check it again.

After another twenty-minute wait, Clark reentered the operatory and began to flirt with Tina once more. When he finally got around to evaluating the tooth he took one brief look, then threw his instruments on the tray. "Now it's way too *low*," he groaned. He gave Grant a C minus on the project and stormed out of the room, as if Grant's poor clinical skills disgusted him.

Grant hadn't touched Tina's tooth, but the gingival seat had miraculously descended from "way too high" to "way too low." Her eyes revealed the fact that she understood the injustice of it all, but she said nothing until Grant had finished the new filling, then suffered through another critical evaluation from Dr. Clark.

"How about if I buy you a drink and we wash this day away? How's that sound?" Tina asked, as she stood up to leave.

"I'd love to, Tina, but Kate's waiting for me, and I've got a ball game tonight. Maybe another time?" Grant sighed.

Operative clinic was completely empty by the time Grant finished up and made his way down to the fifth-floor locker room. The halls were empty and quiet, too, and his footsteps echoed through the locker room. Grant washed his face and stared at himself in the mirror above the sink. He was tired, but he'd cleared one more hurdle. He dried his face, went to the phone, and called Kate in her office on the sixth floor to say he'd pick her up in five minutes. Maybe they could pick up a pizza before the game. It was good to be done for the day.

Outside the locker room, he glanced out the window down onto Washington Avenue, just in time to see Miles Clark walk by with Tina Hilgendorf on his arm. She was tossing her head back and laughing at every clever thing he said. Oh well, Grant thought, maybe they'll both get just what they want.

~:~

The Blue Sox were taking a beating. The score was ten to one in the bottom of the eighth, and it was clear to Grant that town ball was over for the summer. They were about to be eliminated from their sectional tournament by a superior team. There would be no celebrations to end the season, no appearance in the state tournament, and that would be all right. He'd had a fine summer.

The dugout was fairly quiet as his teammates on the Blue Sox played out the string and waited for the drubbing to end. Grant looked right, then left, at the young men sitting close to him, and he remembered the season.

The catcher, a surly kid from Jackson, Minnesota, had been ejected from two games, while he was catching, for arguing balls and strikes with umpires. One of their pitchers had quit the team during the fourth inning of an early-season game; he'd just walked off the mound, got in his car, and drove home, after mumbling something about how pissed off he was about two errors his center fielder had made. No one had seen him since that night.

The second baseman struggled with anger management. Every now and then, after striking out, he'd take a bat behind the dugout and pound it on the ground as hard as he could swing it. Grant remembered how all the Blue Sox had sat there and laughed, shoulders bobbing and looking back and forth at each other while they'd listened to the kid cussing and thumping his bat on the earth.

Danny Austin had been their leader all summer. He'd had a cup of coffee with the Mets, but he'd failed to hit the ball when his chance came and they sent him back to the minors. He said it nearly broke his heart at first. He quit baseball, came back to Minneapolis, and got a real job. Now, after two years to think about it, he was a bit more introspective. What the hell, he'd made the show, and no one could ever take that away from him.

Grant took his spikes off, put them in his duffel bag, and put his tennis shoes on. His season was over. He'd played four innings in left field and two innings at first base. After going hitless in three at bats he'd been lifted for a pinch hitter. It was OK; he hadn't played that well and he'd struck out twice. It was time for the Blue Sox to get every one of their players in this, their final game.

Grant arranged the gear in his duffel, slid it under the bench he was sitting on, and looked over at his teammates in the dugout. There was no sense of gloom or frustration, even though they were about to lose. The other team was just better, and they all knew it. Several reserve players walked about, asked questions regarding the other team's pitcher, and prepared for their chance to play while the others sat quietly on the bench or talked among themselves.

On one end of the bench, Will was chatting with Danny Austin. Grant decided to walk over and sit with his buddies for the remainder of the game. As he wove his way through teammates, he stepped over the other guys' bags and shoes, he overheard small conversations about curveballs and girlfriends, and he wondered briefly if Kate had made up her mind where she wanted to go after the game for a late dinner.

Grant was approaching Will, still about ten feet sway, when something that he never could have predicted struck him. As if a switch had been thrown inside him, he suddenly saw the image of Kate, sitting on her hospital bed and holding their lifeless child. She turned her shattered face toward him and he saw it all happening again. A wave of emotion began to rise in his chest. Where had this all come from? Then the incident from the hospital roared at him like a runaway train and he dropped onto the dugout steps and sat with his face in his hands. All he could do was weep. At first he could hide it, but then his chest began to heave and he started to sob. The vision struck him down like the sudden impact of a heart attack. He saw the child, and he felt, for the first time, the full and complete pain of the baby's death. He'd never hold his son or get to know him. The whole awful experience at the hospital had come and gone before he'd had a chance to truly deal with it. He'd managed to keep a lid on all the raw emotions until this moment.

His teammates stepped back from him and stared at each other, each of them begging for an explanation about what had happened to Grant. A kid wearing a batting helmet and carrying a bat bent over and put a hand on his shoulder. "You OK, Grant?" he asked with a confused look.

Will was at Grant's side in an instant. "What's the matter, Pard?" he asked, with an arm around Grant's neck.

"He died," Grant choked. "He died and I never got to . . ." His voice trailed off and a fountain of sorrow overflowed. Grant was all alone now, but surrounded by a gathering crowd. Kate was holding a lifeless child and staring at him, then they were standing by a lonely grave at Six Mile Cemetery.

Will looked up into the eyes of the baseball players who crept forward, then leaned back and showed them the palms of his hands. Everyone understood the gesture as a request for some space. Nothing was physically wrong; there had been no illness or injury. But Grant needed to be left alone for a while. The players nodded their understanding, and they moved away and went back to what they'd been doing. Will sat with an arm around Grant's neck while the minutes passed.

Finally Grant sighed heavily and steadied himself. He blew his nose and wiped away his tears. "I don't know what happened, Will," he said after a while. "All of a sudden it was just there, all of it. It just boiled over, out of the blue." He stopped and turned toward Will. "I never grieved for my son. I was always trying to keep a stiff upper lip for Kate." He wiped his eyes and relived the worst moment of his life again. "And all that anguish had to get out." He sighed. "I don't get it, it was like a dam busted. I don't know why it chose this moment. Sorry, Pard."

"It's OK," Will shrugged.

"I'm sorry, Danny," Grant said to Danny Austin, and acknowledging a couple of other teammates sitting nearby.

"It's OK," Danny replied. "I've heard of this kind of thing before, and I don't think you're the first one to have this happen."

"No problem," one of the others added.

"You gonna be all right?" Will asked. "You wanna go someplace and talk?"

"Nah, I'll be OK now," Grant said. "I s'pose I should explain all this to the other guys, huh?"

"No, I don't think you need to," Danny said. "Some of 'em already know what happened to you and Kate, and I'm thinkin' that by now everybody knows, and understands."

When the game ended, each of the Blue Sox came over to Grant and offered condolences, or sympathy, or whatever one young man might offer another at a time like this, and then said good-bye for the season.

Grant watched them drift away to their own wives and girlfriends. Then he found Kate and told her what had happened. A baseball season was over, but so much of the game remained.

~: CHAPTER 26 :~

Fall semester of senior year started shortly after the town ball season ended. The days and weeks passed at a steady pace. Some days clinic was an ordeal, and some days it was a great learning experience. There was something new to learn every day. Autumn rolled over into winter, and the future drew near.

The weatherman on the radio said it was twenty-two below zero one morning. The bus ride to school would be a cold one, so Grant decided to linger in a hot shower for a while longer. The steam felt good and he filled his lungs with it.

They'd have a nice home-cooked meal tonight in order to celebrate, well, nothing actually. They just wanted to celebrate. He'd offered to make Mayfly Hatch, or pesto, as the rest of the world called it, but Kate had opted for spaghetti. She'd spent the night before making a special recipe of sauce and meatballs. She planned to cook it all day in the slow cooker. They'd have fresh bread, and a tablecloth, too. Grant asked her if he should pick up some Champagne in order to make the evening a little more romantic.

"No!" Kate had said. "I still can't even stand to smell that stuff!" Then that great smile flowed over her face and she said, "I mean, no thank you. Why don't you buy some romantic beer instead." She was so beautiful, he thought.

Two and a half years of marriage. How could that be? And so much had happened. One thing was for sure, tonight would be fine. The apartment would smell like spaghetti when they got home from school. They'd light some candles. They'd eat. There would be sex, plenty of sex. He breathed in a lungful of the steam and allowed himself to think about the sex for just a moment before he stepped out of the shower.

The bathroom door flew open with a loud crash and Kate burst in. She was crying and holding her face, and through the shower curtain Grant could see that her face and the front of her white sweater were covered in blood. "Oh, God!" she cried.

She'd been shot! It had to be that, there was too much blood for anything else. Grant ripped open the shower curtain and took her in his arms while she shrieked and trembled. His heart was in his throat when the steam cleared. Kate was hysterical.

But the red stuff wasn't blood. It was spaghetti sauce.

The last thing she had planned to do before leaving for school was to take the slow cooker from the refrigerator and plug it in. It would sit on the kitchen countertop and cook all day. But somehow the electrical cord caught on the refrigerator shelf and pulled the entire ceramic pot full of spaghetti sauce from her hands a moment earlier. The thing went off like a bomb when it hit the floor, and Kate received the brunt of the blast, all the shrapnel of meatballs and tomato sauce, right in her chest and face.

"Goddammit!" she screamed. "The whole fuckin' thing blew up!" She groaned and grunted as if she actually had thrown herself on a grenade.

"Are you all right?" Grant asked, but he already knew the answer. She was fine, just extraordinarily, unbelievably pissed off.

He grabbed a towel for himself and followed her "bloody" footprints back across their small living room and into the tiny kitchen. It looked like a chainsaw massacre had taken place. Bits and pieces of meatballs and spaghetti sauce were running down the walls.

The situation was absurd. A small chuckle lifted itself from Grant's chest before he could bite his lip and suppress it.

"It's not funny, goddammit!" Kate screamed. She slammed the bathroom door as hard as he'd ever heard any door slammed. It sounded like she'd fired a high-powered rifle.

Grant laughed, loud and long. He knew Kate had stripped and stepped into the shower, and she couldn't hear him now. The stuff was in her hair, it was everywhere. But the funny part was the way Kate had come off the tracks emotionally. He'd never seen her that angry. He'd never heard such language from her. It was hilarious.

He was still naked, on his hands and knees, cleaning up a spectacular mess, as he chuckled the entire time. He'd never seen anything like it. The mess was world class, and Kate's reaction was so far over the top. He laughed, and cleaned, and laughed, then he scrubbed more bloody footprints from the living room carpet.

Finally, when he felt he could keep from laughing, he dared to enter the bathroom. He kept his eyes turned down while he cleaned more bloody footprints from the bathroom floor and gathered up Kate's clothes, which were covered with the same mess he'd just cleaned up.

He knew she was watching him, searching his face for even the smallest hint of a smile. Jesus, it was torture. It was like trying not to laugh in church when he was a boy. He felt himself losing the struggle. His lips curled just a bit . . .

"It's not funny, goddammit!" she roared once more. Then she burst into tears when Grant fled like a beaten hound.

Kate lay on the couch thirty minutes later. Still nearly catatonic with anger, she stared at the ceiling between the groans and animal sounds rolling around in her chest. She'd called in sick. She planned to spend the day there, apparently.

Grant knew better than to try to kiss her good-bye. He eased his way over to the door and was about to let himself slip out for the day when Kate finally spoke. "Don't you *dare* tell anybody about this . . . until it's funny! Goddammit!" He clicked the door shut and locked it, even as the belly laugh inside him began to bulge into his throat. He hurried to the street and let it out. She'd just spoken the greatest sentence he'd ever heard, and all he could *do* was laugh.

Kate obviously understood that there was humor in what had happened, but the anger still had complete control of her. "Don't tell anyone about this until it's funny," she'd said. What an insightful thing to say. Maybe all laughter did have its birth in sorrow? He'd think about that intellectual stuff some other day. He sure as hell wasn't going to be discussing it with Kate for a while. For now, he was in a hurry to get to school and tell his buddies what had happened.

He called Kate at noon, and she was still surprisingly pissed off. When he called again at three she seemed to be regaining her sanity, and he convinced her that instead of trying to repair the shattered plans for a private dinner they should just have Will and June over for pizza. He'd go pick it up from a popular new place over on University Avenue. They'd have fun. *The Godfather* was going to be on TV that night and they could watch the movie together. It wasn't the evening they'd planned, but it would be like old times.

"OK," she said. "Sounds good. You didn't tell anyone yet, did you?" she demanded.

"Nope," Grant lied, thankful that she couldn't see his face.

The rich smell of pizza followed Will and June into Grant and Kate's apartment several hours later. "Colder'n a well-digger's ass out there!" Will shivered. "Hope the pizza's still warm!" He gave the two large pizza boxes to Kate and threw his coat on the floor by the couch.

June was describing a flu epidemic among the children in the elementary school where she taught while Kate put paper plates and napkins on the table and Grant took four bottles of beer from the fridge.

"Oh, it was a rough day today," June said. "I had two kids barf right in my classroom."

Will took a bite of pizza, then looked over at his wife. "Great table talk, honey. Did it look like this?" He pointed to the combo pizza in front of them.

"That's gross, Will," June replied.

"Well you're the one . . ."

"Let's talk about something else until the movie comes on," June interrupted. "I read today there are some electronic companies doing research on a machine called a videocassette recorder. Apparently, we'll be able to buy tapes, like audiocassettes, only with movies on them, and watch movies whenever we want someday," she explained.

"I'll believe *that* when I see it," Will said. He leaned forward and locked eyes with Kate at close range. "How was your day, Kate?" He brought a glass of beer up to cover his smile, but his eyes gave it away. Kate could see that he knew everything.

"Rat bastard!" she blurted at Grant. "You told him!" She felt herself giving in as the absurdity of the whole day threatened to part the clouds and let her see the humor in the spaghetti incident, too. She could see that Will and Grant had had an all-day laugh at her expense.

Will laughed when he shouldn't have and a swallow of beer shot out his nose.

"He made me, honey." Grant was pointing and laughing at Will now. "I couldn't help it."

When Kate saw that June was also caught up in the laughter she was finally able to let go of the anger and join them in a belly laugh, at her own expense.

⁓ː⁓

Deep in the middle of the frigid winter night, long after their best friends had gone home, Kate sat on the green couch by herself. Wrapped in a wool blanket and wearing some of Grant's heavy socks, she nursed a can of beer and tried to watch an old Charlie Chan movie on TV.

The movie held no interest for her, but Grant was fast asleep and had been for a while. She simply needed someone to keep her company until she was ready for bed, and Mr. Chan would do.

Another great evening with their best friends had come and gone. They'd laughed and joked until their sides ached. She'd never known friendship and laughter like this. "All good things come to an end"—she said the words out loud and surprised herself. This evening had ended because it had to. The boys would graduate soon, too, it was inevitable. Graduation was good, it was what they'd worked toward for four years, but it would mark the end of a special time and place. Most of the time, she looked forward to Grant's graduation. They could get on with their lives. But sitting in the dark of the night, she let herself be afraid of the unknown. This was such a good place to be. She'd been happy here, really happy, and she wondered what surprises waited around the next bend in the river.

～ CHAPTER 27 ～

It never failed. Never. All around the university, the first warm spring afternoon wasn't just a harbinger of change; it *delivered* the change. College girls showed a little more skin. College boys showed a little less maturity, and a lot more attention to the college girls. Everyone seemed to stretch out and throw off winter.

As always, Grant and Kate held hands when they walked from their bus stop to the dental school. Recent spring rains had washed away the grit of a long winter. The green grass smelled good, and buds on all the boulevard trees threatened to open into a summer canopy before long.

Today, however, each of them was thinking of the profound changes carried on the spring wind. Warm breezes did indeed signal new life for everyone, but especially for them. Soon they'd be leaving school behind and starting a life together far away. There was a new horizon for them to sail over and they were excited to set out. Their university years would be over in just a couple of weeks. Kate had given her notice at work; she wouldn't be back next year. They'd put money down on an old dental office and a small home in Walker.

Graduation day had been racing toward them for months, and each day slipped by a little faster than the previous one. The big day was finally so close that they were planning what clothes they'd wear, and how they'd celebrate. But now that the end was finally close, they weren't sure if it was the finish line or a brick wall.

A new life? Certainly, it was time to get on with things. Still, there was a sense of melancholy in all of this. Kate had spent twelve years around the university. Even though she was ready to move on, the place was a part of her now, and this was the end of something good.

And for Grant? He'd been here for eight years. He couldn't help but feel the impending loss of a good thing also. For his whole life, every other spring wind had meant only that summer was coming—girls, baseball, swimming, a break from schoolwork. But this warm breeze meant all that was over. It was time to go to work, like his father.

Each of them dreamed their own dreams and tried to convince themselves that what they'd be taking hold of in a few weeks was better than what they were letting go.

Grant leaned over and was about to kiss Kate good-bye when they reached the fourth-floor coffee shop. Just like every other morning, she'd go to her office for some reading and prep time while he continued on up to clinic. "I love you," he whispered just before the kiss.

"No tongues!" came a loud voice from the coffee shop, followed immediately by familiar laughter.

Ben Pribyl, Andy Hedstrom, Joe Paatalo, Will, Mitch Morgan, and Carol Knutsen were all sitting at the same table, waving Grant and Kate over to join them. These gatherings for morning coffee had become less frequent as their senior year neared its end. The parties and bitch sessions at Stub & Herb's had all but ended sometime during the winter, too. Everyone had been caught up in their own busy schedules while they worked at completing graduation requirements and finalized plans for the next part of their lives.

On those rare occasions when they had been able to sit together and visit, their conversations had been dominated by talk of bank loans, mortgages, and the business of starting a dental practice.

They'd all abandoned the carefree attitude of a college student, for the most part, and they were ready to go their separate ways.

But this morning, by chance, they'd all come together again. Neither Grant nor Kate nor anyone at the table could resist a satisfied smile.

Carol stood behind Ben and rubbed his shoulders, grinning while she waited for Grant and Kate to take a seat.

What a change, Grant thought. The bunker mentality that had brought this group together and galvanized these friendships had evolved into something new. These people had some swagger now, and they'd earned it. They were seniors, about to graduate. They'd done the work and they were all pretty good. Grant looked around and noticed the way the younger students revered the seniors at this table. Everyone at the table was near the top of the class academically, and they were all confident of their clinical skills. They were also pretty sure they were about to change the world. An aura of invincibility surrounded the table. If the university had been an air force base, this would be a table full of fighter pilots.

The pleasure of the spontaneous gathering triggered the need to relive some of the infamous moments from their first semester together. Will retold the story of Grant's threat to stuff Ebby into a beer bottle and of Grant's anger at receiving a C on his own work, while Will got an A for borrowing it. Ben shared his memory of the pathetic look on Will's face when he was summoned to Dean Muckinhern's office to discuss his failing grade in Biochemistry. Carol recalled her shock at seeing the sparks fly from their cadaver's head.

They all still hated Dr. Ebverret Rettig, and they didn't mind that anyone sitting nearby might hear them say it. But the talk of Ebby Rettig had taken on a different tone. They'd overcome him. He was a vanquished foe, something tangled in their hooves as they were about to gallop away.

Dr. Miles Clark was now the most hated person on the dental school faculty. There were several other clinical instructors like him—selfish, arrogant, and condescending—but Clark was the eye of the storm. Like playground bullies, Clark and the others came to school just so they'd have someone to humiliate. Just the mention of Miles Clark aggravated students, and every time they got together and began to bitch, his name came up.

Carol recounted the first Miles Clark story: he'd made her start over on a project that another instructor had already approved. Andy told one about Clark embarrassing a junior dental student, and Mitch said that after clinic that day he'd overheard a couple of other instructors whispering about how the faculty disliked Miles Clark too.

"I was in Clark's section yesterday," Will offered with a sinister grin. Everyone understood that he had a story to tell, and when Will leaned forward and began to speak softly, everyone else at the table leaned forward to hear.

"Remember my patient, Robert Walker?" Will asked Grant.

"The retarded adult?" Grant replied. "About fifty years old?"

"Yup," Will answered. "Nicest guy you'll ever meet, salt of the earth. Anyway, I did a lot of operative for that guy. He was a mess when we met, and we kinda became friends over these last few months while I was doin' the work. That guy tried *so* hard to be a good patient, did whatever I asked. And he was funny! Every time I brought a needle over to his mouth to get him numb he'd get a goofy grin and say, 'Here comes the harpoon!' Then he'd open wide. The guy was a stitch."

Will glanced around him, then he leaned closer to his friends at the table and they responded by leaning closer too.

"So I'm all set to finish his operative. We're gonna do his last filling and then we'd be all done. I saw that we were gonna have Clark for our instructor, but I figured what the hell, everything has gone just fine up to this point, right?"

Everyone at the table was grinning now, filled with expectations.

"So I got him numb," Will said. "And while we're sitting there waiting for Robert's lip to go to sleep, he sorta mumbled something. I asked him to repeat himself and he sorta mumbled again. I said to speak up. He gets his brow all furrowed up like he's doing calculus problems in his head and he wants to talk about the answers, and then he says, 'Say Will, I have to go to the bathroom.'"

The group snickered and looked back and forth among themselves.

"Now I'm a little upset that Robert might have to chop a log and I'll have to help with the paperwork," Will said, which caused more snickering. "But when I took him into the bathroom there, the one in the main hallway, just outside clinic, he went and stood in front of a urinal, so I was pretty relieved." Will paused until the snickering died down.

"But my happiness was premature!" Will started again. "Robert fumbled with his zipper for a few minutes before I realized that I was gonna have to help him . . . you know." Will raised his eyebrows and the apprehensive snickering started again.

"So as I'm reachin' over to help him with his zipper I'm struck by a very disconcerting thought." He paused again. "In addition to not wanting to touch another guy's dick . . . ," Will stopped his story and whipped his head toward Ben Pribyl, ". . . I'm just not like you!" The group was familiar with the story of Ben's encounter with Miles Clark in the bathroom at Petrowiak's and they shared one more laugh over the incident.

"Anyway," Will started again when the laughter died down once more. As he'd done for four years, he was playing his audience like a violin. "I'm not wantin' to be standin' there doin' that with Robert. You know, helping him whip it out, 'cuz what if that was the moment Fred Muckinhern chose to walk into the can, and there I am, fondling my retarded patient in the men's room." Will nodded and let his friends savor the image for a moment before he continued. "So I reached down there and gave his zipper a tug, then I jumped back," Will said.

The group around him was silent, stares fixed with anticipation.

"He flopped out the biggest hog you've ever seen! The thing scared me! What a waste—Robert's never gonna use that thing!"

An explosion of laughter blew everyone back into their chairs, and Will raised his voice over the laughter. "Then as I'm watching him handle that python I started worryin' I was gonna hafta help him stow it away when he was done!" The laughter continued at an even higher level when Will finished with, "I just ran out and waited for him to come back. Then about five minutes later I saw Dr. Clark step in there to toss a whiz. When he came out he was talkin' and walkin' with Robert so I figured they were new friends."

As usual, Will Campbell brought the house down. The friends howled with laughter, then they gradually stood up and readied themselves for clinic.

"Hey, Will!" Carol called out for everyone to hear as they all began a slow walk out of the coffee shop.

"Yeah," Will answered.

"Do you have Robert's phone number with you?"

None of them could have known it at the time, but Carol's quip triggered the last laugh they'd share as a group.

Every experience around school was a final one now. Grant saw his last patient in Crown and Bridge clinic later that week, then had the chairman of the department certify that he was finished. Two days later he finished up in Periodontics, and the next day he completed his final project in the Endodontics clinic.

All that remained was to cement his final gold onlay in the Operative clinic. When that was done, school was over and he'd have nothing to do but clean out his locker and wait for the graduation ceremony. He wasn't sure if he felt good or bad while he sat at his lab bench and polished that last shiny bit of gold.

The onlay glistened. It was fully polished and ready to cement in place, like a gold medal he was about to place around his own neck. Grant arranged his instruments, then rearranged them, while he waited for his final patient to arrive. He'd climbed the mountaintop. He'd won the race. He felt there should be party hats and a cake waiting back in the lab when this day was over. But it was just the same routine as every other day in clinic.

"Feels good, Doc!" the patient said an hour later, when he clicked his teeth together and stood up. He thanked Grant, then added, "So, am I gonna be reassigned to a new student when you graduate?"

"Yup. That's the way it works," Grant replied.

"Well, I'll miss you. You did good!" He pointed to his mouth and smiled. "Good luck, Grant." He shook Grant's hand and left the clinic.

Grant knew he'd never see the man again, or any of his patients from the university. He felt a little conflicted about that, too. He remembered Loretta Klitsche, then smiled and dismissed her from his thoughts. He turned and looked at the instruments scattered about his operatory. All that remained of his time in dental school was to clean this up, return the instruments to the dispensary, and have Dr. Miles Clark put the final grade in his Operative clinic book.

He was surrounded by the voices of others who were trying to finish up for the day, too. But he was finished, forever. All the good times and bad times had led him to this one final chore: cleaning spit and blood and dental cement off these instruments. The others working nearby were all third-year students. None of them knew that this was it for him, and no one cared. They were just anxious to be done for the day.

Thirty minutes later Grant was standing in a long line of students, waiting for Dr. Clark to make the final check in his Operative book. Then he'd walk to the office down the hall and hand his book in to the secretary. After that, the world was just empty: no homework, no deadlines, no requirements, no Ebby Rettigs or Miles Clarks to deal with. It felt strange.

There were a few nice guys on the faculty. No, there were a lot of them. In fact, he'd married one of them, and he'd become friends with Muckinhern and Ruminsky. But the Clarks and the Rettigs were the ones everybody remembered.

This line was moving slow, really slow, Grant thought. Kate was waiting for him up in her office. They'd probably go over to Benny's and celebrate a little.

He looked at his watch, then glanced up at Miles Clark. Clark was doing his best to embarrass a younger student in front of his classmates. Grant made eye contact with the student next to him and both of them rolled their eyes. Everyone hated Miles Clark.

Even today, on Grant's last day, Clark had been severely critical of Grant's onlay. Nothing was right—the tooth had been prepared improperly, the onlay itself was poorly designed, even the polish on the gold was incorrect. Clark had made such a strong effort to irritate and embarrass Grant that on one occasion another instructor, an older guy with thin gray hair, had wandered into Grant's operatory after one of Clark's tirades.

"Hey!" the instructor had whispered, motioning for Grant to step away from his patient. "Can I see your work?" the instructor asked when Grant stood up.

"Sure," Grant replied.

Five minutes later the instructor smiled at Grant. "You do nice work, young man," he said. Then he lowered his voice a bit. "I remember when Dr. Clark there was a student, and on the best day he ever had he couldn't do what you've done here. Don't worry about him," the instructor had said.

It was a nice thing to do, talking to Grant like that, and it had made him feel good. But he'd grown callous to clowns like Miles Clark. There had been a time when Clark's abuse would have infuriated him. No longer. Miles Clark was just a rainy day, and Grant was willing to wait until the sun came out again; it always did.

The line was barely moving. Grant looked at his watch again and waited for Clark to finish his character assassination of the student in front of him.

Finally, Clark held his hand out to Grant, as if taking the Operative book from Grant was a terrible imposition. Grant poised himself for the barrage of insults he knew was coming. But Clark did a strange thing. He flipped the book open, signed the last page, and handed it back to Grant. No bullshit. No mean-spirited criticism.

That was it. Everything was finished. Dental school was over. Grant stood and stared for a second.

"There. You're done at last," Clark sneered. "I'll bet when I die you'll come back and piss on my grave."

Everyone in the line froze, waiting for Grant's reply.

"Nope," Grant started, then he made a point to stare directly into Clark's eyes. "I took a vow that when I left this place I'd never stand in line again."

He turned abruptly and walked away while the students still in line stifled their laughter.

CHAPTER 28

As a boy, Grant had heard his mother say it a hundred times: "Funerals aren't for the dead, they're for the living." Over the last few years he'd come to feel that graduation ceremonies were much the same. They were stuffy, uncomfortable affairs designed for parents and other relatives, and their only value was to signal the official start of a graduation party.

Initially, as his graduation day had approached, he thought he'd just as soon skip the whole cap-and-gown thing and get right to the party. He'd done the ceremony with the mortarboard and gown after high school and again after college. All he could remember from either of those two days was standing around, having his picture taken, and wishing it would be over. But now he was beginning to feel otherwise.

Today felt different than those other days. The ceremony today represented something *way* outside the experiences of anyone in his family.

The graduates stood together in alphabetical order at the back of the auditorium, fidgeting with their caps and gowns and waiting for the orchestra to play "Pomp and Circumstance" so they could march in and let their loved ones see them.

Grant looked into the anxious eyes of his classmates, and the weight of it all began to settle on him. The anticlimactic feeling of his last few days in clinic had changed. This was a moment for him to remember, and he wanted to share it with his family.

The band began to play, and one hundred thirty soon-to-be Doctors of Dental Surgery took a slow walk down a long aisle while they searched the auditorium for their families.

"There he is!" came a little voice when Grant was about to be seated up front near the stage.

It was The Jimmer, nearly six years old now. Seated next to Kate, The Jimmer waved feverishly, holding nothing back, his face pure joy. A missing front tooth and some freckles made him look like a Norman Rockwell character. Grant waved back and The Jimmer squealed. It didn't seem possible that he could be so old. It felt like only yesterday that he'd grabbed Kate's breast and embarrassed her in front of everyone, but nearly four years had passed since then.

Grant scanned the faces of his relatives. His brothers and their families sat together, smiling and pointing when Grant looked at them. Gladys smiled like she had at piano recitals and Sunday school plays when he was a child.

Big Ole Thorson met Grant's eyes and let a satisfied little grin lift the corners of his mouth before he nodded his approval. Grant pointed at his dad and returned the nod. Big Ole was so proud of his boy he was about to burst his buttons.

And then there was Kate. The Jimmer was still leaning against her and pointing at Grant. The Jimmer had a thing for Kate, and she loved it. She was part of his family now as surely as if she'd been born into it. She watched Grant and let her eyes tell him how proud she was.

Grant reached his right hand to his chest, tapped his heart and mouthed the words "I love you" just before he took his seat.

He truly wanted to listen to the speaker, but he couldn't hear much. The speaker was famous and brilliant, and he was up there talking about all the challenges the graduates had overcome, and all the great things they would do. But all Grant could hear was a man's voice making background noise.

Surrounded by his classmates, he stared at his hands and thought about all this: the fall he'd taken on Washington Avenue; the friends he'd made; the Twins game where he'd fallen in love; Benny's Deli; the first night Kate had slept with him; their wedding day; Stub & Herb's; that awful day they'd lost a child; all the laughter and good times in that tiny little apartment; and today. He knew Kate was sitting in the audience thinking about all the same things and probably crying. Out of all the people on earth, how had he been lucky enough to find her? Eventually the graduates were invited to walk across the stage and receive their diplomas. Later they adjourned to the large lobby where the faculty at the dental school had provided coffee and cookies. Classmates wandered about, looking for each other to say a good-bye or to introduce their families to their friends. Grant noticed that no one was there for Ben Pribyl, only Tanya the Mauler, and after some fairly emotional farewells with his friends, Ben disappeared into the crowd.

Fred Muckinhern and Joe Ruminsky came looking for Big Ole and Gladys. Grant was pretty sure neither of them would ever forget the way Gladys Thorson had asked them for permission to tell her son that Big Ole had suffered a heart attack.

Will and June made their way over for something of a good-bye, too. Although Will would be staying at the university for three more years to study oral surgery, they'd see each other often when Will and his family came to stay at Spider Lake Duck Camp, not far from Grant and Kate's new home in Walker. Will Campbell was the one friend and classmate that he was sure to stay close to.

"Best friends!" Will whispered, as he wrapped a bear hug around Grant.

"Best I ever had, Pard," Grant whispered. "You just call me if you have any trouble in oral surgery." They laughed and joked for a while, introduced each other to their extended families, and then drifted off in different directions.

Kate was standing alone by a window that faced out onto Washington Avenue when Grant found her. He put his arms around her slender waist and pulled her close. "We made it! Are you ready to move on?" he asked.

She put her cheek against his and nodded. Then she ran her long, soft fingers down the back of his neck several times and whispered, "I'm pregnant."

∾ CHAPTER 29 ∾

June 1979

The U-Haul was just about empty. Thank god, Grant thought. It was hot, unusually hot. The little house was tucked into a stand of white pines on the western shore of Leech Lake, and the nearest neighbors were several hundred yards away in either direction. A breeze off the lake would have made all the difference in the world. But there was no breeze, no cool air to drive off the fatigue. The air was so heavy that even the shade under the giant white pines was hot.

Grant carried the last kitchen chair out of the trailer and put it down on a bed of brown pine needles. Damn, he was hot. He sat down on the chair and breathed in the smell of the pines.

The sum total of his worldly possessions lay scattered about the front yard, like so much debris after a storm. Kate had used money from her job and purchased them a new bed and a kitchen table and chairs, but other than that, all they owned was used furniture, someone else's cast-off things. Someday they'd have nice things, but not yet.

The old green couch was nearly covered by boxes filled with clothing, small appliances, and odds and ends. A tattered set of golf clubs lay beside the couch. Behind that were stacked a few folding chairs. Two ugly table lamps sat on top of two cheap end tables over by another stack of boxes. Maybe other people wouldn't think it was much, but it would be fine for a couple of beginners.

Grant leaned back and surveyed the grounds once more. He crossed his legs, folded his arms, and, trying to ignore the mess in the yard, he took another look at his new home.

Neither big nor expensive, the place was about thirty years old and not particularly well built. The one-story house had cedar shakes for siding, and the trim around the windows was painted green. It was set back about a hundred fifty feet from the lake, with a great view of Walker Bay. The kitchen would catch the morning sunshine and the hills behind would protect them from the west winds during winter. It looked about right to him. It was all he could afford, but it was all he'd ever hoped for.

The best thing of all had been the look in Kate's eyes the first time they came to look at it with the realtor. She tried not to smile when they looked around, and she tried not to smile when they talked about it afterwards, but she couldn't hide her desire. She definitely wanted it.

She was inside now, cleaning the kitchen so they could start putting their dishes in the cupboards. She'd been working hard all day alongside Grant. They'd left Minneapolis that morning at 5:00 a.m., like a couple of Depression-era Okies setting out in search of a better life. Six hours later they'd rolled to a stop here. After a kiss and a moment to stretch, they went about moving into their new life.

There had been only one moment of remorse, one sad good-bye. When the U-Haul was packed and ready to go, they'd walked through the apartment for a final look around. They were leaving a safe harbor and they'd never be back. From the first moment of their friendship, this place had been their refuge. It had seen the best of times, and the worst. They'd risen together there each morning and set out to conquer the world. They'd returned each day, sometimes like battered ships that had survived a storm and reached a quiet shore. But it was time to go, time to move on. They shared a tear and a kiss, and they drove away.

Grant stood up and walked into the house. There was work to do now; he'd think about the old place some other time. He'd take a minute and see what Kate was doing before he carried the rest of their belongings inside.

The kitchen smelled fresh. The countertops and the floor had been scrubbed with some pine-scented cleaner and Kate had begun to put their dishes into the cupboards. Curiosity drove Grant to peek into the refrigerator. Only beer and Coke were in there. He was tempted to have a beer, but that would only slow him down with the job that remained.

He grabbed a bottle of Coke, then found an opener. "Kate!" he called.

"I'm here," she answered from the bedroom she'd decided would be theirs.

Grant sipped the Coke and walked through the living room. There was no furniture inside the place yet, and his footsteps echoed off the hardwood floors in the small house. He glanced out the window and noticed how still Leech Lake was on this blazing summer day. He opened the door that led out to the screened-in porch, hoping to let in some fresh air, but there was no breeze.

Kate was pulling a bedspread over their bed when Grant walked into the room.

"First things first!" she said with a huge grin, and she put her arms around him. He'd never have known she was pregnant if she hadn't told him a few days earlier.

"It's hot in here," Grant said while he held her. He pressed the cold bottle of Coke against her sweat-soaked cotton T-shirt.

"Mmmm," she said, "a little higher."

Grant brushed her hair aside and put the bottle on the back of her neck. She lowered her head and let him move the bottle around on her neck. "Mmmm," she said again.

They stood and held each other for a minute, then two. "You OK?" Grant asked.

Kate nodded yes, then looked into his eyes and smiled a triumphant smile. There was no longer any trepidation about his graduation, or their new life, or leaving the old apartment. She was thrilled, excited about the challenges ahead. "Can you believe we actually did this?" she beamed.

By late afternoon the heavy lifting was done, and Grant hoped it would start to cool off. The day seemed to have grown even hotter. The inside of the little house was clean, and most of their things were piled into the living room instead of scattered across the front yard. But the place felt like an oven.

Grant sat on the arm of the green couch and rested for a second. "One more box to bring in, then let's take a break," he said.

"There's a lot of work to do yet," Kate replied.

"It's been a long day, honey. I'm about outta gas. You've gotta be getting tired, too," Grant said.

"That porch out there is going to be nice, but it smells like tobacco juice and B.O. You're going to have to scrub that up and put some new stain on the walls," she said.

"Yeah, I noticed that too," Grant interjected. "And there's plenty of other things to be done, I know. But we can't do it all today."

"Yeah, but . . . ," Kate started.

A car door slammed out by the empty U-Haul truck and they turned to look out the open door in the front hallway.

A man with wrinkled, leathery skin on his face and a mixture of gray and black hair beneath his baseball cap was walking around the front of his car and toward the house. Grant guessed he was about sixty-five. "You talk to this guy, whoever he is. I look terrible!" Kate said as she turned away and hurried into the bathroom.

Grant walked out the door and met the man on the lawn.

"Hi," the man said. "Are you the new dentist?" He wore khaki pants that had seen some wear. The cuffs on the khakis hovered about an inch and a half above a pair of black, ripple-soled coach's shoes and white cotton socks. His white T-shirt was brand new and his faded green baseball cap had overlapping capital Ws for a logo. This guy was a coach, a lifer, that much was for sure.

"Grant Thorson," Grant said as he offered his hand. He didn't know what to make of this guy.

"Louie Swearingen," the man said with a happy smile. "I live just down the road a bit." He pointed over his shoulder. "The realtor who sold you this place is a good friend. He said you'd be moving in this week so when I saw your truck, well . . ." Louie Swearingen shrugged. "Welcome to Walker."

"Thanks," Grant replied.

"Your wife's a dentist too, I heard?" Louie asked.

"Yeah, that's right," Grant said.

"Heard you played ball for the Gophers, too," Louie said, and the tone of his voice revealed the reason for his visit.

"A long time ago," Grant nodded, and he smiled. Louie already knew a lot about him.

"Well, I was the high school coach here for thirty-seven years. I retired a few years ago. Mostly I fish nowadays, but I still coach the amateur team here," Louie said.

"Town ball?" Grant said. "You have a town team?"

"Yeah, the Walleyes! The Walker Walleyes. Thought you might be interested in playing some ball." Swearingen smiled. He had the happiest face Grant had ever seen. His eyes drooped a bit, but his rumpled face looked as if he was about to share a funny story. "We have a game tonight, too. Wish it wasn't so hot."

"Playing at home tonight?" Grant asked with rising interest.

"Yeah, the ball field is just a bit north of here . . ."

Kate stepped out the front door and walked toward Grant and the stranger.

"Hello," the man said, as he took his green hat off and extended his hand. His eyes moved quickly up and down from Kate's face to the brace on her leg. "Louie Swearingen," he announced once more. "I'm your neighbor, just down the road.

"Welcome to Walker," he reiterated, as he tossed his hat back on. He stood in the shade and talked for a few more minutes. He talked about the fishing on Leech Lake and about the people who used to live in the house Grant and Kate were moving into. Then he got around to baseball and the Walker Walleyes again. It seemed that the Walleyes were a little short on talent, and since Grant had played for the Gophers, maybe . . .

"Well, I'm a little busy tonight," Grant said. "But maybe when we get settled in."

That was a yes as far as Louie Swearingen was concerned, and his face brightened when he turned to leave.

"Hey, Mr. Swearingen?" Kate asked as he was about to get into his car.

"Yeah," he replied, "and it's just Louie."

"It's really hot in there," she pointed at the house, "and I'm too tired to make a meal. Where's a good place to get a sandwich?"

"Tamarac Chateau," Louie said with no hesitation. "It's just north of here about a mile, right on the Ice Cracking River. Close to the ball field, too." He nodded. "Another good spot would be Emil's Diner, in town, but Emil closes up around three in the afternoon." He thought it over for a second, then added, "You'll like the Chateau. Good food, lotsa young people like you." He was about to slide into the front seat of his car when he stood up again. "I hope you can play ball, Grant. Games are usually Thursday and Saturday nights, and Sunday afternoons, with a couple weekend tournaments."

"We'll see. "Pretty busy right now," Grant replied, and he waved good-bye.

"Small towns, huh? He knew all about us. That was nice, I think," Grant said.

Kate waved as Louie drove away, then she looked at Grant. "Do you want to play ball?" She knew the answer.

"Mmm, maybe." Grant shrugged. "Well, yes. I do. I mean, hell yes!"

"Then you should play."

"I'm gonna think about that some other time. For now, I think we should put a few more things in order, then clean up and try to find the Tamarac Chateau," Grant said.

"Sounds really good," Kate said.

~ː~

Only a handful of stars were visible as Kate and Grant made their way across the gravel parking lot at the Tamarac Chateau. The deep woods surrounding the place had gone black, but the summer sky still held a trace of blue. The blistering sun had set beneath the pine trees on the western horizon a few minutes earlier, and a billion stars would soon be twinkling in the summer sky of northern Minnesota.

"Nice night," Kate said. "But it's still really hot."

"Yeah, but it's nice to be done working for the day," Grant replied. He took her hand and they walked across the parking lot.

Music was pulsing though the dark brown rough-hewn logs of the Chateau well before they reached the door, and when Grant swung it open the ambience inside rushed out to greet them.

Loud music blared from several speakers. The Tamarac Chateau was one large, well-lit room. The interior walls were of pine logs and knotty pine paneling, and a soft orange glow from all the wood welcomed them in. About two dozen patrons were spread about at booths and tables, eating and drinking beer. Several young men laughed and carried pool cues around a pool table.

"Just the two of you?" asked a pretty young waitress.

"Is there someplace a little quieter?" Grant asked.

"Sure," she replied. "Follow me." She led them toward a large picture window on the other side of the room and then out onto an open deck overlooking the Ice Cracking River and Leech Lake. "It's a little warm out here. Is this OK?" she asked.

"Perfect," Kate said. The first stars were beginning to appear and they were the only people seated on the veranda. "Just perfect." They seated themselves at a picnic table near the deck railing. Kate asked the waitress to bring a Coke for her, a beer for Grant, and some deep-fried cheese balls, and a couple of hamburgers.

"Ahh. Cheese balls and longnecks," Grant said when the waitress served them. He tapped the neck of his brown beer bottle against Kate's Coke bottle and took a long swallow.

"Wow. Is that good!" he said. "Long day, huh?"

Kate nodded and took a long swig of Coke, then she held the cool glass bottle against her forehead.

"Tired?" he asked.

"A little," she replied.

"Well, try to save some energy for when we get home." He flicked his eyebrows and hinted at sex.

"Sounded funny to hear you refer to it as home," she said with a gleam in her eye.

"Yeah, it did," Grant agreed. "And there is that one special thing we could do to make it feel like our home."

"I was thinking that very same thing," she replied. She held the beer bottle against her chest and let the cool sweat from the glass bottle drip down the cleavage that her cotton dress exposed. "Got some throbbin' started here," she said playfully.

Her appetite for sex had never diminished, except for that one awful time when they'd lost the baby. She was always willing, no, enthusiastic about lovemaking, even on a hot summer night after a long day. She loved the little tease that made him smile, and she loved the way the teasing and playfulness rolled over into something urgent and overwhelming.

Grant knew that Kate's friends would be shocked, flabbergasted, if they ever heard the things she said to him, the little things she whispered in his ear. There was a side to Kate that she could share only with him, and it was thrilling when she chose to do so.

He leaned across the table over his hamburger and beer and whispered, "Well, when we get home, I'm gonna . . ."

"Are you Dr. Thorson?" said a man with a big voice, standing close to him.

"Uh, yes. Well, we're both Dr. Thorson, actually," Grant stammered. He was glad he'd been interrupted before he'd said what he was about to say, and he was embarrassed that he'd almost explained some pretty detailed plans in front of a stranger.

"My name is Pearly DeMoore." The man stuck out a huge hand.

Pearly was a hard man, twisted steel. His hand was about the size of a garbage can lid and it was heavily callused. His arms were big and thick and he'd cut the sleeves off his baseball uniform to reveal the bulging muscles. He was a working man, that much was clear. He had salt-and-pepper whiskers, and Grant guessed he was in his early forties.

"Grant Thorson," Grant said.

"Kate Thorson," Kate said, when her turn came to shake Pearly DeMoore's hand.

"You look like a baseball player, Pearly," Grant offered, when it appeared that Pearly didn't know just what to say next.

"That's right. We just had a ball game." Pearly gestured at the other men wearing baseball uniforms and sitting at a nearby picnic table.

"Yeah, we talked to your coach, Louie, a couple hours ago. So how'd ya do?" Grant asked.

"Took it on the chin pretty good." Pearly shrugged. He couldn't keep his eyes from darting down to Kate's brace several times before he continued. "Louis said he'd had a little visit with you, and that you'd played for the Gophers?" Obviously, Pearly was able to identify them because Louie Swearingen had already told the baseball players that he'd met the new dentist who played baseball and who was married to a pretty lady dentist with the steel brace on her leg. Pearly had just made the obvious connection when he'd walked onto the deck.

"Long time ago," Grant replied.

"Well, we could sure use some fresh arms," Pearly said. He turned toward the other men at his table. "This is Milburne Carrigan, and that's Melbourne Carrigan. They work for me." The two young men had ruddy complexions and red hair. There was no mistaking that they were brothers. They both smiled and nodded.

"You guys related?" Grant asked, then smiled at his own joke.

"Twins," they said at the same time.

"Who's older?" Grant asked.

Milburne raised a finger and said, "Two minutes. I'm the smart one, too."

"Neither one of 'em is exactly a brain surgeon." Pearly laughed along with the twins, then gave Milburne a twenty-dollar bill and said, "Get a coupla pitchers, why don't ya, and we'll talk some baseball." As he sat down at the table with Melbourne he lit a cigarette and added, "Nice meeting you Grant, and Kate. Welcome to Walker, and remember that we can use you on the Walleyes."

"Sure thing." Grant smiled and turned back to Kate.

Kate and Grant finished their hamburgers under the stars while Grant eavesdropped on Pearly and the Carrigan boys' conversation about the baseball game. Grant had another cold beer, and he and Kate discussed the passing of one of the special days in their lives while they planned for tomorrow.

"Oh my God!" Kate gasped a few minutes later, when she swung open the door of their home. "It's still so hot in here. It's like an oven." They'd left windows open when they went to dinner, but there was still no breeze, and the little house refused to cool off. Very few of the older homes in

Minnesota's lake country had air-conditioning because they never needed it, especially homes so close to a large body of water like Leech Lake. But every now and then during a hot stretch, even those who lived on the lakes suffered in the heat.

"Tell you what," Grant said. "Let's put some fans in the windows, try to move some air around, and go sit by the lake for a while." He went to the garage and rummaged through the pile of things that hadn't found a place yet. Ten minutes later they sat on the shore of Leech Lake, side by side in the two rickety lawn chairs Grant had been saving since Kate first visited his apartment.

"It's still pretty hot, even out here," Kate sighed. She pulled her cotton dress away from her chest and fanned herself with it. "It's gonna be tough tryin' to sleep in there." She pointed back to the house.

A silver moon hung over the stillness of the lake, and they sat together, alone. Now and then a dog barked far off in the distance, then a loon somewhere out on the lake would answer with a haunting call.

Grant took her hand and squeezed gently. "Ever been skinny dippin'?" he asked.

"No," she scoffed.

"Well . . . ," he said when he stood up, "tonight will be the first time for you."

"I'm not gonna . . ."

"Sure you are." He pulled his shirt over his head and tossed it in her lap.

"What about the neighbors?" she protested.

"They're five hundred feet away, on the other side of a forest! It's dark, and they're asleep, and they don't even know we're here." He kicked off his tennis shoes and socks, then stepped out of his shorts and threw them in her lap, too.

Kate covered her face with her hands, "We're not really . . ." Before she could finish her sentence Grant was unfastening her brace. Then he stood her up and lifted her dress over her head. "Are you sure? The water's going to be really cold, you know." She tried to protest, but he could hear the excitement growing in her voice.

"That's the idea," he said, as he slid her panties down. Then he held her by the waist and looked at her standing in the moonlight. "Look at you," he sighed. He slid his arm around her waist and prepared to carry her into the lake.

"Wait a minute," she said. She reached both hands up to remove the rubber band that was holding her long hair in a ponytail. She then tied her hair up on top of her head to keep it dry, while he looked at the moon shadows on her naked body.

When they finally stood nose to nose, the moonlight was sufficient for each of them to recognize childish mischief mixing with teenage lust in the other's eyes.

"Ready?" he asked. The soft grass beneath their feet was warm and damp.

"OK," she giggled.

She put her arm around his shoulder and he gently lifted both her feet about an inch off the soft grass and carried her at his side, toward the shimmering black water.

"Ooo, it's gonna be cold!" he laughed, when his toes splashed into the water. His feet settled slowly into the small rocks and gravel on the lake bottom and he took another step.

"Feels good," she said, as the water rose up over her knees. She had both arms around his neck now.

Small waves rippled away from their bodies in concentric circles as he carried her farther into the lake. The water was above their waists now, and the cool water made their skin feel prickly.

"Know how your hands kinda sting on a winter day when you take your mittens off and make a snowball?" Grant asked while he inched out into deeper water.

"Yeah," she replied.

"That's how my nuts feel right now," he said.

A moment later the flat surface of the lake lapped at their chins, and if any neighbors were listening nearby, they'd have heard only the muffled laughter of two lovers.

"This is great," Kate said softly. "It's so cool. I've never felt anything like this, the water feels so good, and I can feel mud and sand, and little plants between my toes." She marveled at all the sensations of walking naked in a cool, clean lake. "How're your nuts?" she asked, giggling at her own absurd question.

"Nuts are fine!" Grant replied. "Just needed some time to get used to the cold water. There's a question I bet you never thought you'd ask anyone." He laughed too, then pulled her close. After a soft kiss on the lips, he stepped back away from her. He was buoyant, or nearly so, and he let the cool water lift him for a moment. Kate felt the water lifting her, too. She held her arms out to the side, then reached toward Grant with a puzzled look on her face.

She walked toward him, chin-deep in the lake, for two steps before either of them realized what she was doing. "Look!" she said, as if she'd found a treasure. "Look at this!" She let go of him and raised her hands out of the water, then took a step on her left leg. There was no bobbing of her shoulders, and no lurching over in preparation to throw the left leg forward with the next step. She walked right up to him, then turned and walked away, then back again, held up by the cool dark water.

"You look like a ballerina," Grant said. "With your hair pulled back like that, and the way you're walking. You don't need to wait till you get to Heaven."

She walked back to him, wrapped her arm over his square shoulders, and said everything she had to say without speaking another word.

❧ CHAPTER 30 ❧

Grant sat by the window and watched for the mailman every day now. Racked with anxiety, he waited for notification that he'd passed his state board examination. He couldn't go to work and start his practice until the people at the Minnesota Board of Dentistry sent the results of his state board exams.

Kate, on the other hand, was busy with patients at the new office, and all Grant could do was bide his time and check the mailbox. He was getting tired of answering questions about why his wife was working and he wasn't.

"Jeez, Kate! What if I flunked the state board exam?" he'd said over coffee that morning. Everybody in town will think I'm an idiot."

"Relax," Kate replied. "You know you did just fine. Your license will be here in the mail any day now." Her words were reassuring and he was pretty sure she was right, but he couldn't relax until he knew for sure.

"Look," she said, when she read the doubt in his eyes, "today you need to look through some of those boxes we haven't opened yet and find your baseball outfit."

"It's not an outfit, it's . . ."

"Whatever," Kate shrugged. "You need to go play ball with Louie and Pearly. Go play with the Walleyes. It'll take your mind off all this. It'll be good for you and you'll have a chance to immerse yourself in the community, maybe meet a few new friends, too. Do it!"

❧

The Walleyes were already stretching and warming up when Grant drove up to the chain-link fence by the ballpark. His legs seemed to move a little faster on their own as he walked across the grass behind the grandstand. He had no control over it. He never had. As a child, if he rode his bike to the park and there were already other boys playing, he'd jump off a moving bicycle and sprint over to join them. As a high school and college player he felt his heart beat a little faster every day when school let out and he could hurry out to play ball. Now he was a grown man with a wife and a job, sort of, and a little hop came into his step on the way to play ball once again.

Louie Swearingen was the first to notice him. "Glad you could join us," Louie called out.

Louie's face looked like a bag of rumpled laundry, a really happy bag of rumpled laundry. His droopy eyes twinkled and some new wrinkles appeared as his smile stretched clear across his face.

"Hope you've got room for one more," Grant said, as he began shaking hands and introducing himself.

College boys home for the summer, young men who'd taken jobs and stayed around town after high school, and a few young businessmen—these were the guys gathered here for baseball. They didn't have much else in common. Nobody here was on their way to the next level, either. This was a far different group than he'd played amateur ball with in Minneapolis or at the university.

Pearly and the Carrigans were the only ones Grant had met before. The Carrigans' faces were covered with sweat and smudge from a long day working in Pearly's plumbing business, and they were happy to be here. Pearly smiled through his two-day growth of gray-and-black whiskers, and he wrapped a huge hand around Grant's once again. "Glad to have you here, Grant. Louie says you can pitch?"

"I can play wherever you need me," Grant replied.

The last of the dozen or so ballplayers to shake Grant's hand introduced himself as the head coach at Walker High School, and said his name was Ray Rivers.

He seemed like a nice enough guy; he was friendly and polite, but the moment he started talking, the other players began drifting off to finish dressing or talk among themselves.

"C'mon Grant. I'll warm up with you," Pearly offered. He led Grant to the right field foul line, where they began stretching their arms and throwing to each other. Unlike all the other players, who wore gray baseball pants and stirrups, Pearly wore baggy blue jeans rolled up with two-inch cuffs. His green baseball cap was more beat up than the green hats worn by the other players, and he wore a gray T-shirt with yellow armpits that couldn't hide the thick muscles in his back and shoulders.

Pearly had a strong arm and a fluid throwing motion in spite of his thick torso. He could play ball. Grant could see immediately that Pearly DeMoore's strength and experience made him the anchor of this bunch.

While he and Pearly warmed up with some long toss, and then took batting practice, Grant scanned some of the other players and made a quick evaluation of the talent on the field.

Milburne Carrigan was a kid with some talent. He ran well and had a nice batting stroke. His own shortcomings and failures seemed to infuriate him, though, and he was quick to fire off colorful combinations of multisyllabic Anglo-Saxon swearwords.

Melbourne could hit some, but he couldn't catch a cold. Grant watched him for a while and couldn't help but wonder if there was something wrong with Melbourne's glove. Melbourne Carrigan was tough, a grinder. Things came hard for him, but he worked until he got the job done, and everyone liked him.

Several high school boys kept to themselves and joked about girls. One of the high school kids didn't belong on this or any other baseball team. Two of the boys were fair, and one of them was a pretty good player.

A young banker who was new in town, like Grant, warmed up with a guy who owned a marina on Leech Lake, and half a dozen college boys who'd come home for the summer made up another little clique.

Ray Rivers walked about with a stern look on his face. He held his chest puffed out while he overanalyzed everything and dispensed unsolicited and unappreciated coaching tips to his teammates.

Maybe one or two of these guys had played ball in college, but none of them, with the possible exception of Pearly, had any significant experience.

"All right, bring it in, guys!" Louie Swearingen hollered. "We'll have a little fungo scrimmage. Then you can take some extra batting practice before you head over to the Chateau."

"Ladies night!" yelled one of the college boys, as he raced out to his position in center field. "Yeah!"

Grant looked around the infield and waited for instructions from Louie. A fungo scrimmage was an excellent idea, he thought. Fungo bats were designed with a long, skinny barrel that was not meant to hit a thrown baseball, but rather to aid coaches in hitting pop flies to infielders and outfielders. The long bats gave an extra dimension of control and accuracy to a coach, and in the hands of an expert, a fungo bat was a great teaching aid. Nine players would take their positions in the field, then Louie would stand in front of home plate and call out a specific situation, such as "Top of the ninth! Tie game! Runner on second! One out!" He would then hit the ball where he wanted to hit it to test the reactions of his players. Fungo scrimmage was a great learning drill for a team like this with only twelve players.

Pearly stood at home plate wearing catcher's gear while he smoked a cigarette and talked with Louie, who had a fungo bat resting on his shoulder.

"OK, Grant," Louie said when all the defensive positions were taken. "You're a base runner to start out. We'll work you into the field after a couple minutes."

Grant jogged to home plate and stood next to Milbourne and one of the college kids who would also start out as base runners. Louie picked up a ball and shouted, "Nobody out! Nobody on! Top of the first!" so that all the players in the field could hear. Then he hit a hard ground ball to the shortstop and hollered "Go!" to Grant. The shortstop fielded the ball and threw it to first base. Grant was out by two steps.

"Runner is out," Louie barked. "Stay there, Grant," he added, then he bent over and picked up another baseball from the pile of balls at his feet. "Runner on first! Two outs. Tie game. Bottom of the eighth!" Louie hollered, as he tossed the ball into the air and hammered it sharply between the center fielder and the right fielder.

Damn, Louie Swearingen meant business, Grant thought, as he raced around second base. There would be no standing around during one of his practices. It didn't matter that Grant had been out on the previous play. Louie told him to stay on first base to set up the next situation he wanted to practice. Now he'd hit the ball exactly where he wanted to, testing all nine of the players on the field. Louie intended to create a play that would result in a close call at home plate, and he was about to see how the position players reacted.

The second baseman ran out onto the grass in shallow right and held both arms up so that the outfielder who picked up the ball could see him immediately when he turned around and needed to know instantly where to throw the ball. The second baseman was identifying himself as the cut-off man. But his back was now turned to the infield and he didn't know what was going on behind him as Grant rounded second base and the other base runner reached first base.

Pearly tossed his cigarette to the ground and bellowed, "Cut four!" He'd just told the infielders all they needed to know; the play would be at home plate. Cut four meant that he was instructing the cutoff man, who was currently standing on the outfield grass facing center field with his back turned on home plate, to catch the ball and then as quickly as he could turn and throw the ball to home plate. A call to cut three would have instructed the cutoff man to turn and throw the ball to third base.

Grant steamed around third base and in the corner of his eye he noticed the cutoff man catch the ball and wheel around toward home in one fluid motion. This would be close, Grant thought. He looked at the plate and tried to read Pearly's body language. Would the throw be late, or high, or in the dirt? Pearly gave nothing away. He stood with his left foot in front of the plate and held his catcher's mitt as a target for the cutoff man. The position of Pearly's feet indicated he was planning to tag Grant with his glove hand as Grant ran by him. This was only a practice drill, so there would be no blocking of home plate and no collisions, but Grant was certain that if this was a real game, Pearly DeMoore would block the plate and challenge a base runner, or a truck, or a train, to run over him.

The throw popped into Pearly's mitt an instant before Grant arrived, and Pearly swiped his glove against Grant's shoulder as he ran past.

"Runner is out! Nice throw, Mike!" Louie yelled to the second baseman who'd served as the cutoff man. "Good hustle, Grant," he added, as Grant walked back toward home plate.

Then Louie Swearingen defined himself. He still held the fungo bat in his hand as he walked out toward the kid who'd been defending the pitcher's position as Grant ran the bases.

"Watch this," Pearly said softly so that only Grant could hear him.

"Butch! C'mere!" Louie said to a timid-looking kid standing on the pitcher's mound. Louie began speaking in a patient tone of voice, but just loud enough that everyone could hear him. "Butch, did you see what Milburne did on that play?" he asked.

The kid stared blankly.

"He followed the base runner down to second base. Do you know why?"

The kid stared again, so Louie answered his own question.

"'Cuz after the runner had rounded first and we were all yellin' 'cut four' he knew we were gonna throw the ball home, right? So he just ran on down to second base."

The kid nodded that he understood that much.

"So at that point we don't need a first baseman anymore, do we? So

Milburne just ran on down there to second base too, so he could be there in case the throw in from the outfield got away from our cutoff man, and he could back up that throw. Understand?"

The kid nodded.

"OK, now think about it. Once that ball was hit to right field, do we need a left fielder anymore? No. But is there a chance for him to help the team if he goes somewhere else? Sure there is! So he sprinted in from left field and took a position over there behind third base just in case something went wrong and the base runner would end up going to third base and maybe the throw to third got away from our third baseman. If he was over there backin' up that throw maybe he saves a run, maybe he saves the game. With me?"

The kid nodded.

"Now, what did you do on that play?" Louie asked.

The kid looked at his feet.

"You stood right here, watching, didn't you?" Louie smiled a stern smile.

The kid nodded.

"Do you know what you should have done?"

The kid looked at his feet and mumbled, "Back up the throw to the plate."

"Exactly!" Louie exclaimed. "Once that ball was hit into right center, we don't need someone to stand on the pitcher's mound anymore do we? You should have hustled back about thirty feet behind Pearly, so just in case Mike's throw got past Pearly you could back *him* up and keep the runner on second base from advancing." Louie nodded to the kid. "You with me?"

The kid smiled for the first time.

"OK then, next time that's the way you play it. Nine men in motion, that's how you play the game!" Louie said as he walked back to home plate.

"Helluva coach," Pearly whispered to Grant. "Every one of those young guys out in the field learned something and Louie didn't have to wipe his feet on anybody, like a lot of coaches would." He glanced up at Ray Rivers, standing by third base.

Before anything else could be said, Louie raised the bat to his shoulder and barked, "Runner on second! Two outs! Bottom of the ninth." He hit another ball into the outfield and watched as the kid on the pitcher's mound raced behind Pearly to back up the throw.

"Perfect! Just perfect, Butch!" Louie hollered to the kid after the play was over. He winked at Pearly and barked out another situation as he tossed another ball into the air.

After a thirty-minute fungo scrimmage the players split up into small groups and Grant went with the outfielders. Each player in Grant's group took his turn while a teammate hit fly balls for them to catch. He'd only caught a few balls and was talking to one of the college boys in the outfield when they heard angry voices begin to rise up from the infield.

Ray Rivers had been throwing batting practice, and now he stood on the pitcher's mound with his hands at his sides while an animated young man stood in the batter's box by home plate. "Goddammit, Ray! This is batting practice!" the kid screamed, and everyone stopped to watch.

Ray pointed at the kid and said something that the outfielders couldn't hear clearly, then he laughed.

The kid at the plate dropped his bat and started walking for the dugout. "Fuck you, Ray!" the kid yelled, then he turned to Louie Swearingen. "I quit, Louie. You can take this town team, and Needledick out there, and cram it all up your ass! I don't need this!" He picked up his duffel bag and stormed off the field toward his car with another player in tow.

"What was that all about?" Grant asked the college boy standing next to him.

"Aw, shit," the college boy sighed. "That was classic Ray Rivers, and there go our two best young players."

"I don't get it," Grant said.

"Ray likes to make those guys look bad in batting practice. He pitches to them like it was a game, instead of just throwing easy strikes so they can work on their swings. He likes to strike 'em out and then ridicule them."

"Why?" Grant asked.

The college boy shrugged. "He likes to make good players look bad. He's just a stupid prick. I guess it makes him feel like he's better than some-one." The kid looked into Grant's eyes, smiled, and added, "We had a phys ed teacher when I was in elementary school who always made the retarded girl in our class be the goalie when we played soccer. Then he'd join in the game so he could score a goal against the retarded girl and then celebrate like he'd just won the World Cup for his team. You figure that out. I don't get it either, but that's the kind of shit Ray does."

Everyone drifted back into their practice routine as the two ballplayers who'd quit the team drove away.

An hour later Grant stood on the pitcher's mound as the summer sun dipped below a stand of pine trees out beyond the left field fence. Practice had been fun, in spite of the incident with Ray Rivers. Mantle had been there again, and Koufax and Killebrew and all the others. Every ground ball that came his way during infield practice was part of the same old fantasy that played itself out in Grant's imaginary World Series. Every outfield fly ball had given him reason to run through the green grass of Yankee Stadium, or Fenway Park, or Wrigley Field, again. Every pitch in batting practice flew off his bat and triggered dreams of thunderous ovations from a large crowd. He loved this stuff; he always had, he always would.

"Glad you came tonight, Grant," Louie offered as he strolled toward the mound. "You'll fit right in."

"He'll dominate in this league," Pearly said. He'd been catching Grant for the last few minutes of practice while Grant worked on his pitching mechanics. "He still throws hard and he can move the ball around. Nice hook, too. Really nice!" Pearly added, referring to Grant's curveball.

"That's great. You're pitching on Sunday then," Louis smiled. "And ask your wife if she'd like to work in the concession stand," he added, before Grant could register an objection.

"OK," Grant shrugged, and the three men began picking up the bats and balls lying around in front of the dugout.

"Hey. Gotta ask you guys something," Grant said, while he stuffed the last of the seven bats into a canvas bag. "What's the deal with Ray Rivers? He's the high school coach, right?"

"What do you mean?" Louie asked without looking up from the bag of baseballs in his hand.

"Well, he talks all the time, but nobody ever answers him or listens to him," Grant said.

"Ray," Pearly scoffed, as if Ray's name left a bad taste in his mouth.

Louie remained silent.

"He seems to offer a lot of unwanted coaching tips to the other players," Grant said.

Pearly started talking while he was still looking through his duffel. "Well, all of the high school boys who've played for him hate his guts, and the college boys who have some talent have defected; they play over in Windigo now. They just won't be around him." Pearly lit a cigarette, sat on the bench in the dugout, and leaned back before he continued. "He doesn't know shit about baseball, and he knows even less about dealing with the boys who play for him."

Grant stole a glance at Louie, who hadn't looked up yet.

"Louie's too much of a gentleman to say anything," Pearly said, continuing a conversation he knew Louie wouldn't touch. "He doesn't even like to hear me say this kind of stuff." Pearly took a long drag and exhaled a cloud of smoke. "But think about what you saw tonight." Pearly pointed the cigarette at Grant. "Remember when Butch . . . what's his last name?"

"Metcalf," Louie answered.

"Yeah, Butch Metcalf. Remember when we first started the scrimmage and Butch didn't know enough to go back up the throw at the plate? Well, he's a senior in high school! He's been playin' for Ray Rivers for two years, and he didn't know what to do! Back when I played for Louie Swearingen we learned that stuff in elementary school." Pearly finished the cigarette with one more enormous drag, then he threw it on the floor of the dugout. "On top of that, if it had fallen to Ray to instruct the Metcalf kid he'd have gotten it all wrong and then blamed the kid for not knowing what to do." Pearly shook his head in disgust, bent over, and began removing the catcher's shin guards from his legs. "The thing that really chaps my ass is that Ray really thinks he's all it! He thinks he really knows his baseball and everybody likes him. What a fool."

"He's still learning, too," Louie Swearingen said, like a true gentleman.

"Pretty slow learner, Louie," Pearly groaned.

~:~

Kate was in the shower when Grant got home after baseball practice. He took a cold beer from the refrigerator and made his way through the darkened house toward the screened-in porch.

The smell of tobacco juice and body odor was gone from the little porch now. He'd scrubbed it and covered all the decking with a new coat of stain. A summer breeze whispered through the tree boughs and carried the fresh scent of pine through the screens. Grant turned on the radio next to his Adirondack chair and waited for the voice of Herb Carneal to fill the dark night air on the porch. The Twins were playing out West tonight and the game was just starting. He popped open the beer, kicked off his shoes, and listened. The Twins had traded Rod Carew, a sure Hall of Famer, only a few months earlier because they couldn't afford to keep their best player. The days of Killebrew and Zoilo Versailles and Mudcat Grant were over, long gone. The Twins would never be any good again. But they were his team, they always would be, and Herb was still around to fill his summer nights with pleasant dreams.

When Kate appeared at the screen door several minutes later, she was carrying an envelope. She wore an oversize gray sweatshirt and baggy shorts over her leg brace.

"Look what the mailman brought," she said, as she waved the envelope at him. "I found it in the mailbox, after you'd left for baseball practice."

"From the board of examiners?" Grant asked, then sat straight and reached for the envelope.

Kate nodded and smiled. "I thought you'd want to open it."

This was it, Grant thought, the results of his state board exam. If he'd passed, he could get on with his life and start seeing patients immediately. He'd finally be a grown-up. If he'd flunked, well, that would be catastrophic. He'd have to take the boards over again in a few months, he'd be ashamed that he'd flunked such an important test, and he'd have to suffer the indignity of letting Kate support him while he waited for a second chance. This was a big deal.

Grant set his empty beer can down on the end table next to the radio and took the letter from Kate. She flipped a switch and turned on a small lamp beside the radio so Grant could see to read the letter. Her face glowed with expectation as she watched him open it.

"What if I flunked?" He stopped with the envelope half open.

"Open it up!" Kate demanded, as if he'd just said the dumbest thing she'd ever heard. Grant tore the end all the way off the envelope, pulled out a single piece of stationery, and stared blankly for several seconds. Then he read one word, "Congratulations . . ."

Kate jumped to her feet and screamed as though she'd hit the jackpot. She pulled Grant up from his chair and hugged him. She squealed and laughed and kissed his cheek.

The joy and enthusiasm in her celebration moved him. He was thrilled to receive the news. A piano had been lifted off his back. Now, and only now, could he actually get on with his life.

Kate kissed him and stroked his back. She told him over and over again how proud she was, and he began to see something in all this that was far more important than passing the state board exam. It was the thing that held them together, the thing that made her his wife; his joy was her joy. Only someone who really loved him could understand something like this. She was ecstatic for one simple reason: he'd just had a great moment of success. It was his moment, but she was living it also. What was going on between them right now was more powerful than sex; it hinted at the mystery of how two people loved each other.

It was too late for them to call anyone when their little celebration died down, so they sat in the dark and talked about the future while Herb Carneal described a baseball game halfway across the country. They talked about their work schedule at the office and what new equipment they should buy, and they dreamed about the day they might be able to make enough money to pay off their student loans, and their huge loan for a dental practice, and their mortgage. The future was spread out before them now, and for the first time the path seemed well marked. Tonight they could dream all their dreams.

"I want to tell you something," Grant said, when the pauses in their conversation began to lengthen.

"Hmmm?" Kate sighed. She was slumped in the Adirondack next to his.

"A long time ago, I think I was about fourteen, I got moved up to play ball with the older kids. I was bigger and stronger than some of them even though I was three years younger than a couple of 'em."

"You're gonna tell me a baseball story? Now?" she asked.

"I'm getting at something, honey, bear with me for a minute."

Kate ran her soft fingers along the back of his hand and waited.

"OK, so I got to play with the older kids for the first time, and the coach made the huge mistake of letting me bat fourth. The guy who bats fourth is called the cleanup hitter; he's supposed to be one of your best hitters . . ."

"I knew that," Kate interrupted.

"So anyway," Grant continued, "the kid pitching for the other team was a senior in high school, and a pretty good pitcher. I took a called strike on his first pitch, then I fouled a pitch off. I hit that second one hard, it just went foul. So then the count was no balls and two strikes, and that kid threw me a big old curveball. I thought that thing was gonna hit me right in the head, so I bailed out, dropped to the dirt to get out of the way." Grant stopped and laughed softly.

"What happened?" Kate asked.

"That curveball broke right over the plate! Strike three!" Grant laughed again. "The catcher laughed at me. The guys on the other team laughed at me. The umpire laughed at me. Hell, my coach was laughing at me when I moped back over to the dugout. I'd never had a good curveball thrown at me before. Scared the shit outta me." Grant sighed. "The pitcher who threw that ball? Nice kid. I still remember his eyes. He felt sorry for me. But he struck me out four more times anyway."

"And the point is?" Kate asked.

"I'm still getting to that. So it turns out that my brother Paul was there that day. He was just home from college and he came to watch me play. Well, after the game, Paul gave me a ride home and I cried in his car. I was so embarrassed. I asked him not to tell Dad about any of this stuff, the striking out and the crying. So the next day Paul took me out and threw me about a thousand curveballs, and after a while I started to hit one every now and then. Later on he showed me how to throw a curve. We had a great day. He was just my brother that day; all he wanted to do was help me. 'Bout two years later I hit a home run that won a game and Paul was there that day, too. It was just a meaningless American Legion game between two scrubby little towns, but it was still pretty cool to hit a walk-off home run. Anyway, as I was rounding third base I saw all my team-mates gathering around home plate, and there was Paul standing there with 'em. He had the greatest smile on his face. I'll never forget it, and he was just happy for me, not because we won the game, but because I did a good thing."

Grant squeezed her hand. "That's how you know who your friends are," he added. "That's how you know who really loves you . . . when something good happens to you and they're just as happy as you are." He paused. "That's why I told you that story, Kate. Because I saw that same look in your eyes tonight when I opened that letter. I've seen it there a hundred other times, too. I just wanted to tell you how that made me feel."

"Well, you're my best friend," Kate smiled.

CHAPTER 31

"What are you doing?" Kate asked. "Trying to stare the print off that page?" She'd found the door to their small private office open just a sliver, and when she peeked in she found Grant standing there with an open book in his hands.

Grant looked up from the book and smiled sheepishly. "Just reviewing my oral surgery technique," he said with a puzzled look.

"Let me guess," Kate said. "You're about to try something you've never done before, right?"

"Pretty much," Grant replied. "I've got a woman back there getting numb, waiting for me to come and extract her tooth." His eyebrows furrowed with self-doubt. "But I've never even seen one like this before, maxillary first molar, broken off right at the level of the bone." He reached out, pulled Kate into the office and gently closed the door. "What do I do?"

A smile spread across Kate's face as she picked up a scrap of paper and a pencil, then drew a picture of a fractured molar. "First of all, you section it into three separate roots." She held up the picture and added, "Like this! Then you go get the trusty 301 elevator and put it right in here." She used her index finger to approximate the correct angle. "A little twist, and the roots will lift right out." Kate smiled and nodded.

He stepped forward and kissed her softly on the lips. "Turns me on when you tell me what to do," he teased.

"Do you want me to come in there and show you?" Kate asked, ignoring his joke.

"No. I already told her I do these kinds of extractions all the time, but I had to get up and leave the room so I could explain something to *you*," he teased again, and he tried to inch past her and move out the door.

"Well, at least you didn't flip through the book while she was watching." Kate stepped in Grant's path and added, "You're welcome for the lesson, too."

"Oh, I intend to reward you, later." Grant's eyes sparkled. "You might even get a nice tip! Did you catch the sexual innuendo . . . ?"

"Get to work," Kate said. "Come and get me if you need some help." She stepped out of his way.

"Sure thing, Doctor," Grant said without looking back.

He came to her often during the first few weeks after he started practicing. They spent every noon hour drawing teeth on the napkins at the tables of the restaurants and coffee shops where they shared lunch. Grant had new questions every day about techniques and materials he was just learning to use.

"What would I do without you?" he laughed one day over lunch at Emil's Diner in downtown Walker. "I actually thought I was ready for the real world when I graduated. But I don't know anything." He used a French fry to push some ketchup around on his plate, and he let her see the frustration on his face.

"Oh, that's not true. You know all the basics. You'd figure out all the rest. You're a thinker." She waved at a waitress and asked for more water, then added, "You'll learn more in the next six months than you did in four years of dental school. Then you'll learn twice that in the next six months."

"So then I'll know as much as you?"

"No, you'll never know that much." Both of them laughed for a moment, then Kate said, "That's the way it is . . . you just keep learning new things. You wouldn't want it any other way, you know. The real losers in life are the ones who think they know everything on the day they graduate, so they make it a point to never learn another thing."

Grant was looking down at his French fries when he replied. "Well, I know I've got a lot to learn in the next few months so I can run our practice after you have the baby. It'll be really awkward if I have to ask my patients to put a finger on their bleedin' tooth while I run to the phone and ask you what to do next." He looked up expecting to see her smiling, but she had no smile to give.

"What is it? What's the matter?" he asked. Her moods had been a bit fragile, he was aware of that much. Maybe he'd put too much pressure on her by suggesting that she was responsible to lead him through the first year or two of private practice.

"Oh, I just get a little overwhelmed sometimes," Kate replied. "I don't feel very good in the morning. Some smells, usually smells in the kitchen, make me sick to my stomach." She paused and looked around the restaurant. "And I'm just not used to this small-town stuff yet. Everybody knows who I am, and where we live. It wasn't like that in Minneapolis."

"Do you think that's a bad thing?" Grant asked.

"I don't know yet, but I'm sure having a time getting used to it. People just walk up and start talking to me. It's odd," she said.

"It'll be fine, Kate. These are good people. I guess I don't notice those things like you do because I grew up in a town like this. I knew every kid in my high school. I knew where they lived and I knew their parents. That's not a bad thing. It's just what it is. People in small towns know each other, it's OK. Look how I turned out!" he said, trying to draw a smile from her.

Kate looked up, nodded, and tried to smile.

"It's something else, isn't it?" Grant asked.

Kate nodded. Grant waited.

"You're afraid of having this baby, too, aren't you?" Grant finally asked. "You're afraid that something might go wrong, like before?"

"Yeah, that's been on my mind," Kate answered. "I'd be lying if I said I didn't think about that. But that's not it."

"What is it, then?" Grant asked.

Kate looked a bit tortured, as if she was about to confess a terrible sin. "I don't want to work after the baby is born," she said. She never raised her eyes up from her plate.

"So?" Grant said.

"I mean I want to stay home and be a mother, full time, for now," she explained.

"Yeah?" Grant said. He knew he'd have to choose his words carefully from here on. There was a lot going on in Kate's head, a quantum shift in her values and self-image. The modern woman was supposed to work outside the home. Recent social changes dictated that a woman get an education and then go to work. Stay-at-home mothers were regarded as just a little bit less, a little bit shallower than working mothers. No one wanted to claim that attitude as their own, but it was out there. And now his wife, who'd struggled with self-esteem issues her whole life, was talking about leaving her career and all that she'd worked for behind so she could be a stay-at-home mother.

She was struggling with some old demons again. Kate had acquired success and self-esteem through hard work. She'd finished at the top of her class in college and dental school. She'd landed an impressive job at a young age and had been looking at a fairly certain climb though the academic hierarchy at the university.

Then, only a few months ago, she'd turned away from the promise of a successful career. She left it all behind so she could live and work in a tiny town by an Indian reservation. Now she was telling him she wanted to finish the complete about-face and stay home with her child.

Actually, the idea made perfect sense to him, and he was happy to have her bring it up. But he knew very well that she was conflicted by it all.

"Sounds like a good idea to me," he said with a shrug.

"We can't afford this, not now." Kate invited her conflict into the discussion. "I should never have gotten pregnant . . ."

"Kate, don't do this to yourself," Grant interrupted. "We both know the numbers from the office, and we both know that we *can* afford to do this. 'Sides that, Walker is a *little* town. They don't need two new dentists here right now. Maybe in a few years when the kids are older and the practice is really busy you'll want to come back." He shrugged.

"Kids?" Kate smiled. "That sounded funny . . ." She reached across the table and took his hand. "Our *kids,* our family." She repeated the words and Grant knew she'd chased the demons away for a while.

"There's something going on in here that I can't really explain." She tapped her hand on her heart. "I want to be a good mother. I want to give our children a home like the one you grew up in, not like mine. I want to be there when they learn to talk, and walk, and I want to be there when they come home from school so I can make cookies, things like that. I want our children to know that I love them." She hesitated for a second. "My mother told me over and over again that I was just a bother and she didn't know why she ever had children."

"Are you asking for my permission?" Grant asked.

"Maybe," Kate replied. "It's just that we may never pass this way again and . . ."

"We'll make it work," Grant said.

CHAPTER 32

A thin, smoky cloud carried the rich smell of bratwurst and hamburgers cooking over a charcoal grill. Two dozen baseball fans had gathered at the Walker ballfield for an evening game between the Walker Walleyes and the Menahga Deerflies. Kate Thorson, the new lady dentist, was making friends while she tended the concession stand, about fifty feet from the grandstand.

When she'd arrived at the ballpark, Louie Swearingen had dropped what he was doing and hustled over to the concession stand. He had opened the doors and swung open the service window. He'd given her some quick instructions about the operation of the charcoal grill, the electric frying pan, and the cash box. Then he'd given her the keys and dashed back to his duties on the baseball field. At that point it was clear that she wasn't just working at the concession stand. She was the entire concession staff.

Two high school girls with long, tan legs and very short shorts stood together by the grandstand, talking to an old woman with a dachshund on a leash. Players wandered about in their uniforms, preparing for the game and visiting with fans who straggled in, one and two at a time.

Twenty minutes earlier Kate had watched an old man get out of his car and walk slowly over to the concession stand to introduce himself to her. "I'm Woodolf Waysno. You must be the new wady dentist?" She smiled while she shook his hand and deduced that he had a pretty impressive speech impediment— his name was actually Rudolph Roesner. While he talked with her, Kate looked Rudolph Roesner up and down and guessed that he either got dressed in the dark or didn't have a mirror at home. He wore a green baseball hat with overlapping W's, a paisley shirt, and plaid Bermuda shorts. Spindly, hairless gray legs connected the plaid shorts with black wingtips and black socks. He was a sweet old man, and he explained to Kate that everyone just called him Speed, and he'd been in charge of the public address system *and* the scoreboard for twenty-seven years. He told a few stories about the rich history of the "Waweyes," then ascended a wooden staircase that led to a decrepit plywood press box above the Wall-eyes dugout. Several minutes later the scoreboard in left field came to life and "The Clarinet Polka" began scratching its way out of the army surplus public-address speakers hanging from two light poles near home plate.

Kate placed mustard and ketchup and a few condiments on the countertop beside the window of the concession stand, and she was about to go check the brats she was cooking when a man's voice said, "Hi. What's for supper?"

She turned back to the window and saw a very round man dressed as an umpire smiling at her.

"Hi," Kate said.

The man's eyes darted down to the brace on her leg, then back to her face. "You're the new lady dentist!" the man said. He thrust his hand out and added, "I'm Tubby Voss, nice to meet you." Tubby felt like an old friend the moment he smiled at her. He was polite and soft-spoken, and she guessed that he weighed three hundred fifty pounds. She sold the friendly umpire three brats and watched him smother them with sauerkraut and onions.

"This here's my partner, Bud Pearson," Tubby said, and he started cramming the first of the brats into his mouth.

Tubby's partner was dressed as an umpire, too. He had a ruddy sunburned face and a friendly smile, just like Tubby. But instead of a left hand he had a stainless steel prosthetic hook. "Nice to meet you," Bud said.

"Bud, this here is Kate Thorson, she's the new dentist in town. I just seen Louie over there and he told me Kate's husband would be pitching tonight," Tubby said between bites.

Kate sold Bud Pearson a hamburger, chatted for a moment, and then watched the two umpires seat themselves at a nearby picnic table and talk about fishing on Leech Lake, while the players continued to warm up and a few more fans wandered in.

During a lull in the pregame action at the concession stand, Kate rested her elbows on the windowsill and looked about. Approximately three dozen baseball fans, mostly girlfriends and parents of the players, walked around on the grassy area between the grandstand and the concession stand. They talked about everything, and nothing. They bought treats from her, and introduced themselves. Several players did the same. This small-town stuff was still pretty new for Kate and she wasn't sure what to think. But as people returned to her window a second and then a third time, she found that she remembered their names, and she liked that.

She was still staring out the window when she noticed Grant walking her way. He looked good in his green-and-gray uniform. He stopped and sat down at the picnic table with the umpires. They shook hands and laughed when somebody said something about Pearly DeMoore. Then Grant stood up and said, "Yeah, that's right, I'm pitching, so pay attention." The umps laughed and went back to their dinner as Grant walked away.

"Do you know those guys?" Kate asked when Grant stepped up to the window.

"Just met 'em," he answered. "Thought I'd say hello."

"I thought umpires were the enemy," she whispered.

"Works out that way sometimes," Grant said. "But usually they're trying just as hard as the players are to get things right." He reached out and pulled Kate close enough to steal a kiss. "Summer was invented so you could wear that dress," he said. "I gotta start throwing. I love you." He started toward the bullpen. "Prettiest girl in the ballpark," he said over his shoulder.

"You look really nice in your baseball outfit!" she teased when he was thirty feet away. Grant simply covered his ears and kept walking.

Twenty minutes later the Walleyes were assembled in their dugout, waiting for the boys from Menahga to finish their infield practice.

"You ready?" Louie asked Grant.

"He's got it workin', Louie. They won't touch him," Pearly answered before Grant could.

Louie Swearingen turned his attention back to the scorebook in his hand, and Pearly lit one last cigarette.

"Menahga's a good baseball town," Pearly offered. "Lotta Finlanders down there. Those guys are tough as hell." He exhaled a cloud of smoke.

"What does that have to do with anything?" Grant asked.

"Nuthin'." Pearly smiled. "I guess it don't mean shit."

Grant chuckled and looked at the row of players sitting next to him. Some were making final adjustments to their uniforms or their gloves. Some sat quietly and chewed sunflower seeds. A couple of the college boys were talking about girls and what they planned to do after the game. Ray Rivers offered inane insights and incorrect information while everyone tried to ignore him.

"Wanna know how this is gonna play out tonight?" Pearly asked Grant. The Deerflies were nearly finished with their infield practice. Their coach was standing in front of home plate hitting ground balls to the infielders and calling out just what he wanted them to do when they fielded the ball.

"Tell me," Grant said.

"OK. Numbnuts Ray over there has got one of his high school players playin' third base . . ."

"Doesn't Louie make out the lineup and decide who's playin'?" Grant interrupted.

"Yeah, pretty much. But Ray's really pushy, and he thinks because he's the high school coach he should be able to use this amateur team to help develop his program. You know what a nice guy Louie is, so he gives Dingelnuts a little say-so with the Walleyes."

"OK, I can understand that," Grant nodded.

"The thing is, Ray is always wrong and everybody hates him. He's the most universally disliked and disrespected person I ever met." Pearly grew more animated as he spoke.

"He takes himself pretty serious," Grant offered.

"Just wait till you see him in action." Pearly shook his head in disgust. "He actually dislikes good players."

"C'mon, Pearly, no coach dislikes good players," Grant objected.

"Just wait, you'll see," Pearly said again. "Like I started to tell you, here's how it works. Every so often he'll have a player that's pretty good. He starts to reason that the kid has already had enough good things said about them, and enough praise. So he sets out to diminish him. I'm guessing he was just a shitty player himself, and now he's using his position to get even with all those guys who were better than him. You know, right some old wrongs."

Grant stared at Pearly.

"It's true! Just watch. He'll try to reduce the better players by elevating some kid of his own choosing who has no talent, then giving that kid unlimited praise while he's unmerciful in his criticism of the better players. You know, like if he says stupid shit over and over again it'll come true?" Pearly tossed his last cigarette onto the dugout floor before it was the Walleyes' turn to take their pregame infield drill. "Just listen to Dipshit when we're taking infield. I can hear it already." Pearly shook his head in disgust. "He's got some kid penciled in over at third base. I haven't seen the kid play in a game yet, but I'll bet the farm he's weak, he's afraid of the ball, and all during the infield chatter Ray is gonna be over on first base

yammering about how 'hard-nosed' the kid is. It's his favorite thing to say."
Pearly's face soured up like he'd just sucked a lemon. "I hate that guy."

The coach for the Deerflies waved to Louie when he was done hitting infield for his team, then followed his team back into the visitor's dugout so the Walleyes could take the field for their practice.

The Walleyes grabbed their gloves and ran out to take their positions for infield. Only Grant, who would be pitching to start the game, and three substitute players remained in the dugout.

What a scene, Grant thought. An orange sun was about to set behind a row of pines out in left field. The Ice Cracking River rolled smoothly along beyond the right field fence, then it emptied into the big water of Leech Lake. All that natural splendor stood in sharp contrast to the polka music, the PA system, the scoreboard, and the Walleyes.

Pearly DeMoore held a burning cigarette between his lips while he caught the baseballs that were thrown back in toward home plate. Grant had never seen anyone smoke during pregame infield practice, and he studied Pearly for a moment. Pearly resembled somebody, but who? Li'l Abner, maybe? No, Pearly looked good in his uniform, it fit him nicely, he exuded power and strength with the sleeves cut off his uniform to reveal those biceps. Pearly caught a ball and flipped it to Louie, and Grant made the connection; Pearly looked like Ted Kluszewski, the powerful first baseman of the Cincinnati Reds during the 1950s. "Hmph, Ted Kluszewski," Grant said to himself before he diverted his eyes to Louie Swearingen.

Louie wore the usual khakis with cuffs, a gray T-shirt, his ripple-soled shoes, and his ancient green hat. He hit ground balls and called out exactly what he wanted to be done by the player who caught the ball. "OK, take it to first base!" Louie hollered before he hit a slow roller to the third baseman.

The ball rolled between the third baseman's legs.

"Bad hop!" came the alibi from Ray Rivers over on first base.

"Again!" Louie said, as he gave the third baseman a second chance with another easy ground ball.

The ball bounced about waist high, a Sunday hop, as the players called it when a ball jumped up to their glove and made the play painfully easy, but this time the ball bounced out of the kid's glove. He picked it up in a clumsy stumbling motion, took too long to set his feet, and then threw the ball about fifteen feet short of first base.

"Hey! Hard-nosed! Atta way to stay with it, Todd," Ray Rivers yelled from first base. The kid had done everything wrong, and Ray was praising him for the only thing he could, for finally picking up the ball and throwing it in the general direction of first base.

Pearly turned as deliberately as he could toward Grant, lowered his hands, and looked at Grant as if he were trying to peer over the top of imaginary bifocals. See what I mean, Pearly said with his gesture.

Grant shrugged his shoulders and nodded his understanding for Pearly to see. But he didn't really care about the kid at third base right now. He was just happy to be playing ball.

When Grant went to the mound for his final warm-up pitches, the bleachers held maybe thirty Walleye faithful and a dozen fans who'd driven over from Menahga. Speed Roesner played a scratchy old cassette tape of the national anthem over the public-address system, and the game was underway.

When the Walleyes tumbled back into the dugout for the bottom of the first inning, Milburne Carrigan was barking, "Shit! Bastard-ass rat fucker!" He was so angry that his shoulders twitched like he was having a back spasm when he cussed. The Menahga Deerflies had scored six runs without getting a base hit, and left the bases full in the top of the first.

"Dammit!" Melbourne Carrigan added. "Bad defense is like the flu. When one of us gets it, we all catch it!" He started sorting though the bats on the bat rack and added, "We gotta score some runs!"

Pearly sat down next to Grant and sighed, "I told you so."

The third baseman had made three errors and probably could have been charged with two more. "This guy takes the cake! He's the worst one Ray's come up with yet."

"Maybe he's just nervous," Grant said.

Pearly grimaced and looked away before he lit another cigarette. "You know that's not the problem," Pearly said, adding, "I told you it was gonna happen."

Grant could only nod in agreement. The kid playing third base was terrible, and Ray's blathering was beginning to bother him, too. To make things worse, bad defense *was* like the flu. Everybody in baseball knew that. But it worked the other way also. Sometimes a great defensive effort lifted the level of play for an entire team. However, as Grant looked at the faces in that dugout, he got the feeling that no one in there had the talent or desire to play at a higher level. They were already beaten.

~:~

Milburne and Melbourne were slowly raking the dirt around home plate and the pitcher's mound while Pearly sat in the dugout and stuffed his catcher's gear into a large duffel bag, twenty minutes after the game ended.

Louie stood next to the bat rack on one end of the dugout and made notes in the scorebook. Grant sat by himself in the middle of the dugout, staring at the tops of his shoes.

Everyone else had wandered away within minutes after the final out, and now only this handful of Walleyes stayed behind to rake the infield and stow the equipment away until the next game. The ballpark lights were still on, but the bleachers were empty and Speed had turned off the scoreboard and, mercifully, the polka music. The Carrigans were talking softly between themselves while they smoothed out the bumps and ruts in the dirt.

"Grant, you threw a three-hitter and we got beat twelve to nine. That might have been the worst defensive effort I've ever seen," Louie said, analyzing the scorebook.

Now that the concession stand was closed, Kate walked around the corner of the dugout and made her way over to Grant. She adjusted the knee joint of her leg brace and sat down beside him without a word. She opened a beer and gave it to Grant.

"I don't think the kid on third base could catch a cold," Grant said after a swig of beer. "I'll bet he had seven errors."

"Actually, it was eight," Louie said, without looking up. "I was just checking the scorebook. I always have to go back and check it after Ray's had his hands on it."

"Lemme guess," Pearly grumbled. He was walking around the dugout and putting the Walleyes' batting helmets in a large canvas bag, one at a time. "Ray tried to protect ol' Hard-nosed over there at third base, so he decided that those three grounders that rolled between his legs should be recorded as base hits, instead of errors on his boy, so he just doctored the scorebook?"

Louie nodded.

"Did you have fun?" Kate asked Grant.

"Sure did," Grant replied.

"I think you were the best one," Kate teased, and she put her arm around Grant's shoulder.

Louie looked up from the scorebook and grinned at the way she'd said the words.

"And you did look really cute in your baseball outfit," she teased again.

"So what about you?" Grant asked. "How was your evening in the concession stand?"

"Oh, I had a little conversation with every person who walked up to the window, mostly girlfriends of the players and a few parents. We talked about the weather, and the fishing, and just about everything else. Several strangers walked up to the window, stuck a finger in their mouth, and started telling me about teeth that had been bothering them. I didn't know if they were asking for advice, or if they thought I just liked to hear about dental pain," Kate said.

"Yeah, people do that all the time," Grant said. "When they find out you're a dentist they stick a finger in their mouth and tell you some awful story about a toothache."

"Well, maybe you should just be thankful you're not a proctologist," Louie replied without looking up from the scorebook. He chuckled at his own joke.

"The umpire was a good customer!" Kate offered.

"Tubby?" Pearly guessed, then he laughed along with Louie.

"Tubby's a good umpire," Louie said while he laughed about Tubby's appetite. "So's Bud Pearson. I'd have 'em for every game if I could, but I need to mix it up a bit and have a few other crews in here from time to time."

"I met Speed, too," Kate said, and she turned and waited for Pearly or Louie to respond.

"Was he the guy in the press box?" Grant pointed his index finger at the ceiling of the dugout. "Hard shoes? Hard socks?"

"Snappy dresser, ain't he?" Pearly chuckled.

"Did you make any money tonight, Kate?" Louie asked. He chose not to offer a comment on Speed's wardrobe.

"Yeah, I sold a couple packages of brats, and a bunch of pop and candy. We made about fifty bucks," Kate answered.

"We've done worse," Louie said as he closed the scorebook and climbed the steps out of the dugout. "See you Sunday, Grant. G'night, Kate! We'll play better on Sunday afternoon." Louie stepped around the corner of the dugout and walked toward the parking lot where only five cars remained. "I'm gonna take the boat out and see if I can catch a fish. G'night, Pearly! See you Sunday, boys," he called to the Carrigans.

Pearly finished bagging the batting helmets, the bats, and the balls, put them into a small storage shed that was attached to the dugout, and then called to the Carrigans. "Shut the lights off when you're done, boys!" He turned to Kate and Grant and added, "I think everyone except Louie is gonna be over at the Chateau for a while. You comin'?"

"Maybe later," Grant said. "It's such a nice night I think we'll just sit here for a while."

"OK, see you later. Thanks for working in the concession stand, Kate," Pearly said. He had cleared the top step of the dugout and was turning to leave.

"Any time," Kate replied. "I had fun."

Milburne threw the lever on the breaker box attached to a light tower over by the visitors' dugout and the ballpark went black. "See you Sunday!" he called across the suddenly dark infield. Kate and Grant listened to Melbourne and Milburne's cars crunch over the gravel in the parking lot and roll away into the night.

In a moment their eyes began to acclimate to the other, softer lights in the summer sky. A half moon threw enough light across the field to turn the trees and grass into blue shadows. Then the surface of the Ice Cracking River began to shimmer in the moonlight, and in the distance Leech Lake did the same. Soon enough, a billion stars began to twinkle.

"What are you thinking about?" Grant asked after several minutes of silence.

"Everything . . . and nothing," she said. "And wondering how I wound up here."

CHAPTER 33

Baseball was over, long over. The Walleyes' season had evolved into a string of bland losses, separated by the occasional emotionless victory.

The green leaves of summer had changed color in September then sailed away on the cold winds of October. Two inches of November snow covered the northern forests now.

Kate lowered herself awkwardly onto a small air mattress on the floor of the gymnasium at Walker Elementary School and waited for instructions. Along with seven other pregnant couples, Kate and Grant had assembled on the cold floor for the final in a series of classes designed to help them find their way through the birth experience.

In her eighth month now, Kate was large and uncomfortable most of the time.

The group had been meeting every Tuesday night for the month of November, and Grant was glad this would be the end of it all. He knew the material they were learning would help with the delivery, but he found the woman who was teaching the class to be insufferable. "She should be teaching in medical school," Grant groaned. He was sitting on the hard floor next to Kate's air mattress. "She knows everything. Who'd guess she's the bookkeeper at a lumber yard for her day job."

"Shhh," Kate scowled as she narrowed her eyes. "Just be quiet and listen." She didn't care for the woman either, but she didn't want anyone to hear Grant's complaints.

"If you could buy her for what she's worth, and then sell her for what she thinks she's worth, you'd make a hell of a deal," he whispered in her ear.

Kate refused to look at him.

The woman in charge of the class stood up and paced around the room while she spoke for about twenty minutes. She summed up all the previous meetings and covered things like focal points and proper breathing techniques for the mother, and all the things that the father would need to do to coach the mother through the birth experience.

Grant tried to listen to her, but his mind began to wander and disjointed thoughts drifted though his head. Things at the office were going well. The accountant said that in a couple of years they might actually be making a good living. Their little house on the lake was comfortable. They'd been lucky to find such a bargain. Will Campbell had called earlier in the day. He'd been telling about a professional boxer that he'd treated in the oral surgery clinic. The guy was Mexican and he'd . . .

"OK moms!" the woman called, when she was ready to move on and review some techniques for relaxation. Grant yawned and rejoined the class. "Let's roll onto our left sides! Dads, you help your gals roll over and then we'll talk about some ways to make them more comfortable during a long labor." Back to the task at hand, Grant thought.

The shuffling and sliding and small groaning noises made by eight very pregnant women trying to shift their significant weight across the small air mattresses was just loud enough that the woman in charge of the childbirth class stopped talking and let the mothers finish rolling over.

"Jeez," Grant whispered into Kate's ear. "Look at that couple way over there. I think the guy is inspecting his wife for harpoon marks before he rolls her back into the sea."

A smile appeared briefly at the corners of her mouth, but Kate stifled it, then hissed, "Shut up! Somebody will hear you."

She lifted and turned her leg brace, then shifted her weight onto her elbow and prepared to raise her right leg over her left. That's when it happened; a sudden and volcanic fart. Its surprising violence was exceeded only by its magnificent baritone tremolo. The air mattress and the gym floor seemed to amplify it. Every head in the gym spun toward Kate.

She was mortified. She whipped her face toward Grant and her eyes cried out for him to save her from the embarrassment of what she'd done, or at least give her shelter so she could hide. No such luck.

Grant began to smile, and Kate could see a tsunami of laughter rising just behind his glowing eyes.

"That happens all the time, moms and dads," the teacher said, as several of the dads began to snicker. "There's a lot of pressure down there . . ."

Grant's eyes were locked onto Kate's for a brief and horrifying lull, just before the moment shifted from excruciatingly embarrassing to unbelievably funny. A peal of laughter even more sudden and powerful than Kate's flatulent outburst exploded from both of them.

He rolled onto his back and howled while Kate did the same. Kate's ample belly shook and she cried out with great long bursts of laughter. All modesty was banished from the room and Kate let go completely. She covered her face with her hands and let herself be carried away with the absurdity of the moment, and the other class members did the same.

Eventually Grant raised himself onto one elbow and kissed his wife while they were still laughing hysterically.

"It's nothing to be embarrassed about!" The teacher called out over the din. "It happens all the time," she said in a futile attempt to regain some order, and a little of Kate's dignity.

"It sure does!" one of the pregnant women responded. "But it's usually *him* that does it!" She pointed to her husband and the group's laughter grew to a new level.

Ten minutes later, after the laughter had spontaneously rekindled several more times, Kate wiped her eyes dry and concluded, "Well I guess we all know each other better now."

∼:∼

Kate was exhausted after they got home from birthing class that night. She'd been in bed for several hours when Grant turned off the reading light at his desk. He made his way to the kitchen by the glow of two small night-lights, opened the refrigerator, and took out a can of Hamm's beer. Then he groped his way into the darkened living room while he waited for his eyes to readjust after the bright light inside the fridge.

It was the end of a long day, a good day, and now he'd have a moment to himself. He wore a gray T-shirt, plaid boxer shorts, and white cotton socks.

The old green couch was beginning to sag, he thought, as he settled into it. He crossed his feet on the coffee table in front of the couch and opened the beer. He stared out the picture window, watching the clouds roll by above Leech Lake, and wondered about, well, nothing, really. The beer was cold and it slid wonderfully over his tongue, and that was enough to think about for the moment.

Eventually, he thought of Will Campbell, and he began to smile. Will and June had come to visit several times since he'd moved into his home and started his practice. He'd always be friends with Will. They'd grow old together. Will would move back to Duluth and the two of them would hunt and fish together for the rest of their lives. Maybe he'd buy a boat next summer. He wondered what Will was doing right now. Everyone else from school, even Ben Pribyl, had moved out toward the periphery of his life.

The second swallow of beer was better than the first. He leaned back, looked out the window, and let a few fleeting thoughts pass through as his mind slipped into neutral. The leaves were all off the trees now. The lake would be freezing over soon. The Walleyes might win a few more games next year. Town ball had been a lot of fun, in spite of Ray Rivers. Louie and Pearly were his first friends in his new town. How 'bout that? Mmmm, the beer was good. Big Ole had given him a sign that read Dr. Grant Thorson to place on his desk at the office. It was nice to see the pride in his father's eyes. Kate was getting pretty uncomfortable. The baby would be here soon. The last of the Hamm's slid over his tongue. Damn, that was good. Felt like bedtime now.

Grant eased himself into bed, then slid close to Kate and put his arms around her so they could spoon for a while. She smelled so nice. He moved his lips close to her neck and kissed her softly. When he remembered the panic-stricken look on her face as she had lain on the gym floor several hours earlier, his face curled into a smile. No matter what she said, farts were funny. Maybe she could understand that now.

The bed rocked ever so gently as Kate began to laugh. She was awake, she'd felt his lips stretch into a smile, and she knew what he was smiling about. "Shut up," she sighed. "It's not funny yet!"

∾ CHAPTER 34 ∾

A powerful force, just on the other side of his eyeballs, was daring him to wake up, but he wasn't ready. It was so nice to be asleep.

Reluctantly, he let his eyes blink open, and there was Kate, pressed against him nose to nose, staring, defying him to wake up, and smiling. She was still wearing her pajamas and lying next to him under the covers, but grinning like a child on Christmas morning.

"Today's the day!" she said when Grant's eyes cleared and some recognition came onto his face. "The labor pains are about twenty minutes apart! I've been timing them for two hours. They started real small, and they've been building steadily."

After a call to alert the staff at the hospital, they packed an overnight bag for Kate and made the short drive across town. Kate's contractions were growing in intensity when a nurse led them into a labor room.

"OK, honey, you just slip into this." The nurse rolled her eyes when she held up a standard blue cotton hospital gown. "Not very flattering, is it? Anyway, make yourself comfortable and I'll be back in a minute to have a look."

Kate put on the gown and removed her leg brace, then slid herself onto the bed. She held Grant's hand and grinned as if she had a secret. "This is it!" she said, squeezing his hand.

A contraction began and Kate's face tightened immediately.

"OK, breathe, Kate. Now's the time to remember all the stuff we learned in class," Grant said. He stroked her arm and added, "Breathe."

An hour went by, then another, as the labor pains grew. By the end of the second hour Kate looked haggard. She was sweating and the hair around her temples and forehead was matted.

With each contraction her face grew more desperate. She looked as though the powerful contractions were about to pull her through a knothole and into a terrible void.

"C'mon, keep breathing," Grant coached during each contraction. He tried to let her hear something calm and reassuring in his voice. When the contraction let up, Kate appeared to fall asleep while she waited for the next. Grant rubbed small ice cubes across her forehead sometimes while she rested. Then, with no warning, she'd catapult forward with terror in her eyes and grab at his shirt when the next contraction started. A few minutes later she'd lie back in bed and close her eyes when the contraction let up. Just when he was certain she didn't even know he was in the room, she'd lurch forward and clutch at him again, like a drowning woman holding onto a lifeline.

"She's dilated to nine centimeters," the nurse announced after the second hour of hard contractions. "I think we'll call the doctor down here and roll her into the delivery room. Are you ready to have that baby?" she asked Kate.

Kate only nodded, and squeezed Grant's hand.

The doctor was talking about the cold weather when he strolled into the delivery room and let a nurse help him put on a gown and gloves. "How are you doing, Kate?" he asked with a smile.

Kate lurched forward as a powerful contraction struck.

"OK, I know what that means," the doctor said. He moved to the end of the delivery table and examined Kate while the nurses put her legs in the cold steel stirrups. "She's just about ready," the doctor said, after a quick look at Kate. Then he glanced to his right to check one of the monitors beside the bed.

"Do you feel like you want to push, Kate?" the doctor asked.

"Yes," she replied.

"Well, don't. Not yet, anyway. You're not ready to push yet."

The doctor didn't seem to be worried about anything. This did seem to be going about as the doctor and the nurses expected, but the situation was so similar to . . . Grant tried not to think about it.

Kate cried out again when another powerful contraction came.

"Don't push, Kate," the doctor ordered.

The nurses closed in a little, and the doctor readied his hands. Please, God, please don't let it happen again, Grant thought.

"All right, Kate, this time you push! Push hard when the next contraction comes."

Kate was on her own now. Grant was simply a spectator from here on. Her head jerked forward with a mighty contraction and Grant thought the veins in her face might burst.

"Push!" the doctor ordered. A nurse standing next to him exhorted, "Push again, Kate!"

Grant peeked to the other end of the table and saw something black and wet in the doctor's hand, then a tiny bluish red arm appeared.

"Ahhh!" Kate cried.

The nurses cheered. The doctor had something in his hands and the longest moment in Grant's life passed.

"You have a perfect little girl! And look at all that black hair!" the doctor said. Kate laughed and wept at the same time. She tried to see the baby, then reached her hands out. "Let me hold her!"

Grant looked back and forth between his wife and his daughter, and tried to understand what he felt.

"All right, honey. I'll take that beautiful little girl of yours and clean her up a little. Then I'll bring her right back to you," said a nurse.

Kate took Grant's hand in hers, and she wiped her eyes dry with her other hand.

"Kate," the doctor said, "I have a little repair to do here. Just a couple sutures and we'll take you up to your room in the maternity ward."

The maternity ward. How about that? They were going to the maternity ward.

"You OK, honey?" Grant asked her.

"We did it!" she said.

"Do you have a name for your daughter?" asked a second nurse, who stood with a paper and pencil as though she was asking for an autograph.

"Ingrid. She's Ingrid Thorson!" Kate announced. Grand nodded his agreement.

~:~

Ingrid Thorson was thirty minutes old when she was brought to her mother's bed wrapped in a cotton blanket and wearing a tiny pink stocking cap. She tried to open her eyes several times but that seemed to require far more energy than she could muster.

"All right, Kate, let's see if she understands how to take nourishment," the nurse said. Then she took Ingrid and held her for a moment while Kate exposed her breast.

Grant stood openmouthed, and he stared with wonder. Kate held the red-faced infant with her left arm and used her right hand to guide her nipple toward the baby's lips.

The tiny pink borders of Ingrid's lips looked exquisitely soft, and when Kate's nipple touched those little lips they began to search for something. Ingrid's mouth clamped around the nipple and she began to suckle.

"Success!" the nurse said to Kate.

Grant watched another small miracle happen before his eyes. He stood there trying to understand what he was seeing, trying to catalog this moment, but there was no similar experience. Ingrid began to make tiny squeaking noises, as if she was truly enjoying her first meal.

Kate lifted her eyes toward him and revealed her ecstasy at the bonding of mother and child. A keystone in her life had just dropped into place and her joy was palpable.

Kate had been his constant companion for several years, and he thought he'd seen everything with her. But just now those blue eyes had told him of love he was only beginning to understand.

∾:∾

Grant had been unable to let his weary body drift off to sleep until almost 3:00 a.m. And he hadn't begun to sleep soundly until just before sunup. It was always hard to get up and get moving when that happened, even today. He was thankful for the January cold that jolted him full awake when he scurried across the parking lot at 8:30 a.m. With some flowers and a couple of doughnuts to share with Kate in his left hand, and a cup of gas station coffee in his right, he crossed the hospital lobby, then skipped up a flight of stairs. He was in a hurry to get to Kate's room, until he reached the nursery.

There she was, lying in her little plastic tub with a label that read Ingrid Thorson. Grant stood with his nose pressed against the glass window and watched Ingrid sleeping peacefully while a baby in the neighboring plastic tub screamed.

That child lying there was his. His! He'd be taking her home in about twenty-four hours. He was somebody's father now, and it was more than he could get his mind around just yet. He stood there and stared until a nurse on the other side of the glass smiled and waved.

"How'd you sleep?" Grant asked when he peeked into Kate's room. She was watching TV and picking at her breakfast.

"Not so good," Kate smiled. "All the excitement didn't wear off until a couple hours ago."

Grant placed the flowers on her windowsill, then kissed her and put the bag of doughnuts on her breakfast tray. "How do you feel?" he asked.

"A little sore. I had a shower about half an hour ago. The doctor says everything is good," Kate said. "Ingrid should be ready to eat pretty soon," she added.

Grant looked at the doughnuts for a second and then he turned back to Kate. He looked like a timid third-grader asking his teacher for permission to go to the bathroom when he leaned forward and asked, "Can I hold her?"

"C'mere," Kate ordered him. "You look just like The Jimmer!" She locked her arms around his neck and laughed as she reassured him he could indeed hold his daughter. She kissed his cheek and stroked his back and allowed him to laugh right along with her. This was the man who'd introduced her to sex, the man who'd made her laugh a million times, the man who shared her best and her worst day, and now he'd revealed himself again, as a little boy. She loved him more than ever.

Visiting hours came without much notice. They were so new in town that they didn't have many friends yet. Some of the staff from the dental office dropped by for short visits. Louie Swearingen came and sat for a while. Pearly DeMoore came to the hospital after church. He wore a brown suit that he'd bought at JC Penney sometime when Kennedy was president. It was his best attempt at formal attire, but he still seemed to be wearing blue jeans and a gray T-shirt.

Grant bought a Sunday paper and read it to Kate after visiting hours ended. They'd started work on the new domed stadium in Minneapolis. Metropolitan Stadium, their special place, would be history soon. The hostages were still in Iran. It looked like the Republicans might select Ronald Reagan as their candidate for the presidency in 1980. The economy looked really shaky. Grant tossed the paper on the floor and wondered just what kind of a world they'd brought a child into.

Not much he could do about that, Grant thought. He stood up and walked to Kate's bedside. "Would you like me to go out and get you a treat? Maybe a little ice cream?" he asked.

"Yeah, that sounds good . . ." Kate replied, as they heard footsteps outside the room. Someone tapped on the heavy wooden door and it began to swing open.

"Hey, Pard! Hi, Kate! Congratulations!" Will Campbell stepped into the room. June peeked over his shoulder, then darted past him and ran to Kate.

"She's perfect!" June squealed.

"What're you doing here?" Grant asked, incredulous.

"Just took a Sunday drive and wound up here," Will replied. "So tell us about everything."

An hour later Kate and Grant were all alone once more, and Kate was nursing Ingrid. Will and June had made a five-hour drive so they could share in their friends' joy for one hour and then drive another five hours back home.

"Remember the day you passed the state boards?" Kate asked, while she looked at Ingrid.

"Sure," Grant said.

"Remember the story you told me about your brother Paul, and home runs and curveballs, and what you said about how your real friends will be there to celebrate the good times?" she said. "Well, the guy who used to put your instruments in the fire just drove ten hours to give you a hug and see our daughter. Is there any doubt who our friends are?"

~: CHAPTER 35 :~

She slid her bare toes across the chilly spot between herself and Grant until she found his legs. She wouldn't wake him now—he'd been asleep for hours—but she wanted to touch him and know that he was there and perhaps draw strength from him. The bed sheets were so soft and comfortable. A blanket and a heavy quilt covered the bed and sealed the warmth about her while she listened to a north wind whistle through the winter night outside her window.

They'd brought Ingrid home from the hospital on Monday, and the past week had been grand. Every day had been like Christmas. Grant's mother had spent the entire week to show her the ropes, answer all her questions, and help with household chores. Every time Ingrid opened her eyes or soiled her diaper they had a celebration. Gladys knew what to do in every situation.

But Gladys and Big Ole were gone now. They'd returned to the farm. Tomorrow morning, after Grant went to work, she'd be all alone with Ingrid and she'd have to figure everything out for herself. She looked out the bedroom window and watched the pine boughs sway in the wind while she tried to reassure herself that she could actually take care of her child without any help from Gladys.

She was awake and ready to get up when the alarm sounded. Grant didn't seem to notice her apprehension as he prepared for work and had a quick breakfast. As the minutes ticked away and the time for him to leave drew closer she began to envy him. She was afraid of the responsibility he was about to leave her alone with.

Grant finished his coffee, gave her a hug and kiss, and left for work.

Suddenly the house was silent. Grant wouldn't be home until noon, and

Gladys wouldn't be there at all. Kate walked to the doorway of Ingrid's room and peeked inside. What now? She tiptoed into the room and stood beside Ingrid's crib. Her tiny features were so perfect. Kate leaned closer to look at those hands, and that peaceful slumbering face. She stared at her child for several minutes, then she sneaked out of the baby's room and waited for her to wake up.

A pile of baby gifts sat on the kitchen floor. Kate unwrapped them and wrote thank-you notes at the kitchen table. She looked over her shoulder and checked the clock every few minutes. Maybe something was wrong? She walked back to Ingrid's room to make sure she was breathing, then returned to the table and wrote a few more thank-you notes before she checked the clock again. It was almost 8:30 a.m., nearly four hours since Ingrid's last feeding. She'd never gone this long. Something had to be wrong.

A moment later, Kate heard Ingrid's first cries of the morning. She hurried to the baby's room, swept the child up, and chirped a mother's greeting while she carried Ingrid to the changing table beside her crib.

The soft and unmistakable scent of baby powder hung in the air when Kate fastened a dry diaper around her child. Ingrid lay on her back and tried to focus her eyes while Kate talked to her and kissed her round white belly. Her hands and feet pumped with no particular pattern, and Kate was certain that she smiled several times.

When Ingrid got hungry and began to fuss, Kate carried her into the living room and sat down in the rocking chair where she usually nursed the baby. Ingrid's cries were still just the little squawks of a newborn, but she was growing more and more impatient by the time her mother's nipple touched her face and triggered the reflex to turn and begin nursing. She fed aggressively and in just a moment Kate noticed the familiar tiny contented squeaks coming from Ingrid while she nursed. A soft "mmm, mmm" rose gently from her with each swallow, as if she couldn't help but signal her contentment and compliment her mother on the fine meal.

This little ritual at Kate's breast was timeless. It hinted at the meaning of love, and revealed the hand of God. While she cradled Ingrid in her right arm, Kate used her left hand to touch the exquisitely soft black hair on Ingrid's head. She marveled at the delicate and perfect shape of Ingrid's ears, then her tiny fingers. Kate exposed Ingrid's feet and stared at her legs. There were no joints, only sausage links, and Kate thought Ingrid's feet, like her hands, were tiny and perfect.

What have I done, Kate wondered. The child at her breast would rely on her for everything. "Will I be a good mother for you?" she whispered, as she tucked the child's feet inside her blanket once again, then watched and listened to the miracle in her arms.

Minutes later Ingrid went silent. Still at her mother's breast, she'd drifted off to a contented sleep.

Kate placed a clean towel on her shoulder and then gently shifted Ingrid so that her face rested against the towel. She cupped her fingers around Ingrid's head, let her cheek rest against Ingrid's soft hair, and smelled the baby shampoo. She'd walk the floor with her child and try to coax a burp from her before she laid her down for another nap.

Ingrid nestled perfectly against her mother's shoulder and made no sound for a few minutes. But the gas in her stomach built and she began to cry and fuss. Kate stroked Ingrid's back, and walked, and hummed a gentle lullaby. When she walked through the kitchen she glanced at the table and noticed a newspaper opened to another article about the destruction of Metropolitan Stadium. Suddenly she found lyrics for the song she'd been humming. In the soft, soothing way that a mother sings to a sleepy child, the Minnesota Twins Fight Song morphed into a lullaby.

"We're gonna win, Twins," she sang, ever so softly and slowly. "We're gonna score . . ." She walked into the living room. "Knock out a home run, watch that baseball soar." She walked slowly back into the kitchen and the gentle motion of her uneven footsteps rocked the cranky infant. "Cheer for the Minnesota Twins, today." Ingrid's crying intensified and Kate let her sweet, soft voice mingle with Ingrid's cries while she took another lap, than another. ". . . Knock out a home run, shout a hip hooray. Cheer for the Minnesota Twins, today."

Ingrid burped on the next trip through the kitchen and then fell silent.

"You sound like your daddy," Kate said, as she laid Ingrid down in her crib. Instead of returning to the pile of thank-you notes at the kitchen table, she stood beside the crib for a moment and watched her daughter sleep. Where would this fork in the road take her, she wondered?

❦ CHAPTER 36 ❧

February 22, 1980

Five-week-old Ingrid Thorson had recently discovered her fingers. She reclined in the plastic baby chair/car seat atop the kitchen table and studied them while Kate moved about the kitchen. The fingers appeared to be fascinating. Every time she got a good look at them she began to pump and flail with her arms and legs as if she was swimming. She seemed like she wanted to speak to her fingers, but since she couldn't make words or even many sounds just yet, she was content to look at them and try to put them in her mouth.

"Daddy's home," Kate said when she saw Grant's car roll into the small driveway. She watched him step out of his car with a paper bag full of groceries under one arm. He looked over at the silvery aluminum hull of an old fishing boat, which lay upside down on top of a snowdrift in the front yard. Then, when he saw Kate looking at him through the kitchen window, he smiled and gave her a thumbs-up signal as he walked to the house.

"I see Pearly dropped the boat off," Grant said as he shut the door behind him. He kissed Kate and then he walked to the kitchen table and kissed Ingrid.

"Yup," Kate said. "Why did he put it in our yard?"

"I made some dentures for his mother-in-law."

Kate looked out the window and reexamined the boat, then scowled.

"Yeah, I know," Grant said. "It's not much, but it's a Lund. I'll put some new seats in it and paint it. It'll be a fine duck boat."

Kate raised her eyebrows to let him know, once again, that she thought he'd made a bad bargain.

"It was either that or not get paid at all," Grant said as he lifted a six-pack of Hamm's from the grocery bag and changed the subject. "It's Friday night. I got us some beer. Thought I'd make supper tonight, too. Seemed like a good night for Mayfly Hatch; we haven't had that for a while." He placed a bag of spinach on the kitchen counter, then reached into the brown paper grocery bag again and retrieved basil, salad dressing, and ravioli. "We can have a romantic dinner on the couch while we watch the hockey game!"

"Sounds good," Kate said as Ingrid started to fuss. "You're in charge of dinner, then." She lifted Ingrid from her seat and walked into the living room, where she sat down and began to nurse the child. "So who won the game?" she called.

Earlier in the afternoon the United States Olympic hockey team had played the Russians in the first game of the medal round in the Olympic Games in Lake Placid. The game had not been broadcast live by ABC TV, but a tape-delayed broadcast was scheduled for 6:00 p.m.

"I don't know!" Grant called back to her as he began preparing his Mayfly Hatch. "I think it was on TV in Canada, but since I planned to watch it with you tonight I made a point not to find out who won, so don't turn on the radio or answer the phone or anything, OK? I don't wanna know until we watch it." He paused for a moment, then asked, "Where's the blender?"

"Under the cupboard to the left of the sink," Kate replied. "They probably got pounded. I mean, it was the Russians."

Twenty minutes later, Grant shut off the blender and the aggravating motor noise ground to a stop. Inside the blender a thick green paste gurgled once. The spinach, basil, and salad dressing had been whipped into pesto. "Jeez, it does look like something I scraped off the bumper of my truck," Grant mumbled to himself.

"What'd you say?" Kate asked.

"Supper's ready," Grant replied. He poured the pesto over a plateful of cheese ravioli and carried a plate and a glass of milk to Kate. He returned for his own meal and then sat down next to Kate on the green couch just in time to hear ABC sportscasters Al Michaels and Ken Dryden mention that the same two teams had met only a few days earlier, and the Russians had won in a rout, 10–3.

"I love you, Kate," Grant said, and he leaned over and kissed her. Their social lives had taken an abrupt turn with the arrival of Ingrid. They had a family now, and they'd be spending their free time right here, on the old green couch, for the foreseeable future. "This is OK, isn't it?" Grant asked, when he realized that Kate was contemplating that very same change in their lives. He pointed to the TV, and the pesto, and the couch. "This is good, right?" There would be no gathering of friends at Stub & Herb's, no stories and laughter over a crowded table, no romance. Just two tired young people sharing dinner on the couch, a Friday night at home, watching a hockey game.

"Sure is," Kate replied. "No place I'd rather be. I love you too."

Life had eased them around another bend in the river. They were happy to be eating by themselves in a quiet little house in the woods. They had each other.

"Hey," Kate said, when their attention drifted back to the talking heads on TV and the pesto on their plates. "Remember a year ago when June was talking about a new invention to play movies at home? Well, I read an article today, some Japanese company is about ready to introduce a thing called a videocassette recorder. They're gonna put complete movies on tape, like the cassette tapes in our car, so we can watch movies on our own TV, whenever we want. *And* there's a new cable TV channel called ESPN, and they'll have only sports, twenty-four hours a day."

"Hmph. What'll they think of next?" Grant sighed.

At first, the hockey game was simply the thing that was on TV, background noise. They expected another massacre at the hands of the Russians, so while they ate, Grant told Kate about his day at work, and Kate told him about her day with Ingrid. "I took Ingrid to the doctor's office today," Kate started, and she shook her head in disbelief. "I didn't take any extra diaper or diaper bag or anything. Of course I didn't anticipate that a baby might require some accessories. Naturally Ingrid filled her pants right away, then she spit up on my sweater. I had to borrow a diaper from one of the nurses. I just didn't think . . ." Kate stopped herself and seemed truly embarrassed. "I'll bet they think I'm a bad mother. I was a mess."

Grant shrugged. "Well, you won't do that again. How would you know about diaper bags and such?" Then he added, "My sports coats all smell like her vomit, too."

"It's not vomit," Kate corrected. "It's spit-up."

"Whatever," Grant said, as he stood up and went back to the kitchen for more pesto.

While he was leaning on the refrigerator he heard Kate groan. "Shit! The Russians just scored!"

Grant brought another beer when he returned to the couch. "I met some of those guys on the Olympic hockey team over at Dommy's place. Met Herb Brooks once, too."

Kate had heard the story before and she chose to ignore him instead of commenting, and she listened to the unabridged version of Grant's encounter with Herb Brooks yet again.

"Hope they don't get their asses kicked," Grant sighed.

"Remember what we used to think about our friends who were married with kids when they talked about poopy diapers and spit-up, like we just did?"

Before Grant had a chance to reply, Buzz Schneider scored a goal and Kate clinked her glass of milk against his can of beer in a small celebration, and they watched the game with a bit more interest as they finished the Mayfly Hatch.

The Russians scored again and Grant carried their dishes out to the kitchen sink. "Well, shit," he sighed, as he rinsed the plates, then returned to the green couch. It was deep in the first period and the USA was only behind two goals to one, but they were up against the Russians, after all, and they had no chance.

As the first period was drawing to a close, Grant leaned forward on the couch. He'd get up and finish the supper dishes during the intermission between first and second periods, but he'd watch this final rush down the ice before he went to the kitchen. Dave Christian fired a shot, there was a flurry in front of the Russian net, and Mark Johnson slapped in the rebound! He scored on the last tick of the clock as the period ended. The Russians looked like they all suddenly had the flu, and the Americans were ecstatic!

Grant sneaked a sideways glance at Kate. They were tied with the Russians. Maybe? Nah!

Grant stood at the kitchen sink, doing dishes between the first and second period, when Kate came and stood behind him. "Tell me I'm a good mother," she said after she pressed herself up against his back and wrapped her arms around him.

"Now why would you say something like that?" Grant asked. He clinked the dishes around in the soapy water for a minute and said, "Of course you're a good mother."

"I felt so stupid today," she said with her lips against the back of his neck. "I don't know how to take care of a baby, my own child." She sighed.

"They don't come with an instruction manual," he replied as he stacked the dishes in the other side of the sink.

"It's harder than I thought it would be," she said. "You know how she starts to cry sometimes at night, usually just a minute or so after we lie down in bed? She makes that tiny little noise, and I'm so exhausted, but I know I have to get up and feed her and probably play with her for a while."

"Sometimes I pretend I'm sleeping," Grant confessed. "But I hear it, too."

"Yeah, I know that," Kate said. "In case you thought you were fooling me. But it's me she really wants anyway. But I have to confess something, something that makes me feel terrible. Sometimes I get angry. I get angry, angry at my perfect child. Then when I straggle into her room and she's so beautiful and so happy to see me, well, I feel terrible because I'm angry."

"So let me get this straight," Grant said, and he turned around to hold her. "You don't like to get out of bed when you're really tired, and you love our child? Is that the problem? Sounds pretty normal to me."

"It's more than that," Kate sighed. "I feel so helpless, so overwhelmed. How do I know I'll be any good at this? She counts on me for everything, and I don't know what I'm doing." Kate looked like she was about to cry.

"Well," Grant said, as he held his cheek against hers, "you've been good at everything else you've ever done. I know you'll be good at this." He held her close and added, "You're the best person I ever met."

It was the kind of thing he'd said to her from the very beginning, and she loved it. Nothing was changed, no great illumination was granted, just a shared moment of support, and unspoken resolve to stay the course. They'd come this far together; they'd go the distance together. A patient and comforting embrace ended when the talking heads on TV called them back to the green couch.

The tempo of the game grew furious. Kate and Grant gradually lost themselves in the little TV screen, twitching and flinching with each deflected pass and collision. The Russians scored again, but they just couldn't pull away. It was still close after two periods. Maybe? Nah.

A minute into the third period something special was in the wind.

"Look at their faces!" Grant said to Kate every time the camera zoomed in on the U.S. hockey players. "They know something. Can you see it?"

Mark Johnson scored to tie the game at the 8:39 mark of the third period and Grant turned to Kate. "Can you see it?" he asked. He stood up and went into Ingrid's room. A moment later he returned to the couch carrying his sleeping daughter. "She needs to see this!" he said, and he held her in his arms while they played on.

Then it happened. With exactly ten minutes left in the game, Mike

Eruzione scored to put the United States ahead 4–3, and the Olympic ice arena exploded with excitement.

"They're gonna beat the fuckin' Russians," he gasped, and he turned to his sleeping child, who was oblivious to everything. "Never talk like that!"

Grant sat back in the green couch and continued to squirm with each deflection of the puck until the end of the game.

"DO YOU BELIEVE IN MIRACLES?" Al Michaels called out, as he put an exclamation mark at the end of the moment.

"Can you see it?" Grant asked softly, when he realized that Kate was staring at the TV too.

"See what?"

"They're just little boys," he answered. "Look!" At that moment the TV camera captured Jack O'Callahan's joyous face. He was missing a front tooth, like any other little boy might be, and then he was rolling around on the ice, laughing and wrestling with a teammate.

"Look at their faces," Grant gasped.

Two hours later, after all the replays and postgame interviews, and commentary and analysis by members of the media, Grant switched the TV off and plopped back onto the green couch next to Kate. The dishes were done, Kate had put Ingrid back to bed for the night, and the house was quiet.

"It's too cold to sit on the porch and think about all this," Grant said. He reached over and turned off the lamp beside the couch. A thick layer of snow covered the forest floor around their home and the entire lake in front of their picture window. The night was silent and still.

Grant leaned over and rested his head on Kate's lap, then stretched his legs down toward the other end of the couch.

"You know," he began, as Kate ran her soft fingertips over his whisker stubble, "people are gonna try to make a statement about politics, and whose system is best, and good and evil, and stuff like that." He sighed and thought for a moment. "But that's not what I was thinking about."

"Oh?" Kate said. She ran her fingers through his hair.

"Those boys out there on the ice tonight? They spent countless thousands of hours skating on frozen ponds and parking lots and empty ice arenas. And you can bet the farm that every time they played with their buddies and dreamed about the future . . . ," he paused and looked up at Kate, "the Russians were there. Every time they brought the puck up the ice in a pickup game or a scrimmage, or even when they played all by themselves under a streetlight, I'll bet they dreamed they were up against the Russians, and they were about to score the game winner."

Kate stroked the back of his hand and waited for him to continue.

"It's the same for every little boy," he said. "I used to throw a rubber ball against the barn wall, and when it came back at me I imagined that I was playing shortstop in the World Series, and I had to make a diving catch and a perfect throw over to first base in order to save the game and win the Series against the evil New York Yankees." His gaze was fixed for a moment, then he added, "Every batting practice home run, every warm-up pitch I took as a boy; I was mowing down Yankees." He nodded his understanding of what he'd seen. "Tonight those boys lived out their dreams, and we all got to share them for just a moment there. We saw them as little boys. More than that, we saw our own childhood, and our own dreams." A crescent moon showed itself between pine boughs every so often while they sat together in the silence of a winter night. "I always thought it would be *me* doing something great while the whole country watched. I wonder if my dreams will ever come true," he added, after a silent stretch. His words didn't seem to be directed at Kate, but rather into the night or to some distant spirit.

"Wanna know something else?" Grant asked, yawning, a few minutes later.

"What's that?" Kate replied, expecting more about the Russians or the Yankees, but he'd already closed that book.

"Sometimes when you leave me alone with Ingrid, I'm afraid," Grant said.

"Afraid of what?" Kate asked.

"I guess I'm afraid she'll start to cry or she'll need something and I won't know what to do. I always feel safe when you're around, because I know *you'll* do the right thing. You'll be a good mother."

Kate smiled to herself and used her fingertips to make tiny circles by his ears. "I love you," she said after a few minutes. When he didn't respond she looked down and saw that he was fast asleep, drooling on her leg.

~: CHAPTER 37 :~

June 1985

Another hot summer day. It was too hot to paint the boat, that much was certain. Oh well, the new seats were finally fastened in, the removable duck blind made of aluminum conduit and chicken wire was finished, and the thing was ready to be painted, maybe. Five years had passed since Pearly had dropped this thing off, and it still wasn't ready for action.

Grant wiped the sweat from his brow and stepped back from the boat. It would be ready soon enough, but he was done with it for today.

"Honey," Grant said to Ingrid, "Would you go get your daddy a can of Coke from the fridge?"

Five-year-old Ingrid Thorson looked up at her father, then used the palm of her hand to sweep her dark hair from her eyes. "Can I have one too?"

"Sure. Maybe we should have a tea party out here," Grant replied, as he pointed to the shade underneath several huge white pines beside the garage.

Ingrid turned and sprinted toward the house. Tea parties were her favorite thing, and Grant knew what was about to happen. While he was waiting for his daughter to sprint back, he turned his attention to the aluminum boat sitting on the trailer in his garage. How could it have taken five years to restore this thing? He lifted his tools from inside the boat and hung them on the Peg-Board over his workbench.

The Walleyes had a game in just a couple of hours. He'd relax and enjoy some time with his family before the game.

This was already his fifth season with the Walleyes, too. Where had the time gone, he thought, as he straightened up the tool bench. Baseball was still fun, and he'd grown to be good friends with Pearly and Louie and the others. But Ray Rivers had all but about destroyed the Walleyes. Everyone hated Ray. All the players did anymore was bitch and make fun of Ray behind his back. The only thing that kept Grant coming back was that Will Campbell had decided to play for the Walleyes these past two summers since he'd finished graduate school and started his oral surgery practice in Duluth. Will and June had three daughters now, and they drove over to their family cabin at Spider Lake Duck Camp every weekend.

Grant smiled to himself when he thought of Will. The guy still made him laugh. Hell, he made everything more fun. Will and his family were little more than an extension of his own family. The Campbells usually arrived at the ballpark just before game time, and that's when the weekend started. They always had fun together, and today would be no different.

Minutes later, Kate and Ingrid emerged from the house. Kate carried a large tray covered with Ingrid's pink plastic tea party dishes, some cookies, and three cans of Coke.

Ingrid wore a straw sombrero, a brightly colored cotton shirt, and some pink high heels that Kate had bought for her at a garage sale earlier in the summer. She struggled to stay upright as she clattered across the garage toward Grant. She'd rummaged through the box of dress-up clothes that Kate had accumulated for her to use at occasions like this one, and now she felt she was properly dressed for this social function.

"Let's have a tea party! I'll be the beautiful one!" Ingrid hollered as she wobbled along. She never looked up from her feet, and she carried an ugly handbag in the crook of her arm.

Kate set the serving tray on a bed of brown pine needles, not far from the garage, then invited Grant and Ingrid to sit down on the ground and join her. She placed a pink plastic saucer and a matching cup in front of each of them and then she turned to Ingrid and said, "OK, honey, you're the hostess, and the beautiful one. You serve the cookies and the tea to your guests."

Both her shoes fell off when Ingrid stood up, so she left them on the ground beside her cup and saucer while she walked around and placed a chocolate chip cookie on her mother's plate, then Grant's, then her own. Next she poured some Coke into each of their pink teacups. Ingrid talked the whole time, narrating every move she made. "Here's a cookie for this gentleman," she said when she gave Grant his cookie. "And here's a cookie for this lovely lady," she said as she put the cookie on Kate's saucer. She talked continuously and gave detailed instructions about proper behavior and etiquette during these pine-needle tea parties.

During Ingrid's first couple of years her relationship with her mother had been so close that she often sought Kate and excluded Grant. But over the past year or so, she'd discovered a fine playmate in her father. He let her use the hammer and the screwdriver when she helped him work on the duck boat. Sometimes they just sat in the boat while it rested on the garage floor and went on make-believe adventures. One day they might have a dangerous trip down a winding river surrounded by wild Indians. The next day they'd have a tea party in the boat and imagine themselves on a luxury ocean liner. Ingrid always dressed herself for these adventures from the box of garage-sale dress-up clothes, and she preferred to be recognized as "The Beautiful One."

"So are you the queen of this whole kingdom?" Grant asked, pointing to the front yard.

Grant loved their conversations because he never knew what she might say next, and he tried to infuse new words into her vocabulary just to see where they might reappear.

"No. I'm a princess!" Ingrid replied.

"That's for sure," Kate said. She smiled when Grant looked over at her.

"So what does a princess do here in Walker?" Grant asked Ingrid, still probing for a colorful answer.

"Oh, I like to go fishing with my daddy," Ingrid said, after she sipped from her teacup. She held herself as if she were a member of high society. Her head was tipped back and she tried to hold her cup with her pinkie finger extended, as she'd seen on TV. "I like to play with the minnows. They're elusive."

Grant flashed a prideful smile at Kate. His five-year-old daughter had just used the word *elusive*. Earlier in the week, while at a routine visit to the medical clinic, she'd watched her doctor put a cough drop in his mouth and mention that his throat was very dry. Ingrid then suggested that perhaps the doctor had xerostomia, a word she'd heard her parents use at the dinner table. When the surprised physician asked her for a definition of xerostomia, she calmly replied, "dry mouth," as if that was common knowledge for all five-year-olds.

Now Kate sipped from her pink teacup and asked Ingrid to elaborate on the fishing experience. "Do you put the minnows on your own hook?" Kate grinned and waited for her daughter's answer.

"No. The sonsabitches are too slippery! Daddy does it for me," Ingrid announced, with the same aloof mannerisms she'd been using all along. She even had the correct snarl in her voice when she said "sonsabitches."

Kate's mouth fell open, and she turned an accusing scowl toward Grant.

His first inclination was to laugh, then he recognized the fact that Kate found no humor in Ingrid's cussing.

Using the calmest voice he could summon, Grant asked very softly, "Where did you hear that word, honey?" He could feel Kate's angry eyes burning at the side of his head.

"What word, Daddy?" she replied innocently.

Great! He'd really stepped in it now. He had to repeat "sonsabitches" just to ask the question.

"Sonsabitches," Grant said with a soft lilt in his voice as if he were referring to a bouquet of flowers. He squeezed his eyes shut after he said it.

"The baseball men say it all the time," Ingrid replied. She took a bite of her cookie and smiled at Grant with a chocolate chip smeared on her chin.

"Well, it's sort of a bad word, and you shouldn't say it anymore, all right, honey?" Grant said calmly, so as not to emphasize the word again and drill it into her impressive memory any further.

"OK!" Ingrid replied.

Kate stared at Grant for a second and then rolled her eyes.

∾∶∾

When Kate and Ingrid opened up the concession stand later in the day, before the game with Menahga, the sound of white ash on horsehide echoed across the empty ball yard. Somebody was taking batting practice in the batting cage.

Grant kissed Kate good-bye and walked slowly to the dugout where Pearly DeMoore was arranging the batting helmets and the bats, as Louie Swearingen searched for a new bag of lime so he could mark the base paths.

When Kate lifted open the concession-stand window, a familiar figure was already standing outside, waiting.

"Hi, Speed!" Kate said while she locked the window open.

"Hehwo, Kate," Speed replied. "Got anything weddy yet?" He stood there and smiled expectantly, hoping she had dinner ready for him. The wingtips and black socks were gone now; replaced by tennis shoes and white socks. But he still needed some fashion tips about clashing colors and patterns: he wore a striped shirt with his favorite pair of plaid shorts.

"Just opening up. Would you like me to bring something up to you when it's ready?" Kate liked Speed Roesner. Everybody liked Speed Roesner, even the small handful of young people who came to Walleye games. Kate would have expected the high school and college kids to make fun of Speed because of the polkas he played and the way he talked and dressed, but the younger crowd, such as it was, liked him.

Speed Roesner was what the locals called a character. Hearing his name mentioned, anyone in Walker could summon an image of Speed's face in their mind's eye, and they'd hear him talking, and they'd smile at the thought of him. Over the years he'd come to see himself as a pretty important fixture at Walleye Field, as the guy in charge of the scoreboard and the public-address system. Ever since the position of concession-stand manager had been dropped into Kate's lap he'd taken a special liking to her; she was a colleague in charge of another important part of Walleye baseball.

"Could you bwing me a bwat, and a Docto Peppo?" he asked.

"Sure thing," Kate said, as she dumped some charcoal briquettes in the grill.

Speed didn't move. He rested his elbows on the countertop of the concession-stand window and waited for some more conversation with Kate.

"So how's the family?" Kate asked.

"Pwetty good," Speed replied. "Wowaine is betto, she had the fwu wast week."

"Sorry to hear that," Kate said, as she opened a package of bratwurst.

"Yeah," Speed sighed. "Wicky and Wandy both got mawied wast summo, you know, so we don't see them too much. And Wonny, he wives in Denvo." Speed nodded his agreement with himself. "But Winda wives in town, so we get to see the gwandkids awot!"

"That's always nice," Kate replied. She'd had so many conversations with Speed over the last five years that she barely noticed the speech impediment anymore. The fact that he'd married a woman named Lorraine, had children named Ricky, Randy, Ronny, and Linda, and couldn't pronounce any of their names, didn't even register with Kate now. She rolled the grill out onto the deck, struck a match to the coals, and promised to bring Speed a brat and a Dr. Pepper in a few minutes. By the time she had a fire going in the grill, the scoreboard was lit up and Jimmy Dorsey was playing the "Clarinet Polka."

"Listen to that," Pearly said, with an edge to his voice. He sat up straight, cocked his head, and waited for Grant to notice something after he'd secured his shin guard.

"What?" Grant asked, while Louie poked around through the shovels and garden hose and all the tools in the little shed. He thought Pearly was complaining about Jimmy Dorsey.

"Listen to Ray run his mouth!" Pearly said.

"Oh, that," Grant sighed. "I thought you meant Speed, and the polkas."

Other voices could be heard across the expanse of green grass now. The boys from Menahga had arrived and were warming up in left field, talking and laughing among themselves, as were the Walleyes. But Ray's voice, as usual, swelled above the others and ground itself into their heads.

"No, it's Ray. I just can't decide if it's the stupid shit he says, or just the way he struts around and acts like a little general," Pearly growled.

Louie closed the shed door and ignored Pearly's remarks.

"C'mon, Pearly. Let's get me warmed up," Grant said.

As Pearly and Grant stood up to walk to the Walleyes bullpen, Will Campbell walked around the corner of the dugout.

"I'm here, boys, you can stop worrying," Will said. When he noticed Grant walking with Pearly, he added, "You pitchin' tonight, Pard?"

"Yup," Grant replied. "Did you bring some hits with you?"

"Is a pig's ass pork?" Will answered, as he dropped his pants and started to get dressed for the game. Then, with his pants at his ankles, Will called to Grant and Pearly. When they turned to look at him he posed like a body builder trying to display his biceps. "Do these look swollen?" he asked.

"That guy makes me laugh," Pearly said to Grant, as they walked around the corner of the dugout.

Grant looked to his right and saw Kate and June chatting beside the smoking barbecue grill while Ingrid and the Campbell girls played together nearby. "Hi, Grant!" June called when she noticed him. He waved and smiled at June, as Frankie Yankovic started in on the "Too Fat Polka." What a great way to end a summer day, he thought.

"I'm feelin' sharp tonight, Pearly. Gimme the ball," Grant said.

Pearly flipped a baseball into the air and Grant caught it with his bare hand. "I still love this," Pearly sighed.

Grant nodded. "Me too."

"But I wouldn't piss on Ray Rivers if he was on fire," Pearly offered.

Grant smiled but said nothing while they walked together to the bullpen. He had come to view Ray with the same disdain as everyone else did.

Twenty minutes later, when Grant walked to the pitcher's mound to start the game, he glanced at the concession stand and noticed both umpires lingering there and laughing.

"Oh for Chrissakes," Pearly groaned, when he saw what Grant was looking at. "We've got the Irish mafia tonight."

Two tall men, both of them over six feet three and wearing umpire gear, were talking with Kate and June. Both of them were handsome, with some gray at the temples, and both of them were charming and gregarious. Grant knew them well by now; they umpired six or eight Walleye games every summer. Jack Fitzgerald and Tom Murphy were both local coaching legends. Murphy was the football coach at a small school just up the road and Fitzgerald was the head basketball coach at a different high school about thirty miles away. They always had a clever and gracious way about them and they were quick with a joke and a compliment when they arrived at a ballpark. They knew how to ingratiate themselves into every local good ol' boys' crowd.

Grant disliked and distrusted both of them immensely. During his first season with the Walleyes, Grant had been the recipient of a little "home cookin'" during a game in Windigo. For the first eight innings he'd mowed down Windigo hitters easily. But in the ninth inning, Tom Murphy, who was umping behind the plate, suddenly stopped calling strikes. If the Windigo batters didn't swing, it wasn't a strike. Grant walked the first three batters in the ninth inning. Even Louie Swearingen was livid. He stood in the dugout and screamed at Murphy for squeezing his pitcher. Murphy just smiled contemptuously. Fitzgerald proceeded to make a couple of bad calls on the bases, and Windigo won.

"I've seen 'em do worse," Pearly had confided to Grant after that game. "They're both pretty well known for that stuff. During the football season Murphy likes to hire Fitzy to come over and officiate the games with his tougher opponents, then Fitzy likes to hire Murphy to help him win the close ones in basketball. One hand washes the other. Visiting coaches know they're about to get fucked when they roll into town and see one of those guys officiating for the other." Then he'd added, "They're both a coupla poon hounds, too. They're always on the prowl. They like to use these ball games to get away from their wives and meet new people, if you know what I mean."

As Grant finished his warm-up pitches he could still hear the way Pearly had said "poon hounds," and a smile crossed his lips.

When the umpires finally took their positions to start the game, Pearly walked to the pitcher's mound for a little visit with Grant, and Will wandered over from his position at shortstop.

"Man, Fitzy and Murphy were really puttin' the press on your wife over there at the concession stand," Pearly said when he dropped the ball into Grant's glove. "Doesn't that bother you?"

Grant took the ball, glanced at Will, and shook his head. Kate and June didn't dislike Fitzgerald and Murphy as much as the players did, but they saw right though the flirting and the suggestive behavior. Kate had told him several times that she wouldn't trust Murphy as far as she could throw him, and that she liked to help him make a fool of himself.

"Nah," Grant replied to Pearly. "Kate and I . . ." He thought for a moment and decided Tom Murphy wasn't worth any more discussion. "Nah," he said, then started rubbing the game ball and turned his attention to the situation at hand. "Let's do this."

You couldn't get entertainment like this in the big leagues, Grant thought, as he took his final warm-up pitches. The manager of the home team had to drag the infield and chalk the base lines, the forty-six-year-old catcher for the home team wanted to fight his teammate, and one of the umpires was trying to hustle up the pitcher's wife. "Town ball," Grant said to himself just before the first pitch, and he waved to Kate over in the concession stand.

From the outset, this game was never a contest.

Will raced across home plate to give the Walleyes a 7–0 lead in the bottom of the fifth inning. "How 'bout that, Pard?" he huffed when he sat next to Grant in the dugout. "I'm three for three tonight! Three piss ropes in the gap!" Then he raised both arms and flexed as if he were a bodybuilder posing alongside other muscle-bound men in a shirtless competition. "Hey Louie?" he called. When Louie looked over at him he asked once again, "Do these look swollen?" and looked at his own biceps, then showed them to his chuckling teammates. "I've still got it," he said. He took a drink of water and added, "I could eat the ass end out of a dead skunk, Pard. Hope the kitchen is still open over at the Chateau when we wrap this up. I'm fuckin' hungry!"

"Can you read?" Ray said with a disgusted sigh, then pointed to a No Swearing sign that he'd stenciled onto the back wall of the dugout.

Everything lurched to a stop in the dugout. All the lighthearted esprit de corps that Will had created a moment earlier had been sapped with Ray's reprimand. Ray was a stopper, he always had been. He took every opportunity to stop or redirect the flow of a conversation, as if it somehow gave him standing to correct the small mistakes of others or change the discussion in some way.

This time Will had heard all he could stand. He put both hands on his hips and replied, "Well, yes, as a matter of fact I can read, Ray. Is there something you'd like me to help you with?" He made a point to let his tone imply that Ray might, in fact, be too stupid to read.

Several of the boys on the bench laughed openly. Ray puffed himself up like a fat songbird and walked to the far end of the dugout without a response.

"What the hell is it with you, Ray?" Will called to him. "That shit might work when you're trying to bully the high school kids around." Grant caught Will's attention and signaled for him to calm down, but Will ignored him and raised his voice a bit more. "But you've got a bunch of grown men here, Ray, and it's not your place to lecture us." Will's anger at Ray Rivers was about to boil over, but he stopped himself in time. He plopped down on the bench next to Pearly and sighed. "What is it with that guy?"

"Well," Pearly replied in a clear voice, unafraid that Ray might hear him, "I think he's just afraid somebody will get wise to him. He likes to stand there on the dugout step with an intense look on his face, so people will think he's analyzing his opponent's weaknesses and preparing a brilliant and complex strategy." Pearly paused. "But actually he doesn't know shit about the game and he's terrified somebody will figure that out, so he hides his ignorance behind all that bluster and puffery."

Will nodded his agreement.

"And he's a prick," Pearly added.

Pearly and Will were laughing at their own jokes when yet another Walleye batter got a hit and Louie called out, "Grab a bat, Ray! You're on deck."

The Walleye players watched silently a moment later when Ray strode to the batter's box. He stood stone-still for a few seconds while his third-base coach flashed him the prearranged hand signals, and then he took his place at bat. His team was ahead 9–1 in the fifth inning of a meaningless amateur game, and yet his eyes were set so hard an observer might think the World Series was on the line.

The pitcher took his sign from the catcher, came to his set position, and delivered a fastball that struck Ray between his shoulders. He arched his back like he'd just taken a bullet from a sniper, then he fell to the ground.

Not a single Walleye came to his aid or uttered a threat of reprisal to the opposing pitcher, who actually seemed to be pretty happy with what he'd done. Several Walleyes glanced back and forth at each other and smiled about Ray's pain. After a moment on the ground, he climbed to one knee and rested briefly. "Get up, you pussy!" Will hollered. "It's a long way from your heart," he added. The Menahga infielders had to cover their faces with their gloves while they laughed.

"Ever think you'd live to see the day that none of your boys would stick up for a teammate?" Pearly said to Louie Swearingen. Louie ignored him.

Pearly turned back toward Will. "See the kid pitchin' for Menahga?" Pearly asked, as he lit a cigarette. "He played for Ray last year, went to high school right here." Pearly took a long drag and watched Ray wobble down to first base. "He had a college scholarship to play basketball at some Division II school in Wisconsin." Pearly interrupted his own story suddenly when Ray arched his back and moaned on his slow journey toward first base. "C'mon, Ray!" Pearly shouted. "Let's see summa that hard-nosed shit!" Then, just as suddenly, Pearly lowered his voice and returned to his story about the Menahga pitcher. "So anyway, the kid is all set to play basketball in college, until Coach Rivers took the boys into the outfield one day in the spring of his senior year and had 'em do sliding drills, with their cleats on, in the grass!"

"Jeez, every bonehead knows you don't do that," Will replied.

"Exactly," Pearly scowled. "So, after Ray shows 'em all the wrong way to slide, the kid caught a cleat in the grass and shattered his leg. No scholarship for him. Now he makes a point to drill Ray every chance he gets."

~:~

The jukebox was blaring and Tamarac Chateau was rocking about an hour later. Baseball players from both teams sat together at several different tables, eating and drinking and laughing. "I don't know if I can take much more of this," Will said when he raised a beer to his lips.

"What do you mean?" Kate asked him.

"I mean I hate Ray. He just drains all the fun from this." Pearly raised a beer and clicked glasses with Will.

"You had four hits! You had a great day! How can you bellyache after that?" Grant replied.

"That guy just ruins everything. I hope he dies in prison!" Will shot back.

"Will!" June chastised. "Sometimes you scare me. And if Ray's so bad, why don't you just get rid of him?"

"You mean have him killed?" Will perked up at his own suggestion and June turned away. Her husband was hopeless.

Pearly raised a glass to click with Will's once again. "Louie thinks it's important to have the high school coach involved," Pearly explained. "And maybe he's right, but . . ."

"Well, I was quite stellar tonight, if I do say so myself," Grant interjected to change the subject, and he stole a kiss from Kate.

"Yeah, you threw a two-hitter with fourteen strikeouts!" Pearly answered. "You had the curve working tonight! You were dern near unhittable. You struck out their shortstop four times. He . . ." Pearly lost his train of thought completely when a group of young women walked in the front door. They were all attractive college girls and they were showing plenty of skin.

"By the way," Melbourne Carrigan announced for Will's information, "the one right there, with the nice shorts and the light brown hair? That's Brandi Rivers, Ray's wife."

"Wow!" Will said.

"Yeah, rumor has it that she's a little bit more than Ray can handle. If you know what I mean," Melbourne said with a wicked grin.

"Looks like she'd be plenty for any one man to handle," Will laughed.

Melbourne bent close to the group and pointed out something else that everyone had already noticed. "Looky there. It's the Badenovs, too!"

"Who?" Will begged, leaning forward for an explanation.

"Look over there, by the pool table. See those two girls with black hair? That's the Badenovs, Boris and Natasha," Melbourne said.

Will, Grant, Kate, and June all scanned the group of girls to locate the dark-haired ones Melbourne was trying to point out.

"There they are!" Kate said, and she covered her mouth and laughed. "I see them now!"

Standing by the pool table, talking to a couple of Menahga ballplayers, was a tall, sultry, angular-looking young woman with very long black hair. Next to her stood a much shorter woman with a round face and black hair. Both of them were dressed in black and wore T-shirts that were designed to feature some impressive cleavage.

"Oh, yeah!" June exclaimed, as the lightbulb clicked on in her head and she understood. "The Badenovs, as in Boris and Natasha from Rocky and Bullwinkle, right?" Will stared openmouthed and marveled at the young ladies' uncanny resemblance to the two cartoon characters.

Grant put an arm over Kate's shoulders and laughed out loud. "I love playing with those young guys. The Badenovs! That's a good one."

Pearly grimaced and shook his head, and the Carrigans grinned at each other.

"Actually, only Boris's last name was Badenov. Natasha's last name was actually Fatale," Will offered.

"Shut up, Will," June scolded. "He just does that to show off," she said to the Carrigans.

"Well, they sure command a lot of attention when they show up here at the Chateau," Pearly said. "Last summer our second baseman spent the entire season trying to take 'em both home on the same night. Said he was trying for a Menahga trois!"

The absurd collision of the English and French language took a moment to sink in, and then another flood of laughter washed over the table. Kate was holding her ribs, trying to stop her side ache, when Pearly stood up to leave and the Carrigans joined the younger crowd on the other side of the Chateau.

A waitress was clearing dishes and empty beer bottles from their table when Will leaned forward. "This probably isn't a very good time to tell you this," he said, pausing to let Kate and Grant see the sudden change in his eyes, "but Carol Knutsen was killed in a plane crash."

Grant's expression turned sour and Kate covered her mouth with her hand. "Say it ain't so, Pard," Grant said.

Will nodded. It was so.

"What happened?" Kate asked.

"Apparently she was flying in a small plane with her new boyfriend and something went wrong," Will replied.

"When?" Kate asked.

"'Bout three months ago," Will said.

"And nobody called?" Grant said.

"We just found out today too," Will said. "I think we'd all sort of lost track of each other. I hadn't talked to her in a couple years."

"Me neither," Grant sighed.

"Her parents didn't know us, and how close our group was, so they didn't call anybody, and it happened in California," Will explained.

"Oh, this sort of thing isn't supposed to happen," Grant said, as the reality began to sink in. A good friend was dead. Maybe she'd just met the love of her life, then suddenly she'd been denied the chance to go on. It made no sense, and that little chapter of *his* life was now closed, too.

"Can you imagine the last two minutes of her life?" Will asked. They all sat, thinking about her. "I was gonna tell you before the game, but it just didn't seem like the right time."

"It's OK," Grant said.

"You know, I feel kinda bad," Will said. "I heard the news earlier today, then when I got here and started playin' ball I was having fun and I actually forgot about her for a while. How could I do that? But I did it."

∽:∾

The steamy shower felt good to Grant. He stood in the shower stall and let the hot water cascade over his head and shoulders while he thought back over a long day.

They'd stayed later than they should have at the Tamarac Chateau. Ingrid was cranky and tired when they finally got home. Then he'd sat up with Kate for an hour and tried to put Carol Knutsen's life and death in perspective. It didn't seem right to just go on after he'd received the news of her death. But what else *could* he do? Her funeral was over. Her life was over. All he could do was just go on. Right?

He let the hot water run over his body and thought about the other friends he'd lost track of: Ben Pribyl, Andy Hedstrom, Joe Paatalo, the others. They were once such an important part of his life, and now they'd pretty much drifted away. They'd gone on with life, too.

Maybe after the shower he'd sit out on the porch with the lights off and think about all this for a while. He was about ready to turn off the water when he found the lump on his testicle.

∾ CHAPTER 38 ∾

Grant let his feet dangle over the side of his hospital bed. He looked around at the gray shadows on the walls. More outrageous fortune. Kate and Ingrid were staying at Will's house, not far from the hospital, tonight. They'd just left his room an hour earlier. Kate would be back early in the morning, before surgery.

A few muffled sounds came from the nurses' station down the hall; otherwise, the place was silent. Tomorrow was the day. He hadn't seen this coming, and he was afraid, more afraid than he'd ever been.

Friday night, forty-eight hours earlier, he'd played baseball with his buddies. He played pretty well, too, and had so much fun afterwards. Life had been so good, so easy. And then while he was still trying to understand the incomplete life of a friend, this had happened. After he'd found the tender lump on his testicle, he said something to Will over coffee on Saturday morning and he saw the concern in Will's eyes immediately. Will drove him to Duluth for an emergency visit with the urologist who practiced just down the hall from him. At first, Grant had convinced himself that it was nothing, but the thing seemed to be growing and getting more tender with every passing minute. It had to be just some strange inflammation that would go away. This stuff happened to other people, not him, not now.

"It's malignant, no doubt about it," the doctor told Grant after some tests. The only thing to do was remove the testicle and hope the cancer hadn't metastasized already. Then some chemotherapy, maybe radiation, too. It felt like the doctor had punched him in the chest.

Testicular cancer was bad, really bad, and this was overwhelming. After all those fireside bullshit sessions about forks in the road, he'd assumed that his road would be a long one. Now he felt so powerless against this thing that might take away all that he had, and all he'd ever have.

Grant slid off the bed, walked to the window, and looked out into the night. A few cars moved along on the highway a mile or so away, and two nurses stood under a streetlight in the parking lot, smoking on their break time. Nobody knew about him or his problem. And if they knew, they wouldn't care. Not really. Even his best friends would greet the news of his sickness or death with indifference, just like Carol's plane crash. "Oh, Grant Thorson died of cancer. That's too bad," they'd say. Then they'd shake their heads in a show of regret, and go on with their lives without him.

And Kate, what about Kate? If he died, would she find someone else, someone better? Ingrid would have almost no memory of him, either. She'd know him only from old photographs. Kate's second husband would be Ingrid's father, not him.

Grant closed his eyes as hard as he could and tried to push these ugly thoughts from his mind, but they circled above him like vultures.

A knuckle tapped softly on his door and startled him. He hoped whoever was there wouldn't be able to see the fear in his eyes when he spun to greet them.

But it was Kate, and she had plenty of fear in her own eyes. No greeting. No smile. She just walked into his arms and held him close. He should have known she'd return after Ingrid was asleep. She'd never let him spend this night alone.

As always, her touch was soothing. But tonight there was a mysterious honesty in the way she held him. "I'm so afraid," he whispered. It felt good to tell someone.

Kate made no reply. She stroked the back of his neck and waited for him to go on.

"I'm afraid of dying, Kate."

"You're not going to die," Kate said through tears she couldn't hold back. "The doctor went over all that with us a couple times. You heard him."

Earlier that day they'd both sat in a small office while the doctor laid it all out for them in not-so-subtle terms. He knew they both had medical backgrounds and they had a pretty fair idea how serious this was. "I won't candy-coat this for you," he began. "I know you've both been reading up on testicular cancer over the past twenty-four hours and I'm sure you both know that fifteen years ago this type of cancer would have been a death sentence—you'd have died a brutal death." Grant would never forget the way those words weakened him. "But we have a new drug now, it's called Cisplatin, and when we mix it up in a cocktail with a few other nasty-sounding chemicals it's yielding a cure rate of about eighty percent." He stopped, pointed at Grant, and added, "I said *cure*, as in 'You're *cured*,' so I want you to understand that your odds are pretty good, Grant."

Kate and Grant now stood with their arms around each other, both reliving the unforgettable exchange with the doctor.

"I'm tired," Kate said finally. "Can I stay with you tonight? I didn't think you'd be sleeping much, so I thought I'd just stay with you. But if you'd be more comfortable I can just . . ."

Grant walked to his bed, threw the covers back, climbed in, and motioned for Kate to join him. She slipped her blue jeans off, then her brace, and lay down beside him. "It's been a while since we spent the night together in a bed this small," Grant said when he turned off the light.

Kate nestled her head against his shoulder and held him close while he lay on his back and stared at the ceiling. "I know what they're gonna do, you know," Grant said after a few minutes of silence. "I know what's gonna happen." He brought a hand down and covered his crotch. "About two minutes after they put me to sleep some nurse is gonna shave me. The operating room will be real quiet at first. Then one of the nurses will say something about the weather. Maybe someone will mention what a nice weekend they just had. About that time the surgeon will pick a scalpel with a number fifteen razor blade. Maybe he'll say something about his golf game . . ."

"Grant, don't . . . ," Kate interrupted.

"Then he'll make an unkind cut," Grant said coldly. "He'll open up my scrotum and snip out my swollen and malignant testicle . . ."

"Grant . . ."

"It'll make sort of a splat when he drops it in the little steel pan they use for stuff like that. Then before he sews things back together, he'll poke around some and try to be sure that everything else is OK." He stopped and thought about what he'd just said. "I know what they're gonna do. I wonder what it's gonna feel like to reach down there and not feel all of me still there."

"We're all missing something, Grant. We've all got scars," Kate said.

"I'm afraid I won't be the same . . . for you . . . sex . . . you can't imagine how that makes me feel."

"The doctor says that'll all be fine," Kate whispered.

"I'm still afraid . . ."

"They're going to cure your cancer so we can go on with our lives," she said.

He'd given a voice to his fears. He'd heard himself say the words. That was enough. Any more talk of it would be more than he could bear.

Kate held him and whispered to him until morning.

~: CHAPTER 39 :~

May 1986

Two March blizzards kept Leech Lake frozen until the second week in May, and it had begun to feel like the world would never be young again.

But the sun broke through as it always did. Spring came in a rush, and the ice was off Leech Lake now. The green canopy of the northern forest hadn't blossomed yet, but today a bright sun moved through the clear sky and seemed to rest a warm, comforting hand on Grant's shoulder. The gentle, regular splashing of waves along the shoreline in front of his home was the only sound Grant could hear as he stood in his backyard and studied the large expanse of open blue water.

Chemotherapy had been worse than he'd expected, far worse. Near the end he'd been so sick he almost gave up. He'd never forget the conversation he'd had with his doctor. "I can't take any more chemo," Grant had protested weakly. "Look at me. My skin is gray and I look like a cadaver. I didn't know a man could feel this sick. I can't do it, doctor. The chemo is gonna kill me. I'd rather take my chances with the cancer."

"Well, Grant," the doctor had replied. "That seems to be how chemotherapy works. In order for the drugs to kill the cancer they have to almost kill you, too. The chemo will save your life, but at some point, before you get well, you might wonder if it was worth it."

The doctor was right. The headaches and the nausea and the pain had been unbearable for a while there. It nearly consumed him.

But it was over now. He'd had summer, autumn, and then a long winter, almost a year now, to rest and regain his strength. His color was back. So was his hair. No one would use the word *cured* yet, but he felt good enough to let himself believe that was the case. Grant filled his lungs with the soft spring wind blowing in off the lake. It was good to be alive; it just wasn't as easy as it once had been. There was a little more to think about now.

Pearly and Louie had stopped by quite a bit after the surgery, just to have a laugh and keep him informed about the latest of the Walleyes' troubles. Will had been there to offer support from that first day. Sometimes he'd just sat beside Grant at the kitchen table and listened to Grant talk about the chemo, or his recovery, or his fears. He listened and laughed and encouraged and scolded Grant, but he was always there when he was needed. When Grant's hair began to grow back, Will helped with physical therapy, which included throwing a baseball. Now, after all he'd been through, Grant didn't have the heart to tell Will that he wasn't sure where the cancer had left him, and that he might just retire from baseball.

When he heard a commotion on the porch behind him, Grant turned in time to see Ingrid burst out through the screen door. Kate stayed on the porch and waved as Ingrid raced across the grass toward her father.

She'd been in the dress-up box again, that much was obvious. She wore a straw sombrero that bobbed when she ran, and a brightly colored cotton shirt that hung to the ground and nearly covered her yellow rubber boots.

As she drew closer, Grant noticed that she was wearing eye makeup and lipstick, and by the look of this, she'd applied it herself. He knew immediately that she'd been having a tea party with her mother and she'd talked Kate into letting her wear some makeup.

Grant looked up to the porch and questioned Kate with his eyes. She answered with a shrug, then smiled and went back inside the house.

"Dad!" Ingrid hollered as she ran toward him. She carried an empty ice-cream bucket in one hand. "Let's work on my rock collection. I'll be the beautiful one!"

It was time to comb the beach with a beautiful geologist in search of rare specimens. Grant took her by the hand and led her to the lakeshore. Yeah, it was good to be alive.

Every rock Ingrid picked up was the subject of intense scrutiny, and then before it could be saved in the ice-cream bucket they tried to invent a theory about how it came to rest on their property. Ingrid jabbered continuously and moved from one fantasy to the next every few paces. Some stones were probably blown there by volcanoes on far-off tropical islands where the natives hunted monkeys with blowguns. She could tell by the way some of the bigger rocks had been piled up that pirates had buried a treasure somewhere near the house and marked the spot with those rocks.

Some of the rocks were just so pretty they needed to be brought into the house and displayed on her nightstand.

A dead fish rocking in the waves along with some other flotsam stole her interest for a few minutes. She was pretty sure it was a baby shark.

"Dad?" she asked during a lull in her own monologue, as if a deep philosophical issue was weighing on her.

"Yeah," he replied, while he studied a small black-and-white stone.

"What's the worst word there is?" she asked.

Now the topic had shifted to swearwords, and he tried not to show his surprise. "Well, there are a lot of bad words," he started. He wondered where this line of thought would carry them. "I don't think there is any one word that's worse than the others." He knew he certainly wasn't about to help her compile a list of dirty words.

"I know what it is!" Ingrid boasted. Her voice turned serious, and she pointed a finger at him.

"Oh?" Grant said, and his curiosity demanded that he ask, "OK, what's the worst word there is?" He braced himself for her answer.

Ingrid looked right, then left, to be sure no one was listening, especially her mother, before she answered his question. She hunched her shoulders over, peeked at him from under the brim of the sombrero, and said firmly, "It's the D word." She nodded to underscore the terribleness of the word.

"Oh?" Grant said, relieved by her answer. The list of bad D words was pretty short. He thought it over for a moment and decided to take his chances and ask for a more precise answer. "So, what's the D word?" he asked casually.

Ingrid scouted the terrain in all directions once more. When she was sure no one else was listening, she stared intently at her father and announced it: "Shit!"

Grant used his left hand to cover the smile tugging at the corners of his mouth. "Yeah, that's a bad word, honey, but there's no D in shit."

"Oh!" Ingrid gasped. She held her forearm across her brow like a silent movie actress trying to show her despair. "I get all those letters mixed up!"

Ingrid's brief theatrical display came and went before Grant could respond. Then she turned away and continued her search for trophy rocks. He watched her for a while as she wandered along the shoreline and talked to herself about pirates and swearwords and dead fish. Childhood, what a great place, he thought.

Will would be here in a few hours for a weekend visit, and Grant couldn't wait to tell Will about the D word. Maybe the cancer had been just another fork in the road, and he'd been lucky enough to take the path that led him here. Will surely would have something to say about that.

~:~

A soft, steady rain fell through the night sky and tapped a soothing beat on the shingles above Grant's garage. Now that spring was finally here, Will had driven over from Duluth to mark the opening of *two* walleye seasons: fishing and baseball. Minnesota's fishing opener was scheduled for this weekend, and the Walker Walleyes would have their first practice of the new season tomorrow night.

"OK, close your eyes," Grant said as he raised his garage door that evening.

The restoration of the small boat he'd taken on trade from Pearly's mother-in-law was complete and it was time to show Will. The thing had been lying outside Grant's home in varying states of disrepair for five years. Something, maybe it was the cancer, maybe it was Kate's continuous complaints about the eyesore that was always in the way, had inspired Grant to finish the project he'd begun so long ago. Whatever the reason, he'd attacked the project with a renewed vigor when the doctor gave him permission to resume a normal physical workload. The physical exercise had helped him regain his strength. But more than that, each little accessory that he customized and restored came with an expectation of use that reached into the future. Hours spent working on the boat had been mental-health time after his brush with cancer.

"Wow!" Will offered when he stepped inside. Raindrops slapped gently into the gathering puddles in the driveway, and Herb Carneal's voice crackled faintly through a small radio on Grant's workbench as he described an early-season Twins game.

Grant had painted the entire boat olive drab—inside, outside, the plywood seats, even the old Johnson motor. Then he'd used a pipe bender to shape eight-foot sections of aluminum conduit into the frame for a removable duck blind, and covered the framework with burlap and swamp grass.

"Really nice, Pard," Will said. He stepped closer, rested his elbows on the gunwales, and peered into the boat. "This'll be great for duck huntin' over on Spider Lake, and it'll be a fine fishin' boat when we lift this blind off." He sniffed once, and added, "It smells like new."

Three sixty-watt bulbs suspended from the rafters provided the only illumination in the garage, and the yellow light cast gray shadows while the men walked along the sides of the boat and inspected Grant's handi-work. Soon the two empty seats in the newly remodeled duck boat grew irresistible, and when Will could stand it no longer he stepped up on the boat trailer, then threw his leg over the gunwale and climbed into the boat. Grant followed close behind and they each laid claim to the seats that they'd occupy for the next couple of decades. Within minutes they'd decided where the duck decoys should be stored and where the sandwiches could be stashed to keep them dry and out of the way. The natural order of this advanced child's play demanded that they begin to scout the ceiling of the garage for imaginary ducks and then shoot them with their fingers.

Sitting in the little boat, surrounded by the burlap walls of the duck blind and pretending to hunt ducks, Grant found himself on a child's adventure, just like the ones he took with Ingrid. There were no pirates or wild Indians today, however, only ducks. This little boat was simply a playhouse, just like the forts they'd built with scrap lumber and used nails when they were boys. The atmosphere inside the boat was perfect for secrets and confessions.

Grant leaned back and tapped his hand on the outboard motor beside him. "This old Johnson still starts on the first pull, too," he bragged.

"You OK, Pard? I mean, the cancer?" Will asked, uninterested in any more talk of boats and motors and ducks for the time being. He wanted to know about Grant's health. The truth.

"Yeah, sure. I feel good. The doctor thinks I'm cured, but they won't actually say 'cured' until I've survived for five years." Grant shrugged.

Will stared into Grant's eyes, demanding a better answer.

"Don't believe me?" Grant asked.

"Just asking," Will replied. "Your color is back, and your hair. You gained some weight back, too. But there's something on your mind. What is it?"

"Ah . . ." Grant sighed and then leaned forward so that his elbows rested on his knees. "I dunno." He was reluctant to confess what he planned to do about baseball.

"How 'bout that little Johnson right there?" Will pointed between Grant's legs. "Does he still start on the first pull? 'Zat the problem?"

Grant's eyes narrowed and a smile stretched over his face. Only Will would ask a question like that. Only Will would sit with him in a little boat on a trailer in a garage and pretend to shoot imaginary ducks, then bluntly ask about his sex life.

"You're inquiring about the Johnson who lives down there?" Grant asked as he pointed at himself.

"Yeah, you know . . . ," Will started, ". . . little short guy? Wears a Nazi helmet and turtleneck? Does he still start on the fist pull?"

"Sure does," Grant nodded. "In fact, sometimes he still starts up on his own, then he calls to me every twenty-three seconds and wants to know if there's any work for him to do." No one except Kate had been willing to talk with Grant about such things. But Will would, and he made Grant feel better just because he'd asked such an outrageous question.

"Wanna see my scar?" Grant asked.

"Thought you'd never ask," Will replied.

Grant stood up and unzipped his blue jeans. "I hope Kate doesn't walk in right now," he said, as he lowered his jeans and his boxer shorts.

Will leaned closer and stared for a moment, then said, "Move Mr. Johnson out of the way, would you?"

Grant lifted things to the side, then sat down on the boat seat to reveal the full extent of the scar.

"Jeez," Will gasped, then he grimaced as if the sight of Grant's scar made his own scrotum ache. "Sorta looks like Loretta Klitsche with her teeth out. Does it hurt?"

"Nope," Grant said while he pulled his pants up. "It's hard to explain. Maybe it's like when a woman has breast cancer, and then a mastectomy. You know, they just never feel whole again, and they think everybody knows. I used to feel around down there while it was healing. Felt kinda swollen and mangled. I thought about it all the time, too. Then I was so sick with the chemo; I didn't really think about much of anything, except how shitty I felt. But it doesn't hurt now, I'm getting used to the way things are," he said, while he tucked his shirt into his blue jeans and zipped up.

When he sat down on his boat seat once again, he dismissed the cancer and asked, "You ever hear from Ben Pribyl, or Joe Paatalo, or Andy Hedstrom?"

"Nope. I do see Dommy Sabetti though, but that's 'cuz he practices about two doors down the hall from me." Will sighed. "Sorta lost track of the others. I guess I was just busy with other stuff, new stuff. How 'bout you?"

"Me neither. Maybe a Christmas card that first year or two after school, but nothing since then," Grant said. "I never thought that would happen. I thought we'd be close friends forever." He shrugged. "I still feel bad every time I think about Carol. But lately I find myself smiling when I remember her. I couldn't do that at first."

"Remember that discussion we had about old girlfriends on our first trip up to Spider Lake Duck Camp?" Will asked.

"You mean when you forgot the food, and we sat by a fire and got drunk? That trip?" Grant asked.

"That's the night I'm talking about!" Will pointed a finger at Grant. "Well, I guess Carol, and the others from school, will sort of fade away from our lives and exist only in our memories, just like those old girlfriends. But their deeds will live on and we won't have to watch them get old and ugly."

"Well . . . that isn't *always* how it works!" Grant grinned and shook his head as the conversation took another turn. "Remember my old girlfriend, Anne?" His eyes hinted at the irony he was about to reveal.

"Only met her once, but yes, I remember. Pretty girl," Will said.

"Well, Anne and her husband just moved to Walker. He's the new football coach and she's the girls' basketball coach. You believe that?" Grant asked, marveling at the uncanny coincidence that they'd wind up living in the same small town.

"So do you still have feelings for her? Like . . ."

"No," Grant said. "Not at all. But it was pretty odd to watch her just stroll up to Kate and introduce herself. I guess I was really impressed by the way they both acted toward each other, you know, 'Hi, I'm the other woman. See you around town.' It was all pretty cordial."

"They're both nice people, what'd you expect?" Will said. "Do you think Anne still has feelings for you?" Will asked.

"Never really thought about that," Grant said with a shrug. "But I doubt it."

"Do you think Kate's jealous?" Will asked.

"Yeah, I know she is. It wasn't so bad until Anne moved here and everyone started raving about the sexy new woman coach. Then one dark night when her demons were back, Kate asked me if Anne and I had been . . . lovers." He smiled sheepishly.

"What'd you tell her?" Will asked.

"Mmmm." Grant thought for a moment. "Some of the truth."

"Bad move." Will smiled.

"Aw, she already knew the truth," Grant replied. "Wanna know what else I told her? Something way more powerful that had nothing to do with sex?" He didn't wait for Will to respond. "I tried to explain something to her. Shortly after we'd started dating and that fire in our bellies was white hot, she walked up to me at school—you and Ben were standing nearby, and Ebby and Joe Ruminsky were on the other side of the room—and Kate put her hand on the small of my back and held me sorta close. She moved her hand around a little bit, and let me put my arm around her. She claimed me in front of her friends, and mine. She let everyone know that I was hers."

A lump had suddenly formed in Grant's throat and he had to stop. Then he swallowed hard and finished. "Felt like I'd just won the World Series. Kate Bellows was mine! Still feels that same way every time she touches me like that. Wish I could make her understand."

"I think she understands," Will said.

A moment later Grant turned to Will and asked, "Have you ever been jealous, Pard? I mean jealous in that sick, bottomless way that you can't do anything about?"

"Once," Will replied after a long pause. "You?"

"Oh yeah. 'Bout a month ago we were sitting on the couch reading the Sunday paper," Grant sighed. "I noticed Kate was spending a lot of time on one long article so I looked a little closer. There was a whole big feature story about her old boyfriend, Rod Muir, and what a great man he is. The guy is a philanthropist, Will. All he does, full time, is give away his family's money. The story went on and on about his interesting life, and there were a couple photos of him. I watched her read the entire article. I just watched her eyes while she read. Pretty soon I began to feel terrible. I wanted her to toss it on the floor and then tell me how much she loved me. But she just kept reading. The cancer never made me feel that impotent."

"It was just a newspaper story," Will said. "Big deal."

"Yeah, well, we've all got dreams, and when I saw the look in her eyes I just wasn't sure what I was looking at," Grant said. "Don't think I ever felt like that. There she was, sittin' on the same green couch we had when we were in school, cuttin' coupons so she could buy groceries. Then she found the article about her rich and fascinating old boyfriend. I felt like it suddenly dawned on her that she coulda had him. But instead she has me: the guy with the used duck boat and one nut."

"Jeez, you're being a little hard on yourself," Will said. "She loves you because of who you are, not because of . . ."

"Oh shit," Grant scoffed. "Now I s'pose you're gonna tell me I'm cute, too. Kate says that kind of stuff all the time and I hate it. I don't wanna be cute. I wanna be her hero. I want her to think I'm ten feet tall and bulletproof, and I don't think I can share that ground with Rod Muir or anybody else."

After five and ten years of marriage, Will's other friends complained about nagging wives who weren't interested in sex. But Grant Thorson was still confessing his infatuation with Kate.

"Well, I've known her as long as you have," Will began, "and I'd have to say that your status as her hero has never been in doubt. But there's something else going on here that you're not grasping. You need Rod Muir! She needs him, too. She needs to feel that someone else, someone good, found her desirable. But she had her choice, and she chose you."

Grant stared at him for a second and tried to understand what Will was saying.

"Think about it," Will said. "Kate had her own job. She was standing on her own two feet, she was having some success on her own. Somebody else wanted her, somebody besides you. That was huge for her self-esteem, and you had nothing to do with it. She needs him. He's the fork in the road, the one she didn't take. Hell, you just mentioned Anne, your old girlfriend, a couple minutes ago. It may be all over with her, but she still means *something* to you, doesn't she?" Will tapped his heart and smiled. "And it's something good, too, isn't it?"

"Yeah," Grant conceded.

"So are you willing to let Kate hold on to Rod Muir like that?"

Grant nodded. "I guess so," he sighed. "How'd you get to be so insightful?"

"Well, a couple years ago when I was still in grad school we had a rough stretch. June and I got married real young, you know. She was the only girl I ever dated, and I was the only boy she ever dated. All those issues about self-esteem and independence had to be worked out a little differently for us, and I guess I started to take her for granted." Just then they heard footsteps outside the garage.

"Hey! Where are you guys?" Kate called out from the doorway. She stepped into the garage carrying a six-pack of Hamm's beer.

"I'll tell you all about it some other time," Will said quietly. He stood up to show himself above the swamp grass and burlap that surrounded their fort. "Over here, Kate!" he said.

The dark rain pelted all the little puddles in the driveway outside the open garage door and tapped a steady soothing rhythm on the shingles above them. When Kate saw Will stand up and reveal himself from inside the boat she knew she'd caught them at play, and a smile spread across her face.

Kate *was* prettier than other women, Will thought. She had some inner beauty that flowed from her at times. Tonight she wore her long hair pulled back in a ponytail. Even in the dim light her blue shirt borrowed some of the pale blue from her eyes, and her black V-neck sweater curved perfectly around her breasts.

She held the beer up to announce that she'd come to join the party. Her eyes always offered something, Will thought. Maybe it was friendship, or humor, or the hint of a joke she was about to share, he couldn't say for sure, but it was grand. "C'mon over," Will called to her.

She started to walk toward the boat, still smiling and holding the beer for him to see. Her shoulders bobbed a bit as she swung her stiff leg and shifted her weight. He watched her labored stride and felt shame for noticing it, and for thinking that some of her beauty had vanished with it.

But at the same time, Will glanced over at Grant and recognized the remarkable phenomenon he'd been witnessing for years. Grant wore the expectant grin of a small child waiting for Santa Claus, and when he swung open a flap of burlap and found himself nose to nose with Kate, he showed her the same lovesick smirk he'd been unable to disguise since their first conversation at the fourth-floor coffee shop.

"Got room for one more in there?" Kate asked. Only Kate Thorson would want to come and sit with them, Will thought. Anyone else's wife would stay away, or maybe deliver the beer and then leave them to their play. Only Kate would want to join her lover and his buddy for a pretend duck hunt and bullshit session in a little boat resting on its trailer in a small garage on a cold and rainy spring evening. Grant and Kate did indeed share something that he and June had lost. They were still sweethearts after all they'd been through, maybe because of all they'd been through, and Will envied them.

"C'mon in, honey," Grant said. Kate handed the beer to Will and then prepared to climb into the boat. Grant stared like an old woman gloating at her grandchild's piano recital.

Kate threw her stiff left leg forward and then stepped up onto the boat trailer with her other leg. It was hard for her to do this, and she looked terribly awkward, but she showed no sign of being self-conscious. The leg brace made it especially difficult for her to climb over the gunwale and under the rail of the duck blind in the same motion.

While Kate was doubled over and clutching at the side of the boat,

Will noticed Grant's eyes turn devious. He waited until she was hovering over the gunwale at the most vulnerable moment and then reached around from behind her and clutched her breasts as he assisted her passage into the boat. He tried to pretend that his action had been offered purely to aid her balance and insure her safety.

"Thank you," Kate said sarcastically, when she sat down next to Grant.

"You're welcome. Here, let me help you brush that dust off your sweater," Grant said, and he began to softly sweep his hands over her breasts once more.

She pushed his hands away, smiled at Will, and took one of the beers from the six-pack. "So what are we talking about?" she asked. "Are you boys pretending to shoot ducks?"

"No. We both bagged our limit a long time ago," Will answered. Thunder rumbled somewhere far off, and the rain outside came down a little more quickly. Will remembered something. "Hey, I forgot to tell you! I've a couple ringers lined up to play for the Walleyes!"

"Who?" Kate asked immediately.

"I don't think I'm gonna play anymore," Grant blurted. "It's time to retire. I'm ready to be done with that. That's what I was gonna tell you earlier."

"Huh?" Will and Kate said in unison. Neither of them tried to hide their shock.

"It's time to be done with that," Grant said.

"You love baseball. You love the Walleyes!" Kate said. "And the doctor said you can go ahead and play." She was incredulous at Grant's announcement.

"Aw, Ray's driven off all the good players. The young guys all moved up the road to play for the Dragonflies. There's only six of us left, and five of us hate Ray. It's no fun anymore. I think the Walleyes are gonna fold anyway."

Kate reached her arm around Grant's shoulders and shook him gently, then stroked the back of his neck. "Don't you remember, honey, at the very end of the season last year when the Twins went to Cleveland with a chance to win the division? They lost all four games. Remember how awful it was? You said if they only had one more right-handed pitcher they'd have won the division." She reached her other hand over and turned his face until he looked at her. "Well, how are the Twins supposed to find you if you quit now?"

Will started to laugh, then he realized that Kate might not be joking. She shook Grant gently once more and tried to coax a smile. Had

Grant actually convinced Kate that he still had a shot to make the big leagues? Will studied both of their faces and wondered. It was one of those moments between a husband and wife that outsiders don't usually get to witness. She still seemed to think he was bound for the big leagues, or did she?

"Just a minute here, Pard," Will finally spoke up. "I told you, I've got three guys lined up, and all three of 'em can play ball. We're not gonna fold!"

"Who are they?" Grant asked without looking away from Kate.

"One of 'em is Dommy's little brother, Paladin Sabetti. Remember him?" Will asked.

"No," Grant said.

"Sure you do," Kate said. "He's the one who got in the fight at Dommy's party. You remember . . . the same day Tanya the Mauler cleaned your teeth!"

"Oh yeah. The wiry little kid who beat the shit outta that football player at a frat house kegger?" Grant asked. "He's just a kid." He blinked to jog his memory.

"Not anymore!" Will replied. "He went off to play hockey at Dartmouth. Played varsity baseball, too. After college he gave pro hockey a shot and bounced around in the minor leagues for a while. He got sick of that after a while. Now he's a freshman in dental school."

"No shit?" Grant said.

Kate put her arm around Grant's shoulder and leaned close to him. "See? You can't quit," she said.

"Yeah," Will continued, "I see him every so often when he's in Duluth to visit Dommy. Anyway, he's got a couple buddies from dental school who wanna play ball this summer. I lined up summer jobs for all three of them over at Totem Lodge; you know, the posh corporate retreat that IBM owns over on Big Bear Lake. They'll be cutting grass on the golf course during the day and maybe doing some other maintenance jobs, and then playing ball at night. And they're still college boys," Will added. "So I'm sure their evenings will be filled with other activities, too."

"Really?" Grant seemed interested for the first time. "And you said the other two guys can play? They're good?"

Kate grinned at Will and rubbed Grant's back to show her enthusiasm for the upcoming season.

"That's what Dommy says," Will replied, "All I know is that they all played college ball for four years, they can all pitch if we need 'em to, and they'll be here tomorrow for the first day of practice."

~: CHAPTER 40 :~

Several families of mice had spent the long winter living in the barbecue grill in the concession stand at Walleye Field. Kate dragged the grill over to the tall grass behind the small wooden building and dumped out the remaining ashes from last summer's final game, along with an impressive mouse nest. Her face was still twisted with a squeamish scowl when she returned the grill to its summer place alongside the concession stand to begin washing it.

She'd come along with Grant to the first practice session of the new season for the Walker Walleyes. Town ball games were just around the corner and she needed to get the concession stand ready. Off in the distance, a handful of men's voices mingled with the sound of baseballs popping into leather gloves.

The refrigerator came to life when she plugged it in. So did the frying pan and the popcorn machine. She placed a clipboard with a yellow legal pad on the countertop by the customer window and began to make a list of things to buy for the upcoming season: brats and buns, condiments, peanuts . . .

While she was writing, Kate noticed some movement in the corner of her eye, and she glanced up from her work. Over in the short grass by the batting cage she saw Grant running alongside Ingrid's bicycle. He was dressed and ready for baseball practice, but for the time being he was teaching his daughter how to ride a bike.

Ingrid sat on the seat, rigid with fear, clutching the handlebars and staring at some fixed point in front of her. Grant ran along, bent over and holding the back of her bicycle seat with one hand and the handlebars with the other. "That's it. That's it," he reassured her.

Kate was spellbound. She leaned out the window to get a better look.

"OK, honey. I'm gonna let go of the handlebars. You steer. I've got you. You won't fall," Grant said. He moved one hand away from the handlebars but kept the other on the seat.

Ingrid clung to the handlebars with the intensity of a fighter pilot.

"OK. Here you go," Grant said, releasing his daughter. "That's it," he said as he ran along beside her. Whenever Ingrid began to tremble and overcorrect, he grabbed the seat and steadied her. "Good, that's good. Now pedal your feet." He ran a few more steps. "I'm gonna let go again. Ready?"

Ingrid still seemed catatonic, but she began to pedal. Then Grant let go and watched her sail away. She rolled along for about thirty feet, and then her maiden voyage ended the way they all do.

She was lying in the grass trying to decide whether or not to cry when Grant swept her up in his arms and exclaimed, "Nice one! You had it! Now you just need to keep going."

Even from her distant vantage point in the concession-stand window, Kate could read exactly what was going on in Ingrid's mind, and Grant's. This was all new for Ingrid, and even though she wasn't injured it seemed like a good time to start crying. Kate wanted to run to her and be the one to hold her while she cried.

But Grant was holding her, laughing, and assuring her that she'd done a good thing. He was removing failure as an option and reassuring her that the crash had been part of a successful ride.

This was a singular moment for Kate. She'd never had an experience like this with her own father, and she could only watch as this one unfolded.

A minute later Ingrid was back in the saddle, a little less rigid, but still pretty serious. Several crashes later she had scrapes and stains on both knees and both hands, but she was beginning to stay upright for extended distances and actually pedal the bicycle.

"Watch me, Mommy!" she hollered, when Grant guided her for a pass in front of the concession stand. Grant smiled and waved too.

Who was that man, Kate wondered. She watched as he ran along in his gray baseball uniform and stood guard over Ingrid. This was a moment Kate could never have anticipated. Her lover, the boy who couldn't keep his hands off her, was teaching their daughter how to ride a bicycle. They'd come far together.

She'd seen him display supreme confidence, and complete despair. He made her laugh, and he made her thumbs go numb. He was her best friend. He was the one she needed. But she'd seen him sick with jealousy, worried that an old boyfriend might still own something that he wanted. She wished he'd come close so she could hold him and tell him.

All the remaining Walleyes from last year's team, except Will, were gathered by the dugout when Grant finally escorted Ingrid to the concession stand. Only the skeleton of a baseball team survived.

"OK, honey," Grant said to Ingrid. "I have to go to practice now. Can you play over here by Mom?" Ingrid made no answer. She was already busy searching for candy among the boxes inside the concession stand.

"I think we're out of players," Grant said to Kate. "It might not matter if I want to retire or not, we're down to a handful of guys." He shrugged and turned to walk to the dugout. "See you later," he called to her.

"Hey, come back here," Kate said. When Grant returned and leaned inside the window of the concession stand she put an arm around his neck, kissed him, and whispered, "I love you."

"Yeah, I love you too," he replied. He looked at her and squinted, questioning her sudden display of affection.

"Go play ball," Kate said. "We'll talk later."

Grant shrugged and turned to join his teammates, glancing over to the parking lot in time to see Will's car rolling to a stop. Will jumped out and jogged over to meet Grant, while June and their three daughters walked to the concession stand. Grant could hear Ingrid squealing as she ran to show off her new bicycle-riding skills for them.

"Hey, Pard. Is everybody here?" Will asked when he caught up to Grant.

"Just the regulars from last year," Grant said. "I think we have a numbers problem."

"We'll have ten guys," Will replied.

"How do you figure?" Grant asked.

"You, me, Pearly, the Carrigans, Ray . . ." Will held up six fingers.

"Yeah," Grant nodded.

"The college boys . . ." He held up three more fingers. ". . . and the Christopher kid, a high school senior, I think his first name is Theodore. That makes ten!" Will held up ten fingers.

"What's the story with the Christopher kid?" Grant asked. "None of these young guys want to play with Ray, they all go up and play for Windigo. Why would he want to play with us?"

"Well, he wants to up and play for Windigo, too. He really hates Ray, I guess Ray really has it in for him. But his dad wants him to play for Louie. He's a big lanky kid, and Louie says he has some talent. He's gonna graduate high school in a couple weeks. Doesn't say shit, really quiet."

"Ray," Grant sighed. "What a dick."

"Yeah, I keep hoping his whole body breaks out in boils," Will said.

"Sure your guys are coming?" Grant asked.

"Yup," Will replied. "I just talked to 'em yesterday."

When Grant and Will stepped around the corner of the dugout they were greeted by a somber collection of Walleyes, looking like a jury about to vote on the death sentence. Louie stood at the far end of the dugout with his hands in his pockets. Pearly sat next to Louie, arms folded and a scowl on his face. Ray was pacing with his chest puffed out, as usual. The Carrigans were sitting on the grass in front of the dugout, and a tall, skinny kid sat on the bench by himself, staring at his feet. No one was speaking.

"Whoa! You guys are gonna hafta channel some of this energy!" Will joked. "Calm down."

"We only have seven guys," Ray replied. "We need to find a couple players or we're going to fold."

"No, we have ten guys," Will declared. "I've got three more coming. They should be here any minute, and they're good players. We're OK." Will turned toward the skinny kid and shook his hand. "You must be Theodore. Welcome to the Walleyes."

"Thanks," Theodore said, barely raising his eyes. He was clearly uncomfortable, a stranger, ten years younger than everyone else in the dugout, and he looked lost.

Grant plopped down next to Theodore and said, "Grant Thorson." He shook the boy's hand and added, "Welcome."

"Well, ten guys isn't exactly . . ." Pearly started, but the slam of a car door stopped him.

"There they are," Will said. "My guys are here!"

Everyone straggled out onto the grass in front of the dugout as three strangers stepped through an opening in the chain-link fence by the on-deck circle.

Eleven men, ten ballplayers and Louie Swearingen, formed in an oval and stared at each other for a moment before anyone spoke. The three newcomers were all dressed for baseball practice, and each of them carried a duffel bag slung over one shoulder. The tallest of the three carried a large cardboard pizza box and the other two were stuffing pizza in their mouths.

"Glad you could make it, boys," Will said.

The shortest of the three, a wiry, bowlegged young man with a square chin and sharp eyes, looked about the group quickly. He wore a green baseball cap that shaded his dark features and a two-day growth of black whiskers. "Jeez, Will," he said sarcastically, "I hope this isn't the admissions committee or some shit like that, they all look kinda pissed off. Do we hafta take a personal interview or something?"

"No." Will laughed along with the others. "This is the team: the Walker Walleyes," Will said proudly. He went around and introduced everyone by name.

The kid who'd spoken first took a step forward and raised one finger in the air. "Paladin Sabetti," he said.

Then the kid on his left, a handsome young man, much taller, with long blond hair and a blond mustache, raised a finger and said, "Dave Johnson."

The last to introduce himself had short dark hair, dark eyes, and a round face. He held the pizza box in front of him and swallowed as he was about to speak. "Dave Johnson," he said.

The Walleye players stood there for a moment as if they were waiting for a punch line. Then Louie spoke up. "Two Dave Johnsons?"

The Dave Johnsons both nodded.

"So what do I call you when . . ."

Paladin Sabetti leaned forward and took center stage. He pointed a piece of pizza at the dark-haired Dave Johnson. After a brief pause for emphasis he said, "Dave the Jew." Then he pointed his pizza at the tall blond Dave Johnson with the mustache and clarified things completely with, "Dave the Fag."

Sabetti continued chewing his pizza as if nothing more needed to be said on the matter.

The Daves grinned and looked about while the Walleyes laughed. Even Theodore laughed. Ray Rivers looked around for anyone who'd make eye contact with him so he could frown a little to show the others that he thought Sabetti's words were inappropriate.

All eyes turned to the blond kid, the one Sabetti had labeled Dave the Fag when he raised his hand. Dave the Fag had clearly heard it before and grown comfortable with the nickname. Still smiling, he shrugged and said, "Not gay."

Dave the Jew took his turn and did the same. "Not Jewish." He smiled.

"Yeah, right," Sabetti scoffed in order to push the joke a little further, then he stuffed the entire pizza crust in his mouth. "Just look at 'em," he added, the words muffled by his mouthful of pizza. "You can tell!"

Paladin Sabetti and the Daves were best of friends. Every one of the men standing in the circle saw that immediately, even though they hardly knew the three college boys. This Dave the Fag and Dave the Jew thing was nothing more than an inside joke they were willing to share with everyone else.

"Can any of you guys pitch?" Louie asked.

"Yeah, we can all pitch, if you run short on pitching," Sabetti replied. "The Daves are pretty good outfielders, I'm a middle infielder."

"You all played ball in college?" Louie asked.

"Dartmouth," Paladin said with a nod.

"North Dakota State," Dave the Jew said.

"University of North Dakota," Dave the Fag said.

"Neither one of 'em could get into college," Paladin Sabetti quipped, and he took another piece of pizza from the box Dave the Jew was holding.

"OK then, let's get warmed up and get some work done," Louie said, as he exchanged a sideways glance with Pearly.

The players split up in groups of two and moved into the outfield to warm up with some long toss.

Sabetti noticed Theodore Christopher staring at him. "Need someone to warm up with?" he asked. He stuffed one last bite of pizza into his mouth and wiped his hand on his gray sweatshirt.

"Sure!" Theodore replied.

"So where you from, kid?" Sabetti asked as they wandered off together.

Grant and Pearly strolled out to the pitcher's mound and waited for the others to drift away in the outfield.

"I thought you were all done, finished with baseball," Pearly said when the others were out of earshot.

"Yeah, I was thinking about retiring . . . you know, being sick for so long?" Grant paused. "I've had it with Ray, too." Then he added, "I thought you might be ready to hang it up too, Pearly."

"I was. I was gonna tell Louie a few minutes ago. But then I got out here and saw his face and thought I might break his heart. It'd kill him if the Walleyes folded." Pearly pounded his fist into the catcher's mitt on his left hand. "'Nen the other thing is that I still kinda want to play. I don't know if I can be done with this yet."

"Me neither," Grant smirked. "Let's throw a little bit, you and me."

Twenty minutes later, after warming up with some long toss in the outfield grass, Grant stood on the pitcher's mound once again and watched Pearly trudge from the dugout to home plate. Pearly wore his catcher's gear and carried a white plastic bucket full of baseballs in one hand. When he reached home plate he tipped the bucket upside down and threw a few balls out to Grant.

Grant found a decent white ball among the grass-stained ones lying at his feet and smelled it, then rubbed it with both hands. He used his shoe to rearrange some dirt in front of the pitching rubber, and while he pawed at the dirt he listened to sounds all around him. Kate and June and the girls were talking over in the concession stand while the other players were taking batting practice and shagging fly balls in the outfield. Another hour of sunlight remained, and then they'd all go over to the Chateau for beer and pizza. This was all good, but one question remained: Could he still do this?

He stepped onto the pitching rubber and lifted his eyes toward home plate. What a sight.

"Ah, town ball," Grant said, as he stepped off the rubber and laughed at the ridiculous sight behind home plate.

Pearly was wearing shin guards, a chest protector, and a face mask, but he was sitting on the plastic bucket and holding one hand over his crotch, and cigarette smoke swirled out from his mask. He extended his catcher's mitt and shook it, ordering Grant to start pitching, then explained, "I'm too old to squat behind the plate this early in the season, and I'm not wearin' a cup, so don't you dare bounce one up here!" He shook the catcher's mitt again and added, "C'mon, let's see what you've got left after a year off." The challenge was muted, however, by the cigarette still dangling from Pearly's lips.

"Let's just stick with fastballs first," Grant said, as he stepped back on the rubber.

He took one small step to the side with his left foot—just enough to shift his weight—then planted his right foot in front of the rubber and felt the effortless closing of his hips and shoulders as he came to his balance point. His mind locked out everything but his target: Pearly's mitt. He spread his hands like a maestro and then let his left foot stride toward Pearly. His shoulders and hips sprung open and he delivered the ball. Pop! Nothing like it. The rhythm, the motion, the feel of the ball, and the sense of guiding it home—there was perfect symmetry here, like life.

Pearly tossed the ball back to him. He could still do this. Why had he wanted to give this up? It was *so* fine.

He worked from a windup for a while, then a stretch. He threw some curves and a few changeups. He didn't need anyone to tell him how he looked. He could feel that his strength was still there. He could hear the ball slam into Pearly's mitt. He threw a few pitches to Mantle, and Mays, and Killebrew. They still couldn't hit him, they never would. All the dreams came back.

"Let's wrap it up," Pearly called to him. "You've still got it."

Louie brought the team together in the dugout just before sundown when practice was over. "I think we're gonna be OK!" he announced. "As long as nobody gets hurt or sick we'll have enough to play, and I think we just might be all right. Remember, our first game is next Saturday, so everybody be here an hour early." He looked around him and smiled. "Now behave yourselves over at the Chateau. I'm gonna go home and try to catch a fish tonight. See you fellas on Saturday."

Ray Rivers and the Daves were the last ones to pack up their gear and leave the dugout after practice, and as they were stuffing shoes and baseball gloves into their duffel bags, Ray asked, "Don't you find it offensive when he calls you Fag and Jew like that?" Then he stood there and waited for an explanation.

"No. Not at all," Dave the Jew replied cheerfully while he zipped his duffel shut.

"It's an inside joke," Dave the Fag said as he tied his tennis shoes. He leaned back on the dugout bench and explained, "The three of us were at a bar one night and some drunk asshole wanted to fight someone, anyone, everyone, it didn't matter. Anyway, the guy gave me a shove and called me a fag, then he took a swing at Dave and called him a Jew—like those were the two worst things he could think of." Dave the Fag stood up and adjusted his shirt. "Then the guy shoved Tark and spilled his beer. Called him a pussy, too. Bad move on that guy's part." He chuckled and looked over at the other Dave.

"So what happened?" Ray asked.

"Well, Tark doesn't back down from anything, so he poked his finger on the guy's chest and warned him. Naturally the guy took a swing. Tark ducked, then hit the guy so hard it scared everyone in the bar. One punch. He dropped the guy like a bad habit. The guy just laid there and bled for a while." Dave shook his head. "You don't wanna fuck with Tark Sabetti." Dave chuckled and added, "Tark thought it was so funny that the guy had called me a fag and Dave a Jew, so he just kept on doing it too."

"I don't think it's funny. It's offensive," Ray huffed.

The cheerful countenance on Dave the Jew's face wavered for a second, then returned. He was irritated by Ray's willingness to preach and his need to correct a stranger, but he felt obligated to keep his first conversation with a new teammate pleasant. "Well, I can tell you that he doesn't mean anything by it," Dave explained. "His mother is Jewish, and his roommate at Dartmouth, a good friend, a guy he chose to live with, is gay." Dave the Jew looked Ray in the eye and let his words sink in before he declared, "Tark is a good guy. Complicated maybe, but a good guy."

The Daves locked eyes for a second, and exchanged a message. In only the briefest of conversations they'd come to dislike Ray Rivers, just like everyone else.

∾: CHAPTER 41 :∾

As always, the Tamarac Chateau was rocking when the ballplayers rolled in. Bruce Springsteen's "Glory Days" thumped its way out of the jukebox while a large crowd of young women sipped at their beers and flirted with the young men who were always happy to buy more beer.

Will, June, Grant, and Kate sate on one side of a table covered with empty beer glasses and several pizzas. They'd hired a babysitter, some-thing they seldom did, so they could all go out together as they had a few years earlier.

Tark and the Daves sat on the other side of the table and watched the crowd grow. As the ladies had been streaming in over the past half hour, it had been growing more difficult for the young men to keep their attention on the conversation with Grant and Will and their wives.

"So, you guys all met in dental school? It that correct?" June asked.

"Yup," Tark answered, but his eyes followed a bulging T-shirt and a pair of cutoff blue jeans that walked by just behind June.

"That's how we met, too," Grant offered, "'cept Kate was a teacher at the time."

Tark quickly refocused on the group at his own table. "No shit? Oops, I mean, really?" he said.

"Yeah," Kate said, and she put her arm over Grant's shoulder. "We met when he came up to the hygiene clinic to have his teeth cleaned and meet girls." Before she could explain the rest of the story, Tark and the Daves all whipped their heads around to look at each other.

"I never thought of that," Dave the Jew confessed. Then he pointed his beer glass at Tark and Dave the Fag. "Write that one down, boys," he said with a smile.

"So how did you three come to be such good friends?" Kate asked them.

"Gross Anatomy lab," Tark said. "We were partners."

"Really!" Grant said. "Well, one day . . ."

The floodgates opened when Grant retold the story about the steel plate in his cadaver's skull, then everyone had a few Gross Anatomy stories to share.

"Well, how about Ebby? How'd you get along with him?" Kate eventually asked them.

"Whoa, what an asswipe!" Tark blurted, and for the next few minutes all three young men stumbled over themselves, each of them in a hurry to share another anecdote illustrating their hatred for Dr. Ebverret Rettig.

"OK, so what did you guys think of your first practice with the Walleyes?" Grant asked, when Ebby had taken enough of a beating.

"Well," Dave the Fag started, "aside from the obvious problem of a lack of players, this could be a decent nine. But there are two glaring weak spots." He paused and used his eyes to ask for permission to share his opinion.

"Go ahead," Will said.

"One of those Carrigan brothers, the one who can't catch a cold. What's his name?" Dave the Fag asked.

"Melbourne," Will and Grant said in unison.

"It's Milburne Rio and Melbourne Leo, actually," Will added.

"Yeah, Melbourne. Jesus, what the hell was their mother thinking to name those two Milburne Rio and Melbourne Leo?" Dave grimaced, shook his head, and continued. "Anyway, he can't catch, or run, he's a shitty outfielder, but he's tough as nails. Tark started calling him Clank after he dropped about a dozen fly balls. His glove must be made of cast iron."

"Clank, I like that," Will said.

"Yeah," Dave the Fag added as an afterthought. "Milburne, the other one, you know how he wanders around cussing all the time? Well, Tark started calling him Pissed, 'cuz he always seems to be pissed off, just so he could tell 'em apart. I think Milburne likes it, too."

"Clank and Pissed, the Carrigan brothers. Has a nice ring to it," Will grinned.

"Yeah, well anyway, you gotta get Clank outta right field. Every ball hit his way is an adventure," Dave the Fag said. "'Sides zat, he runs like Frankenstein."

"All right," Grant said as he raised a beer to his mouth. "What's the other glaring weakness?"

"Ray Rivers!" Tark blurted. "He's the heart and soul of all your problems. I can't believe he's the high school coach here. Theodore absolutely hates his guts! That kid can play, by the way. Theodore, I mean. He's good. So what's the deal with Ray, anyway? There's gotta be eight or ten high school or college boys from town who could play for this team, but Theodore says they all choose to play up in Windigo to get away from Ray."

"Gotta tell you, I didn't think he was so bad a few years ago when I first started with the Walleyes," Grant said. "So either I was just blind to it all or he's getting worse. But it's like Pearly told me way back then: Ray doesn't seem to like the better players, especially the ones who might require a little coaching with the finer points in order to really bring out their talent."

Tark and the Daves stared, openmouthed.

"OK, here's the way I see it." Grant began a more thorough explanation while he emptied a pitcher of beer into his glass. "Ray just doesn't have the technical knowledge to teach the finer points of the game. You know, hitting, position play, pitching mechanics, hell, everything. So when he's required to do that he just gives up on the kid. He tells the other coaches that the kid is uncoachable in order to cover up his own poor coaching skills. Then he turns to some other kid, hopefully a kid with some natural talent, so he won't have to coach him, either."

Will nodded his agreement while Tark and the Daves tried to understand.

"On top of that," Grant went on, "he was obviously a shitty player himself and he has some lingering resentment toward people who are better than him." Grant shrugged and sipped his beer. "As the high school coach, he has the power to destroy anyone he chooses."

"'Zat what he did to Theodore?" Dave the Jew asked.

"That's what Pearly says," Grant replied. "Apparently Ray went out of his way to get Theodore; put him in impossible situations, doctored the scorebook to make him look bad, gave wrong information to the local newspapers when it was time to phone in game results—all that in order to justify the ass-pounding he gave the kid. What was it that Abraham Lincoln said? 'Nearly all men can stand adversity, but if you want to test a man's character, give him some power.'"

Even as he was finishing his own sentence he began to grin, then he turned to Will and said, "Sounded like I was talking about Ebby, didn't it?"

Everyone at the table knew Dr. Ebverret Rettig and saw the truth in Grant's comparison of Ebby and Ray. While they were laughing and pouring more beer into their glasses, Kate noticed Tark's eyes dart over to the far side of the room. She turned around to look at whatever Tark had noticed, then turned back to Tark.

"That's Ray's wife," Kate said.

"Which one?" Tark replied.

"The pretty one with the red hair and the long legs and the short dress. The one you were staring at," Kate answered. "That's Brandi."

Now the Daves were staring, too. "*That's* Ray's wife?" Dave the Jew said. He looked and sounded like he was choking on something. "She's . . . she's . . . attractive." He wore a hungry smile when he looked into the eyes of the others at his table.

"Who're the two others?" Tark asked. "Who are the dark-haired ones she's talking to?" His eyes were fixed on a group of women standing by the dance floor. He never looked away, as if he was a predator, measuring his prey. He'd lost all interest in baseball and Ray Rivers.

"They're from Menahga," Kate answered. "They're the Badenovs."

"Huh?" the Daves asked in unison.

"You know, from Rocky and Bullwinkle. The Badenovs, Boris and Natasha. I don't know their real names. A couple years ago our shortstop started calling them Boris and Natasha, and the names stuck. Natasha is the tall one and Boris is the short one," Kate explained.

"Natasha's not bad," Tark said as he stared at her. "She's really pretty."

"Boris isn't bad either," Dave the Jew opined.

"She wears a little too much makeup," June said, looking at Boris. "She thinks she needs a lot of makeup to look pretty."

"That's what the beer is for!" Dave the Jew announced for everyone to hear. Tark and the Daves chug-a-lugged the beer in their glasses, poured themselves refills, and then stood up to leave.

"It was great to meet you all," Tark said. "And we'll have a great time this summer. But my friends and I have some business to attend to." And with that, Tark and the Daves were off to mingle with the crowd of women over on the dance floor.

"Remember when we were that age?" Kate asked, her arm again over Grant's shoulder.

"Sure do," Grant and Will replied at the same instant, and before another word could be said the Daves were both chatting and smiling with Brandi Rivers. A moment later Natasha's eyes brightened when Tark introduced himself.

"So, I gotta ask you something, Pard," Will started, suddenly energized by a new line of thought. "You were talking like you were ready to be done with baseball. Still feel that way?"

"No." Grant watched Tark put his arm around Natasha's waist, and even though he couldn't hear their conversation he knew there was some serious flirting going on over there. He remembered other bars and other teammates, and he remembered how fine he felt earlier at practice when he'd been pitching. Mantle, Mays, Killebrew, and Kluszewski drifted through the other images. "No, Pard, I don't know what I was thinkin'." He put his arm around Kate. "I need this. I wanna play."

CHAPTER 42

Brilliant golden light splashed across Leech Lake early on Saturday morning. Grant shuffled into the kitchen, wearing boxers and a gray T-shirt, and started some coffee brewing. Maybe it would be a nice warm day for the Walleyes' season opener. They'd had two productive practice sessions during the week and they were anxious to play ball.

When the coffee was ready he poured a cup and walked to the picture window facing the big lake. Really windy out there, he thought, and the thin clouds had a wispy, gray look. Not good. People who live in the north can feel when winter is still about, and Grant knew there was a cold front coming.

Kate stepped out of their bedroom wearing long pajamas and a pink robe. She walked directly to the coffee pot without a greeting for Grant, but he turned and watched her every step. It never failed—just watching her do the simple things caused him to take notice. She was leaning against the kitchen counter, no makeup, first thing in the morning, and he thought she was pretty. He turned away from the window and stared at his wife.

She finally noticed him when she raised the coffee to her mouth. Her eyes smiled and then her lips curled. "Don't even think about it," she said. She'd caught him fixed in a familiar amorous trance. "Ingrid will be awake in a few minutes."

"Was it that obvious?" Grant asked.

Kate nodded and walked to him. "Yeah, you don't hide it very well," she said, putting her arm around his waist.

"Sorry," Grant sighed.

"It's OK, I like it." She kissed his cheek. "Ingrid is going to stay over-night with the Campbells tonight, you know. So we can make some noise."

Ingrid stumbled out of her bedroom, sucking her thumb and dragging a blanket. She walked directly to the TV, turned it on, then collapsed on the couch and announced that she was bored.

When the phone rang an hour later, Ingrid was still sitting on the couch, watching cartoons, eating a Pop-Tart and talking to herself, or maybe to the Pop-Tart.

"Thorsons," Kate said when she answered the phone. Her face bright-ened an instant later. "Hi, Ruth," she said. It was Ruth Saathe, Ingrid's Sunday school teacher. "What's up?"

Grant guessed that Ruth was about seventy-five years old and had been everyone in Walker's Sunday school teacher at one time. She kept her hair in a little bun at the back of her head, and she resembled the tiny old woman in the Tweety Bird cartoons. Grant thought it was odd that she would call his home on a Saturday morning, and he listened to Kate's con-versation with her while he read the sports page.

"Sure, yeah, go ahead," Kate said into the phone after a few minutes of small talk. When Grant looked up he saw Kate's expression turn pensive. "Yes, by all means. What happened?" she asked.

"Uh huh," Kate said as she listened. "Uh huh. Uh huh." Kate's eyebrows tightened. She closed her eyes and put her hand over her face. "You're kid-ding." She shook her head. "You're kidding!" she said again. "I'm so embar-rassed," she said, and she turned a hard, accusatory look toward Grant.

Grant could hear Ruth Saathe laughing on the other end of the phone, and Kate attempted to laugh with her, but her angry eyes never moved from Grant's face. "OK, thanks for calling. We'll have a talk." She hung up the phone and used her index finger to signal Grant that he should fol-low her out of the kitchen, immediately. Ingrid was still visiting with her Pop-Tart when Grant joined Kate in their bedroom.

"That was Ruth Saathe," Kate said.

"Yeah?" Grant replied.

"Want to guess what your daughter did in Sunday school last week?"

Grant shrugged. He could hear the anger growing in Kate's voice.

"She turned to her friend, Melanie Willette, and pointed her finger."

"Yeah?" Grant shrugged again.

"Then she said, 'Pull my finger,' and Melanie did."

Grant knew what was coming next, and tried not to smile.

"She farted when Melanie pulled her finger!"

"That's my girl!" Grant said proudly. Pretending to be appalled at this point was not an option. He'd already been smiling for ten seconds, and the embarrassment Kate displayed only made it more difficult not to laugh.

"It's not funny!" Kate scolded.

"Sure it is," Grant chuckled.

"Everybody in town will think we're just white trash!" Kate whined.

"No. They'll smile and think we're just like they are," Grant answered.

"You talk to your little girl!" Kate said with no trace of humor in her voice. "Make it clear that all the 'Pull my finger' stuff is over. Understand?"

Now it was like laughing in church. Grant simply couldn't hold back the laughter. He nodded his understanding, but clearly felt no remorse.

"You think this is funny?" Kate asked. "Just wait till she embarrasses you in public!"

Grant nodded. Kate turned to walk away. "I'll talk to her," Grant said. "But . . ."

"But what?" Kate said, when she spun to face him again.

"Women just don't know what's funny and what's not," he replied.

Kate shook her head and walked away. "Talk to her!" she demanded.

~:~

The midday sun was warm, but not warm enough. A chilly breeze promised that an unkind change in the weather was not far off. It would be a cold Saturday night for baseball, but he'd have a tea party with Ingrid before the front came through.

Grant lifted Ingrid into the little fishing boat first, then he loaded a cooler filled with all the things he could think of to keep Ingrid busy for a couple of hours on the lake. They'd fish for a while and eat for a while, and he'd let her run the motor for a while. Eventually he'd find the right time to talk to her about having other people pull her finger.

"I'm kinda hungry, Daddy," Ingrid said shortly after one o'clock. She probably wasn't very hungry, Grant thought, but she'd watched him fill the big cooler with sandwiches and cookies and several cans of Coke, and of course her pink dishes. She was just ready for a tea party.

Preparations for the fishing trip had taken nearly two hours. Father and daughter carried a shovel into the woods and dug up some worms for bait. They'd made sandwiches together and they'd packed some warm jackets, several fishing rods, and a tackle box.

Now they'd been fishing for about ten minutes. The boat was anchored perhaps four hundred yards from their backyard, and Grant hadn't had enough time to wet a line yet, he'd been so busy taking the sunfish and perch off Ingrid's line.

"You're hungry already?" he asked, smiling but not surprised.

"Yeah." She furrowed her brow as if she'd given the question serious thought.

"Well, you have another fish on your line. Why don't you reel him in first?"

Ingrid glanced down and saw her bobber darting under the surface. She set her jaw in an even more determined stare and began to turn the handle on her fishing reel.

"Nice one," Grant said when he reached over and grabbed the sunfish, which was almost as big as his hand. He held the fish in one hand and removed Ingrid's fish hook with the other. Then he tossed the fish back into the lake and smiled at Ingrid while he wiped his hands on his blue jeans.

"Dad?"

"Yeah."

"That fish peed on you."

"Oh?"

"I think you squeezed him too hard."

"Well, maybe he just had to pee?"

Ingrid thought for a moment and then asked another question. "Dad?"

"Yeah."

"Where do fish go poop?" She looked as though she was probing the mysteries of the universe.

"Right in the lake, I guess," Grant said.

That was just too much for Ingrid to think about. She looked over the side of the boat and said nothing more.

Grant opened the cooler and set places for himself and Ingrid on the boat seat. He laid out place settings of the plastic dishes and put a sandwich and a cookie on each plate. Then he placed a pink cup and saucer on the seat for each of them, and he filled their cups with Coca-Cola.

While he arranged the party treats, Grant watched Ingrid out of the corner of his eye. Her feet dangled above the floor of the boat and she began to sing something in a tiny voice.

"What're you singing?" Grant asked when he closed the cooler.

"Cadillac Wrench," Ingrid replied.

He realized she meant the song "Cadillac Ranch" by Bruce Springsteen, but he didn't bother to correct her.

"Where'd you hear that?" he asked.

"Mom plays it all the time," Ingrid answered. "The baseball men play it too." "Who's your favorite singer?" Grant asked.

"Raffi," Ingrid replied. "I'm thirsty, Daddy." She reached for her pink teacup full of Coke.

"You mean the guy who sings 'Baby Beluga' and 'Bathtime'?" he asked.

"Uh huh." She was talking about Raffi, a popular children's performer, and looking at her chocolate chip cookie, when she started to sing "Baby Beluga."

This seemed like the moment. She was distracted by the talk of Raffi, and Bruce Springsteen, and cookies. Grant decided to address the farting issue now. "You know that thing you do when you have your friend pull your finger and then you pass gas?" he asked in his calmest voice, so as not to draw undue attention to the act.

"Yeah."

"Well, you probably shouldn't do that anymore."

"You do it," she said.

"I won't do it anymore either," he replied, thankful that Kate wasn't around to hear this.

"Grampa does it. Really loud!" Ingrid giggled. "Uncle John does too."

Grant had to bite his lip. All the Thorson boys had learned the game from Big Ole, and their Grampa Gustav had played it pretty well too.

"Well, we shouldn't do it anymore," Grant replied, barely able to keep his composure.

"OK," Ingrid said, and that seemed to be the end of it.

Grant nodded and felt a sense of relief. He reached for his peanut butter sandwich and accidentally knocked it onto the floor of the boat, where it settled into a small puddle with a layer of nasty flotsam. Dirt, part of a dead minnow, and a paper label from Will Campbell's chewing tobacco stuck to the sopping wet sandwich when he picked it up.

"You wanna trade sandwiches?" he asked.

Ingrid giggled and said, "Mom dropped a piece of toast on the kitchen floor yesterday, and the peanut butter stuck to the floor."

"What'd she do then?" Grant asked, not really expecting an answer.

Ingrid looked to the right, then to the left, then directly into Grant's eyes, before she told on her mother. "She said the D word!"

"Oh really?" Grant said. "Well, just be glad she didn't spill spaghetti sauce."

⁓: CHAPTER 43 :⁓

The Walleye players were gathered in their dugout almost two hours before the game. The plan had been to take plenty of batting and infield practice before the Dragonflies from Windigo showed up. Louie Swearingen was passing out green-and-gray uniforms to the new guys, while the veterans who already had their uniforms sat on the grass in front of the dugout and stretched their arms and legs and joked with each other.

"All right, you new guys, here's your uniforms," Louie said, as he bent over and dug around in a large cardboard box. "Hope you brought something warm to wear underneath 'em; it's cold tonight. Chance of snow later, how 'bout that?" Louie still hadn't looked away from the box. He fished around for a moment longer and then he stood up with an armful of gray and green.

"Here you go, Tark." He tossed Sabetti a bundle. "You're number twenty-four, should fit."

"Thanks, Louie," Tark said, while he inspected the uniform. "Willie Mays," he mumbled under his breath.

"Dave, here's yours. You're number thirty-one," Louie said as he tossed a bundle to Dave the Fag.

"Good, a prime number, indivisible by any number except itself," Dave the Fag said, as he examined the jersey.

"Jesus," Tark sighed. "He's thrilled to get a prime number." Tark rolled his eyes when he looked over at Pearly. "I told you so, Pearly. He's light in the loafers."

"And the other Dave, here you are, number twenty-one," Louie said when he threw the uniform to Dave the Jew.

Tark leaned back in his seat on the dugout bench and launched a sarcastic stare at Dave the Fag, daring him to find some obscure mathematical significance to Dave the Jew's number.

"Math is the universal language," Dave the Fag explained as he pulled his pants up. "I think the number twenty-one means . . ." He paused, searching for a reply to Sabetti, then gave up and mumbled, "Fuck you, Tark!"

"Theodore, I hope your mother can sew, or do some alterations here." Louie tossed the last bundle to Theodore Christopher. "In order to get you into a uniform that fits a kid as tall as you are, I had to give you a size that was made for somebody a little thicker through the middle, too. It's just a big uniform. It's a little baggy and it's gonna flap in the breeze when you run. Maybe your mom can take it in a little?"

"Thanks, Mr. Swearingen," Theodore said.

"And you're number nine," Louie added.

"Ah, the Splendid Splinter, Ted Williams," Tark mumbled, as he adjusted his stirrups. He was a student of the game, and he was obviously familiar with the heroes of past generations.

While he was still only half-dressed, Tark chose to steal away on an errand. He crept up the stairway behind the dugout and made his way into the press box. "Looks like a deer stand—a really shitty deer stand," Tark breathed as the door to the press box above the Walleyes dugout creaked open. The rickety tower overlooking the infield did in fact resemble the sort of thing that a deer hunter might build in a tree in order to hide from a wary buck. A dozen empty Coke cans and another dozen empty Hamm's beer cans littered the floor, along with a million or so sunflower seed shells. The place smelled like an armpit.

The dented and well-worn control panel for the aging scoreboard, which hung from a chain-link fence out in left center field, rested on a plywood countertop in front of two folding chairs. Next to the control panel lay a microphone and a beat-up Radio Shack audiocassette player.

"Nice! Really nice," Tark said sarcastically, as he swung open the plywood shutters that protected the press box, letting the breeze off the Ice Cracking River blow the stale air out. He turned on the power switch to the cassette player and the scoreboard, and then he noticed a shoe box on the floor. Four cassette tapes, all polkas, two by Frankie Yankovic and two by the Six Fat Dutchmen, had spent the winter, maybe several winters, in the shoe box, along with a bottle opener.

"That shit's gotta go," he said as he kicked the shoe box into the corner and put his own cassette tape in the cassette player. He clicked the microphone and tapped it with his finger, then raised it to his lips. "Good evening, ladies and gentlemen!" His voice crackled across the empty ball field. "And welcome to the ballpark this evening for the Walker Walleyes' season opener. For those of you who are just arriving or who may not be aware, during the off-season your Walleyes acquired the contract rights to hard-hitting, slick-fielding Paladin Sabetti." He paused for a second, then added, "Sabetti, a native of Eveleth, and a very handsome lad, is currently pursuing a career in the custodial arts at the Totem Lodge." When he switched off the microphone he could hear his teammates chuckling in the dugout below him.

"Gear Jammer" by George Thorogood and the Destroyers was rumbling out the army surplus public-address system when Tark strolled back into the dugout. "Sorry, Louie, but those fuckin' polkas had to go," Tark said with no hint of apology. "'Sides that," he added, "you just can't take infield practice without the Destroyers!"

"'Bout time," Pearly said. He lit a cigarette while he stretched his legs. "I hate those polkas."

"I thought you guys liked my polkas," Louie said, feigning indignation. He knew everyone hated the polkas. Tark had simply been the first one to do anything about them. "I'll have a little talk with Speed Roesner about the music selection," he added.

"So what do we know about Windigo? Who do they have back this year?" Grant asked. "Is that Peoples kid still around?"

"Ah, they're no better than we are," Louie said, while he arranged the bats along the dugout wall. "But they do have that Peoples kid back."

"So, he's some big stud or something?" Dave the Jew asked, while he sifted through his duffel bag.

"Miller Peoples has been the best player in this league since he was a ninth-grader," Pearly said casually. "He just finished his junior year in high school. He's six foot three, about two ten, physically mature, has been for two years, the kid is a horse. Nice kid, too. I don't think we got him out last year."

"That's not true. He popped up a couple times!" interjected Melbourne, who actually liked it now when his teammates called him Clank. "Good news is that this will be his last year in this league. He'll be playing for money the day after he graduates high school. The pro scouts have been all over him."

"Really?" Tark said suspiciously. Every player in the dugout recognized the skeptical tone in his voice and understood that Tark was about to make it his personal mission to test Miller Peoples.

"Well, I know one thing for sure," Will Campbell said from his seat by the bat rack. "I still look handsomer than shit in my Walleye uniform." He struck a pose and displayed the light gray uniform with dark green piping down the shoulders and legs and around the belt loops and pants pockets. His green hat featured two large offset Ws, for Walker Walleyes. "Hell, even Pearly looks good in one of these," he said. He slid his glove over his left hand and winked at Theodore.

"Know what we need now?" Dave the Fag said, as he tore the top off the pizza box he'd left in the dugout a few days earlier.

No one answered. Several of the Walleyes watched as he hustled into the utility shed at the end of the dugout. Then, with a hammer in one hand, he scurried back to the place where he'd been standing.

"A booger board!" he announced. He pressed the cardboard against the wall of the dugout with the back of his left hand and used his thumb and index finger to hold a nail while he hammered the booger board in place.

"Good call!" Tark said when Dave was finished. He stuck a finger into his nose, pulled it out, and smeared a large booger across the middle of the cardboard. "Well," Tark said as he stared at his work, "it's not a trophy, but it's a start. The bar has been set. You now have a goal to strive for. Can you beat that one?" He seemed satisfied with his work as he smiled and backed away from the booger board.

Louie shook his head and chuckled when he made eye contact with Pearly. "Does it feel like we're back in dental school" Grant asked Will, as he stared at the booger board.

"It's not bad, Tark," Dave the Fag said. He was leaning over and tying his shoes. "But conditions are just not optimal for booger production tonight. It's too cold. We need some hotter, dryer weather." He spoke as if he'd dedicated years of meticulous scientific research to the proper temperature and humidity required for optimal booger production.

The rest of the Walleyes finished dressing, and they all stole a glance at the booger board as they walked past it and out onto the green grass. Some were laughing, some were shaking their heads. All of them were primping and admiring their uniforms.

"We're not gonna have that kind of stuff in the dugout," Ray Rivers said with some authority, and he reached up to tear the booger board off the dugout wall.

Tark's left hand shot forward and made a slapping noise when his palm collided with Ray's wrist. His fingers clamped an iron grip around Ray's arm. "The board stays," Tark growled, nose to nose with Ray.

Ray tried to move his right arm but Tark's hand was a vice. "The board stays," Tark hissed once more, and he threw Ray's arm back at him.

Ray took a tentative, challenging step toward Tark, but when he saw the malevolent look in Tark's eyes he thought better of it and turned to Louie. "Louie, we can't . . ."

"The board stays!" Louie chastised Ray, with an angry tone in his voice. "The board can stay. It's just those young guys having fun and . . ."

"It's not Walleyes baseball," Ray whined. "It's . . ."

"It is *now*!" Louie barked. For the first time in anyone's memory, Louie Swearingen was angry. "And don't bring it up again, ever!" Louie seemed to have finally reached his limit with Ray, and everyone, including Ray, knew that Louie had heard enough.

Every Walleye in the dugout turned away and let that be the end of the discussion. Theodore Christopher, however, found it impossible not to smile at Louie's put-down of Ray Rivers. Ray saw Theodore smile, too, and he watched as Theodore exchanged glances with Tark Sabetti. Tark rolled his eyes and returned the smile while the others stood and wondered what might happen next.

Dave the Jew put an end to the uncomfortable silence. "Oooo!" He stood up and held his hand over his rear end. "Somebody's knockin' at the back door." He made an uneasy face and looked over at Dave the Fag, "I gotta find the shitter pretty quick. I've got one about a half-inch out and startin' to stink here." Then he ran stiff legged and frowning for the men's room behind the bleachers while Dave the Fag and Tark smiled at each other.

Pearly leaned back and laughed out loud while the others chuckled. Ray snatched the scorebook and clipboard off the bench and stomped down to the far end of the dugout in a display of disdain for the conversation. Tark and the Daves did not fail to notice that Ray had revealed a raw nerve for them to pick at.

Will ambled over to Grant and whispered, "I thought Ray was about to get his ass kicked for a minute there."

"Too bad. I think we'd all like to see that happen," Grant whispered back.

The Walleyes all wandered away from the dugout and began to long toss with a partner, swing a bat in the batting cage, or run in the outfield grass to stretch their legs. Louie and Pearly were chalking the base paths as they always did just prior to games.

Only Ray, Tark, and Dave the Fag remained in the dugout when Dave the Jew strolled back in. Ray was making out the lineup for the upcoming game, oblivious to the way Tark and Dave the Fag sat like vultures circling above a fresh kill over at the other end of the dugout. Both of them had a clear vision of the disgusting remarks they expected to coax from Dave the Jew when he returned from the men's room, and the negative response these comments would draw from Ray.

"Nice turd?" Tark inquired when Dave returned.

Ray looked up from the scorebook immediately.

"Oh yeah! It was a dandy. Sorta looked like Richard Nixon on the one end," Dave the Jew replied. "I couldn't get a good look at the other end. But I thought I saw a resemblance to Theodore Roosevelt, without those little glasses, of course."

"Mt. Turdmore, eh?" Tark asked.

"Yeah, sorta," Dave the Jew replied. Then he dismissed Mt. Turdmore from his immediate thoughts and added a profound insight. "You know, taking a dump is much like a love affair." He slid his left hand into his glove and pounded his right fist into the pocket several times.

"How's zat, Dave?" asked Dave the Fag.

"Well, all we really hope for is a clean break at the end," Dave the Jew said seriously, and he laughed along with his buddies.

Ray tossed the scorebook onto the bench in an exaggerated display of disgust and stormed out of the dugout while the college boys chuckled. "Jeez, that prick needs to go," sighed Dave the Jew.

"Yeah, what a hosehead," Tark agreed.

Minutes before the start of the season opener, Grant was standing on the bullpen pitching mound taking his final warm-up pitches when he noticed that the cold breeze carried the smell of charcoal and brats and popcorn. The smells of the ballpark were as comforting as his mother's cooking, drifting through the old farmhouse. He raised his glove to his face and breathed in the friendly scent of worn leather, too. Then he welcomed Mickey Mantle back for the season opener.

Kate and June were happy to be inside the concession stand for tonight's game against Windigo. With each passing minute the north wind grew a bit colder, and the cozy little building offered shelter that none of the players or fans would find tonight. Kate decided to plug in the coffee pot as she watched the players for both teams making their final preparations. They'd sell some hot coffee tonight.

"Hehwo, Kate!" came a familiar voice. Speed Roesner leaned on the concession-stand window and greeted her. "Hehwo, June," he added.

"Hi, Speed," they chirped in unison.

"Gonna be a cold one tonight," Kate offered.

"Sho is!" Speed replied, then he quickly changed the subject. "How do you wike the music?" "Bad Moon Rising" by Creedence Clearwater Revival was playing at full volume, and Speed seemed concerned that the new music might alienate some of his longtime fans.

"I love it!" Kate replied. "Nice work!"

"Weewee?" Speed was shocked at her reply. "You wike it too, June?"

"Love it!" June said.

Speed struggled to understand the way the world had changed. He shook his head slowly and said, "Woowee just told me to go ahead and pway the stuff that the new guys bwought up to the pwess box." Then, to double-check their opinions, he asked, "What about Fwankie Yankovic? Don't you wike the pokas any mo'?"

"Always hated 'em, Speed," Kate said. "Creedence is much better. The Destroyers, too."

"Me, too," June added.

Boris Badenov chose that moment to reach into the window and slide fifty cents across the windowsill. "Could I have some popcorn, please?" she said. While she waited for the popcorn, she said, "Nice to see they finally started playing some decent music at ball games." She had no idea that Speed had been responsible for the polkas.

It was perfect timing. Kate pointed to Speed and said, "He's the man in charge. Tell him!"

"Oh," Boris Badenov said with a pretty smile. "Nice work!" She touched Speed's arm and nodded.

Speed was confused, deeply confused. He'd always suspected people came to ball games just to hear his polkas. Now this. He turned and walked back to the press box as if he was dragging a bag of rocks. Someone else called to him and said they liked the new music, too. All he could do was nod and keep on dragging.

"Got any hot coffee?" boomed a large voice a moment later, while Kate was tending to the coffee pot. Tom Murphy and Jack Fitzgerald, the umpires for tonight's game, were standing at the window with their shoulders hunched over to keep out the chill when she turned to look at them.

"Hi!" Murphy said when Kate faced him. "Gonna be a cold one tonight, eh?"

Murphy and Fitzgerald were always affable and friendly toward Kate and June, but Kate knew that Grant detested both of them. She'd heard Grant and the others talking about the "Irish mafia" and their lack of integrity. She knew that Louie liked to hire Murphy and Fitzgerald for several home games each summer just to bring in different umpires now and then, which made everyone happy. They umpired town ball during the summer because they were old friends and they liked to hang around together. They each made about twenty dollars per game, and were both middle-aged, has-been jocks that liked baseball. It gave them a chance to visit many of the local watering holes in search of young women after the ball games, too.

"Hello, boys! Got your long underwear on tonight?" Kate asked, while June poured hot coffee into two Styrofoam cups. Kate had always thought Murphy was pretty impressed with himself, and she found Fitzgerald to be distant and aloof, but she'd tried to cultivate their friendship.

"No long johns," Murphy laughed. "Should have, though. I heard it's supposed to snow later." He looked out at the gray dusk and added, "Maybe I'd have a brat if you girls have any ready yet?"

"Sure thing, Murph," Kate said. She stepped to her left, plucked a brat-wurst off the grill, placed it on a fresh bun, and slid it across the countertop to Murphy.

"Grant pitchin' tonight?" Murphy asked while he waited.

"Yup," Kate replied.

"Everything OK? I mean with the cancer and everything?" Murphy asked.

"Yeah, he feels great," Kate said. "Nice of you to ask." On the surface Tom Murphy's questions seemed sincere. But Kate had known others like him, and she recognized the insincerity in his words. He was the type of man who actually liked to hear bad news about others. He didn't really care about Grant's health; he probably hoped that something was still wrong. He wanted to pick at an open wound. And just maybe he wanted to hint that he'd be there if she ever needed any comfort.

Kate was putting Tom Murphy's dollar fifty into the cash box when she noticed him spread ketchup all over the brat. Fitzgerald had turned away to look at the players on the ball field, June was stacking Coke cans in the refrigerator, and Murphy was lost in thoughts of his bratwurst.

Kate watched him slather ketchup over the whole thing and then slowly raise it to his mouth.

"Wait!" she yelled at the last second. "Don't eat that!" Kate barked as if she'd accidentally handed him poison and was now trying to save his life.

Murphy froze with his mouth open, just about to shove the brat in. His eyes were opened wide, with white showing all around them.

Fitzgerald whipped his head around to see what was going on, and so did June.

"This is a ballpark!" Kate said sternly. "Nobody, I mean nobody, puts ketchup on a ballpark brat. There are rules. Proper decorum must be observed."

A smile pulled at her eyes, then at the corners of her mouth. She'd scared him, and she loved the fright in his eyes.

"Oh Jesus," Fitzgerald laughed. "She really got you, Murph. You looked like she caught you stealing. I thought you were going to hand that brat back over to her for a minute there." Fitzgerald bent over and grabbed his knees when he laughed.

Murphy laughed too, a huge belly laugh, but he was embarrassed and a bit angry. He didn't like to be teased; that was for other people. He quickly regained his composure, then took a bite and walked away with his chuckling sidekick, but not before he winked and pointed at Kate and tried to pretend that he thought her joke was funny. She saw the truth in his eyes.

"I don't like those guys," June whispered when they were out of earshot.

"Well, I think Murphy knows that," Kate said.

"Did you see the way Murphy looked at us?" June replied. "It's like we're standing here naked. Look in their eyes, they're both the same. Those two are good to go, and all it would take is for us to say the word."

"You think so?" Kate asked. "They're married, aren't they?"

June rolled her eyes. "You think that means anything to those two?"

Several Walleye players were pacing in the dugout. A few others sat quietly and stared straight ahead. Tark and the Daves were standing in a small circle, laughing among themselves.

Ray Rivers was busy with the scorebook. "I'm gonna have a hard time getting you any playing time," he said to Theodore. Ray, engrossed in the scorebook, implied that his complex game plan didn't include young Theodore.

Tark stopped laughing when he heard Ray's remark. He clenched his teeth and glowered over the top of imaginary bifocals before he rolled his eyes in disgust. He was struggling to hide his dislike for Ray.

"OK you guys, let's take the field," Louie said when it was time. As the Walleyes started to stand up, Tark stopped them.

"Hold it!" He held up his hands and waited until they were all silent. "We're gonna have some fun here," he said. He picked up a bat and banged it against the ceiling of the dugout. "OK! Hit it, Speed!" he said.

There was an audible click in the PA speakers, and a second later "Who Do You Love" by George Thorogood and the Destroyers began to play. Tark nodded his head with the drumbeat while he pounded his fist into his glove. Nodding and pounding, he began to smile. He pointed his index finger at Dave the Fag while he nodded with the beat. "Ready?" he asked.

Dave nodded.

Tark pointed at Dave the Jew. "Ready?"

Dave nodded.

Tark nodded a bit longer, then pointed at Grant, who by this time was wearing a grin. "You ready?"

Grant nodded.

"Well then, let's play ball!" Tark said, and he turned and led the Walleyes' rush onto the field.

Pearly nudged Grant with an elbow and chuckled. "I love that guy."

Grant walked to the pitcher's mound with a new white game ball in his hand. He stood with both feet together on top of the pitcher's rubber and surveyed his surroundings. Speed Roesner waved to him from the press box above the Walleyes dugout, and Grant waved back. Ingrid rode her bicycle in foul territory, out in right field, oblivious to the baseball game that was about to start. The Badenovs were standing by the chain-link fence, next to the Walleyes on-deck circle. That was a bit of a surprise, and there were several other college girls with them. The rest of the crowd, maybe three dozen people, mostly wives and girlfriends, were scattered about in the nearly empty bleachers and the grassy area in front of the concession stand. Tom Murphy would be umping behind the plate, and he stood there talking to Louie. He was dressed in his umpire gear and holding his face mask in his left hand while he chuckled at something Louie said. The Windigo players were lined up along the front step of their dugout, chirping at Grant, suggesting that he was about to get hammered. Pearly stood behind the plate, clean-shaven, no cigarette dangling from his mouth, ready to do this.

Grant's eyes moved to the concession stand and he saw that Kate was looking back at him. She'd been standing in the window, watching him, and now she smiled and waved. Grant tapped his heart with his throwing hand.

"Play ball!" Tom Murphy cried a moment later from his position just behind Pearly, and he slid his face mask down as Windigo's leadoff hitter walked to the plate.

Grant was making the last of his preparations with the dirt around the pitching rubber when Tark surprised everyone in the ballpark again. The Walleyes' second baseman arched his back, turned his face up to the cool evening sky, and let go a rebel yell. There was no English vocalization to it, just a scream from far down inside him. When the yell left his throat and burst into the cold air it condensed into a cloud above him so that it could be *seen* by everyone, too. The other Walleye players grinned and looked at each other. Louie even smiled at Theodore, while Theodore sat openmouthed on the Walleye bench.

When he'd ground his feet into the hard-packed dirt beside home plate, the first Windigo hitter raised a bat to his right shoulder and cast his eyes to Grant. Holding the ball in his glove and using the glove to cover his face, Grant peered over the webbing while he took the sign from Pearly. He went into his windup and delivered a crisp curveball that buckled the hitter's front leg before it snapped across the plate and into Pearly's mitt. Strike one. So sweet. Nice to be back, Grant thought.

Grant struck out the first two Windigo hitters, then he gave up a monstrous home run to Miller Peoples. Ray Rivers committed two errors at third base, and two runners were stranded on base when Grant struck out the last hitter.

"C'mon, Ray!" Tark groaned when the Walleyes jogged into the dugout for their first turn at bat. "Your pitcher is out there workin' hard and he gets you two routine ground balls, and you can't handle either one of 'em? Get in front of the ball! You afraid of something?" Tark stood and waited for a reply. Apparently he enjoyed confrontation. He'd only verbalized the things everyone else wanted to say, and no one came to Ray's defense. Then, just because he couldn't hold his tongue, Tark added, "Was that ball barkin' at you when it rolled by? You looked like a mailman who was afraid of some old lady's poodle."

Ray was fuming but chose not to reply. No one had ever spoken to him in such a manner.

In an attempt to calm the troubled waters in the Walleye dugout, Grant broke the silence. "Man, that Peoples kid is solid! I threw him thirteen straight curves. He just laid off the ones that weren't strikes and fouled off the others. Then I thought I'd sneak a fastball by him. Bad idea. I'll bet that ball had scorch marks on it when it left the park." Grant sat down next to Theodore and threw an arm over the young man's shoulders. "Don't worry, Theodore, We'll get you in the game. But when you get in there, just remember not to throw Miller Peoples a good pitch."

"Yeah," Pearly agreed. "That kid won't be seeing another fastball anytime soon, not anything in the strike zone anyway."

Dave the Fag walked to the booger board and tried to make an offering. "Damn cold weather," he said after he'd smeared a watery mark on the pizza box top.

He was still looking at the booger board when Will started the Walleye half of the first inning with a base hit, and the Walleyes proceeded to score five runs in their first turn at bat. Tark and the Daves hit three consecutive doubles and Clank followed with a home run. The cold weather didn't seem to be bothering anyone.

When the Walleyes came to the dugout for their half of the fourth inning, the score stood at 7–2, and their entire season was about to change before any of them left the dugout.

"How're you feeling?" Louie asked Grant when he reached the dugout steps.

"Good. Really good," Grant replied. He put on a jacket and tried not to bump into his teammates, who were all milling around the dugout, anxious for a turn at bat.

"He looks strong, Louie," Pearly offered. Then Pearly stood up, glanced at the booger board, nudged Grant with his elbow, and chuckled.

When Grant looked over at Pearly, he happened to notice a forlorn Theodore Christopher staring at the dugout floor. Theodore was the only Walleye who hadn't played, and everyone was ignoring him.

"Louie!" Grant said over the chatter in the dugout. "I've pitched four innings after a long winter. I'm tired, and it's cold tonight. Get the kid up and throwing. Let's see what he's got."

Theodore sat up straight and looked at Louie.

"He's not ready for this level yet," Ray shot back at Grant. "And who're we going to take out of the lineup in order to put him in the game?" Ray's tone was defiant, and it triggered a volcanic response from Tark.

"Take yourself out!" Tark said, as he stood up at the far end of the dugout and pointed a finger at Ray. Every other conversation in the dugout stopped immediately and all the players moved out of the developing cross fire between Tark and Ray.

"You made out this terrible lineup," Tark continued. He was a large cat that had been waiting to pounce. "You've got everybody in the wrong position, and *you're* the weak link! What's going on here? You get to say and do all this stupid shit and everyone just gives you a free pass. Why?"

The Walleye dugout was absolutely silent.

Ray bristled but remained seated. Louie, however, was standing by the bat rack at the end of the dugout. He folded his arms across his chest and looked at Tark, and he seemed to be waiting to hear what Tark had to say. Will Campbell had confronted Ray in the past, but never like this.

"Chrissakes!" Tark started when he was certain he had Louie's attention. Everybody else was staring and waiting too. For the first time, someone was about to verbalize all their misgivings and disdain for Ray Rivers. "Ol' Hard-nosed here is afraid of the ball!" Tark again pointed at Ray. "I'd sit his sorry ass down right now and put Clank over at third base!"

Ray scoffed, and the rest of the Walleyes looked over at Melbourne "Clank" Carrigan.

"Don't like the idea of playing Clank at third base?" Tark pointed at Melbourne Carrigan. "Well, the fuckin' guy is twisted steel. He might not catch everything that comes his way but he sure as hell won't jump out of the way. He'll get in front of it, maybe play it off his chest, but he'll get people *out*!"

Tark turned to Ray and repeated, "Out!" He said the word *out* as if he were trying to head-butt Ray with it.

"Yeah, right," Ray scoffed again.

"You know why Clank is such a shitty outfielder?" Tark continued, growing more and more agitated. He looked up and down the bench, waiting for a reply. "'Cuz he runs on his heels! That makes the ball appear to bounce when he's chasing it." Tark looked directly at Clank. "When you're chasing fly balls they jump around in the sky, don't they?"

"Yeah," Clank said, with wonder in his voice. Tark had just solved a lifelong riddle for him.

"Told ya so," Tark nodded, and he looked at Ray. It was his turn to scoff now. "I'm surprised that a coach of your caliber hadn't figured that out," Tark said sarcastically. He turned and pointed at Clank. "There's your third baseman."

"I play third," Ray objected.

"You suck, Ray!" Tark yelled, which triggered a rash of spontaneous laughter from the Walleyes. "Where did you learn that bullfighter defense, anyway? 'Bout the only thing you don't do is holler olé and wave at the ball as you let it trickle into left field."

The Walleyes, including Louie, were all laughing now, waiting for Tark to continue his tirade.

"You wanna win?" Tark dared them all, then he caught Louie's eye and silently asked for permission to continue. "This could actually be a pretty salty bunch, but here's what we gotta do." He looked around to be sure everyone was listening.

"OK, you want your swingin' dick, your best player, at shortstop. That's me. You need to move Will over to second base. Sorry, Will, you've got great hands but you're about three steps slower than me. Everybody knows you want your two best glove men up the middle. That's Will and me.

"Then you move Pissed out to right field and play him shallow. If anybody hits one over his head, well, good for them. Pissed'll catch everything that's hit in front of him, and he'll throw some runners out. He's kinda slow, but Dave the Fag covers a lotta ground out there in center field; the Fag can cover for him.

"Grant Thorson is a complete player, and the best pitcher in this league, they say, and whenever somebody else pitches, Grant can go play whatever position the new pitcher was playing. We're lucky to have such a versatile guy.

"Last," Tark paused, "you put Theodore at first base. He can do it."

"I told you he's not ready for this," Ray whined. "He never even got the job done in high school . . ."

"Hey!" A voice interrupted from just outside the dugout, breaking the spell. Tom Murphy, the umpire from behind home plate, had walked all the way to the Walleyes dugout. "You gonna send a batter up here or what, Louie? Everybody's waiting."

The Windigo Dragonflies were all assembled at their defensive positions and had been standing there for a couple of minutes while the Walleyes had been distracted.

"Sorry, Murph." Louie glanced at the scorebook. "Will! Grab a bat, you're up. Dave the Fag, you're on deck."

Murphy shook his head when he heard Louie say "Dave the Fag," then he walked back toward home plate wearing an odd smile.

"All right," Louie continued. "Theodore, get up and start throwing. We're gonna see what you can do."

"But Louie!" Ray protested.

"I'm the skipper of this nine!" Louie barked. "Ray, you sit the rest of the way. Melbourne, you go to third base, Grant, you take first base, Will, second base, Milburne, right field, Tark, shortstop. Your changes all sound good to me. Now we'll see if they work."

Ray stood with his chest puffed out, and he poked his index finger into Tark's chest. "You guys have it in for me," he growled through clenched teeth.

That was it for Tark. Nobody ever touched him like that. Ever.

Everyone froze, waiting for Ray Rivers to meet with a sudden and violent end, but Tark chose not to strike Ray. He leaned forward and smiled when he replied, "Well, that's partly true." He knew all the Walleyes were listening, and he squeezed the moment with a pause. "Your wife was over at the Chateau the other night, and I'm pretty sure both the Daves had it in for you. And from what I hear, everybody else around here has had it in for you too. If you know what I mean." He winked at Ray.

Ray's face reddened and he shoved Tark.

"You sure you want a shot at the title?" Tark tilted his head to the side and dared Ray to challenge him again.

"Right now!" Ray demanded, and he walked out the back of the dugout toward the grass beyond the batting cage.

"Ooo, bad move on Ray's part," Dave the Jew muttered to Clank, but Clank was suddenly interested in Brandi Rivers, not Ray.

Clank cast a sideways glance at the Daves and whispered, "Did you guys . . . Brandi . . . a Menahga trois?"

Dave the Jew turned away as if smoke had been blown into his eyes while Tark followed Ray to the batting cage.

"OK, where would you like to fall?" Tark asked, when Ray raised his clenched fists. A heightened sense of anger flashed across Ray's eyes, and he tried to throw a punch as he lowered his head and charged Tark.

Tark danced backward two steps and used an open hand to push Ray's head down and then to spin him into the ground. "Don't get up, Ray. I'm gonna hurt you," Tark said.

Ray jumped to his feet and swung wildly at Tark's head. Tark used his left hand to deflect Ray's right, before launching his own right hand. The punch flattened Ray's nose with a thud. Ray's hands dropped to his sides, his knees buckled, and he crumpled in a pile of elbows and knees.

Two college girls who'd seen the fight were holding paper napkins on Ray's face to stop the trickle of blood from his nose a minute later when Tark stepped away. "He might need some help drivin' home," Tark said. "But he'll be OK." Then he walked back to the dugout.

Tark calmly reentered the dugout and sat next to Pearly. "What happened to Ray?" Pearly asked.

"He's gonna need some time off," Tark replied.

"Well where'd he go?" Louie asked.

"He's just layin' there bleedin', over by the batting cage," Tark replied.

"Is he OK?" Louie asked. "I mean, did you hurt him?"

Tark shrugged. "Turns out he wasn't so hard-nosed."

Pearly stood up, walked to the back door of the dugout, and saw the two college girls tending to Ray's wounds. "He's sittin' up, Louie, but I don't think he knows if he's afoot or horseback," Tark chuckled.

Louie grinned, then told Milburne to go over and inform the umpire and the Menahga coach that Theodore Christopher would be entering the lineup in Ray's place in the batting order.

Theodore pitched the rest of the game and did just fine, baggy uniform and all. He struck out six Dragonflies and walked only two batters. Unfortunately, the two batters he walked were both on base when Miller Peoples hit another thunderous home run. Grant was the first to congratulate Theodore, and then he reminded him never to throw Miller Peoples another fastball. The rest of the Walleyes played well in their new positions also, and they won, 8–5, as thick wet snowflakes began to settle out of a black sky and swirl through the yellow glow under the ballpark light towers in the ninth inning. Walleye field looked like a paperweight snowstorm when the last Menahga hitter struck out to end the game.

Ray Rivers dropped off a blood-spattered uniform at the concession stand while the Walleyes were in the field during the seventh inning, so that none of his teammates could see his swollen face. His Walleye career was over.

CHAPTER 44

"Look at the snow coming down," Kate exclaimed. She was sitting on her living room floor, an hour after the game. "Who'd have thought we'd get heavy snow like this on the same night we had a baseball game?"

Ingrid was spending the night with the Campbell girls at Spider Lake Duck Camp and Grant and Kate had the house to themselves. After a hot shower, Grant had piled wood in front of the hearth and he was about to build a fire.

"Yeah, it's a little unusual, but it's springtime in the north. We've had plenty of snow in May," Grant replied. He bunched up several sheets of newspaper and placed them in the fireplace. "Worked out pretty well for us, I'd say," he added with a grin. "We get to share a fire."

Kate popped open a can of Hamm's beer and took a sip. "It's too bad Ray had to find out about his wife like that," she said.

"Oh, I think he knew." Grant stacked several pieces of cardboard and some kindling on top of the newspaper in the fireplace. "He just didn't know that everybody else knew," Grant added. He reached over to the pile of firewood and selected several pieces of poplar, which he stacked on top of the kindling.

"The thing about Ray," Grant continued, taking a book of matches from his pocket, "is that he affects everyone the same. He makes their lives worse." Grant struck the match and held it by the newspaper. A little yellow flame sent a wispy cloud of smoke up the chimney, and the flame billowed into a crackling fire in a few seconds. Grant sat on the hearth and turned to face Kate. "He needed to be humiliated and dismissed. I'm glad he's gone. Guys like that never seem to figure it out. Know what I mean?"

Kate nodded yes, but she was done talking about Ray. "I saw the young guys looking at you tonight," she said. "They admire you. You're the one they look to, you and Pearly. They all like Tark, but you're the leader."

"Yeah, I know," Grant said. "Funny how we just keep on changing, huh? Now I'm an old guy all of a sudden. Gimme that other beer, will you?" he asked as he extended his hand.

"So how did you feel tonight?" Kate asked, as she gave him the can of beer.

"Good, really good. I got a little tired at the end, but overall I felt good." He waited for a second after his first swig of beer. "The cancer is gone, Kate. I just know it. I'm gonna be fine. We're gonna be fine."

"Told you so." Kate smiled and held her beer can out.

"Yeah, you did." He clicked his beer can against hers. "So much has come and gone for us. We've crossed some rough water together."

"Oceans." Kate nodded.

"Do you ever wonder how we wound up here, together, like this?" he asked.

Kate nodded. "Just lucky, I guess."

The kindling and the poplar logs settled a bit and sent sparks up the chimney. Grant leaned over and found two bigger pieces of oak. "These'll burn for a while," he said, as he placed them on the fire.

"Think about it," he resumed. "Don't you wonder sometimes about the way we met—and all the people who had a part in it?"

Kate nodded. "Fred Muckinhern retired, you know."

"Time keeps on passing," Grant said.

"The Jimmer is in third grade now," Kate added, and both of them laughed at the thought of The Jimmer.

Then Grant reached over and lifted Kate's right foot off the floor and began to rub it as he took her sock off. "What're you doing?" she asked.

"I think you know." He grinned. "Remember the time we got naked in front of a fire, at Will's cabin, and the dog . . ."

"Yes," Kate laughed. "Why do boys think that stuff is so funny?"

"It just is." Grant shrugged. "You're smiling, look at you. You tell me."

"I'm smiling at you, not the dog," Kate said. "You looked so happy tonight."

Grant took his socks off and tossed them on the floor next to hers. "I was happy," he said. "I have this great fantasy that's always there when I'm playin' ball. I'm mowing down the Yankee hitters, and . . ."

"Wasn't Mickey Mantle a Yankee?" Kate asked. "And don't you wear number seven because he was your favorite player?"

"Yeah," Grant nodded.

"So you hate the Yankees, but Mickey Mantle is your hero . . ."

Grant sighed, then grinned as he tried to explain. "He was a Golden Boy with unlimited talent, and I was just a boy. I had no idea about his problems or his demons, and I didn't care that he was a Yankee. He was just the best player. He could do anything. Now that I'm older I still want that Mickey Mantle of my childhood to come and play with me. It's a little complicated, I guess, but as long as I understand it, you don't need too." He leaned forward, stole a kiss, and then unbuttoned her blue jeans. When he'd removed her jeans she sat before him wearing only cotton panties and her red sweater.

He sat down on the hearth again and looked at her. With both legs bare now, one withered and one muscular, she smiled and waited for him to continue.

"Still having the same fantasy?" she asked.

"No, the Yankees are drifting away here," Grant said.

"Maybe you're dreaming about the Twins winning the World Series?" she teased.

"That'll never happen," Grant said as he stood up and removed his clothes.

"Well, maybe the young guys like Puckett and Hrbek . . ." She knew Grant had lost interest in any further conversations about baseball, but she kept talking just to tease him. Grant lifted her sweater over her head and laid it down beside her. When he pulled her close, she purred and left the Twins and the Yankees behind too. "I have a fantasy. One that I need you to help me with," Kate whispered as he kissed her neck.

"Yeah?" he replied, expecting an X-rated request.

"Teach me how to ride a bicycle?" she asked.

Grant stopped the kissing and raised himself to one elbow. "Really?"

"Really," Kate nodded.

"You can't ride a bike?" he asked.

"How would I learn? Who would teach me?" she answered.

"Sure," he shrugged. "I can do that. But maybe for now we should go back to some other fantasies."

Thirty minutes later Kate rolled onto her back and began shaking her thumbs. "Wow," she sighed. "What do you suppose the rest of the Walleyes are doing right now?"

~: CHAPTER 45 :~

"This'll never work!" Theodore whispered as Tark dragged him out of the swirling snowflakes in the parking lot and into the Tamarac Chateau.

"Sure it will!" Tark replied. "Just stick with me."

Far across the long building, on the other side of a large rectangular bar, dozens of other young people were dancing and drinking. The Daves and the Carrigans were there, still dressed in their Walleye uniforms. Tark waved to Natasha Badenov and began to lead Theodore through the crowd.

"Can I see some ID?" asked a buxom young waitress. She'd appeared from nowhere and stopped Theodore in his tracks.

The kid froze. Tark wrapped an arm around the boy's shoulder and smiled at the pretty waitress.

"I'll vouch for this young man," Tark said. "He's of age. You can take my word for it."

"Let's see some ID," the girl demanded, extending her hand.

Theodore didn't move until Tark shook him. Then he grimaced like he was about to pass a kidney stone and reached into the right hip pocket of his oversize Walleye uniform. He pulled out a small piece of paper that Tark had given him in the parking lot, and after some hesitation he gave it to the waitress.

The girl studied the paper for a moment and her eyes began to tighten as if she was looking at a bright light.

"This is a Minnesota nonresident fishing license," she said.

Theodore nodded seriously.

"It says you're twenty-eight years old and you're Japanese," she said.

Theodore nodded again.

"Do you speak Japanese?" the girl asked.

"Sí," Theodore said.

"There you have it!" Tark bluffed, as if Theodore had used the correct password and explained everything. He started leading Theodore to the back of the bar.

"Not so fast." The waitress held her hand up to block their path. She took a hard look into Theodore's nervous eyes.

"Is there a problem?" Tark asked, and he winked at the waitress.

The girl had short, dark hair. She was cute. She was nobody's fool, and she was familiar with bullshit artists like Tark. She folded the paper and gave it back to the nervous boy. "I know who you are, Theodore."

"There must be some mistake," Tark said. "Mr. Aoki is visiting from . . ."

"Save that crap for your buddies." The waitress scowled at Tark, then she turned to Theodore. "Can you behave yourself if I let you in?" she asked.

Theodore nodded, and the waitress turned back to Tark. "Can you keep him out of trouble?"

"Sí," Tark said with a wink.

The girl rolled her eyes and stepped out of their way.

Natasha Badenov had one arm around Tark's waist before he reached the dance floor and suddenly Theodore was on his own. He stood alone in his oversize baseball uniform and wore a forlorn expression, until someone called his name.

"Hey, Theodore!" Dave the Fag hollered. "C'mere! I've got someone who wants to meet you."

Standing beside Dave the Fag was a short, dark-haired girl wearing all black; she was the one they called Boris, Boris Badenov. He'd seen her from across the infield earlier that evening when Clank had pointed her out, standing with Natasha and the other girls. He'd thought she was kind of pretty from a distance, and now she wasn't too bad up close, either. She had a lot of makeup on, but she was OK, and she was smiling at him!

"Theodore, this is Pamela Macek. Pamela, this is Theodore Christopher," Dave said. Then he was gone, back to his conversation with another girl.

"Hi," Pamela said.

"Hi," Theodore nodded.

"I saw you pitch tonight. You did good!" Pamela said.

Theodore had to bend over to hear her, she was so short. She couldn't be much more than five feet tall, he thought. And he was nearly six feet six. "Thanks," he said. "I got two base hits, too."

Boris Badenov wasn't interested in base hits. Even the naive Theodore

Christopher could see that much. "Let's go sit down someplace so we can talk," she suggested.

Theodore found a small booth along a bank of windows and seated himself.

"You want a beer?" Boris asked, as she slid onto the seat beside him instead of the seat on the other side of the booth.

"Sure," Theodore said. Boris raised her right hand to signal a waitress, and in the same instant she put her left hand on his leg. High up on his leg. She was gently stroking his thigh when the waitress who'd checked his ID appeared at their booth.

"What can I get you?" the waitress asked. She scolded Theodore with her eyes.

"A beer?" he said tentatively.

"What kind of beer?" she asked, still scolding him.

"Can I have a Hamm's?" he asked.

"Sí," the waitress said as she turned away.

"Do you know her?" Boris asked when the waitress left.

"A little bit," Theodore said.

Although Boris didn't grab a good hold on anything else, she certainly held Theodore's attention for the next few minutes as she stroked his leg and talked with him. She didn't really like baseball but she liked baseball players, she said. She went on to point out all of her friends over there in the crowd. She told Theodore where they liked to party, who was dating who at the moment, and who liked to smoke pot. She drank two more beers herself and then she bought Theodore another. He thought she was getting prettier.

"Hey, how's it goin', eh?" Tark said when he plopped into the seat on the other side of the booth and pulled Natasha in after him.

"Hi, Theodore, my name is Melanie. Pamela is my baby sister," Natasha said as she extended her hand. She was even prettier than Pamela, and she impressed Theodore immediately as someone who was a bit older, and wiser, and maybe a bit harder than any woman he'd ever met.

"Hi," Theodore said as he shook her hand.

"You know the roads around here pretty well, right?" Tark blurted before Theodore could say any more.

"Sure, I grew up here," Theodore replied.

"Well, good. 'Cuz we're going on a road trip. Finish your beer!" Tark smiled.

Theodore finished the last swallow of his second beer and Boris chug-a-lugged the fourth beer she'd ordered since they'd sat down at the booth.

They all stood up and walked across the noisy, crowded Chateau in single file. When they reached the front door, Tark leaned on it and they burst into a silent, Hollywood snowfall. Giant wet snowflakes fell steadily, noiselessly. Over the past hour they'd covered the north woods with a white blanket almost two inches thick. It was a spectacularly beautiful night.

"Here's my car keys," Tark said as he tossed a key chain at Theodore. "You're driving." He put one arm around Natasha and he raised his other hand to show Theodore the twelve-pack of beer that he was carrying. He flicked his eyebrows and announced, "Road buddies."

"Good!" Boris said. She let herself into Tark's 1972 Ford LTD and slid so far across the front seat that there was barely any room for Theodore in the driver's seat. Before Theodore could start the engine he heard a beer open in the backseat.

"Hey, gimme one too," Boris said.

Theodore eased the silver Ford out onto the quiet highway, and then he turned off on the first secluded road he came to. It was nothing more than an abandoned logging trail and he was certain they'd see no police, or anyone else, for that matter. He was pretty sure that's what Tark had in mind, too.

Most of the conversation came from Tark and Natasha in the backseat. They laughed and joked and giggled while Theodore guided the car on through the snowflakes, down more deserted roads and logging trails.

"You *sure* you know where you are, Theodore?" Tark asked when the conversation began to dwindle.

"Sure, I've been hunting grouse and deer on these trails my whole life," he replied.

That was all the reassurance Tark needed. In the next moment he started out on another mission, and things got real quiet in the backseat. Theodore tried to sneak a peek in the rearview mirror, but he couldn't see much. He could hear clothing rustling, and from time to time he heard Melanie giggle and whisper something to Tark.

He was trying to stretch his neck for a better look at the backseat when Boris threw an empty beer over to the floorboards on the passenger side of the LTD, then in the same motion she brought her hand back over and rested it firmly on his crotch.

The car lurched to the right and blasted through a small patch of wild raspberry bushes and poplar seedlings before it veered back onto the logging trail. It wasn't that Theodore objected to the new grip that Boris had taken, she'd just surprised him. Really surprised him.

"What was that?" came Natasha's muffled voice from the backseat.

"Nothing," Boris answered. "Yet." She turned her drunken eyes to Theodore and smiled fiendishly. In only a moment her nimble fingers identified several strategic pressure points just underneath his Walleye uniform, and he suddenly needed to keep both hands on the steering wheel in order to control the Ford.

Theodore had no idea what their destination was but he'd acquired a pretty clear idea regarding Boris's intentions. While he was trying to visualize several potential endings to all this, she surprised him again. Boris suddenly shifted her weight and swung her right leg over his lap so that she was straddling him and looking into the backseat. Miraculously, she'd placed herself on one of his favorite pressure points, and she began moving her hips in a way that prevented him from thinking of much else. Her cheek was pressed against his and she began describing what she was going to do in a few minutes. Then she began to narrate the wrestling match going on in the backseat, too, since she had such a good view.

"Hey?" Boris interrupted her own narrative. "You wanna smoke some pot first?" she asked.

"No thanks," Theodore said.

"Hey, Mel, you got any weed?" she asked her sister.

Natasha didn't seem too perturbed by the interruption. She sat up and began looking through her purse until she found a marijuana cigarette, then she gave the joint to Boris.

"Got a light?" Boris asked with the joint between her lips.

"Sure," Natasha replied. She flicked her small butane lighter and flooded the Ford with yellow light.

Theodore stole a quick glance over his shoulder and noticed that everyone in the backseat was still fully clothed, pretty much. He also noticed that Boris looked a lot drunker than she seemed. Before he had time to think about much more, it happened. He rolled the Ford through a puddle and Natasha's flaming cigarette lighter drifted a bit too close to Boris's hair. The excessive hair spray she'd applied ignited in a shocking and brilliant *poof.*

In the brief instant just before anyone understood exactly what had happened, Boris looked vacantly at Theodore. With a joint dangling from her lips and her eyes fixed at half-mast, her head was ablaze and the whole incident seemed surreal.

Theodore stomped on the brakes, slammed the Ford into park, grabbed Boris, and leaped from the car. He then shoved her flaming head into the wet snow in the ditch along the remote logging trail they'd been cruising.

Boris didn't yet seem to understand what was happening. She was making sounds, but not words, as Theodore swept up handfuls of wet snow and smeared them over her head to extinguish the sizzling hair. The smell of burning hair hung heavy in the silent forest when the flames finally went out.

Natasha and Tark had jumped from the car too, and they stood over Boris, wavering, as if they were struggling against some unseen turbulence. Ankle-deep in the snow, with their clothing mostly unbuttoned and unzipped, the alcohol and the sudden commotion were playing hell with their equilibrium.

"Whoa!" Boris said as she pulled her head from the wet snow and took a look around her. "What was that?" Her hair was badly singed, wet, and matted against her head, but there were no burns on her face or scalp. She'd unfastened her bra to give Theodore better access, and now her sweater and bra had ridden up under her armpits, exposing her breasts. She looked around and at herself and tried to establish her bearings. She felt her head, and when she realized that everything was intact she began to smile. Theodore reached over and adjusted her sweater to cover her breasts, and they all began to look back and forth at each other.

Two baseball players, the lovely Natasha, and the now not-so-lovely Boris—with a still-smoldering head—all gaped at each other while the wet snowflakes drifted down around them. Theodore didn't know what to do next. He brushed the snow off his cold hands and looked at a stunned Tark, hoping for some direction. Boris Badenov was too drunk and disoriented to stand up, so she stayed on her knees for a moment and stared blankly at the ground in front of her. Natasha looked about the scene too, unsure of what to say or do. "Whoa," Boris said again, and a smile came to her lips. Tark was the next to smile, then Natasha, then Theodore, and the faint smiles billowed into belly laughs in the same way that Boris's head had burst into flames. In the next instant the silent woods were filled with their laughter.

On the way back to the Chateau, Tark and Theodore sat in the front while Natasha did what she could to repair Boris's hair and reassemble her clothing. Boris threw up twice.

∾ CHAPTER 46 ∾

The May snowstorm blew itself out in one dark night. Warm weather followed on its heels, and Theodore Christopher graduated from high school. The Walleyes were undefeated after two games at home and two on the road, and they'd begun to catch the community's attention.

"All right, Kate," Grant said one Thursday evening. "Would you like to learn how to ride a bike today?" He had gotten home at five o'clock and immediately changed into his Walleyes uniform. "We've got a couple hours before the game tonight. Let's take Ingrid's bike, and that old one in the garage, and head for the ballpark."

"But . . . what if . . . ?" Kate halted.

"C'mon, honey. Ingrid loves to ride around there. Today's a good day for you to learn. We'll be the only ones there for the next hour," Grant coaxed.

Ten minutes later Kate was straddling the seat of an old Schwinn bicycle that Grant had picked up at a garage sale two years earlier. Ingrid was already riding around in the empty space by the batting cage and Grant was about to start the lesson.

"Can you pedal with your bionic leg?" he asked.

"Not very well," she replied. "I'll have to leave the knee joint on my brace unlocked so I can keep it bent and just rest my left foot on the pedal." She grew hesitant. "Maybe I'd better not . . ."

"Bullshit," Grant blurted. "You need to do this. Don't worry about pedaling, not at first, anyway. You have to learn to balance yourself before you start pedaling. Once you have the balance figured out we'll work on the pedaling."

"But . . ."

"Hang on, honey." Grant said as he eased the bike forward. "Just rest your feet on the pedals. I'll be holding you up."

"Grant! I don't know . . ." She'd lost all confidence and she was growing rigid, like all beginners.

"I'll be right here," he said calmly into her ear. His left hand rested beside hers on the handlebars and his right hand steadied the bicycle seat. He began to jog alongside her. Then he let go of the handlebars with his left hand.

"Grant!" she pleaded.

"I'm right here," he said softly. "You steer this thing. I'll hold you up." He ran a little faster. "You're doing great!" he said. "It's not so hard, is it?"

"What if I crash?" she asked.

"Can't happen." He ran alongside her, then said, "I just let go of you. You're on your own now."

"Grant!"

"I'll be here," he said as he ran along beside her. "You're doing fine."

And she was doing fine. She had the balance figured out right away, but as she began to decelerate it grew more difficult to balance the bicycle.

"How do I stop?" she asked.

The bicycle began to wobble as it slowed to a near stop. "Grant!" she cried, but he was watching from a distance. She began to lose her balance and the bike rolled to her left. In an instant she lay in a pile on the soft grass with her bicycle wrapped around her.

Grant was there immediately.

"You said you wouldn't let me fall!" she said.

"I said I'd be here for you. There's a difference," he said.

Kate glowered at him.

"We all gotta fall at least once," he said. He was kneeling beside her now. "Didn't hurt, either. Did it?" he asked.

She glared and then struggled to move the bike off her leg brace and stand up. Grant lifted the bike and helped Kate to her feet. He knelt again and picked several small clumps of sod from her leg brace, then he examined a small scratch on her other leg.

"You're OK. Let's do it again. This time when you come to a stop remember to lean it to your right and put your right leg out for balance," he said.

"Are you gonna let me fall again?" Kate asked, still upset that he'd let her take a tumble.

"Maybe." He grinned and softened. "I love you, Kate, I'll protect you. But everybody has to fall down some. If you don't, well, you never really appreciate this." He nodded his agreement with his own words. "You just get up and keep going." He shrugged. "Did it hurt?" he asked as he prepared for another run.

"A little. Not much. Scared me, though," she confessed when he began to push once more.

A minute later he was running alongside her, but not touching her or the bike. "I think you've got it," he said. "Now try to pedal. Just use your right leg. See if you can drive the pedal down hard enough so it'll push the left pedal over the top with the down stroke on the other side."

He steadied the bike while she tried once, then a second time, and finally both pedals were turning. He let go of her again and watched her ride by herself.

She used the brakes and stopped without tipping over. She demanded another start, then another.

"OK, so how do I ever get started on my own?" she asked eventually.

"I think you'll need to start over on the pavement in the parking lot. This grass is a little soft for you to learn to start pedaling with just your right leg—it'll slow you down too much. But once you've learned, I think you'll be fine starting out on soft grass, too."

There were several close calls over on the pavement, but in a few minutes Kate was starting and stopping on her own. She had it. She rode in straight lines, then circles, then figure eights, while Grant stood and watched.

Ingrid noticed her mother and father in the parking lot and brought her own bicycle over so she could join in.

As Kate made a smooth pass in front of Grant he noticed the breeze blowing through her hair and the look of exhilaration on her face. He saw her eyes fix on Ingrid, and then he heard something magical.

"Hey, Ingrid! Look at me!" Kate called out. The little girl from right field, the one with the French braids, was back. He hadn't seen her this clearly since the Twins game ten years earlier when he'd fallen in love with her. The happy girl with the French braids and the brace on her leg was simply calling out to another child, wanting recognition for mastering a two-wheeler and unlocking a bit of her spirit. The other child just happened to be her own daughter.

Kate's face glowed with joy. She was captivated, fascinated by this freedom and the sense of flying. She'd never felt this before, and now she owned it. It wasn't the same as rounding third and heading for home, but it was close. She laughed and talked and pedaled about for twenty minutes, until some of the Walleye players drove into the parking lot so they could prepare for the game.

Eventually, Kate rode her bicycle over to the concession stand and let it rest against the building while she prepared things for the game, and still the smile would not leave her face.

~:~

Except for Kate and Ingrid over in the concession stand, and the handful of Walleyes getting dressed in the dugout, the ballpark was still empty. Tonight's opponents, the Nevis Shysters, hadn't arrived yet, and the only noise in the park was the soft conversation of the players.

"Jeez your car stinks, Tark," Dave the Jew exclaimed while he pulled his pants up. He knew what had happened after the Windigo game. Everyone knew by now. He just wanted to see how Tark would respond.

Tark cast a glance at Theodore and the kid returned a smile.

"Well, as you may have heard via the rumor mill," Tark said as he pulled his green stirrups over his white stockings, "Theodore's new girlfriend . . ."

"She's not my girlfriend," Theodore interrupted.

"I believe you're all familiar with Miss Badenov," Tark continued, as if Theodore hadn't spoken. "She was seriously overserved by the bartender at the Chateau. You can all rest assured that I've spoken to the management about this problem," Tark said seriously. Then he added, "I'm also concerned that young Theodore's delicate psyche may have been scarred by Miss Badenov's improper sexual advances, and subsequent head fire and vomiting."

His teammates chuckled, and Theodore covered his face with his hands.

"Hey, Theodore. Come with me," Grant said as he stood up and tucked his jersey into his pants. "I'd like to work with you on a coupla' things." Grant took his glove and a ball and walked toward the pitcher's mound. Theodore was only too happy to leave Tark and the others behind.

When they reached the pitcher's mound, Grant flipped a baseball to Theodore. "Show me how you hold a runner on first base," Grant said.

"Why?" Theodore asked.

"'Cuz you got called for two balks the other night. You must be doing something wrong," Grant answered.

"OK." Theodore shrugged and took his stretch position, as if there was a runner on first base.

"So far, so good," Grant said. "Now check the runner."

Theodore glanced toward first base, over his left shoulder.

"Good," Grant said. "Now pick the runner off. Make a quick throw to first."

Theodore shifted his feet and pretended to throw the ball to first base.

"Your footwork is all wrong," Grant said with a grimace.

"That's the way Mr. Rivers taught me," Theodore replied.

"OK," Grant started. "He's gone now. Forget everything he told you. Now show me your stretch position again."

Theodore stood with his right foot just in front of the pitching rubber, and he looked toward home plate.

"OK, Theodore, you're right-handed, and when there's a base runner on first base he'll be watching your heels because he knows the instant you lift your left heel you have to throw to the plate. That's when he'll break for second base if he plans to steal. If he sees you raise your *right* heel he knows you're gonna step off the rubber and then you can throw wherever you want." Grant paused. "Are you with me?"

"Yes," Theodore replied.

"All right, here's one way to pick a runner off first base. You have to step off the rubber with your right foot, *then* turn and throw to first; and you'd better be quick about it. Another way . . ."

"Mr. Rivers said to . . ."

Grant held his right hand up, closed his eyes, and shook his head. "Forget Coach Rivers," he said. Then he went on with short lessons about a pitcher's balance point, hip rotation, and follow-through. Ten minutes later Grant said, "OK, now show me how you grip your changeup."

A small crowd was beginning to gather on the grassy area between the bleachers and the concession stand twenty minutes before the game was to start. There were new faces in the crowd, mostly young people, and quite a few of them were women. Several of the Walleye players were in full uniform, talking with their new fans, when Tubby Voss and Bud Pearson walked into the park.

"Hi, Kate," Tubby said. "What's with all the people?"

"Hi, Tubby. I think the new players have drawn a fan base from the Chateau," Kate replied.

"Grant pitching tonight?" Tubby asked, as he placed $4.50 on the countertop. He didn't even have to ask for the usual three bratwursts anymore. Kate knew his routine and she had them ready.

"Yup," Kate said as she slid the brats toward him and then took his money. "Thanks, Tubby."

"How's he feelin', Kate?" Bud Pearson asked. "I mean after the cancer and all."

Even after six years in a small town, Kate was still surprised when someone who was a friend, but a friend who existed on the periphery of her life, could walk up and ask a question like that with such heartfelt concern.

"Good! Really good," Kate said. "He feels strong, and the doctor gave him the all-clear."

"Well that's great," Bud said. "The guys up in Blackduck said he was real sharp the other night. Just like before."

"Yeah, we feel pretty fortunate," Kate said.

Just then Speed Roesner walked past. "Hi, Tubby. Hi, Bud. Hi, Kate," he said as he hurried by. He was five minutes late and he was certain that the crowd was growing restless because he hadn't turned on the scoreboard or started the music yet. He took two steps at a time on his way up the stairs to the press box. A moment later the Six Fat Dutchmen started into the "Beer Barrel Polka."

Ten seconds after that a voice from inside the Walleye dugout hollered, "Speed! Turn that shit off!"

The Dutchmen stopped with a loud click, and Bruce Springsteen boomed through the speakers with the next click.

Two of the Nevis players wandered over, said hello to the Walleyes, and then made their way to the concession-stand window. One of the men looked to be in his mid-forties and the other one was young, really young.

Kate recognized the two. She'd seen them at ball games before but didn't know their names.

"Heard Grant was pitching well again," the younger one said to Kate as he paid for his brat. "That's great. Well, it's not so great for us," the kid corrected himself.

"Oh," the kid said, when he looked into her eyes and realized that he hadn't introduced himself. "I'm Steve Petersen, and this is my dad, Gordy."

Both men talked with Kate for a few minutes at the window, and she had two new friends. Steve said he'd never been able to get a hit off Grant, but Gordy had gotten a couple off him two years ago. Gordy seemed pretty proud of that. They chatted about a few of the other teams in the league until someone hollered, "Hey, Pete!" And both of them whipped their heads around to see who was calling.

"Gotta go. See you later, Kate," Gordy Petersen called over his shoulder as he and his son jogged over to join their teammates.

"Good luck," Kate said to them.

Steve Petersen grinned and said a muffled "Thanks," with half a brat stuffed in his mouth.

Kate put their money in the small cash box and wondered if the concession venders at Metropolitan Stadium ever got to make friends with the players and the umpires.

Starting time for the game was still a few minutes away, and the Shysters were finishing their pregame infield practice while the Walleyes sat in their dugout and watched. As the players made last-minute preparations, the usual inane and obtuse conversations sprang up.

"I almost shit my pants at work today," Pissed said while he tried on a new batting helmet. "I was just gonna fart and I felt some heat down there. Changed my mind at the last second. You never wanna trust a fart when there's some heat with it." He offered the insight as if it had moral value or intellectual merit for everyone in the dugout.

Without looking at him, Tark replied, "Yeah, your asshole is an amazing organ. It can tell the difference between solid, liquid, and gas in just a fraction of a second." He paused and cocked his head to the side before he completed his thought. "But sometimes that's not fast enough, eh? Heh, heh, heh."

"That guy cracks me up," Pearly said to Will.

"Hey, Theodore!" Dave the Fag said from the top step of the dugout, as he looked into the bleachers. "Boris is here! Looks like she has a new hairdo." Several players jumped up to have a look, and Theodore covered his face again.

A moment later Grant noticed Dave the Jew sitting by himself at the far end of the dugout, softly singing his own version of a popular song, "My Sharona." He tapped his right fist into his glove in time with the beat and sang, "Ma-ma-ma-ma- my sca-ro-tum . . ."

Grant calmly turned and made eye contact with Will. "Sounds like the fourth-floor coffee shop back in dental school," he said, and they each nodded their recognition of a turning point. The Walleyes had a new sense of esprit de corps that could never have existed in the presence of Ray Rivers. They were smiling, they were eager to play ball, and Tark Sabetti's enthusiasm was infectious.

An hour before the game, Tark had taped a ping-pong paddle to Clank's wrist so that the flat side covered the palm of his hand. Then he'd taken Clank to third base and hit ground balls to him for thirty minutes. The idea was to teach Clank to play with soft hands, to gently stop the ball on the ping-pong paddle and not to stab at it with his glove. Ray would never have come up with such a learning tool. Now Tark was chatting with Theodore about the theory of hitting.

"Ray taught you what?" Tark blurted in amazement. Every head in the dugout spun to look at him.

"He said to swing *down*, to chop down on the ball. Said we'd hit more ground balls and force the other team into making errors."

"That's the dumbest fucking thing I ever heard! All you ever do that way is hit weak ground balls, pop up, or strike out!" Tark screeched. He stood up, overcome by the need to explain. "OK, I'm the pitcher. I'm standing on the pitching mound, fourteen inches higher than the batter's box." Tark raised his right hand, which held a baseball. "I'm six feet tall and when I release the ball it's here . . . ," he pointed to his right hand, ". . . eight and a half feet in the air." He nodded at Theodore, then added, "And your bat is already belt-high, and you're gonna chop *down*? Jesus! Think about it. If you wanna hit line drives your swing plane has to be roughly parallel to the flight path of the pitch. You *must* have a slight uppercut. Do the physics! I'll take some extra batting practice with you after the game." He turned away and punctuated his lesson with yet another shot at Ray Rivers. "Jeez, what a dumb ass . . . 'chop down on the ball.'"

"OK, Louie," Tubby Voss said. "Your guys can take the field."

"OK, boys . . . ," Louie started, and the Walleyes all stood up to run onto the field.

"Hold it, Louie!" Tark interrupted, and all the Walleyes stopped in their tracks. Tark pulled a bat from the bat rack and pounded on the ceiling of the dugout.

Several seconds later there was a click on the PA system, and "Who Do You Love?" began to rumble out of the speakers. Tark slid his glove onto his left hand and began to nod his head with the beat while he looked at his teammates and began to grin. He waited until the drums began to thump, then he said, "OK, you hosers, let's go!" And he led them onto the field.

To the surprise of everyone, including Tark, a small cheer arose from the crowd. The spectators had lined up along the chain-link fence when Speed started the music and they were waiting for the Walleyes to take the field.

Speed had never heard anything like it. He stood up and craned his neck to the side when he stuck his head out of the open press box window. Several dozen young people were standing below, clapping along with the music. He stared for a moment, trying to comprehend. Then Natasha looked up at him and waved. She smiled and gave him a thumbs-up.

He slumped back into his chair and shook his head. Natasha Badenov had just smiled and waved! The people over there were having fun! This was all new.

A moment later, as the game was about to begin, the leadoff hitter for the Nevis Shysters was walking to the batter's box when Tark let loose with his signature rebel yell. The hitter was so startled he dropped his bat and jumped. For a second there, the kid had been sure he was under attack. When he picked up his bat he was laughing, along with everyone else at Walleye Field.

Tark Sabetti was emerging as the catalyst for a great transformation.

⌣∶⌣

The Walleyes led 9–0 in the top of the seventh inning when Tark gave his last lesson of the day, and it was a special one.

Grant had thrown three scoreless innings, then Theodore had done the same. When Tark took his turn on the mound the game was all but over. The second Shyster batter of the seventh inning hit a high pop-up in foul territory about fifty feet past first base. Theodore drifted toward the chain-link fence by the Walleyes dugout, but he got turned around and let the ball drop.

When the half inning ended and the Walleyes were walking back to the dugout, Tark got up in Theodore's face.

"That's your play, Theodore!" Tark growled loud enough for everyone to hear. "You gotta catch that pop-up. I don't care if you fall down and land on a pile of scrap lumber fulla nails, you gotta keep working till you catch that ball. That half-assed stuff might work in high school when Ray is in charge, but it won't work anywhere else. Understand?"

Everyone knew that Tark and Theodore were becoming good friends, and the combative nature of Tark's message surprised them initially. Theodore's feelings were hurt, and he lowered his head half in anger, half in shame, before he said, "Yes."

In the next moment Tark had an arm around Theodore's neck. "OK then, now here's how you play that ball. You keep it over this shoulder as you run . . ." Tark explained how to play the high one over first base. Then he told Theodore what a good job he'd done while he'd been pitching. He'd made a point for the others to hear, and he'd raised the bar for all of them.

Theodore Christopher, more than any of them, had been waiting for someone to demand excellence from him, and his eyes grew steely as the game ground to an end. He never wanted to hear Tark talking to him like that again. He'd never do anything like that again.

∽ CHAPTER 47 ∽

Father-daughter Saturday afternoon tea parties in Grant's little green boat had evolved into regularly scheduled events, and Ingrid was packing her things for another one while Grant loaded the cooler and fishing gear into the boat.

"Beautiful day," Kate said, as she shaded her eyes with her hand and watched Grant finish preparing the boat.

"Sure you don't want to come along?" Grant asked. "We have some interesting conversations out there."

"No thanks." Kate smiled. "I'll attend the tea parties on land. You two can have a special time with the ones at sea."

The screen door on the porch slammed and Ingrid raced across the lawn. She was carrying a pink vinyl suitcase that had come with an extensive collection of Barbie doll accessories. She was breathless when she finished her sprint across the yard.

"What's in the suitcase?" Grant asked, as he fastened a personal flotation device around her.

"I brought Kimberly Kay Johnson along," Ingrid said.

Her favorite Barbie doll had long blonde hair and Ingrid had named her Kimberly Kay Johnson. It made no sense to Grant, but he didn't need it to make sense.

"C'mon, Kate," Grant coaxed. "Join us."

"All right," Kate shrugged, and Grant helped her step into the boat.

Some Saturdays Ingrid wanted to fish a little bit before they started the tea party, and Grant hoped that today would be one of them. He anchored the small boat just off the shoreline, about two hundred yards from the house, and reached for a fishing rod.

"You want to put the worms on your own hook?" he asked Ingrid.

"No, you can do it," Ingrid replied. She wore a red-and-blue Twins cap, a green T-shirt, and a pink skirt, and Grant could see immediately that she had no interest in fishing today. She was already talking to her doll. "Kimberly Kay Johnson, you can sit here beside my dad." She was animated as she opened her pink suitcase and began explaining the seating arrangements to everyone.

"Dad, would you please set the table?" Ingrid said. She'd issued a command in the form of a question. Grant stashed the worms and the fishing rod behind him near the motor and then lifted the pink tea party dishes from the cooler.

Ingrid hadn't assigned her mother any particular chores yet, so Kate simply watched as her daughter rifled through all the Barbie accessories in the suitcase at her side.

Both Kate and Grant happened to be looking at Ingrid, just watching to see what she might say or do next, when she lifted Kimberly Kay Johnson from the pink suitcase. They were both taken aback by what they saw. Ingrid had used two Band-Aids and two silver ballpoint pens to fashion a leg brace on the doll's left leg. She sat the doll on the boat seat next to Grant and then used a tiny hairbrush to straighten the doll's hair. She then began searching through the pink suitcase for something else.

Kate and Grant both looked up from the doll at the same time and locked eyes. What to do? What to say? They hadn't seen this coming.

"Mom?" Ingrid asked while she dug through the doll clothes in the suitcase.

"Yes, honey," Kate replied.

"Will my leg be like yours when I get older?" Ingrid asked matter-of-factly. She turned to Kate and waited for an answer.

Grant waited for Kate's answer too.

"Oh, no, Ingrid, I hope you never have something like this. I got very sick when I was about your age, and my leg never got better. I wouldn't want this to happen to you," Kate said. She was startled by the sight of Kimberly Kay Johnson, and by Ingrid's question.

Ingrid stared at her mother now, only half understanding. Her great unspoken expectation, until this moment, was to be just like her mother when she grew up. She didn't understand.

"Oh, sweetheart," Kate started to explain. "This has been so hard. I wish I could have lived my life without it. My life would have been so much better without it."

Before those words had left her lips she knew she'd stung Grant. She knew he'd always felt that her polio was the thing that brought their lives together. Now she'd just implied that her life would have been better without him. She didn't have to look into his eyes to know that he was hurt.

Kate hadn't expected all this: the sudden surprise of Kimberly Kay Johnson's leg, Ingrid's innocent question, and then her own fear that she'd hurt Grant's feelings. A lump formed in the back of her throat as her emotions began to collide, and soon enough her eyes filled with tears. She reached for Grant's hand. "I'm sorry, I didn't mean . . ."

"I know," he interrupted.

What's the matter, Mommy?" Ingrid asked.

"Nothing, honey." Kate sniffled as she wiped her nose.

"Why are you crying?" Ingrid asked.

"I don't know," Kate replied. She laughed, then she sobbed in the next instant and pulled Ingrid to her breast while she let the rest of her tears come.

Grant put a hand on his wife's shoulder. He understood, sort of. Kate had just had a fairly candid look at the way her only child expected life to unfold, and the vision had been bittersweet. Then she'd found herself wondering about the path her own life was taking. There was a lot going on in her head.

Eventually Kate blew her nose, chuckled, took a deep breath, and urged Ingrid to resume the tea party. Their moment was over.

The three of them talked and laughed while they shared Coke and cookies with Kimberly Kay Johnson. Grant never did get a chance to catch a fish.

The warm sun felt good on their shoulders as they packed up the tea party dishes a half hour later. As they motored home, the little Evinrude droned along and Grant remembered the look on Ingrid's face during her exchange with Kate. She'd seen something she couldn't understand yet, but it had definitely been imprinted in her memory. She'd seen her mother crying. She'd stared at Kate and wondered just what sort of thing could make her mother cry. She'd be recalling it over and over again throughout her life, and she'd try to understand, just as he remembered Little Ole and his father sprawled out on that dirt floor in the machine shed all those years ago.

∾ ∶ ∾

The Walleyes usually took several cars and rode together in a caravan when they played away games. Tonight they were playing in Windigo, and they sat together in the late afternoon heat while they waited for Tark and the Daves to roll into the parking lot at Walleye Field. They'd be the last to arrive; they always were.

Grant and Will sat together in the front seat of Grant's car. The engine was turned off and the doors were open. Will was reading a fishing magazine, and Grant was staying in the shade while he remembered Ingrid's tea party.

Pearly had parked his van next to them. The sign on the side of the vehicle read "Pearly's Plumbing," and Pearly drove it to all away games so he could write off his baseball expenses as advertising. Theodore and the Carrigans stood outside the van and talked quietly. Louie's car was parked nearby, also with the engine off and the windows open.

"Hey, I heard Ray's gonna play for Windigo. 'Zat true, Louie?" Clank asked.

"I gave him his release a while ago," Louie answered. "I heard he'd caught on with the Dragonflies."

"S'pose old Hard-nosed will be playing third base tonight?" Pissed asked. He was leaning on Grant's car, looking around at the others. "Rotten prick."

"Probably," Louie sighed. He got out of his car and parked himself on Grant's hood, next to Pissed. "I know he's got some family connection up there. Good news is that he'll probably just get the Dragonflies all screwed up now."

Clank had slid Pearly's side door open and was sitting on the floor of the van with his feet on the ground when he threw a question out for the others to think about. "Think we'll see the Irish mafia tonight?"

"Hmph," Pearly scoffed. "Bet on it." The Windigo Dragonflies had a long-standing reputation for hiring friendly umpires whenever the Walleyes come to town. Tom Murphy and Jack Fitzgerald had grown famous for blatantly one-sided umpiring in critical situations. They didn't cheat all the time, just at Windigo, and only when it really mattered.

The sun had grown a bit hotter and the ballplayers went silent for a minute. This was usually the point in the conversation when one of the players would mention a particularly bad call by Murphy or Fitzgerald, then someone else would recite another familiar anecdote, and then there'd be twenty minutes of Irish mafia stories. Fitzgerald had made some shaky calls over the years, but Murphy earned most of their scorn. The players all hated him, and as they sat in the sun they began to remember outrageous bad calls by Tom Murphy. Each of the Walleyes began to notice hard feelings swelling in their chests.

But Theodore Christopher spoke up first. Louie had just informed Theodore that he'd be pitching tonight, and after a few minutes to think about things, a little anger had boiled over inside him, too. He didn't know anything about Murphy and Fitzgerald, but he'd suffered unfairly at Ray's hand, and he had revenge on his mind. Even during the short time since Ray had left the Walleyes, they'd all seen Theodore begin to change. He'd been a timid schoolkid when the season began. Now he was a young man in search of himself. He reached into his hip pocket and withdrew the tin of tobacco that he had begun carrying several weeks earlier. He placed a brown pinch of finely ground tobacco between his cheek and gums and announced, "I'm gonna drill Ray. Every time!"

"Here they come," Will said, as he pointed to Tark's silver LTD. The Walleyes all turned and watched as the big Ford barreled into the parking lot and lurched to a stop next to Pearly's van with a cloud of dust billowing behind it.

The Daves were both holding their noses with one hand when they stepped out of the car. They grabbed their duffel bags and hurried toward their teammates.

"What's the matter?" Pearly asked.

"Tark hasn't found the time to clean Boris's vomit out of the backseat yet," Dave the Fag said with his fingers still holding his nose shut.

Dave the Jew shook his head in disgust and added, "Smells like we hit a skunk."

Tark was the last to join them. Partially dressed in his baseball uniform, he walked toward them wearing his jersey, checkered boxer shorts, and sandals. He carried his duffel in one hand and a gas station hot dog in the other.

"Hey, you hosers! Ready to go up there and kick some ass tonight?" He circled to the back of Grant's car and threw his duffel into the open trunk. When he walked back around to the front of the car they all noticed that he wore something around his neck. Suspended by a shoelace from an old hockey skate, Tark wore an evergreen air freshener as if it were a magical emerald amulet.

"Glad you're drivin'," he said to Grant when he slid into the backseat. "My car kinda stinks. C'mon, let's go!"

The Windigo Dragonflies were dressed and waiting for their opponents when the Walleyes arrived. The players on both teams were familiar with each other by now. Most of them had played ball against each other since high school. Some of them were good friends, but a few harbored hard feelings. The rivalry between Windigo and Walker went back for years and when the two teams met, even the best of friendships were put away for nine innings.

The Walleyes straggled in, single file, walking from their cars toward the visitor's dugout. Some of the Dragonflies called out greetings to Pearly and Louie. Miller Peoples jogged over and spoke to Theodore for a moment, and Tark made a point to glare at Ray Rivers.

"How do you know the Peoples kid?" Tark asked Theodore when they reached the dugout.

"From high school. We've been playing sports against each other for-ever," Theodore said. "He's a good guy."

Tark looked away. As far as he was concerned, everybody on the other side of the infield was the enemy and they were not to be spoken to.

As always, the first few innings would be played in twilight, and the game would be finished under the lights. While the players got ready to play ball, a warm summer sun drifted toward the western horizon.

Just before game time, Tom Murphy and Jack Fitzgerald stood at home plate with Louie and the Dragonflies coach, going over the ground rules, while Theodore and Pearly finished their pregame warm-ups in the bull-pen. "I feel good, Pearly," Theodore said.

"Well, you're not gonna get any help from these umps, so you'd bet-ter be sharp," Pearly replied. "Just keep the ball low, and don't give the Peoples kid anything to hit. Make him hit your pitch, or just walk him. Understand?"

"I'm gonna drill Ray," Theodore added, this time defiantly. He was ready to argue about his unkind intentions if Pearly objected.

"Looking forward to it," Pearly said as he bent over to get a drink of water from the fountain near the Walleyes dugout.

"Hey, look at that," Theodore said while Pearly was still drinking.

Eight cars filled with regulars from the Chateau pulled into the parking lot. A moment later, young people started to get out of the cars, laugh-ing and joking with each other. Natasha was the first person Theodore noticed, then Boris. There were almost thirty Walleye fans walking into the ballpark together.

Clank and Pissed stood up, leaned on the chain-link fence by the on-deck circle, and watched their friends approaching. They'd never seen such a strange thing. They had fans, fans willing to travel.

Tark left the dugout and walked right into the crowd of fans. He was standing with his arm around Natasha's waist when Louie walked back to the dugout after his meeting with the umpires at home plate. He caught Tark's eye and motioned for him to return, then hollered for the leadoff hitter, Will Campbell, to pick up a bat and get ready to hit. Louie couldn't remember the last time that so many Walleye fans had made the effort to come along for a road game, and he'd never seen his boys so energized by a crowd.

A baseball game lasts for nine innings. There is always ebb and flow, and there will usually be ample opportunity for failure, and redemption. Like many other contests, baseball doesn't create character, it reveals character, and this matchup was about to reveal plenty.

Will hit the first pitch of the game into the right field corner for a double. Grant hit the second pitch sharply for a single that scored Will. Tark homered on the third and the score was 3–0 before the Walleye fans had settled in. They stomped their feet, shook the fence, and hollered as the Walleyes surged ahead of the Dragonflies.

The Daves both got base hits, as did Pearly, and the bases were loaded with no one out when Clank came to the plate and struck out. Pissed popped up for the second out, and it was Theodore Christopher's turn to hit, with the bases loaded.

As Theodore walked to the plate with his oversize uniform hanging from his shoulders and waist, the Dragonflies and their fans began to exhort their pitcher to put an end to the inning, but one voice rose above the others. Ray Rivers, ol' Hard-nosed, playing third base for the Dragonflies now, began a verbal assault on Theodore. "C'mon now," Ray barked to his pitcher. "Just throw strikes. This guy can't hit . . ." He went on and on in one long grating rant about all of Theodore's failures in high school. His voice stung Theodore, as Ray explained to everyone in the ballpark that Theodore had never done it, could never do it. The attack was personal and it began to anger the other Walleye players.

"Looks like he might explode," Will said to Grant, while they watched Theodore at bat. Will would be the next hitter if Theodore got on base, and the two of them were standing together in the on-deck circle.

"Yeah, Ray is definitely in Theodore's head," Grant sighed.

Theodore struck out on a clumsy swinging third strike, and Ray made a point to laugh out loud and crow about the awkward way Theodore had failed as he ran to his own dugout when the inning ended. Will placed his bat in the bat rack and started to walk out to take his position at second base for the bottom of the first inning, but he stopped short and turned to Grant. "You better go talk to him, settle him down," Will said.

Theodore was standing on the pitcher's mound when Grant approached him a minute later, and when Grant got a close look at the kid's face he was glad he'd made the trip. Theodore's eyes were swollen with rage and he seemed about to cry.

"You OK?" Grant asked.

"Gonna drill that fucker," Theodore replied through clenched teeth.

"Well good, you know we'd all like to see that." Grant tried to draw a smile from Theodore, but there was no smile forthcoming.

"Look, Theodore, here's what's about to happen," Grant started. "You're all pissed off and you're gonna start throwing way too hard. You're gonna be wild, and walk some guys, and Ray is gonna be standing on the front step of that dugout ridin' your ass."

Theodore stopped his warm-up pitches and looked at Grant.

"If you wanna shut him up you must throw strikes," Grant continued. "So be sure to come to your balance point, then fire. You have to trust in your mechanics here, you have to believe that the velocity will be there if you do the things we've practiced. If you have to think about anything, think about bringing your face right into Pearly's mitt. The ball will follow." Grant stopped, then asked, "Are you listening?"

Theodore nodded.

"One more thing," Grant said.

"Huh?" Theodore asked.

"Don't miss Ray."

Finally Theodore smiled.

Grant left Theodore standing with both feet on the pitching rubber, about to go into his windup, when Tark arched his back and unleashed his pregame holler.

Pearly was crouched behind home plate holding his catcher's mitt for a target, and when Tark yelled he heard Tom Murphy groan slightly. Murphy's face mask was nearly touching the back of Pearly's head, so Pearly could hear anything Murphy wanted to share with him. The groan was not a good sign.

Theodore's pitching motion was flawless. His balance and footwork were perfect and he delivered a fastball that sizzled all the way home then popped into Pearly's glove.

"Ball one," Murphy said softly, into Pearly's ear.

Pearly hesitated briefly before he threw the ball back to Theodore, then he caught another blazing fastball when Theodore returned it over the heart of the plate.

"Ball two."

Pearly grimaced.

Next came ball three, and the Walleye faithful began to chirp in protest. Everyone in the ballpark had just watched three blistering fastballs thrown over the center of the strike zone. Theodore wound up and delivered another.

"Ball four. Take your base," Murphy said.

Pearly never turned to look at the umpire, but Murphy knew he was waiting for an explanation.

"Your dago shortstop has a big mouth," Murphy said to Pearly's back while he checked the clicker in his left hand.

OK, Pearly had the picture now. He could read between the lines. Murphy didn't like Tark, and that was no big deal. But it was a lame excuse. The fix was on, that much was clear. Murphy had never been opposed to helping the home team, and this *was* town ball, when umpires often served up some home cookin' to visiting teams. This, however, was something more, and each of the Walleyes had their own idea about the dark side of a man's character that would allow him to do this.

Theodore was coming unhinged. He was certain this was all Ray Rivers's doing.

Louie shook his head in disgust. He knew that Murphy had always been jealous of his reputation as a coach, and he knew Murphy liked to do whatever he could to take him down a bit.

Will saw Tom Murphy simply as a self-important, washed-up, small-town jock who was too stupid to differentiate between winning by cheating and winning straight-up.

Pearly had been around Tom Murphy for years. He'd seen Murphy do this before, many times, and then retell the story with himself as the hero and everyone else as frustrated whiners.

Grant knew that Murphy liked to flirt with Kate, and he understood the perverse logic that a dented can like Tom Murphy brought to a situation like this. Murphy felt he could somehow lift himself above Grant by witnessing Grant's destruction. He'd throw this game in favor of Windigo, and the next time Louie hired him to work a game in Walker, he'd stand at the concession-stand window and tell Kate how, despite his efforts to call the game fairly, Grant's team just lacked the talent to compete. Murphy was devoid of personal integrity. He didn't mind standing behind the plate and giving the appearance of authority and impartiality while his actions were totally self-serving and mean-spirited. Grant looked on from his position at first base and understood what was about to happen. He remembered Abraham Lincoln's quote once again: "Just about everyone can handle adversity. If you want to test a man's character, give him some power." Grant despised Tom Murphy.

Theodore walked the next batter on four pitches, then gave up a moon-shot home run to Miller Peoples. He seemed about ready to break down when his catcher paid him a visit on the mound. "Hang in there, kid. You're pitching just fine. Murphy is just sending us a little message," Pearly said. "Come on now, keep workin'."

A pop-up and two ground balls to Will finally brought the first inning to an end, 3–3. Game on.

When the Walleyes assembled themselves in the dugout between innings, Pearly went directly to Tark. "Don't expect any favors from the man in blue," he warned Sabetti. "And keep your mouth shut if things don't go your way. I think Murph would like a reason to toss you out of this game. Do you understand me?" he asked firmly.

Ten minutes later, Tark walked slowly back to the Walleye dugout after a disastrous at-bat. His lower jaw was set tightly and his eyes burned with rage. Tom Murphy had just called him out on strikes, three called strikes, to end the half inning. The first two pitches were high, nearly over his head, and the third one, a slow curveball, had bounced a foot in front of the plate. Tark understood the message from Murphy too. He bit his lip, walked silently back to his dugout, and then took his defensive position at shortstop. Keeping his mouth shut wasn't easy for Tark.

Tensions were running high among the Walleyes when Ray Rivers took his turn in the batter's box to start the Dragonflies' second inning. A moment later he was writhing on the ground near home plate. Theodore had unleashed a whistling fastball that struck Ray squarely on his left elbow.

Normally the sight of Ray Rivers thrashing around in the dirt would be a source of laughter for the Walleyes. Not tonight. The Walleye players all stood with their hands on their hips and waited unsympathetically for Ray to stand up and wobble on down to first base. They were glad to see him rolling around on the ground. They hoped it hurt. They were angry, and growing angrier by the minute.

Murphy and Pearly were standing shoulder to shoulder, watching as Ray tried to get up off the ground, when Pearly said, "Looks like the kid is still a little wild, you know he walked all those other guys." He looked directly at Tom Murphy's eyes. Both of them knew that Theodore had plunked Ray deliberately. Murphy chose to let that one go, then he continued to call the game with one strike zone for the Walleyes and another one for the Dragonflies. Murphy seemed to be telling the boys from Windigo that if they chose not to swing, the pitch wasn't a strike.

Two more innings passed while a sense of anger and frustration swelled among the Walleye players.

The scoreboard read 6–3 in favor of Windigo when Theodore took the mound in the bottom of the fifth inning, and the bad dream started all over again. He sent seven pitches through the heart of the strike zone. Tom Murphy said he'd issued a base on balls to the first batter and taken the count to three balls and no strikes on the second batter.

The crowd from the Chateau was groaning with every pitch now, and some unkind insults began to litter the air.

Pearly took a deep breath and held one finger down for Theodore to see, the signal for a fastball. When Theodore delivered the pitch Pearly never moved his mitt. Like the others, it was right down the middle.

"Ball four. Take your base," Murphy said to the batter.

A collective groan rose from the Walker fans.

"Jesus! How can you sleep with all these lights on?" shouted an angry female voice from the midst of the Chateau crowd. The voice was followed by peals of laughter from both Walker and Windigo fans.

Tom Murphy found no humor in the moment, however. He was fumbling with the umpire's ball and strike clicker, and fuming. The idea that so many young women were making fun of him was almost too much to bear. Then, when he saw Tark smile and point to Natasha, Murphy began to grumble about that smart-assed little dago shortstop and his bitch girlfriend.

"Time out!" Pearly squawked. He walked to the pitcher's mound. It was time for drastic action. "All right, Theodore, I've seen enough o' this shit," he growled. "Here's what we're gonna do. Gimme the next pitch right where I ask for it. Make it a fastball. Then on the second pitch I want you to take aim for Murphy's facemask. I want you to reach back and put a little extra cheese on it. Really bring it! We're gonna turn his lights out. You understand?"

Theodore nodded.

"But just to make it look good, I want you to shake me off a couple times; make it look like we got our signals crossed and you threw a heater when I called for a curve." Pearly dropped the ball into Theodore's glove and said, "OK, now's the time for you to step up. Let's see what you can do."

Theodore's first pitch, as expected, screeched over the plate and slammed into Pearly's glove for ball one. Pearly made no complaint; he simply tossed the ball back to Theodore and waited for the next pitch.

"C'mon kid," Pearly whispered to himself, as he settled in position behind home plate and set himself to receive Theodore's second pitch. "Put a little mustard on it, and make it a good one."

The pitch was going to be accurate. Pearly could see that much as soon as the rocket left Theodore's hand. As the ball rifled toward a spot just above his own head, Pearly lowered his catcher's mitt ever so slightly and let the ball go by.

The ball struck Murphy's mask flush in the center. Murphy's head snapped backward, his mask bounced up over his head, and his knees locked. He fell backward slowly, like a boulevard elm after a chainsaw bite. He was out.

Players and coaches jumped from their dugouts and stood over the stricken umpire for a few minutes while his lights came back on.

"Sorry, Murph," Pearly said when Murphy finally sat up in the dirt behind home plate. "Guess my pitcher and I got crossed up. I was expecting a curve." That, of course, was a lie. Jack Fitzgerald stood next to Pearly and said nothing. Pearly couldn't say for sure if Fitzgerald, the other umpire, realized that Murphy had been beaned on purpose, but he was fairly certain Fitzy had received the message.

Tom Murphy's lights may have come back on, but nobody was home yet. His eyes were vacant and his legs wobbly when he stood up.

Windigo fans applauded. The bunch from the Chateau chuckled.

"You're gonna have to finish the game by yourself, Fitzy," Louie said to Jack Fitzgerald, who'd actually been doing a good job umpiring the bases.

"I can do that," Fitzgerald said. "I've done it before." Then he stripped the chest protector, shin guards, and face mask off his injured partner and ordered play to be resumed. When umpire and catcher were standing alone together at home plate, Pearly chose his moment to say what was on his mind.

"Had enough home cookin' for one night, Fitzy," Pearly said.

Jack Fitzgerald ignored him.

"Not shittin' you, Fitzy," Pearly warned. "I'm gonna take it *real* personal if . . ."

"Play ball," Fitzgerald said, and he signaled for the Windigo batter to step into the batter's box and for Theodore to get ready.

Theodore proceeded to strike out the side in twelve minutes to end the fifth inning. As the Walleyes were leaving the field, Pearly turned his back on the umpire and said, "Nice job, Fitzy," as he walked away.

Jack Fitzgerald ignored Pearly once again, but an understanding had been reached. The umpire couldn't acknowledge Pearly in any way; it would be tantamount to an admission of cheating on his part, or Murphy's. He just did his job fairly, turned his back, and let the ugly emotions of a few minutes earlier give way to the rhythm and flow of town ball. At least for a few minutes.

Dave the Fag led off the sixth inning with a base hit, and Dave the Jew followed with another. Pearly drew a base on balls and Clank followed that with a hit. When Pissed drove a double into the left field corner the score was tied at six with runners on second and third with nobody out, and Theodore Christopher was up next.

Windigo's catcher called for time out, and he slowly walked to the pitcher's mound for a conference with the pitcher who'd given up four hits and a walk.

Theodore stood alone by the chain-link fence and looked around the ballpark while the Dragonfly infielders gathered at the pitcher's mound.

The Walker on-deck circle was only a few feet from the fence, and Theodore was so close he could hear several conversations on the other side. There were girls over there talking and laughing about a lot of things that had nothing to do with baseball. But there were also several young men who'd apparently played for Ray when they were in high school and didn't like him either. Walker hitters had been standing near the fence for several innings and sharing their growing anger and frustration with their friends who were pressed against the other side of the chain links.

While he waited for his turn at bat, Theodore let his eyes wander from the Dragonflies standing on the pitcher's mound over to the crowd beside him. Boris was there, holding hands with some guy. That was fine; he didn't think he wanted to know her any better, anyway. Natasha was there. She and Tark had become an item. Theodore thought she was smart, and he liked to hang around with Tark and Natasha whenever he could.

"Hey, Theodore," said some college kid when he noticed Theodore looking his way. "Help yourself out here, buddy, rip a shot, drive in a couple more runs!" He didn't know the college kid, who was several years older, but Theodore had seen him around town for years. It was pretty cool that the older guys from the Chateau knew his name.

"All right, let's go, batter!" Jack Fitzgerald barked at Theodore when the conference on the mound was over. He'd been swinging a heavy bat while he warmed up for his turn at the plate, but the one he intended to bat with was leaning against the chain-link fence behind him. He dropped the heavy bat and reached for the one he wanted.

"Hi, Theodore," came a heavenly voice from the other side of the fence.

It was the waitress who'd demanded to see some ID at the Chateau! Her delicate fingers were clinging to the chain-link fence and the bat he intended to use was almost touching her. She was smiling, and she was so close he could smell her perfume when he grabbed his bat!

"Hi . . ." He paused, and his eyes went blank.

"Krista," she said. "My name is Krista Hesby. I'm the one who . . ."

"I remember." He smiled sheepishly and nodded.

"Are you coming to the Chateau after the game?" she asked.

"Well, I . . ." Theodore stammered.

"C'mon, kid! We're waiting!" Jack Fitzgerald barked from home plate.

Damn right I'm coming to the Chateau, Theodore thought, as he turned and walked to the plate. She looked so fine in her T-shirt and shorts. He'd just received a special invitation to a party he wasn't about to miss. Krista Hesby's legs were so tan, and her smile was so pleasant, and there just wasn't enough room inside her T-shirt for those . . .

Ray Rivers chose that instant to throw gasoline on a fire. "Hey, Boy Wonder!" Ray crowed. "Here comes an easy out. He can't hit." The other infielders were chattering in the same way. Ballplayers chatter to reassure their pitcher and put a little doubt in the batter's mind. They'd been doing it for a hundred years. It was just infield chatter.

But as always, Ray's chatter was different. It was personal and malevolent. Ray wanted to hurt Theodore. His voice grated a bit more than the other infielders', and his words carried the sting of a personal insult.

Theodore forgot all about Krista Hesby, the waitress with the nice T-shirt and the pretty smile. He forgot everything except his hate for Ray Rivers.

"Theodore!" Tark's voice snapped in an effort to capture Theodore's undivided attention. Tark was coaching third base, at least for the moment. The Walleyes didn't have any coaches other than Louie, so they all took turns coaching third base and first base.

Tark could see the anger in young Theodore's eyes, and he wanted the kid to focus it on one thing only. "Theodore!" he snapped again, this time louder and in a harsh tone that was intended to challenge the young ballplayer to pay attention to what he was about to say. "Just look for one you can drive, a fastball right here." Tark held his right hand about belt-high, and Theodore nodded.

Ray was still jabbering when Theodore took his stance in the batter's box.

"We oughta put one in your ear for hittin' Ray twice," the catcher said from his crouch.

"Yeah, well, you do whatever you want," Theodore said defiantly, without taking his eyes off the pitcher. "But that prick is going down every time." He knew Jack Fitzgerald had heard him and he didn't care. He was angry, really angry. Ray Rivers was the only infielder still chattering when the pitcher went into his windup and released the ball.

Theodore heard the ball hissing when it was still about forty feet away. He'd recognized what the pitcher planned to do almost from the instant the ball left his hand. The idea was to try to blow a fastball by him, but this was exactly the pitch Tark had told him to look for: a belt-high fastball. Everything was perfect—the ball seemed to be frozen in time, sitting on a tee. Theodore turned his hips open and drove his hands through the strike zone.

The ball jumped off his bat. He'd just released a bolt of lightning. An immense feeling of power, mixed with sublime euphoria that only a well-struck baseball can provide, surged through his system.

Will and Grant were standing together in the on-deck circle when Theodore hit the ball, and they watched it rocket into a huge expanse of green far out in right center field. "Wow, the kid ripped a piss rope," Will said, then he spit a gob of tobacco juice.

Theodore was gliding as he swung around first base. He'd just hammered something open inside himself. His drive was clearly a double, but no more. He could see the ball rolling way out by the fence, and before he reached second base he knew he should hit the brakes and stop there. But he knew who was playing third base for the other team, and instead of slowing down he lowered his head and lengthened his long, loping stride. His uniform flapped behind him like a parachute.

Then he did it. He hollered, "Cut three! Cut three!" and shifted into overdrive.

Will and Grant stared openmouthed. Theodore was going to third base, by God, and he wanted the opposition to know it. The Walleyes sitting on the dugout bench all stood up and began cheering. They'd never heard a base runner announce his intentions by hollering to the defense. They understood exactly what was about to happen. There would be a reckoning at third base.

Long before he reached second base Theodore felt something unstoppable erupt from his chest. "I'm comin', Ray! And I'm gonna cut you! You rat bastard!" He bellowed to let Ray Rivers know that he intended to spike him when he reached third base.

In that moment all the Walleye players realized that Theodore Christopher was no longer running through space. He was galloping through their collective souls like a wild horse. In the heart of every one of those grown men there still lived a little boy who wanted to make a defiant dash through his enemies. Now Theodore was doing just that, and as he hollered an angry promise to Ray Rivers he was calling out for his teammates to join him. Somewhere out there by second base, the joyful spirits of nine other men joined Theodore in the wild race.

Windigo infielders hurried to position themselves. All of them were now yelling "Cut three!"

Walleye players were screaming for Theodore to hurry up. The contingent from the Chateau pressed up against the chain-link fence and shook it. Windigo fans were shouting. The handful of Windigo players sitting on the bench were standing up and yelling. Tark Sabetti, coaching at third base, was jumping and hollering for Theodore to hurry up.

Theodore's long stride had closed the distance faster than anyone would have guessed, and he was about to turn an easy out at third into a close play. The Windigo cutoff man took the throw from the center fielder, then spun and threw the ball to Ray Rivers, who was waiting nervously at third base. The ball popped into Ray's glove an instant before Theodore dropped to the ground and kicked up a cloud of dust with his slide.

The bottom of Theodore's shoe was bearing down on Ray Rivers. He intended to use his cleats and cut whatever part of Ray was nearest to third base when he arrived.

Ray waited for an instant, then he jumped out of the way.

"Safe! You missed the tag!" Jack Fitzgerald hollered as he spread his hands in the safe signal. He'd hustled all the way from home plate to third base to be in position for the play.

The Walleyes and their fans screamed their approval.

Theodore bounced to his feet and glared at Ray with his hands up, ready for fisticuffs if Ray was interested.

Tark raised both hands above his head, leaped into the air, and hollered, "Teddy Fuckin' Ballgame!"

The Walleyes began hollering "Hard-nosed!" to taunt Ray Rivers about his cowardice. A moment later Natasha and some of her girlfriends joined in the chant and Ray Rivers was vanquished. Forever.

Tark shook Theodore's hand and gushed, "Teddy Ballgame! Teddy Fuckin' Ballgame! Jesus, you even look like the Splendid Splinter! That was the greatest thing I ever saw!"

Order was restored in a few minutes. Will popped up. Grant grounded out. Tark hit a long fly ball to Miller Peoples in center field that ended the inning. But while Tark's fly ball sailed back toward earth, Will and Grant stood side by side in the dugout and watched for a moment. They watched as Tark raced toward first base, and then slowed up when he saw the ball settle into the outfielder's glove. They kept watch as Tark gave up and trotted in a lazy circle over toward Theodore, who'd been stranded at third base.

Tark and Theodore jogged together for a couple of steps and then Tark put an arm over Theodore's shoulder and said something to him. Theodore Christopher's face blossomed into a joyful, exuberant smile and he nodded his agreement to whatever it was that Tark had said. When they reached the first base line, Theodore actually skipped over the base path.

"Hey! Teddy Ballgame!" a woman called from the Chateau crowd, and Theodore turned his beaming face toward her and waved.

"Oh," Grant sighed to Will, "I wish Kate could have seen that."

Theodore mowed down all the remaining Windigo hitters except for Miller Peoples, who collected two more hits, and the Walleyes won 8–6.

The labor pains had been long and difficult, but Teddy Ballgame had been born at third base.

❦ CHAPTER 48 ❧

Dental appointments almost always began with small talk about the weather, then kids or grandchildren. Maybe a patient would mention fishing, and someone would share a story about a big fish, or a stringer full of big fish, that had been caught on Leech Lake or one of the many smaller lakes in the area. Patients would wave their hands and make Grant remove his fingers from their mouths so they could tell about the big one that did or didn't get away.

But this summer, more than any other in anyone's memory, there was a buzz around town that involved baseball. "Hey," someone would start out. "Did the Twins win last night? And how 'bout that Kirby Puckett? How'd he do?" Invariably a short discussion of the Twins would be followed by, "How 'bout the Walleyes? How'd they do last night?"

Grant Thorson wasn't just the town dentist anymore, he was the best pitcher in the league. Now when strangers approached him in the grocery store, they didn't always ask him about sore or broken teeth. More often than not they asked about his pitching arm.

Kate Thorson wasn't just the lady dentist with the brace on her leg anymore, either. She was the woman who was married to Grant Thorson the pitcher, and she loved that. People approached her in church or on the street and asked about Grant and the Walleyes now.

The Walleyes traveled to such exotic destinations as Blackduck and Motley. Grant threw a one-hitter in Nevis, then another in Staggerford. Teddy Ballgame pitched well in Nimrod and again in Menahga. Tark hit three home runs in a game in Staggerford. They lost two close games over in Wolf Lake, but those guys were always good. The Walleyes were turning into a salty nine, just as Tark said they would. They expected to play well now, and they were having fun.

Crowds were not exactly overflowing, but they'd swelled from a handful of wives and girlfriends to nearly a hundred local spectators for home games. The following of young people from the Chateau had grown significantly too. Some were baseball fans; many were there just for the party.

Natasha Badenov was never far from Tark anymore. They'd grown close after that snowy road trip back in May. Both of them were a little more worldly than the other college-aged people in the Chateau group, and their relationship had a special heat. He'd started referring to her as Melanie, not Natasha.

∾: ∾

The final Saturday in June seemed to be weighed down by the still, humid air of summer. Walleye Field was lush and green from regular spring rains, and the yellow sun burned its way through a steamy blue sky.

Kate hoped for a cooling evening breeze off the lake, but that never seemed to happen after such long, still days as this. She moved the grill a bit farther away from the already uncomfortably hot concession stand and went about her preparations for the evening's game with Staggerford.

Ingrid and Kimberly Kay Johnson were having a private tea party in the cool shade of several red pines over by the Ice Cracking River just before game time while Kate and June began serving cold drinks to thirsty fans.

Grant made his way through the milling crowd and approached the concession stand shortly before the game. He nodded hello and spoke to many of the people. Tubby Voss stood at the concession-stand window holding a paper plate with three brats, all covered in sauerkraut, and Bud Pearson stood beside him, nursing a cold bottle of Coke. Both of them were already sweating.

"Hi, Tubby. Hi, Bud," Grant said. "Gonna be a sticky one tonight."

"You got that right," Bud replied. "You pitchin' tonight?"

"Yup," Grant said.

"Should be an easy night for you, Grant," Bud offered. "We did the Wolf Lake–Staggerford game on Wednesday. Those guys can't hit."

"It's never easy, Bud," Grant replied. "That's what makes it fun."

Then Grant leaned through the concession-stand window until his face was nearly touching Kate's. "Prettiest girl I ever saw," he said softly, just before he kissed her. He didn't seem to care who heard it or saw it. He just wanted a kiss before the game.

"That was nice," June said as Grant walked away, as if she'd never seen anything like it before. Kate smiled and opened another pack of bratwurst.

Bud Pearson and Tubby Voss were still standing by the window when Kate noticed Speed Roesner descending the rickety stairway that led from the press box.

Speed was wearing his customary plaid Bermuda shorts, along with his polyester golf shirt and Walleyes cap. Speed never left the press box before a game. Never. But he was walking slowly through the crowd now, and Kate grinned because she knew why. Speed had come to see himself as one of the celebrities at Walleye games. People had been telling him how much they enjoyed the ball games, and the music. The crowds were bigger, and they made some noise. People knew him, and he left the press box every so often to give them a chance to compliment him in person. He loved the attention, and he'd gone so far as to click the microphone on and introduce batters as they came up to bat. He was the Voice of the Walleyes.

Speed made his way to the concession-stand window and struck a confident pose while "Run Through the Jungle" played over the PA system. "Wooks wike wots of peepo dwove ova fwom Staggofood," he observed.

"Yeah, it's big crowd tonight," Kate replied. "Can I get you anything, Speed?"

"Some sunfwowa seeds and a Coke, pwease," he answered, and he slid his money across the windowsill.

"It's on the house," Kate said, and she slid his seeds and Coke and money back to him. "Really enjoying the music!" she added.

"Thanks, Kate. It's Cweedence," Speed informed her, in case she didn't already know, and he turned and actually seemed to strut back to the press box. June and Kate both giggled when he was out of earshot.

The Staggerford team wasn't very good, and that was irrelevant tonight. Tonight town ball was simply the vehicle that carried lives from one station to the next. Maybe that's all it ever was.

The first Staggerford batter walked toward home plate to take his turn at bat and the PA system clicked to life. Speed said the batter's name and the PA system clicked off. Three names, all mispronounced, and three outs.

Grant retired those first three Staggerford hitters easily. He'd come all the way back and maybe he was better than ever. One thing was for sure: he loved every bit of this. His arm felt strong. His teammates were a joy to play with. The smell of fresh-cut grass was everywhere, and a huge silver moon rose above the lofty pines and balsams on one side of the field at the same time a dying orange sun withered behind the red pines on the other side of the field. The deep greens and blues of a summer evening were highlighted by the sparkling surface of the Ice Cracking River and the first few stars that appeared in the gray sky.

As always, Mickey Mantle was here too, along with all the other faces from those old baseball cards. He saw them running in black-and-white film footage. And he saw them walking back to the dugout, filled with frustration after he'd struck them out. The dreams were still alive; they drifted along and wove themselves through the reality of town ball.

In the bottom half of the first inning, Speed Roesner raised the bar another notch. As Tark walked to the plate, with Grant standing on second base, the PA system clicked but there was no announcement from Speed. Several seconds went by and suddenly the first six notes of George Thorogood's "Bad to the Bone" blared through the speakers. Speed had been listening to the cassette tapes that Tark had left in the press box, and he'd customized this player introduction.

The crowd began to cheer, and Natasha raised both hands in the air. Even Paladin "Tark" Sabetti laughed. Then he hit the second pitch into the Ice Cracking River for a home run, and he pointed at Speed when he rounded third base.

There would be no player feuds or home cookin' from one-sided umpires tonight, just town ball and all that went with it.

Grant and Will were standing together on the top step of the dugout in the bottom of the second inning when Teddy Ballgame walked past them to the on-deck circle. He stood there for a moment and then reached his hand toward the chain-link fence. Several delicate fingers reached through from the other side of the fence and Theodore brushed his own fingers against them.

Will leaned out for a closer look and saw Krista Hesby standing there smiling at Theodore. "Hey, Teddy Ballgame's in love," he said to Grant.

Grant leaned out for a closer look too, and replied, "She's a nice girl. I know the family."

Dave the Fag noticed Grant and Will staring at something, so he craned his neck around for a look. He wandered over and studied Krista Hesby from a distance, then spit tobacco juice on the ground and said, "Nice tits." Before he sat down again he walked over to Dave the Jew and borrowed some more tobacco.

After walking the leadoff hitter in the third inning, Grant retired the next three batters on easy ground balls. When it was his turn to bat in the bottom of the inning, he hit a ball off the fence and wound up with a triple. He couldn't remember a night when things had been more perfect. He sat down on the bench next to Will a few minutes later and took a deep breath and looked out across the infield. A giant yellow sun hid behind the red pines and took its last few furtive peeks at them before it sank below the western horizon. It seemed to Grant that this was a good time to say something profound to Will, or at least make an observation about the good lives they were living. He looked over and made eye contact with Will, but there were just no words for the moment. He turned his palms up, looked about, shook his head and smiled.

"Yeah, I know what you mean," Will said.

Tark, however, had something to say. He studied Tubby Voss for several minutes, then, when the dugout became silent, he nudged Dave the Fag and in a cerebral, almost reverent tone, he asked, "Can you imagine what it would be like to be the next one to use the shitter after Tubby?" The way in which he'd spoken gave the question weight, as if only a team of scientists and theologians could truly understand the implications of such a thing.

"Yeah," Dave the Fag nodded in wonder. "And I'll bet the toilet seat is just one giant wet spot, too." He reached over and borrowed some Beech-Nut from Tark while everyone pondered the question.

Dave the Jew stood up, used his index finger to harvest his nose, and showed the trophy to Tark.

"Nice one," Tark said after a quick inspection.

Dave the Jew placed a giant snag on the booger board and sat down without saying a word.

"Hey, Tark?" Theodore asked. He was done thinking about Tubby Voss's explosive gastrointestinal potential and Dave the Jew's booger. "Do you ever guess when you're hittin'? I mean, do you guess what the pitcher's gonna throw you? Curve, fastball, changeup?"

"No, I try not to do that," Tark replied. He stood up and took a bat in his hands to illustrate his answer. "You always want to look for the fastball, 'cuz if you get it, then you'll be ready. If you're lookin' for the fastball and you get a curve, well, you just keep your hands back and wait a bit. It's possible to slow your swing down. But, if you're lookin' for the curve and you get the fastball, you're screwed; you just can't speed up your swing and catch up to it." He nodded at Teddy Ballgame. "Always look for the fastball."

"But if you're guessin' curve, and you get a curve?" Teddy Ballgame asked.

"Then you win." Tark shrugged. "But it's risky business."

"OK . . ." Teddy Ballgame started off on another long question about hitting. He asked questions all the time now. He hollered support to his teammates and heaped insults on his opponents. He barked at umpires. He came early for extra practice. He'd made a complete transformation from the meek Theodore Christopher to the brash, outspoken Teddy Ballgame, at least when he crossed the white lines.

Away from the ballpark he was still Theodore Christopher, the lanky, mild-mannered, nice-looking young man with the pretty girlfriend. But when he got to the ballpark he morphed into Teddy Ballgame, the abrasive competitor with an attitude.

When Teddy Ballgame finished his question about hitting, his mentor in baseball and in life grinned for a second, then started his answer with, "That's a good question, Teddy, and now I'm gonna tell you right where the bear shits in the buckwheat." With that poetic preface, Tark explained, in detail, how to hit the ball to the opposite field. When he was finished with a thorough explanation, he added a question. "You takin' that pretty little girl over to the Chateau after the game, Teddy?"

"Is a pig's ass pork?" Teddy Ballgame answered without looking up.

Will looked over and caught Grant's eye and both of them began to chuckle. Senseless and gross dugout conversations were a cherished tradition throughout baseball, and the Walker Walleyes were Hall of Fame senseless and gross.

When they took the field for the top of the fourth inning, the Walleye players began to hear a low hum emanating from way out past the center-field fence, in the vicinity of the Ice Cracking River. The night sky was turning black, and all that remained of the day was a dim orange glow behind the pines. The sound grew louder and more ominous with each passing minute.

"What's that noise?" Tark asked Clank while they waited for Stagger-ford to send a batter to the plate. "Sounds like a squadron of bombers comin' this way."

"You're gonna wish that's what it was," Clank answered.

"Whadaya mean?" Tark asked.

"It's mosquitoes. They're just coming out of the swamp over there for an evening raid."

"Can't be," Tark replied. "Mosquitoes don't sound like that."

"Just wait," Clank grinned.

By the time the inning ended, all three Walleye outfielders were nearly hysterical. They sprinted to the dugout together, swatting and slapping as they ran, each of them desperate to get their hands on some insect repellant.

"Shit!" Dave the Fag hissed. "Every time I took a step out there I kicked up a hundred mosquitoes."

"Little peckers are hungry!" Dave the Jew said while he slapped his neck and face several times.

"Bastard! Fuck! Cocksucker!" Pissed said as he rifled through his duffel bag in search of a can of mosquito repellent. He was so upset that he was trembling and he spoke in complete sentences made of swearwords only, but that wasn't so unusual for Milburne "Pissed" Carrigan.

"Try some tobacco!" Tark suggested. He was swatting mosquitoes on his arms and legs now, sometimes two and three at a time. "I think it makes you give off a chemical that drives skeeters off. Really!" He opened a new package of Beech-Nut and began passing it out to his teammates.

Stomping, swatting, and cursing the cloud of mosquitoes while they frantically rifled through their duffel bags in search of bug spray, none of them noticed June Campbell appear from around the corner of the dugout and stand on the top step holding two huge spray cans of mosquito repellent. She'd come on a mission of mercy, but the players were all so busy that no one noticed her while she waved the spray cans at them.

"Hey, Louie!" Tark called out over all the cursing and swatting in the dugout. "You know why baseball players don't get circumcised?" He was bent over and scratching his ankle.

Still, no one noticed June. She thought maybe she should leave quickly and come back later, but she froze.

"No, Tark. How come?" Louie replied as he slapped his own left arm and squashed three bloody mosquitoes.

"So they'll have someplace to put their tobacco when they go to the dentist!" Tark blurted while he was still bent over and swatting mosquitoes.

Every one of the Walleyes burst into laughter at the word picture Tark had painted in the midst of the crisis. His timing had been perfect. Almost.

June stood on the top step of the dugout with the aerosol spray cans of mosquito repellent in her hands and a flabbergasted look on her face. She'd come to deliver their salvation, and she'd overheard Tark's joke.

All she could do now was close her eyes, shake her head, and laugh along with them.

She tossed one can to Pearly, then she carried the other into the dugout and spent a few minutes applying the spray to thankful ballplayers' ankles, backs, and necks. "OK, you guys are on your own," June said. As she left the dugout and rushed back to the concession stand, she could hear the Walleyes laughing even harder.

When June returned to the concession stand, Kate was hurriedly securing a screen over the window and Ingrid was sitting on the floor, crying. The onslaught of mosquitoes had come at dusk, like a biblical plague. The bugs were everywhere. Ingrid was covered in welts, and most of the fans had given up and run for home.

"How were the boys doing?" Kate asked while she closed all the doors, sealed the window, and began to swat any surviving mosquitoes in the concession stand. Then she picked up her exhausted child and held her on her lap.

"They were a little frantic when I got there," June replied. She shared Tark's one-liner about tobacco and the dentist. "I felt like a phys ed teacher who'd stumbled into the locker room and discovered . . . well, something I wasn't supposed to discover."

"Yeah. Grant sure loves this," Kate said. "I do too." The concession stand was free of mosquitoes now, and Kate looked out at what was left of the baseball crowd. "Looks like everyone left for the Chateau." Ingrid was drifting off to sleep and Kate began to sway back and forth while she sang, ever so softly, the fight song that she'd converted into a lullaby. "We're gonna win, Twins, we're gonna score . . ." until Ingrid was asleep in her arms.

"Well, the boys are having fun. They won't mind finishing the game with no fans in the stands." June stared out at the players and the ball game that was continuing under the lights. "Will loves this, too. He talks about it all week." A moment later she went on as if she was speaking to herself. "He loves Grant, too. He's so happy about the way Grant has recovered, and he talks about how much Grant loves you." June's voice had a funny lilt at the end, and Kate looked over at her.

June glanced at the sleeping child in Kate's lap to be sure that Ingrid wasn't listening to them. When she saw that Ingrid was fast asleep, she turned a pair of desperate eyes to Kate. "I have to tell you something," she whispered as her lip began to quiver.

Kate shifted in her chair and waited for June to tell her whatever it was she had to say. The agony on June's face intensified for a moment and Kate knew it wasn't a good thing that she was about to learn.

"I had an affair," June whispered. Her lip trembled even more, and she wiped a tear from each eye.

Kate reached over and held June's hand and waited for her to go on. Her lip still trembled and she blinked back tears for nearly a minute. She looked at Kate several times, as though she was about to tell the story. Then suddenly she was unwilling or unable to speak. She'd worked up the nerve to jump off the mountain, but now she wasn't so sure if she wanted to tumble all the way to the bottom.

Kate had never been down this road before. Here was a close friend, perhaps her closest friend, confiding in her about an infidelity. She'd never imagined that she'd be in this situation. Now what? She held June's hand and waited. The ball game had become distant and irrelevant now, someone else's playtime. From the corner of her eye she could still see the game, but now it was nothing more than men running and yelling across a green carpet.

"It was after you and Grant had moved up here," June finally said. She drew in a huge breath and then let it out. "Will was always busy, never home. I felt like a single mother. Molly was a toddler." June wiped her tears and sighed once more. "I felt I'd become invisible. We hardly ever saw each other, or spoke to each other, or had any time—fun time, together. The only time he ever seemed happy was when he was talking about his friends from school. Some of his friends were women, and that made me feel so bad." June finally let it all go and sobbed for a minute.

"It's OK," Kate said several times while June cried.

When the tears stopped coming, June's face lost all expression and she said, "Then I guess I felt nothing for him. We'd grown apart, just like his father had warned us. He was doing his thing, and I was doing mine." June shrugged. "So about that time there was a nice, handsome young guy, younger than me, who got his first teaching job and was teaching just down the hall from me. When we met in the hall he'd smile and chat. He'd tell me how nice I looked, how pretty I was. He'd ask me questions and then listen to the answers. He made me feel good about myself."

June stopped and shook her head as if even she couldn't believe the next part of the story. "Then one night after some meeting at school, we . . . you know."

Kate nodded. June lowered her eyes before she continued. "The sex was really exciting, wild and forbidden. I knew it was wrong, but I wanted it, and all the attention that came with it."

"Did you love the guy?" Kate asked.

"No, but I tried to convince myself that I did. Down deep, though, I knew it was all wrong. I began to feel really bad about the whole thing and I broke it off."

"So, what happened? Did Will ever find out? You two seem so happy now," Kate said.

"Well, about the time I broke it off with Brad, that was his name, I think Will started to notice just how bad things were between us. We had some awful fights, too. He really went to work to fix things, we got some counseling, and, well, here we are," June said. "But I never told him. I think he suspected something, but he never asked and I never told."

"Why did you tell me about it now?" Kate asked.

"I had to tell somebody. You're my best friend, and . . . I wanted you to hear it first," June said.

"First?" Kate questioned her.

"It's been gnawing at me for a couple years. I have to tell Will or I'll never get it behind me," June said.

Now it was Kate's turn to sigh and collect her thoughts for a moment. She was hesitant to say all that was on her mind. June could see that much. Kate stood up and carried Ingrid over to a corner and laid her on some cushions. Then she rearranged a few things on the countertop near where they'd been sitting. "How do you feel about it all now, looking back?" Kate finally asked her.

"Well, it was something that I did, and I can't take it back . . ."

"Exactly," Kate interrupted. "And do you still have any feelings for the guy?"

"No, not at all," June replied, "But I have to tell Will because . . ."

"Wait a minute, June," Kate interrupted again. She squeezed June's hand to emphasize what she was about to say. "We love our friends right where they are. We don't judge them or try to change them. I guess that's how they got to be our friends in the first place. So rest assured that I don't feel any different about you because you told me all this. You're my friend and I love you. That's not gonna change, ever. Maybe someday I'll need to come and tell you a similar story."

"That'll never happen. You and Grant have something . . ."

"Well, you never know about things like that. I'm no different than you," Kate interrupted yet again. "People do this stuff. It happens. It could happen to anyone." Kate reached over and took both of June's hands in hers. "I know you didn't ask me for advice, but I'm gonna give you some."

Kate sat and looked into June's eyes while she recalled the conversation she'd overheard between Big Ole and Grant on her first visit to the Thorson farm. She'd never forgotten the way Grant's father had spoken about the disparity between honesty and integrity. He'd said that Little Ole's wife was the only one who told the truth, and she was the only one who had no integrity.

"Whatever you do, do *not* tell Will about this," Kate said.

"But . . ."

"Look, June, *you* did it! *You* did the crime, now *you* have to do the time. *You* bear the pain. Don't make him do it," Kate said.

June stared as if her best friend had slapped her face.

"I love you, June! I'm with you here," Kate tried to reassure her. "But think about this. You're about to abuse the concept of honesty in order to give yourself an excuse to dump your pain and guilt on Will's shoulders. You'll just break his heart in order to assuage your own pain. You're the one who needs to feel bad about this, not him. Just keep your mouth shut. This is a time when integrity demands that you live a lie."

They looked at each other for a long moment.

"Don't tell him, June. It's the wrong thing to do. If you need to talk to someone from time to time, call me. I'll be there for you. I'll love you just the same, you know that. Grant will never know about this either, just you and me."

June had plenty to think about all of a sudden. She hadn't expected to hear all this from her friend, and she sat for several long minutes while she considered everything.

"I didn't say it would be easy, June, and it'll never go away, so you'll always have it there in the back of your mind. Just forgive yourself and move on," Kate said.

Not one customer bothered them for the last four innings of the game. They talked, and cried, and talked some more as the players ran and hollered under the lights. Eventually the conversation moved to other things, but it returned to the affair several more times. June didn't find the relief she'd been seeking, but she began to understand that there probably would never be complete relief from her guilt. She said she understood what Kate was trying to say, and they talked of forgiveness, and redemption, and secrets, and June began to agree that maybe she should just keep it all to herself.

A raucous overflow crowd milled about the Chateau after the game while Kate, Grant, Will, and June sat together in a corner booth.

Walleye players, still dressed in their gray-and-green uniforms, drank beer with their buddies, or danced and flirted with girls.

Louie Swearingen had gone straight home after the game so he could sit on his dock, and maybe catch a fish while he listened to the Twins on his radio. Everyone else, even Pearly DeMoore, was at the Chateau tonight.

"What a great night!" Grant said. "'Cept for the bugs."

"Yeah, that was the worst insect hatch I ever saw," Will replied. "Did you hear Pissed when he sucked one down his throat and started to cough?"

The four friends sat at the little booth and talked and ate pizza and drank beer for several hours. Will and Grant re-created all the situations of the game, and their wives pretended to be interested. The boys shared all the strangeness that they'd heard in the dugout. Tark and Natasha came and sat with them for a while. Other players and other friends stopped by for short visits and then moved along. A smitten Theodore Christopher brought Krista Hesby over and introduced her. When he and his girl crept out of the Chateau together well before the party was over, Grant exchanged a knowing smile with Kate.

Kate kept an arm over Grant's shoulder most of the night. She watched him laugh and tell stories as she had since the very beginning, and he still made her laugh.

She watched June, too, as she sat beside Will. There was a peace in her eyes that hadn't been there earlier. Kate looked back and forth between the faces at her table and wondered whether she'd overheard Big Ole and Grant talking on that cold morning for a reason. So many lives had bumped into hers and then skidded away. She wondered if June would keep her secret, and then she wondered what she'd do if she found herself in the same situation.

~: CHAPTER 49 :~

A warm and pleasant June drifted seamlessly into July, and the summer found a familiar routine that seemed endless. After long days at work, the ballplayers and their friends and families met at the ballpark several days a week. Road games, almost as much as the home games at Walleye field, were met with anticipation.

The time spent in their cars on the way to neighboring towns was always a rich source of bizarre anecdotes from each of the players' workdays or private lives. Pearly and the Carrigans told stories of plugged toilets. Grant and Will shared recollections of colorful characters, past and present, like the King of Me and Loretta Klitsche and Ben Pribyl. Since cutting grass and doing odd jobs at a resort didn't provide much in the way of amusing anecdotes, Tark and the Daves regaled their teammates with stories from their night lives. Hangovers and fast women were the topics that dominated their tall tales. Theodore Christopher just listened.

Along the way, the Walker Walleyes developed into a good team, and at times they were downright impressive. Although they lost a few games they shouldn't have, they also had two second-place finishes in weekend tournaments, one in Fargo and one in Duluth, both coming against solid competition.

The arrival of Tark Sabetti had marked a new beginning for the Walleyes. He and the Daves had saved the team merely by their appearance on that first night of practice, and then they'd driven off the hated Ray Rivers. Tark's combative and confrontational style, along with his rebel yell at the start of every game, had endeared him to his teammates. Some of his opponents embraced Tark's style too, and they became fast friends. Others disliked him immediately. He made friends and enemies in equal numbers, and his teammates could never accurately predict which of their opponents would love or hate him. There were many nights when Tark and the Daves lingered in the darkened ballpark parking lots long after road games had ended, drinking beer and talking with members of the opposing team. There were other nights, however, when he left a neighboring town's ballpark with the silver Ford spinning its wheels and churning an angry cloud of dust into the night, his middle finger up in the air, shouting a promise to kick somebody's ass.

Tark had supervised the emergence of Theodore Christopher into Teddy Ballgame, too, and what a transition it had been. Theodore, the timid boy who cowered when Ray Rivers chastised him, and then smirked when Tark confronted Ray, had morphed into Teddy Ballgame. He chewed tobacco with the older guys, and he joined in the dugout discussions of baseball, turds, and boogers with enthusiasm. He also had worlds of talent that Ray had chosen to overlook or suppress. With each passing week Teddy Ballgame grew more aggressive and confident. Although he threw the ball harder than anyone else in the league, including Grant, he was just learning to be a pitcher, to mix finesse and control with his power. Grant supervised Teddy Ballgame's development as a pitcher and he came to view Theodore Christopher as the little brother he never had.

Theodore loved all the comparisons to the baseball icon Ted Williams, and he did indeed bear a strong resemblance to the Splendid Splinter, or Teddy Ballgame, the Boston Red Sox Hall of Famer. He made a point to leave his uniform baggy as the style had been in the 1940s and not alter it to the tight-fitting style that current players preferred, and it became his signature. He studied Ted Williams, read what he could find, and kept an eye out for old film clips. Once, after a late-season home run, Theodore clapped his hands and galloped on his way to first base, just as Ted Williams had in a famous newsreel clip from the 1946 All-Star Game. His teammates loved the deliberate re-creation of a celebration by the original Teddy Ballgame.

Even Speed Roesner found something new inside himself that summer. He was a bit of a showman. "Who Do You Love?" had become the Walleyes anthem as the season progressed, and he played it during infield practice and just before the boys took the field for all home games. Speed made a point to listen to the tapes that Tark left with him so he could customize some other players' introduction as he'd done with Tark and "Bad to the Bone." He brought the house down on one sweltering Sunday afternoon when the Windigo Dragonflies made their final regular-season visit to Walker. Almost three hundred people attended that game, and they all heard the PA system click on when Ray Rivers made his way to the plate for his first at bat. In a monotone voice, Speed introduced him, "Way Wivas," then Sammy Davis Junior began to sing "Candy Man." For Ray's second at bat Speed used Helen Reddy's "I Am Woman" and the place went crazy. Ray took himself out of the game after that.

Perhaps the only indication that there might be a downside to all this came one afternoon near the end of July when Grant and Ingrid and Kimberly Kay Johnson were fishing together during a tea party on Leech Lake. Ingrid's feet were dangling from the boat seat as she shared an Oreo and a Coke with Kimberly Kay Johnson when Grant felt a tug on his fishing line. A moment later he lifted a two-pound walleye over the side of the boat and Ingrid squealed, "Way to go, Daddy! You got the cocksucker!"

When his pulse slowed and his breathing returned to normal, he had another chat about bad words with his daughter. Then he decided to keep her as far away from Milburne Rio Carrigan as he could for the next decade.

This summer of town ball had saved Grant Thorson, too, in a way not even the love of a good woman could have. Real life, a mortgage, a family, and a business to run had combined to distance him from the simple joys of his early life. Then the cancer had given him all the reason any man could need to leave the dreams of youth permanently behind.

Now he'd been able to fill himself up with all those dreams once again. Will Campbell, his best friend, picked him up for road trips about once a week, and while they drove to Nimrod or Blackduck or Wolf Lake they had a chance to catch up on each other's lives, maybe talk about dentistry a little bit, and have a few laughs. The laughter and the absurd conversations in the dugout always gave him reason to look forward to the next game, too. For the first time he was one of the older guys. That was OK, just a little different. And the young guys on the team? They weren't much different than the boys he'd grown up with, or the boys from college.

∾:∾

"OK, explain it to me again," Kate said. "I still don't get it." She pedaled her new bicycle around the Walleye parking lot in large figure eights and waited for Grant's explanation.

He followed behind her, cruising slowly on his own bicycle and wearing his Walleye uniform, and Ingrid followed behind him. They'd all brought their bicycles to the parking lot so they could ride together for a few minutes before the one o'clock start of that day's game. It was the first Saturday in August, seventy degrees and calm, not a cloud in the midday sky, and it would be the last day of baseball at Walleye Field this season, no matter what happened.

The Minnesota State Amateur Baseball Tournament would be held in St. Paul later that month, and no Walleye team had ever made it that far, so no one on this team had even given it a thought, until today.

"All right, one more time," Grant began. "Today we'll determine the winner of our sectional tournament. The winner goes on to play in the state tournament in St. Paul."

"I know that," Kate said. "But how come you don't know if you're playing one game or two today?"

"OK, here's the deal. It's a double-elimination tournament, which means you have to lose twice before you're out. We lost our first game, to Windigo, then played our way back and won the losers' bracket, while Windigo won the other bracket. Now the winner of the losers' bracket has to play the winner of the winners' bracket. If we win the first game that means we've both lost one game during the tournament, so we'd have to play a second game; winner take all. If we lose the first game the season is over and there's no need for a second game. Got it?"

"Yup," Kate answered. "Are you nervous?" she asked while she pedaled.

"A little bit," Grant said. "The Walleyes have never made it to the state tourney, so that's sort of a big deal." Three motorcycles with extremely loud exhaust pipes roared past, out on the highway, and when Grant turned to see them go by a great memory from his childhood came back to him. "Hey, Ingrid," he called out when the motorcycles were gone. "Would you like to make your bike sound like those motorcycles?"

What a bizarre question, Kate thought, especially at a time like this, and when she turned to look at Grant he returned a fiendish grin. Before Ingrid could answer his question he'd stopped his bike and was jogging toward his car. "I'll be back in five minutes," he shouted over his shoulder. He didn't seem very nervous about baseball as he ran to the car.

"C'mon, Ingrid," Kate said a minute later, when she steered her bicycle toward the concession stand. "Let's get ready for Daddy's ball game." She was rolling the barbecue grill out when Louie drove into the parking lot, followed by Pearly. The Carrigans drove in next, then Theodore. Louie and the players were in the dugout, talking about what lay ahead of them, when Grant returned to the parking lot.

Grant was obviously pretty happy with whatever he was about to do, and he jumped out of his car and ran to Ingrid's bicycle. "OK, honey," Grant said when Ingrid came over and stood next to him. "These are baseball cards. They have pictures of baseball players on them." He began to unwrap a pack.

"Is your picture in there?" Ingrid asked.

"No, honey. These are really good players, the ones you see on TV." He kept unwrapping.

"Mom says you're the best one." Ingrid spoke as if she was quoting scripture.

Grant smiled, but stayed focused on the job at hand. "OK, honey, here's what you do. You look right down here in the corner, and if the card has an N and a Y on it, then you put it over here." He started a separate pile of cards. "These are New York Yankees, and the Yankees all belong in the spokes of your bike 'cuz they're all sonsabitches." He flinched at his own cursing, then when he realized that Kate hadn't heard him, he showed Ingrid the other items he'd purchased while he was away on his errand. "These are clothespins, and this is how we use a clothespin to fasten a baseball card to your spokes."

A minute later, ten New York Yankees flapped against Ingrid's bicycle spokes as she pedaled around the concession stand. "Mommy, look at me!" Ingrid yelled as she rode past the window. The harder she pedaled, the louder the baseball cards slapped.

"That's really nice!" Kate called out the open window. She turned to face Grant, who'd let himself in the back door of the little shed. "I hope she had as much fun with that project as you did."

"It's one of those rites of passage," Grant beamed. "I'll put 'em on your bike later too." He stepped forward quickly and pulled her close before he stole a kiss. "Still the prettiest girl I ever saw," he mumbled as he turned away. "I gotta go warm up."

Kate watched from the window as her husband walked to the Walleye bullpen. Ingrid rode past him once just so he could see and hear how loud her bike was, and Grant made a point to plug his ears and grimace as if the loud noise was painful. Ingrid laughed and pedaled faster.

A moment later Pearly stepped around the corner of the dugout and met Grant by the narrow gate in the chain-link fence. "Jesus, Pearly. I feel so good . . . if I felt any better there'd have to be two of me!" Grant said.

Kate watched Grant stroll out to the first base line where Louie was preparing to chalk the base paths and the batter's box and then put the bases in place before he raked the pitcher's mound. She couldn't hear what they were talking about, but they were still smiling when Pearly walked over and took Grant to the bullpen for his pregame warm-ups.

In a few minutes her friends from Walker and Windigo would come up to the concession-stand window and order something to eat. They'd talk about the weather, and their kids, maybe the fishing, maybe even baseball. But they were her friends now, not small-town strangers who knew too much about her. These people said hello to her on the street, sat next to her in church, and spent their money at Grant's dental office. They were *all* her friends; the people sitting in the bleachers who'd come to watch their sons, and friends, and husbands and fathers, and boyfriends play ball. The Walleyes players, the Windigo players, and even the umpires were now good friends.

She watched Grant throwing a ball with Pearly. He looked so strong. Only a year earlier she'd been afraid for his life. That seemed so long ago now.

They'd been married for only a few years, but they'd been through so much together. They'd lost a child. He'd survived cancer. She'd left her home and all her friends behind so they could go off on this adventure together. So many people had meandered into and out of their lives. For a moment, she let some of the faces roll across her mind's eye. Ben Pribyl, Joe Paatalo, Darcy Wilhelm, Carol Knutsen, the King of Me, Miles Clark, Rod Muir, Dominic Sabetti, and all the others. They were all there for a second and then they were gone.

She watched Grant catch another ball over in the bullpen. He said something that made Pearly laugh, then he threw another warm-up pitch. She remembered their first date and the look on his face when he'd told her that he couldn't pay for her cantaloupe. Out of all the men in the world, how did she ever find him? He was a good man, just like his father. Just like she knew he'd be. How many extraordinary twists of fate had wound through their lives to bring them to this moment? And what else did life have in store for them?

"Hi, Kate!" June's voice startled her back to the concession stand. "What can I do to help?" June asked, as she let herself and her girls in the back door and began arranging things in the refrigerator. Kate kept her thoughts to herself and went about preparing for their customers.

~:~

Will Campbell sat alone in the Walleye dugout, lacing his shoes and allowing his senses to take in all that the ballpark had to offer. Like everyone else, he usually arrived at the park half dressed, straggling into the dugout to finish dressing in his game uniform and chat with his teammates. He was ready to go out and warm up now, but he chose to wait for a minute.

Louie was still chalking the base paths. He'd dragged a garden hose and a rake onto the infield grass and he was fussing with the infield as he always did.

Pearly and Grant were warming up in the bullpen beside the dugout and Will could hear the regular pop of Grant's pitches slamming into Pearly's mitt.

The Carrigans were taking some batting practice in the batting cage. It sounded like Clank was pitching to Pissed. After each crack of the bat echoed across the park, a short combination of Anglo-Saxon swearwords followed close behind.

Teddy Ballgame was sitting down, stretching his long legs in the outfield, and he seemed to be floating in a sea of green.

When he'd first arrived in the dugout, all Will could smell was a faint odor of tobacco mixed with the stale, musty air from the little shed where Louie kept the lawn mower and the infield rakes. Then, while he'd dressed, the soft breeze had carried the odor of lighter fluid and charcoal over from the concession stand. Now the air was filled with the smoke from bratwursts cooking, and it made his mouth water.

George Thorogood and the Destroyers were pounding out "Gear Jammer" over the PA system. Will slipped his glove onto his left hand and slammed his fist into it, then he held it to his nose as he'd seen Grant do a thousand times. It was great to be part of all this, he thought. He took one more moment to drink it all in before walking out to long toss with Teddy Ballgame.

Tark and the Daves staggered into the dugout as Will was about to leave. The three were wearing sunglasses and they seemed to be in too much pain to speak. Tark still wore his emerald amulet. Dave the Jew bent over and tried to spit on the dugout floor, but all he could gather was a small, cotton-like bolus of saliva.

"Tough night, boys?" Will asked.

Dave the Fag turned a surly face to Will, said nothing, and looked away.

"Well, get some water in you, stay hydrated. When your head hurts with a hangover it's from dehydration, you know," Will offered.

"You got any aspirin?" Dave the Jew groaned without looking at Will. "Sure," Will replied.

Will was hunched over his duffel, rifling through the T-shirts, socks, practice uniform, and assorted bandages he always carried, when George Thorogood stopped playing with a sudden click. A second later Frankie Yankovic started in with "Beer Barrel Polka."

Tark leapt to his feet and slammed a bat against the ceiling of the dugout. "Speed!" he hollered. "Nunna that shit today!" Then he winced, clutched his ears, and collapsed onto the dugout bench again. Will could see the pain etched on Tark's face, despite the sunglasses. The yelling had nearly caused his head to explode. Both the Daves had their index fingers in their ears too.

There was a click on the PA system and Frankie Yankovic was no more. Another click was followed by Creedence and "Bad Moon Rising." Neither Tark nor the Daves had any more to say about the pregame music selection.

"Here's some aspirin," Will said. He tipped the small bottle and gave each of them three aspirin tablets.

"Got any hand lotion, Will?" Tark asked after he'd washed the aspirin down with a long drink of water.

"No, but I'm pretty sure June has some in her purse," Will replied. "What do you need that for?" Will studied Tark's hands while he waited for an answer.

Tark stood up and unbuttoned his well-worn blue jeans, then dropped them to his ankles. Both his knees appeared to be burned. They were bright red and looked raw. He stood in his boxers and let Will inspect his knees.

"Jeez, Tark, what happened?"

"Melanie got some new carpet for her trailer," Tark replied. He let Will figure out the rest.

"'Zat hurt?" Will asked, not trying to hide his smile when he pointed at Tark's knees.

"Whaddya think?" Tark replied.

"I'll be right back," Will said quickly, and he turned to leave. "June will have something for that." It was time to get ready for the game and one-third of the starting lineup didn't look very good.

"Hey, June!" Will called while he was still twenty feet away from her. "Do you have any hand lotion?" He leaned on the concession stand windowsill as he spoke, and was startled to see Natasha Badenov inside, chatting amiably with Kate. She must have decided to help Kate and June on a busy day. That was nice, Will thought. But now he couldn't explain the reason why he needed the hand lotion.

"What do you need that for?" June said as she started looking through her purse. Will was thankful that she didn't push him for an answer.

"Hi, Kate. Hi, Melanie," Will said. Some of her friends called her Natasha, but not the Campbells or Thorsons. She was well aware of her nickname, however, and didn't mind it. Will couldn't help taking a close look at her knees. She was pretty, no doubt about it, and she sure didn't mind showing plenty of that well-tanned skin. Her knees looked fine. Will could only imagine where . . .

"Nope," June said. "All I've got is Noxzema. It's the stuff I put on the girls when they get sunburned."

"That'll do," Will said. He took the blue plastic bottle from her hand and turned to leave. He'd keep an ear open and hope that Tark might give some details.

"Hey, Will," June said. "Do you have any aspirin? Melanie has a headache and I'm all out."

"Here you go," Will said when he gave the small bottle to June. He managed not to smile until he turned away. It must have been a rough night for everyone.

When Will returned to the dugout, Tark and the Daves sat together like three blind mice. The Daves were fully dressed in their Walleye uniforms, hands resting on their thighs and staring straight ahead. Tark was dressed, but his uniform pants were at his ankles and he seemed desperate for some relief. Will gave the Noxzema to Tark and then stood back and watched him begin to apply it. As the cool white lotion dripped onto Tark's flaming skin he sighed "Mmmm," then he began to spread the soft cream over his knees.

When Tark stood up to button his pants, Will had to ask the question. "Was it worth the carpet burns?"

For the first time since he'd arrived, Tark smiled. He nodded slowly and said, "Oh yeah. Definitely."

Hangovers, sore knees, and the exact location of Natasha Badenov's carpet burns were all forgotten as the four men emerged from the shade of the dugout into the afternoon sun. This would be a glorious day for baseball.

Several car doors slammed in the parking lot, and the Windigo Dragonflies made their way into the ballpark. Like the Walleyes, they were all half-dressed and carrying duffel bags. They intended to finish dressing in their dugout too. Several of them waved to friends on the Walleyes. Two of them walked slowly to the concession stand, said hello to Kate, and purchased a bratwurst. Miller Peoples made a long walk out to say hello to Theodore, and Tark glowered at Ray Rivers. Business as usual.

"Did I hear that the Peoples kid hit .650 for the season?" Dave the Fag asked. "Is that possible?"

"He hit .657," Will answered. "You believe that?"

Tark glared across the diamond at Miller Peoples.

Louie was finally finishing the chalking of the batter's boxes at home plate, and thin clouds of smoke drifted away from the bratwurst cooking at the concession stand. Baseballs popped into leather gloves and wood bats cracked in the batting cage. The voices and intermittent laughter of the players carried across the field, as did the purring of the baseball cards on Ingrid's spokes. Game time was drawing near.

"You guys better get warmed up," Grant said as he walked past Tark and the Daves. He was obviously looking for something. "You look like shit, by the way," he added indifferently. "Tough night?"

"Tell ya later," Tark said.

Grant had already lost interest in Tark's pain, and he kept on walking when he noticed Louie finishing his chores at home plate. "Hey, Louie! Where'd you put the game balls? I'd like to use one to warm up."

Louie stood straight, arched his tired back, and pointed toward the concession stand. "I put a dozen new game balls over in the concession stand when I came in. I forgot 'em over there, I think. Sorry."

"No problem," Grant said. "I'll find 'em." He turned toward the concession stand. "Kate!" he called. "Are there some game balls in there?"

, and reappeared in the window with a new white baseball in each hand. "I'll bring 'em over," she called out.

Everyone in the ballpark was busy with something, yet everyone seemed to keep one eye on Kate as she walked from the concession stand toward home plate. Maybe it was the way she moved, maybe it was just that Grant stood and waited for her.

Tark and the Daves never took their eyes off her. She walked through the narrow opening in the chain-link fence next to the on-deck circle and then turned toward home plate. Her left leg swung awkwardly as it always did, and her shoulders bobbed a bit. But when she noticed Grant standing in the dirt by home plate, waiting for her, she did something that none of them would ever forget. She began to smile as though she was walking down the aisle on her wedding day. The college boys wouldn't, couldn't, look away now.

She was still thirty feet away from Grant when the the PA system clicked. Bruce Springsteen had been doing most of the work for the past few minutes, and now there was a silent moment between songs.

Suddenly the song "Legs" by ZZ Top began to pulse through the army surplus speakers hanging from the press box and light poles.

Oh my god, Tark thought. What a time for "Legs" to play. Kate was certain to be embarrassed by this song about a woman with beautiful legs. His bleary and bloodshot eyes flashed a panicky look at Will. Both of the Daves did the same.

Will noticed everyone's apprehension, but he grinned and nodded to reassure them that everything was going to be fine. "Don't worry," he said to Tark.

Teddy Ballgame chose that moment to look over toward home plate, too, as did June and Natasha and a few of the Windigo players. All of them held their breath and waited for an uncomfortable moment to pass, and a few of them had to look away.

But Kate did exactly what Will knew she would. She showed them all the face of unconditional love.

She began to nod her head right along with the throbbing rhythm, and when Billy Gibbons and Dusty Hill began to sing "She's got legs, and she knows how to use them," Kate spread her arms and walked directly into Grant's embrace.

"You look so handsome in your baseball outfit," she beamed.

"It's a uniform," he corrected.

"I love you," she purred.

Some of the players stared, some tried not to. Grant and Kate Thorson moved into another dimension there by home plate. They were all alone, oblivious to everyone around them.

With a new baseball in each hand, she put her arms around his neck and began to move her hips with the beat. She raised her face into the light blue sky and let her head move with the music too. Her long hair swished behind her.

Grant's teammates pretended to go on with their pregame rituals but watched from the corners of their eyes. Theodore stared and took note of something good, really good, happening between Kate and Grant, but it was far beyond his understanding. He filed the moment away in his memory to be reanalyzed at some later date. Then he looked around to see if anybody was watching.

With her forearms resting on Grant's broad shoulders, Kate brought her eyes to his and smiled a seductive smile. Her hips moved with the music, her head bobbed, and she continued to smile.

Tark and the Daves hadn't looked away since Kate left the concession stand. This little scene certainly wasn't playing itself out as they'd expected, and they were relieved about that. Kate sure wasn't embarrassed about anything; she seemed to like the song just as much as the rest of them. All those who'd been watching began to sense something more here, something they couldn't comprehend. It was complicated, and yet it was simple.

Kate's feet never moved, but she was gliding across a ballroom floor. She wore blue jeans and a green T-shirt, but her mood and movements suggested a black evening gown. They were making love over there by home plate, and all she'd done was deliver a couple of baseballs to the starting pitcher.

"I never noticed just how pretty Grant's wife is," Tark said while he watched Kate stand with her arms around Grant's neck.

"Best friends, and jealous lovers," Will whispered to himself.

"Huh?" Tark said.

"I'm getting a boner here," Dave the Fag said.

∿ CHAPTER 50 ∾

All of Grant Thorson's baseball dreams clicked into place when the first game started promptly at 1:10 p.m. He was sharper than ever. He struck out the side in the first inning, then he homered in his first two at bats, took a no-hitter into the sixth inning, and lost it when Ray Rivers dumped a fluke base hit into right field, inches over Will's glove.

"Goddammit. Sonsabitches and cocksucker!" Pissed groaned when he sat down on the bench after the inning. He'd been the one to field Ray's base hit and he was angry that he hadn't caught it.

"Helluva way to lose a no-hitter," Tark grumbled. "Some weak-hittin' shitbird like Ray drops a duck fart in for a hit! Sorry, Grant."

The score stood at 8–0 when the Walleyes came to the dugout for their half of the sixth inning.

Clank walked to the booger board with his finger in his nose and stood there until his teammates were sure to notice, then he harvested another trophy and placed it on one of the few remaining open patches of the booger board.

"Nice one!" Tark said as he walked past Clank on his way to the bat rack. Small patches of red blood were beginning to appear on Tark's knees, but he'd said nothing about pain since he'd arrived at the park. His hangover had vanished and he'd played well. He selected a bat and then walked to the plate and singled on the first pitch. Dave the Fag promptly drove him in with a double into the gap in left center.

"Gimme some chew," Tark said when he returned to the dugout. He sat next to Pissed and extended his hand. Milburne Carrigan opened his pouch of Red Man tobacco and held it out for Tark.

"Thanks," Tark said. "I use Red Man when I want to hit for a high average, but I switch to Beech-Nut when I'm going for the long ball."

Pissed folded the pack of tobacco shut, put it back in his pocket, and waited for a moment before he added his own insight. "I use Red Man 'cuz it makes me shit."

Will turned to smile at Grant. They both knew this game was over. The Walleyes were pounding Windigo, they were confident, and they were on a mission. They'd finish up with this ass-whipping and then play one more game with the season on the line.

Thirty minutes later they were shaking hands in the dugout. Grant had thrown a complete game three-hitter, and they'd won 12–0. Walker and Windigo had played each other four times during the season and each team had won twice. They'd played twice during the tournament and each team had won once. After a thirty-minute break they'd do it all again, one more time.

~:~

It still seemed odd to Kate. She'd come to enjoy it, but nonetheless it surprised her every time a baseball player wearing a dirty, sweaty uniform would wander up to the concession-stand window and slide a buck fifty across the counter for a brat, then sit down at a picnic table with his girlfriend and chat for a few minutes between games of a doubleheader. But that was the nature of town ball, and today was no different.

Bud Pearson had umped the first game from behind the plate. Now he sat at an orange picnic table in the shade of some red pines and relaxed with a Coke and a brat. Tubby Voss sat next to him and cradled a plate piled high with his usual three brats. They talked about the things they'd seen in the first game until a middle-aged couple they seemed to know came and sat with them and redirected the conversation to the fishing on some lake north of Walker.

Three smiling Dragonflies walked toward the concession stand, and when they passed by the picnic table on the way, one of them nudged Bud's arm and said, "Nice job, Bud. You called a good game."

"Thanks, Tony," Bud replied.

When the ballplayers reached the concession stand, the one Bud had spoken to leaned against the countertop and asked for a hamburger and a Coke, then added, "Grant really had it workin' today. Best I ever seen." Like everyone else, the young man knew who Kate was.

"Thanks," Kate said when she took his money. "He sure loves it." The boy said thanks, took his lunch to an empty picnic table in the shade, and waited for his buddies to join him.

When Kate turned to wait on the next customer she found herself face to face with Miller Peoples.

"Hello, Mrs. Thorson," the boy said.

"Hello, Mr. Peoples," Kate said with a smile. "What can I get for you?"

"A brat and a Coke. Please," he said. The kid was taller than Grant, with a man's shoulders. His hands were big and coarse and his face was dirty. "Grant was really good, again," he said while Kate was preparing his bratwurst.

"Have you looked at any colleges yet?" Kate asked when he handed her two dollars for his lunch.

Miller Peoples's face spread into a smile and he said, "Yeah, Minnesota and Texas." Then he lowered his voice and added, "But if I get drafted by the pros I might play baseball right after high school."

That information wasn't exactly a scoop, and Kate smiled at the way he was willing to share his secret with her. "Well, good luck with your decision," she said.

"Thanks," the polite lad said. He turned to go join his friend at the picnic table in the shade.

Perhaps a hundred people stood around talking and eating on the grassy area in front of the concession stand when Kate noticed Will and Grant walking toward her. Will had an arm around Grant's shoulder and gave the appearance of a bodyguard leading a celebrity through a crowd. "Helluva game!" someone said to Grant. "Outstanding!" someone else called out. Grant smiled and waved to friends.

"My boy needs a brat," Will said when they reached the window. Then he hustled Grant around to a picnic table in back of the concession stand so they could have a few minutes of privacy.

Kate brought them each a brat, and she leaned close to Grant and whispered, "You were the best one!"

"I felt strong, honey. Really strong," Grant replied.

Louie Swearingen spent the entire time between games of the doubleheader alone in the dugout. He filled out the lineup card for the second game, then he sat down and watched while Clank and Pissed dragged and raked the infield dirt and then watered it. He was still sitting with his feet crossed, staring into the outfield, when Grant joined him. All the other players were still enjoying a few minutes more in the shade by the concession stand.

"It's been a helluva season," Grant said when he sat down.

"I wish you could have been here to see what town ball was like in the fifties," Louie said.

"I've heard some stories," Grant replied. "My dad played."

"We drew crowds of three and four thousand people, in tiny little towns," Louie said. "We had players that were only a step down from the big leagues." He chuckled. "Everybody did a bit of cheatin', too. Players got paid to play amateur ball. The lumber yard, or one of the car dealers, or maybe if a town had a small factory, they'd advertise that they had a position open, then hire some kid from outta town to work there. Then all of a sudden they'd find out that the new guy just happened to be a helluva ball player. How lucky." Louie laughed again.

"What position did you play, Louie?" Grant asked.

"Infield, but I could play anywhere. I was a glove man." Louie grinned.

"I bet you were," Grant said.

"Never hit a home run," Louie offered. "Not one. Never." He looked far into the past.

"Nothing like it," Grant said.

"I wouldn't know," Louie replied, then his countenance changed entirely. "But I know I never had more fun than this summer. These guys sure make me laugh. We never had booger boards back then."

The Walleyes began drifting back to the dugout as time drew near for the second game to start. Teddy Ballgame sat next to Louie and announced that he was ready to pitch. Tark dropped his pants and applied some more Noxzema to the carpet burns on his knees. The Daves lugged a large cooler of beer into the equipment shed as discreetly as possible in case there might be a postgame celebration.

Tubby Voss would be the umpire behind the plate for the second game of this doubleheader, and he made his way over to the Walleye dugout to remind them that according to the prearranged tournament format, they would be the visiting team for the second game, even though they were playing at their own park.

Game two started at 4:20 p.m., when the heat of an August afternoon was at its peak. Although game one had been a rout from beginning to end, the outcome of the second game seemed to swing back and forth with each pitch.

Will Campbell led off the game with a base hit. Then Grant hit into a double play. Tark followed with a double, then tried to score on a base hit by Dave the Fag, but Miller Peoples made a strong throw from center field and Tark was out at the plate by the narrowest of margins.

Teddy Ballgame walked the leadoff hitter for the Dragonflies, who stood on second base a moment later when the second batter singled. Miller Peoples followed with a fly ball that triggered the first in a series of memorable plays. Dave the Fag caught Peoples's fly ball in the deepest part of center field with his back against the outfield fence. The runner at second tagged up and tried to score all the way from second base. But he was thrown out at the plate, just as Tark had been a few minutes earlier, only this time it was Tark who made a spectacular relay throw to Pearly. Then, in all the commotion, the runner at first had scampered back to the bag, tagged up and tried to advance to second base during the play at home plate, and Pearly threw him out at second base. A triple play! Miller Peoples had come to the plate with a chance to break the game open and Windigo came away with nothing.

"Put that one in the book as 8–6–2–4!" Pearly laughed when he walked back to the dugout. "Never seen a triple play like that one!"

Louie was recording the unusual triple play in his scorebook when he peeked out from under his Walleye cap and said, "They say that every time you go to a baseball game you'll see something you've never seen before."

The bizarre first inning was a harbinger of things to come. Both teams hit the ball hard for the first three innings, but neither of them could score. Both pitchers settled down in the fourth inning, and neither team could put a bat on the ball for the next two innings. Then base hits were followed by strikeouts and double plays at the most critical times. Every pitch seemed to change the situation entirely and give one team a huge advantage over the other, but no one scored, and they labored on in the afternoon heat.

"Jeez, Pearly. You look like the dogs had you under the porch all day," Tark said when the Walleyes trudged into the dugout after the seventh inning. Pearly found the shade as quickly as he could, then he poured ice water over his head and the back of his neck.

"I'm too old for this shit," Pearly groaned.

The oppressive heat and the stress of a scoreless tie began to weigh on the players, and it seemed that no one would ever score a run. Then, as Teddy Ballgame prepared to lead off the top of the eighth inning, he stopped in his tracks on the way to the bat rack and set an amazing event in motion. "I think I can bunt for a hit, Louie," he said. He probed Louie's eyes and waited for a reply. None came. "Look for yourself, Louie. Ol' Hard-nosed is playin' way back over there at third base. He'll shit his pants if I lay one down."

Louie glanced at Ray Rivers, who, inexplicably, was far out of proper defensive position, standing behind third base. "Do it on the first pitch, and make it a good one," Louie said.

Ray had remained mostly silent since his midseason confrontation with Theodore, and he wasn't about to inspire the lad any further. He kept his mouth shut and waited for his pitcher to deliver the first pitch of the eighth inning to Theodore. But he took his position way too far from home plate. His heels were resting on the outfield grass, and Theodore tried not to stare at him when he stepped into the batter's box.

The pitch appeared to be halfway to the plate when Theodore finally squared off to bunt, and he laid down a perfect one that rolled slowly out toward Ray. Ray was so surprised that he didn't get off his heels in time to make a play, and Theodore stood at first base with a bunt single.

Will Campbell drew a base on balls, and Tark Sabetti left the on-deck circle with a chance to be a hero. A base hit would score at least one run and maybe start a big inning for the Walleyes. It was time for something to happen, and the crowd came to life after the Dragonflies convened at the mound to discuss their defensive strategy.

Speed played "Bad to the Bone" as loud as he could over the PA system while the Windigo players talked.

A moment later, when his teammates had returned to their defensive positions, the Windigo pitcher came to his set position and the crowd grew even louder. He delivered a fastball and Tark took a mighty swing.

"Shit!" Tark bellowed the instant he hit the ball. He'd popped it up, a mile high. It had been a belt-high fastball and he knew right away that he'd just missed a chance to hit one in the river. He slammed the bat against the ground.

Bud Pearson immediately raised his right hand and the prosthetic hook on his left, and called, "Infield fly rule! The batter is out!" As the umpire working the bases, it was Bud's job to make the call and he did it correctly. In a situation like this, with bases loaded or runners on first and second and no one out, it was the umpire's obligation to invoke the infield fly rule and call the batter out immediately on a fly ball hit to the infield. If he failed to make that call, an infielder could simply let the ball drop and then start a triple play, because the runners would naturally retreat to their bases, expecting him to catch the ball.

Now Tark was automatically out, and the ball was still rifling straight up into the afternoon sky as Theodore retreated to second base and Will retreated to first.

As Bud was shouting about the infield fly rule, Theodore decided to plant both feet on second base and simply wait for the play to be over. He stood on the bag straight-legged, with his arms folded.

But the shortstop was looking up into the sky and edging closer to Theodore. There was no need to catch the ball, everyone knew that. But the shortstop was nearly touching Theodore now, and looking up directly above him.

Good infielders will sometimes drop an infield fly such as this one in an effort to trick an inexperienced base runner into making a break for the next base and giving up a foolish out on the base paths, and Theodore guessed that the Windigo shortstop was pretending to grow frantic and trying to trick him into breaking for third base. He was having none of that. He stood his ground and waited for the play to be over so Dave the Fag could take his turn at bat and try and bring him home.

Suddenly the shortstop jumped back away from Theodore and the fly ball struck him on the top of his helmet. It didn't hurt, but it surprised him, and everyone else.

The ball glanced off the side of Theodore's helmet and rolled far out into the outfield between Miller Peoples in center field and the guy in right field.

A stunned silence fell over the whole ballpark. Theodore looked into Bud Pearson's eyes and was the first to understand what had happened. The ball was still in play! Tark was out—everyone understood that much—but now the ball had rolled way out into the outfield. No one had called time out, and there was apparently no stoppage of play. Every one of the Dragonfly infielders looked around and wondered what to do next.

Still, Bud Pearson stared back at Theodore, but made no call.

Theodore suddenly knew what he had to do, and he broke for third base while everyone else remained straight-legged and stunned.

The infield fly rule is clear about the fact that even though the batter is automatically out, base runners are free to advance at their own risk. But everyone in the park assumed that since the ball had struck Theodore it was a dead ball. Theodore knew better now, when he read Bud Pearson's eyes, and he knew that Bud was telling him to run like hell.

Bud still made no call, and the ball kept rolling, and Theodore kept running, and Bud watched while the rest of the players began to figure things out.

Finally the Windigo shortstop realized he'd better do something and then argue about it later. Every voice in the park was screaming when the shortstop finally picked up the ball, but Theodore was dashing across the plate by the time he was ready to throw it.

"Teddy Ballgame!" Tark roared as Theodore dashed across home plate.

The ensuing argument lasted for nearly ten minutes. The Windigo coach looked like he'd swallowed a bug. His arms flew in different directions and his face turned red from yelling. Ray waved his arms and jumped up and down. Louie stood and shook his head, then nodded his head, then shook his head.

Finally Bud Pearson was able to quiet the hostile mob. "Here's the call," Bud started. "Runners on first and second, nobody out, batter pops up. Infield fly rule. The batter is out." Pearson looked around the group to be sure they understood. "All right," he said when no one argued. "The ball strikes the base runner who was standing on second base . . ."

"He wasn't standing on second base! He was way off the bag!" the Windigo coach yelled. "That's interference on the runner! He's out too!" And the argument erupted once more.

Bud Pearson calmly raised both hands to demand quiet. "No! That's not true. I watched him the entire time. He was standing on second base. He's safe, it's a live ball, and he can advance at his own risk. The runner scored from second and his run counts!" Essentially, Bud had challenged the integrity of the Windigo coach, then he'd made it plain that he was done explaining things.

The Windigo players and coaches grumbled and whined as they turned away, but Tark reenergized them when he blurted, "Nice try, Asshole, you can probably flush a turd that big when you've got a 'homer' like Murphy in your pocket! But not here!"

Several Windigo players jumped at Tark like they were about to start swinging before they remembered Tark's reputation with regard to fisti-cuffs, and they decided to continue the retreat. "Fuck you, Sabetti," one of the Dragonflies said.

"Any of you pussies want a piece o' me, c'mon! Right now!" Tark dared them all, then he waited at home plate. "That's what I thought," he said when no one answered his challenge. "All you pussies can all kiss my ass, right where da sweat makes it red," he added to tempt any or all of the Dragonflies to request a shot at the title.

"Well, that was a colorful word picture I haven't heard for a few years," Will said to Grant on the way back to the dugout. "I'd say that a line has been drawn in the sand, eh?"

The Walleyes could do no more damage in the eighth, and then Windigo went down quietly in their half of the inning. The Walleyes made three more quick outs in the top of the ninth and a tense 1–0 ballgame rolled into the bottom of the ninth.

Theodore took a deep breath and walked to the pitcher's mound. "Just throw strikes, and keep 'em low," Grant said as Theodore brushed past him. "Don't change a thing."

Kate and June closed down the concession stand, locked the doors and window, and hurried over to the chain-link fence by the Walleyes on-deck circle so they could watch the end of the game with everyone else. Everyone in the ballpark was either sitting in the bleachers or pressing up against the fence. Men hollered encouragement, either to the Windigo batters waiting for a chance to bat, or to young Theodore. Wives, mothers, and girlfriends crossed their fingers while their insides twisted.

All eyes were fixed on Teddy Ballgame while he pawed the dirt on the pitcher's mound, then finished his warm-up pitches. There was no hint of a smile when he finally stood on the rubber, back straight and peering in to take the sign from Pearly. He went into his windup and delivered ball one, then ball two, then ball three.

"Oh, God, don't let this happen," Kate whispered.

Every player and fan in the ballpark knew that the Windigo hitter wouldn't swing at the next pitch; he'd let this one go for sure, hoping Theodore would issue a base on balls. Theodore went into his windup once more and threw a fastball down the middle. "Strike one!" Tubby cried.

Again, Theodore wound up and delivered a pitch, and the batter fouled it off. He fouled off the next three pitches too. On the ninth pitch the Windigo batter drilled a solid single to left field.

Walleye faithful began to feel their stomachs tighten. Windigo fans sat straighter in their seats and wondered if a miracle might happen.

Theodore threw three straight balls to the next hitter before he worked himself back to a full count. Once again the hitter fouled off several pitches, and with each new pitch the tension mounted. When Theodore delivered his eleventh pitch, the batter turned and hammered a screaming ground ball between Tark and Clank. The ball jumped off the bat like a lightning bolt and every Windigo fan thought they had their miracle.

But Tark made one step to his right, caught the lightning bolt, backhanded on one hop, and started an easy double play.

Kate allowed herself to breathe again. With a sudden reversal of fortune, it was the Walleyes who got the miracle. Instead of Windigo base runners everywhere, there were two outs and nobody on base.

One more out, oh God, just one more out. Kate could barely watch now.

Theodore walked the next batter on four pitches, and Walleye fans started swallowing hard again.

Louie Swearingen called time out. He made an agonizingly slow trip to the mound, as did Grant, Pearly, and the other infielders. "You OK?" Louie asked Theodore.

"Sure," Theodore replied.

Louie turned his eyes to Pearly and waited for the catcher to give his opinion. "Give him one more hitter, Louie," Pearly nodded.

Louie had planned to do just that, but he wanted to see the look in Teddy Ballgame's eyes before he made a final decision. "OK, Theodore," Louie started. "This guy who's coming up to bat has one hit off you all year, you've struck him out twice today. Just keep the ball low. If he hits a ground ball the game's over. If he pops up, the game's over. Let him get himself out." Louie nodded and smiled at Theodore. "Go after this guy!"

As Louie walked back toward the Walleyes dugout he glanced to his right and saw the same thing everyone else did. Miller Peoples stepped out of the dugout and into the on-deck circle. If Theodore couldn't get the guy at the plate to end the game, he'd have to pitch to Miller Peoples.

It happened almost before Louie had settled into his seat. Theodore delivered a pitch and the Windigo hitter drove it far into the gap between Dave the Fag and Dave the Jew. The ball rolled almost to the fence before Dave the Fag picked it up and threw it to Tark, the Walleye cutoff man.

The Windigo base runner who'd started on first base happened to be particularly slow-footed. Nonetheless, Tark expected to see the runner rounding third when he turned to relay the ball home. But the third base coach for Windigo had held him up. Bad coaching, Tark thought; he was pretty sure he couldn't have thrown the runner out. He raced back to the infield, ready to throw if the runner changed his mind.

Windigo fans stomped their feet on the planks in the bleachers and shook the chain-link fence while they screamed their approval.

"Time out, Tubby!" Louie hollered when Tark had the ball back in the infield. Then he stepped out of the dugout and walked into his nightmare. After thirty-five years of town ball he was one out from his first state tournament. His two best pitchers were used up and the best player any of them had ever seen was up next, with the winning run standing on second base. Now what?

When Louie arrived at the mound, Pearly and all the infielders were waiting for him.

"I'll get him out, Louie," Theodore said.

Louie held his hand out and demanded that Theodore give him the ball. "Teddy Ballgame . . ." Louie sighed. "You pitched a helluva game today, young man, but you're done."

"I'll get him . . ." Theodore pleaded.

"You're done, Theodore," Louie said again, this time with no doubt regarding his decision. Theodore handed the game ball to Louie, and his pitching duties were done for the day. "You got us here, but somebody else is gonna take us home," Louie added.

Five seconds passed in silence. It seemed like an hour. Louie's eyes drifted over to Grant, and Pearly's eyes followed.

"Got anything left?" Louie asked Grant.

Grant held his hand out, asking for the ball, and said, "Thought you'd never ask, Louie. I'll get him."

Louie, Pearly, and Grant stood together and shared something for a moment. Then Louie nodded when they'd reached an unspoken agreement, and he handed the ball to Grant.

"Wait a minute!" Tark blurted. "Do I have to explain this shit to you guys? Chrissakes, look over there!" He pointed to first base. "First base is open! Walk this fuckin' guy! Take the bat out of his hands! His run doesn't mean anything anyway. If he comes around and scores we're already beat. Take him out of the picture! Put him on first base and pitch to the next guy." Tark paused and quizzed Pearly and Louie with his eyes. "In case you haven't noticed, ol' Hard-nosed is up after this guy. He's over there shittin' in his pants right now." Tark pointed to the Windigo on-deck circle. "Look! He's terrified you're gonna walk Peoples to get to him, and then make him look like a fish!"

Tark paused again and looked at Pearly, then Louie, then Grant, while he waited for a reply, but none came. "This is a fuckin' no-brainer, guys. You never let the other team's superstar beat you! We walk Mickey Mantle over there and pitch to Tinker Bell. Game over! Don't you get it?"

Grant rubbed the game ball for a second, then he finally spoke to Tark. "You don't understand what's going on here, do you, Tark?"

"I sure as hell don't!" Tark replied.

"Look, Tark," Grant said softly. "We live for moments like this, and they don't come along very often. Three weeks from now you're gonna be back in dental school, you and the Daves. Will and I will be doing dentistry and getting ready for the duck season. Pearly, he'll be crawling over cat shit in some old lady's basement tryin' to fix a leaky pipe." Grant stopped and locked his eyes on Tark. "Everybody is gonna move on. Even Theodore here, he'll be off to college—another great adventure. But today, well, like you said. Today we have a chance to go after Mickey Mantle. So let's do it."

Tark stared back at Grant and refused to understand.

"Think about it, Tark. Someday that Peoples kid is gonna be standing behind the podium in Cooperstown and you can tell your grandchildren about the day . . ."

"But if they put a crooked number up there on the scoreboard—anything other than a one, we're finished," Tark interrupted.

"A crooked number?" Grant scoffed. "Is that what you're afraid of? Well, don't be." Grant pointed a finger at Tark and added, "Lotsa things worse than that . . . like lettin' somebody steal your dreams." Grant looked over at Miller Peoples in the Windigo on-deck circle. "He's just another boy, like me, like you, and he just wants to make his dreams come true. Well, today *my* dreams are comin' true!"

The deal was done. Tark nodded a grudging acceptance of Grant's explanation, then he finally grinned at Will, who'd stood there and listened to it all.

Theodore was just glad to be relieved of the responsibility for the final out. He took the first baseman's mitt that Grant had been using and gave Grant his glove.

"Let's play ball, guys," Tubby Voss said after his slow walk to the mound.

"Gonna change pitchers," Louie said to Tubby.

"OK, have him take his warm-ups now," Tubby replied as he turned back toward the plate.

"OK, here's the deal," Grant said to his teammates, suddenly all business. "I don't need any warm-ups. I'm ready. But the rules allow me eight pitches, so I'm gonna take 'em, and I'm gonna let those guys see me throw seven wild pitches. I'm gonna be all over the place, in the dirt, back to the screen, everywhere. Number eight will be a curve, just to get the feel of it. Peoples will be watching all this and he'll assume I'm wild and can't find the zone, so he'll be takin' on the first pitch. I'm gonna startle him with a heater. He'll let it go, and I'll be ahead oh and one. Then I'm gonna give him a straight changeup, right down Broadway. If he swings he'll either miss it or be so far in front of it he'll jerk it way foul." Grant paused. "Then I'm gonna finish him with a yakker, and his front leg is gonna buckle 'cuz he's afraid it's goin' in his ear. It's gonna snap over the plate for strike three. Good morning, good afternoon, good night!"

"What if he swings at that first pitch, the fastball? Tark asked.

"Then we'll have to think of something else to tell our grandchildren about," Grant smiled. He started pawing at the dirt in front of the pitching rubber and dismissed his teammates with, "Let's do this, Pearly. Remember to cover your nuts for the first seven," he said without looking up.

Pearly walked back to the plate. Louie walked back to the dugout. Tark walked back to shortstop. Clank and Theodore walked back to third and first base. But Will stood by the mound with his arms crossed, and Speed Roesner chose the moment to switch the music. After the speakers crackled for a second, Norman Greenbaum's "Spirit in the Sky" began to throb its way through the park.

"Ah, what a great song!" Grant said as he wound up to deliver his first warm-up pitch. He never looked at Will, but he kept on talking to him. "Remember, Will, it was the summer of '69." Grant bounced a pitch six feet in front of home plate and the Windigo players made a point to laugh out loud, then they began taunting Grant.

"I got my driver's license in the spring. Dad bought me a piece-of-shit '58 Ford so I could drive to baseball practice," Grant said when Pearly threw him a new ball. He stepped on the rubber again. "Mets won the Series that year. The Miracle Mets!" he added with some satisfaction.

"Spirit in the Sky" played on and Grant sailed a pitch five feet over Pearly's head all the way to the backstop, and the Windigo players howled again.

"I remember," Will said. Both of them were oblivious to the catcalls from the Windigo crowd.

"Mighta been the best summer of my life," Grant said while he waited for Pearly to throw a ball back to him. "Except for that first summer with Kate."

Will stood with his arms crossed and waited for Grant to continue.

"I got a letter from the Twins that summer," Grant announced when he stepped on the rubber again.

"Really?" Will said, as Grant went into his windup. "You never told me about the letter." Grant bounced another pitch, this time far to the left of home plate. Even the Walleye fans groaned over Grant's terrible warm-up pitches. Both Grant and Will heard the groans and they knew that the deliberate errant throws were achieving the desired result, but they were busy with their own conversation.

"I never even told Kate about that," Grant said while he waited for Pearly's return throw.

"So what did the Twins have to say?" Will asked.

Grant moved some more dirt with his shoe, then he stepped back on the rubber and looked at Will. "Said they'd heard a lot of good things about me and they'd be watching my development." He delivered another terrible pitch and a few Walleye fans covered their eyes. "How 'bout that?" he added.

"So whatever happened?" Will asked, over the groans coming from the bleachers.

Grant was looking at Pearly when he answered Will's question. "I think they're still watching," Grant said. Then he stared directly into Will's eyes and declared, "Not shittin' you, either!"

Will could only stand there in the summer sun and wonder. He thought he knew his best friend. He thought he understood Grant's thoughts and could read Grant's mind. But not now. Was he serious or was he joking? For the very first time, Will didn't know.

Over by the Walleye dugout, all Kate could do was pray that this would end well. She stood at the fence and watched Grant warm up, her fingers clinging to the chain links. June was crowded next to her right side, holding to the fence like everyone else, and Natasha stood on her left. Just a moment earlier, Ingrid had sensed all the tension building and she'd edged her way alongside Kate's right leg. Now she pressed her face against the fence too.

"Spirit in the Sky" played on and Kate watched her husband finish his warm-up pitches. He was terrible, and the Windigo players were taunting him unmercifully. But he seemed so caught up in his conversation with Will that he didn't notice them. Grant was beginning to move a little differently after each pitch. Something was changing. She pressed her face against the fence and stared. That's when it happened.

Her grown-up husband, the love of her life, stood out there on the mound. But he was ten years old now, maybe fifteen—it was so hard to say—but he was young and unbowed by the weight of life. He was wearing his Walleye uniform with Mickey Mantle's number seven on the back, but he was a little boy. He pawed at the dirt with his shoe and tried to emulate his big-league heroes, but he was just a boy. He had some swagger, too; he was preparing to mow down some Yankees. Kate covered her mouth and stared.

"Batter up!" Tubby Voss called out, and Miller Peoples stepped up to the plate. The fans in the bleachers stomped their feet, and those lined up along the fence cheered, but all Kate could see was the little boy about to throw a pitch. He stood, stone-faced, and stared at home plate for a moment. Then he went into his windup and delivered a pitch.

Just as Grant predicted, Miller Peoples kept the bat on his shoulder and took the first pitch. "Strike one!" Tubby barked. Miller Peoples had let that first pitch get by him for a called strike and he looked away in disgust, because *that* was the pitch he wanted. He knew he'd been set up. Kate kept staring as the grim-faced little boy on the pitcher's mound caught the return throw from Pearly and then went into a little ritual before he threw another pitch. He rubbed the ball with both hands, hitched up his pants, and then stood straight with both feet on the rubber, peering over the webbing of his glove as he took the sign from Pearly. When he threw the ball he grunted and strained and convinced the batter that he intended to blow another fastball past him, but he held the ball back in his hand and pulled the string . . . a lovely changeup.

Miller Peoples lunged and the crowd gasped when he drove the ball far out into foul territory in left field. It was just a long strike, about a four-hundred-fifty-foot strike. Grant had sold Peoples a fastball but delivered a changeup. The count was no balls and two strikes. No one in the crowd knew, but this was going exactly as Grant had planned.

Kate was aware of crowd noise, and she felt the fence shaking, but her attention was fixed on the face of a little boy. She'd seen him in old photos, and now he was right here. The boy stood there once again, feet together, back straight, glaring at Miller Peoples over the top of his glove. Then he stepped sideways and went into his windup. There was no sound anywhere in the world when the ball left his hand.

Miller Peoples's left leg wobbled, his shoulders twitched, and the baseball looked like it rolled off a table before it snapped into Pearly's glove. Strike three! The little boy beamed for a second. His teammates jumped with joy and the fence shook. Miller Peoples was out. Game over.

But Tubby Voss shook his head. "No!" he said. He pointed his right hand at the outside of the plate. "I didn't like it! Outside," he said loud enough for most of the crowd to hear. "Ball one."

Walleye fans groaned. Windigo fans cheered. Miller Peoples took a deep breath, and when Pearly threw the ball back to the pitcher's mound Kate saw that the little boy was gone.

Grant rubbed the ball and circled the mound, unable to hide his frustration. He'd made his best pitch and Tubby had missed it. Now what?

For the first time in anyone's memory, Louie Swearingen's angry voice boomed from the Walleye dugout. "Everybody in the goddamn park saw that was a strike!"

Tubby shook his head and mumbled. "Didn't like it."

A tiny but very angry female voice called out from the Walker crowd. "You'd like it if it was a bratwurst!" Peals of laughter rippled through the ballpark, and the laughter grew louder as heads turned to discover a sheepish Krista Hesby covering her face. The unexpected dose of laughter supplied by Teddy Ballgame's pretty girlfriend had drained away some of the unbearable pressure.

Filthy and soaked with sweat, Pearly began what seemed like a thousand-mile march to the pitcher's mound. He'd spent seven hours behind the plate during the heart of a scorching summer day. He'd been struck on the head and shoulders by foul balls, and he'd used his forearms and thighs to block pitches that bounced in front of him. The catcher's gear he'd worn all day only served to amplify the afternoon heat, and he'd worked harder than any of his teammates. But when he reached the mound his eyes were clear and bright. "Now what?" he asked Grant.

"Well," Grant shrugged. "I'd say we throw him two fastballs, high and tight, then finish him with another hook."

"Sure you don't wanna walk him?" Pearly asked.

"Losin' your nerve, Pearly?" Grant smiled.

"Nope, just wanted to be sure we were still on the same page," Pearly replied. "Keep the cheese right under his chin, then be sure not to hang the curve . . . nice and easy." Then Pearly turned and dragged himself back to squat behind home plate.

Grant pawed at the dirt around the pitching rubber and thought things over while his catcher returned to his position. Maybe he should just go ahead and walk Miller Peoples so he could pitch to Ray? It was still an option. Nah, he couldn't do that. Never.

When Pearly was ready, Grant took his sign, went into his windup, and delivered a fastball that nearly hit Miller Peoples's chin, then another, and the count stood at three balls and two strikes.

A crescendo of stomping and screaming and clapping began to rise into the afternoon air when Pearly threw the ball back to Grant, and Kate's stomach twisted around itself. She knew he'd never walk the Peoples kid on purpose. The only way Miller Peoples would get a base on balls would be if Tubby Voss missed another strike. Grant would challenge Miller Peoples. For sure.

Everyone in the park screamed or stomped or clapped their hands when Grant put both feet on the rubber one more time, stood straight, and glared at the Peoples kid. Kate could hear none of the cheering, though. A part of her, the best part of her, stood out there with Grant as he bore the weight of the world on his shoulders. For the first time in all these years of watching Grant play ball, she raised her voice and hollered to him, louder and louder with each passing moment. "Blow him away, Grant! BLOW HIM AWAY!" She screamed over and over and shook the fence along with the others.

Grant stood tall and took the sign from Pearly. It would be a curve. Grant reminded himself not to throw it too hard. It had to be a jaw-dropping, leg-buckling curveball.

He wound up and let it fly, and it was a good one. He'd set it up well by throwing two fastballs just under Miller Peoples's chin, and this pitch was headed for Miller Peoples's head. There would be a moment of hesitation when the hitter feared for his safety. He'd wobble, then freeze, and Pearly would cradle the final out in that old catcher's mitt. Maybe he'd swing and miss, but Miller Peoples was going down.

Miller Peoples's front leg didn't buckle. His hands stayed back. He never flinched. He waited. Grant saw his eyes grow large, and he saw that Miller Peoples wanted something too. He'd guessed curveball, and he got one. Peoples uncoiled. He sprang at the ball like an angry cat, and he made a perfect swing.

Everyone there saw the powerful young man crush the ball. Kate knew in an instant that the ball was a home run, and the ball had barely left the bat when Kate turned to look at her lover.

Grant didn't need to turn and look; he knew the ball was outbound and there'd be no recovery. He closed his eyes, bent at the waist and rested his hands on his knees while he looked straight down at the infield grass and listened to the celebration that was erupting all around him. Somewhere high up in those red pines out there beyond the fence, Grant Thorson heard all his baseball dreams bouncing around in the tree boughs.

Pandemonium spread across the infield of Walleye Park as Miller Peoples made his lap around the bases. Windigo players rushed out to wait for their hero when he reached home plate. Some fans raced onto the field to join them.

Ingrid Thorson cheered wildly too. Her daddy was out there doing something and everyone seemed to be appreciating it. She jumped up and down and yelled right along with all the Windigo fans. Then she looked up and saw that her mother's eyes were swollen with tears, as were June Campbell's and the tall woman standing by her mother. Kate and June and Natasha Badenov cried together, then laughed together when they saw Ingrid cheering, then cried some more when Ingrid joined them in sorrow.

For a moment it seemed as if Grant was struggling to hold himself up. He braced his hands against his knees and stood there, bent over. He was all alone out there. When he finally stood up straight, Kate read the abject disappointment in his hollow eyes. He was broken.

Grant watched Miller Peoples finish circling the bases. Teddy Ballgame nodded his forlorn congratulations when Peoples rounded first base and ran past him. Will Campbell actually shook Miller Peoples's hand when he passed Will at second base. Tark stood with his arms folded and made damn certain that Peoples touched every base. Clank was already off the field when the home run hitter reached third base. Pearly looked like he'd seen a ghost as he walked away from the crowd of jubilant Dragonflies gathering by home plate.

After Peoples rounded third base, the last leg in his home run journey would be nothing but a celebration with family and friends. But just before he reached third he glanced over his left shoulder and sneaked a look at Grant, who'd been watching him. They locked eyes and Grant nodded a salute, then tipped his cap. Peoples returned the nod, rounded third base, and the party was on. Only Kate saw the exchange between victor and vanquished.

Tubby Voss and Bud Pearson made a hasty retreat, as umpires always do. They ran to their cars in the parking lot. Somebody would be certain to offer them unkind advice if they waited around at the field.

The final score was 3–1, and Speed let it linger on the scoreboard for a few minutes. The Windigo Dragonflies had hung one last crooked number on Grant Thorson.

Kate made her way through the crowd and found Grant still standing by the pitcher's mound. She cried openly and buried her face in his chest. "Oh, I wanted you to strike him out!" she said, her voice muffled by his chest.

"Me too," Grant sighed. "Thought I had him, too, but . . ." His voice trailed off. "Shoulda walked him, I guess."

"I saw something," Kate said. "I saw the little boy who was up against the Yankees, or the Russians, or whoever it is little boys fight in their dreams."

"How'd I look?" Grant knew exactly what she'd seen.

"You were just a boy!" Kate laughed and sobbed at the same time.

"That's why I do this."

"I wish your dreams could come true, just once . . ." Kate sobbed into his chest.

He ran his hand over her long hair and down her back. "Maybe next time," he whispered.

The Walleyes made their way to the dugout while they watched the Windigo celebration move from home plate to their dugout, to the grassy area in front of the concession stand, to the parking lot, then to disappear out on the highway, heading back to Windigo.

The last of the remaining baseball fans had trickled out of the ballpark when the Walleye players assembled in the dugout like a platoon of shell-shocked marines. A long day and a long season had come to an end, and the red pines beyond the outfield fence were casting great shadows.

Kate raised her lips so they were touching Grant's ear, and she whispered, "Thank you."

"For what?" he asked.

"For this place in the world. It's perfect," she said. Then she turned to look at the beaten men wearing the dirty, sweaty uniforms in the dugout, and she took his hand when he walked over to join them.

"Sorry, I guess I shoulda walked him," Grant sighed when he sat down on the dugout steps beside Kate.

"Bullshit! You had him, once. Fuckin' Tubby," Tark groaned, and the dugout fell silent.

Louie Swearingen moved slowly onto the grass in front of the dugout and raised a hand into the afternoon shadows. "Wait a minute, boys. We had a helluva summer!" he said. He gestured for June and Natasha and Krista Hesby, who'd been standing quietly by the dugout steps, to join them. As the women inched into the dugout, Louie raised his voice to

Speed Roesner, who was about to close down the press box for another year. "Speed! Clear the scoreboard and then put some appropriate music on, will you? Then c'mon down here and join us."

A moment later the "Beer Barrel Polka" clicked on, and Speed stepped around the corner of the dugout.

"I saw Tark and the Daves sneaking some beer in here between games, for a celebration," Louie said. "Why don't you guys drag that cooler out and we'll have a little private party of our own right here before we go over to the Chateau for pizza?"

The Daves carried out the cooler full of ice and Hamm's beer and Natasha sat down next to Tark. Will saw her glance at the blood on his knees and then smile sheepishly and kiss him on the cheek.

June sat down beside Pearly and put her arm around his powerful shoulders, and her small gesture seemed to release much of the anger and frustration from the dugout. Then she looked at the players on the bench and said each of their names slowly, "Dave the Fag, Dave the Jew, Clank, Pissed, Tark, Pearly, and Teddy Fuckin' Ballgame . . ." She shook her head and listened to a murmur of laughter from the players. Then she looked across the gathering of players sitting in the dugout, and she shared an exchange with Kate. She'd make a point to share the good times with Will, just as Kate had said, and keep her secret.

Will opened a can of beer and put his arm around Grant's shoulder. "Well," he began, "my Pard had a helluva day today! And if that *one* pitch had just looked a *little* bit more like a bratwurst . . ."

Another murmur of laughter spread among the players and all eyes turned to the darling young Krista Hesby who sat on the dugout steps between Theodore and Kate. Krista covered her face and laughed with the rest of them. The anguish of a few moments earlier was ebbing quickly. This group had weathered a storm together.

Kate rubbed her hand across Krista's back while everyone remembered her angry outburst over Tubby Voss's missed strike three, and Theodore leaned forward to explain something. "I found her out in the parking lot after the game," he said. "She was standing out there by Tubby's car, cryin' and apologizing!"

"What a nice thing to do," Kate said, but Krista kept her face buried in her hands, still trying to hide her shame.

"You never apologize to an ump . . . ," Tark started to explain, but he was interrupted by a small crash. Ingrid had ridden her bicycle around to the front of the dugout to see where everyone was. But she'd run over a coil of garden hose and was soon crying and draped over the tangled wreckage.

Grant jumped to his feet and lifted his daughter off the bicycle. After a quick inspection he told her she was OK and that she should watch where she was going. While everyone in the dugout watched, he stood her bike upright, lowered the kickstand, and then began to replace the baseball cards and clothespins that had been knocked off in the crash.

Ingrid walked to her father's side and put her hands on her thighs. She made a point to squat next to him as if he needed help with the rebuilding of a complicated machine. She looked up at him once, then back to the bicycle, then, while everyone was listening, she said, "The Yankees go on your spokes, don't they Daddy? 'Cuz they're all sonsabitches!" Then she got on her bike and rode away.

The exhausted Walleyes laughed and cheered, and they raised their beer cans in a weary salute to Ingrid.

Grant rejoined his teammates in their dugout, took a seat on the top step, and studied his friends while he looked around. Sunset was only moments away, and Walker's boys of summer found themselves looking out over the gloamin' while another season of town ball disappeared behind the red pines where Miller Peoples's home run had landed. The devastating loss was already just another fork in the road. They'd all taken this road together, and they'd be fine.

The Walleyes were still laughing at Ingrid when Grant turned to look at Kate. Her eyes were red from crying a few minutes earlier, and her soft white cheeks were streaked with the tracks of her tears. Now she was laughing, and exchanging smiles with the baseball players seated around her. She shook her head, wiped her eyes, and chuckled while she denied any role in the development of Ingrid's vocabulary.

Grant felt the anguish of another crooked number begin to subside. After all, Kate Bellows, the prettiest girl he'd ever seen, was still sitting beside him. He let his eyes wander over her legs, her long delicate fingers, and her hair. The love they shared had left both of them totally vulnerable and completely secure. He couldn't help but wonder just what it was that held his life so close to hers. She was the dream that had come true. He raised an arm over her shoulder and claimed her as his best friend one more time.

Down on the far end of the dugout, Teddy Ballgame leaned back, sipped his beer, and crowed, "Wait till next year!"

∼: EPILOGUE :∼

Ben Pribyl married Tanya the Mauler and they moved to Oregon. Grant and Kate never saw Ben again; they just lost contact. Years later they heard that Ben and Tanya had five daughters, all of them scrappers, and that Ben had struggled mightily with nightmares of Vietnam.

Joe Paatalo, Andy Hedstrom, Jimmy Drahota, and Mitch Morgan all stayed in contact with Grant and Kate periodically, and they saw each other from time to time at dental conferences and conventions. They laughed and joked and told the same stories over and over, but they were never close again.

Darcy Wilhelm was never able to practice dentistry. She tried several times and failed. She simply lacked the intellect to analyze a complex problem and then solve it. After six terms in the Minnesota state legislature she was elected to the United States Senate.

Joe Ruminsky and Fred Muckinhern both retired several years after Grant and Will graduated. Ruminsky keeps bees and Muckinhern is writing a book about the micropathology of periodontal disease and its implications for heart disease. They still meet for lunch twice a week at Stub & Herb's.

Ebby Rettig died alone. Ruminsky and Muckinhern were the only U of M faculty members present at his funeral.

Miles Clark is now the head of preclinical studies at the dental school.

Louie Swearingen coached the Walleyes for six more seasons, then he died in his sleep on a cold New Year's Eve. He never made it to the state tournament.

Pearly DeMoore, Milburne (Pissed) Carrigan, and Melbourne (Clank) Carrigan are still plumbers, although the Carrigans own the business now.

Pearly played another year with the Walleyes. The Carrigans each played six more.

Paladin "Tark" Sabetti played another year for the Walleyes. After a stormy, on-again, off-again courtship that lasted for six years, Tark married Natasha Badenov. They remained good friends with the Daves, and they named their first son Theodore Christopher Sabetti.

Dave the Fag and Dave the Jew each became Dr. David Johnson and they practice dentistry together in Duluth, just down the hall from Dr. Paladin Sabetti and his brother Dominic. Their patients differentiate between them by using their middle initials F and J.

Theodore Christopher went off to college but returned every summer to play ball for the Walleyes. He broke Krista Hesby's heart several years later when he married someone else.

Miller Peoples did make it to the big leagues. He hit 128 home runs in the majors before arm and shoulder injuries derailed his career. Then he returned to the University of Minnesota and graduated from law school. On the rich walnut bookshelf behind his desk, he displays only one memento from his baseball days: the home run ball he hit off Grant Thorson.

Will and June Campbell remained best friends with the Thorsons for the rest of their lives. June never shared her secret with anyone but Kate, and Will played with the Walleyes for six more years.

In 1986, not so long after Miller Peoples' home run and Windigo's trip to the state tournament, the Minnesota Twins did acquire the services of an aging right-hander with a Hall of Fame curveball and a reputation for allowing crooked numbers. The next season, Bert Blyleven led the Twins to a World Series championship.

Kate and Grant shared a passionate love affair for twenty-three years. Each of them went to bed every night and thanked God that the other had chosen them first. Sometimes, on quiet evenings, they'd sit together on the darkened porch and talk about the child they'd lost, and the unhappiness of Kate's childhood, and Grant's cancer, and a thousand other crooked numbers they'd endured. But they laughed, too, when they remembered good times, and the good friends. In the deepest, darkest moments of these quiet nights, each of them looked back and wondered about all those things that held their lives so close together. Kate died of heart disease when she was forty-nine, still the prettiest girl Grant ever saw. They remained best friends and jealous lovers to the end.

Grant Thorson played fourteen more seasons with the Walleyes. He played on because he loved the game, and the banter with new teammates, and the retelling of old stories. But more than that, he played because even though someone might hit his dreams over the fence from time to time, they always returned to him.

On October 13, 1995, Will Campbell called Grant to tell him that Mickey Mantle was dead. Grant went out to the little porch where he listened to Twins games with Kate, put his face in his hands, and wept. But that's the great thing about dreams; they live forever, and Mickey returned soon enough, just like the little girl with the French braids and the brace on her leg.

Grant Thorson is still waiting for that call from the Twins.